Real People Love This Book…

"It moved me so much that I wept. I was so excited I took it downstairs to read certain passages to my mom and dad! Then I urged my best friend to read it. The themes come right out of my own life. I love it!"

Molly Winters, Lake Bluff, IL, College Student

"I really got into Nathan Payne—he's such a great character that I couldn't wait to find out what happened to him next. I feel like I know the guy personally—Nathan and the others remind me of real people I know."

Martin Maher, Tully, NY, Financial Professional

"I don't read many novels and I had low expectations. All I can say now is that I couldn't put it down. It had me turning the pages. It really moves fast. It's great!"

Tom Baugh, Akron, OH, Businessman & Father

"The passage where Father Chet and Becky Macadam talk about celibacy is one of the most insightful that I've ever read on the subject—all this interwoven into a story with a great plot. I'm very excited about this book!"

Eileen Biehl, Westlake, OH, Mother & Writer

"The climax of the book was creative and mystical, and really gave me food for thought regarding my own life. Bud Macfarlane has a real gift for dialogue and characterization."

John Madigan, Chicago, IL, Father & Lawyer

Characters so real you'll swear you know them.
A plot that twists and turns so fast you'll lose
sleep to find out what happens next.
A riveting story that whisks you from Salt Lake
City to Chicago to Rome to Notre Dame.
A supernatural thriller that will rock your world.

PIERCED BY A SWORD

A savvy drug dealer from the meanest streets
of Cleveland…

A no-nonsense Irish Pope who drives his own car
and travels in disguise…

A beautiful, unmarried pregnant woman with a
quick wit and quicker temper…

A relentless, aging tycoon from Utah…

A mysterious Dark Man who sees the future before
it happens…

A handsome, hard-drinking, hard-living securities
broker…

A soft-spoken, shy, gigantic former NFL football
star from Louisiana…

A fast-talking young priest from New Jersey with a
penchant for causing trouble…

…And the Mother of God.

IF YOU REALLY
LIKE THIS BOOK

Consider Giving it Away.

Saint Jude Media, the nonprofit publisher of this novel, invites you to send for copies to distribute to your family, friends, and associates. We are making it available in quantities for a nominal donation. We will even send a free copy to individuals who write to us directly. There is no catch. It's a new concept in book distribution that makes it easier for everyone to read great books.

See the back pages of this book for more details, or write to us for more information:

Saint Jude Media
PO Box 26120
Fairview Park, OH 44126-0120

www.catholicity.com

Discover a New World.
Change Your Life Forever.

Published by Saint Jude Media
PO Box 26120, Fairview Park, OH 44126-0120
www.catholicity.com

© 1995, 1996 by William N. Macfarlane, Jr. All rights reserved,
including the right to reproduce this book or portions thereof in
any form whatsoever without permission. First edition 1995
Second edition 1996

ISBN: 0-9646316-0-1
Library of Congress Catalog Card Number: 95-68985

> This book is a work of fiction. Names, characters, places,
> and incidents either are the product of the author's
> imagination or are used fictitiously, and any resemblance
> to actual persons, living or dead, events, or locales is
> entirely coincidental.

PRINTING HISTORY:
May 1995 (75,000)
November 1995 (75,000)
December 1996 (75,000)
April 1998 (35,000)
February 1999 (25,000)
January 2000 (15,000)
July 2000 (20,000)
May 2001 (25,000)
June 2002 (25,000)

Cover Design by Ron Wiggins
Cover Art by Benjamin P. Hatke, MI
Typesetting by Joe Vantaggi on a Power Macintosh 8500
Printing by Offset Paperback Manufacturers, Dallas, PA

Printed in the United States of America

To my mother, Patricia I. Macfarlane, the
consecrated wife who sanctifies her spouse.
Among many other wonderful things, I received the
artist's urge to create from you.
Thanks Mom.

ALSO BY BUD MACFARLANE JR.

CONCEIVED WITHOUT SIN
HOUSE OF GOLD

PIERCED BY A SWORD

BUD MACFARLANE JR.

SAINT JUDE MEDIA
CLEVELAND, OHIO

Foreword

Long after our century is over, long after the fifty thousand titles that are published in English each year are forgotten, you and others will turn to tattered copies of *Pierced by a Sword* and smile, and puzzle over it, and wonder how it was written, and thank God for it. You will remember the darkness of our times and realize that God prepares, that He always sends us his messengers the prophets, his truth-sayers, his servants.

You may be cracking open this book just to please a friend or neighbor or aunt or son or mother or father or pastor who gave it to you. You may be asking yourself whether it's worth the effort to invest time to begin reading it.

You should.

The supermarket tabloids are flooded with "end times" prophecies these days, predicting disasters of all kinds, promising saviors of all kinds, and stirring into the mix a distorted version of what Catholic prophets and mystics have been warning us about for centuries. Although *Pierced by a Sword* plunges us into an exciting roller coaster ride through the coming years, it is not that kind of prophecy. It does not attempt to predict what the future will be—rather, it is a superb story of what the future might look like, feel like, and how each of us might fit into the drama. In this book, you will not find **the** future, but you will find **a** future.

Pierced by a Sword is the story of a group of ordinary men and women who change the world, and do so at a time in history when the powers of darkness appear to have fatally undermined the political, economic, and cultural landscape. The characters in this book are more than just fascinating and believable. They are real. You will meet poor men and yuppies, investment brokers and drug dealers, parish priests, housewives, native Americans and Irish nuns, bad Catholics and good Protestants—and vice versa, atheists and agnostics, college professors, saints, popes, an antipope, a Russian general, U.S. Marines, a New Age guru, jaded street-kids, suburbanites, corporate magnates, a hot-shot pilot, a pro football star, a grade school teacher, authentic visionaries, hit men, and both shades of angels. And many, many more. This is our world. This is your world.

Let me tell you a little about the storyteller, the author of *Pierced by a Sword*. Like so many readers of this novel, I first heard of it when it was sent to me by a friend. She thought that since I had written a novel about a fictional apocalypse, I would enjoy reading something by another "end times novelist." My curiosity was aroused, but I was simply too busy to spend precious time on a paperback that was two inches thick and looked like it came from the pulp fiction rack at the local corner store. Who has the time to read nowadays? Besides, I didn't need another book chock-full of bad news. (I was especially wrong about the last item.)

Eventually, unable to sleep one night, I picked it up and thought I would just skim through it, in order to be able to tell my friend that I had read it. After the first few pages I was no longer skimming. Despite myself, I was reading it. A few more pages after that and I was hooked. After a chapter or so, I was completely *inside* the story, living its startling events as if I were there. The story was tremendously satisfying! It was wild and humorous and moving, and full of powerful insights. The characters breathed. The author's imagination was buzzing with life. The writing was fresh and captivating, even though it was a first novel written by a young man. I realized that this was no cheap potboiler. It was something more. Much more.

I took the publisher's invitation to write in with my reaction, and even included a few pointers for the young author. I tried to be as diplomatic as possible, for I too have made mistakes over many years of writing fiction. To my surprise, Bud Macfarlane Jr. phoned me after the letter was passed along to him. (My novel *Father Elijah* had not been published at the time. As the editor of a small, Catholic family journal in Canada, I was virtually unknown in America.) We chatted briefly, compared notes on the state of the world, writing, and the difficulties of apostolic work. From the start it was obvious that Bud Jr. was a very funny guy, a man with a fabulous sense of humor. And that struck me as odd, considering he had written a book about a very serious topic. I went back to his novel and reread it, and found many examples of his wit, and many more examples of his deeply reflective nature. What reconciled these two traits, what made them work together, was Bud's great gift of hope. His novel seemed to be saying that, yes, modern people are in pretty rough shape, and yes, there is darkness growing in the world, but the darkness cannot overcome the light. Especially when we are laughing.

A few months later, I was invited to speak at a conference in Chicago. I phoned Bud, who was going to be in the area that weekend, and we agreed to meet. The day before my flight, it began to storm. A freak blizzard appeared out of nowhere in late spring and dropped two feet of thick snow on us within twenty-four hours—a very unusual occurrence in my part of Canada. As I shovelled off the steps, I recalled one of Bud's last comments about the "coming tribulations," as he called it. He had mentioned that in all probability the next stage in unfolding world events would be an increase in the frequency and intensity of natural disasters. I argued with myself that weather in Canada is unpredictable, and one shouldn't read too much into the snow I was shovelling. As I was lifting one last heavy shovelful, there came a tearing pain in my lower back and I collapsed to the ground. I had suffered from a sore back a few times over the years, but nothing like this. I was in agony, paralyzed, unable to move.

I desperately wanted to phone Chicago and cancel my speaking engagement, but knew I had given my word that I would be there. I assured myself that I would probably be able to walk a little after I reached the airport, which was a two hour drive away. I crawled on hands and knees to the car, somehow managed to drag myself into the seat, and backed the vehicle out of the partly cleared drifts onto the treacherous highway. The drive to the airport was one unending torture session, during which I remembered what I had so often forgotten during my twenty years of lay apostolic work: every time I was to give a talk or do a significant work in the service of God, I was struck by severe sickness, car troubles, or any number of similar problems which arrived in waves with uncannily bad timing. I had always chalked it up to coincidence, but now I could no longer ignore the pattern, and it was a perfectly *consistent* pattern. If you do a work for Our Lord, you're going to take some flak; you're going to be hassled. Stop doing the work, and your troubles will just melt away like a late spring snowfall under a hot sun.

That stiffened my resolve, and it seemed a miracle when I managed to board my flight and arrive safely in O'Hare Airport in Chicago. As I hobbled out of the arrival gate, I was met by a huge, grinning bear of a man, who introduced himself as Bud Macfarlane Jr. I was almost doubled over and having trouble walking. I told him my tale of woe. He smiled again and explained that only a few hours earlier he had been released from jail. Driving to the city the previous evening, he had been caught in a speed trap by the local police. The officer had checked Bud's license on the computer and found that it had been suspended. The car was impounded and Bud was put in jail for the night. He was totally perplexed by this surprise turn of events because he knew that there was nothing out of order with his license. There would be fines and a trial and no end of inconvenience getting it all straightened out. Weeks later the police bureaucracy discovered that the computer had made an error, and that Bud was completely innocent. But in Chicago that weekend, the hassles were mounting.

"Looks like Ol' Sparky's giving us some trouble," Bud said. "It's a good sign! Nah—it's a really great sign!"

A great sign?! I was not convinced.

We spent the remainder of that day driving around Chicago and going to the University of Notre Dame, a couple of hours away. We saw first hand the places where many of the events of *Pierced by a Sword* take place. We sat in Bruno's, the Italian restaurant in the novel, eating pizza (which is a staple of Bud's diet), and discussing books. Gradually our excitement grew as we compared notes about the craft of writing and spiritual truths. So many of our experiences, especially ones regarding the faith, were identical. We were citizens of two different nations, had come from different backgrounds and cultures (he from suburban New Jersey and me from the Great White North). I was fifteen years older than he. Yet we shared the same vision of supernatural realities and had come to the same conclusions about what is happening in the world. Later, we drove back to the conference center in Chicago, carefully parked in the lot, and called it a night. The next morning Bud awoke to find that the car had been towed away. He was *laughing* when he showed me the empty spot. We decided to walk together (despite my back!) the few miles to the towing garage, and hours later and a hundred dollars lighter, he was restored to his car. This time I laughed, too, reinforced by a new understanding of the nature of the battlefield we all fight upon.

"This is a good sign," I said to him. "In fact, it's a really great sign!"

He smiled at me, nodding.

So began a friendship that should last forever.

Bud Macfarlane is thirty-four and in love with his wife and two sons. He took a degree in History from Notre Dame, taught high school, drove a UPS truck, travelled the nation as a successful executive in two different industries, played all your American sports, cooked in restaurants, and is now the founder of the Mary Foundation, which is the world's largest producer of Catholic audio tapes. Millions of people have heard these tapes, and millions more will hear them as the work of the foundation continues to grow at an astounding rate. Yet, for all that, Bud remains a humble man, is quite "normal," and is more dedicated to his family than to his work, only a part of which is writing novels. He has devoted his life to conveying heaven's messages to the world. He doesn't bowl anybody over: he trusts that most of us are open-minded, and will respond to the truth if presented in a respectful and straightforward manner.

These messages are of the greatest importance, and we ignore them at our own risk. In *Pierced by a Sword,* the author has blended them into a fascinating, compelling story. This third printing of the book boasts a beautiful new cover, and the text has been fine-tuned by careful editing. The story is largely unchanged, although some sections have been expanded in order to enrich the tale and to clarify certain points that might have been misunderstood in the first version.

A novel which attempts to imaginatively express the spiritual drama of our times may take many forms. It can be populated by saints or sinners, or both. It can be situated in times of war or peace, or both. It may be well-written or not so well-written. It can show how low man is capable of sinking and how much in need of redemption he is, or it can restrict itself to pious platitudes and cardboard figures trotted through simplistic morality plays. It can err in the direction of being too explicit in describing sin, thus glamourizing it; or fail to show us the urgency of the struggle over every human soul. It can make the mistake of overestimating the power of darkness or underestimating it. The underlying theology of a work can all too easily veer slightly off track and cause damage to an unknown reader; alternatively, it can pull back so far from realism that it loses credibility and ceases to touch the heart. When writing about the things of God and the things of man and the things in between them, the dangers are great. The author faces a minefield of choices.

Even though I have been through every line of this book with Bud during the rewrite, I'm still not certain how he managed to avoid all the dangers listed above. I believe this is the gift of inspired storytelling. Many have used this gift for good or for bad, or for personal gain, or for fame, or even let the gift atrophy while pursuing other things. The author has given Catholic readers much that is familiar and much that is new. Our Protestant brothers will be pleasantly surprised to find farseeing insight into spiritual warfare and the Bible. Those who think the End Times are hogwash can read it for fun (you'll find that it offers more page-turning pleasure than Stephen King or Tom Clancy!). And I would challenge the reader who is skeptical about the things of God, but is sincerely questioning, to jump in and try to find your own story in one of the characters.

The universe is big—much bigger than we suppose. Don't be afraid. This book is not a trite put-down of sinners. In fact, sinners are the protagonists of this novel. Perhaps this is because the author knows that we all struggle with darkness. It is obvious from the opening lines that Bud is in love with his characters. Maybe that is what makes them so real. They are *us*. They stumble through the confusing temptations and stagger toward the enticing mirages that dominate our culture; they are imperfect, they fall, they are in pain, and they long for something better but don't know where to turn for help. Sound familiar?

And as the author reveals to us the destruction we bring upon ourselves in so many ways—carnal, ideological, spiritual—he steers carefully away from obsessively focusing on our sinfulness. At every turn he demonstrates that grace is more powerful than evil, divine providence is always going ahead of us preparing the way for moments of choice, moments of conversion, moments of light.

"Private revelation" is a tricky thing, controversial to say the least. Wisely, the author entrusts the final decisions on these matters to the discernment of the Church. Those who have met him know he is quick to point out that this novel is a piece of fiction. The purpose of prophecy is not to give an inside track on the future: that would merely be a kind of "baptized" fortune-telling. Genuine prophecy, by contrast, is concerned with the timeless truths as they apply to the current situation. One hundred years from now, virtually every person alive today on this earth will be dead. In this sense, we are always in the End Times.

Pierced by a Sword is an imaginative apocalypse. It is more concerned with raising the question:

What if?

What if it turns out this way? What would I, the reader, do in such a crisis? Where would I place myself in this vast landscape of chaos? How would I personally resolve the dilemmas faced by the men and women in this novel? What choices would I make if I were in their place? And most importantly, will I be ready?

As you read this book, you will gradually come to understand the principles at stake whenever good and evil confront each other. I will not spoil the story by giving away even the smallest part of the plot. Plunge in! Discover it for yourself. Get ready for a journey of epic proportions—rather, *cosmic* proportions. You hold in your hands a little treasure, a marvel. This is an adventure, a comedy, a tragedy, a turbulent odyssey and a peaceful stroll. Most of all, this is a love story like no other I have ever read. A new kind of love story. I'll see you inside…

MICHAEL D. O'BRIEN
12 DECEMBER 1996

Acknowledgments

I thank my lovely and brilliant bride, Bai, for putting up with me while I wrote this.

My dad, Bud Macfarlane, Sr., who is my greatest inspiration, for twelve years of unparalleled background research, and for his peerless example of *faith in action*.

Bill Merimee, John Kernan, Helga Duffy, Michael O'Brien, and Meg Winn for priceless editing—this book wouldn't have been completed without you. John Klee for the idea. Ted Flynn for encouraging me to *start*. Joe Vantaggi for typesetting. Father Witt for his "papal" blessing. Jim Walsh at Verona High School (NJ) for teaching me how to write. Sister Anthony Mary and all the dedicated nuns who taught me at Our Lady of the Lake Grammar School. Dan Tekulve for his stunning generosity. Bill Whitmore for getting it done at Saint Jude Media.

All the Mary Foundation "Prayer Corps" priests and religious for the grace merited on behalf of this book. Professor Richard J. Thompson and the Reverend Edward O'Connor, CSC, for introducing me to Aristotle and Aquinas, respectively. Phil Stein for reasons only you know. Paul Deininger for aviation tips. Daniel J. LaPorte. My brother Joe Macfarlane. My nine sisters (yes, nine!). Tom "Huck" Heaslip for predicting this 16 years ago. John and Jen Madigan, Eileen Biehl, Susan and Greg Radzialowski, Tanis Merimee, Michele TePas, Tom Baugh, Uncle Joe Mack, Sister Deb at *Signs of Our Times,* Joanie Hasser, Mary Pat Wagner, Carol Baugh, Joe Koopman, and all of my many "pre-readers." For my "bad guy" friends. Marty Maher, not because you helped much, but because you'll get a kick out of being here. All friends and benefactors of the Mary Foundation around the world. It's an old cliché, but I can't thank everyone. Please don't be offended if you're not in here. I thank God when I think of you.

Preface

I believe that most novels get read because readers find them entertaining. Hopefully, you won't be able to put this book down once you get a few chapters into it because you are enjoying yourself and are pulling for the characters. And you'll feel disappointed when the story is over because you'll want more. *And* you'll like it so much you'll recommend it to a friend. That's the greatest compliment you can give me as an author. No amount of marketing can replace a good story.

My friends and relatives may notice fictionalized scenes from their lives in this book. Some of the characters are very loose composites based on people I know. Thanks for the material. I'm sure most readers would be surprised to find out that many of the more outrageous and improbable events in this book are "based on true stories." It's still fiction, though—remember that. I'm not a prophet.

Strap on your seat belts and enjoy the ride. Trust me— I may drive fast but I know where we're going. Nathan Payne, Becky Macadam, Father Chet, and other friends are waiting for you. *Oremus*.

BUD MACFARLANE JR.
13 MAY 1995

Regarding This New Edition

Do not lose courage in considering your own
imperfections, but instantly set about remedying them.
Saint Francis de Sales, Patron of Writers and Editors

Beep beep!
The Road Runner

There is a myth: it takes one person to write a book. While
I certainly thought up most of the stuff in this book, it takes
many people to get a book—any book—into your hands. This
second edition is in *your* hands because over two hundred
thousand people read *Pierced by a Sword* and passed it on.
This is humbling. I suspect that millions more will read this
book before it's all said and done, and you might be a big
part of that. If there are millions more, this is the edition they
will read.

It was the talented Catholic novelist, Michael O'Brien,
who first suggested a complete rewrite of *Pierced by a Sword*.
In case you've read the first edition and are worried that this
is a different book, rest easy. Nothing different happens. The
plot and the characters are the same. It's not *revised* so much
as *fixed up* here and there. Michael and I spent many, many
hours retooling just about every line in this book, and if we
did our job well, and I believe we did, this version will read
easier and have more emotional impact, but won't be different in any essential way. Thousands of people have written to
me or told me that they've read the first edition more than
once. I'm curious about what your reaction will be to this
version if you have read the first version. Drop me a letter.

Why rewrite a bestseller?

You must understand that I never wrote a word of fiction
before I started *Pierced by a Sword* in the fall of 1994. In
fact, almost one-third of it was written before I was convinced
that I was doing anything more than killing time on Sunday

afternoons. I was having some fun, I told myself, and didn't think it would ever be submitted for publication.

I can't even claim that I had the original idea to begin this book. This story started on a dare from my wife, who overheard me giving writing advice to a friend during a long phone call. That evening, I wrote—as a lark—a few character sketches. In my mind's eye, I saw

…a man driving a Mustang—a troubled man—and then I saw him light a cigarette with his Zippo. He turned to look at a sleeping, slender woman in the passenger's seat…

and I was hooked. I never bothered to plot out the book—I just wrote down what I saw in my head. This must be a gift I have, and I'm chagrined that I had never used this gift before. When friends read the first rough draft chapters, they asked me, "What happens next?" My only answer was, "I don't know; I'll have to write it down to find out myself." I'm not recommending that young writers refrain from plotting their novels, but it sure does help if you want to keep the reader in suspense. How can you know what happens next if I don't?

On my wedding anniversary, December 8th, a few months after I began, my wife looked up from her xeroxed manuscript and casually observed, "I have a lot of friends who would love to read a book like this." A light bulb went off. At that moment, *Pierced by a Sword* ceased to be a diversion, and became a *real* book. I started to write with my friends in mind. And because I have a lot of great friends from all walks of life, I started writing it *for you, too.* I was thinking of you, the reader, as I wrote every word. If that's bragging, then it's bragging. But I don't write for myself. I don't write to express profound inner feelings. I write for you. You're my judge and jury. All I ask is that you give this book three or four chapters to warm up. Then, if you're bored, give me and this book the death penalty: stop reading.

I was trying to help you "discover a new world" and hopefully, "change your life forever." I was trying to help you enjoy every word, and spur you on to the next word, and the next sentence, and the next page. I wanted to get you to laugh, to cry (even us tough guys), to think, to put off daily chores, to stay up way past your bedtime, go to work groggy-eyed, and then continue reading during your lunch breaks. I want you to fight with your wife over who gets to read it first.

After all, these same things happen to me when I get lost in that magical yet mysteriously real "world" of a good novel. I hear the best words a writer can hear when auto mechanics, ninety-year-old nuns, doctors, teenagers, moms, atheists, Howard Stern fans and Dittoheads, English teachers, single women, folks who "don't read novels," non-Catholics, those who do and don't like King/Clancy/Grisham, Bible thumpers, Canadians, Libertarians, liberals and conservatives, "regular guys," or any other kind of person you can think of tells me they "couldn't put this book down." I'm a Catholic (and a guy, and a Notre Dame grad, and a New Jersey native) and this book reflects that. But a good story knows no religion. We turn the page or we don't.

I never had ambition to be a writer, much less a novelist. I never trained. I never studied fiction writing (though I do come from a family of natural-born storytellers). I read a lot, but I don't generally read different stuff than most people. The more I wrote this book, the less fun it was and the more plain old hard work it became. Despite valiant efforts by the people I thanked in the acknowledgments of the first edition, I didn't have the experience to write a book without technical flaws. I did the best I could at the time. Many people helped me do a better job this time around. There are a couple of new twists, a few loose ends tied up, especially at the end. Hundreds of readers wrote to my publisher with help on minor grammatical errors and a few fact-checking mistakes. We've done our best to fix them. There won't be a third edition, though, no matter how many printings we go through. Twice is enough.

Michael O'Brien is a fitting choice for writing the Foreword to this edition. He knows this book better than any person I know. You can trust him. I did. There were others who slaved over the new version, especially Tom Case, author of *Moonie-Buddhist-Catholic* and one of the finest writers walking on this earth. I also want to thank the folks at Saint Jude Media, especially Rosanne Hawley and her brother Andrew. Each is a talented editor, but together they're stunning. Dan Davidson, Jamie Hickey, my sister Cathy, and Holly Deliduka also burned the midnight oil for your reading pleasure.

Finally, I want to thank Dave Baugh, who is a fine man and an inspiration. Bill Whitmore, who was so instrumental in bringing you the first edition, is also responsible for the new cover. Our typesetter, Joe Vantaggi, returned to the scene of the crime for this version, and also made editorial contributions.

Finally, despite what Michael O'Brien says in the Foreword, I'm not a prophet. But I still drive fast. Fasten your seat belts. Put the top down. Grab a cup o' Joe and adjust the pillow under your neck. We're going for a ride.

And if you enjoy this ride, and even if you're not the praying type, say a prayer for my wife, Bai. This book really was her idea.

BUD MACFARLANE JR.
8 DECEMBER 1996

And Simeon blessed them, and said to
Mary…"Behold, this child is set for the
ruin, and for the resurrection of many in
Israel, and for a sign which shall be
contradicted. And thy own soul a sword
shall pierce, that out of many hearts
thoughts may be revealed."
Luke 2: 34-35

Prologue

24 R.E. (Reign of the Eucharist)
Marytown, Indiana

The lone bell of Immaculate Conception Church rang in the distance as Denny Wheat sighed, then leaned forward and cut the motor of his battered John Deere. Noon.

Time to whisper into the ear of my Lord.

He bowed his head. Denny's son Zack, silhouetted in the October sun, stopped working on a Cessna 172 fifty yards to the west and also bowed his head. The entire population of Marytown was praying the Angelus.

Denny finished his prayers and turned the old tractor back on. *We're not much different than simple farmers hundreds of years ago in Christian Europe,* Denny thought. *Except now, every person in Marytown feels like they are whispering into the very ear of Jesus. The Eucharistic Reign of Christ, we used to call it in the Dark Years, not knowing what it meant. It turned out to be so simple! What took years of discipline for the great mystics like Saint John of the Cross is like breathing for the residents of Marytown.*

Denny looked at his son Zack, who was twenty-two.

The 1990s, the Dark Years, are to Zack like that movie Star Wars was for me in my youth—sheer fantasy. A time so evil that it can barely be imagined by those who were born in the Eucharistic Reign.

Denny was reminded of the role he played during the Dark Years. He remembered the heroes and heroines he knew during that horrible and strangely exciting time of suffering and redemption—Nathan, Becky, Father Chet, others.

And Lee Washington! I knew them—I lived through it. I lived to tell...

PART ONE

The Remnant

There is nothing that does not participate in beauty and
goodness, because each thing is beautiful and good
according to its proper form.
Saint Thomas Aquinas

Called up my preacher; I said, Give me strength
for round five. He said, You don't need no strength,
you need to grow up, son.
John Cougar Mellencamp

Each man has his own vocation. The talent is the call.
Ralph Waldo Emerson

Well I'm goin' out, I'm goin' out lookin' for a cynical girl,
who's got no use for the real world.
I'm looking for a cynical girl.
Marshall Crenshaw

But then, O Immaculata, who are *you?*
Saint Maximilian Kolbe

Chapter One

1

Mid 1920s, Summer
Woodland Section
Cleveland, Ohio

Father Greg walked through the courtyard of Saint Nicholas Church with Sister Susan, the principal of the parish grammar school. They were saying their daily Rosary together for the parishioners. Father Greg was meditating deeply on the fourth Sorrowful Mystery—Jesus Carries the Cross—so he didn't notice when his Miraculous Medal slipped out of the hole in his pocket down to the ground. The medal had been a gift from his mother on the first anniversary of his ordination twenty years earlier. He carried it in his pocket because he didn't like wearing medals around his neck.

After weeks of searching, Father Greg gave up looking for the medal, praying: *Dear Mary, let someone who needs it find it. I had it for twenty years—that's enough for me. I'll make you a deal! I'll trade you the medal for a bigger church and a new school for Sister Susan.*

In the 1920s the Woodland Section was still a vibrant community, and many new parishioners were joining Saint Nicholas. The steel mills and car factories of Cleveland were running at full steam. It was a safe and wonderful place to raise a family.

2

Early 1980s, Summer
Woodland Section
Cleveland, Ohio

The heavyset kid swung mightily and whacked the tennis ball.

Lee Washington turned and ran as fast as he could, looking over his shoulder. The black youngster was straining to catch the tennis ball off the broomstick of LaPhonso Mack. LaPhonso was already a legendary power hitter in the rough and tumble annals of Woodland stickball. Part of a three-man team, Lee Washington was the lone outfielder. He was an expert at dodging the abandoned cars, wild dogs, and old tires that filled the back of the empty lot which served as an illegal dump in the ghetto neighborhood. Lee strained his eyes against the setting sun while his teammates cheered him on. He prepared to dive headfirst for the dirty green ball.

I'm gonna catch it!

Lee tripped on a rusty bumper from a 1965 Chevy pickup and missed the ball. Dirt filled his mouth. Game over. His teammates cursed in a good-natured way as the laughing LaPhonso rumbled around the makeshift bases.

Lee, who was not a particularly good or bad player, was not disappointed. The shy, fatherless boy had given chase with supreme effort—as usual. Despite their perfunctory curses, he knew his teammates appreciated the hustle. No one else but Lee would have been crazy enough to dive for a ball in the debris. Summer was only half over and stickball would resume tomorrow.

He spit the dirt out of his mouth. Then he waved to his friends, hollering brightly, "I'm okay! See you tomorrow!" He put his hands on his hips and surveyed the dump.

His friends called back their good-byes and turned to go home. He continued to dust the dirt and grime off his pants and suppressed an urge to kick the truck bumper. He looked again at the twisted, rust-covered hunk of metal.

Must be a new piece of junk, he mused. *What's that gleaming there? A quarter?*

Lee Washington took a step and bent over to pick up the quarter. But it wasn't a quarter. He didn't know what it was. He had never seen a Miraculous Medal before. It was mostly caked with dirt.

It was made of silver, like a quarter, and Lee thought it might be worth some money. *Maybe I could sell it? Get some candy for it. Yeah, I'll get a couple Marathon bars.*

Lee, despite being soft-spoken and shy, was known by his schoolmates as a deal maker. The little entrepreneur loved to buy and sell. He also had a reputation for fairness. Fairness was good for business. *I'm gonna be a mill-yanair someday.*

The dirty Miraculous Medal was large—almost as big as a quarter, but oval shaped and thicker. He spit carefully on the medal and wiped it off with the flap of his shirt. His brow furrowed with curiosity as he studied the sculpted images on both sides. He liked the picture of a woman stepping on a snake on the one side and the two hearts on the other. One heart had a crown of thorns upon it, and the other heart had a sword going through it.

Cool! Wonder what the round thing with the points on it is? He didn't know it was a crown of thorns.

He tentatively sounded out the words on the front side, "O Mary, conceived without sin, pray for us who have recourse to thee." When he pronounced *conceived* he said: Consee-ive-ed. *So it's a religious thing. Cool.*

Lee had been abandoned by his father before he was born. He had no religious training from his mother, Shawna Washington. He figured that "Mary" must mean the mother of Jesus. He had seen the Christmas crèche in front of the local Baptist church during Christmas time. Lee was an intelligent boy, and correctly deduced the words to be a prayer.

What the hell. Might as well say it. He took a deep breath. "O Mary con-see-ive-ed without sin, pray for us who have recourse to thee." *Cool.*

When Lee got home to the tenement, he found a sturdy steel chain in his mother's huge costume jewelry collection, and attached the medal. He hung the large silver medal around his neck, looking at himself in the mirror. None of the other boys had medals. He liked it. He decided not to sell it after all.

Over the years the Miraculous Medal became his good luck charm. He did not attach any religious significance to it beyond the one prayer he said in the sandlot the day he found it. That prayer was the first prayer of his life. His second prayer would come years later.

Lee never discovered, however, that the sandlot where he had found the medal was on the former grounds of Saint Nicholas Church, which had been demolished right before the Great Depression. Old Father Greg had done well as a pastor and he eventually decided to sell the lot and the church to build a bigger, better church several blocks away. The original building was deconsecrated and demolished with the blessing of the bishop. Sister Susan was thrilled to get a bigger, brand new school in the mix. And Lee eventually got a Miraculous Medal. A good deal all around.

3

The Late 1990s
Saturday Afternoon
7 October
Chicago, Illinois

Cities are full of beautiful women. Becky Macadam was more than beautiful. She was *achingly* beautiful. She was blond, twenty-six, and in trouble.

"My Grace Kelly with dark brown eyes," as Daddy used to say, Becky thought rather miserably. Bad news on the horizon. The little red plus sign she was looking at said so.

She was quite stunning—despite the sweat suit hiding her athletic limbs as she knelt on the living room floor. Her simple but elegant short haircut was all in a mess. Had she been a bit taller and thinner, Becky might have been an extremely successful model. As it happened, she was a mildly successful advertising executive.

Her eyes focused again on the square piece of plastic on the expensive throw rug on the wood floor. She read the result of the home diagnostic test and knew for certain what she had already guessed by feeling. *I'm pregnant. I can't believe it. A muffin in the oven,* she thought with a mixture of sadness and distant jubilation.

Condoms! They don't really work, now do they?

Becky suddenly thought of her father. Walt Macadam had died of lung cancer when she was in grade school. An only child, Becky had been devastated. *Why do you keep popping into my head at a time like this, Daddy?*

Anger and frustration flashed inside her. She stared at the red plus sign on the little plastic square. She threw it across the room. Becky had a strong arm and it glanced off Sam's picture. *There, now I feel better.*

She thought of Sam, who had been her domestic partner for over a year.

*That's the sixty-four thousand dollar question, isn't it? Will Sam want me to keep it? It? Try **him** or **her**.*

She got up, went to the kitchen, tiny as all kitchens are in the apartment world of Chicago, and poured herself a giant plastic cup of wine. The logo of the Chicago Cubs was on the cup. It was not expensive wine.

Cubs. I'm going to have a cub of my own. She lit a cigarette. *I'll be okay. I'll be just fine. I'm a big girl.*

Outside she heard a random car horn. A fly buzzed around the apartment ceiling and followed her into the living room where she collapsed on the couch. Becky inhaled deeply on her cigarette and exhaled a long slow mist of smoke.

Hi little Cub! I'm your mom. What's it like in there?

Then, the most beautiful woman in the whole city began to cry like a little girl in soft, reluctant sobs. Her domestic partner was due home from shopping in less than an hour. Both were then supposed to get ready for a party at Nathan Payne's later that night.

4

Sunday Morning
8 October
Indiana Tollway, Indiana

The black convertible Mustang sliced through the air, top down, at eighty-five. Nathan Payne scanned the horizon for state troopers. The rock music on the CD screamed "Three Strange Days" by a group called School of Fish. In the passenger seat a young lady with wavy, shoulder length auburn hair and a snow white complexion was sleeping deeply. She had been out like a light since way before the Skyway.

God, she's different, he thought wistfully, gripping the steering wheel more tightly, keeping one eye on the road. *Inside and out different.* Her name was Joanie Wheat.

As if she could read his thoughts in her dream, she gave a low moan, adjusted her position on the gray leather seat, but didn't wake up. She was wearing baggy jeans and an oversized gray sweater which hid her thin figure.

I wish she would open her eyes. She had the clearest blue eyes Nathan had ever seen—and he had looked closely into many a woman's eyes. Joanie Wheat was not the most beautiful woman Nathan had ever been with, but she did have the most enchanting eyes.

He decided against waking her up and turned his complete attention back to the highway, which was whizzing by in a blur. Chicago was now seventy miles to the west. The rolling hills of western Indiana were starting to level out into good old Hoosier flatlands.

Nathan was a slender, handsome man with inscrutable green eyes that made him seem older than his thirty-one years. He glanced at the young lady again before taking another sip of the Jolt which was keeping him awake after the big party last night in Chicago.

I've got to call my voicemail and let Chet know where I'm going.

Nathan had given Chet the number.

Chet was Father Chet Sullivan, Nathan's boyhood friend visiting on vacation for a week in Chicago. Chet was a parish priest from New Jersey. He was the same age as Nathan. Despite Chet's protests, Nathan had thrown a big party on Chet's second night in town. Forty people had been crammed into Nathan's large high-rise apartment, which was located on the lakefront—Chicago's chic Gold Coast.

Nathan had met the girl in his passenger seat for the first time at the party. Coincidentally, Joanie had been an acquaintance of Chet's ten years earlier during his undergraduate days at the University of Notre Dame. Chet had been pleasantly surprised to see Joanie there.

She was a friend of a friend of a friend who heard about the party. I was pretty wasted before she even showed up. What number would she have been, forty-eight? Nathan was suddenly aware of a strange emotion. It was far away, like the sound of a ship's foghorn.

*What is that? **Guilt?** That's not like you, Fat Boy. Not like you at all. The Fat Boy does not feel guilt! She was a consenting adult, even if she was a somewhat drunken one. You didn't even go all the way with her, though you got pretty close.*

Nathan's tongue-in-cheek nickname for himself was Fat Boy. He had called himself that since high school. At the time, Nathan had been overweight by forty pounds. He had been overweight for practically his entire life up until the summer before his senior year at Fenwick High School. Fenwick was a Catholic school run by dedicated Dominican friars.

The guilt over last night was still there.

A dry little voice spoke to him: *What have you become that you're trying to seduce drunk girls, especially nice girls like Joanie? She cried so sadly before passing out last night. For heaven's sake, she knew Chetmeister! If Father Chet had seen you sneak away with her, he would've barged in to break it up, claiming to be looking for his keys or something.*

Chet had been out on the open air deck trying valiantly to bring Christianity to Nathan's many heathen friends while making them laugh at the same time. *Good old Father Chet. Mr. Missionary. My friend through thick and thin. Why does he still waste a week on me every year?* Chet was the only person from New Jersey who Nathan still kept in touch with since moving to Chicago.

Probably going to get one or two to church today, if I know the cagey Irishman. Nathan's thought was not very far from the truth. In fact, it was right on the money.

Forty-seven. Nathan had been keeping track of how many women he had slept with since the first, a girl he would forever remember as Sally the Waitress. In a way, he couldn't help but number them because he had a special gift for numbers. During his freshman year of college, Sally the Waitress had been serving him drinks at a bar near his apartment at the University of Illinois. Sally had told Nathan that she wanted to see his room, and one thing had led to another. *How long ago was that, twelve years? I've been sleeping around for over a decade?*

Almost against his will Nathan divided forty-seven women by twelve years and instantly came up with 3.916666—on to infinity. Two numbers had presented themselves and his mind automatically called forth their mathematical relationship.

His ample mathematical skills gave Nathan the edge—along with his voracious appetite for competition—that made him the top trader in the smallish but respected brokerage firm for which he worked. Over the last two years he had earned well over three hundred thousand dollars per year. Nathan invested most of his money right back into his own daring trades.

Let's round it off to four women per year. That's not that many, really. Nathan wondered why it seemed that somewhere around number seventeen his sexual activities started to feel more like running on a treadmill than a day at the amusement park. *The word you're lookin' for is empty, Fat Boy. Sex gets old, like playing Pac Man over and over again.*

Nathan did not consider himself promiscuous. He was relatively inactive compared to some of the other men in his circle. *Only four a year, and not as many in the last few years,* he told himself, trying to assuage his guilt. *Old Charlie goes through that many every month, easy.*

Charles "Charlie" VanDuren was the owner of Nathan's firm, VanDuren, VanDuren, and Brooks—known as VV&B on the exchange. VanDuren had inherited the firm from his father and relied heavily on Nathan's abilities, even though Nathan was not a partner. Charlie had promised Nathan a stake in VV&B two years earlier when he lured Nathan from another trading house. Nathan was somewhat bitter, but not surprised that VanDuren had strung him along about becoming a partner. He didn't trust VanDuren. He trusted very few people in this world except for Father Chet Sullivan—and he didn't even trust Chet on morality. He took pride in finding his own way through life. He even held the VanDurens of the world in disdain for needing to conquer women to puff themselves up.

Don't need no woman, he thought. *I'm the captain of my own ship. A veritable master of my own destiny, an island—a rock. A rock! And a roll. A donut, really. A jelly donut. With sprinkles. **Chocolate** sprinkles—jimmies.*

Nathan took another sip of Jolt as he chuckled numbly at the strange stream of humorous flim flam that sputtered from his mind like stock numbers slipping silently across the big board. Only he could read the numbers.

For Nathan, sleeping with women was more a form of relaxation than anything else. He never got emotionally involved with the women he slept with, and was always perfectly clear about his intentions towards them beforehand. At least he thought he was.

A modern version of a gentleman.

Did this nice girl really want to sleep with you? The voice was back, asking questions Nathan didn't want to answer. *Shut up!* He ordered. *I'm a rock, remember? With jimmies.*

By his own lights he was a moral person. He didn't lie, he didn't cheat on his taxes, and he didn't mess with people's heads like Charles VanDuren often did. He knew for a fact that VanDuren had a knack for juggling several women at once. An image of Charlie juggling buxom starlets on the Ed Sullivan Show—replete with circus music—popped into Nathan's head. He let up on the gas a little and looked queerly at the can of Jolt. *What are they putting into this stuff?*

A moment passed. *And I don't sleep with married women like Charlie does.*

For Nathan this somehow made sleeping around okay. He had told Father Chet just that several times over the years during their infrequent discussions on sexual morality. Nathan didn't like to talk about those kinds of things with Chet. Moral conversations made Nathan uncomfortable. *Old Chetmeister made a lot of sense, even if he was wrong.*

How can Chet make sense and still be wrong, Fat Boy? His little voice mocked him.

Don't go using logic with me, he shot back. *I'm a numbers man.*

Nathan was also living his life under a burden which the vast majority of men never carry. Women were *extremely* attracted to him. It was not uncommon for him to enter a nightclub and within an hour have three or four women make it clear to him that they wanted to sleep with him.

It's like they smell something on me, he often thought as they lined up before him at the bars and pool tables in loud smoky dance clubs. *They don't even know me. It's like they think they can sign up for me like signing up for Little League.*

His ability to attract women was legendary among his party friends. Even Charles VanDuren held him in a kind of awe. VanDuren tried much harder than Nathan to add women to his own list, which ran into the hundreds. Most of Nathan's friends assumed he seduced many more women than he actually did.

He was also much less promiscuous than his own father, who had been more like Charles VanDuren. Harry Payne had given Nathan the distinct impression that being a man meant sleeping with a lot of women. His father had also been cruel, distant, and lacking in all affection. Nathan hadn't talked to him in years. He couldn't—Harry Payne had been murdered in jail.

Okay, when this chick wakes up, just ask her. If she didn't want to get started with you, she'll tell you. If she did want to, fine. If not, say you're sorry. End of story. Now shut up, Fat Boy!

Fat Boy, Nathan thought, and remembered George the Animal. George Moore had given Nathan the nickname Fat Boy at Fenwick High School in Oak Park, Illinois, during Nathan's freshman year. Although Nathan wasn't thrilled with the nickname, he was very shy and not many students at Fenwick had noticed him enough to tease him, much less call him Fat Boy to his face.

Nathan tried to avoid the Animal. George Moore was not a mental giant. He also had the annoying habit of teasing all the students who were smarter than he was—which is to say, practically the entire student body. Students were terrified of the Animal. George Moore was over six feet tall and weighed a muscular two hundred and fifty pounds. Everyone expected him to get a football scholarship to some Big Ten school. Even teachers looked forward to the day of his graduation.

During Nathan's junior year, George saw Nathan chatting with Betty Gabelli at a football game. Even as a somewhat pudgy teenager, women were attracted to the painfully shy Nathan. She had struck up a conversation with Nathan, who happened to be standing next to her so he could get a better look at the field. Like George, Betty was no rocket scientist. Betty was not even a rocket scientist's *assistant.* Nathan was quite uncomfortable. He failed to see George glaring at him from the huddle on the field. He didn't even realize that the Animal had taken offense until a couple of days later, before gym class.

Two days after seeing Nathan talking with Betty Gabelli on the sidelines, George lingered in the locker room and asked Nathan to stay behind and help him "with something." He naïvely waited next to George as the room cleared out, figuring the Animal was going to ask for tutoring help in math.

George stood, pushed Nathan into the locker and punched him in the stomach. Nathan doubled over. Then the Animal kneed Nathan in the forehead, barely missing his nose. Nathan, dazed, collapsed on the cold concrete floor of the locker room. He could still remember seeing George's shoelaces from his prone position.

George leaned over and spoke menacingly, "Stay away from Betty, Fat Boy."

Then George spit on the floor next to Nathan and walked out. It took Nathan a few minutes to regain his wind, and a few more to figure out what George was talking about.

Betty who? Betty Gabelli? He suddenly remembered talking with the airhead cheerleader during the game. He hadn't even known that Betty was George's girlfriend!

Three minutes after he figured out the reason for George's violent warning, Nathan formulated a plan to get revenge. He made up his mind to follow through with it. It would take about ten months to accomplish, he figured, and it would do the entire school a favor. Nathan mentally dubbed his plan Nathan Payne's Personal Bequest to Fenwick High School. Someone had to tame the Animal before he killed somebody.

The next day Nathan went for a jog. He also signed up for Judo classes at a dojo in Elmwood Park. He took a job after school at McDonalds to pay for the Judo classes. Within four weeks he was running five miles a day and lifting weights in his basement for two hours a day, three days a week. He often played the theme to the movie *Rocky* when he lifted weights—not for inspiration, but because it struck him as funny. *Yo Adrian! You don't understand! I gotta fight dis guy! Gotta fight da Animal!*

Nathan decided the Fat Boy wasn't going to be fat ever again. He didn't have any close friends so there was no one to miss him after school. His only extracurricular activity was the Math Club, which met twice a month.

Nathan took up cigarettes despite his running because he associated smoking with mental toughness—and his father. His chain-smoking father was doing ten to fifteen for grand larceny at Rahway State Prison in New Jersey at the time of Nathan's little high school project.

He surfaced from his reverie about George Moore. His Mustang had rapidly caught up to a truck laboring up a long, low hill. Considering the speed at which he was traveling, Nathan guided the Mustang around the truck with a deftness that belied the difficulty of the maneuver. He pulled a cigarette out of the pack with his lips, expertly popped his Zippo in the wind despite the top being down, and stepped on the gas pedal. The needle shuddered up to ninety. The edges of a green sign glimmered as the sun rose beyond it: Notre Dame 7 Miles. *Notre Dame. Knute Rockne. Rudy. Fighting Irish—the whole nine yards. Chet says it's the most beautiful campus in the country and Joanie here is from South Bend. Maybe I'll drop in, see the place. Need gas.*

Nathan's high school memory persisted. George the Football Animal. Ten months after taking up his bequest, Nathan patiently waited for the big football player near the back of the school building.

"Hey Fat Boy!" George sneered when he spotted Nathan, who was smoking a Kent. "See you ain't so fat no more." George laughed at what passed for a joke in George's book.

Nathan casually flicked the butt down and ground it under the heel of one of his Converse All Stars. *You can do it, Rocky!* Burgess Meredith's gravelly voice rang in his head.

The two loners were alone together in an alley of sorts, with a cyclone fence on one side and the red brick wall of the gym on the other. Nathan stood in the middle of the path. Some brown leaves from the previous autumn scattered the dirt path that was a favorite shortcut through the woods for some students. Senior year had started a month before. Nathan had been studying George's habits for weeks. Every day the Animal walked alone down this path after football practice. Nathan felt a mixture of fear and anticipation.

He had imagined walking up to George and insulting him, picking the fight, beating on him for several minutes, and then calmly telling him something like, "Watch who you decide to beat up for the rest of the year, you animal." Now that the moment of revenge was upon him, Nathan waited until George was a stride away before speaking to the massive football player.

"Stop," Nathan stated calmly but firmly.

George stopped, looked at what he thought was a now pitifully thin Nathan, and came up with this brilliant retort, "What's your problem, Fat Boy?"

George was in a hurry. He wanted to get home and watch his new pro wrestling video.

With one economical but powerful motion, Nathan cracked the fingers of his left hand crisply onto the small but sensitive area just below George's nose and above his upper lip. George collapsed in pain, completely surprised by Nathan's blow.

The Animal goes down! Just like they taught me in the dojo, Nathan thought absently. *Wax on, wax off.*

Nathan stood over George's body. No insults. No kicks. Still writhing in pain on his back, George comically tried to kick Nathan, who easily grabbed his ankle and twisted it just so, knowing George could feel pressure at the knee. George screamed again, more out of fear than actual pain. A scream echoed off the brick wall of the school.

"Don't hurt me, Fat Boy!" George begged in a whiny voice.

What a moron! The dumb bastard is still calling me Fat Boy!

For months Nathan had imagined he would be elated at this moment, and now, almost like a surgeon observing a new procedure, he felt nothing but cold surprise. And then boredom. He dropped George's leg, which made a small thud on the dirt path.

Nathan leaned over and put his mouth next to George's ear. George had his eyes squeezed tightly closed, and was whimpering.

"Stop," Nathan repeated, softly, coldly. He turned and retrieved his books, which he had stored next to the brick wall.

Let him figure it out for himself, Nathan thought. Then he walked away. It had been the last time he struck anyone in violence.

Neither George nor Nathan ever mentioned the incident to anyone at Fenwick. Keeping it a secret gave Nathan a certain satisfaction. George had his own obvious reason for keeping silent. He had been humiliated by a nerd and the fewer people who knew about it the better.

Happily, the Animal seemed to have figured out Nathan's cryptic command and immediately ceased teasing and bullying other students. Nathan avoided the Animal but gave him a look across the lunchroom the next day.

Stop being a bully or I'll really hurt your knee next time. No knee. No scholarship. No football career. I can destroy you, George Moore. It's our little secret. Down boy!

To the surprise of both Nathan and George, a kinder and gentler Animal made a few friends as other students realized that George had somehow changed. Nathan's outlook on life also changed. Feeling good about himself and his bequest to Fenwick, he became slightly more outgoing in the Math Club, and struck up friendships with some of the other shy students. It was the beginning of his new social personality, which he quickly built upon at the University of Illinois the following fall.

In his Mustang over a decade later, Nathan was pleasantly surprised to find that he held George's memory with nostalgia, not rancor. *Before the fight, nobody knew either one of us, really. Maybe we had that in common. I wonder if George's dad was a first class jerk like mine was? We changed each other.*

After Fenwick, George Moore got a full ride to the University of Iowa, but ironically, hurt his knee during a practice in his junior year and never amounted to much of a player. Nathan lost track of him after that. *Wonder what the Animal's up to nowadays? He'd probably laugh if he knew they call me Feel the Pain Payne on the trading floor.*

The Notre Dame exit approached.

Notre Dame it is. Why did I decide to drive Joanie home anyway? She came on the train. I could have put her on the South Shore Railway.

He looked at Joanie for a long time and almost missed the exit.

5

Three Months Earlier
Woodland Section
Cleveland, Ohio

Lee Washington was slightly buzzed on three Colt 45s. His most distinguishing characteristic was his brown skin. Lee was neither tall nor short, thin nor heavy, handsome nor ugly— but he was surprisingly strong. He had a loaded pistol tucked under his thigh as he drove his aging Oldsmobile Cutlass down a dark side street in one of what the white folks in the suburbs would call "a bad neighborhood."

Where is that boy? Yeah, there he is. He better have his money, Lee thought coldly.

He pulled the Cutlass up to the curb. A black man in a tan and white t-shirt ambled up to the car after a furtive glance to check for the police. Lee powered the window down and quickly exchanged the vial with the white crystals for the right amount of rolled up cash.

Easy does it.

Slowly, Lee pulled the car away. He was only twenty-five years old, and a small-time pusher. Lee made his money on the margins—not unlike Nathan Payne—only in a different market. A dangerous market.

Careful. Don't wanna get the big boys ticked at a small-timer like me. Get this stuff in Toledo and drive all the way back here to make a lousy fifty per gram. Better lay off for a few days. Why blow my big deal on the odd chance of getting busted? Now, should I go see Tawana or Kristianne?

Lee couldn't keep his mind on either girl, as luscious and willing as they tended to be toward him. He was more interested in real estate. Five months earlier, half serious and half high on Colt 45s, he had called the 800 number after watching one of those late night infomercials. He bought the whole "Make Millions Through Real Estate" home study course for a hundred bucks using a stolen credit card number. Lee had the package sent to an abandoned house in his neighborhood. He tipped the UPS driver to keep his mouth shut—the driver knew the house was abandoned.

It took him a month to listen to the tapes. He found he could understand the books if he took his time and skipped over the bigger words. Lee quickly grasped the concepts—after all, he had been in business for himself since he was in grade school. From personal experience, he understood the concepts of cash flow, strategic planning, and how to get the most out of people. He had a knack for making deals. The young entrepreneur probably knew more about corporate espionage than a typical Fortune 500 CEO.

Starting with five grand he had saved from his drug trade, Lee began to buy up distressed properties. By the end of his third month as a big time real estate dealer, as he now thought of himself, he had quietly bought and sold several properties just outside of his immediate neighborhood—some at tax delinquency auctions downtown, most with little or no money down.

He avoided buying properties owned by the big drug dealers. Despite his efforts to hide his activities, a few of his friends reported that his name was circulating in what Lee considered the wrong circles. One of the meanest crack dealers, Elmer "Fudd" Matthews, had been asking around about him. That wasn't a good sign.

But Lee had just executed a plan that would make the downtown real estate specialists jealous. Without a doubt, his deal would baffle the neighborhood drug dealers, who were more interested in whores and cars than houses and contracts. Tawana, who liked the milder drugs Lee supplied her, and who worked in the mayor's office downtown, had heard rumors that the Cleveland Clinic was planning a major expansion. The Clinic was a huge medical complex located in the center of the most dilapidated part of Cleveland.

Apparently, a lot of the money was coming to the Clinic Foundation from HUD, HHS, and Federal AIDS Research Grants. The Clinic was planning to expand south toward the Woodland and Cedar sections. The deal was still in the planning stages—and not a done deal by any stretch. It was months away from any public announcement, but timed nicely to coincide with the mayor's re-election campaign.

Most of Lee's properties were right smack in the middle of the expansion. Lee had already been offered $150,000 for all of his properties by a major development company, which had sent a slick, pony-tailed lawyer in a fancy suit to his mom's tenement. He didn't even shake hands with Lee. The lawyer smiled furtively at Shawna Washington, who was watching

Wheel of Fortune on television. She seemed oblivious to Lee's deal.

During the brief meeting, the lawyer had mistaken Lee's lack of social graces and ghetto vocabulary for stupidity. After a minute or two the lawyer made a lowball offer.

It's worth three times that, you ugly freak! Lee had wanted to scream. Instead, he quietly told the lawyer that he wanted $345,000 in cash plus lawyer's fees (just like Lee's real estate books suggested) or he would go to MBM Management, a major competitor which probably didn't even know about the Clinic Foundation's plans.

Just like a dealer, man, Lee thought, steadying himself. *The richest—and oldest—dealers always stay cool, man. Scream inside, whisper out. Then I can take me and Mama and get out of this dump.*

The Ponytail Man called up the next day with a final offer of $335,000 and half the lawyer's fees. Lee was going to roll the legal fees into the deal anyway, so it didn't matter.

After putting the phone down he took a few minutes to add and subtract the numbers. *After paying off the paper I'm holding on these properties, I'm goin' to clear over $112,000! Later, Woodland!*

Elated, he tried his best to fake indifference when he called back the next day and took the offer. Lee had gone big time.

That had all occurred three weeks ago, and now he made his drug runs more out of habit and for cash flow. The papers were signed but the lawyers were still hashing out final transfer details, tying up Lee's cash. Lee did not trust the lawyers, or anyone else for that matter. No one in the neighborhood knew about his fledgling real estate empire. If everything went right, no one would.

Lee and his mom were planning on flying to Los Angeles in four days. Then they would spend a couple of weeks in a posh hotel while Lee bought them a nice house—with little or no money down, of course. Then he would start a new empire. The general idea was to try to forget he ever set foot in the Woodland Section of cold, stinking Cleveland, much less grew up there his whole damn life. The legal eagles, following Lee's explicit instructions, were going to transfer all the money into a Los Angeles bank.

Screw this drug dealing from now on. It's too dangerous. Be dead before I'm thirty. Who would take care of Mama?

He pulled into the parking lot of his mom's tenement. He sighed as he got out of his car and shuffled to the back door. *I hope Mama bought the plane tickets just like I told her,* he thought as he climbed the ratty steps of a stairway that smelled faintly of urine and marijuana.

6

Saturday Morning
7 October
Walcott, Wyoming

Manuel knew he had no business in Karl Slinger's garage. The little Mexican groundskeeper said a quick Hail Mary under his breath as he tried the door to the limo. It was open. He quickly pulled the audio tape on Marian apparitions out of his coat pocket and placed it on the center of the plush passenger seat. He closed the limo door and silently padded out the back door of the big garage.

Manuel glanced over his shoulder at the huge summer residence of Karl A. Slinger, Chairman of the Board and CEO of SLG Industries, one of the two or three largest agricultural corporations in the United States.

Señor Slinger is a nice man. He always says hello and calls me by my first name. He's even a Catholic, although he never leaves to go to church on Sundays. He'll probably just throw the tape away. I'm a fool. Will Señor Slinger guess it was me and have me fired? Who knows?

Manuel thought of Diego Baerga, who also worked on the grounds of the Slinger Ranch. *Diego didn't go to church on Sundays before hearing the tape by Professor Wheat of Notre Dame. Now Diego goes every day—and says a daily Rosary.* It had been Diego's idea to plant the tape in Slinger's limo.

"Hey, hermano," Diego had reasoned, "just because Señor Slinger is rich doesn't mean he don't need to hear this stuff. Think of his soul, 'mano."

Aw, he'll probably just throw the tape away, thought Manuel as he walked to the tool shed. *Then again, maybe he won't.*

Chapter Two

1

Saturday Morning
7 October
Walcott, Wyoming

"Nice game, Lenny," Karl Aquinas Slinger told his tennis partner and attorney, Leonard Gold. Lenny grunted. Slinger continued, "You taking the later flight back to Salt Lake City? I'm taking the limo to the airport myself in thirty minutes."

Karl wiped what was left of the hair on his balding scalp with a towel in the opulent shower room in the bath house near the tennis court on the Slinger Ranch.

Lenny Gold picked up his racket and waved it regally. "I'm going to sit around on my duff and relax after letting the boss beat me again at tennis. I'll take the rental car to the local airport, Karl. I have to take the corporate jet to Portland to check that new deal in Oregon you've got me working on for Monday, and I want to go over the numbers again before I leave this hovel. You'll have to drive to the real airport in Cheyenne and fly commercial."

Lenny Gold had been Karl's lawyer for over thirty years. Lenny got a kick out of calling Karl's multimillion dollar ranch a hovel.

"Fine with me, Lenny," Karl replied cheerfully. "And what do you mean, 'letting the boss beat me'?" Karl gave Lenny his best poker face before continuing, "I can kick your skinny little lawyer butt whenever I want. I've got an all around game."

It was a true statement.

"Come on, Karl, I was only kidding," Lenny protested mildly. "I've never met a man more focused on winning than you in my whole life. My brains and your guts. You've got to admit, it's gotten us far, hasn't it?"

Karl nodded, then smiled at his friend, "And we're just getting started, Lenny!" Karl echoed his favorite phrase. He had said that hundreds of times to Lenny following all their deals. Most of the deals had worked out pretty well. Karl was worth hundreds of millions of dollars, not including his SLG stock and options. Lenny was worth millions.

"Indeed we are. This skinny lawyer will see you back in Salt Lake City on Tuesday." Lenny finished dressing and picked up his bag. He headed out the door toward the guest house, which was quite spectacular, although small compared to the main ranch house. Beautiful Elk Mountain outlined the diminutive lawyer in the distance.

A few minutes later, Karl finished dressing and then walked to the garage where the limo driver already had the car warmed up. The driver jumped to open the door for him. Karl climbed in and almost sat on the audio tape on the seat.

"What's this all about?" Karl asked his driver, holding up the tape.

"I have no idea, sir," the driver said, a hint of nervousness creeping into his voice. Mr. Slinger was known for his volcanic temper, although he seldom vented it on the help.

"Hmmn. 'Marian Apparitions.' I wonder what that means?" Karl asked, holding up the tape. He hesitated, as if he was about to hand it to the driver and tell him to throw it away.

"Are we going to the local airport or do we have to go to Cheyenne?" Karl inquired.

"Cheyenne. A little over two hours, sir," the driver responded, a slight note of relief in his voice.

"Very well. Let's go then."

Karl's tone dismissed the driver, who quickly pulled out, heading away from the mountains toward Interstate 80.

Karl looked at the tape and thought of his mother with not a little bit of guilt. The last time he had given religion a thought was at her funeral. Karl had been devout as a boy, even entertaining thoughts about being a priest in eighth grade.

I don't know why. Our parish priest, Father Wyznieski, was a mean old coot. Why did I ever want to be like him?

Karl had stopped attending Mass during college. That had deeply disappointed his mother. He could still remember her chiding him in her thick Polish accent from time to time, until her death ten years ago: *"I don't care how much money you make, Karl Slinkowicz, or how many houses you buy me! You are a poor man if you have no faith in Holy Mother Church. What will become of you, Karl? Look at your mama when I talk to you! What will become of you?"*

All he could ever reply was, *"It's Karl **Slinger** now, Mama, not Slinkowicz!"*

It wasn't that Slinger hated the Church or the faith. He was just too damn busy. *Let Dottie go to Mass. If I don't believe, why should I go? Is it as simple as that? I don't believe in God? Well, now that I think about it...I guess not. So what?*

Karl was suddenly overwhelmed with a strong urge to toss the tape out the window. But he didn't. He hated long car rides (in fact, he hated to be silent, still, or alone) and he was big on listening to business book tape summaries during his numerous trips in cars and planes. But he didn't keep the tapes in *this* limo (SLG Industries had several limos located around the country). And there was no one to call on business on a Saturday.

Oh, what the hell, he thought, *maybe it will pass the time. Marian Apparitions, eh? Maybe it'll make me laugh like those money-grubbing televangelists on late night TV!*

Slinger tapped the window separating him from the driver and handed the tape through.

"Play it," Slinger ordered tonelessly.

Without saying a word, the driver reached back, took the tape, and inserted it into the tape deck, adjusting the controls to send the sound into the passenger compartment. The driver made sure he could not hear the tape. Mr. Slinger, who didn't even have a laptop computer, hadn't considered learning how to use the sound system installed in the back of his limousine. Slinger preferred to delegate such trivial matters to his driver. Karl barely knew how to use his car phone, which was ironic because SLG Industries was one of the most technologically advanced companies in the world.

As the first ten seconds of the tape crackled, Karl saw in his mind's eye an image of his mother in her casket. That serene look on her face had seemed just a little bit too serene to have been arranged by the body baggers at the funeral home. Mrs. Slinkowicz had her rosary beads in her hands. He looked at her face in the image and half-expected to see Mama's eyes open.

They didn't. But the corners of her mouth seemed turned up in a little smile. Little did Karl know that in the next hour and ten minutes the eyes that would be opening were going to be his own.

2

Early Friday Morning
6 October
Amsterdam, The Netherlands

His eyes were coal black. They opened.

New York. Yes, it will be New York first.

He closed his eyes again, and smiled while he slept. His room was exquisitely appointed. The beautiful blond woman who had slept with him had left earlier. She was the finest money could buy. No matter how much they cost, no woman could bear to sleep next to him in his cold bed. He was a prime agent of the Prince of this World. In his cobblestone drive sat a Jaguar. In the garage, a Ferrari. In the morning, he would arise and don the most finely tailored suit of clothes that good European taste could select. He would comb his perfectly coifed hair with oil that cost over fifty dollars a bottle.

He called Amsterdam his home, but he had lived in many cities during the past five decades. He was a highly placed official in a powerful international banking institution. Although completely anonymous in a public sense, his name was well known in certain elite, secret circles—circles of men who sat at the green, felt-topped tables of power in the purple-marbled halls of international affairs, beyond the influence of any democracy.

The dark man was handsome. He photographed extremely well. He dressed and acted European, but his sharp features and lightly tanned skin suggested a hint of his Semitic forefathers, who had migrated to the continent before most histories were written. It was rumored that his lineage was traced to one of the finest noble families of Russia—bankers who wielded influence even before the days of Ivan the Terrible. But no one in the elite circles he now navigated seemed to be directly related to him. It was also whispered that both his parents died while he was young. His *real* parents were the headmasters of the finest boarding schools of Europe; it was further rumored that he descended from the Czars themselves, not their bankers.

This was not true.

Actually, he was of royal lineage of a sort, from a kingdom that no longer existed except in the dry, dusty tomes of libraries. If one could—and one certainly could not, for records of this particular man's lineage were not kept, or were destroyed, or simply didn't exist—one would trace his blood to the Kingdom of Babylon. In fact, his mother had been a whore, and he had been born in Egypt.

The dark man opened his eyes again. The room was perfectly opaque. The plush, thick curtains were drawn to seal off even a tiny beam of moonlight penetrating the murky sky of the Netherlands. His eyes were like black creatures merging with the darkness.

New York. Gone. Just like the others—only much worse.

He had been told about Hurricane Andrew the same way in 1993. Bosnia and Rwanda in 1994. Kobe, Japan, in 1995. The explosion of TWA Flight 800 in 1996.

His eyes closed and the smile returned. He needed to rest because he was scheduled to fly to Rome in the morning.

Over one thousand miles away, a fault that lay dormant since before science recorded such things trembled slightly. The tremor was not strong enough to be noted by the technicians who monitored the seismic instruments.

The microquake did nothing more than cause ripples in the several small, man-made lakes that surrounded the outskirts of a certain city in the Middle East. Ripples in the lakes —as if a huge, rough beast approached their banks. And Jerusalem slept.

3

Saturday Morning
7 October
Interstate 80, Wyoming

The tape finished and Karl Slinger was perfectly still. The limo driver, worried when he saw the blank stare in Karl's eyes, lowered the compartment window and inquired, "Is there anything the matter, Mr. Slinger?"

Life came back into Karl's eyes so quickly the driver was reminded of the water turning hot during his morning shower when his wife turned on the cold water in the sink.

"I'm quite all right, thank you," Karl replied distantly, then somewhat forcefully, "Rewind and play that again. I bet I can get most of it in again before we reach the airport."

Wow, the driver thought, *the old man never listens to a tape twice. Marian Apparitions? Must be pretty hilarious.*

Then again, I don't recall Mr. Slinger laughing very much. He looked like he was having a heart attack back there.

"Pretty funny tape, Mr. Slinger?"

"What? Funny you say?" Karl sounded distant again. "No, not at all. Quite the opposite. Is it still rewinding?"

The driver nodded. "Yes sir."

"Good. Listen, when we get to the airport, see if you can buy me one of those portable tape players, you know, the ones that kids are always glued to—"

"—a Walkman, sir?"

"Yes. A Walkman. That way I can listen again on the plane back to Salt Lake City."

The tape stopped rewinding. Within a few seconds, the deep-timbred tones of Professor Tom Wheat filled the passenger compartment of the limo for the second time. The driver debated turning the sound up in his own compartment. That was against the rules. One didn't become Karl Slinger's personal driver without a certain amount of discretion.

That's right, he didn't even know where the tape came from before he got into his car. First thing I do when I get back is ask around. Maybe the old man would like to know who planted that tape on his seat.

4

Sunday Morning
8 October
Chicago, Illinois

Becky Macadam had a hard time sleeping after last night's party at Nathan Payne's apartment. She tossed and turned all night. Finally giving in to insomnia, she left her bed and tried to read a Clancy novel until after the sun came up. She fell asleep on the couch at eight.

The phone rang, waking her up. She walked to the kitchen to pick up the portable phone. She wasn't in a good mood. Her eyes were bloodshot. It hadn't gone well when Sam came home last night before the party.

It's probably Sam. Calling to apologize for being such a coldhearted jerk.

She decided to answer the phone.

"Hello, is this Becky Macadam's residence?" the friendly male voice on the other end asked.

"Yes it is," Becky replied warily. "Who are you?"

"Chet Sullivan. *Father* Chet. We met last night at Nathan Payne's party. Remember me, the priest from New Jersey?"

An image of Father Chet Sullivan surfaced from her memory. *The priest at the party!* She also remembered her vague promise to show him the Art Institute. She had been more than a bit surprised to see a Roman collar on such a young-looking man, much less at one of Nathan Payne's parties. The young padre had been drinking liberally, although he was obviously able to control his liquor. Like many people who don't know priests personally, Becky was somewhat shocked to see a priest act like a normal person. Chet was charming and friendly. Funny, too.

"Oh, yes Father, you must be calling to take me up on my promise to show you the Art Institute." *Oh no! Why did I ever promise such a thing?* she asked herself. *Because he was so decent, despite that New Jersey accent.*

"Father, listen, I never meant—"

"Look, if it's not convenient, I'll understand. You mentioned that you knew it well, and I've never been to the Art Institute in all these years. I just thought, well—"

"No, no, it's not that, it's just that it's not a good time for me right now…" she stopped herself short of sharing details of her problem with Sam. *Don't tell him anything—don't even hint at it.* "…but I found out some very, ah, disturbing news last night before the party." *Now why did I say that?*

Chet's voice changed noticeably. It became lower, almost professional. "Look, I'm on my vacation but I'm always a priest. Actually, what I'm trying to say is, if you need to talk about something, well, I *am* a priest, and sometimes it helps to talk with someone you don't know very well. Please, if my offer isn't welcome, just say so. No big deal."

"Oh…no, Father, I'm glad you offered. It's sweet of you." *I'm recovering nicely,* she thought. *No way I'm going to talk to this, this—stranger. Blow him off.*

"Maybe we could just get a cup of coffee and skip the museum. Are you with anyone, Father?" she heard herself say despite her resolution. Something inside told her to trust the man.

"As a matter of fact, I was planning on inviting Nathan Payne along," Chet answered, "but the man was last seen headed east toward South Bend with a lovely girl named Joanie Wheat. I'm staying at his apartment." The young priest paused. "Just coffee?"

Father Chet now sounded relaxed and confident, as he had sounded at the party. In reality, he was quite nervous and silently began to pray another Hail Mary for Becky, prepared to wait a long time for her reply.

Indeed, Becky paused for a long time.

"There's a coffee shop just down the block from you near the lake, on Sheridan, next to a pizza place named Leona's," she suggested finally, but nervously.

"Got it. I'm walking now. Ten minutes?" he confirmed.

"More like twenty. I have to do my makeup." She hung up by pressing a button.

My makeup! I sound like a ditz. I'll just go have coffee with him and catch up on Nathan's secret past with his boy-hood priest buddy and find out all about that lovely girl he spent so much time with at the party last night.

Becky went to the bathroom to get ready. *I don't really wear much makeup, do I? Dad's right. He always used to say that wearing makeup is like putting chrome around the Mona Lisa. "And the frame God gave you ain't so bad either, like your mother's."* She could still hear her father's easygoing laugh.

Maybe if you didn't have such beautiful brown eyes, Sam wouldn't have bothered to fall in love with you. Love you? He doesn't even know you.

Suddenly, the emotions of last night's fight came back to her, followed quickly by the memory of Sam's cold words, couched as they were in such warm tones:

"Oh honey," he had said, "it's going to be all right—I'll even help pay for the doctor."

Her heart had jumped. *He wants the baby!*

Then he had gone on with the phoniest tone of compassion Becky had ever heard from him. It was almost a whine and had reminded her of a whimpering dog. "I know a guy at work whose girlfriend went to a clinic where they have counseling and everything before they, you know, take care of the problem. He drove her and stood by her the whole time. You know I'll do the same. I'm here for you, honey."

At that precise moment Becky Macadam had ceased to be pro-abortion and became prolife. *Abortion isn't for women,* she had decided, *it's for the stinking convenience of men!*

She had replied slowly, seething, "You can be so cold, Sam. This is your baby, too."

"Baby?" Sam had laughed nervously. "What baby? It's a blob of tissue. Look, when did you become such a prolifer?" He visibly caught himself, knowing that he had crossed some kind of line with her.

"Oh honey," he said with false sincerity, "it's your choice. I know that. I'll stand behind your choice either way." The way he said "choice" sounded like he was describing dirty linen.

"Even if I decide to keep little Sam or Samantha?" she rejoined, looking at him, her brown eyes narrowed to angry semicircles. *Daddy always said I made snap judgments,* she thought now. *Later on he told me that I was a "choleric." Some kind of medieval psychology thing. Why am I thinking about Daddy again at a time like this?*

Somehow she had known what Sam's reply would be. A lie. She put her hands on her hips, waiting.

"Sure," he had said, flatly. Sam was staring over her head, beyond the couch, to the window. "Sure," he repeated, "whatever you decide. I'll stand by you."

Thoughts rushed into her head like the broken remains of a ship crashing in on a huge wave during a storm.

You're lying, Sam! My God, you're already wondering where your next apartment is going to be! You sound like the Robot on Lost in Space. What did I ever see in you, Mr. Robot? Why, I oughtta smack you back into last Tuesday.

She still had her hands on her hips.

*Who sounds like that? God, now I even **think** like Daddy!*

Somehow that thought had made her even angrier. Then she did slap him. Hard. *Just like in the movies, Rhett Baby,* she thought wildly.

"Get out. Now," she hissed softly.

When he hesitated, Becky began to throw things. Sudden Sam scurried out the door like a scared cockroach. After he left she started breaking things. His things. First in the living room. Then she went into the bedroom and pulled all the drawers out of his dresser, whipping the clothes all over the room. She had worked her way to the bathroom by the time the landlord came by to find out what the racket was.

It had still been early and even though she didn't feel like going to Nathan's party, she felt like hanging around her apartment even less.

When Becky got to Nathan's party, she didn't talk much except to the nice young priest. And she didn't breathe a word to anyone about her brave new life as an unmarried, pregnant woman.

✝ ✝ ✝

The smell of cologne brought Becky out of her funk. She looked at herself in the mirror, seeing no beauty, only sadness.

A fly landed on the mirror, distracting her from the memory of the big fight with Sudden Sam. Surprising herself, she smacked the fly dead so fast and so violently that she cracked the mirror. Disgusted, she quickly washed her hands in a sink filled with broken bottles of Sam's cologne.

It stinks in here. Oh, Daddy, why did you have to die?

She threw on some black nylon tights and a big rumpled, white sweater. After donning her Keds she grabbed the keys.

Hi Father Chet! I'm Rebecca Macadam. You know, Macadam like in asphalt? By the way, I'm pregnant. You Father. Me Mother. Ha ha ha. Jeeze. Get a grip—you're just going to get some coffee.

She closed the door behind her and started down the stairs, headed for the coffee shop and Father Chet, a Catholic priest.

5

Sunday Morning
8 October
Notre Dame, Indiana

Nathan Payne took a left off Angela Boulevard and turned onto Notre Dame Avenue, which was lined by enormous oak trees on either side. He saw the famous Golden Dome at the end of the street, topped with a statue of Mary. She was crushing the head of a snake with her heel. The statue itself was over two stories tall. Nathan was so distracted by the dome that he almost drove directly onto the campus lawn where the South Quad intersects with Notre Dame Avenue.

So that's why Chet always goes on and on about this place. She is impressive.

The Notre Dame campus is unique. It has no streets except an access road that circles its campus proper. Nathan was forced to park the Mustang in the lot of the Morris Inn.

Time to wake this girl up and find out where she needs to go next.

He looked at her. *She looks like that actress, Bridget Fonda, only with wavy, auburn hair.* Nathan was still troubled by his newly assertive conscience. *She definitely didn't have much experience doing what we did together, and she was more drunk than I was. Probably has a heck of a hangover coming.*

He looked at her for a full two minutes and decided not to wake her. He grabbed a Kent and lit up. As he looked at the pack of Kents, the cigarette triggered a memory of his dad.

Still smoking that bastard's brand.

✛ ✛ ✛

Suddenly, Nathan was four years old again, sitting on the floor in the hallway next to the kitchen, with salty tears in his eyes, trying not to cry. It was Bloomfield, New Jersey. His dad had just snapped at little Nathan to get back to bed *or else.*

The men in the kitchen didn't know that the little boy could hear them. Nathan could smell the cigarettes and cheap cigar smoke. His dad's friends were enjoying their weekly poker game. Mostly they talked about sports or work. Sometimes, politics. There was a lot of foul language and some drunken laughter.

Nathan's dad was a postman, and this particular time, the old man was relating one of his many stories about seducing or being seduced by one of his several "regular" women on the route. Two of the other men were also postmen and shared their own crude stories.

Nathan only vaguely understood what they were talking about, but he knew it was about women, and Nathan knew his mom was dead, and that he didn't have a woman like those men had women.

His mom had died when Nathan was three. He didn't know why. Some kind of cancer. His dad didn't beat him as often after Sarah Payne died. Not getting smacked around made him feel happy his mother was gone. His father had beaten Mom, too.

Then, feeling happy about his mother being gone made Nathan feel terrible, worse than ever.

He gave up crying a few months after his mother died because it didn't make him feel better. More often than not, his tears earned him a slap from the old man.

Life was a dark, silent hell until Nathan went to school a couple of years later. His only consolation before school started was his Babsie, his Polish grandmother on his mother's side. Babsie lived in Nutley. She came over once or twice a week to look after him. She also took Nathan to Mass every Sunday.

The tender old woman taught little Nathan how to pray and told him stories he could only vaguely remember now. One story was about a painting of Mary where some soldier died when he struck it with a sword. The other was about a priest-dude named Max who died in a Nazi concentration camp. (Nathan mistakenly thought concentration camps were places where there was no food except bread and everyone had to try to concentrate on math problems or else bad guys would kill you. This lasted until Nathan was in fourth grade and learned about real Nazis in social studies class.)

Babsie often told Nathan that he descended from noble blood, insisting that he was from a line of kings. At the time, Nathan thought noble blood was blood that did not come from bulls.

God, talk about the fairy tales a grandmother makes up to console a pathetic little kid, Nathan thought as he took another drag on his cigarette.

Babsie died the day the boy went to school for the first time. No one bothered to tell Nathan about Babsie's death. When he asked his father where she was, his dad said Babsie went away, and told the boy to shut up.

Nowadays I would've ended up in some special class for the emotionally disturbed.

Young Nathan started to eat too much (his dad's favorite meal was boiled hot dogs and lots of potato chips) and by second grade he was considered chubby by teachers and classmates. Nathan wasn't quite fat.

I probably didn't eat one vegetable outside of school until I was fourteen years old. By the way, what's going on here, This Is Your Life, Nathan Payne? Must be the booze from last night. God, how depressing! Weren't you ever happy as a kid?

The answer was yes. On the first day of school, an Irish kid sat behind him and immediately started whispering in Nathan's ear about the teacher, Sister Leonardo Mary. The Irish kid kept calling her Sister "Lardo" and would puff out his cheeks like a bullfrog—intimating that the good sister was less than svelte. Indeed, she weighed well over two hundred pounds. Nathan giggled.

By the third day of school, Nathan surprised himself by trying to come up with his own jokes to whisper to the Irish boy. Although he was never quite as funny as the skinny Irish kid with the gleam in his eye, Nathan got off a few good ones. They sat next to each other at lunch, then began to hang out on the playground.

The Irish kid's name was William "Chet" Sullivan. The nuns called Chet "William," but all the kids called him Chet, which wasn't a common nickname in Catholic schools. In third grade Chet told Nathan that Chester was his mother's maiden name.

Presently, Nathan wondered if he would ever have had any friends if a funny Irish kid named Chet hadn't sat behind him on that first day of school. With a capacity only children seem to have, Chet decided instantly that the shy, portly kid with the green eyes was his best friend in all the world, and that was that.

Chet was Nathan's ticket to a normal life. Chet had three older brothers who protected both their youngest brother and Nathan from bullies. The Sullivan boys all played together after school. Chet and Nathan shared a somewhat sarcastic, wry sense of humor. Chet was cool. Therefore Nathan was cool.

Even though Nathan was not the biggest or fastest kid on the playground, he was deceptively quick and coordinated. Most kids wanted him on their team for boxball, stickball, team tag, and all the other games kids played on the asphalt playground.

It's amazing how important playing games was in grammar school.

Nathan was an exceptionally adept game player. He was usually chosen captain of the team because he had a knack for picking players. He knew which ones would mesh into a winning team.

Nathan also had the uncanny ability to see everything and everyone in the field of play and could guess what was going to happen next. He was almost prescient. On the playgrounds of grammar schools, these were highly valued traits, and seemed to make up for Nathan's quiet demeanor in the eyes of his classmates.

Why did I forget all this? Nathan asked himself now, exhaling a plume of smoke in the direction of the dome. *Those were great days. I never even think of them anymore. Why did I stop playing sports?*

He didn't know. Then he remembered.

Oh yeah, my dad the felon, he thought sarcastically. *Harry Payne, number 12345-whatever at Rahway State Correctional University.*

When Nathan was in seventh grade, his dad was sent to prison for trying to steal something expensive from the post office. *Was it the safe?* Nathan wasn't sure of the details. Within days of his father's conviction, Nathan had been put on a bus to Chicago. He didn't like his new "family." They were distant cousins on his mother's side. A social worker had recruited them to take him in.

*Or was it I didn't **let** myself like them? The Wojtals. Jeeze, I can't remember doing anything with them but eat dinner.*

They both worked all the time. No kids. Back to the depressing part of The Life of Nathan Feel the Pain Payne.

He never really found friends in the public grade school he attended in the Chicago suburbs. *I was the invisible kid.*

Before moving to Chicago, he had practically lived at the Sullivan home, eating dinner there a couple of times a week and generally getting into harmless trouble playing pranks with Chet. His grades didn't reflect it, but the teachers knew Nathan was smart and treated him kindly. Especially the nuns.

Although he considered himself an agnostic and carefully avoided setting foot in church after his Babsie died (except for required Masses at Our Lady of Lourdes Grammar School), it always bothered Nathan when comedians made jokes about cruel, heartless nuns.

Old Sister Lardo used to look at me with such gentleness, and seemed to sense I was troubled. She never pushed me, but always told me how intelligent I was. Most of the other nuns were the same way. Next to Chet's family, nuns were the nicest people I ever knew.

One day in fifth grade, Sister Leonardo held Nathan after school. She was now the principal of Our Lady of Lourdes. She threw him for a loop that day: *"You know, Nathan, you've always been my favorite student. Don't look so surprised young man! I know you and the Sullivan boy called me Sister Lardo in first grade. The elephant never forgets."* The big woman laughed cheerfully, letting him know that the joke was okay in a strangely adult way. He was particularly confused after the elephant crack.

Sister Lardo had continued: *"Nevertheless, I'm entering you in the diocesan math contest. I know you can do better at math, much better. We have tests."*

God! She must have been referring to IQ tests! Nathan now realized.

"I have a feeling that you'll do quite well if you consider math a game. I'm going to help you after school. Don't look so long-faced, young man. Just fifteen minutes a day. Then

you can run along to the Sullivans' house and play. The elephant has spoken, young man, and you shall obey."

The gigantic nun did tutor him—every day for two years. And Nathan won every math contest he ever entered. Nathan was doing college level calculus by the end of eighth grade. In Chicago, his math skills earned him a full scholarship to Fenwick High School. The scholarship was sponsored by a math-whiz alumnus who had made millions manufacturing drinking straws. It was called the Straw Man Scholarship by Fenwick students. Nathan aced his SATs (in both Math and Verbal) and won a full ride to the University of Illinois.

Chet got into Notre Dame, and the two friends made a ritual of meeting in Chicago on weekends a few times a semester. Chet had been a faithful pen pal since the move. Only now did Nathan consider that Chet might have been deeply saddened when he moved away. *I was so selfish that I shut everybody out—and I almost shut out Chetmeister. Chet used to write to me four times before I ever wrote him back.* By the time they got into college, both young men were more interested in partying than anything else.

We were a killer team until old Chetmeister got religion. Ten years ago. Funny, I never came to visit Chet here at Notre Dame. Not even once. Was I avoiding this place?

If a stranger could see Nathan sitting in the Mustang with the sleeping woman next to him, it would seem like he was having a telepathic discussion with the statue of Mary on the dome.

Yeah, I used to love you, Mary. Babsie said you knew Mom and I would get to see you both together someday. Babsie would never tell me when someday would come. Well, there you are. Where's Mom?

He tasted salt.

Have I been crying?

He looked over at Joanie. She was wide awake. For a brief moment Nathan saw empathy in her eyes. It disappeared quickly.

"Hi Joanie," he said softly, awkwardly. He looked down at his lap, embarrassed by his tears. He closed his eyes for a heartbeat, and looked back to the pretty, silent woman next to him. This was his first sober look into her eyes.

Nathan Payne fell in love. Just like that—much in the same way Chet had decided to be Nathan's best friend on the first day of school so many years before.

"I want to get as far away from you as I can as soon as I can!" Joanie Wheat came down on each word slowly and distinctly, as if she had practiced them. "And I'm going to start right now. Thanks for the ride, Mister."

She didn't even open the door. She hopped over it instead and stormed away, toward a brown statue of a guy who was wearing a funny hat.

6

Sunday Morning
8 October
Notre Dame, Indiana

Professor Thomas Wheat finished collecting his lecture notes and left his office in O'Shaughnessy Hall—known as O'Shag to students and teachers. He had come in on Sunday to gather the notes so he could review them for his class the next day. He had a crew cut, was average height, with rough good looks. He looked more like an NFL quarterback than a History professor, except for his typical professorial uniform of khaki pants, oxford shirt, and herringbone jacket. One month past his sixty-first birthday, coeds still seemed to get infatuated with him. Their crushes barely registered on Tom—he was a happily married man and a father of seven.

He had eight grandchildren already. His wife Anne got a kick out of his tradition of making grandchild projections at the family Christmas gatherings. Last Christmas, he had predicted two more grandkids—and was thrilled when three were born. Tom and Anne lived in a modestly large farmhouse in Mishawaka, ten miles from campus.

Unlike his politically correct and research-oriented peers, Wheat taught for the sheer love of it. He was deeply satisfied when his students finally grasped that history was more than a recitation of facts. Most of his peers considered him a relic for the simple reason that he believed one could discover objective truth in history. Surely he would never have gotten tenure in this day and age of Political Correctness. As for his students, they loved the way Wheat told stories.

He had an avocation outside of academia. Fourteen years earlier, he had become entranced by William Thomas Walsh's book, *Our Lady of Fatima.* He had dedicated his spare time and research to finding out all he could about the alleged apparitions of Mary, the Mother of God. These apparitions had multiplied around the world in recent decades. Soon he was giving talks on the subject at local parishes. His natural storytelling ability and his flair for the dramatic had made him famous in a small subspecies of the huge body of Catholics in the United States: Catholics who actually believed that Jesus had the power to send His Mother to the world as a prophetess—just as Yahweh had sent Noah to warn the world before the Great Flood.

Joe Jackson, an enterprising member of the local Knights of Immaculata group recorded one of Wheat's talks and—against Tom's mild protests—started distributing the audio tapes freely to anyone who asked for them. Jackson never charged for the tapes, but free will donations seemed to cover the costs.

That had been almost five years ago. Millions of audio tapes had been distributed by Jackson's Kolbe Foundation in the meantime. Now Wheat was considered the foremost English-speaking expert on Marian apparitions—but only by those few Catholics who were predisposed to listen to him. There were almost sixty million Catholics in the United States.

Relatively few—perhaps several million—knew of the reported messages from the Mother of God in any detail.

His colleagues, had they known about his secret career, would have laughed. "There goes that old dinosaur Wheat—on and on about superstitious and deluded children seeing the Mother of God!" Wheat wouldn't have bothered to point out to his learned colleagues that Mary had predicted at Fatima the rise of Communist Russia before the Revolution in 1917. She had also predicted when World War II would start—thirty years before it began.

Not to mention her predictions to children in Rwanda of the wholesale decapitations in 1994—ten years before they occurred, Tom mused darkly.

Professors at Catholic colleges like Notre Dame had dropped Marian devotion decades ago. Wheat's colleagues were a microcosm of Catholics in general. Wheat knew the statistics well. Less than forty percent of Catholics attended Sunday Mass. Of those who did attend, less than twenty percent actually believed the teachings of their own Church. This meant only seven percent or so of the entire Catholic population were like Wheat—true believers. It was not uncommon for the remaining seven percent of orthodox Catholics to fight with each other over the authenticity of particular Marian apparitions. Some of the more traditional Catholics, who were understandably embittered by the *de facto* prohibition of the beautiful Tridentine Mass, considered adherents to Marian apparitions to be End Times fanatics. Of course Tom Wheat didn't consider himself a fanatic. He considered himself a sober reporter. If the Mother of God and her Son were saying that the world was about to undergo a period of unprecedented tribulations, who was he to ignore their words?

The whole situation is one giant mess, Wheat thought dejectedly. *It was my generation that dropped the ball. Twenty centuries of faith stopped cold by one generation of baby boomers. Martyrs spilled their blood so my generation could skip Sunday Mass to watch pro football. Communion of Saints exchanged for the New Orleans Saints.*

The majority of Wheat's students were so poorly educated in matters of the faith that they would have had trouble reciting the Ten Commandments.

Ninety-three percent of baptized Catholics rejected part or all of the ageless teachings of Catholicism. This vast majority got divorced, contracepted, aborted, and generally acted like everyone else in nominally Christian America. To Wheat's liberal Catholic friends, these same statistics meant seven percent were still following the "superstitions of Rome."

Liberal Catholics didn't disturb Wheat's equilibrium. He avoided arguing with them—their minds were pretty much closed to the facts. Wheat was secure in his love for the Catholic Church, which he loved more than teaching and more than his wonderful wife, Anne. The Catholic Church was the Mystical Body of Christ. To love the Church was to love Jesus. It wasn't complicated.

Wheat also believed for a logical reason: the Catholic Church was unique in all of history. It was the very measuring stick of history. He could not deny any of its teachings, which he knew with the precision of a dedicated scholar, nor the beauty these truths brought into his life.

More than that, Tom Wheat believed because his prayers were answered, which had been the case since he was a boy. He had experienced first hand what the famous French convert Pascal was driving at when he challenged atheists and agnostics with his famous Wager. Blaise Pascal believed that if a person sincerely acts *as if* he had faith with devotion for a period of one year, the gift of faith will be given to him. After all, if God doesn't exist, you've lost little. If He does exist, then you've gained an eternity filled with infinite reward by making a finite wager of a part of your life. Tom Wheat was well aware of the fact that thousands had converted to the faith after taking up Pascal's Wager. By this stage in his life, he was a lot more worried about his family and friends choosing to forego those rewards than missing them himself.

As Tom studied the apparitions of Mary, he started to respond to what Mary was saying. *My colleagues would say I've internalized it,* he thought with a grin.

He took the Queen of Heaven's advice and began to fast on bread and water twice a week. He made a concerted effort to love his wife and children in the little things. Wheat offered up the small inconveniences in his life for the conversion of sinners. He enlisted in Mary's humble army by joining the Knights of Immaculata. In short, Tom was becoming a saint. He was a preacher who practiced what he preached—a rarity.

Wheat looked at his Longines wristwatch. *Time for Mass.*

For some reason, as he left O'Shag, Tom decided to walk down the South Quad toward Sacred Heart Basilica instead of his usual path by Zahm Hall via the North Quad. Such is the prompting of chance—or grace. For this little detour would bring him into contact with Nathan Payne—and would change the fates of countless people.

Chapter Three

1

One Month Earlier
Hilton Hotel
Los Angeles, California

Lee's mother was really starting to get on his nerves.

Doesn't Mama know I'm doing this for her? God, I'm going to have to cut her off like I used to cut off my junkies when they couldn't pay. She's addicted to clothes, furniture, and lottery tickets! Amazing.

He snorted up another line of coke off the small mirror he had placed on the expansive desk.

What about you? Gonna cut yourself off, boy?

He ignored himself.

A beautiful black woman, a relatively famous rap singer named Raja X, lay sleeping in the bed. It was a king-size bed with fine mahogany posts.

Time to call the office.

The irony, of course, was that Lee would never have done coke while selling it in the Woodland Section of Cleveland. That would have been bad for business. Back then, he held addicts in contempt. He preferred alcohol as his drug of choice. But Cleveland was in another universe altogether.

Lee was now in what he considered a much more desirable universe. In less than three months he had parlayed his minor fortune from the Cleveland Clinic Foundation deal into much, much more. After moving to Los Angeles with his mom, he quickly began to study the landscape for deals similar to the one he pulled off in Cleveland. For a home, he bought a modest two-bedroom split-level in El Segundo—as close to the airport runways as he could find—to take advantage of the lower property values. He quickly moved in with his mother and their few meager belongings. He gave her four thousand dollars and told her to buy some clothes and furniture. It took her less than one day to spend it. Lee leased a new Chrysler Concorde—with practically no money down, of course.

Lee was so impressed with the results from the real estate course that he spent days at the local library studying everything he could find on the subject. He also bought a book on dressing for success (to Lee this meant dressing white).

A clerk at a bookstore recommended a few titles in the Human Potential Movement section. Lee bought a few of those books on a whim and really dug them. Soon he was regularly purchasing audio tapes at the Scientology bookstore after reading in *People* magazine that John Travolta was a big-time member.

He watched CNI and practiced pronouncing words like the white folks. His mother laughed at him but Lee paid little attention. After a few weeks he had to buy Shawna her own separate television set for her game shows and Oprah.

Lee knew instinctively that it was a white world and that he owed his Clinic deal to no small measure of luck.

He spent another five grand on a new wardrobe, relying on the advice of a homosexual clothier named Fabian who got a kick out of Lee's request to help him dress "like a honky lawyer."

Lee doubted Fabian was the homosexual's real name. He suggested in a slightly lisping voice that Lee should visit a certain hair dresser who could supply Lee with a honky haircut. A friendship began. Fabian invited him to a party a few days later and Lee did not decline.

He kept his mouth shut at the party out of fear of embarrassing himself with his ghetto speech, and partly to observe carefully the new world of upper and middle class whites, blacks, and gays of both colors.

So this is where all the money is, he thought.

He was struck by two things. First, (and this was hard for him to admit to himself) he was as smart or smarter than most of the people he met. This was especially true despite his lack of reading and writing skills. He had been sizing people up his whole life, as a survival instinct, and he knew that he could out-think most of the people in the room except, curiously, the gay haberdasher Fabian.

The second thing Lee noticed was a complete revelation. For the first time in his life, he could not smell fear on the skin of whites when they looked at him.

Standing in the corner of Fabian's apartment, Lee put down his glass of watery light beer and looked at himself in the mirror that covered the entire wall of the smoky living room.

I look more like Bernard Shaw on CNI than any of the homeboys back in the Woodland Section. I didn't have to move to LA to get away from Woodland. All I had to do was shop at Tower City! Tower City was an upscale mall in the center of the business district of downtown Cleveland.

These two revelations, namely, that he could disguise his poor background with clothing, money, and manners; and that he was more intelligent than most other people—even white people—added up in Lee's mind more quickly than he added profit margins during his deals: *I'm going to be rich!*

All his Personal Power tapes assured him basically the same thing.

Lee turned down two offers for cocaine that evening, excused himself early, and made sure he got Fabian's phone number before leaving. He drove his Concorde back to El Segundo. Instead of going to bed, Lee stayed up until two in the morning studying.

One week later, he convinced Fabian and two of his gay friends to take options on land in Oxnard near a hospital that was slated to receive huge federal grants for AIDS research.

Then Fabian introduced Lee to a gay soap opera actor. The actor happened to be black and was originally from Akron, Ohio. The two transplants hit it off. Lee discovered the actor was in the market for a condominium in Inglewood. Four days later, Lee passed the California real estate exam by one point and sold the actor a condominium the next day.

Three days after that, he rented a prime piece of office space in downtown Los Angeles across from the Hilton. Lee considered the office in the same category as his wardrobe—a disguise to fool whites and middle class blacks. He also hired a white secretary from a temp firm, and Fabian's accountant to do his books. Then he hired another one of Fabian's friends to resell the smaller properties in El Segundo that Lee had begun to buy. He called his company Washington Properties. Washington Properties broke even or made a few thousand on most of the smaller deals. Lee was so engrossed with his work that he barely noticed he was working eighteen hours a day. Shawna Washington began to complain that her son was too busy and started nagging him for more money.

Lee was investing almost all his Clinic Deal fortune, consciously betting on his own ability, bolstered by the human potential tapes and books he was reading. Financially, he seemed to be a good horse to bet on. When he made Fabian and his friends fifty grand each (and pocketed as much for himself, plus a cut) on the Oxnard properties, word quickly spread about the Boy Wonder from Cleveland.

In the hip and hyped world of Los Angeles, Lee gave halting, low-key presentations, delivered with his calm, quiet voice. His presentations were always augmented by impressive research neatly inscribed on yellow pads in his tiny, childlike handwriting. He was tough, fair, and even generous. Little did his investors realize that this was his practical and relentless way of investing in them. They were more valuable to him than any property.

Lee secretly relished the fact that he had maneuvered himself into a glorious position for any businessman: *Now I'm*

*risking and investing other people's money, just like it says in
all the books.*

He began to chant to himself over and over: *I will have a
million dollars before the end of the year. And after two years
I'll have ten million dollars. By the end of ten years I'll own
the Lakers!*

He put the team photo of the Lakers on his desk, just as
the tapes advised him, so he could visualize owning the sports
franchise.

Fabian had made a pass at Lee several weeks earlier, and
he didn't seem insulted when Lee turned him down. Lee decided that if he didn't want to collapse from exhaustion, he
had better take a few hours off to relax with a woman. He
was pleasantly surprised when the white women he met at
the parties were willing to sleep with him. They were even
willing to be seen with him at restaurants and nightclubs.

When Raja X took him to the bathroom at one of Fabian's
endless parties and offered him a line of white powder, Lee
decided one snort might help keep him awake.

One line was all Lee took at that party. After all, he was in
control of himself and in total control of his own destiny. He
was *creating* himself. He could handle one line. Besides, if
all these rich folks could handle it—and afford it—couldn't
he?

Just one line.

Raja was far more beautiful and insatiable than old
Tawana. Lee had to admit that Tawana was a little fat in the
thighs and not as, well, *cosmopolitan,* as Raja.

Unlike Tawana, Raja came from a middle class family
and was well spoken. The rap singer had gone to a local community college before striking out into the music world. Raja
worked out to stay in shape. She affected ghetto slang as part
of her stage persona. Lee had a good laugh when she told
him that.

Raja X laughed harder when he confided to her that he
affected his honky pronunciation by watching CNI. They

shared ambition and belief in creating themselves and more recently, their drug bills. Raja's real name was Ellen Snow.

A year ago I didn't even know the word cosmopolitan, much less understand it.

Lee eventually began to get high before sleeping with Raja. To relax. One night he bought ten thousand dollars worth of coke.

Ten grand? That's a few hours of work on my deal in Oxnard. That's like ten bucks back in Woodland. No sweat. I'll have a million before the end of the year...

Lee shook himself from his thoughts and focused his eyes on the phone again. He decided to put off the call to the office until morning. The drug was quickly taking effect. He climbed off the chair and onto the bed, kissing Raja on the cheek. She opened her eyes and looked at him, smiling warmly. Then she noticed his Miraculous Medal. She remembered a question which she had always wanted to ask him.

"Why do you wear that around your neck?" she nodded at his Miraculous Medal. "What's it called?"

"Oh this?" A puzzled look came to his face as he held the medal in his hand. "I don't know what it's called. Found it in a dump when I was a kid. It's my lucky charm. It helped me find you." Still looking down, Lee smiled awkwardly at his corny, romantic innocence.

He looked up and saw that Raja had raised her eyebrows, showing him her "I'm gonna have an Ambiance night" look. Curiosity about his medal had left her mind as quickly as it came. Lee forgot about his good luck charm.

"Come here, City Boy," she purred.

2

Nathan watched Joanie Wheat storm ＿＿＿＿＿＿ ＿＿＿ ＿atue
of the guy with the funny hat. During ＿＿＿＿ ＿＿＿ ＿＿t life he
had always been the one to walk away, ＿＿＿ ＿y sneaking out
of bedrooms after one night stands. He *never* allowed himself to get emotionally involved with women—even those he
slept with more than once. When they realized this, they left
him soon enough.

Now Nathan felt pulled in two directions. He had always
prided himself on his detachment. He had little use for feelings and despised men who let women trap them emotionally. All his experience since losing his mother had taught
him to feel relieved when women deserted him, or vice versa.

Yet Joanie was somehow different. As she walked briskly
away, not looking back, he felt that she was taking something
with her that was *his*. He felt, no, he knew, that this was a
moment of great importance. It was like the microsecond
before he took a gamble on buying or selling a stock.

It was the time for a decision. Nathan decided.

What do I care? She's not even number forty-eight.

He took his eyes off the auburn-haired girl and put his
fingers on the key in the ignition.

The hell with her.

✛ ✛ ✛

At precisely the same moment in Chicago, the Reverend
William Chester "Chet" Sullivan was patiently waiting for
Becky Macadam to show up at a coffee shop. Thinking of
her brought his friend Nathan to mind.

t Nathan's party where Chet met Becky.
ng habit—decided to say a prayer for Nathan,
a thousand times before in spare moments over the
. Just a simple, short prayer.

Dear Jesus, help Nathan find his way to your mother's Immaculate Heart, like you helped me. He's my friend.

Father Chet quickly forgot his little prayer when he saw the stunningly beautiful Becky Macadam walking up the sidewalk toward the cafe.

A song from a New Jersey group called the Smithereens popped into the priest's mind: *"Beauty and Sadness."*

Then, a line from the Gospel of Luke: *"A sign of contradiction"*—like the *Pieta* in Saint Peter's in Rome. What's more beautiful and sad than the Mother of God cradling her dead Son?

✝ ✝ ✝

As Nathan began turning the key to start the Mustang, he heard a woman's voice inside his head: *"Beauty and sadness, young man. Joanie is a sign of contradiction and so are you."*

"Is that you, Sister Lardo?" Nathan asked aloud, confused.

He looked to the back seat, half-expecting to see his first grade teacher sitting there as if transported through some kind of surreal time warp. The convertible's back seat was empty. He spun quickly to look out the windshield.

Then the voice came again. One word: *"Go."*

Even though he was wide awake, Nathan suddenly felt as if he had woken up from a dream.

One word echoed in his mind. *Go.*

Go, Nathan thought, rather disoriented. *Go where? Leave Notre Dame? Go after her, you stupid moron. Run!*

Nathan turned the car off and jumped out without opening the door. He sprinted toward Joanie.

What are you going to say to her, track star?

He caught up with her at precisely the moment she reached the strange statue.

"Joanie," Nathan called softly, out of breath.

She turned to look at him. Her blue eyes iced over with anger. His stomach pitched like a boat on a wave when he looked at her. He was breathing hard.

Say something, she's waiting!

"Well?" she asked impatiently.

"Uh, Joanie," he repeated desperately, "what's with the chef?" He gestured directly at the statue of Father Sorin above them. Sorin wore a boxed cap common to priests of the early 1800s. It was not unlike a chef's hat. Father Sorin had a long beard, too, which oddly added to the effect.

"What?" she asked as she looked up at the statue of Father Sorin. "Oh, that."

For a moment she forgot how angry she was.

"That's Father Sorin. He's the French priest who founded this place. Sorin came with some Indians when this was all wilderness and looked out and said, 'Someday, a great university will be here,' or something like that. That's his hat. There's a Latin word for it, but I don't know it. Hey!"

Her anger came back like a boomerang. He had humiliated her last night. Joanie Wheat was not *that* kind of girl.

"Listen, Mister. I already told you I don't want anything to do with you." Now her voice was cold.

"Joanie," he pleaded, still lost for words. *God! You idiot!* he chastened himself.

She remained silent, almost enjoying watching him squirm. *How can you look directly into my eyes like that?* she thought. *Aren't you ashamed?*

"What if I said there's been a mistake?" he suggested desperately. Nathan hesitated. Then he heard himself saying, "I'm so ashamed of myself." He noticed her expression soften just a bit. *Such beautiful eyes,* he thought distractedly. He continued to feel for the right words.

"I am..." he stuttered, then more firmly, "...so terribly sorry. You don't even know me and I've hurt you. I'm sorry."

The anger was draining from her eyes now. Then she squinted, appraising him.

Oh really? she thought. *Sure you're sorry. Sound pretty sincere, too. You must practice that line. Off you go, Mister!*

She prepared to drop the hammer on him, but she was stunned to hear her own voice mutter, almost compassionately, "I forgive you."

I can't believe I just said that, she told herself. Then she knew. *You said it because you meant it. You forgive him.*

They looked at each other, silently, for a long moment.

Nathan smiled. Now it was her turn to feel her stomach flutter.

Oh no, she thought.

Behind her, Nathan saw a man walk up. He was pretty rugged looking. Then Nathan heard the older man clear his throat.

Joanie turned to see her father standing there.

"My daughter, I presume?" Professor Wheat winked at Joanie. Tom Wheat gave Nathan an appraising look before continuing, "And who is this fine young gentleman? A student?"

Professor Wheat was surprised to see his blue-eyed daughter's porcelain cheeks flush red. *Red, white, and blue,* Joanie's father thought absently.

Joanie tried to regain her composure.

"Oh, no Daddy! I mean, hi Daddy!"

She's flustered, Wheat thought as Joanie gave him a hug.

After the embrace, she continued nervously, looking back to Nathan as she spoke, "This is a friend of Chet's. I met him in Chicago last night. His name is Nathan…"

Joanie wracked her memory for Nathan's last name. *I get drunk, I spend the night with this guy. **Then** I forgive him. **And now** I'm pretty sure I just fell in love with him—and I can't even remember his name!*

"Nathan Payne, sir," Nathan said as he offered his hand to Tom Wheat. "Do you really know Chet Sullivan?"

Wheat noticed Nathan's unusually strong grip and liked it.

"Not very well, I regret to say. He was a student here a while back. He was an acquaintance of my son Greg. How do you know him? And isn't it *Father* Chet now?"

"It sure is, sir. I mean, it sure is Father Chet, and we grew up in New Jersey." *Why do I keep calling him sir?* "I guess you could say we're best friends."

This news seemed to please Joanie's dad.

Probably thinks I'm okay if I'm friends with a priest. If only he knew the hell Chet and I used to raise back before Chet got religion. If he only knew what I did with his daughter last night!

Nathan felt the blush coming to his cheeks. He looked at Wheat and suddenly realized that perhaps this old guy was well aware of Chet's not-so-priestly habits during Chet's undergraduate days. It was hard for Nathan to decipher Tom Wheat's gaze. He suddenly felt ashamed.

Wheat looked at his watch, then at Joanie. "Look, sweetheart, I'm headed over to Mass at the Crypt." The Crypt was a chapel in the basement of Sacred Heart Basilica, the main church on the campus. "Would you like to join me, Nathan? You're both welcome to have lunch with me afterward. That is, of course, if you're free."

Nathaniel Payne, who hadn't set foot in a Catholic church since seventh grade, looked at Joanie Wheat and quickly decided she still had some of *him* in her possession. He could even endure a Catholic Mass to be next to her for a little while longer. Deciding quickly, Nathan flashed his most winning smile at Professor Wheat.

"I'd love to go! That is, if you don't mind, sir. I'm free all day."

Wheat looked at his daughter, silently asking, *"Do you mind?"*

Men, Joanie thought, *they always dominate conversation.*

Then she looked at Nathan. *I'll give you one Mass and one lunch, Mister.*

"Then let's go," she said somewhat unenthusiastically.

Nathan and the Wheats left the watchful eye of Father Sorin and walked across the South Quad toward Sacred Heart Basilica.

3

Sunday Morning
8 October
Chicago, Illinois

A thin, bushy-haired Irishman wearing a Roman collar and a black cotton London Fog windbreaker walked into the coffee-house next to Leona's Pizza on Sheridan.

Father Chet found an empty table next to the window. It was another cloudy, windy day in Chicago, but not as cold as it looked. Nevertheless, it was good to get out of the wind. He remembered how beautiful Becky was and how she brushed off his attempts at small talk. Chet was a good priest—and he was a chaste man after long, hard years of practicing the virtue of chastity upon entering the seminary at Seton Hall University. But he was still human. Chet said a quick prayer asking Mary to help him remain chaste in mind and action during his meeting with Rebecca Macadam.

Praying about her reminded him of Nathan, who had been more than a little drunk while hanging all over Professor Wheat's daughter, Joanie. Chet hadn't seen Joanie Wheat in years, and hadn't known her well during his undergraduate days at Notre Dame. He had been surprised to see her at Nathan's party. She had not struck him as the wild kind of girl when he was at Notre Dame. He had partied pretty hard with her older brother, Greg Wheat, who was now a happily married lawyer in North Caldwell, New Jersey, not far from Chet's current parish.

Out of long habit, Father Chet added a short prayer for Nathan, too. Chet didn't know it, but at this very moment,

Nathan was sitting in his Mustang at Notre Dame, deciding whether or not to go after Joanie Wheat.

During his college years, and before he rediscovered his faith, Chet had not been an angel with the ladies by any stretch of the imagination, although he had never been as wild as Nathan. Chet was somewhat uncomfortable meeting alone with a woman as pretty as Becky.

Pretty is not the right word for her. Her beauty transcends mere prettiness. In fact, at the party her beauty had reminded him of her Maker. *If she's made in the image and likeness of God, then I can hardly wait to meet God.*

The priest reminded himself how forlorn she had seemed at the party last night and on the phone this morning.

He was only thirty-one but he had been a priest for over four years and had come to trust his instincts about people. He could intuit when a person needed a word of encouragement or a shoulder to cry on. At the party Chet knew in his bones that Becky was hurting. Chet believed in the gifts of the Holy Spirit, one of which was called the gift of counsel—the ability to give the right advice to those in need. He was prepared to exercise that gift now.

He spotted Becky walking down the sidewalk toward the door. Her unique beauty and stark sadness reminded him of a song, and then, the Pieta. He said another quick prayer, this time to Saint Anthony of Padua.

Help me find the patience to listen. Help me find the right words to say.

Father Chet stood up as she approached his table. She had a strong, athletic gait. He pulled a chair out for her.

Becky smiled wanly. "My, my, aren't you a gentleman!"

He laughed good-naturedly. "Sorry. It's the way my parents raised me and my three older brothers. My mom was afraid that four Irish boys growing up together would turn out to be oafs, so she emphasized common courtesy."

"Don't get me wrong. I like it," Becky protested.

There was a long pause. A waiter came and took their orders. Both preferred regular coffee, black.

"So how do you know Nathan Payne?" Father Chet asked.

"A girl who works at my advertising agency who used to work at Nathan's brokerage firm introduced us. I don't know him very well, really. I gather he's quite a lady killer. Tell me, Father," she emphasized the last word, arching an eyebrow, "how do *you* come to know the infamous Nathan Payne?"

This brought a smile to Father Chet's face.

"We go back to first grade, first day of school. He moved to Chicago in seventh grade. We were best friends in New Jersey. Nathan was like an extra brother in my family." Chet thought of Nathan's dad, Harrison "Harry" Payne, and the elder Payne's criminal conviction and subsequent death.

"We raised hell together in college. I went to Notre Dame and he went to Illinois. I spend a vacation week with him every year. I don't seem to have much effect on his, shall we say, bad habits."

I'm talking too much. Ask a question, Sigmund.

But no question came to him.

They both sipped coffee during a long silence. Becky was obviously uncomfortable now that their only common thread, Nathan Payne, was out of the way. Chet believed in quick prayers and prayed one. Two words. *Saint Anthony!*

"Look," he said, "sometimes it helps to just start."

Rebecca Macadam's pleasant smile died. Tears welled up in her eyes. She dropped her gaze, hugged herself with her arms, and let out a small, low sob. Her shoulders shook. Chet was now being guided by the Holy Spirit but he was too concerned for Becky to notice. He quickly made up his mind.

"This isn't the place," he whispered. "Let's get out of here. Get some fresh air."

He threw a five dollar bill on the table and helped her out of her seat, gently but firmly holding her shoulders as he led her out the door.

They walked toward the beach on the lake, a block away, and then right up to the water's edge. He stood back from her and turned toward the majestic Chicago skyline to the south, trying not to hear her gulping sobs over the brisk wind. True to his nature, he kept praying.

✟ ✟ ✟

Though it seemed much longer to both of them, it was only a few minutes before Becky stopped crying. She turned to him with the look of a child. Chet knew she was ready to unload her cross.

On whom is it better to unload a cross than a priest, another Christ? he thought. *The cry was good for her.*

Again, following his instincts, he took a gamble.

"You're pregnant," he said evenly. There was no condemnation in his voice. It was a statement of fact.

Their eyes met. She nodded.

I'm all ears. I'm all ears, Chet repeated to himself.

Father Chet Sullivan, who had come to Chicago to relax on vacation with an old friend, was poised to fulfill his priestly vocation as best he could.

"He…Sam…my former boyfriend…wanted to kill it," she began.

And then it all came out. They walked on the beach as she poured out her troubles. She surprised herself with her candor. Somehow it was easier to be frank with this stranger, this *priest,* than with herself.

Father Chet said little. A nod here and there. Gently asking an incisive question at just the right moment. He avoided physical contact, knowing that it was not what she needed. He was good at his job, although he did not consider his work a job. It was his calling, his vocation, his life.

When she was done, Chet gently invited Becky to follow him, "Come with me. I want to show you something."

✟ ✟ ✟

They got off the elevated train (called the "El" locally) and ascended the steps to State Street. The wind had died down and it was a short walk south to Madison, then west to Saint Peter's Church. Saint Peter's is run by Franciscans and has confessions and Masses on the hour. It stands between skyscrapers. The three-story Romanesque structure has an enormous crucifix above its bronze front doors.

Becky had not said much on the train or during the walk to the church. When she looked up at the large crucifix above the doors, she thought of her dad. A small smile—the first since she left for coffee with Father Chet—came to her face. Father Chet noticed.

She looks like Grace Kelly with brown eyes. Grace! What a wonderful word!

They entered the church. It was relatively empty. Saint Peter's is most crowded during weekdays, when well-dressed lawyers and unkempt homeless men share its pews. Father Chet led Becky to the tabernacle. He knelt and she knelt next to him. He pulled a well-worn rosary out of his pocket.

"Do you know how to pray this?" he asked.

"I know the Hail Mary and the Our Father," she offered meekly. "It's been so long I've forgotten the rest. I was a child the last time I prayed a Rosary."

"That's okay. Just follow along with me. There's no one grading us."

So as not to disturb the other worshippers, they began to whisper the Rosary.

Becky (who would have confidently bet several million dollars before Father Chet's morning phone call that praying a Rosary would not be one of her activities on this day) found herself thinking of her dad and of her first Holy Communion. On that day, Becky's father had done the same thing as Chet was doing now. Walt Macadam had taken her to church in River Forest early in the morning before breakfast, and had knelt with her before the tabernacle. Becky even remembered the same smell of burning beeswax.

Before that Rosary so many years earlier, her father had said, "If you pray this one Rosary well, Rebecca, Mary will always take care of you and make sure you have what you need when you need it."

"Daddy? Won't you take care of me? Why does Mary have to take care of me?"

Her father laughed his gentle laugh and cradled the side of her face with a rough, warm hand.

"Sweetheart, of course I'll take care of you. Mary just helps me take care of you a little bit better than I could by myself, that's all."

And then Walt Macadam said something that seemed strange, "But if I'm ever not around, Rebecca, I'll be with Mary. And I'll make *certain* she takes care of you in my stead."

The seven-year-old adored her father. She was horrified by the mere thought of her dad not being around, and it showed on her face. "Are you going away now?" little Becky's lower lip trembled as she spoke.

"No. Oh no! I'm right here, Becky. Wild horses couldn't drag me away!"

He pulled her off her feet and hugged her tightly. In Saint Peter's Church, almost twenty years later, Becky remembered the smell of 'Lectric Shave on his cheeks.

Her father had leaned back slightly. Her nose was an inch away from his. He added with mock gravity, "Wild *mice* couldn't drag me away!"

Rebecca giggled at the thought of tiny mice trying to drag her big strong daddy toward a little mouse hole. Then her father had pulled his well-worn rosary beads out of his pocket...

✛ ✛ ✛

After the Rosary, Father Chet asked Rebecca if she wished to go to confession. He mentioned that other priests were available for confession along the sides of the church.

"What the hell," she said with a smile, "I've gone this far. I might as well go all the way. But only with you. Do they still cut off your fingers if you tell anyone my sins?"

She raised her chin and looked down at his hands as if searching for a missing finger or two.

Father Chet stifled a laugh. "Believe me, Beck, I doubt you'll confess anything I'll remember ten minutes from now. Most confessions are pretty much the same. You're not talking to me, you know. You're whispering into the ear of Christ. He's also got a bad memory when it comes to sins, or I wouldn't be wearing this collar."

She could tell he meant it.

"Afterwards, I'll buy you lunch," he added, unconsciously sweetening the pot. "I'm starved. Then I'll tell you about my own less-than-saintly past if you want. Just don't tell the cops. I'm a wanted man on Rush Street, even today."

She laughed to herself as she pictured Father Chet in his Roman collar in one of the wild nightclubs on Rush Street.

"Shush," he said with a glint in his eye and a mischievous smile. "No laughing in church."

"But you made me!" she whispered back in feigned anger, holding in her laughter this time.

"No excuse," he added with mock solemnity.

His smile is infectious. I can tell why Nathan likes him so much. I can just see those two together. He's so natural. Father Chet is one of the good guys.

Then his demeanor changed. Chet became the Reverend Sullivan. He was serious, yet relaxed at the same time. He gestured for her to wait, then made his way toward the sacristy to borrow a stole and to get a key to a confessional.

Becky waited. The feeling of peace, which had been with her since the beach, grew stronger.

I feel like I've lost twenty pounds in twenty minutes.

She suddenly thought of her baby.

I'll worry about you when you get here, little Cub. Mommy's going to "whisper into the ear of Christ," so let me concentrate on the matter at hand.

4

Sunday Afternoon
8 October
Mishawaka, Indiana

Wheat walked into his den and immediately recognized the name written in his wife's handwriting on the message pad. It was from Karl Slinger of SLG Industries.

Karl Slinger. I just saw him on the cover of Forbes.

Wheat owned stock in SLG. He had read the article with great interest. Wheat dialed the number.

"SLG, may I help you?" The person who answered the phone was obviously a secretary. It surprised Wheat to have a business line answered on Sunday.

These CEO types work brutal hours, apparently even on Sundays, Wheat thought.

"Professor Tom Wheat, returning Karl Slinger's call."

"Professor Wheat?" He could hear the skepticism in the secretary's voice. "Please hold."

Wheat held.

"Wheat? Karl Slinger here." Slinger was famous for skipping social amenities.

"Yes, sir. I gather you're not calling this SLG stockholder for business advice?"

"Call me Karl, or Slinger, Tom. May I call you Tom?"

"Sure. What can I do for you…" Tom hesitated, "…Karl."

"I just finished listening to your tape on Mary for the fourth time. We need to talk."

"Well, I've got time right now. What do you want to know?" Wheat replied. *It's amazing how far and wide these tapes get disseminated. Wonder how Slinger got one?*

"You don't understand. I want to meet you in person. I can be on a plane to South Bend in fifteen minutes. Can I take you to dinner?"

This isn't happening. Wheat made a decision, then spoke, "Not necessary, Karl. I'll let my wife know we're having a guest for dinner. It's about a three hour flight from Salt Lake, isn't it?"

"Less than three hours in my private jet," Slinger replied.

"What kind of bourbon do you drink?"

"How do you know I drink bourbon?"

"I read Forbes. And don't all Marines drink bourbon?"

Slinger laughed heartily.

"So we're both Marines, are we?" Slinger responded. "Semper Fi, Tom."

"Semper Fi," Tom shot back, using the Marine Corps motto, which means Always Faithful.

"I drink Maker's Mark when I can get it," Slinger went on. "Look, we can get acquainted when I arrive at the airport. Can you pick me up?"

Wheat smiled to himself, adding up hours and subtracting for time zones in his head. "Sure. See you at seven, I suppose. You can stay overnight with us, too, if you want. It just so happens I have a case of Maker's Mark in the basement."

"See you at seven, then. Good-bye." Slinger hung up abruptly.

Wheat thought of Joanie. He was still unsettled by the way his daughter had looked at Nathan Payne at lunch when Payne wasn't looking at her.

Something's going on here.

Wheat had mixed emotions about Nathan Payne. At Mass, Wheat was disturbed to notice that neither Payne nor Joanie left the pew to receive Communion. Payne seemed pleasant enough during lunch at the Oak Room, but Joanie had been curiously silent. Wheat had been surprised when Joanie invited Nathan to dinner.

I better tell Anne to put out two extra plates. I wonder what Joanie and Nathan are doing right now?

Tom Wheat had seven children. One girl and six boys. The oldest five were married, scattered around the country with families of their own. Joanie was his second youngest, the apple of his eye, and the one who took most after himself. *Joanie looks like Anne and thinks like me.* She still lived at home along with her brother Denny, who was also single. Tom, who tried his best to let his children make their own way in life, was nevertheless very protective of his strong-willed daughter.

I guess I'll find out more about Payne tonight when Slinger comes to visit. Should be a lively dinner conversation.

Chapter Four

1

Sunday Afternoon
8 October
Chicago, Illinois

After hearing Becky's confession, Father Chet concelebrated the next scheduled Mass at Saint Peter's Church. Then he and Becky took the El back to her neighborhood and went to Leona's Pizza for a late lunch of Chicago-style deep dish pizza. Chet, who was used to thin crust New Jersey pizza, thought Chicago deep dish was nothing more than a giant lump of hot cheese and crackers. Becky was amused when he ordered *pizza pie,* and figured it was a New Jersey colloquialism.

During the meal, he related stories of growing up in New Jersey with three older brothers in a close knit Irish family. Using properly circumspect language, he told her of his reckless days with Nathan. It was clear that Chet had not been nearly as wild as his friend. Becky listened quietly and showed little sign of shock.

After his second slice he leaned back and lit a cigarette. He was working on his third beer.

Saving souls always works up my thirst. Chet held his liquor well, befitting an Irishman, and was just starting to feel the effects of his beer.

"I didn't figure you for a smoker—are priests allowed to smoke?" she asked quite seriously.

"Look, we're human like everyone else. Pinch me and I feel pain. Cut me and I bleed. Stress me out and I grab a smoke. It's one of the few vices I allow myself. Another legacy of hanging out with Nathan Payne, Hedonist Extraordinaire." He laughed. Then he added in a deep voice, "Chet Sullivan, Patron Saint of Marlboro Lights."

They both laughed.

Then Becky asked the question she had wanted to ask since the party on the night before, which seemed like a year ago.

"How did a guy like you ever end up becoming a priest, for godsakes?"

"For *Christ's* sake." He arched his eyebrows. "I owe it to a guy named Joe Jackson and to my brother, Jimbo—that's what everyone calls him. He's the oldest."

"Okay. I'll bite. Tell me more, O Great Storyteller!"

Ignoring her friendly barb, he continued, "My mother and father were great parents, and very devout. They gave everything they had for me and my brothers, and sacrificed to send us to Catholic schools. Dad was a teacher and my mom worked extra jobs in convenience stores to help put us through college. They were so proud when I got into Notre Dame.

"But I don't think my folks realized how very little of the Catholic faith was taught in the Catholic schools we went to. I mean, did you really learn anything substantial about the faith in your grammar school, Beck?"

"Not that I can think of," she replied. "I remember drawing pictures of Jesus in religion class but not much else. I left for public school in fifth grade. CCD classes were pretty boring and I stopped going. My mother didn't care, and by then Daddy had died. He would have made sure I went. Did I tell you he loved to pray the Rosary? I just drifted away and stopped going to Sunday Mass when I went to the University of Chicago."

"Same with me," Chet concurred. "My faith was never, how do you say it, a *priority* for me, even when I was a kid. I didn't take it seriously and just went to Mass because my folks said I had to. I was at Notre Dame for three months before I realized that I wasn't even saying grace before meals anymore. I didn't miss it, and none of the other students seemed to miss it either."

Becky nodded. "I know what you mean."

"And the theology courses I had to take at ND were pretty dull. They mocked Catholicism, and, as I learned later, distorted the true teachings of the faith. Maybe I never had the faith.

"Anyway, to make a long story short, I was more interested in getting drunk with my friends. When I finally got a Smick Chick to sleep with me, well, that was it, I was hooked. I felt a little guilty at first, but the guilt gradually went away with repeated usage, as they say. Besides, even the priests at Notre Dame were all saying that guilt was bad. Just what I needed to hear. I never slept around indiscriminately, but I thought it was okay if I was, quote unquote, 'in love' with the girl. I was a fool." Chet held two fingers up in each hand as he said the words "in love."

"Smick Chick?" Becky looked puzzled.

"Oh, I'm sorry. We called the girls at Saint Mary's College, which is right across the road from Notre Dame, after an acronym based on the initials S-M-C. S-M-C, 'Smick.' Get it?"

Becky nodded.

"Well anyway, Nathan seemed to attract women like flies to honey when we'd 'go hunting' on Rush Street on weekends. I'm not proud of those days. I probably messed up a lot of Becky Macadams in my time. Sex was like a drug. Worse than drugs. Drugs don't get you pregnant." Chet, who had told this story before, paused for effect.

"Then Jimbo showed up and punched me."

Becky was obviously confused.

Chet explained, "My brother James was always very devout, even as a little kid. He was the oldest, and the toughest out of all of us. We called him Jimbo, did I mention that? He used to stick up for me, Mike, Tommy, and even Nathan on the playground. Tough as nails. Joined the Marines after high school. Said Rosaries every day, too. Still does." He paused to take a sip of beer.

Chet went on, "Anyway, you're an only child—"

Suddenly, Becky cut him off. "My mother had herself *spayed!*" she blurted.

For the first time all day, Chet was completely taken aback. It was her tone of voice—the bitterness as well as the crudeness. *Wow, her emotions turn on a dime. She's holding back tears*.

And Becky held back her tears. *I'm not crying again today*, she thought as she gathered herself.

Then she began to explain the reason for her bitterness, "After Mom divorced Daddy for Rich Guy Number One in California—she's on Rich Guy Number Three at the moment in Seattle—I asked her over the phone once why she never had any more kids. Big mistake!

"She told me that she knew Dad would never amount to anything the day she had me, so she asked the doctor to 'spay' her in her stirrups right there on the operating table!"

Strong feeling had crept back into her voice. Chet watched the play of emotions on her face as she fought for and won control of herself.

"Mom said it so matter-of-factly, like she was talking about having her hair done or something. She didn't even know the word 'sterilized' or the phrase 'having your tubes tied.' She never told my dad, who was heartbroken he couldn't have more kids. Mom let him think it was his fault all those years.

"Maybe that's why I had such a strong reaction when Sam suggested an abortion. I thought I was pro-choice until the moment he suggested we 'take care of the problem.' Spayed! Can you believe it?"

"What a cold bitch!" Chet blurted. "Oops! Sorry about the foul language. Too much beer. I didn't mean to judge your mom—it just kind of slipped out."

He looked at her and realized that she had put the words "spay" and "bitch" together and was holding in a laugh. The twinkle in his eyes did them both in and they laughed. And laughed, almost to the point of tears.

"Parents," he said finally.

Of the kids I see back home, how many are messed up by their parents? He pondered the question to himself for a moment. *Most. It's sad. I was lucky I had Mom and Dad. **Blessed** is a better word for it.*

"Anyway," she said, "you were talking about your brother Jimbo."

Father Chet collected his thoughts. "Oh, yeah. Well, you've got to understand that in most families with lots of boys the older brothers always beat on the younger ones. My friends in school used to brag about it. There was this sick notion going around that beating up your little brother was toughening him up or something.

"Well, both my parents would have none of that with me and my brothers. They simply wouldn't allow us to strike each other or there were serious consequences to pay. It sounds contradictory, but hitting my brothers was one of the few offenses that could bring out Dad's belt. I was the youngest, and don't even remember getting hit one time.

"Dad always told us to hit somebody else's brother if we had to hit somebody. After a while, we all took a kind of pride in it. Sullivans Never Hit Sullivans would be the title of the movie if they ever make one about my family."

Becky smiled, and took another sip of wine.

"Like I said, Jimbo wasn't the biggest Sullivan, but he was the toughest. He was ferocious when he played sports. Even the toughest bullies at school were afraid to mess with him. He had a quick temper and two seconds after he lost it, he was as friendly as could be. I think the word I'm looking for here is 'powder keg.' Am I talking too much? We Irishmen are known for running off at the mouth."

Becky vigorously shook her head. "Please, go on!"

"To make a long story short, during my senior year, Jimbo showed up at Notre Dame to visit me one day when he was on leave from the Marines. Man, he looked like he was carved from marble! I remember kidding him about his haircut. Jimbo and I went out drinking on Saturday night with this huge guy named Joe Jackson. Jimbo met Joe while saying a Rosary at the Grotto."

"The Grotto?"

"Right. It's a holy place at Notre Dame. It's an exact repro- duction of the cave in Lourdes, France, where Mary appeared to Saint Bernadette. It's like a shrine, I guess. A few students and Holy Cross brothers say a Rosary there every night after dinner, and I guess that's where Jimbo met Joe."

"Lourdes? Saint Bernadette?" Becky was obviously lost.

"Look, one long-winded story at a time. I'll tell you about Lourdes some other time. I'm almost done with Jimbo's Right Hook. I guess I'm giving away the punch line." He laughed at his bad pun.

Becky squinted her eyes at the priest. Chet continued.

"I'll take you there tomorrow. It's only a couple of hours away and I've got my car. Can you get the day off?"

"I'm off every Monday. I only work four days a week. The agency said it was either that for everyone or layoffs for a fifth of us."

"Great! Then we'll go. I have a feeling we'll run into our old pal Nathan. He didn't answer the phone at his apartment or have anything on his voicemail when I called before this lump of cheese was served."

Becky gave him a look. It was time to finish the story. *She's beautiful. Better take it easy on the beer, Father Stupid Idiot.*

"Okay okay. So I guess *I got drunk* on a Saturday while Jimbo and Joe had a couple of beers. They stared at me like I was the biggest jerk in the world, which of course I was. The next morning, when Jimbo tried to wake me up to go to Mass, I told him to, uh, 'go away,' but in less gentlemanly terms.

"He grabbed me by the collar, lifted me out of bed, and I swear on my sainted mother's grave—by the way, Mom is alive and well—he lifted me up in the air over his head—and

I'm bigger than he is—with *one* hand, his left, and hit me with a tremendous right hook."

Becky winced.

"Let me just say, this particular treatment by my dear brother James did *not* help my hangover. Knocked me out cold, as a matter of fact."

Becky interrupted, "Why do I get the feeling you've told this story before?"

"It's probably the rehearsed punch lines. Do you mind?"

"Not at all. Priestly violence fascinates me," she quipped.

"He woke me up by lighting his Bic under my ear. He crouched down and looked at me and said quite evenly, 'Idiot brother, I'm only gonna say this one time, so listen carefully. You're going to get your butt cleaned up and dressed up and you're going to Mass with Joe here. Joe is going to make sure you get your sorry butt to confession tomorrow after I leave. And you're never going to miss Mass again. I know you've been drinking and whoring for the last three years like a friggin' moron and you don't realize it, but Mom knows too, and you're breaking her heart.'

"'I've got more important things to do than worry about whether or not you're going to hell. Yes, hell. No, repeat, *no* brother of mine will go to hell, and you can be sure as cotton each spring that you will not, repeat, *not* continue to break Mom's heart or I'll come back here and break both your arms next time. This Catholic stuff is all true, and you know it. Grow up, little brother.' Then Jimbo got up and wiped his hands like he had just cleaned up a pile of dog crap.

"'Sorry I had to hit you, little brother, but you needed it. Joe, get this sorry excuse for a Sullivan ready for Mass. I've got to get out of this dump. I'm so disgusted I can't stand to even look at him.'

"With that, Jimbo left. I looked up through bleary eyes at Joe Jackson, who is over six-foot-six. He simply looked at me and said in that soft voice of his, 'Let's go.'

"It was the first and last time any one of my brothers ever struck me. I didn't see my brother at Mass that morning. At

Christmas break two months later, back in New Jersey, he treated me as pleasant as could be the whole time and never said a word. By then, I was back to the sacraments, and good friends with Joe Jackson, who is as wild about Catholicism as Nathan is about partying. Sometimes I wonder if Jimbo made one of his little motivational visits on Tommy and Mike, because they're both pretty solid when it comes to the faith. I'm too embarrassed to ask them.

"After Mass the day Jimbo hit me, Joe asked if I had ever thought about being a priest. I told him no, but that I would. Next thing you know, I'm in the seminarian program at Seton Hall. And now you know the rest of the story." Father Chet intoned the last sentence like Paul Harvey, the famous radio personality.

"And what's Jimbo up to these days?" Becky asked as she took another sip of her wine. Then she rested her elbows on the table and put her chin in her hands.

"Still a Marine, an officer. Married. Lives in Virginia. He has three incredibly cute and incredibly aggressive boys. His wife Doris is a saint—and just as tough as Jimbo."

"Maybe you should have flown Jimbo in this morning to whack me. It would've saved us some time," she suggested in such a serious tone that Chet couldn't tell if she was kidding or not. *If she is kidding,* Chet thought with admiration, *then she's real good at it.* He decided to play it straight—just to be safe.

"Never crossed my mind. Not my style, though I often think the Jimbo Sullivan Catechetical Method might help Nathan Payne." He could now tell by the faint gleam in her eye that she *had* been kidding. "Later I asked Jimbo what made him do that to me. He told me a story about the great French advocate of the Rosary, Saint Louis Marie Grignion DeMontfort, who preached in the early 1700s—"

"—I can hear another story coming, Father Chet. You Irish priests are full of great stories. Go on, tell me about Saint Louis Greenwhatever de Rochefort."

"Grignion DeMontfort," Chet corrected, chagrined. Becky caught on quickly to his introductions. Not for the first time did he note that there was a pretty sharp "somebody" living in the lovely house before him. Intelligence added to her beauty. *Old Father Duffy was right!*

He cleared his throat and took a sip of beer.

"Saint Louis used to walk from town to town in rags, preaching the faith and teaching people about the Rosary. He was barefoot half the time, and didn't carry any money. He relied on God to provide his meals, if he ate any at all, through the generosity of the people he met. Sometimes I wonder if I shouldn't do the same myself."

"Hey, I'm buying! This is the nineties, you know. Besides, I make more money than you do," Becky interrupted genially.

"You don't have to do that," Chet retreated quickly. "I wasn't hinting that you should buy, I'm sorry. We'll split it. Besides, I'm on vacation."

He paused. "Hey, quit distracting me when I'm regaling you with my fascinating stories!"

"Pardon me, Hans Christian Andersen." She gave him a tiny pout, rolling her eyes as she pretended to be mollified by his lighthearted rebuke.

Chet continued, warming to one of his favorite tales.

"Anyway, one night DeMontfort got into a little village and started preaching in the town square. Back then, the towns weren't that big, and everybody showed up for a preacher. It was like going to the movies.

"Turns out there's a saloon just off to the side of the square with some tables outside, and some drunks were loudly and viciously catcalling DeMontfort as he tried to preach. Saint Louis ignored them as the townsfolk whispered to each other about the discipline and patience of the holy man from Montfort, who had been commissioned by the pope himself to be an apostolic preacher! A lesser man would get angry, they said, nodding to each other.

"So DeMontfort finishes his sermon. He puts down his Bible, and calmly walks over to the saloon. He politely asks the gentlemen to stand, and then he commenced to beat the living tar out of each one of them!

"The next day, the penitent hecklers show up in bandages to hear him preach, and not a peep came out of them. So there you have it, the original Jimbo Sullivan Right Hook Story."

Becky had obviously enjoyed it, and had laughed delightedly at the part where DeMontfort hit the drunken men. She lit a cigarette, took a puff, and raised her wine glass.

"You know what, Father Chester Sullivan?"

"Whatever may it be, Miss Rebecca Macadam?" Their eyes met. They shared wry smiles.

She clinked his glass.

"I think tonight might be the start of a long and satisfying friendship. You remind me of my Daddy the way you make me laugh."

Father Chet blushed innocently.

"Aw shucks, Miss Macadam."

2

Sunday Afternoon
8 October
Notre Dame, Indiana

After lunch at the Oak Room, Joanie surprised Nathan when she told her father that she would like to show Nathan around the campus.

Nathan, who was normally quite self-assured with women, found it hard to make conversation. He debated with himself a dozen times about whether or not it would be safe to take her hand. She was not giving him any physical clues. When she wasn't looking directly at him, Nathan stole glances at her willowy frame and wondered what was the matter with himself.

I've never felt this way before, he thought.

He was terrified that she might abruptly end her tour of the campus and walk away from him forever; he was simultaneously afraid that she *wouldn't* walk away.

He listened to Joanie relate the history of Notre Dame as they strolled about the campus. She seemed to be a walking history book of the place. Nathan soon found out that her six brothers had also attended the university. Faculty members apparently merited steep tuition discounts for their children. Joanie had majored in History like her dad.

Half an hour after starting they found themselves in front of Moreau Hall, looking across Saint Joseph Lake at the rearward view of the Golden Dome. An awkward silence ensued.

"I don't know how to say this," he said tentatively. They were both facing the lake, not looking at each other.

"What is it, Nathan?" she asked softly.

"I feel like a hypocrite going to Mass with your dad like that. I'm not a Catholic," he confessed.

"Then how did you know the responses during Mass?" Joanie didn't seem too surprised by his admission.

"I remembered them from grade school. I haven't been to Mass since seventh grade. I have a hard time forgetting things."

She turned to him. "Why are you telling me?"

Although she was obviously no longer angry at him, her strong gaze had a unique effect on him. *She's boring in on me. I can't lie to this girl.*

"Look, Mister," she continued, "if there's ever going to be anything between us, and I am definitely *not* saying there is, you're going to have to learn to level with me."

Her tone was not unkind. But the determination in her voice was still there.

"Okay," he replied. *She wins,* he thought. "What do you want to know, Joanie?"

"Let me lay out my assumptions first, okay?" she requested politely with a hint of excitement in her voice.

"Shoot." *Assumptions, what assumptions?*

"First," she continued, "I assume what we did together last night, even if we didn't, uh, 'go all the way'—to use the popular phrase—was not a new thing for you. I'm probably one of a long line of Nathan Payne's paper dolls. I also assume that you were not so drunk that you couldn't have stopped yourself. You could have—before I stopped us. If there is ever going to be any future for us, that kind of thing has got to stop. Or else I'm going to walk away and leave you right here to cry in the lake. What I want to know is why."

"Why what?" Nathan stalled. *Boy, she's got me pegged.*

"You know what I'm talking about, Mister Payne."

There's that look of hers again, he thought.

"The truth is," he paused. "The truth is, I don't know. Sex has always been like, you know, recreation for me." He braced himself for a verbal or physical slap. It didn't come.

"That's better, Nathan," she said kindly. She was smiling. "That's the first real thing I've heard you say all day, or last night, for that matter."

Again, Nathan felt his knees go rubbery. *I'm going to fall down,* he thought.

"That's all for today. You can stop squirming. You look terrible. Are you okay?" Joanie's concern was genuine.

"No, I mean, yes, I'm okay. Can we sit down?"

There was a bench behind them. They sat down. He lit up a smoke. He half-expected a protest to come from her. Most women hated his smoking.

*Then again, Joanie isn't "most women," is she? She's— what is she? She's **strong.***

"My turn," she said.

"Your turn?"

"Truth time. Last night was almost my second time. The first and only time was ten years ago when I was sixteen, in high school. The guy was a lot like you—charming, same sad eyes, better looking, and the captain of the football team. I was drunk then, too. I didn't plan on doing what I did—it just kind of happened after the first kiss. I shouldn't have let us get started last night, either."

Nathan said nothing. He was stunned, not at her revelation, but at her tone. *Ten years? I didn't know women like Joanie still existed. She's so different. I've never met such an honest person.*

She continued, "I guess I was rebelling against my strict upbringing. I was curious and it seemed like all my classmates had done it. The next morning, I realized that it was a mistake—no, that *I had made* a mistake. I went to confession and put it behind me. Half the problem was the alcohol. I'm a lightweight, really. My dad once told me that the real sin sometimes is letting yourself get drunk, because you impair your ability to make a moral decision after you're wasted.

"I vowed never to let myself, uh, be compromised, ever again. Until I got married, of course. And it hasn't been hard. Until I saw you standing next to Chet Sullivan last night."

She looked at him tenderly.

I want to look into those eyes for the rest of my life, Nathan thought, light-headed. He was amazed by his own thoughts.

"I guess the real reason why we're sitting here under the shadow of the dome, Nathan, is that last night wasn't all your fault. I knew you were the man for me the moment I laid eyes on you. I can't describe it. I guess I ignored all the signs that you are the kind of man you are because you were friends with Chet—it's so hard to think of him as *Father* Chet!—and because I was so comfortable with you. I was hoping against hope. You've been a long time coming, Mister. All the other men in my life just couldn't cut it. Not that there've been all that many."

He looked at her with a cocked head and a confused look.

"I'm getting to the point," she continued. "The point is, I'm pretty sure I *let myself* drink too much last night. I've got to take some of the responsibility. You know the old saying, It takes two to tango. In the same way, I let you huddle me into your car afterwards and drive me here. If I was so sure you were like all the others, I wouldn't have done that. If I wanted to be a hypocrite, I could have let you go on your merry way after lunch today and blamed last night on you and the booze."

"Why didn't you?"

"It wouldn't be right." She looked down briefly. "At least you were living according to your libertine principles. I'm sorry."

"Don't be sorry. You're so honest with yourself, Joanie. I wish I could be more like that," he heard himself saying. Then he added, "What does libertine mean?"

She laughed to herself.

"It means that seeking pleasure is the highest goal of living. A Roman coined the term, I think."

Joanie looked toward the dome. Her smile faded. Nathan noticed a line form between her eyebrows.

"Nathan, we have to set two ground rules. If you agree to them, we can see each other. If not, forget it. I'm not making any promises, mind you. I just want to start off with a clean slate. Like last night never happened."

"What are the rules?" Nathan asked, curious and terrified at the same time. *I've never been much for anyone's rules except my own.* The image of Sister Lardo suddenly popped into his head. *Where does she keep coming from?* He blinked and focused on Joanie again.

Joanie was now looking at him. *It's like she knew I was daydreaming and is waiting patiently for me to finish with my thoughts.*

"First, what happened last night can't happen again, or I might not be able to stop myself," she told him, rather tenderly. "Ever. I wouldn't be able to live with myself, and I know this might sound crazy, but I don't believe I would ever get to really know you if we slept with each other. We are going to have to follow the Tom Wheat Rule for what's permissible during courtship, as my father terms it."

"And what is the Tom Wheat Rule?" Now Nathan was very curious. And to his own surprise, willing to obey this rule before he heard it.

"Don't kiss anyone you wouldn't marry the next day." She squinted at him, waiting.

"Huh?"

"It means no physical affection except holding hands until we're engaged. And I'm not saying we're engaged or anywhere near it! And then, after we're engaged, nothing more than a kiss like you'd give your mom."

When Joanie said *mom* Nathan's eyes clouded over, which she mistook for disagreement.

"Too tough for you, Mister?" she asked.

"No! Not at all!" For what seemed like the hundredth time today, Nathan surprised himself.

"Then what is it?" she asked sweetly, taking his hand into her own.

"I never kissed my mom," he said as much to himself as to her. Nathan didn't often think about his mother. It was obviously painful for him to even speak about her.

My God, he's on the verge of tears! she thought. *What kind of childhood did you have, Nathan Payne?*

Automatically, she started praying a Hail Mary for him.

"Look, I don't want to talk about her," he said finally, but not defensively. "Not today. Maybe later. Too much is happening to me today. Inside me. I haven't slept in two days, and to tell you the truth, you're blowing me away."

He took a deep breath and fell silent. She waited patiently. The late afternoon sun was beginning its slow slide toward the horizon, glimmering off the statue on the dome. The wind was still. A perfect reflection of Mary was on the lake in front of them.

A long silence ensued. Nathan broke it, "I don't understand the Tom Wheat Rule, but I'm willing to go along with it if that's what you want, Joanie."

She could tell he meant it.

"What's rule number two?" he asked tentatively.

"I don't expect you to understand this one either, Nathan."

For the first time she was a little hesitant.

"I'm a big boy, Joanie. What is it? Do I have to do push-ups in my skivvies in front of the football team while humming the fight song?" Nathan hummed the first bar of Notre Dame's famous fight song.

Joanie did not quite laugh at his forced joke, but she did smile. She broke her grip and tapped him on the thigh with a mock slap. "No, it's actually easier than that and harder at the same time," she answered. She decided to take a plunge. "I want you to seriously consider practicing your faith again. You *are* a Catholic, by the way. You were baptized and probably confirmed. You just don't practice it. I could never get serious with a non-practicing Catholic. Like I said, I don't expect you to understand."

"Don't worry about that," he said. "Go on."

"My dad calls it Pascal's Wager. Ever heard of it?"

"Yeah," he replied. Now Joanie was surprised.

"Chet told me about it," he explained.

"Really?" *This is too good to be true,* she thought.

"Yeah, he's been working on me since he got religion when his brother whaled on him and literally knocked him back into the Church. I have to admit, Chet's one hell of a lot more subtle than you are. About six years ago he gave me a book by Blaise Pascal called *Pensées.* I think it means—"

"—Thoughts," she finished for him.

"Yeah, that's it. I guess old Chetmeister was using reverse psychology on me. I don't read much. I've always been a numbers man, good at math and science. When he gave me the book, I thought he figured I'd never read it, and I read it just to spite him, you know, because I figured *he figured* I'd never read it. He's pretty wily. Never trust an Irishman with a glint in his eye. Anyway, I read it. Most of the philosophical stuff went over my head. Pascal was a brilliant mathematician; I studied some of his math stuff at Illinois, believe it or not.

"I guess I rushed through it—but I remember the Wager. 'Infinite reward is worth a finite wager.' Made sense. But I didn't take old Blaise up on the offer. Funny name for a guy,

Blaise. Reminded me of hell. You know, blazing fires of hell and all that."

"How do you possibly remember the exact words from something you rushed through years ago?" Joanie was more than a little amazed—as if she had just found gold in the backyard creek—by Nathan's memory, and because he knew about Pascal's Wager.

"I can't *not* remember most things," he admitted sheepishly. He looked embarrassed, as if an old secret was out in the open. Many extremely intelligent people hide their intelligence from the world; Nathan was no exception. Smart kids got beat up on the playground.

"Anyway. I'll take up the Wager. I understand it. It's mathematical. Let's see: because you're a practicing Catholic and you're not going to change, you're dead certain you will only get serious with a 'real' Catholic. You want to find out if I'll like being a real Catholic, and the only way to find out is for me to actually do it, not to think about doing it. And I *was* baptized Catholic. Is that how it works?"

"Exactly."

"Okay. I'll have to trust you about the no kissing until we get…" He stopped himself before saying the dreaded word.

"Nathan, darling, the word is *engaged.*"

The determined look was back, although her tone had been loving.

Did she just call me darling? Nathan's stomach did another flip flop. It was not an unpleasant feeling. As a matter of fact, it felt pretty good.

There's no fooling around with Miss Right-to-the-Point. And I like it. Nathan felt a freedom to speak he hadn't felt in a long time. *Admit it, Nathan my boy, you've **never** felt the freedom to talk openly to a woman—**with** a woman. Ever.*

"Can I say something, Joanie?"

She nodded. She took his hand again, holding her breath, waiting for his answer.

"I've never talked to someone who just comes right out and says things the way you do. It's unsettling, but I like it. I don't want to think about..." he hesitated, then smiled, "...marriage, at least not right now, but..." he hesitated again, but not as long this time, "...but I can't stand the thought of having you more than twenty yards away from me. Just *thinking* about driving back to Chicago tonight and leaving you here is making me crazy."

Their eyes met. Tears welled up in Joanie's eyes. Nathan was breathing hard again. The rubbery sensation was back in his legs.

"Don't get mushy on me, Nathan Payne." She laughed and gave out a sob at the same time. He held her, and she let him.

They were both trembling. It was the first time either of them had fallen in love.

Nathan realized that it was the first time he had held anyone (or been held) without sex crossing his mind since— since, well, Babsie, his grandmother, had held him as a child.

What's happening to me? he thought, not for the first time during this strange and wonderful day.

Then, as he held her, he decided to tell her the truth. It seemed so refreshing after living outside of either truth or lies for so long.

I'm in a new universe. What did she call it? Libertine? I was in the Libertine Universe. I'm in the Moral Universe now. This is where Joanie lives. This is where Professor Wheat lives. So this is where Chet lives!

The unshakable feeling that he was breathing new air in a new world was palpable. *Morality is a place, not an idea. Perhaps it's just my mathematical mind-set.*

And so he told her the truth. With her arms still holding him, he pulled away slightly and cradled her porcelain cheeks in his strong hands. He felt her tears on his fingers. He searched to meet her eyes, but Joanie was looking down. He saw her delicate features and eyelids instead.

"Joanie?" he whispered.

"Yes, darling?" she replied quietly as she looked up to him.

"I don't know if I can do it, sweetheart. You know, follow your rules. But I promise that I will try my best. I can try hard. Harder than you know, maybe. Is that good enough for you?"

She could see that he was afraid that she might say *No*. That she could break him like a twig. She was, after all, a very practical woman. Her answer was firm.

"Yes, Mister. Your best is enough for me. Just try. It's a wager, remember. I can't force you to do anything. I'm putting my money on Blaise Pascal." And not for the first time, Joanie surprised Nathan (although he later wondered why what she said should be a surprise, given her background).

"I'll pray for you, Nathan."

"You and Father Chet both. Now I'm outnumbered."

For a long while they embraced in the orange light of the late afternoon sun on the clear fall day at the University of Notre Dame. As they walked in silence the long way around Saint Joseph Lake, they instinctively grasped for each other's hand. It was almost time for dinner at Tom Wheat's house, where Karl Slinger was due to arrive in less than an hour.

Somewhere, unknown to either Nathan or Joanie, a nun was smiling.

3

The Beatific Vision, Heaven

"Somewhere" was in the light-soaked bath of the Beatific Vision—the very Mind of God, in heaven. It was here that Sister Leonardo Mary MacEvoy, baptized Kathleen Marie MacEvoy by her parents in 1933, was permitted to see and hear the conversations of Nathaniel Payne and Joanie Wheat.

Kathleen MacEvoy had been given the name Leonardo Mary by her superior, Sister Anthony Mary, who had been a big fan of Leonardo da Vinci when Kathleen joined the Dominican Sisters of Jersey City.

Kathleen was the youngest of nine children and raised by devout parents. She had first considered becoming a nun in fourth grade. By her sophomore year in high school she realized that she was never going to be elected Queen of the Prom. She was plain and had a weight problem, despite her father's insistence that she was the most beautiful girl in the world.

She didn't hold it against her father—or God, for that matter—that she had not been created physically beautiful. She took it as a concrete sign from God that her desire to be like her Dominican teachers was not merely a figment of her active imagination. This didn't mean that she thought all homely women should be nuns, or that all beautiful women should not be nuns.

She had little trouble convincing the Dominicans to let her drop out of Bishop Walsh High School to enter the convent before her senior year.

For Sister Leonardo, a fact was a fact. Her homeliness and girth would be an asset to living the life of chastity required of the Brides of Christ. She was good at math. She was soon guided by her spiritual director into teaching. She turned out to be an excellent teacher with a knack for administration. Living the Rule of Saint Dominic came easily to her; the years at Our Lady of Lourdes flew by much too quickly. She loved being a nun!

Leukemia eventually killed her. It was in her bones. Before the cancer started to eat away her organs, her five-foot frame had supported over two hundred and fifty pounds. The sturdy nun withstood six long months of suffering before death overtook her.

In purgatory (where Catholics believe the temporal punishment due to sin is measured out in the burning love of the infinite Mercy of God), Sister rejoiced that the cancer had taken so long because it mitigated her time there. (If you could call it "time," for in purgatory and heaven—and in hell, for that matter—there is no human conception of time.) The many sincere prayers of her fellow Dominicans had also helped Sister Leonardo enter heaven sooner.

Not much is known of the Beatific Vision, though one can certainly discover a few things about it in the great mystical works of Saint Teresa of Avila and others. What *is* known is that the Beatific Vision is where the All Knowing Father permits human souls in heaven to "see" tiny portions of the things and events He sees.

And Sister Leonardo was keenly interested in the life and destiny of Nathan Payne. Of course, she had taken an interest in the shy boy when he was her student at Our Lady of Lourdes. She knew all about Nathan's tragic family life, his ne'er-do-well father, and the stratospheric scores he achieved on his second grade IQ test. When he was in first grade, he reminded the good sister of herself. She had always regretted letting herself lose track of him after his sudden move to Illinois, caught up as she was with the lives of hundreds of other children, many of whom needed help every bit as much as Nathan had.

On earth she had prayed for him whenever she was reminded of him (as she often was by other dysfunctional children, as they became known later in her career). She had even felt drawn during her ordeal with cancer to offer her sufferings for the mathematical genius whom she had tutored two decades earlier.

After purgatory, she was finally brought to heaven by the Blessed Mother herself and by Saint Dominic (or at least by Saint Dominic's soul, for very few are reunited with their bodies in heaven. Jesus, who ascended to heaven, and Mary, who was assumed by Jesus into heaven, are notable exceptions. It has long been taught—by Saint Thomas Aquinas, in particular—that a person will not have his soul reunited with his body until the Final Judgment).

Sister Leonardo was pleased beyond comprehension to be given a specific task by the Savior Himself regarding the fate of one Nathaniel Payne. She was not permitted, however, to see his final destiny.

In fact, her work with Nathan during her time on earth had been part of the Divine Plan. She had cooperated with that plan on earth and now she had merited further work in this same plan in heaven. She was allowed to see him (and to know his thoughts) during his brief period of decision as Joanie Wheat was storming away from him while he sat in his Mustang in the parking lot of the Morris Inn.

It was revealed to Sister Leonardo that the Infinite Wisdom had deigned to use *her* voice, which was one of the few feminine voices Nathan had ever trusted, to nudge him toward Joanie Wheat. Sister Leonardo was also aware of at least four other creatures who were working with Nathan during his moment of decision—the Mother of God, Nathan's guardian angel, a priest in Chicago, and Nathan's grandmother.

Awe and other human emotions are not obliterated in the Beatific Vision. She was ardently hoping that Nathan would make the right decision, and simultaneously in awe that God was able to help the confused young man make his decision without ever taking away his free will.

After all, during his moment of decision, Nathan *could* still have decided to drive away and leave Joanie Wheat behind, even after God spoke to him using Sister Leonardo as a conduit of grace. In fact, Sister Leonardo was absolutely certain that the reason why God chose to *not* directly reveal His Divine Self to Nathan was precisely to protect Nathan's free will. In this sense, God is like electricity. Dealing directly with God would have overloaded Nathan. That is the reason why Moses' face changed so dramatically after he saw God on Mount Sinai. Sister Leonardo was being used as a circuit of God's grace—much as people use electrical circuits to down-size current to make it safe for appliances. Nathan's decision to pursue Joanie Wheat was as perfectly and purely free as any other decision in his life. But he did have some extra encouragement before making it.

Opinions are also allowed in heaven. Sister Leonardo was of the opinion that the tide was turned when the casual prayer of one Reverend William Chester Sullivan entered the Beatific

Vision in which she had been participating. Father Chet was also one of her former students, and he had also benefited from Sister's heavenly role as one of God's vast number of circuits.

Because the Divine Wisdom had decided to wipe her voice from Nathan's memory as mysteriously as He had allowed her voice to be used, Nathan would never know of Sister Leonardo's role. Neither would Father Chet, stranded as he was in the murky darkness of his finite body in a Chicago coffee shop.

All lives are passion plays. Sister Leonardo Mary, baptized Kathleen Marie MacEvoy in 1933, had lived her own passion play, and was now enjoying the fruits of her courageous life on earth. She was eager to continue to play a role in Nathan's passion play. And so, as she watched Nathan and Joanie holding hands as they drove to Professor Wheat's home, Sister Leonardo did so with a beatific smile!

Chapter Five

1

Saturday Morning
7 October
Detroit Metropolitan Airport
Wayne, Michigan

He had come to the end of one of his country-hopping tours
to the four corners of the earth. In a sense it was his earth.
This was a business trip. Detroit was the last leg on a tour
that had brought him to Russia, Japan, and then Los Angeles.
Detroit was just a stopover—no big crowds were scheduled
to see him here. He would fly back to Rome this morning.

Pope Patrick, formerly Angus Cardinal O'Hara of Dublin,
descended the steps of the TWA 747 toward the tarmac. Behind the jet, the engine of one of those odd-looking, low
slung refueling trucks backfired, sounding much like a gunshot. Everyone in the entourage and the crowd ducked; a
woman screamed. Police and secret service agents rushed
toward the poor mechanic at the fuel truck, who limply held
up his specialized wrench, which he had been using to open
the fuel cap. A plainclothes Secret Service agent pulled the
radio in the lapel of his jacket toward his mouth.

*"This is Agent One! False alarm! Repeat! False Alarm!
Report Keyholder's status. Check in Three, over."*

Keyholder was the radio code name for Pope Patrick.

*"Agent One, this is Agent Three, Keyholder is okay. He's
laughing, as a matter of fact. Repeat, Keyholder okay. Copy?"*

"Copy that, Three. Condition Green. Resume agenda. Laughing? Keep the editorials off the security line. Over."

Agent One was a stickler for details, which was one of the reasons why he was Agent One, Officer-in-Charge.

"Roger, One. Over and out."

Agent Three, O'Malley, cleared the line. O'Malley, who was a Catholic American of obvious Irish descent, turned toward the pope and broke one of the unwritten rules of Secret Service agents.

O'Malley smiled.

✚ ✚ ✚

The false gunfire incident didn't make the local news. Individuals in the crowd did go home that evening and remark to their families that the only one who hadn't ducked was the slender, wiry pope. Pope Patrick was used to gunfire, they reasoned.

Pope Patrick, still Angus to his cronies in Dublin and Belfast, was the Cardinal Who United Ireland three years before becoming pope. During the final stages of negotiations he had been shot in the neck by an IRA terrorist who didn't take kindly to the Cardinal of Dublin's efforts to end the Troubles.

Public sympathy built up on both sides of the conflict as the entire world waited for three days to see if the courageous and gregarious cardinal would pull through. He lost three pints of blood but the .22 bullet miraculously missed his spinal cord. He was back negotiating in less than three weeks. His strategy was to concede everything to the Protestants except the necessity for religious freedom and civil rights for Catholics. In exchange, the six northern counties were reunited with the Republic of Ireland, now called the New Republic of Ireland.

In return, the Protestants got a clean slate from the Catholics: governmental appointments, guarantees of rights to lands taken from Catholics centuries earlier, special courts, fairly strong laws to suppress Catholic (and Protestant) terrorist movements, and so on.

Many Catholics were not pleased with the deal. The man in the street didn't seem to be too concerned with the details after the shooting. After a few tense months, the treaty worked. Just like that.

Angus kept the real reason why it worked to himself. He had begun his thirty-year, one-man effort to reunite the Six Counties while he had been a seminarian. Over decades he had developed personal (and often secret) friendships with the most publicly anti-Catholic Protestant leaders. Angus had rarely discussed and never argued religion with them. They knew they could trust Angus. He had even gone as far as donning disguises, visiting the Protestants in secret, and drinking more than one under the table. He sent their children gifts on their birthdays. He called them with condolences when their relatives passed away. More than once he risked his life by attending Protestant funerals.

Angus always avoided publicity. He kept at his project so tenaciously for so many years that hatred melted away in the hearts of Protestants for this one particular Catholic. Some kept their contacts with him simply because he was the only Catholic from the Republic they knew with any degree of intimacy. As he rose in the ranks of the Catholic hierarchy over the decades, it became a kind of badge of political prestige to "know" Angus. It helped that Angus had a lion's share of disarming, devastating Irish charm.

It's hard to hate a man when your twelve-year-old daughter calls him Uncle Angus, Angus told himself.

As he grew older, his position teaching languages at Maynooth Seminary gave him more time to travel. Angus began quiet and secret discussions with a few influential Protestants who had by now become close friends. They were convinced, as was Angus, that if they could get over their personal prejudices, then why couldn't both bleedin' sides settle their differences? It wasn't long before he began to enjoy the company of his sincere Protestant friends more than the

often lax Catholics in the Irish hierarchy. When he became a
cardinal, he convinced his friends to open negotiations with
the Republic of Ireland, Northern Ireland, and England. Unknown to the general public, the pope himself had made a
few calls on Angus's behalf to dignitaries at the highest levels of the governments of all sides.

Every night since his ordination Angus had prayed: *I love
my separated brothers, Mary. Help me love them more.*

Work, prayer, and love were his guiding principles. Reading biographies of great men and women who changed the
course of history convinced him that his personal doubts about
his quixotic quest were a temptation from the evil one. *Great
men all seem ordinary up close, and I'm as ordinary as the
next man. Maybe I don't need to be great to get this done.*

But Angus O'Hara was much more relentless than an ordinary man.

His other secret weapon had been Saint Thérèse of Lisieux,
who is nicknamed the Little Flower by her devotees. He was
born on her feast day, the first of October. His sainted mother
had tutored him in devotion to the precocious French
Carmelite nun who had died in her early twenties in 1897.
Angus's mother had been very devout. Angus's maternal
grandfather had converted to the faith from Presbyterianism,
and had come to Dublin from Belfast to work for the Guinness
Brewery. On his father's side, he was pure Irish. His Scottish
ancestors had been "planted" in Belfast from Scotland by the
English during the days of William of Orange. This may explain part of young Angus's implacable desire to reunite the
two Irelands. It also explains his decidedly Scottish first name.

The Little Flower's intercessory power in heaven was
legendary among Catholics. He decided to become a priest
in eighth grade after reading her autobiography, *The Story of
a Soul.*

When he wasn't on his "commando raids" in Northern
Ireland, Angus spent his vacations visiting Carmelite convents in Ireland, Europe, and the United States. He enlisted
them in his private war to end the war in Northern Ireland.

During his triumphant speech at the signing of the Belfast Treaties, as they became known, he attributed the success not to himself but rather to "the generosity of the Protestants, whom I love as brothers, and to the power of God." Angus presented Thomas Jefferson's Quiet Revolution of 1800 in America, and the more recent bloodless coup in the Philippines, as historical precedents for the rarest of historical rarities: a major transfer of geopolitical power that did not cost lives. Ever the diplomat, and to avoid hurting the sensibilities of his Protestant brethren, Angus left out the part about cloistered Catholic nuns fasting and praying for three consecutive decades for the Troubles to end.

Many Catholics were embittered by the Belfast Treaties, which seemed to greatly favor the Protestants, but no one dared question Cardinal O'Hara's motives after the assassination attempt. One year after the Belfast Treaties, many on both sides were wondering what the centuries-old fuss had been about in the first place. Only time would tell if peace would last. The more strident Protestants and the IRA had vowed to continue terrorist attacks. Cardinal O'Hara kept visiting his Carmelites just to cover his bets. He wasn't one to put faith in man-made treaties. He almost flaunted his now public friendships with Protestant leaders.

Angus never neglected two of his personal passions, namely, the study of languages and contemplative prayer. He prayed at least two hours each day in front of the Blessed Sacrament. On the average, he slept less than four hours a night.

He was not a proud man, and despite his success at moving crowds with his legendary Irish wit and aplomb, he was not comfortable in the spotlight. He was more comfortable working with people one-on-one, and his language studies helped this. His goal was to be able to hear confessions in twenty languages before he died.

To the everlasting shock of his longtime spiritual director, who just happened to be the Bishop of Belfast, Angus still considered himself ordinary. Angus knew that the fruit of his lifelong work came from the power of God's grace to change hearts. He scrupulously avoided the ecclesial politics of the hierarchy in Ireland. He was genuinely surprised when the pope conferred the Office of Cardinal upon him. It never occurred to him that he had taken the same tack in bringing peace to Ireland that Saint Patrick had taken hundreds of years before to convert Ireland to Catholicism; namely, the conversion of leaders' hearts.

In sum, as is often the case for a person who is a saint with a capital *s,* Angus was blissfully unaware that he was one of the greatest saints who ever walked the earth. He was just doing his job the best way he knew how, and his job was to be a priest. He wasn't planning to attend the ceremony to receive the Nobel Peace Prize until the pope himself called him up and ordered him to go to Stockholm.

When Angus returned from Stockholm, he found that his schedule was less hectic. He could now spend a great deal of time visiting the parishes of Dublin. Children ran into the streets to play soccer with the spry cardinal, who still wore the traditional black outfit and Roman collar of a parish priest. Angus still drove his own beat up "commando car," as he called his old Fiat. Several weeks after the Belfast Treaties were signed, it became common knowledge that if you wanted to find Father Angus (as he was still known, despite his title), the last place to look for him was at the chancery.

The pope began to call Angus every month. The cardinal developed a genuine friendship with the Magnificent Pole (as Angus thought of him). Angus spoke passable Polish. Sometimes they spoke in Latin. They often practiced languages while discussing Catholic problems. Angus and the pope were like two steelworkers discussing a mechanical problem at a poorly run factory. Indeed, the "factory" which the pope inherited was in extremely bad shape. And, what the pope related to Angus about Marian apparitions was even more disturbing than the dismal state of the Catholic faithful. When the pope failed to make his regular monthly call, Angus deduced that something was wrong. He read in the papers that the Magnificent Pole had died of mysterious causes, much like his predecessor, but the official word put out by the Vatican bureaucracy was that the pope had succumbed to congestive heart failure. Angus had his doubts, but no proof of a conspiracy.

Three weeks later, Angus Cardinal O'Hara of Dublin was elected as the first Irish pope in history—with most of his votes coming from third world cardinals appointed by the man he succeeded.

Angus soon discovered that most Vatican insiders thought the powerful Cardinal Casino of Milan had been favored to win by a close but comfortable margin, but at the very last moment exactly one dozen cardinals had changed their votes due to the "prompting of the Holy Spirit." According to the grapevine, Casino backers derided them as "the Twelve Apostates." Two hours before the controversial vote, another four Casino backers died on their way to the Vatican in a tragic collision with a busload of German tourists.

There was a strong move by the Casino backers to delay the vote, which was barely defeated. Angus was elected by one vote. No canon lawyer could dispute the validity of the conclave.

Despite the whispers of *confreres* during the dizzying conclave that he was "Number Two" after Casino, Angus was as genuinely surprised as anyone by his elevation to pontifical office.

Angus had thought of just one thing the moment the result of the vote was announced. It was an offhand remark made by his friend, the Magnificent Pole, during one of their monthly phone chats: "I watch what I eat, Angus. I brought my own cooks from Poland."

Angus had the distinct impression during the conversation that the pope had not been speaking about the relative merits of Polish and Italian cuisine, but something sinister.

Within two months of becoming pope, Angus had the Catholic world distracted by his controversial appointments to various posts within the Vatican. Angus was up to his old tricks. In a view he kept to himself, he saw the millennial long Schism between the Roman and Eastern Churches as a problem as scandalous as the Irish Troubles, only writ large.

He began to disappear for days at a time, sometimes in disguise. He began to use his tremendous skills to win over the leaders of the Eastern Orthodox churches. Angus sent letters, notes, and gifts. He scheduled informal, secret meetings. The new pope saw nothing wrong with calling Eastern leaders for advice, which they found refreshing. He found it helpful.

A simple form letter to his Carmelite Army, laser printed on handsome papal stationery, deployed prayer troopers in cloistered battlefronts. He thought peace would take years, even decades, but found his entreaties well received from the word go.

Pope Patrick was just doing his job.

2

Sunday Afternoon
8 October
Michiana Regional Airport
South Bend, Indiana

Tom Wheat waited by the private aircraft gate in the small terminal of Michiana Regional Airport. He had seen the corporate jet with SLG painted on the tail land a few minutes before. A large, powerfully built, bald-headed man who was obviously Karl Slinger, Chairman and CEO of SLG Industries, was heading toward the gate in a golf cart driven by an airport worker.

He doesn't look seventy-four. Must have served in the Pacific during Number Two.

Before the cart reached the ground level gate, Slinger recognized Wheat and gave him a huge smile and a wave.

Slinger leaped off the cart and jogged toward the door carrying a leather overnight bag. He practically ran through the open door toward Wheat.

"You're Wheat, aren't you?" Karl boomed.

"Mr. Slinger, I presume?"

Both men clasped hands in a firm, quick grip.

"Are there any more bags—" Wheat began to inquire.

Slinger cut him off.

"Look, I want to tell you two things. Last night I went to confession for the first time since high school. This morning, I went to Mass for the first time since my mother died ten years ago, and I received Holy Communion for the first time in fifty-four years. My wife Dottie just about had a heart attack! In the last twenty-four hours, I've said my first two Rosaries since I was a little boy. I owe it all to you and to your tape. One of my gardeners left it on the seat of my limousine yesterday morning, can you believe it!"

Slinger let out a laugh so loud that several heads turned in the terminal.

"Welcome back, Karl!" Wheat replied, caught up in Slinger's enthusiasm. The smile on Wheat's face was very wide. *This guy's energy is enormous!* Wheat thought.

"I've got my Caravan right outside. Let's go. My wife Anne has a feast ready. Do you like kielbasa?"

Polish sausage was Slinger's favorite meal. He eyed Wheat suspiciously.

"A calculated guess, Karl. I read Forbes, remember. I feel like I know you. The article mentioned that your dad came to America from Poland—"

Slinger smiled and finished Wheat's sentence, "—and you figured all Polacks love kielbasa. Got it. Actually, my doc tells me to lay off it—bad for the cholesterol." Slinger noticed the concerned look on Wheat's face. "But don't worry, my friend, I'll gladly make an exception on account of your wife's putting herself out like that. Who wants to live forever anyway?"

Both men laughed and headed for Tom Wheat's minivan.

3

Saturday Afternoon
7 October
Rome, Italy

Luigi Cardinal Casino was in a jubilant mood. The flight from
Milan had gone quickly and smoothly. Every dog has his day.
Tomorrow was Luigi's day. He was also in disguise: an Oleg
Casini suit, Gucci shoes, and a fedora angled over the dark
Ray Ban sunglasses. No one glancing at the confident gray-
haired man strolling into the Roman bistro would have recog-
nized Casino as the man who missed being elected pope by
one vote eighteen months earlier.

Casino went to the back of the bistro and sat down in his
private booth. The waiter thought Casino's name was
"Giancarlo Tucci" and had no idea that he was a prince of the
Catholic Church.

The waiter's main concern was that "Tucci" tipped well,
liked expensive brandy, and valued privacy. Within minutes
a tall, thin, handsome, and impeccably dressed man who was
also wearing sunglasses came to Casino's table and sat down.
The dark man in a dark suit had neatly combed, greased-
back hair. Unlike Casino, the dark man kept his sunglasses
on. The waiter brought them each a snifter of brandy.

"Are you ready for tomorrow?" Casino's guest asked casually.

"I am. I have done as I was instructed," Casino responded
gravely. "It is fixed—there will be no Twelve Apostates or
unfortunate bus accidents to delay our plans this time!"
Casino, feeling the bitterness of losing the election to Angus
O'Hara, glared at the other man. "Although I sometimes think
there really is a God watching over this damned church!"

At that, the man in the dark glasses laughed heartily. Then
he leaned forward and took off his glasses, looking directly
into the cardinal's eyes. The blood ran out of Casino's face as

he became instantly transfixed by the other man's gaze, like a deer caught in headlights.

Those are the blackest eyes I have ever seen, the cardinal thought. *Am I being hypnotized?* Casino felt the sweat on his back turn cold, and crazily imagined small ice crystals forming along his spine.

The man with jet black eyes picked up the menu and began to speak amiably, as if discussing the weather. One perfectly manicured hand rested gently on the base of the untouched brandy snifter. "You know, Luigi, I did not have to come today. I wanted to look you in the eye before it happens. Angus O'Hara will be much easier than the other one—I lobbied to forgo the use of drugs this time. There will not be any traces.

"The Society has a complete dossier on him. We have been following this Irish fool for over a year. He is a lightweight, a dreamer. Intelligent, clever, charming—yes—but completely naïve when it comes to politics. I am confident that we have waited long enough, and have prepared for this *event* on a worldwide basis. The *event* will go smoothly, and I trust you will follow your instructions to the letter after the event. O'Hara returns from America this evening. You *will* be pope soon."

The dark man looked back to Casino.

"I have to return to Amsterdam tonight," he continued, "so we will not meet in person again. Perhaps after the new conclave. The Society will arrange things and contact you with instructions. Please extend my apologies to the waiter and remain here. Finish your meal." The dark man frowned and put down the menu.

He seemed to be finished speaking, then added, with a smile that was quite charming, "One last thing, Luigi. I'm disappointed you don't believe in God. I do."

Their eyes met and Casino felt like screaming. The man put his black sunglasses on, which seemed gray compared to his eyes. He stood and walked away, leaving the cardinal alone.

He quickly downed both untouched brandies and motioned to the waiter so he could order something stronger.

Just a little to take the chill off.

4

Sunday Evening
8 October
Mishawaka, Indiana

The Wheats owned over sixty acres on the outskirts of Mishawaka. Tom and Anne decided to invest their life savings into the land thirty years earlier when it became clear that they could not support their growing family on Tom's salary. To this day they rented out most of the land to local farmers who grew corn and other crops in the fertile Indiana soil. The Wheats had built additions onto the farmhouse to make room for their seven children.

Tom had also invested his money wisely in stocks, but he was not a wealthy man. He regularly gave more than ten percent of his income to charity. Most of their friends would have been shocked to discover that Tom and Anne didn't keep a monthly budget. They trusted God's Providence to provide for their needs; God had never betrayed their trust.

Anne was Tom's childhood sweetheart; they had been pretty much in love since the days when they played together in the streets of their South Bend neighborhood during the Depression. They got married before Tom left for Korea with the Marines Corps. Anne looked much like her only daughter Joanie, with clear blue eyes, thick auburn hair, fair skin, and a willowy build, although it was a bit worse for the wear after nine pregnancies (including two late miscarriages) and thirty years of coal-filtered Lark cigarettes.

Anne had a kind of homespun wisdom and what Protestants would call an abiding faith. She was solid, steady, funny, and a wonderful cook. She was also a daily communicant.

She was standing at the drive when Tom and Karl pulled up in the dusty maroon Dodge Caravan.

"How do you do, Mr. Slinger? Welcome to the land of the Hoosiers!"

"Quite pleased to be here," Slinger replied, and proving that he was not completely without charm, added, "I'm pleased to see that not all the beautiful Irish lasses are in Ireland." His smile was winning.

"Oh, go on now. I'm a worn out old lady and you both know it!"

"Let Karl and me go in and have a drink before the meal, Annie." Wheat looked past the house to the field behind his home. "Is that Joanie and that Payne fella?" he said, gesturing toward the hill, where two silhouettes stood before the sinking sun.

"It is. Interesting young man," Anne observed. "Joanie seems quite taken with him. Mr. Slinger, I hope you don't mind us having a second guest at the table?"

"Not at all, Mrs. Wheat."

"Do call me Anne," she suggested, smiling. "The Maker's Mark is in the den. I don't know about you, Karl, but Tom's too old and too stubborn to bother with any warning about drinking too much." Anne turned to her husband, squinting her eyes as she spoke, "Just don't embarrass me at the table, Thomas. Dinner'll be along in about half an hour."

She walked to the door and rang the large dinner bell which hung over the old-fashioned milk box set into the clapboard wall of the house. The two silhouettes turned and began walking toward the house.

Joanie and Nathan came into the den. After introductions were made, Nathan excused himself to call his voicemail. He came back to the living room next to the den where Joanie was sitting.

"Well, well. I just called my voicemail," Nathan said to her. "I left a message earlier letting Chet know I'll be back late tonight. *He* had a message for me. He's coming tomorrow to Notre Dame with a girl you met at my party, Becky Macadam. He's on vacation for the whole week, you know."

"Isn't that marvelous! I don't really know Becky," Joanie observed. "We've got a mutual friend, a Notre Dame grad, who works at her agency. Becky seemed pretty mellow at your party. I'll bet Chet's probably going to meet up with Joe Jackson, too. You don't know him, but Joe is the guy who started and runs the Kolbe Foundation, which distributes my father's tapes. It's too bad you'll miss them."

"I could take the day off," Nathan offered.

"Not on my account," she said.

"Why not? We could spend more time together. Get to know each other better. Chet would make a great chaperone, too. And hey, he's *my* best friend! He's here on vacation visiting *me*, remember?"

"I remember," she nodded.

"By the way, Chet sent me one of your dad's tapes a couple of years ago. I threw it away without even listening to it. Mr. Open Mind, right?" Nathan frowned.

Joanie thought for a moment. "I want you to stay. But I can't get off work—I don't have any personal days left."

"Call in sick," Nathan suggested.

"That's lying. I won't do that." Her reprimand was firm, but her tone was not harsh.

She's tough as nails. And I like it. The Moral Universe. I'm an alien. These people don't lie.

"I'm sure Mom would offer to put you up. There are plenty of empty bedrooms," Joanie suggested helpfully, looking toward the stairway that led to the bedrooms.

She's totally forgotten my suggestion that she lie about being sick. Just like that. Forgive and forget? Forgive without being asked?

"I can get a hotel. It's not a hassle, and I can afford it," he replied.

"Okay by me," she said, looking down at her hands.

Nathan was having a hard time keeping his gaze chaste when Joanie was not directly watching him. She was wearing her usual casual uniform—jeans and a floppy sweater, with white socks and black boots—surfing up to the edge of grunge fashion. Her clothes hid her sleek, feline figure. But they could not hide her almost European posture—which was extremely feminine—or her natural physical grace. Nathan found himself stirred by her despite himself—the way she tilted her head; the way emotions quickly surfaced and submerged on her face; the way she now stood up and arched her back, stretching. Nathan half-expected to hear her purr.

This Tom Wheat Rule is going to be tough, he thought.

"But really, Nathan, it's no problem having you stay over. Mom will make sure her room is between yours and mine. She has ears like a hound dog. If you head anywhere out of your room that's not the bathroom, she'll shoot you before Dad or Denny can strangle you."

She giggled, her eyes brightening.

"She's a good shot with a rifle, too," Joanie added, a hint of a playful smile around her eyes.

"You're serious, aren't you?" he asked uncertainly.

"Only half," she said. "Oh, you better call Father Chet on that voicemail and let him know where to meet you. I suggest the Father Sorin statue, for obvious sentimental reasons. I'll catch up with the two of you when I finish teaching tomorrow afternoon. I'll take the bus."

Joanie, like her dad, was a history teacher, but she taught in the local public middle school. Her car was in the shop getting a new transmission.

She got up from the sofa, grabbed his hand, and led him to the country kitchen where the wonderful smell of polish sausage mixed with the fragrance of hot apple pie.

I can't remember being so excited just to hold a girl's hand, Nathan thought as he let himself be led into the kitchen. Karl Slinger and Tom Wheat were just getting seated.

5

Saturday Afternoon
7 October
The Motorman Motel
Santa Paula, California

Sister Leonardo was not the only creature capable of intervening in human events. A dark figure, assigned to his post by an even more grotesque creature from a world without light, was working on a man named Lee Washington, who was tossing and turning on filthy, threadbare sheets in a cheap motel.

The grotesque creature's orders were clear. His superior, who was only once removed from the Supreme Master, had made certain of it, during the earlier briefing on the target.

"If you succeed in your task, countless numbers of these vile humans will cower beneath our Supreme Master's throne. You will be greatly rewarded. Many humans will be your slaves if you succeed in enslaving this one weak, pathetic man. The target is ready to listen to you. You are practically inside his mind. Even now, he is being led to a place where you will finish him. You have all the resources at my disposal at your disposal. The Supreme Master, who is attending most important business in Sector Four, is expecting complete victory, or he would have overseen this oblation himself. Surely, I do not need to explain your punishment if you should fail. But you will not fail. I will be at your side." The demon's superior had laughed wickedly after finishing the brief.

Around them, there was no light, but there was fire.

6

Saturday Afternoon
7 October
San Nicholas, Argentina.

Maria Bonilla knelt before the tiny altar in the nook of her one-room apartment. There was a small, cheap statue of Mary, shaped much like the statue of Mary above the Golden Dome at Notre Dame. Next to that statue was a smaller, expensive marble replica of the Pieta. There was also a set of old rosary beads, three candles, and an arrangement of wildflowers—which are difficult to find in the barrios of San Nicholas. A battered black and white photograph of her only son, Jesusy-Maria, who had died exactly thirty years ago to the day, stood next to the Pieta. Maria picked up the beads, and tried to shake the sleep and sting from her eyes, confused.

Hoy tengo bastante sueños—I have enough dreams for today.

Why am I so tired? **He** *must need my prayers very much or El Diablo would not be trying to make me sleep. Perhaps because it is the anniversary of Jesus-y-Maria's death. Santa Maria, keep me awake for my Rosary for* **him.**

The *he* she referred to was not Jesus Christ. Nor was *he* her son, the dead Jesus-y-Maria. *He* was the son Maria did not know.

In the bed behind her, Miguel Bonilla, her husband of forty-seven years, was asleep, exhausted after working a ten hour night shift at the garbage processing plant.

German surnames are common in Argentina. Maria's father, Gunter DeGraffenreid, a poor farmer and young widower, had emigrated to Argentina from Bavaria, Germany, in 1905. Unable to earn enough money to buy land, he was reduced to a life of backbreaking manual labor in the dingy factories on the outskirts of Buenos Aires. Gunter was ostracized by his few German peers in his factory when he took an Argentinean girl for his second wife. He valued his faith much more than his social standing. Gunter DeGraffenreid moved to San Nicholas soon after he remarried.

His bride Alena, Maria's mother, was a very holy woman. Alena had given Gunter nine children. She lovingly taught her nine children—especially her youngest, Maria—to pray fervently for all things and to bear the burdens of poverty with dignity.

Medical complications had prevented Maria from having any more children. She had poured her heart and soul into raising little Jesus-y-Maria to be a successful man. Maria was therefore profoundly disheartened when the legacy of faith was broken when her only child, her Jesus-y-Maria, had taken up with drugs.

She did not blame Miguel for Jesus-y-Maria's demise. Miguel was a faithful, hardworking, and devout husband, and could he help it if he had to work long hours to keep them from starving?

Although she had very little formal education and did not know the intricacies of moral theology, she did know her faith and she did understand in her heart about human nature. She did not think that Jesus-y-Maria had been completely without blame for his own life. Indeed, Maria believed he had chosen his fate. His death was the result of his driving ambition to leave the barrios; his reliance *on himself.* She knew this. She was not a fool. She had taught him to be this way. She had instilled the ambition into his young heart.

During the agony she experienced after Jesus-y-Maria died of a drug overdose, she had taken an honest accounting of herself. Maria had compared her life to that of her own mother. She realized that if she were to die and face God, He would weigh her and find her wanting regarding the one task He had given her beside that of being a good wife.

She had sinned by relying on herself and her own will to form Jesus-y-Maria. Whereas *she* was content to live honestly and proudly in her own poverty, she had taught her son to seek a way out of poverty *for its own sake.*

She had paid lip service to passing the faith onto her son. She taught him the catechism with little enthusiasm. Yet what energy she poured into tutoring him in language and math! Education would save him! A house on the hill with the middle class would save her Jesus-y-Maria! She had even studied on her own, scrimping and saving to buy textbooks, so as to learn more and more so she could pass on her new-found knowledge to Jesus-y-Maria.

At first Jesus-y-Maria had done well in the one-room shack that served as the school building. The teachers all agreed that he was bright and ambitious. He was popular with the boys and girls alike and could make everyone laugh. After graduating in the American equivalent of tenth grade, he went to the city to seek real work in the factories. He found a job quickly and within two years was promoted to a management position.

Then it had been simply a matter of saving enough money to move them all out of the barrio to one of the few middle class *avenidas* of San Nicholas, which were located on a small hill on the east side of town. Maria did not realize how much she had been looking forward to moving "onto the hill" until after Jesus-y-Maria died. She bitterly recalled bragging to her neighbors about how well he was doing at work and where they were going to live in just a little while longer.

Jesus-y-Maria began taking the amphetamines manufactured in his factory. The uppers helped him stay awake to work the extra hours he needed to get a jump on the other managers. He didn't dare tell his mother, whom he loved with all his heart. He was doing it for her! She would not understand.

He died when he took a lethal pill that was mistakenly manufactured at ten times normal strength by a worker who was trying to conceal his inability to read the mixing instructions at his new job station. It was a freak, really, an accident of chance. Thirty long years had passed since Jesus-y-Maria's burial.

But Maria had not taken his death as an accident. As far as she was concerned, she had put the pill into Jesus-y-Maria's mouth. She had traded the spiritual for the material, and her son had paid with his life in the bargain. If it had not been the pills, it would have been something else, she concluded.

Maria mourned for two years. Miguel could not console her. She went to the church in San Nicholas and knelt before the large replica of the Pieta, wordless, unable to pray, unable to cry. She looked at the immense anguish in Mary's face and contemplated the suffering of the Mother of God, who held her broken Son in her arms. Maria condemned herself. Mary had not killed her own Son.

I have no right to suffer like you, Señora! You did not kill your son!

At three o'clock on October seventh, the Feast of our Lady of the Rosary, two years after Jesus-y-Maria died from the overdose, Maria Bonilla heard the Blessed Mother speak to her as she knelt before the Pieta. The words were clear and distinct. She heard them with her own ears, and even though she knew the church was empty, she turned to see if there was someone behind her. Maria was certain she was alone in the empty church. She thought that it must have been her imagination. Then the words were repeated again. It had sounded as if Mary were sitting right next to her. These were the words Mother Mary repeated:

"Your heart, too, has been pierced by a sword, Maria. My Son Jesus has forgiven you. You will be given another son. You must pray for him. You must pray for him."

The second time she heard the beautiful, soft, yet firm voice of the Mother of God, Maria almost fainted because her mind could not deny what was happening to her.

"Who is this son? How can I have a son? I am barren," Maria had said aloud to the Pieta, stricken with fear and surprise. Intense heat filled her chest underneath her black dress and spread to her limbs.

Am I losing my mind? she asked herself.

The Blessed Mother answered her out loud; and these words were the last words Maria ever heard from Mary on this earth:

"You are not losing your mind, my daughter. You will not know this son. He is one of mine. Now he is our son. He needs you to pray for him. Will you pray for him?"

"Yes," Maria whispered, offering her fiat.

Maria began to pray. She prayed for six hours—the first joyful prayers since her beloved Jesus-y-Maria had died. She prayed fervently, tears streaming down her face, ignoring the people who came and left the church. The pastor had to help her off her aching knees so she could leave.

In the confessional the next day, she told the priest what had happened to her. He did not know if she was telling what had really happened to her or what she *thought* had happened to her. It mattered little to him. He could hear the hope in the tragic woman's voice. It was the first hope he had heard from Maria Bonilla since poor Jesus-y-Maria had died.

He absolved her of the same sin she had confessed over and over during the last two years, and asked her to follow him into the humble cottage that was his rectory. There he gave her the beautiful statue of the Pieta he had bought with three month's stipend while visiting Rome as a seminarian decades earlier.

"You are not to question what happened to you yesterday, Maria. Nor are you to tell anyone else, not even Miguel. Do you understand?"

She nodded. He continued.

"You have suffered much, and I will not judge you. From now on, you will not judge yourself. You will leave that to God. You have been given a second chance by the Mother of God. Do not waste it. Take this statue home and pray a full, sincere, and complete Rosary—all fifteen decades—every day at three o'clock, the hour of Jesus' death. Yesterday was the Feast of the Holy Rosary—it was not a coincidence. You will also start being a wife to your husband again. Miguel has suffered too, and you have been selfish with your grief. He also deserves a second chance. He is a good man. If you do these things, I believe you will meet this 'unknown son' Our Lady spoke to you about when you get to heaven. Will you do all these things, Maria?"

She nodded vigorously.

The old priest walked her to the door. As she went down the path he made a mental note that his own prayers for the ending of Maria's suffering had been answered. He had never known a holier woman in his entire life—with the possible exception of Maria's own mother, Alena.

Maria went home feeling as if the weight of the entire world had been lifted from her shoulders. For the next twenty-seven years, she faithfully kept the stipulations of the bargain the priest had laid before her.

So, the unaccountable sleepiness and the urge to skip her *Rosario* and climb into the warm bed with Miguel was brushed aside by the force of long years of habit. In fact, Maria rejoiced that her heavy eyelids would merit more grace for her unknown son by making her normally joyful Rosary all the more difficult. She turned her eyes toward the Pieta as the words of the *Madre de Dios* echoed down through the years in her mind, as they did every day at three o'clock when she prayed.

"*Now he is our son. You must pray for him.*"

7

Sunday Evening
8 October
The sky over Mishawaka, Indiana

Denny prepared to land the Cessna.

He was one of that rare breed—the natural born pilot. Dennis "Denny" Wheat, twenty-four, gently touched his Cessna 172 down on the homemade airstrip on six acres of land within walking distance of his parent's farmhouse.

Denny was slightly built, yet strong and muscular—not unlike Pope Patrick, Angus O'Hara. Denny spent a lot of time in the air. He had been obsessed with flying since he saw a documentary about the Wright Brothers on television at the age of five.

Even then, he knew that he would spend as much of his life as he could sitting in a pilot's seat. His childhood was filled with memberships in air clubs, endlessly making model planes, and working odd jobs (especially over at Hubert "Huey" Brown's farm) to save for his first plane.

Nevertheless, his childhood had been one long wait until the day when Huey Brown decided to let Denny, age fourteen, take the stick of the old Cessna Huey used for dusting his crops. (Yes, Huey Brown was known by his Hoosier neighbors as Farmer Brown.)

Denny headed toward the thick clouds on his second day up with Huey Brown and flew "on instruments"—that is, without any reference to land and without visibility. It was a skill which Huey himself had mastered only after a hundred hours in the air. Denny, however, performed on instruments like a seasoned pilot. Clearly he also enjoyed it—unlike the most seasoned of pilots.

Kid's a born aviator, Huey thought. *I need a pot o' money to rebuild the Deere—maybe I'll offer him the 'duster. Betcha corn to cotton he's got the money for it.*

Four weeks later Denny bought the Cropduster from Huey. A few years after that, Denny acquired the Cessna 172. The 172 was much faster, held four passengers, and had sophisticated radio equipment. He called the two planes his "fleet."

Anne Wheat had resigned herself to the fact that she couldn't keep Denny out of the air. By the time the boy was ten it had become obvious to her that "the flight thing" was not merely a stage he was going through. But she was still his mother and was darn well going to make certain the boy got a good education, pilot or no pilot. He had spent four interminable years at Notre Dame, where he majored in aeronautical engineering. He squeaked by in classes that did not have to do with flight, while acing any course that did.

The boy was unpredictable. One time his mother wondered aloud why Denny showed no desire to join the armed services to fly jets, or run off to the air shows that toured the cities of America. Denny told her that he preferred small prop planes because they required more artistry to control. As for air shows, he didn't want to be a freak in a circus. He had strong tastes and a purity in his love of flight. He was a prop man and that was that.

Had Denny been born fifty years earlier, Lindbergh might have faced some serious competition.

He now had a job flying freight from Michiana Regional to Midway for a local company. He found flying to Midway boring and much preferred the peaceful freedom of being in the air alone in his Cessna. He also enjoyed dusting crops for the local farmers.

He was now returning from the Henley Farm just outside of LaPorte. He had used Henley's crop duster for the job and had shuttled himself there and back with his 172. He landed, jumped out onto the grass, and made his way across the field to the kitchen door. He smelled the fresh-baked apple pie sitting on the ledge of the kitchen window. Inside he found his sister Joanie, his parents, and two strangers. One was a man who looked to be in his mid-thirties and the other was a much older man sitting next to his dad.

"Hi Mom and Dad," he said. Then, looking directly at Nathan, he added, "Hi Joanie. How was your party in Chicago?"

"The party was very eventful," she replied, shaking her head at her little brother, trying but failing to avoid looking at Nathan. *Very funny, Denny.* She then looked to her dad.

Tom Wheat made introductions before Denny sat down. The young pilot was famished.

Denny looked at Nathan, then at Joanie, and knew the two were in love. He knew all about flying high and feeling free.

Chapter Six

1

Anne Wheat served *kielbasa* in a casserole of onions and green peppers along with a side dish of scalloped potatoes.

When politely asked by Anne, Nathan briefly told about his job trading securities at VV&B, and how he grew up in New Jersey with Chet Sullivan. Despite his quiet voice, Joanie noticed that he had no problem looking either her parents or Mr. Slinger in the eyes.

Tom Wheat told Slinger how he chanced upon the book *Our Lady of Fatima* at a Marian shrine in Carey, Ohio, fourteen years ago. Tom had stopped by the shrine gift shop after giving a lecture to the Historical Society in nearby Findlay. Wheat intended to buy a rosary for Anne as an anniversary gift and happened to see the book at the counter. Having only a faint childhood recollection of the story of Fatima, his interest was perked. He stayed up all night at the hotel reading the book.

When he arrived back in Mishawaka the next day, he announced to Anne that the book had changed his life. At the time, she thought her husband sounded somewhat fanatical. *Dedicated* would be a better description of Tom Wheat. Applying his keen intellect along with an historian's lifetime of training, he devoured all the information he could find on the historical appearances of Mary. There was even more information on contemporary apparitions, which had begun to multiply around the world. He soon began to correspond with experts, authors, and the spiritual directors of alleged visionaries. During his summer breaks he dragged Anne to apparition sites around the world.

Marian apparitions became an all-consuming passion. Before long, experts began to call Wheat for *his* opinions, and to tap into his encyclopedic knowledge on the subject. No one had a better grasp of the big picture.

A few years later, a fellow named Joe Jackson asked Wheat to speak before the newly formed Knights of Immaculata group at Notre Dame. Jackson, Wheat's former student, had enjoyed a brief career in the National Football League. Two years before asking him to speak, Jackson convinced several NFL players to appear in a prolife video. Joe subsequently started a foundation for the purpose of distributing prolife videos and other Catholic materials. He called it the Kolbe Foundation.

Marian groups began asking Wheat to speak at parishes around the state and then at parishes around the country. Wheat discovered what he termed "the Network" of Marian groups. There were dozens of Marian peace centers and literally thousands of Marian prayer groups, as well as a growing number of parishes with perpetual Eucharistic adoration.

Ten years after Wheat began his speaking engagements, Jackson approached him about releasing an audio tape to be distributed for free. Wheat, who had never taken fees for speaking, had no problem with tapes being given away, but he tried to discourage Jackson from releasing the tape. He did not want to appear to be promoting himself. But he didn't forbid Jackson from carrying out his plan.

Jackson distributed four hundred audio tapes with the simple title of "Marian Apparitions" at a Marian Peace Congress in Chicago. Jackson sent free tapes to anyone who wrote in for them after the congress. Over ten thousand tapes were given away in the first year. After two years, one hundred thousand. After four years of distribution over two million

people had heard "Marian Apparitions" with practically no
advertising by the Kolbe Foundation. Tapes were passed
around with glowing recommendations. Jackson told Wheat
that hundreds of families had each distributed thousands of
tapes! Thousands of individuals had each distributed dozens
of tapes. The Kolbe Foundation also distributed several other
audio tapes on Catholic topics.

Wheat and Jackson found themselves caught up in a great
Marian Catholic revival exploding around the world. Besides
the Kolbe Foundation, there were five or six other major
Marian apostolates that fed information to the millions of
people who were rediscovering their faith through the apparitions of Our Lady. One group in Pittsburgh had published
millions of special edition newspapers detailing the same kind
of information that was on Wheat's tapes. Another apostolate
in Philadelphia produced hundreds of thousands of professional videos about approved apparitions. A married couple
in Virginia had published a book—similar in content to
Wheat's audio tape—which had sold hundreds of thousands
of copies.

Both Jackson and Wheat believed that it was primarily
the powerful messages from heaven which fueled the talk's
popularity. Jackson lent more weight than Wheat did to
Wheat's unique speaking style, which was dramatic yet not
offensive. Wheat was more historian than preacher, and emphasized facts over opinion during his talks. The professor
preferred to quote the messages directly and to draw out the
common themes. Non-religious listeners found it interesting—even if most of them rejected the message. Historians
could find no error in any of the well-researched facts, nor
could theologians fault Wheat's precise theological language.
Wheat achieved on a recording what he had done routinely
for over thirty years in the classroom: he transformed a lecture into a dramatic event.

Joe Jackson's part-time project had turned into a full-time
job at the Kolbe Foundation, which was now the largest

producer of Catholic audio tapes in the world. More than two dozen people worked for him.

Jackson was unassuming in person but was a tenacious ball of action when it came to apostolic work, Wheat assured Slinger during the dinner conversation.

"You would like him, Karl. He thinks big. He *is* big—you should see him! I'm speaking tomorrow night at Joe's Knights of Immaculata group, which has over one thousand members in this part of Indiana. Perhaps you could stay another day and meet Joe? It starts at five o'clock," Tom suggested.

Wheat noticed his wife rolling her eyes.

Anne Wheat the Catholic believed in her husband's unusual calling, of course; but Anne Wheat the wife had grown somewhat weary of his obsession. The man she had married, the mild-mannered professor, had become an evangelizing zealot who constantly struggled to balance his family, profession, health, and apostolic work. Anne both cursed and blessed the transformation. On the one hand, he didn't seem to have free time anymore. On the other hand, he had become more humble and considerate of her despite his lack of free time.

A prophet is never welcomed in his own home, Joanie thought when she saw her mother's expression.

Joanie, who also believed in her father's avocation, was temperamentally better suited to tune out her dad. She had heard him speak privately and publicly on the subject dozens of times before. She gave her mom an understanding look.

"I'd love to hear you speak, Tom!" Karl boomed. "I'll call Lenny Gold, my lawyer, and tell him I'm taking another day off. He'll flip. I'm the last person in the world he'd figure would ever become a Christer. I haven't taken two days off other than occasional vacations with Dottie in years."

"Mr. Slinger, what's a Christer?" Nathan asked.

Wheat and Slinger chorused chuckles.

"A Christer is World War II military slang for what you would call a Jesus Freak or a Holy Roller nowadays," Wheat explained for Slinger.

"Did you fight in the big one, Mr. Slinger?" Joanie asked.

"Yes," Karl replied rather crisply, looking down at his plate. Like many veterans who have seen combat, Karl didn't like to talk about his days with the Marine Raiders on Guadalcanal. He had lost many, many friends in those fierce battles.

Then Slinger had a thought which he expressed with uncharacteristic sobriety, "You know, Tom, your tape reminded me of America in the thirties. Everyone knew in their hearts that Hitler was a bad apple and that a war was coming. It was like no one could admit to themselves the stark reality of what was going to happen, even though you could smell it in the air. I mean, if someone suggested to me in high school that the Nazis were going to attempt to exterminate every Jew on the face of the earth, I would have laughed. Hitler was like a big bully you wanted to avoid, but couldn't. This time the bully is darker, meaner, and invisible.

"If it's true that the Mother of God is predicting a great battle between her army and Satan's army, then Hitler is going to look like small potatoes."

"I think I know what you mean," Joanie added. "When I try to imagine Daddy fighting in Korea, it always seems like cartoons to me. When I teach the Battle of Britain to my kids, it's hard to imagine myself living in London in 1943 with bombs dropping on my neighborhood every night. It's like World War II happened in a movie, but not for real. I guess it's just plain hard to believe that Dad's talk is true. To reject what Dad says outright is tempting, but that would mean rejecting a lot of facts. It would mean that God isn't serious when He sends prophets to the world."

This reminds me of eating at the Sullivan house when I was a kid, Nathan thought. *Everybody is free to join in the conversation. I used to stay pretty quiet at the Sullivans' back then, too. I wonder what Joanie and this Slinger guy are talking about?*

Everyone pondered Joanie's observation until Slinger spoke up again.

"That Warning you talk about on your tape sounds like it's going to make it real for people, Tom," Karl observed. "Do you know when it's going to happen? You didn't mention any date on the tape."

"To tell you the truth, Karl, nobody knows for sure. I probably know more about this subject than anyone else in the country, and even I don't know. Most experts think it's going to be soon, but a careful reading of the alleged events at Garabandal suggests that we'll be far along into the Schism and Tribulations before it happens. Only one of the Garabandal visionaries, Mari Loli, knows the year of the Warning, and she hasn't told anyone. No one knows the exact date." Wheat absently swirled his Maker's Mark in his glass as he spoke.

Garabandal is a small town in the Cantabrian Mountains of northern Spain where Our Lady reportedly appeared to several children over two thousand times from 1961 to 1965. Mary told the children of incredible events that would take place in the future, including something called the Warning.

A long moment of silence ensued before Nathan spoke.

"If you'll pardon me, sir, I don't know what you're talking about. Warnings, tribulations?"

"Forgive me, Nathan, of course you don't," Wheat apologized. "In the sixties at a place called Garabandal in Spain, Our Lady told children that the entire world would undergo a 'correction of conscience' called the Warning. All human activity will stop, and each person will see his or her soul as God sees it. It will be a frightening thing to see the impact of your sins on other people's lives, and how your sins offend God. It will be something similar to experiencing your own final judgment, but before you die.

"Frightening as it may sound, the Warning is really an act of God's mercy. If such an event does occur, it will be the first time in history that all people experience the same thing at the same time. It's a stupendous event, really, and quite incredible.

"Garabandal is controversial. There have been two investigative commissions by two bishops over the years. The local bishops have denied a supernatural character to the events, although the content of the messages was not found contrary to Catholic teachings.

"We must always use caution. Garabandal might be a blind alley. Bishops have changed their minds, too, about these things, but we can't hope or count on that in this case.

"Catholics are not even required to believe in Fatima, which has been fully approved. We must always balance belief with caution. God does not send prophets as a joke. God does not joke.

"Let's assume that Garabandal is false. That still doesn't mean there won't be a Warning. Many saints throughout the ages have undergone personal versions of the Warning. Saint Teresa of Avila was actually shown the place in hell reserved for her had she not reformed her life. Apparently, she was a fairly apathetic nun before her great prayerful ecstasies and active life reforming and founding Carmelite convents in the sixteenth century.

"More recently, in the 1930s, Blessed Faustina of Poland underwent a personal Warning, seeing herself as God sees her. She was horrified at the damage even the smallest of her sins caused to her soul, and to her fellow human beings. And Blessed Faustina was a very holy woman. Many believe that she will be canonized a saint.

"Mary is currently appearing to an Irish woman who warns that all mankind will experience an 'inner awareness' of how God sees our souls. Meanwhile, a priest named Father Gobbi of Italy, who hears Mary by way of a phenomenon called a 'locution,' has been writing about a worldwide 'judgment in miniature.' I could name seven more contemporary mystics who have spoken about a Warning.

"Some biblical scholars believe that Simeon's prophecy—given to Mary and Joseph when they presented the infant Jesus at the temple—alludes to this Warning. 'And your heart, too, a sword shall pierce, so that the thoughts of many will be revealed,'" Wheat quoted, finishing his short dissertation.

From the look on Nathan's face it was obvious that he was still somewhat confused.

"Maybe I should give him one of your tapes, Dad," Joanie suggested. "That way he can listen to it on the way back to Chicago tomorrow night."

A smile came to Anne Wheat's face. "Are you planning on staying for the evening, Nathan?" she asked.

"If I can find a hotel nearby, Mrs. Wheat."

"You may call me Anne, Nathan. Why don't you stay with us? You can sleep in Denny's room."

I knew it, Joanie thought. *Staying with Denny is a nice touch, Mom.*

Joanie was not surprised to find herself hoping Nathan would accept her mother's offer. Joanie, thinking of Nathan's remark at the lake, was not comfortable with the idea of having her new boyfriend more than twenty yards away either.

"That's awful kind of you, ma'am—but I wouldn't want to put you out," Nathan answered courteously, wondering if he was laying it on a little thick.

"Not at all, Nathan. Any friend of Father Chet is a friend of the Wheats. You can even borrow one of the boys' pajamas tonight. Then I can give your clothes a wash before you get up tomorrow morning."

Anne Wheat was obviously an experienced mom.

"Thank you. All the same, I'd feel better off in a hotel."

Why don't you want to stay here? Nathan thought. *Because you don't trust yourself, that's why. You're a fish out of water around here, Fat Boy.*

"Whichever you decide is fine with me," Mrs. Wheat said with a note of finality.

Karl Slinger had been lost in thought during Anne and Nathan's conversation. He spoke up. "You know, I'm new at this Marian stuff. I'm not sure what to do next," he said, almost to himself. "Actually, I *do* know what to do next," he added. Making quick decisions was a part of Karl's nature. "I'll ask you, Tom. And you, Anne. What *do* I do next?"

Wheat looked to his wife, who nodded, before he answered Slinger. "It's actually pretty simple, Karl," Wheat replied. "First, get ready for one long Lent. The way things are going—and despite the efforts of Joe Jackson and others to let the country know what's going on—many people are going to need your prayers and spiritual sacrifices before they open their hearts to heaven's messages. That's what it means to be a part of the Mystical Body of Christ.

"Second, concentrate on doing a good job living your state in life as a husband, father, friend, and businessman. In that order. That's where we please God the most—humbly doing the job He gives us when we wake up in the morning. That's your first priority, Karl. It may sound strange, but this battle is not going to be fought on the usual battlegrounds. The first battleground is in our homes. God has to win the battle in our families first. Then we can move out and seize other territory."

A cloud came over Karl's face before he spoke. "That's what I spent the most time on yesterday in the confessional. I always prided myself on being an honest and fair businessman. I'm tough, but fair. I don't lie. I despise liars.

"But the hell I've put Dottie through over the years! All those nights she slept alone when I stayed at the office or traveled on business. I never cheated on her with other women, but I let my business be my mistress. And all that time she was so patient, never complaining while I practically ignored my daughters for decades."

Slinger turned toward Nathan before continuing, "I have two daughters, Nathan, and three grandchildren. And except for their weddings, I never attended one of their graduations, their birthdays, or even their kids' birthdays. Is it any surprise that neither girl lives in Utah anymore? Listen to me! I'm still calling them 'girls' when Marsha and Kathy are both over forty years old!

"They stopped inviting me to family events after a while," the big man said sadly. "I've been a real ass."

There was an awkward silence after the man confessed his flaws. Tom noticed for the first time that Slinger's face looked old.

"Your wife's prayers helped, Karl," Anne said gently, "and that's why your prayers are so important now. There are other Karl Slingers out there who don't have anyone to pray for them."

For a moment Tom Wheat thought Karl Slinger was going to cry. But the blood rushed back into the big Pole's face and suddenly the energetic Karl was back.

"My mother! My mother prayed too! She prayed every day of her life for me! One time I asked her why she only ate black bread on Fridays and she wouldn't tell me why. She must have been fasting for me." Karl was now beaming brightly. "I saw her smile before I heard your tape in the limo!"

"You *saw* your mother?" Tom asked. "You told me on the way home from the airport that she passed away a long time ago—"

"Oh yes! She died over a decade ago. I didn't have a vision or anything. I saw her in my mind's eye. It was quite normal. I thought it was just my imagination at the time, and forgot about it until Anne mentioned Dottie. You don't know how good this makes me feel!"

Nathan looked directly at Slinger and asked a question—or rather, gave Karl a gentle order—without saying a word: *Tell me why, Karl. I need to know. This is important. I don't know why it's important, and I don't know what you and Tom are talking about, but you have to tell me why you feel so good.*

Nathan had been born with a gift. Even though Karl Slinger was decades older, a hardened war veteran, and a tough captain of industry, Nathan had the ability to command him to answer an *unspoken* question with a *look*. Slinger would respond to Nathan's silent command without consciously realizing he had been issued an order.

Perhaps it was Slinger's excitement. Perhaps it was part of Nathan's gift.

It was the same trait that made him the leader everyone looked to for instructions when the going got hairy at VV&B. It was the same trait that had made the other boys follow him during playground sports in grammar school.

Tom Wheat, who had served far away from the bloody front lines during the Korean War, suddenly realized where he had seen the look on Nathan's face before tonight. Tom Wheat had seen it on the face of the military legend, Douglas MacArthur. Wheat had been inspected by MacArthur once during the war.

My God! I'd follow this young man anywhere. And he's half my age! he thought rather disjointedly. *Things are getting curiouser and curiouser. There's more to this boy—this* **man**—*than meets the eye.*

At the same instant Tom Wheat was thinking of General MacArthur, his daughter Joanie was reminded of the first time she saw Nathan standing next to Father Chet in Nathan's apartment.

Before meeting Nathan, Joanie had concluded there was a high probability that she would never find a husband as strong or as smart as her own father. Somewhere along the line she had resigned herself to remaining single the rest of her life rather than marry a lesser man than her dad. She had not dated much since college. She liked her job, but often felt frustrated because she rarely met new men in her teaching circle, much less solid Catholic men. Joanie had almost skipped going to Chicago for Nathan's party when an old college girlfriend (who used to work at VV&B) invited her. Now she saw the handwriting of Providence. She had felt the presence of Nathan's almost completely latent leadership ability the first moment she saw him, and had connected to it in her heart. Her thought at the present moment was almost the same as her father's: *I don't care where you're headed, Mister; I'm going with you.* She felt a flush of heat on her cheeks.

"I'm happy because my mother is in heaven!" Slinger practically shouted it. "My Mama is in heaven, and she's given me another mother—the Mother of God!"

Heaven? The Mother of God? Nathan wondered.

Only Slinger's strength and sincerity stopped Nathan from writing him off. The man obviously believed. Nathan was disturbed by Slinger's faith. *I'll never get faith like his, even if I try Pascal's Wager for **ten** years! I'll lose Joanie, and I don't even have her now as it is.*

"Sir?" Nathan asked.

Slinger nodded.

"Whatever it is you have, I want it. I need it, sir. As long as Mr. Wheat says you should pray, would you mind praying for me?"

"I'd be happy to pray for you. I'd be damned happy. Oops, sorry Anne—about the language I mean. Don't get discouraged, son."

Slinger, who was not without a gift for adding weight to his own words, paused for effect before adding, "Yesterday, I was just like you, Nathan. Just like you."

Nathan, using his gift again, looked around the table. The glance took only a moment. This unspoken command was given with only a fraction of the intensity he had exercised on Slinger. Nathan didn't realize he was using his gift. It was a part of Nathan, as automatic as finding the mathematical relationship between numbers.

No one felt manipulated or resented Nathan. It was simply *clear* to everyone around the table that the subject was closed.

Anne broke the awkward silence, "Apple pie, anyone?"

"You bet, Mom." Denny spoke for the first time, relieved that this emotional dinner conversation was over.

✛ ✛ ✛

After dinner Joanie and Nathan left to get some air outside, holding hands as they walked out the back door toward

Denny's Cessna. Denny helped his mother clean up. Tom and Karl retired to the den for a nightcap of Maker's Mark.

In the den, Tom, who already felt an affinity to Slinger and sensed that he could trust the big man's opinion, asked him what he thought of Nathan Payne.

Slinger, despite his gregarious and seemingly impetuous nature, impressed Tom with his willingness to mull things over before speaking.

"Tom, you know, when I was a boy, I grew up on my daddy's ranch near Butte, Montana. Daddy spoke crooked English, but he built that little place into the largest ranch in Montana by the time I got it and turned it into SLG.

"One time my papa took me out hunting. He shot this huge grizzly bear. He thought the bear was dead, but he wasn't sure. Before walking up to the bear to check, he took me aside and told me to be careful, because a bear is one of the most powerful animals in nature, and even more ferocious when wounded.

"'Don't mess with bear ven hurt, Karl,' Papa said. 'Hurt bear ist trouble. Hurt bear ist like ten not-hurt bear.' Then Papa walked up to the bear slowly, and carefully shot it again with his Springfield.

"That young man your daughter is so taken with may be young, and he may be inexperienced, but he *is* a bear. A powerful bear. He's soft-spoken and quiet, almost like a kid, but he's a bear all right."

"When he gave you that look at the table," Wheat added sagely, "he reminded me of Doug MacArthur."

"I personally know lesser men who run Fortune 500 companies," Karl nodded. "Good men, tough men—I'd bet none of them would last five minutes with Nathan Payne in any kind of contest you could name.

"Nathan's wounded, too, Tom. He's got old bear-wounds he doesn't want to face. If you love your daughter, and I know you do, I suggest you and I *both* start praying for Mr. Nathan Payne."

Both men exchanged looks.

"Another thing my papa told me when I was a kid," Slinger added after a moment's reflection.

Tom squinted his eyes and asked gravely, "And what is that, Karl?"

"Papa used to say the best way to heal an old wound that still hurts is to open it up again and bleed out the pain. I don't know how Nathan's going to face whatever it is he's wrestling with, but it's going to be one hell of a scene when that wound opens."

There was nothing more to say. Tom pulled his rosary out of his pocket and held it toward Karl.

Smiling, Karl pulled out his own rosary, which was given to him by the priest who heard his recent confession in the Cathedral of the Madeleine in Salt Lake City.

Let's get down to work, Karl, Tom thought.

Both men, accustomed to work, got down to it.

2

Saturday Afternoon
7 October
The Motorman Motel
Santa Paula, California

Everything was gone. All his money. His properties. His mother. Raja X. Gone.

Everything was gone except his heartbeat.

His mother was the real problem, Lee thought. She had lowered him to this state, or so Lee's darkened mind told him. It was her fault.

Lee tried to get up from the dirty bed in the cheap motel located near the Ventura Highway, the highway made famous by a song in the seventies. Unable to balance, he collapsed to the floor. His needle-specked arm came into focus. He was too high and too depressed to cry. Then he began having trouble focusing on the needle marks on his arm. One was bleeding—but the blood didn't look red. It looked ghoulish, bluish, almost white, like milk mixed with food coloring.

So much stuff in me that it's blue.

It was a statement. He was too strung out to be shocked. He was afraid of something else, something much worse.

"What are you going to do when it wears off?" he asked himself. The words came out, "Wha…gonna do…wears off."

The addict doesn't fear death. He fears being *clean*. The agony is excruciating, physically and mentally.

"DTs coming, Lee." Was that his voice? He didn't know anymore.

"DTs," the voice insisted.

Delirium Tremens.

The voice was lying, and enjoying the irony of the lie; DTs come to alcoholics, not cokeheads. Lee, who knew this sober, was too wacked out to tell the difference right now.

For the demon, it was the fear that mattered. Lying was just a habit.

Lee began to turn his head toward the ceiling. It seemed to take an hour to do so and the effort drained almost all of his remaining energy. He looked at a black spot on the uneven ceiling. It seemed to grow larger before his eyes. He fell into the hole and his drug-induced state called forth the events of the last month. They flashed by in eerie succession, as if the chronology were the only order in his universe.

The look of horror on the investors' faces when the Santa Monica Hospital deal fell through, taking most of their money and much of Lee's money with it.

Fabian slamming the door in his face at Fabian's apartment. "Get out of here, Junkie!"

Raja X slapping him across the face, shutting Lee up. "We had something special, Lee, and you threw it all away," Raja had added wearily, dry-eyed. He saw Raja walking away, quietly closing the door behind her.

The banker telling him there was no money in his account. "Your mother withdrew a cashier's check on your behalf this morning. She had a signed document with your signature on your office letterhead. You weren't in, so we checked the signature against the one on file. Mr. Washington? Are you feeling all right, Mr. Washington? Mr. Washington?"

Frantically calling all over the Woodland Section. To no avail. His mother was a cokehead, and she was gone. Gone.

The visit by the two burly men and the one smarmy man from the Mafia—warning him of what would happen to Lee if he didn't pay off his enormous drug bill. The shock when he discovered that his own mother had taken up almost one-third of the tab.

Violently trying to burn the Personal Power tapes in his car with his lighter, delirious with anger, as he crashed his Chrysler into the storefront of the Scientology bookstore on Vine Street. The sound of the burglar alarms ringing in his ears while he hot-wired a car a block away after he stumbled away from the demolished storefront.

Scoring enough blow to kill a horse from a dealer who didn't know about his sudden lack of credit on the street...

How did I get here?

Lee fell headlong into the present. Indeed, he did not know how he had gotten here. That information was gone, left behind in the black hole.

There was enough blow left to do the trick on the dresser covered with contact paper next to the bed, along with a spoon, a rubber tube, and a lighter. Nearby, a needle.

In the odd way the mind works when hammered with drugs, Lee became instantly, completely lucid.

Gotta do it now. Gotta do it before you pass out, man. If you don't, you'll live. DTs. No DTs. Is that my voice?

I control my own destiny. Die. Die. Gotta die. I control my own destiny.

Lee was completely certain that his next hit would be his last. If he took it, it certainly would be. If he took it. Lee was not alone. Above him, a battle raged. Lee had given up the struggle below.

3

Monday Morning
9 October
Chicago Skyway, Illinois

Father Chet and Becky were driving in his "priest car," a 1984 Chevy Malibu his brothers had chipped in to buy him when he was ordained. It had over one hundred and thirty thousand miles on it.

He had not been surprised when he got the voicemail message from Nathan asking him to meet up at the Father Sorin statue.

He had an intuition about Nathan and Joanie, but he was still worried about what had gone on behind the closed door of Nathan's room during the party. He had prayed that they had both passed out before anything untoward had happened. He had gone as far as putting his ear to the door and listening. Father Chet had barely been able to make out Nathan's mild snoring.

I'm too late, he had thought, disappointed with himself and with his longtime friend.

Joanie Wheat was a good girl if she was anything like the rest of the Wheats. It was a good family. Chet had resigned himself that there wasn't much he could do for Nathan except to pray.

Maybe nothing happened in there. Maybe she'll be good for him.

Chet had been drinking a bit too much himself and had been asleep on Nathan's couch when Joanie and Nathan left the apartment early yesterday morning.

Chet and Becky finished praying the Rosary in the car. Father Chet had prayed especially for the grace to remain chaste. He was not naïve about the danger that traveling alone with Becky posed to his vocation.

Thanks Adam and Eve, he thought sardonically.

He tried hard, successfully, to keep his eyes on the road and not on the incredibly attractive Becky Macadam. He reached up without thinking and pulled his Roman collar a little bit looser.

Becky spoke up. "Isn't it against the rules for a priest to be, you know, alone with a woman?" she asked with genuine curiosity.

"You mean a beautiful woman, don't you?" he answered, keeping his eyes on the highway. Out of the corner of his eye he saw her blush.

"It's funny you mention it," he continued. "I was just thinking about that. To be perfectly frank, it is against the general rules. Even calling you yesterday was pushing the envelope. I told myself that you needed to see a priest, not a man, so I bent the rules a little. Kinda like when Jesus let the apostles gather food on the Sabbath because they were hungry.

"Turned out I made a good decision, I think, and I'm glad I did it. But technically speaking, I'll be glad when we're in mixed company later. No offense. I'm human, that's all, and you *are* a beautiful woman."

"Thank you," Becky replied. She could think of nothing else to say. *Am I thanking him for the compliment, or for being such a gentleman?*

Like Nathan Payne, Becky had been having the odd feeling that she was not traveling in her normal circle of friends.

This man is different, she thought, unaware that she was echoing the exact words of Jews in Israel who had the same reaction to Jesus two thousand years ago. She was not aware that Catholic theology maintains that priests are "other Christs."

"Anyway," he went on, "I was thinking about what Aristotle wrote about the concept of Beauty, and about my cousin Helen, who is also a beautiful woman."

"I'm very curious, Father Chet, as to what you're going to say next."

"Well, Aristotle and the classical philosophers all pretty much held that Beauty is what they call a transcendental. That's a fancy word for saying that a beautiful thing is a reflection of an absolute principle. I'm butchering his philosophy now, but Aquinas believed that God is All Beautiful, because He is the first principle, or the absolute, of existence, of everything. If there's no God, then nothing exists.

"It follows that anything made in His image and likeness is also beautiful. In this sense, even the Elephant Man is beautiful because he was made in God's image. And so are you. In a way, a person who is physically beautiful, like my cousin Helen and you, even more perfectly reflects God's image. Am I getting too deep, here? Just call me on it, Beck."

"No, not at all," Becky protested. "You have a gift for making complicated things seem simple. Please, keep philosophizing."

"I knew a crusty old priest at Notre Dame—Father Duffy was his name—who used to talk with me about this stuff for hours on end. Most of it went over my head. One time I asked him how all this philosophical stuff related to real life. He gave me an example that has helped me be a better priest."

Chet flicked his blinker and changed lanes.

"I've already told you that I used to be a wildman with Nathan back in my Notre Dame days, before Jimbo's right hook. My biggest worry going into the seminary was that I couldn't hack being celibate. Let's just say I've always been plagued with raging hormones. Anyway, Father Duffy told me what I just told you about Beauty being an absolute principle, but with much more philosophical precision, of course.

"He told me that a beautiful woman is made in the image and likeness of God, and that I could mentally—how did he say it—transcend, yeah, transcend my own nature when I saw a beautiful girl, and think of my supernatural desire to see God, Who is All Beautiful, and is much more beautiful than any woman.

"In practical terms, it's really not healthy to repress sexual desires, as if they're something evil, which they aren't. That kind of desire just comes back later, stronger than ever. It's much better to channel sexual desire into other areas, like work, study, and physical activities. Your physical beauty can remind me of my spiritual desire for God, instead of arousing my natural inclination to, let us say, keep the species going. It's a healthy way of redirecting what comes naturally.

"Father Duffy also told me that the more I develop my desire to know and love God, the easier it would be, and the surest way of doing that is to pray, to talk to God. I also have to watch my eyes, to learn to control them like I control my arms or my legs. To tell you the honest truth, it hasn't been nearly as difficult as I thought it would be   keeping chaste, that is. It's worth it. I can't be a good priest without being chaste. Remember that story I told you about Saint Louis DeMontfort? I read somewhere that the first stop he made when he hit town was the local brothel."

She eyed him suspiciously.

"It's true," Chet continued. "DeMontfort used to go right into the brothel, get down on his knees, and start praying the Rosary. It's like that old saying, 'you can't fight sin without going to where the sinners are.' I doubt Saint Louis could have done that without the virtue of chastity, and without control over his eyes."

"Wow," she said, almost to herself, "that explains it."

"Explains what?" he asked.

"That explains why I'm so comfortable with you and why you remind me so much of my dad, besides the fact that you love being Catholic. I mean, Dad *loved* being Catholic."

"I'm still a little lost," Chet said.

"What I mean is, and I don't mean to sound stuck up or anything…" she was searching for the right words, "…but when men look at me, they don't look at *me*, but at my—parts! That's it! It's like I'm a piece of meat or something. They look at my body. Even when they look me in the eye, it's like they're adding up how much I cost or something."

Chet just nodded. He could see the wheels turning inside her head. *She's pretty sharp,* he thought. *I wonder what she's going to think of Joe Jackson?*

"So I know what you mean about controlling your eyes. That's why I never liked Nathan. He didn't look at me right, although I could never put my finger on it exactly. You, on the other hand, looked at me like my father used to, like I was your sister or your daughter. I know it sounds funny, us being the same age and all—"

"It doesn't sound funny at all," he interrupted gently.

"—but even at the party," she finished her thought, "I knew there was something special about you, Father Chet. And now I know what it is. You're the real thing."

And Chet, who was indeed the real thing, did what most virtuous people would do when confronted with such a truth. He blushed.

A few minutes passed in silence while he pondered her observations.

"Another passing thought about Beauty, as long as I've got such a receptive audience."

"Fire away, O Great One!" she teased cheerfully.

"Hey, cut out the O Great One bit. Do you want to hear this or not?" he asked, then lowered his voice, "I'm always afraid I'm talking too much."

Her look plainly told him to continue.

"Well, something I've always admired about my cousin Helen is how well she *handled* her beauty. What I mean is, she's beautiful on the inside as well as the outside, and it makes her even more beautiful. There's something sad about a beautiful woman with a bad personality. It's almost sacrilegious. Again, I can't help but think of Father Duffy and his transcendentals. He used to say that putting an ugly frame around the Mona Lisa was a sacrilege, and that putting an ugly personality inside a beautiful or handsome person was an insult to the Creator. You could say that being beautiful is a responsibility."

Father Chet noticed that Becky's expression changed when he mentioned the Mona Lisa. She had a look of far away sadness.

"My dad used to say something like that to me when I was a little girl. My mom was very pretty you know. She was Junior Miss Illinois before she met Dad. But she didn't have the personality to go with her looks. Oh! I must sound like a monster talking about my mom like that!"

"Look, Becky, I'm a priest, not a psychologist. Kind of like McCoy in the old Star Trek series, 'Jim, I'm a doctor not a mechanic!'" His impersonation of the actor who played McCoy was right on the mark. Becky laughed.

"Like I said, I'm not a shrink, but it sounds like you've got some good reasons to be bitter about your mom. I don't want you to necessarily spill your guts about her and how she's not Florence Nightingale or anything, but I do want to let you know that it's okay to air it out in front of me. I'm not going to judge you. Or her. Maybe *her* mom was messed up, eh? We could probably trace it all the way back to Adam and Eve."

"I know, I know," she said. "I was just thinking about my dad, that's all, and how horribly she treated him. When they got married, Daddy was supposed to be on the fast track in Chicago politics. He was too nice, I guess, and when he never got past local alderman, Mom dumped him. And dumped me, too."

She paused.

"Look, you're right," she said with a note of finality, "I don't really want to talk about her right now. Let's change the subject. I'm philosophically soaked."

I bet you're not, Chet thought. *I bet you get this stuff better than I do.*

Chapter Seven

1

Monday Morning
9 October
Notre Dame, Indiana

Joe Jackson casually tossed the football in the air and caught it as he walked down Notre Dame Avenue toward the Father Sorin statue. He was early for his meeting with Father Chet and Becky. He was thinking.

His high school football coach had convinced him that tossing a ball in the air while walking to school would help Joe develop his hands. Years later Joe still found that the activity helped him to think. He kept an extra football in his car and another next to his apartment door just in case he ever needed to go for a walk.

He enjoyed pondering things. And he was also singularly good at catching footballs, having spent two years in the NFL before rupturing a disk in his upper back. His career ended, and although his neck often gave him pain, he considered himself lucky to be able to walk and run like a normal man.

If Father Chet were asked to explain Joe's temperament, the priest would surely describe him as a melancholic—a man who needs to think before making up his mind. Once he made up his mind it was hard for him to change it back again.

He had literally *thought* his way into the Catholic Church as a young boy growing up in Metairie, Louisiana. He was raised a Baptist and had embraced the Bible wholeheartedly. Like many fundamentalists, he had immersed himself in Holy

Scripture. He didn't have the awesome memory of Nathan Payne, although he was quite intelligent, but his melancholic nature did help him enjoy meditation on the Bible. As a boy he often found himself distracted during class as the sayings of Jesus echoed in his mind from his Bible reading the night before.

A single word from three passages had echoed in his mind for over three months during seventh grade. He didn't understand the connection among the passages, which perked his curiosity all the more. The word that echoed in his mind was *Woman*.

"Woman, behold thy son. After that, He saith to the disciple, Behold thy mother."

"Woman, what is it to thee and me?"

"And I will put enmity between thee and the Woman, and between your seed and her seed."

He had been forced to look up the word *enmity* in the gigantic dictionary in the local library. It meant "a state of hatred" or "completely without common ground, never touching"—like two magnets that repel each other.

In the first passage from the Gospel of John (which was Joe's favorite gospel), Jesus was talking to Saint John and Mary at the foot of the cross. In the second passage Jesus was addressing his mother before performing His first public miracle of changing water to wine during the wedding at Cana. In the last passage God was speaking to the serpent just after the fall of Adam and Eve.

By seventh grade Joe had two great desires in life—to play professional football and to be a "beloved disciple" like Saint John.

Joe was quite shy; he didn't discuss theology with his parents or teachers. Nevertheless, he had deduced that each passage was pivotal in the overall scheme of the Bible. Most theologians, Protestant or Catholic, would have agreed, although each tradition would give conflicting interpretations to the passages. Joe knew nothing of differing traditional interpretations in seventh grade. He knew just one thing:

The word *Woman* was ringing in his ears.

Joe turned the passages over and over in his mind. He prayed to Jesus for understanding.

*Why does God warn Satan about the **Woman** in practically the first thing He says in the Old Testament? Satan will have no common ground with this Woman. Satan will never touch her.*

*Why did Jesus call his mother **Woman** at the very beginning of his public ministry, before his first miracle? Why didn't He call her Mom, Mother, or simply Mary? It was one of the **first** things He said.*

*Why did Jesus call Mary **Woman** on the cross? It was practically the last thing Jesus said before He died.*

As a Protestant, Joe was well aware that the Old and New Testaments were intricately related. He knew that God often inspired the authors of the Bible to emphasize significant words in key passages.

Joe sorely wanted to ask his pastor about the passages after services on Sunday. But he knew that his pastor would definitely not like his questions. He wanted to know about Mary.

Protestants didn't talk about Mary. Only Catholic Papists talked about Mary and every Baptist knew Catholics worshipped Mary and prayed to her, which was the terrible sin of idolatry.

So he kept thinking. The answer came to him one day while praying between plays at football practice. It was so simple: *The Woman is Mary. Mary is the Woman.*

Joe was so elated that he nearly injured his teammate on the next play. Unlike many players, the young man was always in an extremely good mood during football games. Joe never got angry. Football was sheer joy. The happier he was, the better he played. It was downright unnerving to opposing players, even during his career with the Pittsburgh Steelers, to see somber Joe Jackson laughing and smiling while participating in gargantuan collisions on the gridiron.

The pieces fell into place so easily for Joe that it started a cascade of new "if-then" statements. On his walk home from football practice, the statements came into his head as if infused from another being. In fact, this was exactly what was happening to Joe although he didn't realize it. The other being was the Holy Spirit working with Joe's highly developed sense of logic.

If Mary is the Woman God is talking about in Genesis, then Satan hates her. Because Satan never has common ground with Mary.

If sin is the common ground Satan has with people, as the serpent just demonstrated by his contact with Adam and Eve, then maybe Satan never touched Mary.

If Satan never had common ground with Mary, then maybe Mary has no sin, like the Papists say.

This last thought disturbed Joe, but he was too excited to stop. His thoughts washed over his doubts like a tidal wave.

If I want to be a part of Jesus' public ministry, then I must participate with the Woman—with "thee and me," like Jesus said. The Woman had practically ordered her son to get started! And He did!

If Jesus gave his beloved disciple John his own mother for John to take into his home, then all beloved disciples were given the Woman, Mary, and should take her into their homes.

If I want to be a beloved disciple, then I have to take Mary into my home.

Then came the most disturbing questions: *Why isn't Mary in my home? Whose home is Mary in?*

Joe knew the answers, but uncharacteristically did not want to think about them. Mary lived in the Catholic churches all around him. Her statues were a reminder, he reasoned, just as Joe kept a photograph of his own mother on the desk in his bedroom.

Why, the Catholics love Mary! a little voice added. *Just like John loved Mary. Jesus told John to love Mary.*

That's going a little too far, Joe. Catholics are messed up. Everybody knows that. The Catholic Church is the Whore of Babylon—it says so right in the Book of Revelation. Joe consoled himself with a common Protestant misinterpretation.

The last thing on his mind as he walked home from practice that day was the thought that he might become Catholic. It was unthinkable. Such a thought might have ended his line of reasoning quickly.

But Joe was taking the first steps. He had already taken the most important step. Baptist or not, he had decided that Mary was *the Woman*. This was an unalterably Catholic position, whether he realized it or not.

And, due to his melancholic nature, it would be nearly impossible for him to change his mind. The *Bible* was clear on that subject. And like every good Baptist, he knew that the Bible contained no errors.

Two weeks later, with surprisingly little struggle, at age twelve, Joe decided to join the Catholic Church. Huddled in his room next to the radio with the volume down as low as possible, he prayed a Rosary with the Metairie Family Rosary Program. He had not known what a Rosary was before he happened upon the program by accident (he was trying to find the LSU game). He knew only that praying the Rosary was a bad thing.

The announcer's words seized Joe like a vice: "Welcome brothers and sisters of Southern Louisiana. Show your love for Mary, the Woman of the Book of Genesis who crushes the head of the serpent with her heel. Show your love for the Woman who stood at the foot of the cross and suffered along with her Son. Pray the Rosary with the people of Saint Catherine's Church of Metairie!"

Joe's whole body shook as he asked Jesus to forgive him for wanting to pray the Rosary. Before the Rosary actually began, he tried to anticipate the vile words the Catholics would use to "worship" Mary.

When the Our Father came on, he was slightly confused. *The Lord's Prayer is in the Bible,* he thought.

When the first Hail Mary came on he was stunned.

That's what the Angel Gabriel said to Mary! That's what Elizabeth said to Mary in the Gospel of Luke! That's in the Bible too!

Although it usually took Joe a long time to figure things out, it didn't take him long to feel angry with his pastor.

Pastor Jellison's been lying to me. I've been had. Those aren't "worship" words. "Pray for us?" That's what Pastor Jellison says five times a sermon every Sunday! If he can ask me to pray for him, why can't I ask Mary to pray for me?

He finished the Rosary with delight, disappointed that it had to end, and relieved that his parents hadn't walked in on him while he prayed it.

I'm going to be a Catholic, he thought.

Then, *Okay.*

Joe's mind was made up. He would join the Roman Catholic Church. He didn't worry about breaking the news to his parents; he was already starting to think about how he was going to convert them to Catholicism. He had decided to move on to the next step—evangelization.

I'll have to learn about Catholicism to do that.

Then another thought came to his head: *After all, my mom and dad were born Baptist. It's not their fault. My **real** parents could have been Catholics for all I know. Catholics don't have abortions. Catholics believe in Adoptions Not Abortions. I read it all the time on their bumper stickers, along with Pray the Rosary to End Abortion.*

Joe's reasoning was without fault and his supposition was almost completely true. But the football player had no way of knowing for sure. In truth, his biological parents *had been* Catholics, although they were not very serious ones when he was conceived. His biological mother was a former LSU cheerleader and gymnast named Mary Johns. She had gotten pregnant by a second string defensive tackle during homecoming weekend.

The football player had talked the reluctant girl into getting an illegal abortion. Before the abortion could be arranged, a fellow cheerleader concerned for Mary's health convinced Mary Johns to talk with a dedicated nurse named Jackie Jackson. Deep down inside, Joe's biological mother had *wanted* to be talked out of the abortion. Without much resistance, Mary allowed herself to be persuaded by the Baptist nurse to carry the baby to term. Like Rebecca Macadam, after she got pregnant, the cheerleader discovered that she was more prolife than she had realized.

"What will I do with the baby?" Joe's biological mother, Mary Johns, had asked.

"I'll take it. I already have two girls, and I can't have any more kids. If it's a boy, my husband will go bonkers. We'll even pay the hospital costs," Joe's adoptive mother, Jackie Jackson, had replied.

The cheerleader broke up with the football player, dropped out of school, and returned home to Pittsburgh. The adoption was quietly arranged after Joseph was born during the following summer.

Mary Johns, who had not gone to church since grammar school, found solace praying the Rosary during the long and often humiliating wait for the baby to be born. She had given up her popularity and her gymnastic scholarship. She suffered mental anguish for her son, but she knew that she was doing the right thing. This gave her some comfort.

Believing that it would be better for the boy, she purposely allowed herself no contact with the Jacksons after the adoption. She transferred to Pitt to finish her degree. Eventually she found a good husband, a Catholic, and gave birth to four children of her own. Years later, when she watched Joe play for the Steelers on television, it didn't even begin to occur to her that this was her lost son.

She knew only that her lost son had weighed over twelve pounds at birth, and had been delivered via cæsarean section after eight excruciating hours of labor. She remembered him during her Rosary every day.

Of course Joe had no knowledge of any of this. His parents never told him directly that he was adopted, but he was quite certain of it. By seventh grade he weighed over two hundred and twenty pounds and stood two inches above six feet. He had tanned Mediterranean skin, dark brown hair, and a long Roman nose. His two older sisters were light-skinned, blond-haired, blue-eyed, and under five-feet tall. His family didn't talk about it, though he could tell his parents knew he knew. Even the other kids in school thought Joe Jackson was adopted—it was that obvious.

But no one teased him. Joe was regarded as the gentlest and kindest boy in his school by teachers and students alike. He was also the largest boy his age in the county, and was absolutely ferocious on the football field. Why antagonize a gentle giant?

And that is how Joseph Jackson came to be baptized and confirmed into the Catholic faith during eighth grade, and why he chose Notre Dame from the dozens of Division 1-A colleges that offered him full scholarships to play football.

It was also how he came to be walking down Notre Dame Avenue, tossing a football with a hand that could have been adorned with both an NCAA Championship Ring and a Super Bowl Ring. He was too self-conscious to wear either one. He was looking forward to seeing Chet Sullivan.

He loved to talk with Father Chet. Chet always gave him something interesting to think about—Chet loved to wax eloquent about Aristotle and Aquinas. Joe didn't know Becky Macadam from Adam, but he would soon find himself thinking about her this day and every subsequent day of his life.

2

Monday Morning
9 October
Notre Dame, Indiana

Chet and Becky rode in silence until the Notre Dame exit
approached. Twenty minutes before Joe Jackson began his
stroll down Notre Dame Avenue, the priest and the young
blond arrived at the Notre Dame campus. Chet was allowed
to drive onto the campus and parked behind the Bookstore
next to the outdoor basketball courts.

It was the second clear and unseasonably warm autumn
day in a row. They walked to the Grotto, which is a replica of
the grotto at Lourdes where Mary appeared to Saint
Bernadette Soubirous eighteen times in 1858. Chet told her
the history of Lourdes, and explained how he had prayed at
the Notre Dame Grotto many times during his days as an
undergrad.

He stood back as Becky knelt and prayed for a few minutes. He looked at the burning candles inside the cave, which
is carved out of the hill behind Sacred Heart Basilica. He
prayed that Becky's new-found faith would take a firm hold.

Because it was a Monday morning, there were only a few
students at the Grotto instead of the many tourists and alumni
who crowd the holy place on weekends. Students came and
prayed as they had been doing at Notre Dame for over a hundred years.

Father Chet and Becky sat on a bench near a flower bed at
the periphery of the Grotto.

"Can I ask you something?" Her tone was timid.

"I'm all ears," he said gently.

"Father Chet, I've been so peaceful since we prayed the
Rosary and went to confession at that church with the big
Jesus. I'm afraid that when you go back to New Jersey it's all
going to go away."

Chet said nothing. His priestly instinct, his great gift, told him to keep his mouth shut and his ears open.

Let her express herself. The voice of Father Duffy came back to his mind: *"No thought is complete until it's expressed by pen or tongue." That's what the old guy used to say.*

"What I mean is," she went on, "what do I do next? What's the next step for me? All this Catholic stuff I mean. It's been so long, and I don't know what I'm doing. My friends aren't like you or Joanie Wheat."

"You work in advertising, don't you?" he asked.

"Yes, I'm an account executive. I write ads for magazines, stuff like that. Why do you ask?"

Chet silently and quickly prayed two words, *Hail Mary!*

He leaned forward, putting his elbows on his knees, thinking. He took a deep breath. He started over.

"Well, grace—God's power in your life—is like a good advertising campaign. A good ad doesn't just get your attention, it grabs you so hard you've just got to go out and buy the product, doesn't it? God's love is like an ad—it's emotional, intellectual, and because it's from God Himself, supernatural. God got your attention yesterday. He did it. I didn't. It doesn't matter if *I'm* around any more than it matters if *you're* around when someone's buying a shirt two weeks after seeing one of your ads. It's time for you to buy the shirt for yourself, Becky."

"I get it. It's time to squeeze the Charmin?"

"Yeah, I guess you could put it that way, squeeze it, buy it, take it home, and…" he caught himself before he finished the sentence.

They both finished his sentence inside their heads and burst out laughing.

"Maybe that's not the best analogy," he said finally.

"Maybe not," she agreed, "but I get the gist of it."

Chet found himself praying again for guidance. For the gift of *counsel*. It was time to ask a question.

"Becky, do you change your mind a lot? I mean, you changed your mind pretty quickly about the abortion issue.

Some people are just made stubborn, and have a difficult time changing. Others change it too fast. The ancients called our inborn personalities our temperaments. Cholerics have temperaments that make them likely to make up their minds fast and stick to it. Sanguines make up their minds fast, but switch to another idea as soon as a new one presents itself. You strike me as a classic choleric."

Becky looked at Father Chet strangely, as if he had just slapped her. "This has been a strange weekend, Father Chet. There's no way you could've known this, but my daddy used to call me 'choleric' all the time when I was a kid. That's about the third time in the last two days you've said something he used to say, right out of the blue. Is that what they call a sign from God? I had no idea what Daddy was talking about, by the way, but I guess you could say I'm a choleric. Most of the people at the agency say I'm a stubborn you-know-what, and it begins with a *b*."

Chet and Becky exchanged looks and remained silent. They turned and looked at a kneeling coed wearing a sweatshirt with "1993: Notre Dame 31, National Champs 24" screened on the back.

Becky wondered what it meant. Chet knew. In 1993 the Notre Dame football team had beaten favored Florida State 31 to 24—Florida State's only loss that year. Despite having identical records, Florida State had been voted national champion by the press. Notre Dame fans, with perhaps typical, if not bitter humor, had found a way to both make money and to advertise their resentment.

Father Chet spoke up.

"Beck, you're going to be all right. It may not be obvious to you, but it is to me. Your dad played a big part in what happened to you yesterday. He's watching out for you. So is Mary. Your dad obviously loved the Blessed Mother, very, very much, and still does in heaven. The hard part is over. I really doubt you're going to change back to your old ways.

"Being a Catholic doesn't mean going to Africa to be a missionary. All you have to do is live a sacramental life. That means going to confession often, frequent Communion, and praying every day. It's not hard. It's a joy. Through the sacraments Jesus is able to live inside you, to guide you, to help you through the good times and the bad. It's like being married. 'For better or for worse.' As a matter of fact, the Church has always used the bond of marriage as a metaphor for Christ's love for His Church. You're not out there all alone anymore."

Becky was paying close attention. *She's soaking this up. Grace is such a wonderful thing. The day before yesterday she would have thought I was a religious fanatic, Roman collar or not.*

"Mostly, though, living with Jesus intimately in the sacraments means having the power to choose His will over your own. In your case, it means doing a good job at what He's put in front of you. He'll help you be a good copywriter, a good daughter, a good friend. He'll help you decide what to do with that little life inside your womb."

"He will?"

Father Chet suddenly had an image in his mind of Becky as a six-year-old girl looking up at her daddy. It confused him, but only for a moment.

"Yes," he said as firmly as he possibly could, "He will. The dog years are over for you, Becky. You're about to start a wonderful road trip, and when you get out of the car, your dad is going to open the door and welcome you into his arms."

He could tell that Becky was picturing her father in her mind's eye. Her eyes were just a bit watery but she was smiling.

"In the meantime," she asked, "where do I find more people like you?"

"It's not as big a problem as you might think, Beck. There are lots of good Catholic groups in Chicago. I'll help you get plugged in. There are lay groups like Opus Dei, and the Legionaries of Christ have a movement called Regnum Christi, to name just two. After a while, you'll find good Catholics with whom you'll be naturally inclined to be friends, and you won't feel like an outcast. It's not like we're living in the catacombs, though it might feel that way at first.

"Of course, heaven itself will help guide you to the right people and places. You can always call me in New Jersey for spiritual advice, too. I'm not going to disappear."

"I hope not! That would make you both priest and magician."

"That's a pretty lame joke, Beck."

"I know, but I'm trying to catch up with all of yours. You sound like you get converts every day." At that, Chet's bright eyes darkened a bit.

"Did I say something wrong?" she asked, concerned.

"No, not at all. You don't know how happy I am that you've, uh, seen the light, as they say. It's just that very few people are open to God's grace the way you are.

"Back at my parish, true believers are few and far between. Usually when I run into girls in your position they want me to talk them *into* an abortion, and they turn me down when I offer to pray with them. Or, I'm counseling women who've had abortions years before and can't live with the guilt, even if they won't admit it to themselves. Mostly though, I feel like I'm throwing sand against the tide. I'm not complaining, mind you, because I knew what I was getting into before I did it."

Chet stopped himself from mentioning his worldly and politically adept pastor, Monsignor Timothy Whelan, who persecuted Chet mercilessly. Chet was not one to criticize others needlessly or publicly.

"Thanks," she said evenly, smiling.

"For what?"

"You don't know?" Becky asked, still smiling.

"Know what?" he said innocently, feeling out of touch with Becky's psyche for the first time since they met.

"For being a good man and a good priest, you moron!" She laughed.

Father Chet had nothing to say to that.

It struck him that Becky was already talking like a normal Catholic. Appreciation for priests and the priesthood was a natural outpouring of solid Catholic faith. His parents were that way. His brothers were that way. The little old ladies who went to daily Mass and fawned over him after he led them in Rosaries were that way. They respected him *and* his collar. Somehow Becky was already at this point.

She is a choleric, he thought. *And just about everything I've said to her today seems like it came from somewhere else. **Somebody** else. Just like when I'm in the confessional. Keep praying, Chet my boy, keep praying!*

He knew that it was not he who had spoken the words, but the Father–Son–Holy Spirit his priesthood represented. Even now, he could see the wonderful transformation on Becky's face. It was the look of a person who had just decided to take a chance on the unknown. It was a look of determination to *do the right thing.* He said a quick prayer of thanksgiving to Jesus and then looked at his watch.

"It's almost ten past! Oops! We've got to get to the Sorin statue. Speaking of meeting good folks, I've been waiting to surprise you. We're going to meet a good friend of mine, Joe Jackson, the guy from the Now Famous Story of Jimbo's Right Hook—"

"—any relation to the famous baseball player?" she asked.

"Uh, no—not that I know of. Are you a baseball fan? You know who Shoeless Joe Jackson was?" The surprise showed on his face. They stood and began walking.

"You bet. I love baseball. My dad used to play semipro baseball and took me to see the Cubbies. He tried to teach me how to hit and throw like a boy. I bleed Cub blue as a matter of fact." She looked up, remembering as she lightly bit her lower lip, a smile around her lovely brown eyes. Then she continued, "Shoeless Joe Jackson played for the Black Sox a long time ago. He got banned from the game, but a lot of people think he got the shaft. There was a great movie about it called Eight Men Out. I rented it twice.

"Are you also a fan of our national pastime, Father?" Becky asked, proud of her knowledge.

"I bleed Red Sox red, ever since my first little league team was the Red Sox. My dad is from Boston and he's a Red Sox fan, too. All my brothers and friends are Yankee fans. So you and I are both fans of teams that never win the World Series."

"Coincidence?" she asked dramatically, arching one of her eyebrows.

He lowered his voice, "Maybe. It could be a sign from God," he nodded ominously, squinting slightly.

They both laughed again.

"Anyway," he went on, "I think you'll like this Joe. He's not like you, but he is."

"There's a brilliant description. Wouldn't work in an ad."

"I forgot, you're an adman, always hewing close to the bone with the sharp knife of language and all that."

"That's right. *And all that,*" she said, chuckling.

"Let's go then. And all that," he countered.

They started walking up the hill to the left of the Grotto behind Sacred Heart Basilica, by the entrance to the Crypt Chapel where Nathan Payne, Joanie Wheat, and Tom Wheat had attended Mass the previous morning.

"Are all priests like you?" the beautiful woman asked as he tried to keep his eyes on their shadows on the sidewalk.

An image of the smirking Monsignor Whelan swam to the surface of Chet's mind. He didn't have an answer for Becky.

3

Monday Afternoon
9 October
Salt Lake City, Utah

The woman needed to wipe the tears from her eyes. The small-statured man with dark eyebrows and gray hair offered her a facial tissue.

"Thank you, Bishop Lanning. I know it's going to be difficult, but as you say, I have no other choice."

Lanning tonelessly reiterated his main point. "Divorce is always difficult. It pains me more than you know to counsel it for you. But your husband has been excommunicated. Unless you remarry you cannot be called forth to exaltation. The devil has taken control of your husband," John Lanning said with feigned empathy. *Why don't you tell her what you really think?* a cynical little voice asked him.

Lanning pulled a business card out of his desk drawer and handed it to the woman. "Here, call this man. He's one of us, and has handled divorces for my flock before."

She took the business card and rose from her chair to leave. He gently rested his hand on her back as he guided her to the door. He closed it and returned to his desk. Lanning sat there silently and motionlessly for several minutes. A dam broke inside his soul. He began to cry in heavy, deep sobs. He cried for the woman, for her husband, for their five children. For himself.

I have helped destroy another marriage!

John Lanning was a bishop in the Church of Jesus Christ of Latter-Day Saints, known more commonly as the Mormons or the LDS. A bishop in the LDS was the rough equivalent to a pastor of a parish in the Catholic Church. John was a direct although distant descendant of one of the original apostles of Joseph Smith, founder of the sect in upstate New York in 1830.

In addition to his part-time religious duties as a bishop he was also a full-time professional for the LDS. He and his wife Elena lived in Bountiful, "up on the hill," atop the closest of the mountains that cradled Salt Lake City. It was a posh neighborhood with the most expensive homes in the city. The view of the capitol building, the city proper, and the valley below was breathtaking. Every morning he left his home and walked down East Capitol Boulevard to the largest office building in Salt Lake City—the offices of the LDS. He had a corner office in the skyscraper that overlooked the impressive Temple and the other buildings in Temple Square.

Officially, Lanning was the director of public relations for LDS. Unofficially, he was known to a select few in the secretive organization as one of the most important marketing minds of the fastest growing church in the United States. Depending on the length and goals of the project, Lanning had hundreds of millions—even billions—of dollars at his disposal. For over forty years Lanning had served the LDS diligently and brilliantly.

The LDS had many shadowy levels of influence. There were always two hierarchies: the public and the private. Very few people—even rank and file members of the LDS—knew about the shadow hierarchy. Lanning believed that he was only a level or two from the top of the hierarchy—the real decision makers in the LDS. He had heard rumors about the mysterious Council of Fifty, which had disappeared from public view when the U.S. Army established two military bases nearby to keep an eye on the sect in the latter half of the nineteenth century. Until they went underground, the Council of Fifty had been the LDS equivalent of a shadow government and private police force wrapped in one.

At the top of the public level are the Prophet and the Twelve Apostles of the LDS. Despite his high professional position, Lanning rarely interacted with the Apostles—most of his instructions came to him in the form of written memoranda.

John Lanning's job was simple: foster in the minds of Americans that the LDS was a family-oriented, harmless, and

ordinary Christian church. That's what the Apostles wanted,
so that's what Lanning delivered. In the privacy of his own
thoughts, he had lately come to think of this main goal as
Project Camouflage.

At the beginning of his career in the early 1950s, after
graduating summa cum laude from the exclusive Medill
School of Advertising in Chicago, Lanning had been a sincere, ambitious, creative, and dedicated Mormon.

By the early 1990s, Lanning's public relations campaign
had worked. The Mormons enjoyed widespread acceptance
in the minds of ordinary Americans. It had been an extremely
difficult and painstaking job. Thousands had implemented
the work—but Lanning had conceived the ideas. Subtlety and
long term planning were his strong suits.

Throughout most of its colorful history as a minority sect
in the melting pot of American religions, the LDS had been
barely tolerated as a quirky (and sometimes violent) aberra-
tion by both the government and mainline Christian churches.
The general breakdown of the family unit of recent times
highlighted the sect's clean cut image. Marketing surveys
commissioned by Lanning in the early 1960s showed most
Americans associating Mormons with the idea of polygamy
(multiple wives). Recent surveys showed the number one idea
associated with Mormons was now "family values."

Overseas LDS missions were booming; over fifty thousand missionaries scavenged the United States and the rest
of the earth for new members. The LDS now had almost ten
million members. Lanning had played a hidden but key role
in this area, too. These missionaries used highly effective
presentations—often memorized word for word and always
carefully tailored to fit the culture of the marketing target.
Lanning had spearheaded the use of Madison Avenue consulting companies to help perfect the presentations and methods used by Mormon missionaries.

The Mormons had a practice called *theological warfare*
which makes these presentations more effective. It was okay
for a Mormon missionary to exaggerate, misrepresent, or hide

the true teachings of the LDS in order to avoid losing a prospect. For the ultimate good of the prospect, of course. This
gave Lanning greater latitude when he helped design missionary presentations.

Although finances were not his department, he knew that
the LDS owned large portions of stock in major U.S. and
international corporations. A negative article in the *Wall Street
Journal* in the 1980s had claimed that the LDS owned untold
billions of dollars worth of corporate assets through a complicated web of holding companies. When word came down
the corridor that the higher-ups were not pleased, Lanning
had spent months doing damage control. To this day, Lanning
believed, only the Twelve Apostles knew the true extent of
the LDS wealth.

Where did all the money come from? Most Mormons were
good Mormons. And good Mormons were required to do-
nate ten percent of their *gross* income to their church—or
face excommunication and loss of the incredible reward of
Mormon exaltation: personal godhood and control of one's
own planet! As strange as this would seem to most Americans, Mormons taught and believed that every Mormon who
is "exalted" will become the god and king of his own planet
after death, which he will then populate with "spirit children"
just as the Mormon God populated the Earth.

Millions of prosperous Mormons contributed tens of millions to their leaders *every week*. This money was invested
and reinvested through the myriad of holding companies over
the decades.

A clever series of national radio and television ads—at
the suggestion of the incomparable John Lanning—cast a
glowing light on Mormon activities, offsetting the bad publicity garnered by the refusal of Mormons to accept black
members until 1978. In 1978, the Prophet suddenly announced
a "new" revelation: God now permitted blacks to be admitted to the married priesthood of Mormonism. (All good
Mormons believe that their destiny is to be admitted to the
priesthood through sacred marriage ordinance rituals carried

out in their temples.) A simple, one page memo had instructed Lanning to "ease" the new teaching into the public consciousness. The fact that the new revelation came shortly after a much publicized racial discrimination lawsuit was leveled against the LDS was not lost on Lanning.

That lawsuit and the new revelation had cast the first doubt concerning his faith into his mind. Slowly but surely the doubt grew until he found himself counseling depressed women to divorce their husbands based on theology he no longer believed. At first the doubt was barely noticeable to himself. To reject Mormon teaching was an unforgivable sin "against the Holy Spirit" according to Mormon teaching. Yet Lanning was a keen observer of human nature by temperament and profession, and he couldn't understand why God would change such an important religious law. Humans lived by unchanging natural laws, he believed. He banked on the universality of human nature to design his strategies.

Thousands of Mormons left the sect after the new "black" revelation. Lanning was asked to craft language to prepare missionaries confronted by Protestants who were well informed about the matter. Soon after the lawsuit, a key scripture in the Book of Mormon which described the elect as "white and delightsome" was changed to "pure and delightsome." At the time, he was aware of hundreds of other scriptural changes routinely made in "updated" versions of the Book of Mormon, but this particular change struck him as a matter of expedience.

Lanning was privy to other information not widely known among Americans. For example, Utah—the land of supposedly well-adjusted Mormon families—had a high suicide rate compared to most states, especially among young people. Mormon women had high rates of depression and divorce.

Over time Lanning's attitude toward his religion changed from unthinking acceptance to an exciting search for inconsistencies. He couldn't face the fact that his growing doubts were endangering his "exaltation," and convinced himself that he was merely doing marketing research. A year earlier, he even got permission to conduct focus groups with former Mormons under the pretext of conducting marketing research.

As his doubts increased, his fear of losing his soul and godhood decreased. A few weeks ago, he woke up in the middle of the night, uncomfortable in the "sacred garment" which is required to be worn by Mormons. The temple garment was supposed to be worn underneath one's clothes, touching one's skin, at all times. Some women even wore their bras over the garment. It was supposed to ward off evil spirits.

Lanning tore it off. For a few moments he waited for the demonic attack to begin. When nothing happened, he fell back to sleep with little consternation. Elena woke up the next morning and saw that he was naked. An expression of horror clouded her face. But she said nothing. Lanning believed she was in a state of denial. They never discussed his doubts. Ever.

As John Lanning sat sobbing in his chair in his ward office, he considered suicide. He could not pray because he no longer believed in God—or at least he could not pray to what he now thought were cartoon Mormon versions of gods. Having lost his faith, he had no belief to turn to for solace.

"Who are you!? Are you Lucifer or Jesus or something else? Are you there at all?" John called out, his voice filled with misery, addressing gods he no longer believed in. (Mormons believed that Lucifer was the defiant brother of Jesus.) *Are you real?* The walls of his office did not reply. Lanning looked out the window. At the bottom of the hill he saw Temple Square and the Salt Lake City valley. He closed his eyes and shook his head slowly. He wanted to die but he no longer believed in heaven.

Chapter Eight

1

Saturday Afternoon
7 October
Motorman Motel
Santa Paula, California

The drugs were beginning to wear off. It was time to end it.
Lee was wearing a dirty pair of pants, no shirt. He was barefoot.

"It's time, Lee."

He managed to climb onto the cushioned chair next to
the cheap dresser. As if watching from afar, he saw his hands
working the paraphernalia required to prepare his vein for
the final hit. He dropped the spoon and inserted the needle
into his vein. Before applying pressure to the plunger he asked
himself a question.

Am I in control of my own destiny? I wonder what comes next?

Above Lee an invisible, ugly creature prepared his next
lie. One more deception pushed into the target's consciousness would be all that was needed. This mission was going
quite well. This was easy!

"Light awaits you, Lee. Light awaits you!"

The creature assigned to destroy Lee Washington chuckled coarsely.

Light awaits me! I will join the light of destiny!

Because Lee had always possessed a curious nature the
thought gave rise to questions in his battered mind.

Is that my voice? Who's that laughing? What light? When have I ever experienced light?

Never. Oh well, here goes nothing.

The Miraculous Medal which Lee Washington had found on the Woodland sandlot during his childhood still hung around his neck. It distracted him. He noticed the image of the woman on the medal, her arms outstretched. Before he could plunge the poison into his vein an incongruent image of another woman entered his mind. Like many who are about to commit suicide, Lee thought of the only person he had ever really loved, despite her betrayal of him. Perhaps the thought of light brought her to mind. He remembered one day when he was a little boy. Shawna had been doing the dishes when little Lee showed her an airplane he had made with Legos. She had turned from her dishes and put a warm, wet hand on his cheek, smiling at her son. "I love you, Lee. You're all I have." This memory gave him one last chance to choose a good thing after choosing so many bad.

His choice would set off an instantaneous chain of events. For all his degradation he did not want to punch out on a bitter note. After all, he had been a successful man after a fashion, and however briefly, an optimist. His last thought was for Shawna Washington. He chose the good.

"I forgive you, Mommy. I love you," Lee Washington whispered sadly, tears forming in his eyes...

Grace was unleashed in a torrent, a cyclone, a tidal wave of power. A mighty warrior came directly to his aid. None other than Saint Michael the Archangel was released by Lee's generous, final choice. The angel was also released by the grace merited by a tired, faithful woman in Argentina who was praying a Rosary for Lee at that very moment.

The grotesque creature and his immediate superior were brushed away in the metaphorical sweep of the archangel's mighty wings. Unlike human affairs, affairs in the world of non-corporeal beings have a sharp quality. There is a finality and definition to these affairs which are not found anywhere on the muddy, material coil of men.

Battles in the invisible world are what mathematicians call "zero sum games." There is no partial success for the vanquished, only total annihilation for Darkness when Light confronts it. The two are incompatible—one could accurately describe beings of Light and Darkness as having *enmity* between them. Does it not say in the beginning of the Gospel of Saint John that the darkness cannot overcome the light?

Throughout the centuries, writers have attempted to describe these battles between dark angels and good angels in colorful military terms. These terms are inadequate. It is sufficient to realize that when the Archangel Michael appeared before the two arch-demons bent on the destruction of Lee Washington, the grotesque creatures were instantly defeated and immediately removed from Lee's midst. It was not the first time Michael had swept these two black enemies back into the burning abyss of hell.

Now God directed yet another archangel to come to Lee's aid. Lee's unique destiny required such drastic measures...

Before he could push the needle's plunger, he heard a man's voice. Lee looked up and saw the archangel. He perceived the creature before him to be a man, although Raphael was not a man.

The Archangel Raphael spoke to the confused, stricken man in the chair, "Lee, if you wish to live, remove the needle from your vein. Then, I shall heal you."

"I'm hallucinating," Lee whispered.

Raphael was standing only two feet away from Lee's chair. Lee knew the difference between an hallucination and reality from direct experience. His mind insisted that the man standing over him *could not be there.*

But this man is as real as the chair I'm sittin' on, he admitted. Raphael looked like any other man except his hair was long, red, and curly. He was taller than Lee and well-proportioned. There was a peaceful countenance on Raphael's face but it was not otherworldly. He was wearing a beige tunic and a leather belt which had a small bag attached to it. He wore sandals with leather thongs and tie strings. He did not have wings and his voice was not unusually deep or undulating like the angels in movies.

In fact, Raphael appeared in precisely the same dress and form in which he had appeared to Tobias, centuries before the birth of Christ.

Raphael shook his head slowly, a smile on his lips. There was a gleam in his eye—as if he was mildly amused by Lee's incredulity.

Presently, he spoke again, "Come now, Lee. It is your choice. The needle…" Raphael suggested in a perfectly rational tone of voice, holding his hand out toward Lee.

Lee, whose head was pounding, had forgotten the needle. He looked at it, pulled it out of the vein, and handed it to Raphael, who placed it back onto the dresser.

"You have had a rough time, my friend. You are in no state to see your true mother, who is coming to visit you. I will prepare you. I am Raphael, the Divine Physician." Raphael smiled disarmingly at the stunned man sitting in front of him.

"I am a bruised reed," Lee heard himself say, unaware he was quoting Scripture.

The strange man of no specific age opened the bag and removed a small cloth and vial of oil. Raphael pulled a small cork from the vial. He bowed his head, closed his eyes, moved his lips in prayer, and then dipped the cloth into the vial. He reached forward, cradled Lee's cheek in one warm soft hand, and made the sign of the cross with the cloth on Lee's forehead with his other hand. A soft orange light from the setting sun streamed through the soiled curtains into the room behind Raphael, outlining the archangel.

Lee tried to speak but the only words that came out of his mouth were "What the—?"

Beginning inside Lee's forehead, a soothing heat drained down into his body. Lee looked at the man's eyes and saw a light in his pupils.

The light grew, but did not harm Lee, and then Lee passed out.

✝ ✝ ✝

When Lee opened his eyes a while later he was completely
healed. His shakes were gone. Addictive desire for drugs no
longer wracked his nervous system. All infirmities had deserted his abused body.

The archangel was gone.

Lee was lying on his side, his back to the chair, facing the
door. His muscles were sore but not aching. He had a perfect
recollection of the mysterious red-haired man who had healed
him. He looked at his arms and saw that the needle marks
were gone. He felt an odd sensation in his stomach and was
alarmed, then surprised, by the feeling. Hunger.

Then he heard *her* voice. It was the same voice Maria
Bonilla heard twenty-eight years earlier as she sat before the
Pieta in San Nicholas. It was the most beautiful sound he had
ever heard. It came from the direction of the chair behind
him.

"I have waited so long to be with you, my son. Come to
me and let me hold you."

Lee, seized with a fear of the strange events that were
enveloping him one after another, yet buoyed by the beauty
in the voice he heard, gathered himself and turned to look at
the woman.

She is so beautiful! And young! She's younger than I am!

"Who are you?" he croaked, his throat constricting with
overwhelming emotions: joy, relief, contrition, awe, peacefulness.

The woman was wearing a long beige tunic with a royal
purple shawl covered with stars, but wore no belt. Lee saw
that her skin was brown but lighter than his own. She had a
simple brown cross hanging around her neck. Now that he
was looking directly at her, she seemed older than he had
first thought. She was *ageless.*

"I am your mother, Lee. I am the mother of all mankind.
Do not be afraid. We have time. There is much to explain. I

know you are confused. First, come here," she gently invited as she held out her arms.

Tears welling in his eyes, Lee allowed himself to be drawn into the arms and lap of the beautiful woman in the chair. Huge sobs surged up from the depths of his body as he embraced the woman. She consoled him with tender words, much as she had consoled Saint Catherine Labouré in a small chapel on the Rue du Bac of Paris in 1830.

"Am I not here, Lee? Do I not see each falling tear, my son?"

Lee continued to cry, but calmly—a little boy in the arms of his mother. With each tear he felt more and more the healing of his soul as his mother held his body in her embrace. This suffering son of man would not be lost today.

✟ ✟ ✟

Maria Bonilla finished her Rosary and felt pain in her arthritic knees as she rose. It was time to prepare *chorizo* for Miguel before he woke up. She felt no differently than she had after the thousands of other Rosaries she had prayed for her lost son. The strange sleepiness was now gone from her system. She would learn of her role in Lee Washington's life after her death.

✟ ✟ ✟

Sister Leonardo Mary MacEvoy winced when she was shown the fierce but brief battle between Saint Michael and the arch-demons torturing Lee Washington. Then she saw the visit of Raphael to the decrepit motel room. She did not see Lee's intimate visit with the Mother of God.

"Why am I being shown this man, My Lord?" she asked the ever present Trinity in which she bathed.

"You will help to bring this man to Nathan Payne, who is also a bruised reed," she was told in reply.

✝ ✝ ✝

Providence is not without certain patterns. The first historical account of an event similar to what happened to Lee Washington occurred in Palestine to a Roman citizen named Saul. Who we now know as Saint Paul, the Great Lion of God. Others have been knocked from their horses.

In the late nineteenth century, a Jewish atheist named Alphonse de Ratisbonne visited Rome. Ratisbonne was proud of his atheism and took great pleasure in baiting Catholics and exposing their superstitions. To prove to a friend how superstitious Catholics were, he wore the Miraculous Medal (which had been given to Saint Catherine Labouré by Mary in 1830). Ratisbonne prayed the "Memorare" prayer of Saint Bernard de Clairvaux for nine days. On the ninth day, upon entering the Church of Sant' Andrea della Fratte, Ratisbonne saw a vision of Mary and was instantly converted. Amazingly, he was infused with knowledge of all the doctrines of the Catholic faith.

Eventually, he was ordained a priest. He spent the rest of his life preaching to the Jews and anyone else who would listen to his eloquent explanations of the beauty and wonder of the Roman Catholic Faith.

In the late twentieth century in Kibeho, a town in the country of Rwanda, Africa, a pagan peasant boy named Sagstasha (who was completely without formal secular education, much less Christian religious education) was visited by a woman who called herself the Mother of God. Sagstasha was also visited by her Son. The pagan boy was taught by Jesus the doctrines and teachings of Catholicism. Sagstasha, who later took the Christian name Emmanuel, astounded skeptical theologians with his infused knowledge. In 1988 the local bishop approved the apparitions to Emmanuel and six others in Kibeho.

So when Lee Washington was infused with the Catholic faith by the grace of the Author of Faith, the event was not without precedent. Like Ratisbonne, Lee received his gift instantaneously. Before he was finished crying in the embrace of the mother of the Author of Faith, he was transformed into a new man. But he would always have the experiences, memories, emotions, and temperament of the Lee Washington who had been led to the motel room less than twelve hours earlier.

✝ ✝ ✝

Lee stood before the beautiful woman. She had spoken to him about many things during her visit. After a time which Lee could not measure, the woman gave him mysterious final instructions:

"My son, I will not visit you again like this before you draw your last breath, but I will be with you in the Spirit of God.

"You must go immediately to Salt Lake City to meet a man who will recognize you. You must try to teach this man the Truth you have been taught. This man's conversion is not inevitable in my Son's plan. If you succeed, many souls will be saved.

"Many trials await both you and this man, but you will be led to others who will help you play a role in the destruction of the evil one who failed to destroy you on this very day.

"Later, toward the end of your tribulations, you will meet a man who will give you a new name. Speak to him these words: 'The angel whom God used to rescue you was named *God Conquers*.'

"You are one of many who has been marked on the forehead with the Sign of the Cross as part of my Son's cohort. You are one of the anointed who will fight the legions of the enemy. *He* brands *his* slaves on the hand.

"You will not be able to see with your own eyes the sign of the cross marked by my angels upon the foreheads of my Son's cohort. But you will, on occasion, have an interior knowledge of this Sign of Redemption on others.

"I must go, my son. Remember, I am with you in the folding of my arms."

The beautiful woman, whom Lee now knew was the very Mother of Jesus, smiled at him. She began to float like a vision and ceased to be "real." Mary left quickly. Lee would have been hard pressed to describe the phenomenon.

He had no possessions, not even a wallet. He left the room in the Motorman Motel in Santa Paula without looking back. He had nothing and he had everything.

He walked out of the motel into the receding darkness. He breathed the crisp, cool California air as if for the first time. Lee looked toward the mountain in the east and the rising sun.

2

Monday Morning
9 October
Notre Dame, Indiana

Becky Macadam had been warned by Father Chet that Joe Jackson was big, but she was stunned when she saw the six-foot-six, two hundred and forty-five pound man leaning against the Father Sorin statue. He had a football under his arm. He was wearing cotton Dockers and a plain gray sweat-shirt over a polo shirt.

Joe turned when Chet called his name. Recognition brought a huge smile to the somber expression that normally rested on Joe's face.

"Chet Sullivan, I thought you might have had trouble on the highway or something." Joe beamed. He dropped the football and embraced the young priest, literally lifting him off the ground. Becky noticed that Father Chet's weight was not straining the dark-haired giant in the least. Joe's accent was thick with southern Louisiana twang.

Joe lowered Chet gently to the ground and turned to greet Rebecca Macadam. The smile was only a faint outline now. The somber look, that many mistook for sadness, was back.

"And you must be Becky. You sure are pretty," Joe blurted spontaneously. There was no fawning in his voice—he was merely stating a fact. Becky blushed.

"How do you do?" she inquired formally, but did not extend her hand. *He's beautiful! Beautiful? I've been talking to Father Chet too much!*

In fact, Joe was not a particularly handsome man. His features were too large, too plain except for his prominent Roman nose. His eyes were deeply set.

Joe's physique, however, was worthy of Michelangelo's David, and could be objectively appraised as beautiful. To a lesser degree Jackson was like Nathan Payne: women had been strongly attracted to Joe because of his status as an athlete and because of his tremendous manliness.

"I am doing quite well, Miss Macadam," he replied somewhat stiffly, imitating her formality, looking directly into her eyes.

True to his nature, Joe did not feel an instantaneous attraction to Becky, despite her balanced and breathtaking beauty. He was wary of beautiful women. In fact, having been chased by both plain and pretty women since high school, he had come to distrust their motives, and appreciated the danger they posed to his spiritual equilibrium. It unnerved him to be the object of attraction by a woman who did not know him well.

Becky, however, true to *her* nature, fell completely in love. The symptoms were clear—fire in the belly, dizziness, a blacking out of visual periphery. She quickly wrote off the emotion, having "felt" instant attraction before. She had been burned by similar feelings for the likes of Sam, for whom she had fallen at first sight. She noticed that Joe looked at her in the same disciplined, chaste manner which Father Chet practiced so well. She folded her arms and tried to look at anything but the giant in front of her.

"Well," Father Chet said, "I know I'm being a bad host, but I have to pray the Office."

The Divine Office is a set of prayers, contained in a book called "the Breviary." It consists of scriptures, prayers, and commentaries which are required daily reading by priests. Many liberal priests skipped praying it. Chet had not missed a day in his priestly life, not even as a seminarian, when he prayed the Breviary voluntarily.

Joe gave the Irishman a skeptical look.

"You've got to be kidding, Chet."

"I kid you not, Shoeless." Since college, Chet had been calling Jackson by the nickname given to the tragic baseball player. "We've got a big day planned. Nathan should be getting here any minute, and we're meeting Joanie Wheat around half past two. Then, at five, we're going to Professor Wheat's talk…" the priest turned to Becky, "…and *then,* we're going to get the best pizza this side of New Jersey, at Bruno's out on Prairie! I don't want to put my Breviary off. Sorry, I've got to go.

"Don't let this big lug scare ya, Beck—Joe's really just a harmless fuzzball, like that guy on the radio. I'll be done in a bit. Meet you in front of the dome."

With that, Father Chet walked away. He allowed himself a stealthy smile—which Becky and Joe could not see. His litany of the schedule for the day had been a ruse. He had observed the look in Becky's eyes. His instincts had been right—Becky and Shoeless were perfect for each other.

He unzipped the leather book cover around his Breviary and began to pray the prayers shared by the "other Christs" of the world.

It'll probably take the big lug three years to figure it out though—unless he gets a little prodding.

Prodding was Father Chet's specialty.

Joe watched the priest walk away.

"Well," Joe said, "let's wait here until the famous Nathan Payne arrives. I hear he's quite a character."

"Chet tells me *you're* quite a character," Becky rejoined.

Joe looked uncomfortable. Becky noticed that he was no longer meeting her eyes.

He's shy. It's hard to believe he played in a Super Bowl.

"Tell me about the Kolbe Foundation," she said cheerfully. Chet had described Joe's work to her briefly during the walk from the Grotto.

"There's not much to say. It's hard work, but it's fun. Before coming over this morning, I read a letter from a man who came back to the sacraments after being away from them for over two decades. All because he listened to a free Kolbe Foundation audio tape his wife gave him."

He speaks so softly, I can barely hear him.

Joe continued, "I just kind of fell into it, I guess. Now that I'm in it, I'm going to press the gas pedal to the ground and drive 'til I crash or the race ends."

Despite his soft-spoken voice, Becky couldn't miss the unbending determination in it. She was an intelligent girl and her job required interviewing high-level executives to help formulate advertising campaigns. Most looked at her legs or stared when they thought she wasn't looking. Many tried to pick her up—even the married ones. She took pride in cutting them down like saplings. They were the hard chargers of corporate America. Joe struck her as a paradox: a meek, shy man with the same determination of the executives with whom she had worked. She concentrated on asking questions to draw him out. His chaste gaze was refreshing. Even Sam had been a bit of a lecher, with roving eyes and a stash of porno magazines she once found hidden in his closet.

An awkward silence ensued. Joe looked up at the statue of Father Sorin.

"He's one of my heroes, Father Sorin. He came here with nothing and affected the lives of thousands, hundreds of thousands—probably millions when you count the wives, children, friends, and associates of the men who graduated from here. I think about him a lot. Nobody knows anything about him. If it weren't for his statue here and a dorm named after him, most students wouldn't even know his name. It's like he never existed. Yet no student would be here without him.

"I want to be like him. And I wouldn't mind if everyone forgot my name." Joe finished one of the most personal revelations he had ever made to a stranger. It was also one of his longest.

I must sound like a moron, he thought.

She looked at him for a long moment, until his gaze found hers. *Who are you, Joe Jackson?*

She was about to ask him just that out loud when the sound of screeching tires broke their reverie. Joe felt a tinge of disappointment when Becky looked away from him.

Nathan pulled his Mustang up to the curb, parked it illegally, and walked purposefully towards them. He had stayed overnight at the Signature Inn near the highway. He recognized Becky as the knockout from his party on Saturday night.

When he spotted the football at Joe's feet, Nathan pantomimed for Joe to throw it. Nathan held up his hands, smiling openly. Joe threw the ball twenty yards to Nathan, who caught it nonchalantly, but with sure hands—a skill that comes from either practice or natural ability. For Nathan it was the latter.

"Go out!" Nathan called to the big man.

Joe looked at Becky, shrugged, and ran a post pattern. Nathan motioned for Joe to run farther and farther.

Becky had never watched a college or pro football game in her life. As she watched Joe Jackson run, she had an emotional reaction not unlike those felt by the scouts and coaches who had studied him over the years.

Reflecting the impressive genes of his gymnast mother and his football-playing father, Joe was a study in speed, grace, and power. Most large men are too bulky to be graceful. Graceful sprinters are often permanent klutzes when it comes to catching footballs. Powerful men are often slow and are most often short and stout. Joe was a rare creature who had the best of all worlds: grace, power, speed. Jackson could have been an Olympic decathlete or played any number of professional sports had he dedicated his life to those kinds of achievements.

Becky's mind, trained in advertising, searched for a metaphor to describe him and supplied her with a mixture. *He's a combination of cheetah and locomotive,* she thought with fascination.

She had no way of knowing that Joe's teammates had nicknamed him "the Thoroughbred" years earlier at Notre Dame.

Nathan, who seemed half Joe's size, threw the ball forty-five yards in a perfect spiral which Joe caught with a tenderness and grace that could only be described as *motherly.*

When Joe turned to face Nathan, Becky saw Joe's huge smile for the second time and heard his deep laughter for the first time as it cascaded down the quad. Something stirred in her which was beyond physical sensation.

Watch it. Last thing you need right now is to start thinking about men. She then asked herself dangerously, *Why not?*

Nathan would have been surprised by the thoughts of Joe Jackson. Joe had played football with a few of the most talented quarterbacks of his generation.

I wonder where this guy played, Joe thought. *Must have got lost at some small college. I know several pro coaches who would be glad to give this guy a tryout—if he were a few inches taller. Throws as nice a pass as I've ever caught.*

Joe jogged—*glided* is a better word—back to Nathan and Becky. Introductions were made. Both men were impressed with the other's casual strength when they shook hands.

Neither was aware that a partnership planned by heaven from all eternity had just begun.

"Father Chet abandoned us to pray in his office," Becky observed presently.

"Chetmeister has an office on campus?" Nathan asked Joe.

"Not an office—the Divine Office—priest prayers. He's probably finishing soon. We'll catch him at the dome. Nice spiral, Nathan," Joe said. "Did you play in college?"

"Me? No. Chess club was more my style, Hoss," Nathan said in a friendly way. Joe never particularly liked being called big guy nicknames, but somehow Nathan could get away with it.

Men, Becky thought, *all they think about is sports. Then again, Mr. Super Bowl didn't bring up his former profession when we met. Most jocks would have.*

The blonde walked between the two men, like a modern Dorothy on her way to Oz.

✞ ✞ ✞

Chet was sitting on the front steps of the Administration Building when the threesome arrived. He closed his Breviary.

"Hey Nathan, how you guys doin'?"

"Just fine," Nathan replied, giving Chet a look.

Then he sidled up and started whispering into the priest's ear.

Whispering into the ear of Christ, Becky thought as she watched the two longtime friends.

"Chetmeister, Joanie says I need to go to confession," Nathan began. "Don't laugh, I'm serious. I want to. Something's happening to me. I need to do it now. You know most of my sins already. Whadda-ya-say, Chet?"

Chet nodded, then addressed Becky and Joe, "Sorry to abandon you two again, but you're going to have to excuse Nathan and me for a little while." His tone cut off any inquiry.

Chet and Nathan turned and walked toward Sacred Heart Basilica. The confessional was to the left of the door they entered. Over the next twenty-five minutes, Chet heard Nathan's frank and unemotional confession.

✞ ✞ ✞

"Well, what do we do next, *Hoss?"* she teased lightly.

"Please, call me Joe or Joseph. I'm not offended when you call me Hoss, Becky. I just like how it sounds when you say my real name," he told her almost apologetically, as if he were the one who had done the teasing.

"Okay," she said. *Did I hurt his feelings?*

"Let's pray, Becky. Let's pray a Rosary. If my instincts are right, Nathan is making his first confession since he was a kid. He needs our help."

"Sure. I'd be glad to. I just did the same thing myself—go to confession for the first time since childhood, I mean— yesterday. That Chet is quite a priest, isn't he?"

Joe nodded, conveying agreement with his eyes.

"Chet showed me the Grotto this morning. Let's go there— it's right around the corner, isn't it? If anyone told me last week that I would be saying two Rosaries in one day, it would have given me quite a laugh. Don't get me wrong, Joe. I want to pray for Nathan. I really do."

The thought of her unborn child struck Becky.

"Joe?" she asked tentatively.

He looked down into Becky's brown eyes. That feeling was in her belly again. He told her with his gentle look that he was more than willing to hear what she had to say next.

"Can we pray for me, too?" she asked less timidly.

"Sure thing," he said softly. "For anything in particular?"

"I can't say right now."

"Even better. A special intention—my favorite. I can't tell you why, but Mary always answers my prayers. She's always surprising me, too," he explained, trying to reassure her.

Why do I spill my guts so easily with this girl? he asked himself.

He talks about Mary like he knows her personally. Like Chet, she thought.

"I like you, Joe." The words seemed to come out of her mouth of their own accord. *Oh no! I blew it!*

His skin was too Mediterranean to show a blush, but Joe was clearly embarrassed.

Have I gone too far? she thought, distressed.

"Good," he said after a pause. "I like you, too, Becky. I think we're going to be friends."

"I would like that," Becky assured herself and the soft-spoken giant.

She decided to take his arm. It was like taking hold of a moving piece of rock.

Joe felt warmth run up his arm. He made a halfhearted attempt to ignore the sensation. He knew that taking a man's arm was less common in the North than in the South. *Becky has manners,* he told himself. *Means nothing.*

"Now that we're friends, lets see what we can do for Nathan," Becky suggested casually. "Father Chet calls it the Mystical Body of Christ, doesn't he? I mean, everybody is connected to Jesus. It's all new to me, and he says it's a mystery, but I like it." She realized that Father Chet's prophecy had already come true. She had found her first Catholic friend.

Joe didn't say a word. *Hmmn,* he thought, *she's interesting. I'll have to think about this one. Becky Macadam. Isn't Macadam Scottish? I'll have to ask her. And she's quoting Father Chet on Mystici Corporis. That's a good sign...*

Joe Jackson's mind was jumping from stone to stone. Rebecca Macadam was a word descending into the warmth of his heart, where she would become flesh. There she would stay.

They arrived at the Grotto and knelt to pray for Nathan, and, unknown to Joseph Jackson, for Becky's unborn child.

3

From *Dark Years History*
(New Rome Press, 31 R.E.)
by Rebecca Macadam Jackson

...debate when the Tribulations began. Many believe they began with the rise of Soviet Russia in 1917—as foretold by Our Lady at both Fatima, Portugal, and Hrushiv, Ukraine—and the enslavement and murder of over ninety million citizens in what had been one of the most pious nations of the world before the communist regime.

Other historians point to the period when practically all the governments of the world—communist, socialist, and capitalist—embraced and glorified abortion as a solution to problems of so-called overpopulation. Abortion was also promoted as the primary sociopolitical means for the so-called emancipation of women after the 1960s. While these attitudes horrify those of us who live today, the pro-abortion philosophy was considered socially and morally necessary. Not counting unborn children lost to abortifacients such as the IUD and the pill, surgical abortion accounted for roughly 1.6 billion souls lost in the second half of the twentieth century. Counting nonsurgical abortions, biologists estimate the actual number of immortal souls lost in this silent holocaust at four times that number.

The reader will bear in mind that fewer than five billion souls lived on the face of the earth before 1950. Therefore, at least half as many souls were murdered in their mothers' wombs *in less than fifty years* than ever were born of their mothers' wombs in all of the centuries of known human history before 1950. A case could be made that abortion was both the *cause of* the Great Chastisement as well as a *part of it*.

Other historians hold that the great natural disasters beginning in the late 1980s and increasing in frequency and intensity up until the Three Days of Darkness mark the "birth pangs"—as Jesus referred to them in the Scriptures—of the Tribulations. Certainly this period marks the beginning of unprecedented visits from heaven by Our Lady and Our Eucharistic King to warn us.

Most historians do agree, however, that the attack upon the life of Pope Patrick the Great and the ensuing Great Schism clearly indicate the time when an historical line was crossed…

4

Sunday Morning
8 October
Albano, Italy ("Sector Four")

Pope Patrick tore a piece of cloth from his soaked nightshirt and stuffed it into the bullet wound just below his ribs, in a desperate—and mostly successful—attempt to staunch the bleeding. There was an extremely painful throbbing in his temple where his head had hit the doorjamb of his Fiat. His vision was alternately blurry and clear.

No hospitals. Don't pass out Angus! the pope commanded. *Sweet Mary, help me!*

He fought nausea and blackout. He collapsed on the side street of Albano. His vision slowly returned. He struggled to regain his feet. The narrow cobblestoned alley was empty.

Got to get to Dublin, then...

Then what?

He didn't know.

He thought of poor Thomas Phillips. The lad, his nephew from Boston, had been a champion wrestler in high school. But he had given up a full scholarship to the University of Iowa to enter the Legionaries of Christ.

A disjointed phrase from the seminarian's lexicon echoed back from a conversation the pope had with the boy months earlier: *...and go. Suck it up and go.*

"It means to gather oneself and prepare to fight against all odds to succeed in winning the game," the bright seminarian had explained.

A pained smile formed on Angus's lips. He willed himself to chuckle. The wound in his side suddenly stung him and his faint smile turned to a grimace. He fought blackout again.

Suck it up and go. What was the other one? Walk it off? Walk it off. Dressed like this? Think!

Somehow the pope was able to stand up. The business day had begun and Angus could see people walking beyond the alley. He spotted a small dumpster nearby and stumbled over to it. Inside he found a ratty coat with a large collar. He abandoned his own water-soaked coat and covered his shivering body. He still had his own wallet and the wallet Thomas had thrown to him during the nightmarish chase. The old man combed his hair as best he could with ice cold fingers.

He made his way slowly to the end of the street and into a drugstore he found two blocks away. He tried desperately to walk without revealing his weakened state. Angus's perfect Italian (spoken in the local dialect) helped keep the clerk from becoming suspicious. The indifferent clerk didn't even look at the pope's face during the transaction. Using damp bills, Angus bought several items with the dead seminarian's money, including makeup, hair coloring, some cheap clothes, a large-brimmed hat, bandages, and over-the-counter antibiotics.

There was a lot of money in the wallet. Thomas had come to say good-bye to him. The lad had planned on leaving the seminary the morning of his death, and had carried his traveling money with him to the Vatican. Thomas had loved being a seminarian, but after much prayer and soul-searching, he had come to the conclusion that he did not have a vocation. His spiritual director had agreed.

He's a martyr now, Angus thought.

Angus bought several loaves of bread, cheese, and some fruit at a grocery cart. He devoured the food while he walked, forcing it into his system. He found a room in a cheap *pensione* in a poor neighborhood nearby. It took all of his will to prevent himself from collapsing onto the small sunken mattress. He painfully dressed his own wound—the bullet was still inside him but the hole was small and uniformly round. It took almost an hour to color his hair and change the complexion around his eyes with the makeup. He fought blackout the entire time. The acrid smell from the hair coloring helped keep him awake.

God did not save me only to have me die in this cheap hotel, he reasoned. Angus felt hope open a door inside him and take up residence in his soul.

He sat and ate an apple with some cheese while he waited for his hair to dry. He grieved as he thought about Thomas Phillips. He tried to distract himself by thinking of where to go next and how to get there. *I'll take the trains,* he thought. *The airlines are too dangerous. **They** might be watching them. Too many trains in Europe to watch them all.*

Chapter Nine

1

Tuesday Evening
10 October
Under the English Channel

Angus gingerly sat up in the small bed of the private sleeper car in a vain effort to minimize the pain in his side. *At least the bleeding has stopped,* he tried to encourage himself. *How did it ever come to this, running like a rat?*

He was beyond weariness, sustained by sheer will, steeled by years of disciplining his mind and body with prayer and mortifications. When the pope closed his eyes, instead of peaceful and much-needed sleep, the night of the assassination attempt played before him like a movie…

…On the very evening of Angus's return to Rome from Detroit, Thomas Phillips had greatly surprised his uncle by showing up in the papal bedroom just before three in the morning. The flight to Boston was in four hours. He had decided to visit the pope and used his special pass to enter the Vatican gate. The guard was accustomed to late night visits by unusual guests to the eccentric pope. Once inside the sprawling gardens and past the Swiss Guard, Thomas used a secret stairway installed by a Renaissance pope which Uncle Angus had shown him for fun.

Months earlier Uncle Angus had told him, "Even the Swiss Guards don't know about it. My predecessor, the Magnificent

Pole, discovered it by accident, and showed it to me when I was the Cardinal of Dublin."

Instead of continuing down the path to the second security checkpoint at the door which led to the pope's private suite, Thomas ducked through a hedge and quietly felt his way through the gardens until he found the secret entrance. After fumbling for several minutes he pushed the correct square of marble and a section of the wall opened. The ex-wrestler squeezed through the small opening into a cramped passage which led to a narrow, completely dark stairway.

The whole night had an emotionally surreal feeling to it, which only added to his disappointment over leaving the seminary. As he climbed the stairway, he consoled himself with the thought that he was living a great adventure. This was something to tell his grandchildren—now that he was free to get married and actually have some grandchildren.

As he reached the top, he paused; a wave of fear washed over him. He brushed it off with a brief prayer to his guardian angel. The pope's bedroom was on the other side. He crawled out of the passageway hidden in the carved woodwork of an immense wall of bookcases.

The pope was sitting at his desk, studying his Bible. He looked up and chuckled. "Good evening, Thomas. How nice of you to join me."

"Well, I was just passing through."

Angus laughed, gave Thomas a serious look, then said, "You're not here to borrow money, are you?"

Now they both laughed.

After a moment Thomas said, "I'm here to ask for your blessing."

"Is something wrong?"

"I'm leaving the Legionaries of Christ. In four hours I'm flying back to Boston."

The pope regarded him thoughtfully.

"I... I don't want anyone to know I came here tonight, Uncle Angus." Thomas went on, "No one knows I'm here, except the Swiss Guard who let me through the gate." His emotions caught up with him. He fought to keep tears out of his eyes.

Angus was surprised—but not completely shocked. There had always been something too worldly about the young man standing before him now.

"Well, Thomas, we both know that you gave it your best."

"Do you think so, Uncle Angus?"

"I do," the pope replied somberly, nodding slowly. "I believe it's all for the greater glory of God. At times like these, the best thing we can do is ask Our Lady for help."

Thomas took hold of himself. He pulled his rosary out of his pocket; the beads were already tightly clenched in his fist.

They knelt down beside the bed and began to pray.

They were just beginning the fourth decade of the Sorrowful Mysteries when a man wearing black clothes and a dark mask slipped through the door into the large bedroom.

The assassin had been expecting to find the pope asleep or at least alone; he hesitated before aiming his gun. Then he fired three muffled shots at the old man. Angus dove behind the bed. Then the assassin turned to fire at Thomas who was already charging towards him.

Thomas Phillips took two of five bullets into his burly chest and one into his left arm. He slammed into the assassin. In a series of quick, brutal movements the assassin was trapped in a human vise. Thomas grunted; all three men heard a sickening crack.

Thomas stood and dropped the corpse. Angus would forever remember the unnatural angle of the assassin's neck.

Like a dead crow, he thought. *God have mercy on his soul.*

Angus was hit. The bullet had gone into his left side below the rib cage.

Thomas saw the blood spreading on the pope's white nightshirt. He grabbed a pillow from the bed, tore it open and gingerly jammed stuffing into the pope's bleeding wound, muttering, "…direct pressure stops bleeding, direct pressure stops bleeding—"

"—Thomas! You're wounded!"

Thomas stared at the blood oozing from his chest and felt pain for the first time. He nodded and began to treat his own wounds.

"No, lad! You don't understand, we've *got* to get you to a hospital."

"No way! I'm okay—we've got to get *you* out of here!"

"Out of here?" Angus replied. "No, I'll call Security—"

"Security?! After this? You've got to get out of here!"

Angus's eyes widened as the significance of his nephew's words hit home.

"Uncle Angus, they let that guy in. They didn't know I was here. Who can you trust?" Thomas reached for his wallet. "Wait! Here, I... I've got a ticket to Boston." He held it out in his bloody hand.

Angus reached for it, and stopped.

"The pope cannot leave Rome. I will not leave Rome." He said it to himself.

Despite his pain, Thomas closed his eyes and prayed. He swayed on his feet.

Angus walked over to him and put a hand on his shoulder, whispering, "You're a brave lad, but that doesn't mean we can't go to the hospital now."

Angus was recovering from his shock. A plan formed quickly in his head, part calculation, part gut feeling. The boy was right: there was no one he could trust beyond the walls of this room. He would never leave Rome, of course. But he did know one thing: *We can't leave through that bedroom door.* It was time to act.

And Thomas's prayer was answered.

Angus hastily threw on a coat and heavy leather walking shoes. Out of habit he grabbed three fake passports he kept in the drawer of the ancient night table next to his bed.

"Through the passage, quickly," he urged Thomas, who was just beginning to get his second wind.

The two bleeding men then entered the secret passage-way, using Angus's flashlight.

This boy is strong. He's as strong as an ox even with three bullets in him! Angus told himself, amazed, as they staggered down the claustrophobic stairway.

Once outside, they made their way over to the path by the gate. They hid behind thick hedges. The Swiss Guard who had admitted Phillips earlier was slumped in his chair in the guardhouse.

"He was probably shot by the assassin who attacked us," Angus whispered to Thomas. "Somehow, I don't think we should leave this way, laddie," the pope added before leading Thomas to a tiny shed in the rear of the gardens. Inside the shed was the pope's Fiat.

Angus had arranged to have the old car available for his secret missions. He always needed to be able to leave at any time without being noticed. Now he opened a private steel gate in a wall that led to a back street.

He didn't know that his enemies had bugged the gate months earlier so they could keep track of his movements. As soon as the gate was opened, the ones who had planned the assassination deduced that their attempt to kill Angus had failed.

"Mary had her *fiat,* and I have mine," the pope quipped, trying to cheer up the ashen-faced seminarian. Thomas didn't laugh. He threw himself behind the wheel. A minute after their escape onto the streets of Rome, a black Citroen appeared behind the Fiat. Thomas saw it.

"They're back, Uncle Angus! Time to suck it up and go!" he shouted, stepping on the gas. Thomas was still pumping adrenaline. His left arm screamed with pain.

Thomas tried but failed to pull away from the more powerful Citroen. During the insane car ride that followed, he frantically explained how easy it had been to overpower the assassin. Talking helped calm him while he drove like a madman.

"Guess they don't teach the assassins in Europe how to wrestle, Uncle Angus! Somehow, I'm glad I killed the son of a bitch as a layman and not as a Legionary. He was going to

kill you! Killing the pope, I can't believe it! Here! Money!"
Thomas threw his wallet at the pope.

The chase lasted only a few minutes. As Thomas drove
the old Fiat over a curb at the end of *Via Cola DiRienzo,* the
steering arm on one of the wheels broke and the car careened
toward the small wooden fence at *Lung Michelangelo* which
separated the road from the raging river below.

For a moment, where there had been the screeching sound
of wheels on the wet streets, there was now only the sound of
rain on the hood of the Fiat before it plunged into the roiling
cold water. Phillips started shouting a Hail Mary as the car
quickly filled with water through floorboards riddled with
rust holes. Only the light from the dashboard let the eerily
calm Angus see Thomas's fearful face, which was now bleeding after smashing into the unbroken windshield.

Angus began to pray for the boy's soul and muttered the
Latin prayers for the Anointing of the Sick. The car hit a gully
at the bottom of the river and flipped over on its side, precari-
ously balancing in the strong current. The pope's door was
facing the surface.

Thomas was dead.

The car was completely full of water now. Holding his
breath, Angus prayed an act of contrition and begged Jesus
for mercy.

I have one minute, maybe less, he thought serenely. *I'm
shot and bleeding. I can't swim well. I'm going to die.*

He decided to die with a prayer in his heart. Rather than
form sentences, he prayed to the Christ whom he had served
as Vicar, and for the intercession of His mother: *Jesus...
Mary... Jesus... Mary... Jesus... Mary...*

Then the angel came.

Angus never saw the angel. The bleeding pope was about
to inhale water when the door of the Fiat was pulled open.
Angus felt—but did not see—two hands with superhuman
strength grasp him and pull him through the water at a terrific
speed. He heard four confusing words: *"God conquers is
here."*

The battered old man heard the words inside *and* outside of his head. Angus had no idea what the words meant. He did not know that the angel was saying its *name:* God Conquers (just as the Archangel Gabriel's name means God Speaks). Angus's angel was saying, in effect, "I, God Conquers, have arrived."

The rest of the experience was like a dream with real water in it. Angus wondered if he was being taken up to heaven when he broke the surface and saw the lights of the city above him. He was far downstream from where he had crashed—at least a hundred yards. He saw the smashed fence far behind him. His lungs involuntarily sucked in huge gobs of air while his bullet wound sent waves of pain through his torso.

Angus saw two men dressed in black, wearing masks, peering over *Lung Michelangelo,* the Citroen behind them. In the glow of a street light Angus saw that they were holding rifles and were looking at the location in the river where the Fiat must have entered. They did not see Angus. The pope felt a chill that had nothing to do with his wounds, his pain, the river, and his shortness of breath.

The invisible hands were still holding Angus under his armpits. He was just above the surface. The strong being moved him to a large, floating log. He was held to the log by this invisible creature of God.

An angel! Lord you have rescued me! I have walked through the valley of the shadow of death!

He felt an enormous warm "hand" cover his wound. He suddenly felt safe and dizzy. Remarkably, the log began to move faster than the current. Again, inside and outside of his head, in a kind of supernatural stereo, Angus heard the angel speak to him:

"South Bend, Indiana."

Water streamed by; Angus lost track of time and passed out. He woke up downriver almost four hours later on the cobblestoned alley in Albano, less than a half mile from the Tiber.

✝ ✝ ✝

In the sleeper car of the train the pope shook himself and turned away from the memory. He wished that he had a set of rosary beads to hold.

He felt better, despite the lack of sleep. The bleeding in his side had stopped to a trickle—although it still pained him greatly—and his head was pounding. He felt wide awake, as if he had just "woken up."

Maybe I'm going to make it. At least through today. I've got to get to Dublin. Then South Bend, Indiana. South Bend? Suck it up and go. I wonder what the angel's name was?

Angus had purchased a Walkman at the station in Paris. He turned it on. As he listened to the news, he was not surprised at the half lies in the reports about his death. There was no mention of an assassination attempt at the Vatican Residence. Nor was there any mention of bullet wounds in Thomas's body. Casino was quoted in the reports. Angus was certain Casino was behind the falsehoods. Why was Casino and not the official Vatican spokesman leading the press conferences?

The beleaguered pope looked at himself in the mirror on the door of the sleeper. He did not resemble Pope Patrick. He looked like Carlos Cepeda, a businessman from Milan—the fictitious man portrayed in his false Italian passport.

It was time to find a place to get some blood and to heal. Angus was a practical man, after all, and you couldn't order room service for blood in a moving train.

And I can't go to a hospital. If I surface, they'll just kill me "again." Angus laughed at his own dark humor. Almost despite himself, he remembered prophecies from Marian apparitions predicting attempts on the life of the pope—and the rise of an antipope. His pale face became a shade paler.

So I better stay out of circulation until I get more information about what's going on. Information is the basis for all future action, he said to himself, repeating one of his own favorite sayings.

So where can I go? Before I die for the second time in as many days?

2

Monday Afternoon
9 October
Notre Dame, Indiana

Father Chet absolved Nathan of his sins. For penance Chet asked Nathan to begin practicing the habit of making a daily examination of conscience. This involves taking stock of one's good and bad actions at the end of every day. Chet waited patiently while Nathan prayed his Hail Mary before the French Gothic tabernacle in the center of Sacred Heart Basilica.

Chet smiled when Nathan walked back toward him. Together they left by the side exit of the church.

"How come I don't, you know, feel anything?" Nathan asked Chet outside. "I'm supposed to feel good, or sad, or something, right?"

"Not necessarily, my friend," Chet replied. "Religion is not based on feelings. It's based on supernatural realities. In reality, Jesus absolved your sins through me regardless of what you feel. It means that your soul is different—cleaned up completely. You still have all your bad habits—the Church calls it the residue of original sin, but you are not the same where it counts, in your immortal soul.

"Let's say you stole ten bucks from me, felt sorry, and asked me for forgiveness, then I forgive you. Well, that's what Jesus did on the cross—forgave all sins up to that point and into the future."

Nathan nodded like a grade school student being introduced to a new subject. Father Chet took this cue.

"But let's suppose you've still got my ten bucks, even after I forgive you. Confession is like giving me back the tenspot, and on top of it, my deciding to forget you ever stole it in the first place. After Jesus appeared to the apostles in the upper room, he gave them the, quote, power to 'absolve sins.' It's in the Gospel of John. The word he used wasn't 'forgive.' Jesus used the Hebrew word for 'absolve,' which means 'to settle accounts' or 'to restore to original state.' What we just did was the 'absolve part' of priestly orders. Mass is the death and resurrection part of priestly orders—the forgiveness part. Mass is the timeless supernatural re-living of Jesus' death and resurrection. Confession is the cleansing of your soul—the absolution. Your penance is paying back the ten bucks in a spiritual action.

"So the sacrament has three parts: forgiveness, absolution, and penance. Penance is also known as reparation."

Chet had fallen into a slight tone of lecturing and caught himself.

"The long and the short of it is that God's grace affects your soul whether you feel it or not, based on your free choice to accept it. You've taken Joanie up on Pascal's Wager by choice, but it may be a while before you start 'feeling' like a Catholic, if ever. Grace is a funny thing. It's like electricity—it's flowing through the wires, ready for you to plug into it, but invisible. When grace is working, you don't feel it, you just work right."

"You've got a way with words, Chetmeister," Nathan said with genuine admiration. "You should have told me this stuff earlier. I bet you're surprised I'm going for all this." Nathan added.

"Hey, buddy, I tried to bring it up, but you weren't listening. And I'm not surprised you turned around. I had complete faith that you would come around eventually—really, I did. I always knew you were destined for greatness."

Nathan could tell that Chet wasn't kidding. Nathan put his arm around the shoulder of his best friend. Becky and Joe were just coming back from the Grotto.

"Joe suggested that the two of you give me a tour of this place," Becky said cheerfully. "We've got some time before Joanie Wheat shows up." She saw Nathan's eyes brighten at the mention of Joanie Wheat.

"If Nathan doesn't mind a second go 'round, sure," Chet answered, looking to Nathan. Nathan gave a quick nod of agreement.

"Well then, let's start at Howard Hall," Father Chet added equably, a smile coming to his eyes. "I'll show you where Jimbo Sullivan landed his fateful right hook on his brother, the erstwhile future priest, yours truly." Everyone laughed politely. They all knew about Jimbo's Right Hook.

"Then let's get some lunch," Joe suggested. "I'm so hungry I could eat a horse."

"You look like you've eaten several over the years," Becky chided. Joe reacted to the verbal jab with a smile.

The big lug is already letting Becky kid him, Chet noted. *Good sign.*

The foursome cut by Sorin Hall across the Bookstore basketball courts toward Howard Hall.

3

Monday Edition
9 October
The New York Times

Rome, Italy. Catholics around the world mourn the death of controversial Pope Patrick, who drowned in the Tiber River after a bizarre car chase through the streets of Rome sometime after three o'clock on Sunday morning.

The reason for the chase is not known. The identities of the drivers of the mysterious black Citroen which pursued the pontiff's vehicle at high speeds are also unknown. The pontiff's car crashed through a barrier on *Lung Michelangelo*. The body of the pope has not been recovered. Police also report plans to dredge the Tiber for Pope Patrick's body in the coming days. Authorities speculate the pontiff may have drowned after a desperate attempt to escape from the car, a Fiat, while it was submerged in the Tiber. Noting the unusually strong currents in the Tiber, which was ten feet above normal height due to a recent series of torrential downpours in the mountains surrounding Rome, and the advanced age of the pontiff, authorities give little probability that he survived the violent crash. The crash also killed the driver of the pope's vehicle, Thomas Phillips, a seminarian from Massachusetts.

"Given the condition of Mr. Phillips's corpse, who died from the crash, not from drowning, it is likely that the elderly pope was also mortally injured. The currents were extremely treacherous. Our divers had a very difficult time recovering Phillip's corpse. The dredging of the Tiber River and the recovery of the submerged vehicle will have to wait until the river subsides," according to the spokesman for *Polizia Romano,* Vitorio Graniconola. "We may never recover the body," Graniconola added, speculating that currents could drag the body into the Tyrrhenian Sea in a matter of hours. Hospital emergency rooms within the surrounding area report no sign of Pope Patrick. According to Graniconola, Catholics throughout the world have little hope that "he escaped the submerged vehicle, and then survived probable serious injuries and the deadly currents of the Tiber."

Luigi Cardinal Casino of Milan said in a press conference held in the Vatican several hours after the tragedy that Pope Patrick, formerly Angus Cardinal O'Hara of Dublin, was an exceptionally gifted leader during his eighteen month reign. Casino noted that the Vatican would cooperate in the international manhunt to find the pope's killers, and vowed to continue Pope Patrick's work to reunite the Roman Catholic and Eastern Orthodox churches. Sources within the Vatican report that Cardinal Casino is the most likely replacement for Pope Patrick, and is highly respected in both secular and religious circles.

Observers say the controversial "Byzantium Protocol," a formal agreement to reunite the two churches for the first time since 1054 A.D., was within months of completion. Casino, fighting back tears, had no comment when asked whether the Byzantium Protocol negotiations would continue on schedule. Pope Patrick won the Nobel Peace Prize after reuniting Ireland two years before being elected pope. An unsuccessful assassination attempt was made on then Cardinal O'Hara by IRA terrorists during Ireland's reunification negotiations.

Vatican watchers also noted that the pontiff had drawn fire from critics within the Catholic Church for his elevation of the doctrine of the Mother of God as Mediatrix of All Graces to "infallible" status only three months into his pontificate. He was also criticized for his rigid stand against admitting women to the priesthood, his condemnation of artificial contraception, and his unyielding opposition to a woman's right to choose abortion. A source within the Rome Police Department says that the pope has many enemies in Ireland, Eastern Europe, and even within his own church because of the "Mediatrix issue." Their investigation will have to "start from scratch."

The drowned man and apparent driver of Pope Patrick's car was Thomas Phillips, a seminarian member of the Legionaries of Christ. Phillips was born and raised in Boston, Massachusetts. Authorities do not know how or why Mr. Phillips came to be driving the pope at such a strange hour.

An unidentified *Times* source within the Vatican reports that Mr. Phillips was a relative of the pope and occasionally served at the pope's private masses. Phillips's parents and authorities from the Legionaries of Christ were not available for comment at the time this special report was filed.

A Vatican press agent said funeral services for Pope Patrick would be scheduled pending a final report from the Rome Police...

4

Wednesday Afternoon
11 October
County Galway, Ireland

An Italian man appeared at the huge and ancient wooden doors of the Monastery of the Holy Blood. The Carmelite sister who greeted him didn't realize that he was Pope Patrick. The old man's face was pale, ashen, and there were deep circles under his eyes. It was unusual to have a tourist visit in this remote part of western Ireland.

Angus asked for the prioress, Sister Mary Bernard, then collapsed but did not pass out.

Angus whispered instructions in Gaelic to Sister Mary Bernard when she was brought to him. Sister Mary Bernard ordered her three nuns to bring the ailing man to her office. There had once been over three dozen nuns in residence—now there were four.

"We thought you were dead, Your Holiness!" she exclaimed when they were alone, after Angus had been revived by a nip of Jameson's Irish.

"Me too, Sister Mary, me too!" he croaked in a hoarse voice. His neck wound, healed years before, was giving him phantom pains. "Please, call me Father Angus."

She nodded and looked at him with concern. He made an effort to sit up in his chair.

"It's a long story," he continued in Gaelic, "and I'll tell you more when I get my strength back. First, you must forbid your sisters, under obedience, to breathe a word about my resurrection." He chuckled darkly. Then winced. Every time he laughed the new bullet wound hurt.

"To do so would almost certainly mean all of our deaths. I took great care to come here unnoticed. I took a train from Italy to England using that new Channel Tunnel, sleeping most of the way. The ferry to Dublin was most difficult. I didn't dare fly, as *they* must be watching the airports if they suspect I'm still alive. We can't be sure. As your friend and your pope, I beg you to guard our secret until I figure out what to do next."

"But what *are* we to do next, Holy Father? Look at that wound!"

"Yes, to be sure, I need medical attention, otherwise you're going to have the first pope to die on Irish soil do so in your Carmel. Any suggestions?"

"Sister Elizabeth Thomas used to be a nurse. If we could get your blood type and find some blood, she could do transfusions. I know a doctor who will fill prescriptions if I tell him it's for one of mine," she suggested.

"My blood is B positive. We'll need a television to follow the news—"

"We keep one here unplugged in the closet, Father," she replied with a smile. "For just such an occasion."

He tried to laugh then thought better of it. A long pause ensued.

The prioress, who was almost eighty years old, had been one of Angus's Prayer Warriors for almost forty years. She decided to ask a question. She had known him far too long to be timid. She thought of him as a son.

"Angus, what's going on?"

He looked her directly in the eyes. "It's the beginning of the great trial foretold by Our Blessed Mother, Sister. The world is never going to be the same. We must have courage!

"It's a terrible pity," Angus continued. "We almost had the Byzantium Protocol completed, Sister! We were on the verge of doing for the Eastern Church what we did for the Six Counties! It was so far ahead of schedule; I was getting ready to take aim at the Moslems next. The Easterns are afraid of being overwhelmed by the materialistic atheism of the west and a resurgent Russia in the east. The theological differences over the Holy Trinity are not the hindrance they were a thousand years ago," Angus was warming to his favorite subject, almost smiling. Then a dark look came over his face. *"They* just wouldn't allow it, I suppose. All I know is that I've got to get better and get myself over to South…"

Before he could finish his sentence the pounding in his temple began to pound harder and harder until a final blow, as if by a real hammer, knocked him out cold.

The prioress was wondering who Angus meant by "they" when she saw the pope collapse onto the floor. She rushed to his side and felt for his pulse, urging herself to hold back her tears. His body was cold and his palms and wrists were clammy.

Angus needs you! Don't lose control, Mary Bernard, he's alive! Dear Mother of God, help him live! Jesus Lord, save your servant!

She found a faint pulse. But his wrinkled forehead was icy to the touch.

She left him on the wooden floor as she rushed to find Sister Elizabeth Thomas, who was waiting right outside her door along with the two other sisters.

The old nuns were horrified by his feather-like weight as they carried their pope to a bed.

Three hours later, an IV was attached to his arm—Sister Elizabeth had driven to a medical supply store in Galway to purchase the equipment. She had taken transfusions from herself and the one other sister with the pope's blood type. Two heavy blankets covered him. Sister Elizabeth tamped a hot towel on his forehead. His temperature had finally begun to rise. A huge fire burned in an immense fireplace in the

large room, which had been a nobleman's bedroom centuries
before.

Sister Elizabeth looked to her prioress and nodded her
head, saying, "The Holy Father is in a coma, Mother. There's
not much we can do for him."

"We can pray, Sister Elizabeth, as we have for the last
four decades. And you can study. You know as much about
medicine as most doctors, but you're going to have to find
out everything you possibly can about treatment for coma
patients. I'm sure I can talk Doctor Soames into supplying us
prescriptions without letting him know who our patient is—
at least for the time being. He's an odd duck, Doc Soames
is."

The two nuns exchanged a glance. Sister Mary Bernard
turned her gaze to her dying friend and cursed the dampness
of the castle.

Live! Live, you tough old warrior!
She looked at his face.
Live, Angus.

5

Monday Afternoon
9 October
Notre Dame, Indiana

Joanie arrived on a Transpo bus, fresh from teaching. She
walked across the campus and found her friends lounging
around the "Woman at the Well" courtyard, which featured
sculptures by the renowned Ivan Mestrovic. For a while they
made small talk as the new members of the group felt each
other out. No one knew what to think about the shocking
death of Pope Patrick. Joe was particularly shaken by the
event—he had idolized the diminutive pope from Ireland.

Joanie and Father Chet left the group. He heard her confession as they walked along the South Quad and absolved her in front of the Engineering Building. Nathan, leaning on the well between statues of Jesus and the Woman at the Well, looked on in wonder as he saw Father Chet lay his hands on Joanie's head. Then Chet made a sign of the cross over her. She raised her bowed head and opened her eyes. A lovely smile came over her face.

Wow. Did I just do the same thing? Nathan thought, feeling happy for himself and Joanie, almost light-headed. *This is the Moral Universe.*

Joanie and Chet returned to the group. She headed right over to Nathan's side and took his hand. He gripped her hand tightly. There was a silence among the young group of Catholics, but not an awkward one. Nathan stifled a sudden and incredibly strong urge to shout with joy, but a sheepish grin did manage to surface to his face.

Chet made a joke about an unrelated subject, and everyone laughed. Eventually Joe announced that Karl Slinger was going to meet him to formally join the Knights of Immaculata in the Log Chapel. He invited Nathan and Becky to also enroll in Saint Maximilian Kolbe's worldwide lay association. Father Chet briefly explained the purpose of the Knights of Immaculata to Becky and Nathan. Becky agreed to enroll enthusiastically. Nathan agreed to enroll after looking to Joanie, who nodded at him with a serious look.

Okay, I'll do it. The Wager, right? Nathan thought as he looked back to her.

✝ ✝ ✝

The Log Chapel is a tiny structure. As he looked around the room Nathan couldn't help but imagine the original founders of Notre Dame huddling around a fire in the one room building, surrounded almost entirely by wilderness at the time it was built.

Before the ceremony, which took less than five minutes, Father Chet explained that the Knights were not a fraternal organization, but rather, the supernatural armed forces of Mary.

"You are about to become first degree Knights of Immaculata. There are no official meetings, or dues, or club activities, though you can organize these kinds of things with other Knights if you wish, as Joe has done with the Kolbe Foundation. Any group of Knights working together are second degree Knights. Our founder, Saint Maximilian Kolbe, a Franciscan priest, purposely set up the Knights to be a free-flowing organization that could adapt itself to any situation, time, or place.

"By making the Act of Consecration to the Sacred Heart of Jesus through the Immaculate Heart of Mary, you change your status here on earth. From this moment on, you are the property of Mary and, as such, are the perfect tool of Jesus, who will deploy you to win more hearts for His Kingdom. He is our Supreme Commander, and Mary our General.

"Saint Maximilian often used military terms to describe the Knights, whose Latin name means Militia of the Immaculate Conception, *Militia Immaculatæ*. Kolbe called the Miraculous Medal, which you will receive today as a sign of your consecration, the 'bullet' we Knights use to fire into the heart of the enemy, Satan."

Becky, Nathan, and Slinger were facing Father Chet, who was standing in front of the modest altar. Joanie, Joe, and Professor Wheat were behind them. Wheat had taken time between classes to attend Slinger's enrollment. The professor had been pleased to find Nathan in the chapel.

"The Knights of Immaculata are especially like the Marine Corps in two ways…"

Wheat and Slinger smiled when Father Chet mentioned the Marines. Slinger noticed the easy going yet organized way Father Chet expounded upon the Knights. *This Irishman is smoother than Maker's Mark,* Slinger thought.

"…First, because once you are a Knight, you are always a Knight. It's a one time gift of yourself to Mary—our gracious response to the gift of His mother which He gave us all on Calvary. In this sense, consider your Knighthood a state of being. From now on, it's what you are. Your Knighthood will therefore 'inform' your actions. You will have opened within yourselves a new aqueduct for the grace of Jesus to flow more perfectly to you through Mary. Pope Patrick's elevation of the Doctrine of Mary as Mediatrix of All Graces confirms this Kolbean teaching so well."

A heavy silence fell as Chet paused. He had casually come upon Pope Patrick like strolling around a corner into a brick wall. The pope was dead. Somehow his death made their event more somber, more relevant for everyone in the room. Tom Wheat pictured the first Christians, fearful and excited in the catacombs, knowing that their baptism carried with it the probability of martyrdom. Chet continued in a much more sober tone.

"Secondly, your Knighthood is like being in the Marine Corps because it is the job of the Knights of Immaculata to storm the most difficult enemy beaches in search of souls to conquer. We're the advance forces in Mary's Militia. We do the toughest evangelical jobs with confidence. Remember, we live in times that are highlighted by an unprecedented battle between Satan, the Red Dragon of Revelation, and Mary, the Woman Clothed in the Sun. Mary needs us. We're signed up for the duration of the war. Like Jesus on the cross, and soldiers in battle, our lives are our sacrifice."

Chet looked down at his feet, then looked quickly at Nathan before continuing.

"One final thing. Don't worry whether or not you 'feel' anything. This is a supernatural event, not an emotional one. Your lives will change forever whether you feel anything this afternoon or not. Let's go for it!"

With that Father Chet led them all in the consecration ceremony. Karl was elated, barely able to control his wide smile despite the serious nature of the short ceremony. Becky found

the consecration prayer touching, and despite what Father
Chet had cautioned, felt as if she was beginning an exciting
adventure. Nathan, as Father Chet had warned, felt nothing
out of the ordinary, but considered himself faithful to the
commitment he had made to Joanie when he took Pascal's
Wager. By simply reciting the consecration prayer, the words
were forever etched into his memory.

Joe Jackson solemnly shook each new Knight's hand and
placed Miraculous Medals around their necks.

Professor Wheat begged their leave to return to teach a
class. Slinger asked Father Chet to give him a quick tour of
the campus before they all left for Wheat's talk in Saint Joseph
Church. Chet was happy to oblige the big Pole.

*I wonder which one will be eating out of the other's hand
before their little tour is over?* Nathan thought as he watched
the priest and the older man walk toward the lake.

Nathan looked at his three remaining companions and
suggested a game of touch football, "After all, this is Notre
Dame, isn't it?"

They played the game in front of Howard Hall as the first
students started to leave their dormitories and afternoon
classes to go to dinner at the dining hall. Many recognized
and called to Joe Jackson, who smiled sheepishly at his fans.

Well, if Mr. Super Bowl isn't embarrassed? Becky noted
pleasantly. *How sweet!*

Several students stopped to watch the game. Although
both Joe and Nathan were determined to keep the game light
and fun, it was a struggle for them to do so. Both men wanted
to win—it was part of their natures.

✝ ✝ ✝

Nathan and Becky won easily, which surprised Joe. Becky
and Joanie were about as good as most women are at football—that is to say, not very good. Joe couldn't help but notice
how Nathan coaxed the most out of Becky during the game,
and how accurately and gently he delivered the ball to her.

Joe could catch but he was just an average passer and that
proved the difference. Nathan wore his new Miraculous Medal
on the outside of his rugby shirt.

When the game was over, the Knights of Immaculata were
ready to leave for Tom Wheat's talk at Saint Joseph Church.
Father Chet returned with Karl Slinger. The priest was singing the praises of Bruno's Pizza, where they all would meet
for dinner after the talk.

6

Monday Evening
9 October
South Bend, Indiana

The crowd filled Saint Joseph Church. Joanie, Nathan, and
Chet found seats near the front. Anne Wheat sat with Karl
Slinger. Denny Wheat was not in attendance—he was off
working in the air somewhere.

Nathan and Becky watched in fascination as an older priest
came and began Benediction. The church was filled with in-
cense and beautiful *a cappella* Gregorian chant, "love songs
to the Eucharist" composed by Saint Thomas Aquinas. Neither
Becky nor Nathan had ever seen or heard a Benediction.
Becky, with her trained adman's eye, noticed that the sight
line between priest and Eucharist blurred when the elderly
priest elevated the monstrance. Others bowed their heads but
Becky stared, transfixed. After a period of adoration, the priest
led the congregation in the Divine Praises and then removed
the Sacred Host from the monstrance, returning Him to the
tabernacle. The crowd was completely silent.

Joe Jackson came to the lectern and briefly introduced
Tom Wheat on behalf of the Knights of Immaculata. Joe was
obviously uncomfortable speaking before a large audience.

Tom Wheat left his seat in the front pew and genuflected slowly before the tabernacle. He then walked to the lectern, bowed his head, and prayed with the crowd for the Holy Spirit to come and enlighten their hearts.

"I want to thank the Knights for inviting me back again to speak this year. It's always a great honor speaking before a group that is consecrated to our Blessed Mother. You are such effective evangelizers for the faith. Your work and prayers have helped reach millions with the urgent messages heaven has for this country and the world. God bless you! I'm proud to be known as a Knight of Immaculata!

"Normally I speak about the apparitions of Mary throughout history, and what they have in common, starting with Guadalupe in Mexico in 1531, and building up to current alleged apparitions and the messages almost all apparitions seem to have in common."

Tom Wheat paused for effect and slowly looked out at the crowd, focusing in on a particular person for a few seconds in each section of the church. Up to this point he had used a casual tone but now he began to speak with a deep-timbred voice that came just short of trembling.

"But tonight, to emphasize the importance, to emphasize the urgency, I'm going to tell you now what I usually save for the climax at the end . . ."

He paused before he delivered the punch line.

"The world is about to experience a great chastisement! A punishment from God far greater than the flood! It will be the most devastating tribulation in the whole history of the world, from the time of the Old Testament, to the coming of Jesus and the establishment of His Catholic Church on earth, from the struggle over the centuries to Christianize the pagan world right up to our own bloody century."

At this point Tom lowered his voice and began speaking slowly and deliberately.

"The world is hanging by a thread. These are Our Lady's words, not mine. Mary expresses the same theme in Ireland, Japan, Kibeho in Africa, Hrushiv in Ukraine, San Nicholas in Argentina, and all across the United States, where reports of mystics are so widespread that our bishops don't have the resources to investigate them all. An estimated fifteen million pilgrims have journeyed halfway around the world to Medjugorje, the site of reported apparitions of Our Lady. Mary, the Woman of Genesis 3:15, is coming to tell us what we can do to form—as Saint Louis DeMontfort calls us in his illumined work, True Devotion to Mary—the *heel* that will crush the head of Satan. This heel we form will mitigate these chastisements for our family, friends, and geographical regions, and help save our country from the wrath of Divine Justice!

"The world is hanging by a thread, Our Lady says.

"Many of our own families have already experienced what Mary has called 'the birth pangs.' Some of you and your relatives have lost property during the record-setting, hostile weather of recent years, and during the unprecedented natural disasters—Hurricane Andrew, the Great Mississippi Flood, the California Earthquake to name just a few. Many of you may not know that Europe and Asia have had similar floods, droughts, typhoons, and earthquakes; again, on an unprecedented scale.

"Some of you have experienced internal tribulations as your families suffer divorce and other problems. Many of you have had to deal with your children having abortions, living together, and the general breakdown of family values that even the dominant liberal media can no longer ignore.

"Others have noted the increased crime rate, the wars multiplying around the world, and the growth of the New Age Movement and cults. No one denies that there is a general spiritual malaise in our society.

"Let me tell you, friends, that the birth pangs have just begun. The natural disasters will increase in number and intensity. This will exacerbate an already weak world economy. Wars will increase. Deadly new diseases worse than AIDS have been predicted by certain mystics.

"Worst of all, the Church itself will experience an open apostasy—a falling away from the faith—far worse than the troubles we see today. This morning's news of the tragic death of Pope Patrick is very troubling. Very troubling.

"As these signs of the times increase, we must be prepared. Unlike the Great Depression when economic disaster hit a mostly Christian nation and social unrest was not a problem, economic disaster in our age of no moral values will mean the probable breakdown of law and order. I do not mean that we should be prepared, as some say we should, by storing up food and guns. I mean spiritual preparation. We must prepare to sacrifice our lives for the faith.

"It should not be lost on any Knight of Immaculata that our founder, Saint Maximilian Kolbe, died in Auschwitz at the hands of the Nazis. If what Mary is telling us in these worldwide apparitions is true, then we must be prepared for a *Zeitgeist*—a spirit of the age—far worse than Nazism, if that can be imagined.

"In the coming days, you may no longer be able to go to your own church to receive confession or Communion.

"In the coming days, you may no longer be able to 'buy or sell' and earn your daily bread without renouncing your faith.

"In the coming days, we may see blood spilled on the streets of America for the first time since the Civil War, only this time with greater weapons of destruction at our disposal.

"In the coming days, as the confusion mounts, your neighbors may have only one person to go to for spiritual enlightenment and relief— you."

Leading up to the last several statements, Wheat's voice had grown stronger. No sound could be heard in Saint Joseph Church except for his deep voice. Now Wheat lowered his voice to a whisper.

"Before I begin my summary of Marian apparitions, let me just make one more observation. If an antipope comes, there is an easy way to identify him. The antipope will contradict the universal teachings of the Church in his effort to destroy it. Watch the *teachings*.

"Watch what he teaches about sexuality, chastity, divorce, contraception, women priests, or magisterial authority, even about the doctrine of hell. Especially watch for a watering down or denial of the doctrines of the real presence of Jesus in the Eucharist and the Immaculate Conception of Mary. Of all the wonderful avenues of grace we have at our disposal, these two—Mary and the Eucharist—are the ones which are most effective. Satan hates these the most and will attack them with all he's got. These teachings have never changed throughout history, despite the enormous pressures brought upon the Holy Catholic Church by the governments and the philosophical forces of this godless world."

Wheat was finished with his introduction. Slinger was amazed that the otherwise mild-mannered and genteel professor hit so hard so fast. *He doesn't pull any punches,* Slinger thought.

Many in the crowd, even faithful Catholics, were uncomfortable with Wheat's message. It was very hard to believe that the world would be punished so completely. On the other hand, it was hard to deny the facts of economic uncertainty, social breakdown, wars around the world, and unprecedented natural disasters. The mysterious death of Pope Patrick added to the weight of Wheat's words. On the day after his death, papers were already filled with rumors that the next pope would be Cardinal Casino. Months before Pope Patrick's death, Casino had hinted in the press about the need for vast "changes" and "modernization" in the Church—code words for changes in practice and teaching. Was Wheat predicting these new (but most certainly false) teachings here, as he had correctly predicted natural disasters and wars years before? Wheat left it up to individuals in the crowd to decide for themselves.

A person's first inclination would be to write Wheat off as an end-of-the-millennium fanatic, Joe Jackson thought, *but even some mainline evangelical Protestants are predicting the return of Christ based on biblical prophecy.*

Joe's love for Holy Scripture made it easy for him to dialogue with Protestants. He had many friends among evangelical and fundamentalist leaders around the country. His love for the Bible actually grew after he joined the Catholic Church. He loved how the Scriptures are integrated into Catholic sacramental life, especially the Mass. He also enjoyed having a trustworthy "judge" for interpretation of Bible passages—the Holy Spirit as He guides the Catholic Church. He relished the freedom of no longer getting bogged down in endless disputes over interpretations.

Wheat had finished summarizing five or six historical apparitions and was now explaining the most important of all in this century, Fatima. He told the crowd how Mary appeared six times over a period of six months in 1917 to three young children in the mountains of Portugal. On October thirteenth, Mary appeared for the final time at Fatima. More than *seventy* thousand people experienced the greatest public, predicted miracle in the history of the world: the famous "spinning sun!" The sun gave off colors and danced in the sky, then it plunged toward the earth in a "power dive" toward the crowd. Huge numbers of witnesses thought it was the end of their lives. All those present, including the atheistic reporters from Lisbon, were shocked to discover that the muddy countryside was completely dried. The entire region had been soaked by torrential rains for days leading up to the miracle. Physicists reported later that only the BTUs created by a nuclear weapon could have vaporized so much water instantly.

Wheat explained the stupendous predictions made by Mary *in 1917* at Fatima, including the Second World War, and the as-yet unelected pope during whose reign it would begin! Mary also predicted that Russia would come under the tyranny of the "Bolsheviks" and atheism, and that Russia would become a "scourge of the earth."

In 1917, anyone examining the predictions at Fatima would have found them more incredible than Wheat's predictions on this very night.

Professor Wheat also noted that Our Lady of Fatima's predictions had not yet been completely fulfilled, including the "annihilation of nations."

Quoting from the book that changed his life, *Our Lady of Fatima,* Wheat warmed to his topic…

"Mary brought those children to hell so they could warn us of what was in store for souls who don't respond of their own free will to God's grace. The children were radically changed forever. They were never the same again and voluntarily took on painful mortifications for the sake of others." Wheat repeated the last five words, *"For the sake of others."*

"After all, what is this battle all about? What is Jesus trying to save us from? From hell!

"Now, even in friendly crowds such as this, some do not enjoy references to hell. Let me just remind you that the existence of a physical hell is a doctrine of our faith. No one can be a sincere Catholic and deny hell's existence if you know the teachings of your Church, which are the very teachings of Christ Himself. After all, Jesus mentioned hell over fourteen times in the Gospels. Jesus believed in hell! In this, we have common ground with our separated brothers and sisters, Protestants who remain true to this essential biblical teaching.

"The fact remains that Satan knows that more people are alive today than have lived and died in all of human history. The evil one wants to drag as many souls to hell as he possibly can, and therefore Satan does *not* want us to believe in the place 'where the worm dies not.'"

At this point, Wheat held up a book, *To Hell and Back.*

"Here is a book by a Protestant doctor which documents hundreds of Near Death Experiences that people have had of hell. Many Catholic mystics have visited hell as a warning to them and those who come after them. One nun, Sister Josepha Menendez, used to return from hell with her habit smoking from burns."

Wheat's voice was starting to build again.

"The point is, unless we do something to help Jesus as part of His Mystical Body, souls will go to hell of their own free wills who otherwise would have chosen eternal life in heaven. Whether the Marian prophecies I speak about are true or not, and I do believe many Marian apparitions are true, this central doctrinal truth about the nature and existence of hell remains just as true as ever!

"Imagine the fires of hell. Pain worse than any pain on earth. The accounts in this book describe flames licking up from the ground and searing white hot heat engulfing inside and outside of your body while all the time you are being tormented by horrible demons far more ugly and grotesque than in any horror movie! The torture and pain are unending! And your sentence in hell is not for a day. Or a year. Or a decade! Or a hundred years!"

Wheat was shouting now, but his voice and intonations were still perfectly controlled, like a fine instrument.

"You are there forever! **Forever!**

"Just imagine that forever and ever your brain is seared and singed by unbelievably painful flames as you try to breathe and think! Unending physical pain! *And,* the worst pain is knowing that you have no hope of ever knowing God or seeing heaven, and that you chose your own destiny by refusing His grace during your life and at the time of your death! God doesn't send people to hell, they choose it for themselves by their very lives!

"It's so horrible we don't want to think about it. We wouldn't want our worst enemy to go to hell. Imagine your closest friend or relative in hell forever."

Wheat lowered his voice to a whisper again, so low and soft he could barely be heard.

"Face it, brothers and sisters, my fellow Knights. Our actions affect whether or not other people go to heaven or hell. Face that, and the fact that we are all members of the Mystical Body of Christ, responsible for each other and not unconnected islands, and you will do all you can to respond to the Blessed Mother's desperate pleas, and to the grace Jesus provides for you to change.

"The Mystical Body of Christ reminds me of what Jesus told Blessed Faustina of Poland when He gave her the Divine Mercy Chaplet during a vision in the 1930s..."

As Wheat spoke about hell, Nathan squirmed in his seat. He was reminded of the sins he had confessed to Chet only hours earlier. He grasped for Joanie's hand.

If anyone deserves to go to hell, I do, he judged. *I hope Chet is right about confession.*

Then Nathan Payne prayed.

Dear Mary, if you're up there in heaven like Chet says, show me whatever it is I need to know to avoid hell. Show me how my sins have hurt others. Show me, because I don't want to lose Pascal's Wager!

I'm no fool, Jesus, but I know that I need more than the fear of hell to straighten me out. I need something more and you must know what it is. Show me!

Use any means necessary!

It was the most important prayer of his life.

Nathan's faith was like a mustard seed. It was small, and new. He couldn't feel it inside himself. But he was sincere. He knew he had to do more than just go through the motions. Just two days of feeling like an alien in Joanie's family had proven that to him.

During Tom Wheat's talk, the Mother of God heard Nathan's prayer in the Beatific Vision. She was touched by his honest desire to know the truth. A fearful grace was procured for him at that very moment because of his sincerity, and because of his unique destiny. It would be implemented later.

The reason for his Rendezvous with Grace would not be much different from the reason for the drastic measures God had taken to save Lee Washington. It was required because of each man's special destiny. The *means* of grace would be different for Nathan—dramatically so—as Nathan would find out in less than five days.

Joanie was quite sensitive to the tightening grip of the man she loved. She had been praying so hard for him while he silently prayed his "Show me" prayer that she completely tuned out her father's talk. Joanie was as much a cause as anyone for the Rendezvous with Grace which he was now "scheduled" to undergo. Such is the reality of the Mystical Body of Christ. Joanie's love connected her to Nathan through Jesus.

Nathan's faith was indeed a mustard seed. It would grow into a tree quickly—but not without exquisite growing pains. After all, Nathan had asked Jesus to use *any means necessary.*

Chapter Ten

1

Monday Evening
9 October
South Bend, Indiana

This is better than Father Chet said it would be, Becky thought as she helped herself to another slice of Bruno's pizza. The style was East Coast, and the heaping cheese and crust were perfect.

*Better watch yourself. Don't want to be fat **and** pregnant.*

Becky was thoroughly enjoying the dinner conversation among Tom Wheat, Karl Slinger, Father Chet Sullivan, Nathan Payne, and Joe Jackson, although Joe and Nathan rarely spoke. Joanie Wheat and her mom seemed to speak more often than Joe, but whenever Joe spoke, everyone stopped to listen carefully to his observations, delivered in that soft but clear voice of his.

*My man doesn't waste a word. Am I already calling him **my** man? Joe doesn't even look at me. He pays more attention to Joanie.*

Prodded by Chet, Slinger told some amazing stories of how SLG Industries had been built into such a huge company. Slinger gave credit for the success to the people he had hired, but it was clear that he knew how to get the right people working for him and how to delegate authority. In the 1960s, SLG had pioneered the concept of technological ranching and private agricultural franchising by sending teams of experts to "franchise ranches" to consult with ranch owners. In turn, owners agreed to share profits as legal partners with SLG. The partners remained highly independent, but outpaced their competitors with more modern production and distribution. SLG was the Domino's Pizza of agriculture.

Slinger was fascinated as Joe and Tom explained how Saint Maximilian Kolbe also used technology to pioneer new ways of evangelizing the world. At one point in the 1930s, Kolbe had over seven hundred priests and brothers publishing millions of magazines and newspapers for distribution throughout Poland and the world. Kolbe's Knights of Immaculata used the latest technology of the day—printing presses all over the world still incorporate innovations developed by poor friars in the backward countryside of Poland! The Nazis shut down the presses and took Kolbe to Auschwitz when the saint was discovered hiding Jews, and because he refused to stop denouncing Nazism in his daily newspaper.

"The extent of Kolbe's vision and activities are underestimated by historians," Wheat explained. "The Solidarity Movement which toppled Communism was led by Catholics who grew up reading Kolbe's Immaculata magazine. These humble union workers found their strength in the Catholic Church and in the example of Kolbe's martyrdom."

Both Slinger and Kolbe were technological trailblazers—and Poles—which seemed to please Slinger.

Slinger, excited about the talk he had just heard in Saint Joseph Church, laid out his plans to evangelize the business community in Salt Lake City and beyond. Karl A. Slinger's middle initial stood for Action, it seemed, and he was not going to delay in getting the word out. He had already cornered Joe before the meal and asked him to submit a wish list for the Kolbe Foundation.

Becky noticed, however, that the most attention was paid to the one who spoke the least, Nathan Payne. Becky was a very perceptive girl.

Even Mr. Wheat and Mr. Slinger stop and listen when Nathan says something, or they simply look to him after they suggest a course of action as if they need his permission or something. That's odd.

Denny Wheat arrived late, but there was plenty of extra pizza for him, and he was able to join the others in rousing choruses of the *Notre Dame Fight Song, God Bless America,* and other standards. Chet had started the singing with a beautiful *a cappella* stanza of the Fight Song.

·The owner, Bruno Nepolitano, emigrant to America in 1958, soon had his daughter Tina playing the accordion. The other forty-plus patrons at the old-fashioned family restaurant joined in the singing. Karl Slinger and Bruno himself, arm in arm, were singing the loudest. Large bottles of Bruno's homemade wine appeared on the tables, *gratis.*

Becky and Nathan, newcomers to Notre Dame-Bruno's Pizza traditions, were quite stunned by the exuberance and warmth of the festivities. Notre Dame, the Irish Wheats, and the Italian Nepolitanos—the three cultures intermingling during the meal were all known by their members for a characteristic summarized in one word: family. Nathan was reminded that Father Chet was always talking about "the Notre Dame Family" and Joe Jackson had even mentioned "the Kolbe Foundation Family." Wheat, Slinger, and the younger Bruno openly shared stories about another family the three men shared—the Marine Corps.

Both Becky and Nathan had come from broken homes but had lived in relatively staid environments from then on. Nathan simply felt uncomfortable, and despite his social nature, felt the most out of place—like an impostor, an alien. He felt the same way about his brief stay at the Wheats, despite his attraction to Joanie. He was a man who didn't like to face his emotions, so he didn't allow his discomfort to rise to the surface of his consciousness. He tried hard to play along and to avoid being discovered—as if a family as warm and loving as the Wheats would reject him.

Becky, perhaps because of her feminine nature, was reminded of the LeCarré novel about the spy who was ordered active after years of living undercover. She felt like she had finally come in from the cold. Unlike Nathan, she had once known the warmth and love of her devoted father. Her reaction echoed another word beside family: layers.

*There are so many **layers** here,* she realized, amazed. She began to peel them like an onion. *There's the Wheat family and the Notre Dame family. There's the American family expressed in the patriotic songs, and the ethnic family and food. Even the Catholic family of the Body of Christ has a "Father" here in Chet. There is the Marine Corps family for the men; the Marian family which is so intimate because it has the Christ Child in the center of it! There is so much love here, how could anyone ever fail in a life immersed in so many layers of family?*

For Becky, this realization was an epiphany. Now that she was in from the cold, she didn't want to go back outside again.

She watched Joe singing in his old-fashioned tenor voice and smiled wildly at him. For the third time today she saw his wonderful extra large smile—but for the first time he aimed it *at her* across the table! She began to sing louder herself, uncaring of the fact that she barely knew the words to *Santa Lucia.* Caught up in the moment and deeply attracted to the layered circles of love she felt in the room, she realized that there was more to life than the romantic love between man and woman (which had been her personal conception of the highest form of love before meeting Father Chet Sullivan).

She realized that romantic love had its place as *a part of* a greater Reality of Love. Real Love (as she now thought of it) drew its sustenance from God's grace and could bear much greater fruit than unions such as she had experienced with Sam and her one other domestic partner. The fruit of those stale unions had been bitter emptiness. Both of her serious relationships had ended with emotional violence. Real Love bore fruit such as she was experiencing in this restaurant— growing, ever-expanding, warm, and fertile!

There is no end to the layers of Real Love!

Something Father Chet told her earlier echoed in her mind, somehow sounding like her own father: *"The Mystical Body*

*is Jesus' body and has His heart. The key is to set aside your
own heart for His purposes. That's what the word 'consecration' means—to set aside for a holy purpose. The fruit of the
consecration to Mary is imitation of the Sacred Heart of Jesus.
It's a mystical, ineffable reality, but I know it's true because I
experience it as a priest..."*

I'm becoming such a philosopher! Get a grip, Rebecca.

She tried to brush aside her thoughts and sentiments as
the result of too much wine. Then she looked directly at Joe
again and realized that he was looking back at her with that
sad expression which she already knew was not sad, but simply his natural somber countenance. He nodded at her; her
belly turned over like a marshmallow on a stick.

*You want him, Becky. You want all this. You want it all!
What's so wrong with that?*

She nodded back to Joe, and for a moment they left time,
as if they were alone in the room. A line from a song she
heard somewhere played in her mind:

This one goes out to the one I love.

The moment ended, the music and laughing returned, and
Slinger proposed a toast to Bruno in that booming voice of
his. Everyone cheered and lifted their glasses.

Becky saw Joe sidle up to Father Chet after the toast and
whisper something. Then they both left and walked out the
back door while the party continued. Through the window
Becky saw Father Chet light up a smoke. Becky wondered
what they were talking about out there.

✝ ✝ ✝

Father Chet took a long drag off his smoke.

"Been drinking much?" Joe asked.

"Not really, Shoeless," Chet replied with a gleam in his
blue eyes. "Who needs to drink when so much fun is already
going on? Drinking would spoil it."

The two men, comfortable with each other after years of
friendship, stood in silence for a moment, looking at the few

cars in the small parking lot behind the restaurant. Beyond the lot there was a cornfield. Bruno's, though wildly popular among Domers (as Notre Dame students and alumni are known), was on the outskirts of the industrial section of South Bend, not far from the farmlands. The air had a slight chill in it.

"Those smokes'll kill ya, Padre—filthy habit ya know," Joe observed amiably.

"Don't I know it, Shoeless," Father Chet replied, not at all agitated. Joe often mentioned Chet's "filthy habit." Chet finished the Hail Mary he was praying for Joe and Becky, expecting Joe to bring up the subject of Becky. The priest decided to get down to brass tacks.

"Okay, out with it," Chet finally said.

"It's about Slinger," Joe said.

"Tell me," Chet replied, surprised.

"Before dinner, he asked me to prepare a wish list for the Kolbe Foundation. You know, what we need to buy and all that. He's worth millions, you know," Joe explained.

"I know. So what did you tell him you needed?"

"I told him we needed prayers," Joe said flatly.

"Good. What did he say to that?"

"Well, he said he was already working on that, and that he meant what kind of things could I do with money if I had it. He's a direct man, Karl Slinger."

Father Chet raised his eyebrow and looked at Joe.

"You know, Joe, it takes you a long time to get with the program, doesn't it?" It wasn't a criticism. It was the truth as far as Chet was concerned. "So what I suggest is that you go home and write up the biggest wish list in the world. Slinger's money is only part of what you need, but you still need it."

"But we don't do any fund raising at the Kolbe Foundation," Joe protested mildly.

"I know that and if Slinger has been hanging out with Tom Wheat, then Slinger knows you don't do fund raising. You didn't approach Slinger for money, did you?"

"Of course not! You know we never do that kind of thing. Saint Maximilian treated rich and poor alike, and never coddled the rich for donations. Father Chet, I'm surprised you would ask such a thing!" Joe's tone had a touch of hurt in it, and Joe had actually raised it above his usual whisper.

"Don't get so touchy, Shoeless, I know all that. What I mean is, if you didn't approach Slinger for money, then you didn't fund raise for it. Get with the program, Joe!

"If Slinger has been inspired by God to give you money, then go for it. Who are you to turn him down, especially when the materials you make in that foundation of yours can save souls through Slinger's generosity?

"You may be bright, Shoeless, but you ain't brilliant. When an old lady on social security gives you five bucks and has to skip a meal as a result, your foundation is an avenue of grace into her life. It's good for her to tithe and sacrifice. It joins her to the cross in the Mystical Body. If it's good for her, it's good for Karl Slinger. The amount of money doesn't really matter."

Joe nodded, and paused to think that one over.

It's starting to sink in, Chet thought. *In some ways, he's like a kid.*

Like many people from the East Coast, Father Chet thought anyone who grew up outside of the New York-New Jersey metropolitan area was naïve and lacked a certain toughness—even an ex-professional football player like Joe. It was one of Chet's few faults.

"Joe, are you afraid that you can't handle so much so fast at the Kolbe Foundation? What happened to Mr. Big Thinker with his big plans to reach the whole country before the Tribulations shut us all down?" Chet was goading Joe. From experience, he knew that sharp questions often got the gears going inside Jackson's head. Jackson hesitated before speaking.

"Are you using sarcastic Yankee psychology on me again, Padre?" Joe's southern drawl was a bit thicker than usual.

He's not so naïve after all! Chet thought, and smiled, as if a smile would get him leniency. He held up his hands, then took another drag off his smoke.

"Chet, listen. I've already got pretty detailed plans ready to spend Slinger's or anybody else's millions. I mean, after thinking about it a lot over the past couple of years, I figured she might send me somebody like Slinger after a while. I figured I owed it to her to be ready." The *she* whom Joe spoke about was the Blessed Mother.

It's like Mary's a personal friend of his or something, Chet thought. *I guess she is. They used to accuse Kolbe of speaking too fraternally about Mary way back when. You have so much to learn, Father Stupid Idiot.*

Then Joe, having maneuvered the wily Irishman into a position like a receiver setting up a defensive back on the football field, burned Father Chet for a touchdown.

Here goes, Joe thought.

"So I told Karl—"

"So it's Karl now, is it?" Chet interrupted with a wry smile, finally realizing that Joe had set him up for something.

"Yeah, I told Karl that I had plans ready—radio program, publishing company, more audio tapes, Catholic bookstores for distribution, a professional association of Marian groups, a speaker's bureau, a national network of warehouse and shipping facilities, a television program, a monthly national prayer rally in every major city in every state, national secular advertising campaigns—and a few other modest projects." Joe obviously didn't need to write up a list. It was already in his head.

Father Chet laughed out loud. The two men exchanged high fives. Chet practically had to leap to reach Jackson's hand.

"How did Slinger react? My goodness, Shoeless, you're talking about millions, tens of millions here—all to spread prophesies of Mary that may or may not even be true..." a worried tone crept into Chet's voice.

"He laughed so loud I thought the rafters would come down on me," Joe interjected. "Then he said, 'Fine, send an itemization of whatever amount it is you need on to Lenny Gold in Salt Lake City and have him set up an account to draw out funds on a per-need basis.' Then Slinger handed me his business card," Joe said matter-of-factly.

Father Chet was stunned.

And that's not all, you clever Irishman, Joe thought.

Joe went on, "He also told me to get moving, because if I didn't think I was up to the task, he'd find someone who was. He said, 'No offense, son,' just like that, 'No offense, son, but time's a-wasting. I just wasted over fifty years myself, Joe.' He said it like I had just proposed we buy a chocolate sundae or something, Chet. Slinger's a lightning bolt, man."

Mary works like the tide, thought Chet. *Just like she worked in the Gospels. Silent. Powerful. You don't see her, but come back in a few hours and it's high tide.* Chet's father had always quoted those lines to his family before beginning the Sullivan family Rosary.

"That's not all, is it, Joe? You've got something else up your sleeve, don't you?"

Joe flashed a toothy smile.

"After reeling off my wish list, I told Slinger I would trade any amount of money he could give me for just one thing."

"And what is that?" Chet was confused, but incredibly curious. *He's probably going to say something like a Mass from the pope,* Chet thought. The thought reminded him of the grisly death of Pope Patrick and the priest was saddened.

"I told him I needed a black robe," Joe said, somewhat cryptically.

"A black what?"

"A black robe, Chet—a priest. Like the Indians in that movie about the Jesuit martyrs. The Indians called priests the black robes. I told Slinger I needed you. I can't do all these projects—if I can do them at all, that is—without a spiritual director and a chaplain. We need the Mass said at the Kolbe Foundation—on its premises every day—"

"But I won't—" Chet tried to interrupt but Joe wouldn't let him.

"—but nothing!" Joe insisted. "We need a priest who loves Mary and understands what we're doing. I know all the trouble you've been having with Monsignor Whelan. And Cardinal O'Donnell might be happy to let you go—he understands the Kolbe Foundation. Whelan hates how you hear confessions every day, preach about the pope and Mary from—"

"I won't do it! The subject is closed, Joe. Closed! Period. I won't leave Notre Dame du Lac Parish. End of discussion."

A fierce look came over Father Chet's face. He turned abruptly and returned to Bruno's dining room, leaving Joe alone in the chilled October night.

Get thee behind me, ye Satan! A passage from the Bible came to the stunned mind of Joe Jackson.

✝ ✝ ✝

Joe stayed outside alone for several minutes pondering what had just happened with Father Chet. At first he felt angry that Chet would so quickly trash an offer to be the chaplain of the Kolbe Foundation. Then Joe figured that Father Chet must have his reasons for not wanting to leave his parish in New Jersey. *Then,* Joe thought that if he could just find out Father Chet's reasons, maybe he could talk Chet out of them. Joe was not about to give up. He began to formulate a plan to find out what was bugging Father Chet.

Lost in his thoughts, he was startled to hear Becky's voice behind him.

"Did you insult his mother or something?" she asked.

"Oh Becky, hello." Then he remembered her question. *She's asking why Chet left so abruptly. She must have been watching through the window.*

"Oh, that. I'm sorry. I don't know why Father Chet left. I mean, I asked him to be the chaplain for the Kolbe Foundation, but he won't do it. I'm sure he's got a good reason. I just wish I knew what it was." *Why do I just blurt out whatever I'm thinking to this girl?*

She came next to him and boldly took his hand, which was large but surprisingly delicate.

"You don't talk much, do you?" she asked. He didn't remove his hand from hers.

"It's not that. Chet says I talk too much. I love to talk with my friends and the Kolbe Foundation workers. My problem is that I'm always thinking so hard about something that I don't have time to speak."

"What do you *think* about me, Joe?" Her tone was confident, as if she was not afraid of any kind of answer he would give her.

It was the perfect question to ask Joe. Becky, consciously following Father Chet's example, began to pray a silent prayer asking for Mary's help: *Whatever you want, Mary, is fine with me. I know what I want now. I want Joe Jackson.*

There was something about Joe that neutralized any of Becky's natural inhibition. He seemed so approachable—so calm and reassuring in his bearing. It was not like talking to a man she had just met this morning. He had registered on an emotional level in her heart, but not necessarily on her mind, as if she was reuniting with a long lost friend. Her temperamental boldness fit his inborn steadiness like two oddly shaped but perfectly fitted pieces of a puzzle.

Joe's mind was not slow, despite his ponderousness. He silently prayed for Mary to help him with the answer.

He had avoided thinking about Becky Macadam *as a woman* since he first saw her. Joe was a *fearless* thinker—along the lines of a fearless thinker who lived in the thirteenth century, Saint Thomas Aquinas, who was nicknamed the Dumb Ox in his younger years by peers who mistook his pensiveness for lack of intelligence. Once a line of reasoning started in Joe's mind he invariably followed it to wherever it led him.

"Can you wait for me for a few minutes, Miss Becky?" he asked politely.

His southern manners are touching, she thought.

"I can wait all night." She tilted her head up and smiled with her eyes.

She waited patiently for over five minutes, admiring him, thinking of Joe running after Nathan's pass on the South Quad like a powerful, beautiful thoroughbred. She thought of how chastely he looked at her, and of his gentle voice. She remembered her Rosary with him in the Grotto, listening to him pray the Hail Mary with her in his unhurried, southern accent. Becky also remembered the look she and Joe had just shared across the table during the song inside Bruno's. He finally spoke up.

"Becky?"

"Yes, Joseph."

"I think I should marry you."

"Okay," Becky answered after only the slightest hesitation.

She turned and they embraced before the cars and the crops in the October moonlight. Becky felt the first layer of love encircle her heart and knew there was more to come later.

Time passed.

"Joseph?"

They were still in each other's arms. Becky did not look at him as she laid the side of her head on his chest, listening to his heartbeat through his shirt.

"Yes, my love," he answered softly, ever so slightly tightening his embrace.

"I think I should tell you something before you go off and marry me. I'm pregnant. The baby comes in eight months." She bit her lower lip.

I should have told him sooner! Why did he have to ask me to marry him so fast! Now I'll lose him. He's too Catholic to want damaged goods.

She clung to him with all her strength, certain it would be her last embrace. Then he spoke, matter-of-factly.

"So?" he asked.

"So? So!" she repeated, her voice rising in anger.

Her emotions surged like lightning. *"So* why would you want to marry a pregnant girl? Tell me! Because you feel sorry for me?"

The bitterness in her voice surprised them both. She looked at him with the same look she had given Sam only two days ago before she threw him out of their—her—apartment.

Joe was not disturbed.

"Becky, listen. There's nothing to worry about with a baby. I'd be honored to be the father of your baby, truly I would. I don't care how or by whom you got pregnant. I mean that. Look at me."

She raised her eyes to his.

He began to speak firmly, but tenderly.

"I have decided to love you. I just figured it out. You're the most beautiful woman I have ever seen. I don't know *when* you got your faith back, but I do know it's not going away. I can tell. I can *always* tell."

Becky couldn't believe her ears, but he sounded so—so *certain.* She nodded, and a sob which started deep in her body escaped her. She never broke his gaze.

"I've always been so in love with Mary, that I never thought I could find a woman as beautiful as she is. And well, you are beautiful inside and out, like Mary. It's like Mary sent me a preview or something. I want to look at you every day for the rest of my life. Life needs Beauty. My life does at least.

"This must sound weird. Does this sound weird, Becky?"

She shook her head. "To tell you the truth, Joe, you're starting to sound like Father Chet. No, it doesn't sound weird. I follow you, at least." The edge was leaving her voice.

That's good, Joe thought.

"Well, anyway, I haven't had much experience with women. I've been saving myself for you all my life. I'm like a room nobody has gone into. Only one person gets to go in that room, and that's you, Becky. That's what I was thinking about when you looked at me across the table during the song. I was thinking about the room, and I saw you walk into it, and I thought to myself: that's fine with me. That's fine with me, I thought. I never thought that about anybody, Becky. That's what made me smile. You've probably figured out that I don't smile much. Heck, little kids cry when they see me in the mall!"

She laughed. The single tear that had escaped earlier was already drying. He gave her his handkerchief anyway. The tension was gone. She still couldn't believe it, though. Then she remembered the little Cub in her mitt.

"Doesn't it bother you that I've let someone into my house?" she asked.

"Have you? Has anyone really gotten into your heart?"

He looked at her with a patience and peacefulness that gave her a chance to settle down.

Biting her lower lip and looking up a bit, she took a moment to think of the two men she had thought she loved in her past, and realized that she never did give her whole self to them. Independence had been the whole idea behind "living together." In this setting, the concept of living together struck Becky as such a stupid and superficial way to waste one's time. She looked directly back to Joe and answered his question with a small shake of her head. *No one has ever come into my secret garden, Joseph, my darling.* Another question came to her.

"What about my baby? I don't understand—"

Even though her question didn't have an edge anymore, he cut her off.

"Our baby, Becky. Our baby. I can explain." Even though it wasn't a question, he waited for her to nod again before continuing.

He's so considerate!

"I was adopted, Becky. It's as simple as that. It's a long story and I'll tell it to you eventually, but that's all you need to know right now. Now that I've decided to marry you, wouldn't it be hypocritical of me to want to reject an innocent human life inside you after my own parents didn't keep me? I've been a prolife activist all my life. Nope." He appeared to be thinking on his feet as he spoke, a rare thing for Joe.

"Nope. It would be wrong for me to reject your baby," he said almost to himself, looking up to the stars briefly. "You can tell me about how you got pregnant if you feel like it, but it doesn't matter to me. I mean, I want to know if you want me to know. I'm curious, I suppose.

"But in the meantime, my love, as far as I'm concerned, you're going to be my wife. The sacramental bond will make our marriage unbreakable. There are so many layers to love."

"Did you just say 'layer'?" she asked, with a hint of excitement in her voice. A smile broke onto her face like the headlights of a car turning on. She heard a noise and turned to look at the door.

Two patrons came out the back door of Bruno's. Becky and Joe waited until they passed.

"Yeah, another layer," he confirmed, "like a wedding ring over an engagement ring. Does it mean something?"

"No, I mean yes, it means everything. I can't explain it."

He looked at her again as she shook her head ever so slightly. He saw the very rarest kind of beauty in her expression. The beauty of innocence restored. Becky was not only physically beautiful, but she had a childlike quality that was precious. It was the same quality Father Chet noticed during his conversation with her at the Grotto.

Unless ye become like a little child, thou shalt not enter into the Kingdom of God, Joe remembered a verse from his own innocent childhood as he looked at his future wife.

There was a long pause as they stood holding hands, looking at the cornfield.

"You're going to find it hard to make me change my mind about marrying you, Becky. Ask Father Chet. He says I'm as stubborn as a Philadelphia lawyer and twice as stupid, whatever that means in Yankee talk," he said, not without a note of pride in his voice.

She laughed at his odd joke.

"Joe, darling, you're already making me feel better. It's just that you surprised me so much with your proposal. Everything is happening so fast!"

"I surprised myself, Becky. It usually takes me months to figure things out. Maybe with you around, we could bring it down to weeks! But my dad and mom fell in love and decided to get married on their first date, and so did Chet's folks. It's not that uncommon, I guess. If it's the right thing, I don't really care how much time passes before making a decision. We might want to wait a while before telling anybody for the sake of appearances. But privately, as far as we're concerned, why wait? Now we can talk about what it's going to be like to *be* married instead of whether or not to *get* married. Those are two different sets of conversations. This way, we can skip dating altogether. I've never been much for dating, anyway."

Yeah, why wait? she thought. Becky reflected upon his words, a little bit amazed at how different Joe was compared to any other man she had known. There was a fearlessness about him. After all, weren't men afraid of commitment?

Where is it carved in marble that you have to spend years together before knowing if the other person is the right one for you? I made up my mind about Joe inside the restaurant before Joe even brought marriage up. The idea of marriage hadn't crossed her mind inside Bruno's. She just knew that she *wanted* him. Joe had taken that desire to the next logical step.

She was also amazed at her own lack of fear. *Shouldn't I be afraid that I'm making a mistake? But I'm not afraid.*

After a long silence, she spoke, "I liked it when you called me 'my love,' Joseph."

"And I liked it when you called me 'darling,' Miss Becky."

"We better get back to the party," she suggested.

"Sure thing."

"Oh, by the way, *darling*," she whispered tenderly, taking great pleasure in hearing the words come from her lips with such emotional certainty.

"Yes, *my love*," he said softly, more softly than usual.

"I accept your proposal for marriage. I don't think I did that yet. I was too busy exploding! My father is dead, so there's no one else to give away my hand, as they say. My mom won't care either way."

"Okay," he said, back to his taciturn self, as he put his arm around her waist and led her to the party, which was just beginning to peter out.

2

Monday, Midnight
9 October
Notre Dame, Indiana

Nathan and Joanie stood under the Father Sorin statue where their new life together had begun the day before.

After the party broke up, Denny drove Nathan and Becky back to Notre Dame to pick up Nathan's car, which had a parking ticket on the windshield. The plan was for Nathan to drive Becky back to Chicago. Denny was waiting in his idling car so he could drive Joanie home.

Father Chet had left for New Jersey from Bruno's Pizza after the dinner. Chet had been terse with Nathan when the two friends had exchanged good-byes. After returning from his discussion with Joe Jackson, Father Chet had announced that he wanted to cut his vacation short. Because his bags were already packed in the Malibu, he would head back to New Jersey right away. Chet made it quite clear that he was not interested in discussing the reason with anyone.

"But you'll have to drive all night long to get back. It's over eleven hours of driving. Stay over at my place one more night...or at least stay in South Bend with Joe—" Nathan had reasoned.

"Can't, buddy. Listen, I'll stay at a hotel if I get tired. Don't worry about me. Nothing personal. I've just got to get back, that's all." This was all the priest would say, a determined tone in his voice.

Slinger and Joanie's parents were long gone. Joanie, Denny, Becky, and Nathan said their good-byes to Joe at Bruno's. Becky had given Joe a light, but rather lingering kiss on the cheek, Nathan noted. He deduced that something had occurred outside the back door. Then the remaining four had gone back to retrieve Nathan's car which was parked on the circle at the end of Notre Dame Avenue.

✝ ✝ ✝

"I wish we had more time to talk, Nathan," Joanie said as she looked up at the Father Sorin statue.

He admired her classic Irish beauty. Her skin was more delicate and white in the moonlight.

"The time for talk is over. Now is the time for action," he said, somewhat distantly.

"Are you quoting somebody?" she asked.

"Uh, no. I don't know where that came from. Maybe the good Father Sorin said it. I heard he was a ventriloquist on top of being one hell of a chef, as well as a founder of great universities. All around guy, that Sorin. Real jack of all trades. Pole vaulted, too—1844 Olympics in Moscow. Silver Medal. I saw it on ESPN. The place went bonkers. Thousands of drunken Russians, storming onto the field, lifting Sorin up on their shoulders, singing the Fight Song in Russian…"

"Your sense of humor is bizarre, Mister. And they didn't have cable in 1844—even I know that." She gave him a wry smile.

"I'm nervous, that's all. This Tom Wheat No Kissing Rule leaves me without the usual avenues for saying good-bye to a beautiful woman after a wonderful date. I did have a great time these past two days.

"I know it's only four days until Friday when I come back. And that thing about not wanting you more than twenty yards away still holds, Joanie. I don't even have a picture of you!"

"Hold on Nathan—Denny!" she called, waving to her brother. Denny got out of his car and jogged over to them.

"What, Sis?"

"Do you have a picture of me in your wallet for Nathan?"

"Sure, I have your college photo. It's a few years old." He pulled a photo out of his wallet and gave it to Joanie, who handed it to Nathan. Nathan noticed that the photo had a note to Denny from Joanie on the back.

"Listen, lovebirds," Denny said, shivering, "I've got to get up early to fly to Midway tomorrow. Don't mean to break up a great time but…"

"We understand, Denny," Nathan said. "Joanie?" He opened his arms and she gave him a quick hug.

They walked back to their vehicles, said good-bye again, and pulled their respective cars onto Notre Dame Avenue. Nathan and Becky waved as he turned the Mustang right onto Angela Boulevard. It was too cold to put the top down.

Now what? Nathan thought, as he headed away from the Golden Dome.

3

Early Tuesday Morning
10 October
Indiana Tollway

After ten minutes of silence, Becky said, "What a weekend, Nathan! I never thought I'd be driving back to Chicago from South Bend with you on Monday after going to a party in your apartment on Saturday. I guess we both had a strange last couple days, eh? We also have one Father Chet Sullivan in common now, don't we?"

Nathan, distracted by his thoughts, nodded but said nothing in reply.

Becky felt like bursting out with song. Her thoughts were filled with her memories and emotions associated with Joe Jackson. She looked at Nathan and frowned.

I guess Nathan's not hankering for conversation. Boy, he's a moody one. If he feels the same way about Joanie that I feel about Joe, you would think he'd want to shout it from the rooftops!

In fact, Nathan was in a dark mood. With every mile he put between himself and Notre Dame, the more he despaired of ever being able to win Pascal's Wager. He didn't know it, but he was being attacked in the same way Lee Washington had been attacked in the Motorman Motel in Santa Paula. The enemies of God, realizing that their time and influence over Nathan were running out, had decided to bring out the big guns. For decades the enemies of God had relied on the depraved morals and messages of the world to keep Nathan unknowingly in their camp. Now they found him slipping away. A three day battle had begun.

✛ ✛ ✛

At the Calumet exit Nathan stopped to buy some Jolt to help keep himself alert. As he pulled up to the highway entrance, he saw a large man hitchhiking. The hitchhiker looked very cold.

"George the Animal!" Nathan exclaimed, amazed. "George Moore! I used to know that guy in high school!" He spoke almost to himself.

Although his Mustang had already passed the man wearing only a worn checkered shirt and dirty Wranglers, the car had not yet entered the highway. He made a decision and hit the brakes rather hard.

"Oh Nathan! You're not going to pick him up, are you? What if he's dangerous?" Becky protested, alarmed.

Nathan said nothing as he cracked the gear into reverse and looked over his shoulder at George Moore.

He's got a beard now! Nathan thought.

Nathan stopped under a glowing orange ramp light. The man ran up to the Mustang and stuck his face next to Becky's window. Nathan powered down Becky's window. Becky immediately smelled beer on the man's breath.

The man spoke up, "Goin' to Chicago, Mister?"

It's not George, Nathan thought dejectedly after hearing the hitchhiker's decidedly un-George-like voice. The hitchhiker's voice was way too high.

Oh well, it's too late now, Nathan thought, disappointed that he had stopped.

"Yeah, hop in. No, wait. Becky, mind jumping in the back? It's cramped but I don't think this guy could fit back there."

Becky opened the door, squinted her eyes at the hitch-hiker and climbed into the back. She was not happy. The strange man was intruding on her pleasant thoughts about Joe Jackson. *He stinks! And he doesn't look a day older than eighteen!*

Tommy Gervin got into the car without saying a word. He did stink. Tommy hadn't had a shower in over a week and hadn't slept indoors in over two days. He had just been fired from a job washing cars in Gary that very day—for stealing. He heard there might be work in Chicago on the docks from one of the brothers at the car wash where he had worked for three whole days.

Except for his voice and beard, he could have been the twin of George Moore. Tommy eyed Nathan cautiously. Nathan seemed to be concentrating on the road.

Rich guy and his prissy rich girlfriend, Tommy thought. *He's probably soft and weak after sitting on his butt at some fancy desk in some fancy office. I'm twice his size.* Tommy crossed his arms and felt for the knife resting inside his thick woolen shirt. *Bet he's carrying a ton of cash. And five credit cards.*

Tommy had never robbed anyone before. But there was a first time for everything.

4

Tuesday Morning
10 October
California Highway 190, California

If Randall Knott had not read the passage about the Good
Samaritan that morning, he might not have picked up the
sorry-looking black boy on the outskirts of White River.

*That boy looks like he's a-been dragged down the Sierra
Nevadas by the coyotes.*

Randall Knott was also a black man. He was a janitorial
supplies salesman who had the northwest territory outside of
Bakersfield for Johnco Distribution Company. Johnco's name
was only half-pun. The owner's name was Johnny Johnson.
Johnson and Knott belonged to the First Baptist Church of
McFarland. Randall's next stop would be the Tule River Indian
Reservation. He had an excellent relationship with Chief
Roundrock.

*And they can't call **me** paleface up at Tule River!*

Randall chuckled to himself.

Randall read the Bible for a half hour every morning when
he woke up, and for a half hour every night before he went to
bed. This morning he had meditated upon the story of the
Good Samaritan. Randall Knott had asked himself if he would
have done what the Samaritan had done.

*Well, that boy's your chance to find out, Randall. Sure
looks downtrodden enough. Thank you Jesus for the opportunity to prove the value of your good and trusted servant
Randall!*

Lee Washington was walking alongside the two lane road,
and did not have his thumb out. Randall pulled his dusty 1986
Buick Riviera onto the shoulder, leaned across the seat and
opened the door.

"Need a ride, stranger?" Randall offered, praying silently
to Jesus.

Lee turned. He looked at Randall. "Brother, I was just praying for a ride."

5

Early Tuesday Morning
10 October
Chicago Skyway, Illinois

Becky was trying to stay awake in the back seat. Fear had overcome her need for sleep. The hitchhiker gave her the creeps.

Tommy decided to pull his knife on the Skyway because he figured the driver of the Mustang would have no room to pull over and would have to concentrate on driving. He waited until he was certain Nathan's eyes were not on him, then moved his left arm slowly toward the handle of his knife— Tommy Gervin was a lefty.

In a split second Nathan reached over and grabbed Tommy's wrist. Nathan's grip was like an iron vise. Tommy was frozen. Then Nathan *looked* at Tommy and Tommy was suddenly filled with fear. What began as a physical battle had quickly become a battle of wills. Nathan won.

Big mistake, Tommy thought. *Now I get my butt kicked.*

"Listen friend," Nathan whispered, "that's not what you need. It's not what we need. Hand it over."

Don't break the bruised reed, Nathan thought, wondering where the familiar-sounding words came from.

Nathan had seen the bulge in Tommy's shirt as soon as the hitchhiker had opened the door to get into the Mustang. He had purposely avoided looking directly at Tommy, waiting patiently for over ten minutes for him to make his move— if any move were to come at all.

Thank God he went for the knife slowly, Nathan thought. *It's been a long time since I've been to a dojo.*

A gasp of breath escaped from Becky when she saw the hitchhiker hand Nathan a large hunting knife. She noticed it still had a price tag on its green rubber handle.

Is it stolen? she thought.

Nathan began to speak quietly, soothingly, but Becky could make out the words, "What's your name, buddy? You remind me of a guy I used to go to high school with."

Tommy hesitated as if he couldn't believe his ears. Then he told Nathan his name.

Within fifteen minutes Nathan fished the whole sad story from him. He related in hodgepodge fashion how he had come to Nashville from Houston in the beginning of the summer with a thousand bucks and a guitar, looking to make a fortune in country music. But he didn't have the talent, contacts, and drive to make it. Within a month he was out of money.

Someone had told him he could get work playing the honky-tonks up north. The naïve young man had been too embarrassed to return home to his mom, so he hitchhiked up to Gary in late June. There, he failed again at music and became disheartened. He began to pick up odd jobs bussing tables at bars. He began drinking for the first time. It had gone well for a few weeks, but his increasing drunkenness had gotten him fired several times. Two weeks ago, as the first cold night air of Indiana autumn set in, he stopped kidding himself that he was camping out. Tommy Gervin was homeless.

"What you need, my friend, is to go home to your mom. You're lucky you got one. I don't have one. At least not on this earth."

"With what, man? I'm busted!" Tommy complained bitterly, his voice cracking.

"Don't worry about that. I'll take care of that." Nathan turned to Becky and said, raising his voice, "I know it's late, Beck, but I'm going to drop Mr. Gervin off at the downtown Days Inn. It's on the way. Do you mind waiting an extra twenty minutes before you get home?"

"No, not at all," she said, her first words since Tommy Gervin had gotten in the car.

✚ ✚ ✚

Nathan parked in the covered parking lot at the Days Inn. Tommy got out first. Before Nathan could leave his seat he felt Becky's hand on his arm.

"Give this to him," she said, handing him the Miraculous Medal which Joe had put around her neck at the Log Chapel. She smiled. It was her way of saying "good job." Nathan looked at the medal and gave Becky a wink.

"I'll be back in a bit," he said to her.

It took less than twenty minutes for Nathan to take good care of Tommy. First Nathan bought him a room for the night. Then he tipped the bellhop fifty dollars, telling him to make sure Tommy got a full meal from the kitchen even if the hotel restaurant was closed at this late hour. Using his credit card and a pay phone, Nathan arranged for a plane ticket to be held in Tommy's name for a flight to Houston on Southwest Airlines out of Midway the following afternoon. At the front desk Nathan exchanged a bill for a roll of quarters and handed the roll to the dumbfounded Tommy, who was sitting on the couch in the lobby. He also gave him two hundred dollars in cash.

"Why ya doin' all this, man?" Tommy asked.

"Let's just say I'm making up for lost time. Or better, I made a bet yesterday and I'm trying to win it. Here's enough money to buy yourself some duds. Even if you sleep late, you can still take the El from here to the Watertower Mall downtown and get yourself some clothes and a meal. Then you can take the train or a cab from there to Midway. Go to the Southwest desk. The ticket is in your name. You have a driver's license?"

Tommy Gervin nodded affirmative. "And what about the quarters, man?"

"You'll need somebody to pick you up in Houston. I think you might want to call your mom."

Tommy looked at Nathan, nodded, then stood up. The two men shook hands.

"Thank you, man, thank you." Tears were welling in his eyes.

"You'll get a chance to make it up to me someday. You can call me when you get to Houston if you want, but you don't have to. Thank me by making up with your mom. This is a gift from my friend in the car." Nathan handed Tommy the Miraculous Medal, his business card, and the "Marian Apparitions" tape Joanie had given him earlier in the day.

They shook hands again. Tommy put the medal around his neck as he watched Nathan leave the lobby. The big teenager turned and headed for the pay phone near the elevators.

Becky was back in the front seat and smiling so broadly that Nathan couldn't help but smile back.

"Don't say a word about this to Joe or Joanie. Or Chet. Especially not Chet. Mind? What I just did never happened."

"The word is mum," she replied. After a moment Becky spoke again, "You're one of the good guys, Nathan. Chet's got good taste in friends. Two days ago I thought you were a self-absorbed jerk. Now I feel like the jerk. I'm sorry."

Nathan appeared uncomfortable with her praise.

"No need to apologize," he said flatly, "two days ago you were right on the money about me. Still are, for all I know."

She could tell he meant it.

"You know that's not true," she said.

Nathan didn't reply.

Chapter Eleven

1

Tuesday, High Noon
10 October
Highway J-22, California

Lee looked at the King James Bible that Randall Knott had between them on the bench seat of the Buick next to a yellow legal notepad with the words "Samaritan" and "Faith" written in what was apparently Randall's husky scrawl.

Randall noticed Lee looking at the Bible.

"You called me brother, Brother Lee. Are you a believer?"

Lee smiled broadly. "Yes I am."

"Bible believer or otherwise?" Randall asked, looking back at the highway. *These hitchhikers will say anything to get a longer ride.*

"I believe every word in that book, if that's what ya mean."

"I read the Good Book every morning and every night, Brother Lee. Have you accepted Jesus Christ as your personal Lord and Savior?"

Lee laughed hard. He hadn't laughed much in his life before the visit from the dark-skinned woman and the angel with red hair.

"More than you know, Brother Randall! More than you know!"

After a minute, Lee added, "Can I take a look at your Bible?"

"Sure thing."

Lee took the well-worn leather-bound book, opened it to the Gospel of John, chapter 20. After a few minutes he began to explain verse 21, 22, and 23 to an amazed Randall Knott.

This boy can preach! He's soft-spoken, but there's power in his reasoning. Too bad he's a Catholic. It was clear from the context of the younger man's explanation that Lee believed in confessing sins to priests.

He's making sense, though, Randall thought. *I always kind of skimmed over those words of Jesus before.*

"So you're a Catholic, Brother Lee?" It was more a statement than a question.

"As a matter of fact, Brother Randall, I'm not. I was hopin' you could drop me off at a Catholic church somewhere so I could become one."

"You kiddin'? You never been baptized, boy?"

"My mom might have baptized me," Lee replied. "I don't remember. I'm new to all this."

"Sure you don't want to join up with the Baptists, Brother? I know the Rev at First Baptist in McFarland. That's my church," Randall said more out of obligation than hope.

Lee shook his head slowly.

At least I tried, Randall thought.

"Is there a Catholic church where you're going?" Lee asked after a while.

"Yeah, there's a tiny mission near the Chief's house up at Tule River. We'll be there in about an hour."

He took another look at Lee. *This boy's a mess. Can't be getting baptized looking like that, Catholic or no Catholic.*

"Let's see, there's a surplus store outside of Tule River..." Randall muttered to himself.

"Huh?" Lee asked, confused.

"Nothin', son. You sit tight. I'll get you to church on time."

A big smile came over Randall's face. There were crow's-feet around his eyes from driving in the California sun over thirty-five thousand miles a year for more than three decades.

The Samaritan was the wrong religion, too. Maybe this boy wantin' to be a Catholic is God's will, and the Lord wants me to help him. Okay Lord. You were a-naked and I'm gonna clothe you. Impossibly, Randall's smile grew wider.

2

Tuesday Afternoon
10 October
Tule River Indian Reservation, California

The priest found himself staring at the picture which his eyes had passed over hundreds of times during the last four years. The image of Our Lady of Guadalupe had been in Father Juan Rivera's family for generations. It hung on the wall between the window and the front door of the little house that passed for his rectory.

Father Juan had "retired" to Tule River Reservation to minister to the Indians four years ago. He was in his seventy-eighth year. Before coming to this place of desolation, he had served as a parish priest in the barrios of Los Angeles for over fifty years.

Retirement? he thought bitterly. *More like exile.*

Father Rivera preferred Tule River over the retirement home.

No one had much wanted the old-fashioned priest in LA. And no younger priest had wanted the Tule River mission. Juan's way of doing things had gone out of style. At least Juan was able to say the Tridentine Mass out here. Those few Indians who came to Mass seemed to prefer it, too.

I drink too much. I smoke too much. I live much too much, the old priest chastened himself.

These things were not true, but Father Juan was still very lonely. He had outlived his only brother, Diego. Diego's children didn't have much use for their old priest-uncle, except for a niece in La Jolla who sent him "Season's Greetings" cards with no references to Christmas in them.

He muttered a quick prayer for the Chief's daughter, Alisa, who was dying of leukemia. He offered his daily aches and pains for her, but he didn't have much hope little Alisa Roundrock would pull through. Chief Roundrock wasn't a Catholic, so Father Rivera didn't think he would be allowed to baptize the seven-year-old, much less administer last rites to her.

His mother had given him the Guadalupe image of Mary. *She looks so young!* he told himself. *She was one of us, a Mexican. You gave your life to her, and what have you to show for it, Juan?*

Very much, very much indeed, Juan! You have baptized. You have heard many confessions. You have said the Mass with devotion!

And so the almost daily dialogue the faithful old priest had with himself went on. He shook himself from his dreams when the tea kettle started to whistle and looked out the window next to the image. Rivera saw a young black man wearing chinos and a red checkered shirt getting out of a Buick in front of the rectory. The driver got out and embraced the young black man.

The young man smiled and waved at the older black man, then walked toward Father Rivera's door. Father Rivera wondered if he could get the tea kettle off the stove before the visitor knocked on his door.

3

Early Tuesday Morning
10 October
Salt Lake City, Utah

Long before dawn, the moonlight reflecting off the snow-covered Wasatch Mountains made it seem as if one could read a newspaper on the deck of the house. Lanning was fast asleep.

He was not unhealthy. Like most Mormons he observed the prescriptions of the so-called Word of Wisdom. He led an active life, completely avoided alcohol, didn't smoke, didn't drink caffeinated beverages, and rarely ate red meats. So when the attack struck him, waking him from his sleep, his first thought was that someone had put his heart into a large vise and tightened it suddenly and *hard*. After opening his eyes and realizing that there was no one in his bedroom except for his sleeping wife, his first emotion was surprise.

Heart attack? Me?

Then sharp pain added to the odd collapsing pressure he felt in his chest. He tried to scream but couldn't.

Elena, his wife of thirty-six years, woke up when John grabbed her nightgown with his right hand and the handle of the night dresser with his left. He violently pulled each end of his cardiovascular cross in a desperate attempt to "open" the walls closing in on his heart. His heart was pounding at over three hundred beats per minute and sounded like a stampede in his ears. Adrenaline from fear was downloaded into his system so quickly he felt it roll down his spine like mercury on an incline. The surge gave him hope in the darkening closet of his pain.

Elena screamed. Her sacred garment was now exposed underneath her torn gown. She frantically dialed 911 while John died.

John Lanning's soul floated out of his body. The pain was gone. His soul was hovering near the ceiling. His emotions were oddly flat—considering how fearful he had been a minute before—as he watched Elena's tears streaming down her face as she shouted into the phone. He saw the top of her head; he noticed a bald spot beneath the thinning hair. He had never been one to spend much time looking in full length mirrors, so he noticed that his empty body appeared smaller than he had imagined while "in" it.

Hmmn. Now I get to find out what's real. I wonder if there really is a tunnel of light? Is Joseph Smith going to judge me like I was taught as a child? Good-bye Elena. I loved you.

Just as Lanning finished his thought, a searing light blotted out his view and he discovered the truth.

4

Early Tuesday Morning
10 October
Chicago, Illinois

Before Nathan dropped Becky off at her apartment on Estes Avenue, he stopped at the Food Mart to stock up on milk and coffee, and to grab a snack. He had the munchies and was sure that the party had cleaned out his apartment of everything except for a bottle of beer or two.

He didn't notice the woman with the jet black hair behind the potato chip section (always the largest section in any convenience store). He got back into the Mustang and offered Becky a bite of his Slim Jim and a sip of his Sport Shake.

"Yuck!" she cried, smiling crookedly. Becky was very tired.

"What? This stuff is the best!" he protested. She was still shaking her head as Nathan held the junk food in front of her.

"Suit yourself," he said finally.

He started the Mustang and headed toward Estes.

✠ ✠ ✠

Inside the Food Mart, Jennifer Gower squinted her eyes at Nathan offering Becky the snack in his car.

Nathan Payne, my old friend, she thought sarcastically. *So you've found yourself another pretty girl to abuse. Bet you're going back to your apartment right now, you slime, after another night of wining and dining Little Miss Sports Illustrated Model...*

Jennifer encouraged the bitterness and anger growing in her breast. She hated Nathan Payne. She still lived only five blocks away from Nathan's chic residence on the lake. She shared a shabby two-bedroom apartment with two other women.

Jenny had been one of the only girls to ever see Nathan more than a few times. Three weeks after graduating from high school in Oshkosh, Wisconsin, Jennifer Gower, prom queen and aspiring spokesmodel, had come to Chicago to become famous.

Two years later, around the time of Thanksgiving, she met Nathan in Hang Ups on Rush Street. It was the first time she had fallen hard for a man. The four weeks she spent with him had been the most blissful she had ever known. He told her that he didn't want to get seriously involved with anyone. That's what all the boys in Oshkosh had said, too. Nathan was different. He was rich and self-confident. She loved his eyes. He would come around to her way of thinking eventually, she was certain of it. Jennifer was used to getting what she wanted.

When Nathan abruptly stopped calling her ten months ago, after frankly telling her to get lost, Jennifer Gower had taken it badly. She became depressed and sought professional help. She joined a feminist therapy group after spying a flyer on the bulletin board in her therapist's office. There she learned that Nathan was just like her father and that she had to stop letting men walk all over her.

Some of the girls in the group were lesbians, which was fine with Jennifer. Although she wasn't attracted to these women, she appreciated their insights about men. Feminists did make a few good points. Men used power to dominate women. Women had to fight back. Jennifer was discovering a compelling philosophy. She was also discovering that she had a mind of her own.

Nathan represented the worst kind of man, the "archetype," according to the feminist literature. He was a predator.

With her newfound self-esteem, Jennifer got back on her feet and landed a few commercials and a part or two with experimental theater productions. She was quite pretty and paid her rent by working as a spokeswoman for hire at McCormick Place. She also held down a nice job as a waitress in an upscale French restaurant on weekends.

The week before spotting Nathan Payne in the Food Mart, Jennifer had discovered she had a chance for a great role—a real *femme fatale*. The part was for a character in a feminist play being written by a friend. The character's first name was Jane.

Jane needs a little practice. Maybe I could work on Jane and at the same time have some fun with Nathan the Predator Payne. Give him a little of his own medicine. I bet he still lives on the lake. This will be good for me. I'll check with the group. I'm sure they'll say it would be good to act out my feelings. And my horoscope said I would meet someone from my past today!

A plot formed in her mind.

5

Early Tuesday Morning
10 October
LDS Hospital
Salt Lake City, Utah

Lanning had been dead for over twelve minutes by the time the ambulance arrived at LDS hospital, which was only a few minutes away from his home. Paramedics had already begun standard revival procedures while taking him off the bed. Both paramedics and the doctor in the Emergency Room were Mormons. The doctor who treated him was aware of the identity of his patient; Lanning was the bishop of the doctor's ward on the hill across the way.

✝ ✝ ✝

Lanning entered the tunnel of light traveling at speeds that seemed faster than any jet on earth. A peculiar light, which appeared as a dot at the end of a tunnel, careened toward him. He saw a being standing in the light at the end of the tunnel; the being was a shape of light outlined by even more fantastic light behind it. Lanning was surprised when the shape took on the form of a woman as he floated toward her. She was wearing a seamless hooded garment. It was black.

He was anxious to see her face as he approached her. When he did see her face he began to scream. There were dark holes where her eyes should have been and giant warts on skin as old and dry as the desert floor. Lanning knew her name. She was Death.

Death cackled a sentence, beckoning him toward her with long skeletal fingers, *"Contraception, my sweet."*

She favored him with a ghastly smile. *"Contraception has made you mine!"* Death laughed with high-pitched wicked humor.

The light behind her became undulating—flames licking up from a lake of fire. Behind her he saw grotesque creatures covered with the flames and heard surreal wailing and screaming. Terrified, Lanning realized that the beings were men and women under torture by demons.

"No!" He willed with all his bodiless being. *"There is no hell!"*

Death laughed at him; the sound of her knife-like voice echoed off invisible walls.

"No! I'm sorry for using contraceptives! I didn't think it was wrong! I won't go in there! I will *not* go in there!"

Death spun around and around in a strange hopping dance. He was only a few "paces" from her and the fiery cauldron of terror.

"No!" Lanning screamed again at beckoning Death. He felt the flames begin to lick up off the surface of the lake onto his legs...

✛ ✛ ✛

Dr. Paul Elway continued the chest compressions until he felt a rib crack in the corpse's torso. He was just about ready to stop the violent, last ditch procedure. Tears were in the doctor's eyes and on his cheeks. Lanning had been dead for over eighteen minutes. *Eighteen minutes,* Elway thought, exasperated, *four minutes more than anyone who's ever "come back" in my twelve years in ER. He's gone.*

Elway stopped the procedure and hung his head, folding one arm and putting his thumb and index finger on the bridge of his nose with his other hand. He exhaled a long breath as he shook his head slowly back and forth. Three nurses, Emergency Room veterans all, began to sob.

The corpse cried out, startling Dr. Elway.

One nurse gasped.

"No! Don't stop! They're taking me to hell!" the corpse screamed in a voice that chilled the nurses. "Don't stop you son of a bitch! Hell! The flames!"

"The flames are **eating me alive!**" Lanning shrieked again!

Elway restarted the chest compressions. He heard the first beep on the monitor as Lanning's heart began to beat again.

"Oh! No! I won't go **there!**" Lanning continued to cry out and began to flail his arms at invisible tormentors.

Elway shouted at a nurse, "What are you standing there for? Epinephrine! Now Nurse Connors!"

With shaking hands, the nurse grabbed the hypodermic needle and a vial as the monitor began to register a climbing heartbeat.

The doctor stopped compressing Lanning's chest. Elway was shaken. Despite his joy at his religious leader's return, his medical experience called forth a question in his mind.

LDS leader or not, Lanning was another case from which to learn. In the Emergency Room there was usually little time before the next gurney came hurtling through the automatic doors. He coldly evaluated what had happened even as he injected Lanning with the needle.

That's odd, Doc, he told himself. *Twelve years and over thirty patients who've "come back," not to mention countless dozens more who were conscious during cardiac arrest—and not one has ever told me to restart the chest compressions. They usually scream at me to stop it hurts them so much. Not one in over twelve years.*

Not one. Until John Lanning.

"Thank you. Thank you," Lanning gasped in a hoarse voice. His eyes were still closed. "I'm back. I was in hell." Lanning was afraid to open his eyes for fear he might see Death again, even though he was quite sure he was back in the hospital room. And back in his body.

Lanning bravely opened his eyes.

"Don't speak, Mr. Lanning. We'll take care of you. You're going to be all right." Elway put his hand on the patient's forearm.

Lanning anxiously looked around the room. "Where's the black fellow with the roses?" he asked.

"Which black fellow, Mr. Lanning?" Elway asked, confused. All five workers in the Emergency Room were white.

"The one with the three roses. I saw him standing next to you as I watched you from the ceiling, before I came back into my body." Lanning tried to move his head to look around the room to find the black man wearing a red checkered shirt and chino pants.

Post traumatic stress-induced hallucinations, Elway concluded. *Hell? Indeed! Lanning was hallucinating. Cardiac cases say the strangest things.*

Elway was more relieved that Lanning showed signs of hallucinating than he was that Lanning hadn't died. Lanning had screamed about hell in a quite convincing fashion, and it had caused a sudden but palpable doubt in Elway's mind.

Elway was a devout Mormon. Every faithful Mormon knows that there is no eternal hell. The "No Hell Doctrine" was one of the seminal revelations taught by Joseph Smith and Brigham Young, the founders of Mormonism.

6

Tuesday Morning
10 October
Downtown Chicago, Illinois

"Where the hell have you been, Payne?" Charlie VanDuren screamed at Nathan as he walked into the VV&B offices in the Standard Oil Building.

After returning to his apartment the night before, Nathan had difficulty falling asleep. It seemed like every time he closed his eyes and tried to imagine Joanie's face an extremely erotic image of one of Nathan's former bed-mates would be pushed into his mind. It was so disturbing that he considered calling Chet; but he remembered that his friend was still on the road, heading toward New Jersey.

He let one or two of the images linger. Then he felt vaguely guilty, as if he had cheated on Joanie in his mind. Then he remembered Pascal's Wager and a foggy teaching from the Bible somewhere—something about sleeping with a girl in your head is the same as sleeping with her for real. Maybe he had heard that in grade school as a child.

You mean I've even got to observe the Tom Wheat Rule in my own head? Oh well, a bet's a bet.

Finally, feeling even more guilty for allowing the images to linger in his mind despite his newfound scruple, Nathan began to pray a Rosary. At four, he dropped off to sleep after the fifth Hail Mary.

Nathan overslept his alarm by three hours. He was always at work an hour early. So why would Charlie be so violently upset about his being late for one stinking day?

The least Charlie can do is let me explain, Nathan thought.

"Come into my office, Rip Van Winkle," Charlie ordered with dripping sarcasm.

"So what's the big deal, Charlie? Are you having a bad-hair day? I oversleep one time and you throw a fit!" Nathan was angry.

"It's not that, Payne! Don't you read the papers? Listen to the radio recently?" VanDuren turned and pointed to the monitor on his desk.

The NASDAQ numbers were listed. Nathan looked at the company just above VanDuren's index finger.

"Oh no," Nathan said weakly.

"The war started last night, our time. The Russians took over your can't-miss oil fields in less than sixteen hours. CNI says that they might be going all the way into Iraq."

CNI was an Atlanta-owned company with communications headquarters in Amsterdam. CNI served over ninety-eight percent of worldwide cable services and over ninety percent of industrialized and Pacific Rim homes. Just about every television in the world that was hooked up to cable or digital direct satellite service carried CNI.

VanDuren was pointing to a stock called TDC. TDC was a freestanding consortium formed with the resources of five major oil companies (three American, two European) which had agreed to develop the newly discovered, massive oil fields in the Republic of Georgia. The name of the consortium was the Tbilisi Development Corporation, or TDC. It was named after the capital of Georgia, Tbilisi, where the consortium was headquartered. The former Soviet state didn't have the infrastructure, technology, know-how, or capital to develop the fields. Two months before the consortium was formed, a treaty had been signed by the now-stabilized Russian Republic and its neighboring states. It had guaranteed peace in the region for years to come.

Georgia had access to the Black Sea. Its rail lines connected it to all of Eurasia. It stood at the crossroads of the Middle East and was not far from the capitals of Iran and Iraq.

With environmental regulations preventing the huge oil fields in Alaska from being developed, and North Sea and Mexican fields drying up, as well as the usual squabbles among Middle East countries hindering production, Nathan had strongly recommended that VV&B put risk-approved funds into TDC. Nathan personally put over half his wealth into TDC stock. It was a gamble—closer to speculation than investment, but the pay back had enormous potential.

On Monday, a one-day war featuring a small "theater" nuclear weapon began and ended suddenly. The Russians seemed to have learned a ghastly lesson during the protracted conflict a few years before in Chechnya. The center of Tbilisi was utterly destroyed by a bomb that was roughly one-fifth the size of the one dropped over Hiroshima in World War II. A victorious Russian defense minister had appeared on television and announced to CNI reporters in Moscow that the Russian Empire had just been reborn. It seemed that no one knew who was in charge of Russia. The minister had pointedly remarked that the former prime minister of the Russian Republic was no longer "in office." He refused to comment on his country's use of the small nuclear weapon.

TDC stock had dropped from 90 3/8 to less than 10 1/4 by the time Nathan walked into the office.

"So?" Nathan asked weakly, his face pale. He was trying to recover from the news on VanDuren's screen. It told him that he had personally lost over three hundred thousand dollars in less than two hours.

"So? You arrogant bastard! Ready to feel the pain, Mr. Feel the Pain? I put over eighty percent of our biggest individual investors and over half our institutional accounts into that freakin' consortium. And I played them off your stellar reputation!" VanDuren rounded out his diatribe with a string of expletives.

"You what? I told you it was too risky! TDC was not for low risk capital!" Nathan shouted back.

"Risky?! You put half your life's savings into the damn thing!" VanDuren's neck was red. "It was the chance of a lifetime. Forty-eight hours ago, no political analyst in the world would have predicted the resurrection of Peter the Damned Great and an expansionist, nationalist Russia!"

Nathan opened his mouth and shut it. He looked out the window and then down at the floor. He felt an odd sensation that the room was tilting, and then the floor righted itself.

"When do I go down, Charlie?"

"Look, Nathan, you had a nice run here. It's the board. The trustees. They'll want a head to roll. Which one of us are they going to believe? You or me? I own half the friggin' firm. Somebody's got to take the fall. Even after you go down, our reputation's shot on the street for years." A rare note of compassion crept into VanDuren's voice. "You'll land on your feet, Nathan, why I bet—"

Nathan gave Charlie a cold look, stopping his boss in mid-sentence.

"Save the Knute Rockne speech, Charlie. Have somebody box my stuff up and send it to my apartment. Sally can forge my signature on the resignation."

"What the hell!" VanDuren shouted as Nathan turned and walked out the door.

7

Tuesday Afternoon
10 October
Tule River Indian Reservation, California

Before dropping Lee off at the Tule River Reservation, Randall Knott had stopped at a surplus store.

Randall seemed ready to buy the entire store for Lee. Lee had insisted that Randall restrict his purchase to two sets of identical chino pants and red checkered shirts, a pair of K-Swiss tennis shoes, underwear, and two pairs of socks. Lee also allowed Randall to buy him some toiletries and a leather "factory reject" gym bag. At Randall's suggestion, Lee stopped in a gas station rest room to shave and wash up as best he could. Lee left his filthy Cleveland Browns t-shirt, socks, beat up Gucci shoes, and Levi's neatly folded in the rest room. He kept his leather belt.

The two men now stood by the Buick in front of a tiny cottage next to a small and ancient adobe church. It reminded Lee of a Taco Bell restaurant.

"Well, Brother Lee, here it is, Our Lady Help of Christians Mission. I guess a small portion of the tribe was converted by Spanish Franciscans when Indians owned the whole state—before the white folks took over. Sure was nice talking to you about the Good Book. You opened my eyes on certain passages in the Bible. You've got a gift, boy. I sure hope you use it after you get yourself baptized."

Randall Knott held his hand out to Lee Washington. Lee ignored the hand and embraced the large black Samaritan.

"I promise you, Brother Randall, you'll be rewarded in heaven for being so generous to this unworthy servant of Jesus." Tears were in Lee's eyes despite his smile.

Randall returned the smile but said nothing.

Lee turned and walked toward Father Juan Rivera's door.

8

Thursday, Midnight
12 October
Chicago's Gold Coast, Illinois

Nathan was more than buzzed. He had been drunk for the past two days. After leaving VV&B, he had headed directly to the nearest drinking station. It was a small miracle that he hadn't gotten into an accident while driving home.

He left his apartment only to buy liquor and rent videos. He had been unable to keep his mind on the movies, except for *Aliens,* which he watched three times. Bags of half-eaten chips and empty bottles littered his living room.

He had been a heavy drinker since college, but this binge was unusually severe. The booze helped him blot out the ramifications of his firing. The realization that his drunkenness broke Pascal's Wager inspired him to drink more. Normally, even an event as traumatic as losing half his money and his job wouldn't have shaken his confidence. But Nathan was being goaded by unseen enemies to surrender to despair. Despair—the loss of the virtue of hope—has always been considered the most serious of sins by theologians.

The unseen enemies were, of course, demons. Philosophers and theologians have always debated the problem of evil. Why had God withdrawn His Divine Protection from Nathan? There is no answer and there is only one answer: for Nathan's greater good. God also allowed evil to run roughshod over Job as a test. God later chastened Job for questioning His motives: *Where wast thou when I laid the foundations of the earth?*

Despite Nathan's gifts for mathematics and leadership, he was not by nature an intellectual. Had he been, the attacks might have come in other areas—an appeal to his intellectual pride, for example. His primary weaknesses were his passions—areas where all human beings have strong natural desires such as food, sex, and drink. The first attack, designed to incite violent anger through the agency of a desperate Tommy Gervin, had failed. The second attack, the failure of imprudent investments in TDC had succeeded in turning him to the bottle. He was like a poorly conditioned boxer being pounded during the later rounds. It was time for his enemies to deliver the knockout punch. If this next gambit failed, there was still one more deadly tactic available to them.

✝ ✝ ✝

The phone rang again. The answering machine popped on with Nathan's terse cynical message: "Yeah it's me; you know what to do," followed by a digital beep.

Joanie's voice came on, "Nathan? Are you there? I'm starting to really worry about you. They said you don't work at VV&B anymore." He heard the alarm in her voice. He tried to avoid a temporary blackout as he pushed himself up from the modern leather and chrome couch.

"I love you, Mister. Do you hear me? I'm not going away. Please call and tell me what's going on." Then she left her number for the third time. He had not answered any of her previous calls.

I love you too, Joanie.

His emotions surged, amplified by the alcohol, as he moved toward the phone. By the time he reached the receiver, she had hung up.

The doorbell buzzed. He looked toward the door. After the third buzz he decided to open it, and replaced the handset on the phone.

It can't be Joanie.

He opened the door and saw Jennifer Gower standing there dressed in overalls and a brown cotton turtleneck. She had tears streaming down her cheeks. Her short, almost oriental, jet black hair was in a mess. There was no lipstick on her full red lips.

"Jenny! What are you doing here?"

"Jimmy let me come up when I explained my predicament, Nathan." Jimmy was the doorman of Nathan's building. Her trembling tone betrayed that she was very disturbed by something.

"Really, Jenny, it's not a good time right now—"

"Fine, I'll leave," she interrupted in a hurt voice, straightened her back and raised her chin as if preparing for a blow, "but I don't have anywhere else to go. I need help. I need a friend. I know I haven't seen you in almost a year, but I'm not here about that. I'm completely over you romantically." She turned as if to leave, and broke out into a pathetic sob. Her shoulders shook.

Pascal's Wager, Nathan thought with a heavy sense of obligation.

He stepped out into the hallway and grasped Jennifer's arm. She attempted to pull away but not hard enough to cause Nathan to lose his grip. She allowed him to guide her into his apartment.

Nathan tried to clear the fog in his brain.

"What's the matter, Jenny? Can I help? Did somebody hurt you?" She was really crying now.

You really stuck it to her last year. At Christmas, no less! She didn't have a friend in the whole city. And she really fell hard for you, too.

"Hold me," she said, childlike. He felt awkward but he held her anyway. Her sobs started to subside. He shook off a memory of holding Joanie at the lake at Notre Dame.

"I've lost everything," she began explaining, "I just got kicked out of my apartment today, and I haven't had a job in over three months. I'm afraid to go home to Oshkosh." There was something—fear—in her voice, when she spoke the word *Oshkosh.*

"Why not?" Nathan was genuinely concerned now.

"Can we sit on the couch?" she asked helplessly, raising her puppy dog eyes to his.

He led her to his couch. He swept off papers, an empty bag of Doritos, and crumpled clothes.

What a pig! she thought. *Careful, you're Jane now. Jane doesn't care what's on his couch!*

He sat first and she sat close to him, delicately placing her hand on his thigh as she faced him.

She proceeded to feed him more lies about how she had been a total failure as a spokesmodel and how she lost her waitress job. She had been so depressed after her breakup with him that she sought therapy. Then Jenny's therapist, a woman in whom Jenny had invested all her trust and hundreds of dollars, had tried to seduce Jenny. Jenny told Nathan how she was so naïve when she came to Chicago, and that no one except Nathan had treated her with any kindness. She told him that the way he broke up with her so severely had been an act of charity because he had been truthful with her—but she didn't make this last point with much conviction.

Almost all her lies were based on truth. Jennifer did have a female therapist but the therapist had not made a pass at her. Jenny had lost a waitress job—but she had found a better job at the French restaurant two days later. She was using a classic acting technique. And she was not a bad actress.

This is too much fun! Am I laying it on too thick? Jenny appraised her performance. *No, he's drunk. He's eating this up with a spoon. Maybe I should cry again?*

Meanwhile Nathan was quick to blame himself for the troubles of this girl he barely knew. *Did I help reduce her to this state? This poor, beautiful girl!*

He couldn't help but notice how pretty she was. He had been quite attracted to her from the first minute he saw her down on Rush Street. Hers was one of the erotic images that had been plaguing him during the past two days. He had also been attracted to her innocence when they dated, even if she was a bit self-absorbed. The alcohol was wearing off some, but he told himself that the way she rested her hand on his leg and snuggled next to him was understandable, considering her state. He was beginning to be aroused but he tried to ignore it.

He told himself that hugging her so closely was helping her.

He whispered consoling words, telling her that it would be okay, that he was there for her, that she didn't need to worry.

"Why can't you go back home to Oshkosh, Jen? Is there something wrong there?"

She hesitated.

Always hold a little back, Jennifer thought wickedly. *Mystery is what holds an audience.*

"I've never told anyone. I can't bring myself to talk about what happened to me in Oshkosh."

Was she abused as a child? By her father? Nathan thought of his own abusive father and frowned darkly, feeling the pain of his own childhood.

She hugged him closer. She raised her full lips to his, and began to kiss him.

9

Tuesday Evening
10 October
Tule River Indian Reservation, California

After several hours of questioning and two pots of tea, Father Rivera decided to grant Lee Washington's request for baptism and first Holy Communion. They sat in the kitchen. A Douay-Rheims Bible was open on the table.

"We can get started tomorrow. I think you should find a bishop to confirm you, though. I don't believe you'll have much of a problem. You'll probably know more about the faith than he will."

Not only had Father Juan been impressed with Lee's knowledge of the Catholic faith, but Lee had also taught the old priest a few highly nuanced insights into the Scriptures—

especially those passages regarding the sacraments. But the scope of Lee's knowledge had not convinced the priest so much as the boy's sincerity and his ardent desire to join the Family of God. Lee openly desired above all things to take part in the sacramental life of the Catholic Church.

Father Juan had ruled out a hoax rather quickly. *Who would come to this godforsaken place to play a trick on an old man like me? Why? God works in mysterious ways—but having this young man pull my leg is not one of them.*

Lee had not told Father Rivera about his visit from Mary, although Lee did relate many of the sins of his life, including his failed attempt at suicide in the Motorman Motel. He attributed his extraordinary conversion simply to "the Mother of God."

"Before I could push down the plunger on the needle," Lee recounted, "something or somebody stopped me. It's hard to explain."

"Perhaps it was your guardian angel," Father Rivera suggested. Lee raised his eyebrows. The priest continued, "Tell me, if you were such a godless person two days ago, how did you come to know the faith so well?"

"I just know it. It's a gift from God. When I picked up the Bible in Mr. Knott's car, I just knew what it meant." It was the truth—sort of. Lee might have been changed but he was not naïve. His instincts told him that Father Rivera and others would find it hard to believe that he had been visited by the Mother of God—and the Archangel Raphael to boot! The brown-skinned lady had not commanded Lee to indiscriminately reveal the details of her visit.

Lee changed the subject, "Can we get some fresh air, Father?"

The old priest suspected Lee was holding something back but decided to let it drop. It was obvious Lee was sincere. Why push it?

"Sure. There's only one major street on this reservation, but we can have a nice walk down it as long as a local doesn't run us over by accident with his pickup truck. I need to stop by Chief Roundrock's place again. His daughter Alisa is gravely ill."

The old man got up slowly and led Lee to the front door. Father Rivera heard Lee speak excitedly behind him before they walked out.

"I know her!" Lee practically shouted. He was pointing to the picture next to the window.

"Oh yes, Lee, Our Lady of Guadalupe. How do you know her?"

I cried on her lap, Lee thought. *She's the one I saw!*

"I've seen her before." It was mostly the truth. "Is this the original?" he asked Father Juan.

The old priest laughed.

"The original is in Mexico City on Tepeyac Hill in a church built to honor where Mary appeared to an Indian named Juan Diego in the early 1500s. My mother named me after him. This copy has been in my family for over two hundred years.

"It's funny, I never considered myself an Indian like the ones I'm supposed to be ministering to here in Tule River, but at one time, my people were considered the Indians. We all became Catholic because of this image."

"You've got to tell me more about her," Lee told the old priest.

Father Juan noticed the urgency in the boy's tone. *Ah! Something he doesn't know about the faith! He knows doctrine and the Bible, but he doesn't know history.*

"All in good time, Lee. All in good time."

✛ ✛ ✛

Chief Roundrock answered the door. His face was ashen. He did not look like a "movie" Indian to Lee, who had never been on a reservation in his life. Roundrock was dressed in clean blue jeans and a western shirt with a bolo tie. He was forty-two but looked younger. He was divorced. His ex-wife lived in Santa Monica where she taught windsurfing to suburban white kids.

"Who's this with you, Father?" Roundrock asked warily, looking at Lee.

"A new friend of mine. Lee Washington, meet Chief Roundrock."

"Pleased to meet you, Chief, sir," Lee said in his most friendly "white" voice. He peered beyond the Chief to the living room of the small but nicely kept home. He saw two young children watching Barney on the television.

The Chief grunted and turned to the priest, saying, "They sent Alisa home to die. She's inside. There's no hope for her." Though his tone was gruff, Roundrock's lower lip was trembling.

"For the love of God, man, let me baptize her!" Father Rivera urged passionately.

"I don't believe in your God or your baptism!" Roundrock shouted. "Go away and leave us in peace!" His voice cracked with emotion as he readied his hand to close the door. "I can get the council to kick you off this reservation if I want! Don't push me!"

"You don't want to do that, Chief, sir," Lee's soft voice seemed to drift past the priest to the Chief.

"Lee, don't—" Father Rivera tried to protest, but Lee gently took hold of the priest's forearm, quelling his words.

There was power in Lee's gentleness. He looked at the Chief for what seemed like a full minute before speaking.

"Perhaps we should pray with *you,* sir. Can I pray with you? I know what it feels like to lose someone you love," Lee said calmly, peacefully, seemingly unconcerned about whatever answer the Chief might give.

The Chief didn't reply. The anger lines on his forehead slowly disappeared. He looked back into the room where his two healthy children were docilely watching television. Roundrock opened the door without looking at his visitors. Lee put his hand on the back of Father Rivera and gave a gentle push.

Lee followed the man to the kitchen, and without hesitating, put his hands on top of the Chief's head. Chief Roundrock flinched slightly but didn't resist. Lee began to pray silently, his eyes closed. Father Rivera watched in utter surprise for two or three minutes while the young black man prayed over the Chief. After a moment Father Rivera began to silently pray to Mary in Spanish.

Roundrock felt nothing. No heat. No sensation—only the ordinary warmth of Lee's hands on his head. He waited patiently with his eyes closed while Lee prayed. Lee finally removed his hands, finished. He had not said a word since stepping through the front door.

"There are no words for the suffering we share with Jesus," Lee said finally, compassionately, tears forming in his eyes.

The Chief nodded solemnly.

"We'll go now," Lee said, meaning every word, not fishing for Roundrock to ask him and Rivera to stay.

There was no reaction from the Chief, so Lee turned to Father Rivera and said, "Come with me, Father, we're done for today."

Still stunned, Father Rivera took a step with Lee toward the front door.

"Wait," Roundrock called after them.

They turned.

The Chief pursed his lips, then looked from one man to the other.

"Alisa is upstairs, sleeping. She's only seven. Please pray for her, too?" His tone was filled with uncertainty. Then, glaring at the priest, he added firmly, "But no baptism."

"Of course," Lee said quietly. "Of course."

The two men followed the worried father to his dying daughter.

Two weeks after Lee left Tule River, Chief Roundrock called Father Rivera and asked him to baptize Alisa. One month later, Alisa died. One month after Alisa died, the rest of the Roundrocks of Tule River became Catholics. A small but significant portion of the tribe followed Chief Roundrock's example over the next six months. Father Rivera desperately wanted to write to Lee to inform him of the wonderful news but he didn't have Lee's address.

Sometimes, late at night, when Father Rivera was most likely to feel the loneliness of his exile, he reminded himself of the soft-spoken black stranger who came to Tule River bearing Christ in his soul.

10

Early Friday Morning
13 October
Chicago's Gold Coast, Illinois

Jennifer began to kiss Nathan more passionately when she realized he was kissing her back. He stopped tentatively when he tasted her tears.

"Jenny, maybe this isn't what you need right now—"

She ignored Nathan's suggestion; she began to sob lightly again as she kissed him. Between sobs and kisses she told him that affection was what she needed.

"I need a friend. Friends can express their closeness, can't they? If only for one night?" Her whispers were so needy, so desperate.

She was so beautiful too, and warm, and Nathan had been very lonely and his life had lacked all beauty since returning to Chicago.

Except for Tommy Gervin. You helped him, too. Jenny needs your help right now, he rationalized.

He began to do things. Things his experience taught him women wanted. Things women like Jennifer Gower wanted.

Maybe she doesn't know any better? Who am I to judge this hurt little girl?

Nathan had experience with Jenny. He knew what she liked. Unlike Father Chet, Nathan had not had years of struggle practicing the difficult virtue of chastity. Nathan's enemies knew his path of least resistance.

Like Lee Washington in the Motorman Motel, he was being seduced by more than the lovely creature named Jennifer Gower. Other creatures, far less appealing than Jennifer, were active in his room. He wasn't aware that he was in the midst of a battle for his soul.

She needs me. Maybe I could forget my own troubles for a while. He pushed the image of Joanie Wheat out of his mind for the fourth or fifth time. *Not you, Joanie! Jenny. Jenny needs me.* He couldn't admit it, but he was enjoying himself, both physically and in his mission as Jenny's pocket-sized savior.

PART TWO

The Warning

The crucible for silver and the furnace for gold,
but the Lord tests the heart.
Proverbs 17: 3

And there appeared a great wonder in heaven: a woman
clothed with the sun, and the moon under her feet,
and on her head a crown of twelve stars.
Revelations 12: 1

The Warning, like the chastisement, is a fearful thing; it
is a fearful thing for the good as well as the wicked. It
will draw the good closer to God and warn the wicked
that the end of times is coming.
Conchita Gonzalez of Garabandal, Spain

Chapter Twelve

1

Tuesday Morning
10 October
Verona, New Jersey

"Monsignor Whelan wants to see you!" Sister Margaret called to Chet as he walked into the rectory. Father Chet's slumping posture revealed how tired he was from his drive straight through from South Bend. Sister was the parish Religious Studies Coordinator.

"Monsignor Whelan didn't expect you until Friday—but the Monsignor was adamant. He'll be back from his symposium on Thursday. He'll expect to see you first thing Friday morning."

Oh no, what is it this time? the young priest thought, distressed. Whelan always wanted to see Chet. Usually to forbid Chet to do something most people would consider the normal part of a good priest's life.

"You look terrible, Father," Sister Margaret said with a touch of smugness. She didn't like Father Chet. She had often locked horns with him over the content of the religion classes he taught at Notre Dame du Lac Grammar School. He reluctantly accepted the liberal books she assigned to the courses but never actually used them while teaching. And the children loved him—especially his fascinating Saint Stories.

Sister Margaret considered Father Chet a relic; an oppressor of women. He was polluting the minds of the children with superstitious garbage. In her opinion, *she* would have made a much better priest than the old-fashioned Chet Sullivan. It was Chet's type in the Vatican who were stopping her from being ordained—unless Cardinal Casino became the new pope, as it was rumored.

"I just drove through the night to get here," Chet explained wearily, sorting through the many phone messages in his box.

Sister Margaret rewarded Chet with a sarcastic smile as she shook her head slowly back and forth. *He's clueless. All that time in the confessional is driving him nutty.*

"Okay, schedule me for nine o'clock after I say Mass on Friday. You can tell the Monsignor that for me, can't you?"

"I suppose so," she replied noncommittally as she looked at her desk calendar.

Chet looked down the wood-paneled hallway to the closed door of Whelan's empty office. He turned in the opposite direction and climbed the stairs to his room.

Sister Margaret's mental reference to Chet spending so much time in the confessional was apt. It was a constant source of tension between Chet and Monsignor Whelan. He spent two hours every day except Sunday in the confessional waiting for penitents. If no one showed up, he read spiritual books and prayed. For the first several months in Verona, very few people came to confession. Whelan had refused to let him print his confession times in the parish bulletin—so Chet, during his Sunday homilies, countered by telling his parishioners that he would be in the confessional every day. He still had many devotees from his first parish, Saint Agnes Church in the Ironbound Section of Newark. Many Saint Agnes folks wanted to continue to have him as a confessor. Word of mouth spread about Chet's availability. On most days, faithful Catholics from all over the diocese came to have their sins absolved.

Chet had a gentle way and a gift for explaining things. He had been inspired to start the practice of hearing daily confessions after reading about Saint John Vianney, who spent up to eight hours a day hearing confessions. Vianney was the patron saint of parish priests. Chet also fasted frequently, following Vianney's example.

Whelan had gambled that the young priest would tire of sitting in an empty confessional for two hours a day during dinner hour. The pastor was enraged at Sullivan's popularity. Even a few of the more liberal parishioners had given Chet "a shot" after hearing how kind and effective he was in the confessional. A few women had raved to Whelan that Chet had saved their marriages! Whelan regarded those reports as highly suspect. He knew one of the couples personally and had quietly recommended that they seek a civil divorce—even if it was against the outdated teachings of "the bishop of Rome."

Chet had also embarrassed Whelan by preaching about the evils of abortion and contraception. The worst part about Chet's preaching was that he didn't rant and rave: Father Sullivan *explained*—gently, clearly, and compassionately. He was fooling many of the more ignorant parishioners, Whelan believed. Some of the well-heeled, upset with Chet's implicit condemnation of their behavior, warned Whelan that financial contributions to Notre Dame du Lac would diminish.

That was not all. Chet had embarrassed the entire diocese by being arrested not once, but three times, while picketing abortion clinics. Chet never blocked the entrances, but tough new federal laws made the right to *assemble for prayer* outside of abortion clinics illegal. Chet's activities made all the papers. Even hostile liberal reporters had taken a liking to the humorous young priest. Chet was a pithy, if not eloquent, spokesman for the sanctity of human life. Reporters often called him for witty quotes to balance their mostly liberal articles on abortion issues. Chet made good copy. He was also known to tip a beer with a few of the reporters. A highly placed editor of the Newark *Star Ledger* was so disturbed by Father Chet's relationships with the *Ledger's* reporters that the editor had been forced to rotate assignments to stop the "contamination." The same editor once called Whelan to complain about the young priest.

Perhaps the thing that bothered Monsignor Whelan most was his utter failure to break the boy. Auxiliary Bishop

Brookings himself had given Whelan the assignment. Everyone inside the diocesan bureaucracy knew that Whelan was in line for higher office. Bishop Brookings had been clear that "breaking" Sullivan was a test that would be watched by those in a position to help foster Whelan's career.

Chet had made the most of his first assignment. Saint Agnes was dilapidated and poor, but had a faithful old pastor, Father Montini, who had been thrilled to have Father Chet. Notre Dame du Lac was on the opposite end of the spectrum— liberal and affluent—considered a plush assignment by most priests in the diocese.

At first Chet was inwardly upset when Whelan advised him to tone down the sermons on contraception and the like. Whelan became more strident when Chet's sermons remained the same. During Chet's third call into the office, the Monsignor had forbidden Chet to mention Pope Patrick or any papal teachings on marriage or sexuality. Chet stood silently before him like a prisoner brought before the warden. Whelan didn't look like a warden, however. He was tall and thin, and as always, dressed perfectly. Whelan always had a plastic smile on his face—like a politician.

"And absolutely not one more word about the Blessed Virgin!" Whelan had shouted at Chet. "Your mind is in the Dark Ages on that subject, Sullivan!"

Fire had flashed in Chet's eyes; then the younger priest had laughed. Laughed!

"What are you going to do?" Chet rejoined cheerfully. "Run up to the pulpit and wash my mouth out with soap? You can't forbid me to teach the Truth and you know it. You can ruin my career and maybe I don't get to be a bishop someday, but so what? I signed up to preach the gospel and to administer the sacraments."

Whelan seethed. Father Chet lowered his voice, leaned his hands on Whelan's large desk, and said with more than a little compassion, "Monsignor, I know you don't understand why I like to hear confessions and preach about the teachings of the pope. I wish you did understand, I really do.

"But you've got to try to understand my point of view, Monsignor. You see, your way of doing things—all the so-called modern stuff you've been teaching since the sixties—is doomed for the ash heap of history. My kind of priesthood was around before the so-called Dark Ages, after the Dark Ages, and it'll be around long after we're both gone.

"And there are more priests like me coming down the pike. Most of my liberal classmates dropped out of the program in Seton Hall, and despite the persecution of normal Catholics that goes on there, usually it's only the true believers who can stick it out. While you fret about the lack of vocations, real congregations like the Legionaries of Christ are busting at the seams. I know, I have friends there—"

"Hold it right there—" Whelan interrupted.

But Chet was just warming up. "Your kind of religion—if you can call it a religion—had its chance and failed. You and your cronies might have control of the diocesan bureaucracies, the newspapers, the committees, and the colleges, but you're a dying breed. You emptied the churches! Nobody understands, much less buys, your liberal mumbo jumbo. I know I don't. It's boring, banal, and dull, filled with lies.

"Worst of all, it's keeping people away from an exciting, challenging, and vibrant faith—the Catholicism of the Apostle's Creed. The Catholicism of Pope Peter to Pope Patrick is a lion. We only need to let that lion out of its cage. People love it when it's presented clearly and in a way that respects their free will.

"You guys blew it. Real faith is coming back! Why do you think there's such a big crowd for confessions? Why are more and more people showing up for the Rosary before I say morning Mass? People want Jesus! They love the sacraments when they realize that sacraments truly are the best way to find Jesus!"

Chet paused, breathing hard. He had built up a head of steam. Whelan was stunned.

"I got used to taking heat like you've given me from liberal professors at Notre Dame. Liberal Catholicism was a dead letter when it arrived. You guys just don't realize it yet. It's sad."

Whelan stood up and pointed a thin finger at Chet.

"Don't you lecture me, Sullivan. I'm the one with degrees from Georgetown and Harvard!"

Chet closed his eyes, shook his head, and thought, *This is hopeless.* All his rage dissipated.

"Mark my words Sullivan, you haven't heard the last of this. Get out of my office."

That had been four months ago. Whelan began locking the doors of the church to prevent Chet from hearing confessions. The penitents came to the rectory door instead, waking Whelan up at all hours. Chet had told them to go to the rectory if the doors were locked. As many as ten people would line up in the waiting room outside of Chet's small office during his off-duty hours. After two months of watching the line from the dining room while he ate dinner, Whelan reopened the church.

Chet had not said a word to his pastor about that. Not even a snide remark. It bothered Whelan all the more that Chet took no pride in winning this battle.

Whelan often poured out his troubles to his mistress, who consoled him greatly. She had been taking care of Father Timothy's emotional and physical needs for more than fifteen years.

"The bishop will take care of that little snot, Timmy," she told him, soothing his ego. "You did your best to bring that arrogant piece of Irish trash to heel—no one will blame you."

2

Early Friday Morning
13 October
Chicago's Gold Coast, Illinois

The passion play didn't turn out exactly as Jennifer Gower had expected. But it was close enough. Her plan was to bring Nathan to the point of no return, then stop abruptly and laugh at him, thereby humiliating him as he had humiliated her last Christmas. It was something a strong feminist character like Jane would do. She would exercise her superior feminine power over him—as men had unjustly used brute force to subjugate women.

Before things really heated up, however, Jennifer stopped kissing Nathan to unbutton his shirt, and found his new Miraculous Medal. She looked at it. She was so surprised to find him wearing a religious medal that she dropped her portrayal of Jane long enough to ask a simple question.

"What's this, Nathan?"

He opened his eyes and looked down at the Miraculous Medal given to him by Joe Jackson on Monday afternoon. Father Chet's words in the Log Cabin instantly echoed in his head: *You will never be the same.*

"It's—it's a Miraculous Medal," he hesitated. "I gave my heart to the Mother of God. A few days ago." He was surprised to hear the words come out of his mouth.

Jennifer was confused. "What? How can you give your heart to the Mother of God? You mean you got religion? You? Nathan Payne? From predator to preacher?" She looked at him as if he had come from outer space.

The passion of the moment was now completely broken. Nathan was very confused. Jennifer didn't seem so needy and distraught anymore.

"What do you mean by predator?" he asked naïvely, removing his arm from around her slender shoulder.

Jennifer laughed hard.

"Well," she finally said, "I was going to wait a few more minutes before breaking it to you, pal, but now's as good a time as any."

The expression on his face was pitiful, confused.

Talk about being lost in space, Jennifer thought.

"Nathan, *darling,*" her tone was sarcastic and treacly at the same time. "It's all been an act!"

"An act?" His eyes widened.

"An act! You don't get it, do you? I've been acting, practicing for a part I'm auditioning for in a theatrical play. I never lost my job, or had my therapist try to seduce me, or had mysterious, ominous problems in Oshkosh! As a matter of fact, my real therapist thought this role playing with you would be good for me."

She was feeling gleeful, powerful. She watched playfully while the light of understanding slowly came into his eyes.

Then the light stopped. He looked away. Then he pierced her with *that look* only Nathan had.

"Get out," he whispered flatly.

She was suddenly afraid for her life, even though Nathan was not planning to hurt her. She had delivered an emotional blow to him far greater than any he could physically rain upon her lovely frame. She had practically destroyed him on the inside. She had done what few men had ever done: won a battle of wills against Nathan Payne.

She had nothing to pick up before leaving. She closed the door behind her without making a sound.

Nathan stared at the wall, oblivious. He was absorbed within himself. In his mind's eye he saw Joanie and despaired that she could *never* be his friend, much less his wife. Jenny Gower had proven to him that he was not worthy of anyone as wonderful and loving as Joanie Wheat.

There she was, standing next to the Father Sorin statue, looking at him with that accusing look of hers, her hands on her hips.

"Well?" Joanie accused.

"Well I guess I lose the Wager. Some tramp comes in here and seduces me with a few alligator tears. God! I didn't last three days, much less a whole year. I was ready to sleep with her to help her out! I threw you away, Joanie. And everything you stand for. Gone! You don't deserve me even if you still wanted me. I can't hack it."

He nodded his head and his eyes stared blankly ahead as he spoke, as if she were in the room with him.

He violently ripped the Miraculous Medal off his neck, disgusted, and threw it across the room.

You're wrong, Chetmeister, I am the same. Just worse. I make a lousy Catholic. I was better off being a jerk.

Talking to himself about his utter failure, even thinking about it, was unbearable. He looked around the room for a bottle of scotch, or vodka, or anything.

Follow me down, the words from an obscure Doors song, echoed sourly inside his head.

"Okay," he replied out loud to no one in particular.

Goin' down. Gotta get some fuel for the trip first. How about the Wheat family favorite, Maker's Mark, for old time's sake? Excellent fuel. Maybe bring a buddy along, Jack Daniels. Captain Jack will get me—

The phone rang, freezing his thoughts. It had to be Joanie.

He let the machine answer the phone.

"Nathan, I can't sleep. I've been praying for you all night long. I know something's wrong. I'm coming to get you. Denny's going to fly me to a private airport in Evanston. He keeps a beat-up car there. I'll be at your place in less than an hour and a half. If you're not there, I'll check every bar in Chicago until I find you. Are you there, Nathan?" Nathan could hear her sobs between her words.

He picked up the phone with a shaking hand.

Joanie heard his breathing after the small click of the handset being lifted. "Nathan, is that you?" she asked, panicked and relieved at the same time. "Nathan, what's going on? Are you okay?" Her frantic questions rushed past him like a stiff breeze, yet Nathan was eerily calm.

"Joanie, don't come."

"Nathan, you sound terrible. I'm coming. You can't stop me. What's going on?" she repeated. He tried to ignore the concern in her voice.

It's for her own good, he thought. *Cut the cord.*

"Don't make me say it, Joanie. Don't make me say it."

She ignored him. "Do you love me, Nathan? Do you?" Her voice was falsely confident, as if she knew he *just had to* answer in the affirmative. Joanie was gambling.

His first thought was: *Say yes!*

Then: *She must sense it's over. She's got courage, I'll give her that much. Too bad. Better to cut it off now and give her some temporary pain than to give her far more permanent suffering later. It's for her own good. And mine.*

"No, I don't love you. I don't ever want to see you again. Good-bye darling." He knew it was a lie. He hung up the phone gently before she could answer him.

Nathan looked at his hands as if they were covered with blood. He desperately wanted to go to the couch, curl up, and cry. But he hadn't cried openly since before first grade. His mother was the only woman he had ever cried for—and crying hadn't brought her back. Crying had only made him feel worse. He made a great effort to control himself. He put his emotions back in the box where they had stayed all his life. Before Joanie showed up and opened the box.

Nathan was hard, like an anvil. An anvil does not yield to the blows of the hammer.

His mental equilibrium gradually returned. The effects of the alcohol he drank before Jennifer showed up were now almost gone.

Nathan decided that getting drunk again would not help him feel any better than crying would. His decision made him feel better. In control.

So, what next, Pascal's Fool?

He looked around his apartment and knew he didn't want to be there anymore. *For all I know, Joanie's playing Amelia Earhart with Denny right now.*

He was at a loss for action. Nathan picked up the small leather key holder with his Mustang keys inside, staring queerly at it until inspiration came. *I know. While she's going west, I'll go east. I'll go for a drive.*

He picked up his wallet. The phone started to ring again. He closed the door behind him before the message on the phone machine finished.

She's not going to give up, is she? he thought wearily. Then a question came to his mind in his own inner voice, but the words seemed to be composed by another person:

Do you mean Joanie or the Mother of God?

3

Early Friday Morning
13 October
Mishawaka, Indiana

Joanie hung up the phone. She fought to hold back her tears. *I can't afford tears at a time like this.*

She turned to her brother Denny, who still had sleep in his eyes. Denny was wearing slippers and a bathrobe.

Denny was not so sleepy that he failed to notice the look of determination on Joanie's face. He had seen that look many times over the years. When the vertical line formed on her forehead between her eyebrows, he knew there was no denying his sister. Besides, he kind of liked Nathan Payne. He could tell that she was extremely disappointed with Nathan's answer to her question a moment before. He had watched the battle for control that had played out quickly on her face.

"Are you sure you can get clearance to land in Evanston?" Joanie asked.

"At this time of night, no problem. We'll be in the air less than an hour, Sis. Let me get dressed. We might have to jump start the car. It hasn't been used in over a month, and it's been cold at night lately. I just called ahead—it's available." It wasn't exactly Denny's car. At many small airports an old car is kept for out-of-town private pilots to use as a courtesy.

"Let's do it then," she said with more resignation than enthusiasm.

"What about your school? What should I tell them tomorrow?" Denny was planning on returning to Mishawaka as soon as he got the beater car started up for his sister.

"Tell them the truth."

"Okay." Denny turned to go back up to his room to get dressed.

Nathan lied, she told herself. *Then he called me darling. That wasn't a lie. He called me darling.*

She checked her purse to make sure she had cash. Then she began to pray for Nathan while she waited for Denny to return from getting dressed. Even though she had been praying for him almost nonstop since he failed to return her phone calls earlier in the week, her instincts told her that she was just beginning to pray for Nathan Payne.

4

Three o'clock
Friday Morning
13 October
Indiana Tollway, Indiana

He was playing a Chicago alternative rock station on the
Mustang's stereo as loud as he could stand it. He wore a heavy
leather flight jacket. The temperature had dipped below freezing, but he had the convertible top down.

Showers had fallen around the South Bend area an hour
or so before the temperature started to drop. He had the
Mustang's powerful heater cranked up all the way. The jacket's
wool lining kept his body warm, but his ears were freezing.
Nathan, who was now stone cold sober, was not feeling the
pain. The Mustang hungrily gobbled up the road before it.
He didn't even look at the speedometer, which was register-
ing over one hundred miles per hour.

Lyrics from a group he didn't recognize streamed out of
the speakers: *...don't get it back. The more you want it the
less you're gonna get it back.*

He was only a mile or so from the Notre Dame exit. The
exit had crept up on him. Remembering the last time he had
seen that exit sign, he reluctantly allowed himself a thought
about the girl who had been sleeping next to him on a warm
Sunday morning.

Funny how I ended up here, Joanie, where you live.

Suddenly his emotions stirred and the voice he had been
trying so desperately to repress since her phone call now spoke
to him.

*You want her. You want her. You **love** her.*

As the thought struck him, the Golden Dome, a mile south
of the tollway, came into his view. He saw the statue of Mary
(fully illuminated by Klieg lights) in the clear night. A hopeful

sentiment suddenly filled him from head to toe. He addressed his heavenly mother out loud:

"May I have Joanie? I love her."

Over the din of the music he distinctly heard a voice—a real voice, not a voice in his head—which sounded kind, like Sister Leonardo's, only more beautiful and loving.

One word.

"Yes," Mary, the Mother of God, replied.

Nathan smiled, elated. He was about to say thank you, as if Mary were sitting in the seat next to him, when the words on the radio foreshadowed his own fate:

I'm spinning out. I can't control my car.

The six speakers screamed the words; the musical chords reflected the cacophony that inspired the lyrics.

What happened next took less than three seconds.

The demonic enemies of Nathan, having failed to destroy the anvil they had repeatedly pounded, were allowed to strike one last thunderous blow. The forces of evil did not realize that their actions, designed to end Nathan's life, were part of a Providential Plan set in motion by Nathan's short prayer: *Use any means necessary.*

Providence decreed the necessity.

He was less than a quarter mile past the exit. After he turned his gaze from the Blessed Mother on the dome, Nathan's enemies succeeded in distracting him long enough for him to miss seeing the patch of black ice on the curving road. The car was going way too fast to avoid it.

The Ford Mustang (never a good-handling car in bad weather) hit the ice and hurtled over the shoulder of the highway. It began to turn over in the air as it left the ground, flying awkwardly toward the gully and a thicket of trees beyond the shoulder.

His left leg struck the top of the windshield and snapped in a complete break as he was thrown far ahead of the car. Nathan screamed. As if in a dream, he saw a large oak tree rushing toward him. The image of the living trees from *The Wizard of Oz* popped in and out of his mind. He opened his arms in a crazy flying parody of a bear hug as he struck the tree. Nathan turned his head sideways before striking it, and immediately felt pain everywhere. The air burst out of his lungs. Too much pain to scream.

The Mustang, now slowly skidding on its side, came up behind him. If someone had been watching the car, they would have been certain that it would not stop before striking the tree with force. Yet the Mustang came to a screeching halt just before hitting the tree; the car had turned sideways and its hood pinned Nathan's body before the broken man could slump to the ground.

As paramedics would discover in just twelve minutes, the car did very little damage to Nathan. The lone toll booth worker at the end of the Notre Dame exit did not see the crash, but he did hear it. He immediately called 911.

Nathan had one collapsed lung. He was still awake. He was perfectly lucid. He concentrated all his might and will and energy on one enterprise: the pulling in of a single breath.

After fourteen seconds, which seemed much longer to Nathan, he pulled in that one breath and instantly regretted it as *new* pain exploded through his chest. He thought a bomb had gone off and wondered when the sound of an explosion would come.

The only sound he heard was the ticking of the Mustang's stalled engine block contracting in the cold Indiana night. His breathing had re-started automatically now, and the pain in his chest abated enough for him to feel the excruciating pain in his left leg. He tried to release himself by squirming his torso but was met by more agony—everywhere pain— and the weight of the Mustang. His arms were still in a mock bear hug around the tree. His fingers began to scratch at the bark.

Nathan did not forget the voice of the Woman who had spoken to him seconds before the accident.

It was the Mother of God. She said Yes!

He was sure of it!

God is behind this.

Nathan decided to skip the formalities. He did not pray, *Why me God?* or *God have mercy on me!* He did not even bother with profanities. He had ignored God his whole life; he decided to turn to his Creator now, not in supplication, or confusion. But in anger. Nathan was supremely angry. Knowing deep in his heart that God could hear his every word—as he had believed yet denied since Babsie had brought him to church as a little boy—he fought the pain reverberating in waves throughout his entire body. He forced his neck toward the sky, stiff and defiant. He did not speak. Instead, he looked up at the infinite stars and gave God *the look*.

And Nathan addressed God, spitting and blinking in his fury.

"So *this* is what I have to do to get Joanie—You, you damn sadist?!"

He winced. He shrugged off the spasms in his back.

"So *this* is why you took my mother and my Babsie from me!"

He tried to raise a bloodied fist, but failed. He shouted at the stars again.

"I'm ready! Do you hear me! I'm ready! **Let's go!**

"Is this all you've got for me? **Do it!** Whatever it is!

"I'm READY!"

The suffering which Nathan was enduring was not all that God had in store for the stiff-necked man.

The battle between demons and angels was over.

The wounds of the bear were torn open, pouring forth their bile.

The unyielding anvil would melt in the furnace in which it had been cast.

The heart was pierced by a sword.

Nathan Payne, still perfectly lucid eight minutes before the paramedics would arrive, was about to receive the greatest gift a loving, merciful Father could bestow upon a child born of a mother's suffering.

Nathan Payne was about to experience the event which Our Lady of Garabandal foretold. The entire world would experience it during the Great Tribulations. Nathan was about to experience his own personal version of the Great Warning.

Fortunately for Nathan, the Divine Furnace into which God was about to cast His anvil was fired by the Merciful Love of God—not the fires of His Awesome Wrath.

In the distance, sirens wailed like women keening along a steep, rocky path; but Nathan did not hear them.

5

Early Friday Morning
13 October
Salt Lake City, Utah

Slinger sat in his pajamas in the den of his home, wiping the sleep from his eyes. He didn't mind taking calls from other time zones so late at night.

"Yeah, so you listened to the tape I sent you. What did you think?" Karl Slinger waited patiently for the CEO of Hawaii's largest agricultural corporation to answer his question. The man on the other end of the line had often hunted with Karl on the Slinger Ranch in Wyoming.

The answer came. An expression of frustration came over his open face.

"Thanks... Uh hum. I understand," Karl said, dejected. "Thanks for hearing it out. Yeah. We'll have to do that sometime. Give Kathy my best." Slinger paused. "Yes, Dottie would love that. I'll tell her."

Slinger hung up, exerting effort not to slam the handset down. It was the eighteenth such call in the last several days.

They tell me politely, indirectly. A few tell me straight out— and I appreciate that. But they all say the same thing: "Are you out of your mind, Slinger?" What will it take to convince these guys?

6

Early Friday Morning
13 October
Verona, New Jersey

Father Chet awoke from a sound sleep. He looked at the alarm clock and winced. Before he could fall off to sleep again, he remembered. *Dad used to say that when you wake up suddenly in the middle of the night, somebody needs your prayers. Somebody you know. Wonder who it is? Becky?*

Becky had called him earlier in the day for some spiritual direction, wanting to know if it would be okay to attend daily Mass.

"You don't need permission," he had told her enthusiastically. "That's the Holy Spirit prompting you. Saint John Vianney once said it was the greatest grace you could receive—the desire to receive Holy Communion every day. Go for it Beck!"

The weary priest, clad only in his paisley pajamas—a gift from his mother—got out of bed and lowered his knees onto the kneeler. The kneeler faced a wall with only a crucifix upon it. He began to pray a Rosary for a Catholic he did not know.

7

Early Friday Morning
13 October
Salt Lake City, Utah

Lee Washington thanked the driver as he got out of the car and promised to pray for him. He pulled from his pocket the wooden rosary beads the old priest on the reservation had given him. He was standing on the corner of B Street and South Temple Street. He looked up at the Cathedral of the Madeleine with its twin stone towers. Lee knew it was open at this early hour because he saw a homeless man going into the front door. He entered the Cathedral and found his way to the Blessed Sacrament, which stood alone in a large Gothic tabernacle behind a wooden chancel screen behind the altar. Kneelers surrounded three sides of the tabernacle in an unusual arrangement.

Upon seeing that this Eucharistic chapel was empty, Lee thought to himself, *I'm alone.* Then, looking at the tabernacle, he corrected himself. *Except for you, Jesus. Except for you.*

Lee knelt down and took a moment to look around at the beautiful woodwork on the walls and the painting of Mary Magdalene looking up to the crucifixion in anguish.

He felt a strong urge to pray for a fellow Catholic.

I don't know any Catholics, he told himself, amused. *Oh well. I'll pray for the person who needs my prayers the most.*

8

Early Friday Morning
13 October
South Bend, Indiana

Joe Jackson slept diagonally on the king-size bed he had
purchased at the Goodwill years before. His apartment on
Eddy Street was small and sparsely decorated. Despite the
wealth he earned playing professional football, he owned very
few material things. Most of his money had gone into
financing the Kolbe Foundation. A windup alarm clock ticked
loudly next to the glass of water he kept on the night stand.
He snored. His nose had been broken four times and it was
rarely uncongested, despite two reconstructive surgeries.

On the floor next to his bed were his two oversized, top
quality basketball sneakers—one of the few luxuries Joe
allowed himself. There were two pebbles in one shoe and
there was one pebble in the other. Joe almost always kept a
pebble in at least one shoe as a reminder to himself of the
pain and suffering Jesus endured on the cross for his sins.
Three years earlier Joe had begun a practice—known only to
himself—of offering the pain from a pebble for any new
Knights of Immaculata he personally helped enroll. Each new
Knight would receive nine days of reparation.

On Tuesday he had dedicated a pebble each for Becky,
Karl, and Nathan—making it uncomfortable to stand for more
than a few minutes because he could no longer shift his weight
from one shoe with a pebble to the other as he had done in
the past.

9

Early Friday Morning
13 October
Chicago, Illinois

Joanie punched her credit card number into the pay phone, looking over her shoulder out of habit to make sure no one was trying to steal her car. The gas station was closed for the night, and she was cold and tired. It was time to call Denny on his separate line, according to plan. Denny had his own line for business purposes. Joanie had driven the streets near Nathan's apartment for over an hour looking for him. His apartment had been empty.

"Joanie?" It was a woman's voice.

"Is that you, Mom? Why are you answering Denny's line? Did he make it home okay?" Joanie was too strung out to give Anne Wheat a chance to answer each question.

"Denny's fine, Joanie. He's flying back to Evanston even as we speak to pick you up," her mother paused for only a moment. "You've got to get back to the airport. Nathan Payne's had a car accident. Here in South Bend on the tollway. He's been taken to Saint Joseph Hospital." Anne's voice was soothing. The mother knew that every word hurt her daughter.

Joanie's world began to spin. For the second time this morning she fought back tears, ignoring her emotions, struggling to control herself. *Nathan needs me.*

"When? What happened, Mom?"

"I don't know many details—just that it's serious. We got a call from the state patrol. Nathan was saying your name when they found him. Trooper McDonough knows your father. Denny's coming to pick you up. You've got to get back to the airport, now."

Joanie held back a sob. "I'm on my way. I love you, Mom. I love him, too. Good-bye." Joanie hung up the phone.

She was not able to hold back tears. Her vision blurred as she drove quickly through the empty streets of Rogers Park and Evanston. She ran three red lights. While Nathan had reacted to his accident with anger, Joanie reacted without a trace of that emotion. She was well beyond blaming God for misfortune.

"Please God, don't let him die. Don't let my Nathan die!"

10

The Beatific Vision, Heaven

Sister Leonardo was again called forth by the Mind of God to intercede on behalf of her former student, Nathaniel Payne. She welcomed the young man into the Ocean of God's Love, knowing from personal experience that God's Love could burn as well as soothe.

Chapter Thirteen

1

Early Friday Morning
13 October
Indiana Tollway, Indiana

Moments after challenging God, Nathan fell out of time into the Eternal Now. He was aware that his physical pain was gone. He felt himself turning and flipping, and sensed heat and light in the distance. Then he came to a stop on a ground he could not see, standing on legs he could not look down upon. He saw a swirling cloud which gradually dissipated.

As the cloud dissipated he saw forming in front of him the Cross of Calvary, with his Savior upon it. There was a sound of thunder and whistling wind all around him. Nathan looked upon the man in front of him and comprehended the perfect mathematical symmetry of His limbs. Nathan simply *knew* that Jesus was perfect and sinless. A Man of Sorrows.

Jesus spoke to Nathan from the Cross:

"Do not be afraid. Son of man, behold your sins!"

All of Nathan's awareness and perception became focused on the wound in Jesus' side which poured forth blood and water, and then light. The light grew and Nathan saw things as God sees, not in chronological succession, but all at once, each in particular. What Nathan saw was perceived as a lay-ered field—a field where everything came into his mind completely.

He was aware of God's total goodness and perfection. He was bathed in His awesome love. The young man felt that there was a wall preventing that love from fully touching him, as if it would destroy him; God's love was ready to roll over him like a giant wave. The knowledge of that love overwhelmed him and filled him with Hope such as he had never hoped on earth. Then:

Layers changed, and Nathan saw a field covered with each of his venial sins. He was aware of their venial nature—that these sins had not condemned him to hell. There were thousands of these sins. He saw them not as a human being looks at a field of grass and sees the whole field, but as God sees the field: each and every blade of grass completely and at the same time.

Nathan saw himself in the act of these sins, watching himself commit each sin like watching thousands of movies at the same time. He watched himself steal office supplies such as pens, notepads, and staples from VV&B for his desk at home; he stole minutes of time from his employer during the pizza delivery job he had taken at college; sneaking into the movies alone through the back exit door as a lonely teenager in Chicago. He stole candy from the corner store several times until he was caught by the proprietor. Nathan, who had despised the proprietor at the time, was suddenly filled with gratitude toward the old man, Mr. Cohen. How easily he had forgotten what he had learned during religion class in first grade: that stealing was wrong.

Nathan saw himself as a five-year-old, spitefully refusing to speak to Babsie when she asked little Nathan if he wanted another hot dog at the school fair. At the time, he knew his insolence would hurt her. He perceived hundreds of other times throughout his life when he had taken pleasure inflicting pain on others through his silences—to friends, teachers, fellow workers, girlfriends. He knew his motive for these deeds with perfect clarity: to make sure others felt pain because he felt no pleasure.

Layers changed and Nathan saw a field of images filled with lies. He saw himself telling a lie to Charlie VanDuren to avoid blame for a minor error at VV&B—then slyly placing the blame on his secretary, Sally Mortimer. He saw hundreds of other lies that detracted from others and served to elevate himself in the esteem of others. He saw the many times he had exaggerated his triumphs and downplayed his failures— however slightly—while speaking to others. He saw the times he had shaded the truth while dealing with clients at VV&B— lies that are accepted in the securities industry as a matter of course. He saw himself lying about little facts on his tax return. Nathan even saw two incidents of lying to Joanie. One time he had lied to her about his childhood out of fear that she would reject him. Nathan had considered remaining silent or telling the truth to Joanie, but had decided that lying was the easy way out. (Somehow Nathan was also aware that he had committed few lies compared to others…)

The field layered again. He relived, with more acute perception, every sharp and sarcastic word he had ever spoken to another human being. These words appeared as tiny daggers that cut the skin of those he hurt. He saw a field filled with bleeding people—people he had cut with his sharp tongue.

The field changed again. He was staggered by the largest and longest fields of venial sins—the countless times a small act of kindness could have helped someone else, but instead he had chosen *not* to perform such acts. One in particular caused him great anguish and sorrow: in sixth grade he had a chance to compliment Dewey Johnson during a boxball game on the playground after little Dewey made a great play. The words of praise had almost come out of Nathan's mouth— but Dewey was held in derision by the other children. Nathan, fearful of losing the esteem of those who thought Dewey was a loser, stopped himself from uttering a simple word of praise.

"Sins of omission," Nathan heard his Savior explain.

Nathan was outside of Time; he perceived each sin quickly, yet each and every one with total comprehension.

All these minor offenses against God were plain to Nathan. He now understood that the laws of right and wrong had been written on his heart before he was born. Now that original sin did not cloud his perception, Nathan was horrified by these seemingly small acts.

On and on the sins piled one upon the other as God showed Nathan all the fields *at once,* layers upon layers. His venial sins numbered beyond his comprehension and appeared as endless vistas of offenses. Nathan realized that a portion of these offenses would not be counted against him because he had not willed them completely. Yet the objective fact that they disrupted the perfectly balanced order of God's universe was enough to greatly disturb Nathan.

Suddenly he was spun around and saw another field with a rocky hill. Jesus was before him on the Cross again. Layer folded upon layer. He became aware of the suffering his venial sins caused Jesus upon the Cross. They caused Him such intense agony! Nathan's consciousness widened and narrowed. His emotions were so excruciating that only a "wall" erected by the Trinity saved him from obliteration.

Nathan prayed: "Dear Jesus, if these are my venial sins then what of all the venial sins of mankind throughout the ages? What of my mortal sins? Am I to see these also?"

Jesus looked directly over Nathan's shoulder and replied:

"Son of man—Look!"

Nathan found himself turning to see where his Savior was looking and beheld an enormous cauldron of fire! *Is that hell?* Nathan thought, amazed and terrified at the same time.

Mortal sins, Nathan thought suddenly, still terrified. He tried to turn from the fire and run toward the Cross but found he couldn't move. He had no body.

Then Nathan left Calvary and plunged toward the cauldron of fire! He entered into hell. He knew in his heart that this was the place his mortal sins merited for his eternity. Unlike John Lanning, who had actually felt the fires of hell licking up his legs during the heart attack, he did not physically experience the pains of hell. Nathan was simply "shown" hell—as if he was looking through the bottom of a glass boat. The sight of it was enough. Like Saint Teresa of Avila, Nathan was shown his particular station in hell. He had no eyelids to close out the horror before him and no vocal cords with which to scream!

Nooooo! Nathan cried desperately inside his mind.

Landscapes changed.

Hell disappeared.

Then Nathan saw why hell could be his destiny. He saw the sins which most offended God—field upon field of mortal sins. Stealing, lying, sexual sins, spiritual pride, dabbling in the occult, destruction of reputations, and mortal sins of omission—the mortal fields were not as large as the venial fields, but each offense in each field would have sent Nathan to hell had his heart stopped beating while on earth.

The worst of these sins, it seemed, was the breaking of the first commandment: "I am the Lord thy God, thou shalt have no other gods before me!" All his mortal sins were a variation of a violation of this one law. He realized now that he had made almost every single thing in his life a god before God. He had replaced God.

As just one example, Nathan saw himself visiting a psychic with some fraternity brothers during his college days. He had considered the visit a lark—something to do for fun—and had never gone back again to the strange Hungarian woman in the tiny storefront on Neil Street in Champaign. The woman had made him feel creepy. One of his friends, Eddy Fetzer, had become "addicted" to the woman. Eddy later committed suicide in his senior year. Nathan saw that Eddy's demise was related to the false seer.

Nathan now realized the true danger of a desire to gain knowledge or power through the occult. In this field he saw that the psychic had been guided by evil spirits. Nathan had considered Tarot cards, Ouija boards, reliance on astrological predictions, New Age mysticism, and other such practices as harmless superstitions on earth. He now realized that all these things originated in utter evil. They were devices to fool naïve men and women into serving the evil one. He also saw that his guardian angel had been protecting him in his ignorance from these evil forces.

Another field Nathan saw was different—an unknown portion of this field was hidden from him. Nathan did not know how or why he could not see this unseen portion. He knew only that he would see whatever it contained later. The portion of the field he *could* see related his mortal sexual sins. By now he was not surprised to discover that self-abuse and viewing pornography were grave sins, but this did not reduce the utter contrition he felt. The horror encompassed more than the sins he saw himself committing by himself and with women.

The real horror was the perfect realization of the vastly important *nature* of the sexual faculty he had abused. Of all the powers given to mankind, this power was perhaps the most God-like. For only God can create something from nothing. The universe itself could not refuse God's command to call it forth from nothingness. Nathan realized that the only new immortal creations that come into the universe are human souls. Each and every soul is unique and immortal. He was awestruck at the incredible honor and trust God the Father bestowed upon men and women. The Father designed into human affairs the ability to procreate new human beings. Even angels were not allowed to share in God's creative power!

How callous I've been!

How inconsequential Nathan had treated this tremendous gift…

He turned his view to the portion of the field of sexual sins that he could not see and shuddered at the darkness.

Fields changed again and again, filling him with horror and awe. He was shown mortal sin after mortal sin, reliving each and every one.

Nathan resolved to serve only God the Father, Son, and Holy Spirit. But there was one more field for him to see.

Nathan knew this last field was there, but he could not yet see it. It was the field that until now had been hidden from his view. Again, he tried to close his eyes as he saw the field changing, and the new, terrible field coming toward him. But he could not close his eyes. The Warning was not complicated, really. It was simply the opening of Nathan's eyes to the Truth.

Fields changed and layers folded upon layers. *Is that gold I see?* Nathan asked himself, confused, terrified. Then he beheld his abuse of the procreative power.

It was time for Nathan to meet his children—the children he didn't know existed before his Great Warning began. Nathan was about to see his two sons and three daughters.

A conversation long-forgotten by Nathan, which had taken place soon after Father Chet's ordination, echoed clearly in his mind as he watched its replay. Chet had been visiting Nathan on vacation almost three years ago. They were in Nathan's apartment discussing sexual morality during half time of a televised Notre Dame football game:

"But Nathan, you're much too intelligent to contradict scientific fact. I'm telling you right now as your friend, you might think having sex is simply for your own fun, but the pill is an abortifacient. The pills and IUDs your girlfriends use can kill fertilized human embryos before they can attach to the uterine wall and destroy them even after they attach. It's a scientific fact. You've got to stop. You could be participating in the creation and destruction of immortal human beings— your own children!"

Nathan remembered looking at Chet as if the newly ordained priest was a lunatic. The pill couldn't kill babies. It just couldn't. Therefore it didn't. Babies? Who knows what those cells are? Microscopic cells! I don't even believe in the soul. It's none of Chet's business, anyway. My private life is my own.

How can you be so sure Chet's not right? *The voice that spoke for the laws written in every heart—Nathan's conscience—had answered.*

His memory condemned him in the court of Eternal Wisdom. The scene with Father Chet disappeared and Nathan saw a field with a young man standing next to an angel. The young man with brown hair and green eyes was standing next to his guardian angel in a field of golden grass far more brilliant than any gold Nathan had seen on earth:

The child's mother was Sally Gilchrist, the waitress at college, his first sexual partner. A son. She got pregnant on the only night he slept with her. Nathan was shown that Sally did not realize Nathan was the father. Sally had mistakenly believed another man, Fred Lind, her steady boyfriend, was the father. Lind had willingly paid for the abortion of Nathan's son.

In a vision on the field next to the child with his angel, Nathan saw his son sleeping peacefully in Sally's womb. Then he saw the boychild ripped to shreds by an abortionist's knife-edged vacuum eight weeks and two days into the unborn child's brief life. Nathan tried to turn his head and couldn't as he saw his son ripped into pieces. Then Nathan saw the parts of his son's body deposited in a removable medical bag in the high-pitched, mechanically whining suction machine used for the abortion. His son's remains joined the remains of five other tiny human beings.

The son disappeared. Fields changed and Nathan saw two daughters:

Nathan beheld them next to their angels. He became aware that they were sisters by the same mother, Gail Stein. Gail had been on the pill. Each daughter had been destroyed because the pill did not allow them to adhere to Gail Stein's uterine wall before their second day of life. The first daughter had died seven weeks before the second daughter. Nathan had dated Gail for three months—his longest relationship. That relationship had ended bitterly, broken up by Nathan. During this Warning, Nathan did not perceive any of his children as tiny cells, but in their full immortal potentialities, as adults, without stain of chosen sin, standing in golden fields, looking directly at their father. They did not recognize Nathan as their stricken father. Their pure eyes looked right through him.

Nathan beheld his third daughter, aborted by a girl named Jessica Thomas. She had slept with him during a one night stand. He had picked her up on Rush Street in a nightclub. He had been drunk that night and did not remember Jessica's last name the next morning after she left him sleeping on his bed. Nathan was horrified to realize that his third daughter's death was Jessica's first abortion—the first of three other aborted children by other fathers. Fields changed, and he saw his third daughter next to her three aborted half-siblings. All four stared right through him. It was made known to him that had he not seduced the naïve Miss Thomas, she might not have chosen to continue sleeping with other men. Nathan's skillful seduction of Jessica Thomas had led her to mistakenly conclude that she was powerless before her sex drive. In this way, Nathan was indirectly responsible for not only his daughter's death, but also the murders of three others.

He was aware that he had been a partial "cause" of these children coming into existence but that he was not necessarily culpable for the abortions and the deaths by abortifacients. For these sins (and for other sins he had been shown during his Warning), he was made perfectly aware of the endless connections, permutations, and potentialities those sins set into motion.

He presently saw that Jessica was so depressed that she was now susceptible to being tempted to suicide by demons assigned to torment her in "real time" on earth. He also was permitted to see the valiant efforts made by Jessica's angel and the angels of her aborted children to save the depressed mother from killing herself. Her fate was not fixed. He found himself wanting to help her but he couldn't. Jessica's field faded and then disappeared from Nathan's view.

In fact, no book could catalogue the repercussions of his sins, which themselves were the free-willed repercussions of sins traced back to Adam and Eve. Layers enclosed and enfolded upon layers.

Then, Nathan saw his second son, his fifth child. This son had a name: Nathan Jr.

Jennifer Gower, Nathan Jr.'s mother, had aborted him at fourteen weeks. She had named the son in her womb after his father, guessing correctly that he was a boy. She had initially been excited to be pregnant by the man she thought she loved. Jennifer had naïvely hoped the pregnancy would convince Nathan to marry her. She was saving the news for Christmas day, but never got a chance to tell Nathan, who had severed their relationship over the phone on Christmas Eve. Now God showed Nathan the unborn boy's eyes, heart, and fingers. Nathan saw how perfectly Nathan Jr. was formed. God let him know that Nathan Jr. had inherited the tremendous mathematical intellect of his father. At fourteen weeks of age, Nathan's son already had black hair like his mother. He saw his son's heart beating peacefully, then speeding up as the abortionist's specialized machete came to slice him to pieces. How the boy struggled to live! Nathan was forced to watch as the forceps came and crushed Nathan Jr.'s head so the pieces could be sucked out of Jennifer's womb by vacuum. He saw Jennifer's uterus perforated accidentally by the abortionist and knew that the resulting infection had caused an emergency hysterectomy in July. In a desperate attempt to avoid facing the moral implications of her abortion, she embraced feminist ideology. What is so cloudy to the human intellect on earth—moral distinction—was crystal clear to Nathan during the Warning. He was completely immersed in the Moral Universe now. Layers changed, and a golden field with a man and an angel was before Nathan. Nathan was paralyzed by the blank stare of Nathan Jr.'s eyes.

Nathan regained his voice and was able to turn back to the Cross as he cried out in agony: *I am not fit to dwell in the House of the Lord! Oh Nathan Jr., my son! My son! Nathan my son!*

Nathan was overcome with guilt and grief. He collapsed on the rocks sobbing, his invisible arms covering his head. Without looking at the Cross, he heard the tender words of Jesus:

"They are all my sons and daughters, Nathan. Let the little children come to me. I have given all the nameless ones names! Son of man, Look!"

Landscapes changed. Nathan turned and saw a rolling field of endless aborted souls, flowing and undulating like ocean waves, beyond his sight. The sound of wind blowing filled Nathan's mind. Far away he heard the sound of beautiful music and singing, but neither sound was coming from the aborted ones.

These countless Holy Innocents were facing away from Nathan. The aborted children were between him and the indescribable light of the Trinity. Each and every child he saw; and each and every one was without any sin except original sin, not having had the opportunity to commit even the smallest offense against the Holy Trinity! Some had been slaughtered by the Pharaoh in Moses' time. Some by Herod. Some by Genghis Khan. Most by Nathan's own generation in the name of Liberty!

Nathan found the courage to speak: "I am accursed, My Lord, as is my generation."

The Father replied: "Before which one of these Holy Innocents, Nathan, would thou enter into My Kingdom?"

Nathan answered, beyond any capacity to lie or plead his case before Eternal Truth: "Not one, Master. I am not worthy to stand in your presence. My offenses are always before me." His contrition was total, inside every fiber of his being.

Nathan was prepared to go to hell. Curiously, he was not disturbed by his willingness to accept his choice of eternity in hell. The only consolation in hell would be his certain knowledge that he had cooperated with Divine Justice. Hell was what he deserved.

He held up his hands before Divine Justice, as if to be shackled and led away. He realized that he would indeed be willing to take his place in the burning cauldron. It was not right to take a place in the Kingdom before his own five children or any of the other unbaptized Holy Innocents.

But God's Warning was not over. God did not shackle the young man of sorrows before the Cross.

Layers changed and Nathan realized that Eternal Wisdom wanted him to look up. He looked, and saw how he had unknowingly cooperated with evil spirits who had worked hard to convince him to commit sin. While in the world, Nathan had rarely been aware that his sins were mortal in nature at the time of his willing participation. A word came into Nathan's mind: *Mitigation.*

Then Nathan heard: *"Father forgive them, for they know not what they do."*

It was the voice of the Son on the Cross. Nathan had been decimated without being annihilated for what seemed an immeasurable period of time by his own sins and the effects of his sins. He spun and saw the Cross as the landscape seamlessly changed once more. Jesus spoke directly to him again. Yet, it was not the voice of Jesus coming from the Cross but the voice of Nathan's closest friend, Father Chet. Jesus repeated to Nathan a familiar doxology in Chet's voice:

*"Through the ministry of the Church, I absolve
you of your sins in the name of the Father, and of the
Son, and of the Holy Spirit."*

Nathan knew that these were the very words Chet spoke
to him in the confessional at Sacred Heart Basilica at Notre
Dame on Monday...

And Nathan spun and layers folded and landscapes moved
and he saw all his sins again sprawled across seemingly endless fields. He saw the light streaming from the wounds of
the Man of Sorrows on the Cross. The light from Jesus'
wounds "covered" the sins, blotting them out, making them
impossible to see. The light was so bright that Nathan tried to
cover his eyes with hands he no longer had.

And then the light faded into a light which allowed Nathan
to see. He no longer saw his sins. The fields were empty of
sins. Instead, Nathan saw a Lamb, with a white fleece bright
shining as the sun. It was the Lamb of God Who takes away
the sins of the world!

Choirs (layers) of angels praised the Lamb. Music and
Light and Beauty and Oneness and Perfection were everywhere, in and out and around Nathan. This was the music he
had faintly heard coming from the Holy Trinity while Nathan
looked upon the Holy Innocents! He looked and saw the
Legions of the Elect. He heard the voices of each one as they
praised the Lamb of God. He saw hundreds upon hundreds
of thousands of priests raising the Lamb up to the Father on
the Divine Altar. Nathan was totally convinced that the Lamb
was Jesus and that Jesus is the Eucharist.

Amidst the voices of the Elect, he heard Babsie's voice
and Sister Leonardo's voice, and for the first time since undergoing his Warning, his wounded heart rejoiced. He bathed in
the perfect harmonies of countless angels and saints. He
opened his own mouth to sing praise to the Lamb, but he
could not speak.

Then Nathan saw a Woman Clothed with the Sun, with a
crown of twelve stars suspended above her head. The Queen

stood in the Court of the Lamb. Nathan heard her voice for the second time. It was the Woman who spoke to him in the car before the Mustang crashed:

*Nathaniel Payne, you are **my** consecrated warrior. The angel has placed the cross upon your forehead. My Son has shown mercy upon your soul on this day through the merits of His Holy Cross and Resurrection, through your merits, and through the merits of others. Your sins have been forgiven. The Father has designs upon your soul!*

Landscapes changed and layers unfolded again and the Woman showed Nathan many things in the fruitful fields of heaven where Mary reigned as Queen. She showed Nathan the mitigating acts of goodness he had chosen during his short life. Like his sins, he saw each one at once and in particular, like leaves of grass in a field.

The dinner which he had bought for a homeless man named Brian Stanesi the very afternoon before he conceived his son by Jennifer Gower.

The many grade school friends he had helped by finding a "place" for them to excel and develop confidence during school-yard games. Nathan realized that his little-used leadership skills could help others in much more serious matters later during his life. If Nathan returned to earth.

Nathan was shown the hundreds (yes, hundreds!) of women with whom he had decided *not* to have intercourse. Nathan realized that his motives had not always been selfish in turning them down. Having lived with loneliness and sorrow since childhood himself, Nathan, always a sensitive man, realized from experience that sexual relations would have made the amorous women feel empty, and chose *for their greater good* to turn these women away. Nathan had often charmed them in order to soften the rejection: "You're too good a person to sleep around with a nobody like me." Or, he had often whispered with complete honesty, using his unique gift for convincing others to act: "Find a good man and get married. Don't sell yourself short." Some had been offended. For many, he had been the first man to ever turn them away. A few, feeling guilty about their promiscuous lifestyles, had taken his words seriously. One, a girl named Ellen McMonagle, had started praying again the evening Nathan turned her away and eventually became a nun with Mother Teresa's nuns in the Bronx, New York. Nathan saw each woman he had helped for the better in the satanic atmospheres of nightclubs.

Nathan saw Tommy Gervin, a baptized Catholic, in "real time" on earth. Tommy was attending Mass with his mother in Houston. Nathan was made to realize that he had helped save Tommy's soul on the Skyway. He also saw the potential good that Tommy Gervin could do in the future. Nathan was overwhelmed—*awed*—by God's plan for him.

The Queen of Heaven spoke: "Yes, Nathan, Tommy Gervin came close to losing his soul forever that night, and upon dying, suffering a freely chosen eternity in hell."

Nathan did not question the truth of the Blessed Mother's statement.

Nathan saw George Moore, who had been abused like Nathan as a child by George's brutal father, and how Nathan's episode behind the gym after school had deeply changed George. He was now a happily married accountant in Naperville. He had three children and attended daily Mass, influenced to do so by others whom Nathan did not know on earth.

Nathan saw that his honest dedication to his work at VV&B had affected many lives for the better. He had helped dozens of families grow and protect their material assets. Some of Nathan's investments had procured good educations for the investors' children. One investor had donated almost all his material wealth—tripled in value by Nathan's savvy—to financing an entire group of Catholic missionary nuns in Africa. In turn these nuns were doing great things for God as Nathan watched in fascination and awe. He did not want to stop watching this field of goodness. This field, like all of the fields Nathan Payne saw during his Warning, was a great surprise.

In perhaps the most amazing sequence, Nathan saw Chet's ordination and how the thousands of times Chet had prayed for Nathan's soul had not only merited grace for Nathan's life, but had helped develop Chet into the wonderful priest he was today. Nathan rejoiced for his friend! He became aware of the seemingly endless fields of good that Chet had "started." Nathan's input had not been *the* deciding factor in Chet's decision to become a priest. But Nathan had played a part, especially as Chet's closest friend during the secure childhood Chet had enjoyed. Chet never consciously realized it on earth, but he was influenced to become a priest so he could help people like Nathan. In this odd way, Nathan had *inspired* Chet. (Nathan was also aware that his bad example had been a negative influence on Chet during their college days. Nathan had seen this earlier during the "sin" part of the Warning.)

Nathan now perceived how Sister Leonardo had been sanctified during her entire life (and especially during her bout with cancer) by praying and doing reparation for Nathan.

Nathan understood that no good deed was ever done apart from the influence of others in the Mystical Body of Christ. Nor did a good act come without the freely given gift of grace. God's Universe—the Moral Universe—was much more complex and interwoven than earthbound men could fathom. He was given the intuition that his present understanding was "supplied" by God Himself and that once he returned to his body this full understanding would revert to partial understanding. Like all mortals, Nathan would resume "looking through a glass darkly" upon his return.

Mary showed Nathan all his good deeds and how they merited much favor from the Father because Nathan had "committed" many of them without faith in God. He had also developed a certain measure of conscience, however malformed, with practically no moral formation from his father. This "mitigation" surprised Nathan. The deep mystery of God's judgment, even here in heaven, was beyond him. He did realize, however, that the judgment was *perfect*. It was as perfect as any mathematical equation ever comprehended by Nathan.

Only God could weigh and balance a man's life, taking into account all the good and bad acts, the good and bad influences, the sins of fathers and the sins of sons, and other mitigating circumstances. He understood that the fulcrum between the objective horror of all sin and the culpability for those sins was *free will*. The wheat of Nathan's good actions was separated from the chaff of his immoral ones. He knew it was primarily the sanctifying grace of his confession with Chet which had saved him from perdition.

The Queen of Heaven waved her arm toward another field and Nathan saw the final days of his life before the accident.

Despite his confession, Nathan knew that his drunkenness, his sexual episode with Jennifer Gower, and worst of all, his choice to despair after Joanie had called him—all these would have weighed against him mortally. It was as if someone had taken a photograph of the state of Nathan's soul just before the accident in the Mustang. That final photograph would be the determining factor in Nathan's Judgment. How important it was to end life in a "state of grace"—the state of a soul free from mortal sin.

As Our Lady showed her consecrated son the last days of his life, Nathan saw not just himself in "instant replay," but the savage attacks by the demonic forces conspiring to destroy him. He observed his brief dialogue with Mary on the highway as he passed the Notre Dame Exit. He discovered that his life had been spared by God. Providence had chosen to directly intervene to stop the Mustang from fatally crushing him against the oak tree. He was shocked to discover how many creatures in the Mystical Body of Christ had been interceding on his behalf at the very "moment" of his crash—Joanie, Father Chet, Joe Jackson, a young black man in Salt Lake City, Babsie, Nathan's guardian angel, Sister Leonardo, and especially, the Queen of Heaven, who stood next to Nathan now. There were others helping him, too. He saw all of them.

Nathan did not know them all personally. They were members of the Church Militant, all around the world, offering their sufferings, prayers, and their lives to Jesus to merit grace for redistribution according to the Father's Will. Finally, Nathan saw how his Warning was a direct answer to his own desperate prayer during Professor Wheat's talk on Monday night in Saint Joseph Church: *Use any means necessary.*

Nathan asked Mary: "Why are you showing me these things? Why doesn't Jesus show me, like He showed me my sins?"

Mary answered: "My Son is showing you—through me. You are my special son, consecrated to me. When you see and hear me, you are experiencing a manifestation of the Father's Mercy. You have much to do for my Son's Kingdom. Your grandmother did not lie when she told you that you are descended from kings. Look now!"

Nathan looked and saw a king dressed in clothing that looked like it came from the Middle Ages. The king was wearing armor and flowing garments. The king was not looking at Nathan. The Blessed Mother spoke to Nathan: *"This king's name is John Sobieski, III. I am the queen of his country, Poland. You are his descendant, my son. Look!"*

Nathan looked and saw thousands of blood relations in a heavenly field, all of them interceding on Nathan's behalf before the Lamb of God! Each one was a descendant of King Sobieski. "You have not come here of your own accord, my son. These saints have merited the grace for your journey." The words of the Blessed Mother filled Nathan's being with a joy that he had known in only one place on earth—the joy of belonging to a family. Nathan had felt that joy fleetingly as a child while visiting the Sullivans with Chet. I am part of a family, Nathan thought. The Family of God!

Landscapes folded and unfolded and Nathan was alone with Mary before the Cross, aware that he had returned to the place of the Warning's beginning. The Alpha and the Omega. He felt contrition and joy and awe streaming through his soul before Jesus. Nathan felt immense gratitude toward his Savior. Jesus spoke one last time:

*"Son of man, behold your mother.
Woman, behold your son."*

Nathan turned to face Mary. It was time to return to his earthly body. He did not want to leave the side of his queen. He could not change or protest the will of the Son, but he was still disappointed that he would have to leave her. She was shown his thoughts and responded gently, yet firmly:

"I will always be at your side. My Son will show me your every thought and deed, for you have given them to me through your consecration. You will not remember all you have seen here, but you will remember much of it, especially your sins against the Holy Trinity. You will undergo many trials when you return. You must seek confession again after you go back. My daughter Joanie is waiting for you…"

Nathan tried to turn his head to look at the Queen of Heaven, but as he turned he felt the bark of a tree on his cheek. Intense pain, starting in his lungs, flowed back into his consciousness…

✝ ✝ ✝

The searing pain from the accident, although still just as intense as it had ever been, was not unbearable. He had been "gone" during the Warning for less than a thousandth of a second in earth time. The paramedics found him passed out, pinned against the tree. A police cruiser's lights filled the area with white, red, and blue from the shoulder of the Indiana Tollway. Having no choice, and worried that Nathan might die quickly, the two paramedics and the trooper pushed the Mustang over and away from the broken man with great effort. Nathan crumpled limply to the ground.

"Look, Sarge, he's coming out of it!" the rookie paramedic shouted crazily. "He's trying to say something!"

Nathan was lying on the ground now, flat on his back. A disturbing wheeze was coming from his lungs as he breathed.

The rookie paramedic threw up when he saw the white and dark red patches on the sides of the tree where Nathan had scratched off the bark with his bloody fingers.

Sarge, whose real name was Willy Matthews, put his ear next to Nathan's mouth.

"Joanie Wheat...Call Joanie Wheat...Mishawaka..." Nathan whispered hoarsely. Then, back from his journey to hell and heaven, he passed out.

"What he say? What he say, Sarge?" the younger paramedic asked with a note of intensity, wiping his mouth.

Sarge ignored the rookie, and looked up to the State Trooper standing next to the tree. "Do you know anybody named Joanie Wheat who lives around here?"

Chapter Fourteen

1

Friday Morning
13 October
Verona, New Jersey

Father Chet came into the rectory after saying morning Mass for twenty or so parishioners. He was in a good mood despite the meeting scheduled with Monsignor Whelan at nine. He saw Sister Margaret behind her desk speaking on the phone. Father Chet reminded himself to treat the antagonistic nun with all the kindness and charity he could muster. This behavior bothered her enormously, despite his good intentions.

"Oh, Father Sullivan just walked in! Hold on, I'll give you to him," Sister Margaret said into the phone, looking at Chet with concern on her face. Before handing him the phone, her demeanor changed, and she whispered, "Keep it short. Monsignor Whelan's expecting you in three minutes."

Chet grabbed the receiver, confused by Sister Margaret's contradictory tones. *Does she know something I don't know?* he thought.

"Father Chet here." He paused. "Oh, hi Joe! Look, I'm sorry I drove off so fast after Bruno's without giving you an explanation—" Father Chet added quickly.

Joe cut him off, "Chet, that can wait. Nathan's been hurt. Badly. He got into an accident on the Indiana Tollway early this morning."

"What happened?!"

Joe related the details to the worried priest.

"Chet, listen, they're taking him into the operating room again. The broken leg is set, and he's got four broken ribs and a serious concussion. I called to ask for prayers. There's something wrong with one of his lungs, which collapsed briefly during the accident. They're doing exploratory pulmonary surgery to sew up a few things and to assess the damage. I'm going to pray for him now myself. I thought you'd want to know."

"Yeah, I'll pray. Is he in danger of dying?" Both men knew that Chet was more concerned with Nathan's soul than his body, despite Chet's obvious concern for Nathan's physical condition.

"The doctors don't think so. He's been in and out of consciousness since they found him. Pulmonary stuff is serious, and Nathan was a heavy smoker. The orthopedic surgeon said Nathan was in tremendous physical condition despite that. I'll keep you posted. One other thing—doesn't he have any relatives? There was nothing in his wallet, and the last thing he said before he passed out was 'Get Joanie Wheat.'"

"Both parents are dead, and he doesn't have any brothers or sisters," Chet replied after a moment's thought. "There was a family named Wojtal in Forest Park that he stayed with during high school. Knowing Nathan, he hasn't talked to them in over a decade. You could try looking up the Wojtals in directory assistance." Chet spelled out Wojtal for Joe.

Sister Margaret glared at Father Chet. When she caught his eye, she pointed to the clock over her desk and then down the hall toward Monsignor Whelan's office.

"Chet? I've gotta go. I don't mean to rush you…" Joe said contritely.

"No, that's okay, I've got a meeting starting right now. Give me a call as soon as you hear something new. Thanks, Joe. God bless."

"God bless you too, Father. I'll call." Joe hung up.

Father Chet was reeling with emotion as the news sank in. He remembered praying last night and guessed that his guardian angel had woken him up to pray for Nathan.

This is serious, he thought. Sadness engulfed him. *Oh Nathan! Hang in there buddy!* He began to pray a Hail Mary silently.

Sister Margaret harrumphed. Chet came out of his prayerful daze. She was standing behind her desk with her arms folded. He said nothing and walked down the wood-paneled hall to the pastor's large office.

Chet was surprised to see the assistant bishop of the diocese, Bishop Brookings, sitting behind the pastor's desk. Monsignor Whelan was standing next to the bishop behind the desk, looking out the window toward Verona Lake. Bishop Brookings smiled.

Monsignor Whelan turned from the window and addressed Father Chet, "Don't sit. This won't take long."

2

Friday Afternoon
13 October
Notre Dame, Indiana

Joanie hadn't slept all night or all day. Her eyes burned when her lids involuntarily closed. She tried to stay awake to pray for Nathan. Her wavy hair had flattened to a wet tangle in the steady mist.

She looked at the candles in the Grotto, then rested her forehead on the hard wooden handrail that was attached by bars to the iron kneeler.

Please, Mary. I'm out of prayers. Please keep helping him.

After returning from Chicago with Denny, she had gone straight to Saint Joseph Hospital to be with Nathan. The doctors told her there was not much she could do for him except pray. Her mother and father were already in the waiting room along with Joe Jackson.

The pulmonary specialist had informed them that there appeared to be no permanent damage or internal bleeding in Nathan's left lung. The trauma from the broken ribs was making it hard for the diaphragm and lungs to coordinate. The doctor gave Nathan a cautious but positive prognosis, "Your friend has been through more in the last few hours than most people go through in a lifetime. He's very strong. He'll make it. He's not quite in a coma but the painkillers will keep him asleep for several hours."

Joanie fell asleep while resting her head on the handrail and awoke when she began to lose balance. She picked up her purse and decided to go home. There was nothing more she could do.

3

Wednesday Morning
11 October
Salt Lake City, Utah

Lanning checked himself out of LDS Hospital a day after his heart attack, despite protests from the doctor on duty.

He felt slightly tired but otherwise fine. He had flatly refused his cardiologist's suggestion to have a pacemaker implanted. In Lanning's opinion the doctors were being overly cautious. CAT scans and EKGs had shown no damage to his heart tissue or arteries. There was no medical explanation for his heart attack. This lack of predictive indicators was not uncommon for heart attack victims, however. And there are more than a few "healthy" corpses in the morgue. After going to hell and back, Lanning was no longer worried about his body. He left early in the morning without calling Elena. The hardest part had been convincing the reluctant doctor to lend him some clothes and a coat.

Looking over his shoulder, Lanning pulled his collar up and slowly walked down the hill toward South Temple Street. He made certain he was not being followed. The Cathedral of the Madeleine was only a few blocks away. Before the heart attack he had become indifferent to the mountains which surrounded the city. In the early morning air those mountains now seemed close enough to touch! Lanning was exhilarated. *I'm alive! I live in the most beautiful city in the United States!*

He entered the Catholic church for the first time. Except for his two years as a missionary in Brazil, his four years at BYU, and his two years at Medill in Chicago, the Cathedral of the Madeleine had been within walking distance throughout his life. He knew from his studies that all Catholic churches had a box with bread wafers inside.

They call it a tabernacle. And they—I—don't think it's a wafer of bread. He tried the idea on like a new sweater, almost amused. *It's like pouring new wine into old wineskins.*

He found the Eucharistic Chapel behind the altar. He knelt on one of the four kneelers that surrounded the bronze tabernacle set in a wooden spire. The church was empty except for a married couple who were whispering on the other side of the cathedral near the immersion-type baptismal font. The entire church was stunning—it had been renovated at a cost of nearly ten million dollars in the early 1990s.

Lanning was uniquely aware of a beautiful irony. He had successfully pushed the LDS to help finance a sizable portion of the renovations. He made the recommendation not out of any love for Catholics, but because he had correctly predicted that helping to finance the renovations would both endear and indebt the Catholics of Salt Lake City to the LDS. It had been a minor project despite the millions it cost the LDS. The charade had been a public relations success.

I helped buy this tabernacle. Even though the tabernacle looked ancient, it was brand new. *It's mine in more ways than one.*

He pulled himself away from his thoughts; he was aware that his thoughts were not *prayers*. It was time for him to pray as a Catholic for the first time in his life.

Mormons called it going "Jack." It was short for the generic "Jack Mormon"—a Mormon who does not practice or believe in Mormonism. Most "Jacks" simply dropped out of the sect into religious nothingness. John Lanning was contemplating going a step further.

Jack Catholic. I like the sound of that. Lots of c's and no m's.

He took a deep breath, hesitating—not so much because he was uncertain of his next step, but to meditate upon the implications of his pending act of faith.

With his first prayer he knew that there would be no turning back. He envied the Catholic couple standing in the back of the church. If they were typical—even lax—Catholics, their Catholicism probably provided them with a social network, family, friends, recreation, and even a philosophical world view.

For John Lanning it was just the opposite. If he became a Catholic, his world would instantly disintegrate as soon as his conversion became public:

He would lose his wife.

He would lose his relatives.

He would lose his friends.

He would lose his job.

He would lose everything.

Well, not everything. I could still have my life if I kept my mouth shut. But are you going to keep quiet, John? What's the Body of the real Jesus in a tabernacle worth?

John was smart enough to know that he had the knowledge and skills to do what few Jacks could do: effectively expose the Mormon religion for what it was. He was trained to foresee the long term implications of ideas.

If you can destroy the cult, then you should. It's as simple as that. If you helped build it, you can help tear it down, too. He smiled ironically. *The LDS's worst enemy is a man who knows the truth about Mormonism and is willing to speak the truth.*

Lanning was certain that he might lose his life if he set himself to exposing the Mormons for what they really were—especially if he met with palpable success. Anti-LDS activities by apostate Mormons were considered "sins against the Holy Spirit" which can only be atoned by the spilling of the blood of the apostate. Before Utah received statehood, so-called Avenging Angels—bodyguards of Brigham Young and other leaders—practiced "blood atonement" with alarming frequency. Mormon fathers shot their own sons out of their saddles as their sons tried to flee the Salt Lake City valley. The most famous Avenging Angel of all, Porter Rockwell, was said to have killed dozens—if not hundreds—with the blessing of Mormon leaders.

Such horrific public activities had ceased in modern times—or Utah would never have been allowed to become a state. Lanning knew that certain "true believer" Mormons still believed in the blood atonement doctrine. No one would give a direct order to kill Lanning, of course. That was not the Mormon way. Somewhere in the secret hierarchy someone in charge would gravely say to someone else willing to do "God's will" that "John Lanning has committed a sin against the Holy Spirit. God will punish him."

The rest would take care of itself. Lanning might be found dead of a drug-induced heart attack. Or shot dead by a "burglar." There were many ways it could be done. He believed that such drastic measures would only be taken if he seriously damaged the sect, which would be no small feat.

A scripture echoed in his mind: *Greater love hath no man than to lay down his life for a friend.*

He turned and looked at the tabernacle. Time to pray.

He began, surprised at how easily and casually the conversation started. *Okay, Jesus, you win. You just gave me a second life two days ago. I'll do it. I'll do my best to love and serve you, my Lord and my God. If you want me to tear down their damned temple, I will do so, out of love for my friends.*

*Yes! Love! They are my friends, and I love them! I will de-
stroy the temple for my friends, so they might be delivered
from their slavery. They will hate me, but I will return their
hate with love.*

*Talking to you now is so wonderful, so—easy. My Mor-
mon friends deserve the chance to do the same. You must
help me, though, my Lord. Give me the courage, the strength,
the knowledge to destroy the infernal thing. I will be your
instrument. Just show me how.*

*Another thing. I know the chances of Elena following me
here are nil. Please give her the power to know you and love
you as I do now. I don't want to lose her, even though our
love grew cold during the slavery I was under. If she doesn't
choose to follow you, please console her in her suffering over
losing her husband.*

John stopped and briefly wondered if he was really talking to Jesus in the tabernacle or to unseen wafers of bread in
a brass box. John felt so good. But his faith in the Eucharist
was not a feeling, per se. It was a state of being.

*Is this what faith is? Believing without knowing? Cer-
tainty of uncertainties? Why am I so comfortable talking to
you if you're not there? I wonder what will happen if I just sit
here and listen for a while?*

He sat silently, trying to listen to Jesus for over half an
hour. He heard no words but felt a distant, barely perceptible
peace. His experience was not uncommon for those who pray
to Jesus in the Blessed Sacrament for the first time.

*Do I have an answering machine in my soul? Are you
leaving messages in my soul that I can't hear with my ears or
imagine in my mind? How do the Catholics pray to you here?
I'm new at this, Jesus.*

Then Jesus' answer came. It did not come in the form of
words, but to his soul as a reality that precedes words, for
words are merely spoken or written symbols for the real
things.

John knew with certainty:

The black man with the roses will help you.

He responded aloud, feeling somewhat foolish: "Okay, the black man with the roses will help me. Got it."

He sat in silence, listening to words he could not hear. Then his mind drifted from Jesus to the reasons why, after his experience of hell, he had been so certain that Catholicism was the one, true, holy, and apostolic faith. And he wondered if he was one in a million, the most unique Catholic convert in the history of Mormonism.

Part of his job promoting the LDS was to research other religions, and wherever possible, to adapt their best methods to LDS methods. Lanning had always been professionally fascinated by Catholicism. Until the late 1960s, Mormon missionaries had tremendous difficulty attracting Catholics. As far back as 1958, he had made it his job to know details about the teachings of the Catholic Church in order to solve this problem.

Mormons were taught from childhood that the Catholic Church was the most evil of all Christian churches. It was the "Whore of Babylon," and the Protestant churches were the "prostitute daughters of the Whore." During secret rituals in the Mormon Temple, a Mormon dressed like a Catholic priest was instructed by a temple worker posing as Lucifer to teach "falsehoods" such as the doctrine of the Holy Trinity! The pope was despised. As a young missionary, he had taken special pleasure in converting Catholic Brazilians to the LDS—believing that he was saving them from the worst religion on earth.

Before his visit to hell, he had gradually and imperceptibly found himself admiring the Catholic Church from a professional point of view. Of course he had completely rejected the Catholic Church *theologically*. It *just had to be* what the Mormons taught him it was—the archenemy, a tool of Lucifer. But he couldn't help but appreciate its elegantly simple hierarchical structure. He marveled at its effective pope-to-pew communication network, which was adaptable to any age or technology. He especially liked its missionary zeal in earlier centuries.

Catholicism was, after all, the largest Christian denomination in the world. It was one of the few institutions in the world nearly two thousand years old, and the only institution that old of any size or influence. It was hardy, he often told his subordinates—sometimes down, but never out. Worthy of clever imitation, it had outlasted persecutions, corruption, revolutions, political upheavals, disasters—and even material prosperity, which John wisely recognized could destroy an institution. He knew the Catholic Church was an excellent business model. It was a source of ideas. If Catholicism was the IBM of churches, then the LDS was Apple Computer.

He was also aware that the Catholic Church was the only church which clearly and unequivocally taught two "realities," among others. The Catholic Church teaches that hell exists. It also teaches that contraception is a grave moral evil. John had always reserved a scruple about using artificial contraceptives. But he used them—Elena had insisted.

So after he "returned" from hell, it took him less than twenty minutes to compare his "new reality" to the teachings of all the major faiths. He had always prided himself on being a realist. Catholicism was the only faith that fit the reality.

Before his recent doubts, Lanning had been a man of prayer and good works. However, the Catholic God was much more appealing now that he believed in a new reality. The Mormon god was a piker by comparison.

Before leaving the hospital, he had been somewhat amused to find himself deciding to become a Catholic as easily as he decided which car to buy for the family. His decision to assent to Catholic beliefs had been made with little struggle. The difficult part would come, he knew, *after* his conversion.

•

4

Friday Morning
13 October
Verona, New Jersey

Chet found it hard to keep his imagination from projecting images of Nathan in a hospital bed, his body covered with bandages. He blinked and shook his head before speaking to Bishop Brookings.

"What can I do for you, Your Excellency?" he asked politely.

Brookings looked at Whelan, who was smiling pleasantly. "We had such high hopes for you, Chet, when you were in the seminary," Brookings began, "but even back then, despite your high grades and hard work, your superiors constantly complained that you were too rigid, too stuck in the old ways."

Oh no, Chet thought, *here comes my first official spanking from the brass. Slap on the wrist for not towing the line.* Chet was not surprised. *What can they do? Cardinal O'Donnell's in my corner.*

Thomas Cardinal O'Donnell was the head of the Newark Archdiocese. He had liked Chet from the start. O'Donnell had encouraged him to remain steadfast during Chet's difficult years negotiating the liberal classes at Seton Hall. O'Donnell was a good-hearted man, and a good Catholic, but the diocesan bureaucracy had tied the hands of the somewhat weak cardinal. He had just departed for Rome as part of the conclave responsible for electing a new pontiff.

"As acting leader of the Newark faith community, it saddens me to inform you that your services as priest are no longer needed." The bishop's tone of voice reflected no taint of sadness. Whelan chuckled cheerily.

"What do you mean? 'Services no longer needed?' What does that mean?" Chet was confused. "Am I suspended? And if so, for what?"

"You're not suspended. I can't do that. Only O'Donnell can do that. After much prayer and serious consultation with Monsignor Whelan, we feel it's in the best interests of the faith community of Notre Dame du Lac that we detach you from your duties here. You may no longer live here. We will not pay your salary. You may not publicly hear confessions or say public Mass, or preach in any capacity within the borders of this diocese. You may still say Mass privately, of course."

Chet was reeling. "But why? What have I done?" he croaked, close to tears.

"You crossed a line," the bishop said. "Plain and simple. Don't expect O'Donnell to bail you out this time. Let's just say that he's not going to be a factor now that Pope Patrick is…gone—"

"—O'Donnell's close to retirement," Monsignor Whelan quickly added.

The words flowed over Chet like shock waves. *O'Donnell's not a factor? What does that mean? Brookings is so smug. He's enjoying this.*

"You want specifics?" the bishop asked. Chet nodded weakly.

"First of all, you've embarrassed the faith community with your political activism in the newspapers. Second, you've constantly disobeyed the Monsignor's requests to tone down your homilies. You've been rigid and uncooperative with Sister Margaret in the religious education program. You've disrupted the peaceful atmosphere of Notre Dame du Lac with your insistence on hearing confessions daily—"

"Those charges are not going to hold water with Cardinal O'Donnell, you know. They're trumped up. I've never disobeyed in any real way and you know it! As soon as the cardinal gets back from Rome—"

Brookings waved his hand at Chet. "You're not listening to me. You don't get it. We don't need any charges. We're ordering you under obedience to stop associating yourself with this diocese. If I could suspend you, I would, but I can't. At least not yet. I fully expect to be the next archbishop of this diocese. If you make waves with your friends in the press, I will suspend you then. The matter is closed."

"But—" Chet started. Bishop Brookings waved again, cutting him off. Father Chet was going to ask Brookings how anyone could possibly know who would be appointed to ecclesiastical office ahead of time. *Cardinal O'Donnell is still holding office! What's going on here? Is this the start of the Great Schism? Or am I just the wrong priest in the wrong parish at the wrong time?*

"No buts, Chet. The matter is closed. You've got two days to move out of here. No Mass tomorrow." Brookings turned to Whelan, "Do you have anything to add for Father Sullivan, Monsignor?"

Whelan looked at Chet with disdain. He took a step closer and leaned forward. "You still think my kind of religion is dead?" Chet half-expected Whelan to spit on the floor.

Chet didn't answer. He turned and left the room.

Monsignor Whelan laughed again, louder. Chet made a conscious decision not to have a drink as he climbed up the steps to his room. He had to think. He was already recovering.

No time for self pity. I've heard of stories like this from old-timers in other dioceses. I was playing with fire. The liberals who run the big house in Newark must know something about the new pope and O'Donnell that I don't. Usually they send troublemakers like me to obscure parishes in the boonies. Before O'Donnell came here, I heard that three priests were unofficially "shut down" without suspension. One had to find a job as a lawyer to keep a roof over his head. I'm out. I need advice. I need help.

Official suspension would have meant that Father Chet couldn't say Mass, hear confessions, or otherwise administer sacraments—a suspension of his priestly faculties. He could still administer the sacraments publicly just as long as he did so outside of the archdiocese.

I'll call Dad. He'll have good advice. Where am I going to live? Can't move in with Mom and Dad, though Greg and

Mindy Wheat have an apartment above their garage. Maybe I could move in with them 'til I figure out where to go next. Joanie Wheat's brother Greg was an old friend of Chet's from their Notre Dame days. Greg was a successful lawyer who lived a few miles away in North Caldwell. Mindy often came to Father Chet for confession. Chet's parents lived in a one-bedroom condominium. They had sold the family home after their last son moved out.

Is this a sign that I should be Joe's black robe? I better start praying, too.

5

Saturday Morning
14 October
South Bend, Indiana

Nathan opened his eyes and saw Joanie. She was sitting next to him reading a book titled *The Screwtape Letters.* She sensed his gaze, and looked at him.

"Welcome back, Mister," she said softly, her eyes watering.

It took him a few seconds to find his voice. "It's good to be back, Joanie," he croaked, his voice barely audible. Nathan's heart filled with an emotion that was foreign to him.

"Joanie. I'm so…" his eyes also began to fill with tears, and he couldn't finish his sentence. The emotion choking him was *gratitude*.

"Joanie…" he began again.

She rose from the chair next to his bed and gently put an arm around his neck, so as not to put the slightest pressure on his broken ribs. She put her cheek on his cheek that wasn't covered with a bandage. "Don't say anything, my love. We'll have time to talk later."

But Nathan did speak, "I need to see a priest—and I need you to pray with me. You won't believe what happened to me. Will you pray with me?"

She nodded slowly. "Sure, Nathan. Should I go find the chaplain first?"

Nathan nodded, wincing from the pain.

"Okay, Nathan, I'll be right back." Joanie released her gentle embrace and left the room to find a priest.

6

Saturday Afternoon
14 October
Salt Lake City, Utah

Slinger didn't like going to what he privately thought of as Town Father Events, even if he was the head honcho father at the event scheduled to begin in less than an hour. He was in the den of his home. He was a neat-desk person, so he carefully policed his large desk of any papers or items before departing. He was just about to leave for the opening of the new SLG Communications Institute when the phone rang.

"I need to speak to Sergeant Slinger, now." Karl immediately recognized the voice on the other end.

"Chip!" Slinger cried out in his booming voice. "Aren't you dead yet, Lieutenant Williams!"

"What, and let you outlive me? No way, Sarge," William "Chip" Williams, Commandant of the United States Marine Corps, replied heartily.

"You calling about the audio tape I sent you, Chip? No, wait. Don't tell me. I'll tell you. You're out of your mind, Slinger! Is that about right?"

There was a pause on the other end before Williams spoke, "Not exactly, Sarge. I just finished listening to it for the fifth time. I don't buy it all, but it's really getting under my skin.

I'm not going Christer or anything, like you have. Do you know this Wheat fella?"

"I just spent two days with him last week. He's a regular guy, Chip, a Marine too, in Korea," Karl replied. A *regular guy* was one of his highest compliments. "And he drinks Maker's."

That got a laugh from Chip. "Is that so? Wheat sounded pretty normal on the tape. Very fact-oriented. Too smart to be a jarhead, though—guess I was wrong. Tell me, Karl, do you really buy this Marian stuff?"

"I do, Chip. I do. I'm throwing every resource of SLG Industries plus all my personal wealth into getting that information into as many heads as possible over the next year."

Karl expected Chip to laugh again. *Here it comes,* he thought, *the "you're crazy" part. Chip's just calling to be polite and say hello to an old Marine Corps buddy.*

But Chip didn't laugh. "So you're serious. Well, if what Wheat says is true, then I don't blame you. It wouldn't be like Sergeant Slinger to sit on his butt."

Karl was surprised. Based on recent experience with over two dozen movers and shakers, he hadn't expected Chip to take Wheat's tape seriously. He had almost decided not to send the tape when Chip's name popped up on Karl's computerized list of friends and acquaintances. He sent almost everyone on the list the "Marian Apparitions" audio tape and the two most popular books on the same subject—*The Final Hour* and *The Thunder of Justice*—overnight delivery. He remembered pausing over Chip's name when previewing the list. Then he remembered the young lieutenant attending a field Mass in Quantico where Karl had served briefly as a consultant at the height of the Vietnam Conflict.

Karl was an expert in radio communications over rough terrain. He had consulted with the Marine Corps on ways to improve communication systems. Before his involvement, American radiomen on the infamous "search and destroy" missions had to strap their radios to their backs. The radios had long antennas which stuck up several feet above the heads of the radiomen. The Vietcong had the nasty habit of picking off radio operators by identifying the soldiers with the large antennas. Karl's ranches had been linked by sophisticated radios decades earlier. Back in the fifties, SLG Industries had even purchased a short wave radio manufacturer and a small radio engineering company to help develop custom comsystems for the ranches. Karl had spent several days in the field with Lieutenant Williams; the bright young officer had taken well to the old combat veteran.

Chip had picked the veteran's brains on communications technology and had pushed for some of Karl's recommendations with the brass. New field radios were manufactured by Motorola for the Marines as a result of their work together. At the time, in 1967, Karl had been surprised when Chip invited him to attend Mass in the field during the ten-day test of the new radios. The new radios were a success and saved hundreds of lives during the protracted Vietnam Conflict.

The two Marines had exchanged Christmas cards over the years but had little contact otherwise. Chip had teasingly taken to calling Slinger "Sarge" (Slinger was a sergeant during his World War II days). Karl followed the young officer's rise through the ranks to the top of the elite fighting service.

"Look Karl," Chip added after a pause, "I haven't got much time. I just wanted to call to say thank you. I've been a pew sitter my whole life, and I don't necessarily buy Wheat's thesis that the world is going to undergo a supernatural chastisement from God, but I've got an open mind. In the meantime, I've started to say the Rosary again with Christy, and to tell you the truth, I feel good about that. I used to pray the family Rosary every night with my folks when I was a kid.

"And I'm going to enroll in the Knights of Immaculata, too. I had heard about Saint Maximilian Kolbe before as a martyr, but I never knew he was so ahead of his time in using technology. That makes two Poles I know who are that way."

"I'm glad to hear it," Karl replied, a note of relief in his voice, "and I appreciate your being up front with me. I've sent out over two hundred packs like the one I sent you, Chip, and the only reply I've gotten so far is either silence, or that I'm off my rocker. Maybe I am."

"No you're not, Sarge. I'm still a practicing Catholic— sometimes I feel like the only one in Washington. But you'd be surprised how many good Catholics there are in the military. Half the officers in all the services are nominally Catholic, did you know that?"

"Really? I didn't know that." Karl was genuinely surprised.

"That's right. The service has always been a way for non-WASPs to gain professional status based on merit.

"Back to Wheat's tape. What struck me as I listened to it was the incredibly fast breakdown of the faith in one generation. If somebody told me thirty years ago that over one-third of the children born in this country would be illegitimate, I would have laughed. There's got to be a reason for all this that goes beyond mere human explanations," Chip observed. "The weird way Pope Patrick died bothers me, too. Something's fishy about his death. And I can't say everything I want to on this line…"

Chip's last remark was a cue that he was about to refer elliptically to information that a Commandant of the Marine Corps could not legally discuss in detail with a civilian.

"…but I have been privy to other disturbing information, if you know what I mean, Sarge. Look, I've gotta go. Thanks again. I'll be praying for you. Come visit me in Washington and we'll discuss this over a good bourbon. Bring Dottie. Christy would love to see her again."

"I'll visit within a month. My secretary will call yours, Chip. I'm serious."

"I know you are, Sarge. Fine. See you soon, then. Good luck."

"Thanks." Karl hung up the phone.

Well, I'll be tied, Karl thought, surprised and relieved that at least one person he contacted didn't think he was going senile. *Even if Chip doesn't buy the whole program now, as events predicted by Mary come true with more frequency, he'll catch on. Chip's a sharp cookie. And, he's the Commandant of the Marine Corps.*

7

Saturday Afternoon
14 October
Salt Lake City, Utah

Lee had prayed all of Friday in the cathedral. He had found a motel nearby, then returned to pray this morning.

He took a walk to stretch his legs. Now he stood in front of the new SLG Communications Institute, which happened to be next door to the Cathedral of the Madeleine. Limos were arriving and dropping off tuxedo-clad men and their wives—members of Salt Lake City's upper crust. On the corner nearby, he saw an oriental man selling roses for two dollars a piece. He was obviously a member of the Unification Church—commonly known as the Moonies. Lee remembered Moonies from both Cleveland and Los Angeles.

Lee checked his wallet for money. He had over fifty dollars left. It struck him as funny that fifty bucks seemed like such a fortune after losing almost a million dollars in Los Angeles. Both Randall Knott and Father Rivera had insisted on giving him money for his trip to Salt Lake City. They couldn't talk him out of hitchhiking. He had used most of the money the two Samaritans had given him to stay in economy hotels while hitching to this beautiful city set on a sloping plain at the foot of the Wasatch Mountains.

Lee, acting on impulse, walked up to the Moonie and boldly put his two hands on the Moonie's head. The Moonie was not old—probably under forty. Something about Lee's smile kept the Moonie from rebuffing the black man in the chinos and the red checkered shirt. Lee closed his eyes and said a prayer over the Moonie—a silent Hail Mary.

The Moonie's name was Kim Woo. He had emigrated from Korea ten years earlier—already a member of the controversial cult—and spent most of that time selling roses in San Francisco before being sent to Salt Lake City. Kim Woo was used to having bottles and other debris thrown at him from the windows of passing cars in San Francisco, and enjoyed working in peaceful Salt Lake City. Here, and only on rare occasions, pedestrians would hurl verbal abuse at him, using foul language while calling him a freak and a cult member. No bottle-throwing. Lee's kindness was touching by comparison.

Kim Woo, whose English was very poor, tried to give Lee three red roses. A broad smile came to Lee's face. He offered to pay for the roses, but Kim wouldn't accept the payment. It was a first for Kim. The cult member would have to account for the missing roses at the end of the day when he returned to the communal house in which he lived.

Lee finally accepted the roses and turned to find John Lanning, dressed in a tuxedo, facing him.

"Do I know you?" Lee asked.

"I don't know," Lanning replied. "Do you? I've seen you before, young man." Words from Lanning's prayer before the tabernacle walked through a door in his memory and sat down comfortably in Lanning's mind. *A black man with roses. This is the one I saw after the heart attack!*

Lee shook his head, confused. He was sure he had never met the short man with the gray hair and bushy black eyebrows standing before him. Then he remembered the words of the Blessed Mother: *"You must now immediately go to Salt Lake City to meet a man who will recognize you."*

"We need to talk, sir. My name is Lee Washington. I was sent to meet you. But I don't know you."

"Who sent you?" Lanning, trying to ignore his excitement, eyed Lee suspiciously.

"Mary, the Mother of God. It's a long story." Lee felt embarrassed. *It's the truth, man, don't be embarrassed,* he thought.

Lanning closed his eyes for a moment and bent his head in thought. When he looked up, his mind was made up.

"Then come with me. You can tell me over lunch. I'm sure Karl Slinger won't mind if you sit at our table. There's sure to be an extra seat—my wife wasn't able to come to the opening of the Institute." Lanning paused when he saw the confused look in Lee's eyes. "Forgive me, Lee, of course you have no idea what I'm talking about. I'll explain on the way. We're going inside the new SLG Institute here, which is opening today. Let's go."

It was a strange meeting—but not the strangest of Lee's recent experiences. So when John Lanning put his arm up, gesturing toward the large open doors of the four-story SLG Communications Institute, Lee didn't hesitate to put his arm around the shorter man's shoulders. There was something about John Lanning that made saying "no" to him difficult, Lee noted.

8

Sunday Evening
22 October
County Galway, Ireland

"Tell me again, Sister Elizabeth—are you sure?" Sister Mary Bernard said with fear in her voice.

"I don't know for sure. I'm not a doctor! Even if I was a doctor, without x-rays and proper diagnostic equipment, it's impossible to tell. I'm guessing, Mother!" The pressure was getting to the former nurse, who was over sixty years old. Pope Patrick's life was in her hands. Sister Elizabeth had read all she could find about treating comas and had done what she could for the ailing patient.

Sister Elizabeth had even taught the other nuns in the Carmel how to perform passive physical therapy on Pope Patrick's limbs and fingers. Without such modern techniques, Angus's muscles would quickly atrophy. His ligaments and tendons would shrink. Getting the sophisticated drugs needed to keep the pope stable was a more difficult matter. Sister

Mary Bernard had risked contacting the local doctor, Barnard Soames. Doc Soames, who was almost as old as the prioress, was definitely not a devout Catholic. He only reluctantly agreed to obtain the prescriptions from Galway as a personal favor. He had known Sister Mary Bernard for a long time and had asked questions that the abbess refused to answer.

"I could lose my license over this," Soames had informed her.

"Believe me, Doctor, if that occasion should arise, it would be worth it. I can't tell you more," she had replied evenly. Doc Soames had been looking after the sisters for over thirty years. He trusted Sister Mary Bernard, but grudgingly.

Now there was a problem with Pope Patrick far worse than finding ways to obtain prescription drugs.

"I don't think the bullet was poisoned, Mother," said Sister Mary Elizabeth. "And thank God there's been little internal bleeding or the Holy Father would have died a week ago. I think it's infected. The redness around the wound is a telltale sign. In his weakened state, an infection could do great damage, and could do it quickly. We need a doctor. The bullet must be removed."

"Dr. Soames?" Sister Mary Bernard suggested.

"Whether we can trust him to keep quiet is your concern, Mother. Whether he can get the bullet out is another problem. He's only a country doctor, and not a true surgeon. Back in the States, we used to take bullets out of Emergency Room patients like prescribing aspirin. It's not that complicated unless it's lodged directly in an organ. Again, I'm way out of my league."

"I suppose we have no choice, then," the prioress conceded. "I'll call Dr. Soames. He already guessed that we were caring for a comatose patient. The look on his face when he finds out our patient is the *real* pope will be rich." She said the word *real* with great irony and a raised eyebrow.

Beneath her gentle facade, Sister Mary Bernard was a tough customer. She had to be. She had more pressure on her than Sister Elizabeth. Assuming they could keep Angus alive,

how long should she hide from the world the fact that whoever the new pope turned out to be, he had not been validly
elected? Could prudence dictate that she disobey Pope
Patrick's direct pre-coma order?

9

From *Dark Years History*
(New Rome Press, 31 R.E.)
by Rebecca Macadam Jackson

...so were the Conspiracy Theorists correct in holding that
a worldwide conspiracy existed to establish a one world
government through control of currency and the destruction of national sovereignty? It is not within the scope of
this work to answer that question in great detail or de-
finitively. Written records from the Dark Years are scarce.
Many of the most important documents are lost under
the ashes of Europe. The very nature of conspiracy means
that traditional historical records were not kept if a conspiracy was indeed in place. Certainly the Catholic Church
had publicly and officially identified Freemasonry as a
secret enemy of the Church many times during the centuries leading up to the Dark Years. As Professor Wheat
frequently stated during the Dark Years: If you believe that
Jesus is God and established a church on earth—the Catholic Church—then it is absurd to hold that Satan would not
have his own version of a "church."

From accounts of former Society members it is clear
now that the antipope Casino was a member of a secretive group calling themselves the Society of Builders, or
simply, the Society. The Society's ties to Freemasonry are
not well established, but probable.

Let us suppose that Thomas Wheat was correct in assuming that Satan had his own earthly church with dedicated members doing his evil bidding (*She Shall Crush Your
Head*, New Rome Press, 17 R.E., page 274). The mark of
the demonic is the mockery and ersatz imitation of the

Catholic Church. For example, satanic masses mocked and copied the real Mass. In the same way, the so-called church of Satan had a hierarchy, but unlike the Catholic hierarchy, it was secretive. Unlike the Catholic Church, where a common layman can know whatever the pope knows in a theological sense, the church of Satan was a deceptive web of confusion. Certain satanic agencies were obviously completely unaware of other satanic organizations. Only the brilliant angelic mind of Lucifer could coordinate a worldwide group of agents working unaware of each other. Pope Leo XIII's 1884 vision of Satan bragging to Jesus that he (Satan) could destroy the Church in one century sheds much light on this thesis. According to Leo XIII, Jesus granted Satan one century and more control over those who were willing to serve the evil one.

In this theoretical construct, the New Age Movement and the Society, with few outward "human" ties—and unbeknownst to each other—were working for the same master. Toward the end of the Dark Years, there were hundreds, perhaps thousands of disparate organizations serving the evil one.

Whereas the Catholic Church is one, holy, and apostolic, the church of Satan was many, unholy, and tyrannical. In a real sense, members of Satan's forces were in the dark. It is no wonder that many reasonable men rejected the Conspiracy Theory before the Dark Years. Both the Conspiracy Theorists and their detractors were searching for purely human historical causes. While it might seem obvious to those born after the Dark Years, only a supernatural construct could explain the events the world experienced. Perhaps the members of the evil one's organizations overestimated the power of their cruel master. At first it seemed that the forces of evil would gain control of the world without much struggle. Yet in the darkest hours good men and women were raised up to form the heel which crushed the serpent's head, as foretold by Saint Louis DeMontfort at the end of Chapter One of *True Devotion to Mary*...

10

Saturday Afternoon
14 October
Salt Lake City, Utah

Karl Slinger was surprised to see a nondescript black man
attired in a red checkered shirt, chino pants, and K-Swiss
tennis shoes, accompanying John Lanning to the head table.
Lee Washington was definitely not dressed properly for the
gala event.

Slinger's multimedia Communications Institute was the
first of its kind in the world. It was going to be as much a
communications hub for SLG as an institute of learning. The
SLG Institute would not limit itself to training its partners in
the use of the latest communications technology available. It
would house the world's most modern communications
school. Slinger planned to train professionals from any
industry willing to pay a reasonable fee. The SLG Institute
had access to every imaginable information highway in the
world. Especially the Internet. SLG even had a large Intranet
connecting all its ranches. Lenny Gold loved to surf the Net,
and was pushing SLG hard in that direction.

Many in the academic world had derided SLG Industries
for building it—what did capitalists know about education?
Characteristically, Karl Slinger had ignored the experts. He
suspected that the academics feared competition from its
efficiency and low cost. Two-year postgraduate degrees cost
over sixty thousand dollars at Harvard or Stanford. The SLG
Institute was planning on conferring one-year degrees for less
than fifteen thousand.

Lanning's amazing, Slinger thought as he looked at
Lanning and the young black man. *Probably a publicity stunt
to help portray the Mormons in a better racial light. Hey!
Wasn't Lanning in the hospital two days ago? I read it in the
papers—heart attack?*

Slinger had a grudging admiration for the public relations director of the LDS. The two leaders had known each other for decades and got along well enough for Karl's purposes. They were not close friends, however. The SLG Institute had brought them together. Lanning had convinced the LDS to contribute $200,000 to the Institute's building fund.

The Mormons were also technologically savvy. Lanning had already hooked up almost all the Mormon temples in the world using satellite teleconferencing. Over the years Slinger had felt the charismatic pull of the man, and in a corner of his mind, he feared Lanning.

Elena Lanning had decided to stay home. Lanning had not yet told his wife about his decision to become a Catholic.

There was a short cocktail hour before the scheduled dinner. Slinger found himself confronting Lanning and the young under-dressed black man out of earshot of other attendees.

"Aren't you supposed to be in the hospital, John?" Karl asked, his usual forward self.

"Yes and no. The doctors say yes. I say no. I feel great. It was only a mild heart attack, Karl."

"Really?" Slinger was skeptical.

"Yes, really. Karl, how rude of me. Let me introduce you to my friend, Mr. Lee Washington. Lee, this is Karl Slinger, the founder of the SLG Institute."

"Pleased to meet you, Mr. Slinger. This is a nice place."

"Call me Karl. What brings you here today, son?"

"The Blessed Mother, sir," Lee heard himself say. He felt prompted to be honest with Slinger.

Slinger's eyes bulged. "You've got to be kidding!"

Lanning was following the strange conversation carefully, intrigued.

"Not at all, sir," Lee said softly, but not without confidence. "It's a long story. But the Blessed Mother was involved with bringing me here today, and helping me meet Mr. Lanning. I was just beginning to tell him about it. It seems like we have a lot in common. Are you a Catholic?"

That's an odd question for a stranger to ask, Karl thought. Less than two weeks ago, he would have quickly replied, "Not really."

"As a matter of fact, son, I am, and I've recently come back to the sacraments. This was the second Sunday in a row that I've gone to Mass in years. In over fifty years, in fact."

"That's great, Mr. Slinger! I just came to the faith a few days ago myself! This is weird," Lee volunteered happily.

It sure is, Lanning thought. *What's going on here?*

Slinger saw a rare look on Lanning's face—surprise.

"Karl, after this event is over, can we talk about something personal, in private, with Mr. Washington? I need to tell you something that is strictly confidential. But I don't want to distract you from your triumph today."

"I'd be happy to meet with you, John. There's bound to be an empty office somewhere in this shiny new building. And I've got an audio tape I want to give to you," Karl added mischievously.

"Great! I can get to know Mr. Washington better during the meal. What's the tape about?" Lanning asked.

"The Blessed Mother," Karl replied evenly.

"Interesting. In that case, I am looking forward to our meeting more than ever."

Lanning didn't even bat an eye when I mentioned the Blessed Mother. Strange, Karl thought. *Lots of strange stuff for one conversation.*

"John?" Slinger asked.

"Yes?" Lanning replied.

"I thought you said Lee was your friend. Why would you want to get to know him at the table?" Karl was not beyond asking a discomfiting question, no matter what the circumstances.

"Lee *is* my friend, Karl. I just met him on the corner before walking into the building. It will all come clear when we meet afterwards, I assure you."

"Okay. Sorry, I guess I'm still confused, but it can wait. By the way, the SLG Communications Institute isn't my triumph. I delegated the whole thing to Lenny Gold. He did all the work, probably by delegating it to others. I just approved a good idea when one of my research guys came up with the concept. I gave the concept to Lenny. I love technology—SLG is built on it—but I doubt I could figure out the keyless entry system to get into this place!" With that, Karl Slinger launched his trademark booming laugh.

Behind Karl, Lenny Gold tapped a glass with a spoon, then asked the small crowd of influential people to enter the temporary dining room set up in the institute's meeting hall.

Karl excused himself, walked over to Lenny and whispered in the lawyer's ear. Lenny looked over to Lee and nodded.

Fifteen minutes later, between the first and second course, a waiter came up to Lee Washington's seat and whispered in Lee's ear. Lee followed the waiter to a men's room where a rented tuxedo was waiting for him, including adjustable shoes. As he dressed, a scripture that Randall Knott had paraphrased came to Lee's head: *"Look at the lilies of that there field, boy! Solomon in all his splendor didn't have better duds than them there flowers! The Lord is gonna put clothes on your back today. And I'm gonna help Him do it."*

Lenny Gold, fearful of guessing wrong, had guessed large, so the tuxedo fit Lee loosely.

"You got some pretty powerful friends," the waiter observed, referring to Gold, Slinger, and Lanning.

"If you're talking about Jesus and Mary, you're right." Lee smiled. "Are you a Catholic?"

After five minutes of gentle questioning, he let up on the waiter, a Jack Mormon utterly uninterested in Catholicism. The waiter seemed to be afraid of Lee. Lee got back to the table in time to enjoy the main course and a rousing address on the importance of technology by Karl A. Slinger.

Slinger's even working in a Catholic saint! Saint Maximilian Kolbe, Lee thought excitedly. *Kolbe? I wonder what he did?*

✦ ✦ ✦

The subsequent meeting was more than a bit odd. It was less of a conversation than a briefing. After everyone else had left, Slinger, Lanning, and Washington met in the small waiting room outside Lenny Gold's office. There were three comfortable padded chairs and the inevitable potted plants, along with a modern glass coffee table.

Slinger undid his bow tie and collapsed onto one of the chairs. Lanning sat down, relaxing, but did not appear as fatigued as Slinger.

Lee Washington sat upright on the edge of a third chair, praying silently. He noticed that Karl looked a bit like that guy on the household cleaner bottles his mother used to use. *Mr. Slinger looks like Mr. Clean!*

A very long silence ensued. Lee began with a prayer: "Father of Eternal Truth, we are your servants. Send the Spirit of Truth. Amen."

Slinger and Lanning echoed, "Amen."

Lee then turned to Lanning and said soberly, "Welcome to the Catholic Church. Though you didn't say anything at the dinner table, the Blessed Mother has given me a certain knowledge that you have been marked on the forehead with her seal. Is this not true?"

Lanning was stunned. During the meal, he had not given any indicators to Lee Washington of his inner conversion. "I don't know about any seal on the forehead, Lee, but yes, I have become a Catholic in my heart. How did you know?"

"I just know, sir," Lee replied honestly.

Another long silence.

"Karl?" Lanning asked.

"Yes," Slinger replied.

"If you know anything about the LDS, then you know that I need to keep this under wraps for a while. I need to plan things out. I need to get my bearings. Can I trust you?"

"Yes, of course!" Karl said with somewhat muffled enthusiasm. Karl knew that no one could be listening in on their conversation. Nevertheless, he still had an urge to whisper. "What happened to you, John?"

"My journey to the freedom of the Catholic faith started a long time ago, and ended, thank God, with my heart attack. I know you'll find this hard to believe, but I woke up in the middle of the night with unbelievable pain…"

And so Lanning told his story. John spoke quickly and succinctly, summarizing the theological problems he had with the Mormons, as well as his role in building the sect's image. He spoke about his harrowing trip to hell and his first prayers in the cathedral less than a block away. He talked for over two hours with only a few interruptions. Karl Slinger asked several clarifying questions during Lanning's story.

Slinger, who had lived and worked with Mormons for decades, had no idea how influential and powerful the sect really was financially, socially, and politically around the country and the world. Almost one-third of the SLG staff were Mormon and Slinger respected them as trustworthy workers and solid citizens. Normally, a higher percentage of workers in a Salt Lake City company would be Mormons, but SLG recruited heavily on a nationwide basis. At times during Lanning's long monologue, especially at the parts describing the true nature of Mormonism, Karl felt his hands go clammy with fear.

After Lanning spoke, Karl related his return to the Catholic faith. Retelling the story of his change of direction was still exciting for Slinger, who couldn't hide his enthusiasm or joy. Lanning had been much more somber.

Finally, Lee Washington, who had barely uttered a word during the first three hours, related his own incredible story. Karl felt goose bumps when Lee revealed his commission from Mary to find "a man who will recognize you" in Salt Lake City. It made Lanning's vision of Lee in the Emergency Room all the more stunning and believable.

They were tired, and soaked with information.

Lee accepted Karl's offer to stay at the Slinger home for the evening. A limo was waiting in front of the building when they emerged onto South Temple Street. All three piled in. From there, they were driven to State Street and then up East Capitol Boulevard to the exclusive homes of both Slinger and Lanning.

✟ ✟ ✟

To the security guard, who could see but not hear the conversations among the three unusual men, the scene had looked like three friends conversing about old times. The only strange part was that each was wearing a tuxedo.

In the room, however, the atmosphere was electric, as if a supernatural field of grace was enveloping the area occupied by the three men. Each responded in his own fashion. No verbal commitments were made that night among Karl, Lee, and John. But a commitment was made nevertheless. Each man was distinctly different in experience, temperament, and talent, but none of them lacked the most important attribute: an open, generous, and unselfish heart.

This troika was the culmination of a Divine plan that was finally coming to fruition. The group the Mother of God was assembling in Utah was not unlike the team she was gathering in South Bend. Both groups would merge into one eclectic team. A humble, small, but powerful corps.

The members of this Marian Corps—Chet, Nathan, Becky, Joanie, Tom, Lee, Karl, John, and Joe—were brought together in answer to the prayers and sacrifices of millions of people around the country who had responded to Mary's call. For decades Jesus and His mother had begged Christians to pray, evangelize, and sacrifice. A portion—a small portion—had responded. Now God was responding.

Chapter Fifteen

1

Friday Afternoon
27 October
South Bend, Indiana

A week after Nathan's accident, Becky Macadam quit her
advertising job in Chicago and moved in temporarily with
the Wheats to be closer to her fiancé, Joe Jackson. Becky and
Joanie had become best friends. Becky spent her days volunteering at the Kolbe Foundation. Joe had delegated to her the
daunting job of implementing the prodigious media campaigns needed to offer Tom Wheat's "Marian Apparitions" to
all Americans. On most days after work she ate dinner at
Joe's apartment. Joe was a terrible cook and she was not much
better.

"Bruno's is sending someone over tomorrow with a plaque
honoring us for being the number one customer for home
delivery in South Bend. We're supporting three delivery men
and their families," she told Joe with a straight face.

"That's nice," he played along with nary a hint of a smile.

They had delayed dinner in order to meet Nathan at the
hospital—Nathan was finally checking out. It had been two
weeks since his fateful Warning. He had agreed to move in
with Joe temporarily.

Joe now kept a stock of Klondike bars in the freezer. Becky
had just finished one. "The baby likes them," she had explained a few days earlier while urging him to stock up. "Next
week he or she will want onion sandwiches or some other
weird food." Becky had also been feeling quite tired in the

early afternoons. "At least I'm not throwing up—yet," she had added dryly.

Becky Macadam sat at the clean but modest kitchen table in Joe Jackson's apartment, looking at her man, patiently waiting for him to speak. She was wearing a blue Laura Ashley dress that demurely covered her to the nape of her neck. Joe had replaced the Miraculous Medal she had given to the hitchhiker, Tommy Gervin. Her new medal was smaller, more refined, and made of sterling silver. The silver medal was set off by the navy blue fabric with a small red flower pattern. Joe was gradually learning how to find jewelry that complemented her beauty.

She took another drag off her cigarette and noticed the big man wince. Becky decided to beat him to the punch and speak first—not a great challenge while conversing with Joe Jackson.

"What? You don't like me smoking?"

"Aren't you worried about the baby or your health?" he replied.

Becky thought for a moment and took another puff, her expression coming just short of defiance.

"I haven't had time to think about it. I've been smoking since I was in high school. Mom smoked. Dad smoked. Sam smoked. It seems like all my friends at work smoke—the copywriters especially. It helps you relax when you have a creative deadline and are strung out on caffeine, or worse. I never did drugs myself, Joe Kid."

Joe smiled at her use of the goofy nickname.

"I suppose I read somewhere that smoking increases the chances of low birth weight in babies. Of the few gals I know who've had babies, most ate healthy, exercised, laid off smokes, caffeine, and alcohol so much that their babies were too big and they had to have C-sections. Why didn't you tell me before that my smoking bothered you?"

She squinted. She had not given him the desired response. He was obviously struggling to avoid saying what was really on his mind—his desire to have her quit smoking.

Becky continued, "Is smoking against Catholicism or something? Father Chet smokes more than I do."

"It's not that, Beck. I don't want you to die before your time," Joe told her with childlike sincerity. "I just want to be with you for as many years as I can."

"Jesus! You're a sweetheart!" she exclaimed, genuinely touched. There was something about whatever Joe said to her which had the power to burrow into her heart. She noticed Joe wince again.

"Now what did I do, Joe Hunks?" She could tell he was offended by something.

When he responded, she noted that he did not revert to a sugary sweet tone. His answer was firm but not unkind.

"Becky, I know you don't realize you're doing it, but you've got to try to stop taking the Lord's name in vain. God's name is holy, and isn't meant to be used as filler for conversation. I know it's just a habit for you, and that you don't intend to offend Jesus."

Becky quelled a sudden urge to defend herself. She realized that Joe was genuinely concerned for her soul. She cut off a sharp reply before it escaped her mouth. Her face turned red. *He really cares about me. I guess I've got a lot to learn. I didn't even realize I said Jesus just now—using it like Joe said, like filler.*

"Oh Joe! Can you put up with me while I catch up to you with all this Catholic stuff?" Then Becky admitted rather contritely, "not only do I curse and smoke, but I have a snotty sense of humor. Sister Bertrill I'm not. And I guess I came on pretty strong about smoking, too, when you were just concerned about me and the baby." Becky paused, trying to think of something conciliatory. "Tell you what, Joe DiMaggio, I'm not promising anything, but I'll consider quitting smoking for the sake of the baby. I'll *consider* it. Deal?"

"Deal," Joe accepted evenly. "Catch up with me? You don't have to catch up with me. I'm not ahead of you. I'm next to you, shoulder to shoulder, Becky. I feel uncomfortable correcting you about taking the Lord's name in vain, but it grinds against my ears like scraping a fork across china. As a general rule, I don't believe in pointing out other's faults before considering my own. As for your sense of humor, I like it just fine. It makes me think."

"It's supposed to make you laugh, sweetheart," she said with just a touch of exasperation, making him think—and then laugh.

"There you go again! I never know what's going to come out of your mouth, and even though I don't always laugh, I'm sort of laughing inside. I'm usually trying to figure out where the pun or turn of the phrase is lurking. You've called me over twenty different kinds of Joe since you got here—Joe Kid, Joe Hunks, Java Joe. Where do you get them all?"

With a serious look, she fixed her gaze across Joe's small apartment, and nodded toward an empty corner near the couch. "Over there. I get the names over there." She even pointed helpfully toward the empty corner.

Joe turned to look, then realized that she was teasing him. When he looked back at her, she was taking another drag off the cigarette, smiling her wry, wonderful smile, one eyebrow raised. He laughed easily and showed his own big smile.

"Ha! That's what I mean, I like your oddball sense of humor," he observed with perfect seriousness.

"I'll run out of my best material in less than two months, Jo Jo. Then you're back to loving me for my cursing and smoking again," Becky remarked, somewhat relieved that Joe liked her most prominent qualities. Her beauty, humor, and strong will intimidated most men.

"And don't forget your Sherman tank personality, Beck. That's what I like the best. Sometimes I get the feeling that your inner reserves are stronger than mine. I like that in a woman…" Joe paused to think for more than a minute.

Becky was now quite used to Joe's pensive interludes, as she thought of them. She used the time to admire his strong features and enjoy her cigarette. They were perfectly comfortable with each other. Several new Joe Names popped uncalled into her mind, including: Joe College, Hey Joe, Joe

Camel, and Cup o' Joe. Presently, Joe came back from his brief journey into the world of thought.

"Yeah," he continued, as if he had paused for only a second, "I am completely certain that your strong will is your most attractive trait. I can't push you around, and you can't push me around. We cancel each other out. I don't know how to say this, but most girls were either in awe of my football prowess, or too tame for my tastes. I think it's safe to say that neither one of us cares about my football past. You're like a dog whose bite is worse than its bark. I like it. Keeps me on my toes."

She snorted softly. *He doesn't realize that he just compared me to a dog. Jesus! I mean, Gee Whiz—sorry, Big Guy,* she prayed quickly. *I guess that's a Southern boy's version of a compliment.*

"So I'm like a good hunting dog?" she asked with feigned innocence.

"Yeah!" he concurred enthusiastically, confirming her thesis and endearing himself to her all the more.

"I'm like a dog?" she repeated, a playful smile coming to her lips.

"Yeah, you're like a really good dog. The best dog in the whole world!"

He still doesn't realize what he's saying, the dear, she thought. Becky stuck out her tongue and panted, holding her hands up like paws.

Joe turned red.

"Beck, I didn't mean you were a dog!"

"Then why did you call me a dog, Cup o' Joe?"

"You're teasing me again, aren't you?"

"Yes," she said simply, letting him off the hook.

Relief showed on his face. He got up from the table and stretched, his hands touching the ceiling. He shook his head and eyed her again. Her beauty was new and striking from every angle. He was a man in love.

"Oh, before I forget…" Joe went over to the refrigerator and pulled a large book down from the top. "This is for you, Becky." It was the *Catechism of the Catholic Church.*

"The Catechism! Thank you so much, Joe! Chaplain Chet just told me to get a copy a couple of days ago."

"I know," he said with his usual soft voice, "I called him last night. He suggested I get you a copy. He brought it up—I wasn't spying on you or anything. You know Chet, he's always working an angle."

After being suspended from his parish at the time of Nathan's accident, Father Chet had agreed to become the chaplain of the Kolbe Foundation. Joe was already expanding it with the advice and resources of Karl Slinger.

She carefully placed the book on the table, got up and embraced the gentle giant. "Thank you, Joe, thank you. I really do want to read it." She reluctantly left his embrace and picked up the book, affectionately running one hand slowly over the cover.

"I know you'll love it," Joe added. "Sometimes I find the Catechism dry, except for the scriptural references that support doctrine, which fascinate me. I've read it several times since it came out. That's just me, though, Bible Thumper that I am. I get the feeling that you'll find it right up your alley, the way your mind works. I really do. Father Chet agrees. He thinks you've got the makings of a theologian."

She looked at him. "Me? A theologian? Not likely. Father Chet is a real card—"

"—a wild card?" Joe offered tentatively, taking a stab at humor.

"Please, Mighty Joe, leave the witticisms to a professional like me."

Joe smiled, unhurt.

"Anyway, we've got to get ready to go before Joanie shows up," he said.

"Okay. I think it's wonderful Nathan agreed to work at the Kolbe Foundation! Joanie says he's itching something awful to leave the hospital. The doctors are amazed at his recuperation." Becky grabbed her jacket.

"Karl Slinger agrees wholeheartedly with bringing Nathan into the mix," Joe pointed out. "Nathan's a real genius with numbers and a natural leader. The Kolbe Foundation is going to get too big too fast for me to run the thing. Slinger also wants me to bring in this Lee Washington guy to run our new western division. More and more, I get the feeling that the Blessed Mother wants me to be less of a hands-on leader and more—how can I describe it—more of a philosophical leader for the Kolbe Foundation. Nathan doesn't know it yet, but I'm going to put him in charge of the whole thing as soon as he learns the ropes. He's not the same since the accident—"

A horn beeped outside as Joe finished his sentence. He looked out the window and saw a dusty maroon Caravan. "There's Joanie now."

Becky confirmed his observation about Nathan. "It's like he aged or something, but in a good way," she said. "By the way, when is Father Chet arriving in South Bend?"

"Three days. Look, we can talk in the car, we've got to go."

"Then let's go, Philo Joe."

"Philo Joe?"

"Joe Jackson, Philosophical Leader of the Kolbe Foundation," she explained as she led him out the door.

"Oh. I get it," he said as he grasped her left hand.

There was a simple, modest engagement ring on her finger.

2

When Joanie, Joe, and Becky arrived at Nathan's room, Nathan was already in the wheelchair required for patients checking out. His left leg was still in a cast, but he could limp around without the help of crutches. Nathan's collapsed lung had recovered with amazing speed and his broken ribs were mending after the extremely painful first week following the accident. He had been forced to forego cigarettes during his recuperation and had taken the opportunity to quit the habit. He still had a large scab on the side of his face. The doctors had warned him that there would be a permanent scar.

Nathan would move in with Joe. He had already broken his lease in Chicago. The apartment was in such a prime location that the landlord had been more than willing to let him go—the landlord was planning on raising the rent substantially on a new tenant. No one but Nathan knew that he couldn't stand the thought of living in the apartment where so many of his more serious sins had been committed. Since the Warning, he had prayed a full Rosary with Joanie every day, and had taken Communion from the Eucharistic ministers who served Saint Joseph Hospital.

Joe visited Nathan every day in the hospital and the two men solidified a friendship that had barely begun before the accident. He didn't relate specific details of his Warning to Joe, but Nathan did have a lot of questions. He found that Joe was a good listener and could answer his questions about the faith with a subtle simplicity. There was something about Joe Jackson—holiness, really—that lent weight to what he told Nathan about the spiritual life.

Two weeks earlier, when Joe had approached him about working for the Kolbe Foundation, Nathan had balked at the idea. Joe outlined the ambitious plans for the Foundation and convinced Nathan that his financial expertise was desperately needed. Finally, he agreed to "help out"—but flatly refused Joe's offer of a modest salary. He planned to privately invest what was left of his savings along with the generous "golden parachute" from VV&B to support himself.

Joanie was the only person to whom Nathan confided any details of his Warning (except for Chaplain Davis, who heard his confession the day after the accident). Nathan could not bring himself to tell her everything he remembered—most notably the fact that Nathan had fathered five children during his lifetime. Their haunting images were burned into his memory.

Joanie had borrowed her father's minivan for the occasion of leaving the hospital. Nathan surprised everyone by asking to see the little church that the Kolbe Foundation had just purchased from the Diocese of Fort Wayne.

Before Slinger's generous financial support, Joe had run the Kolbe Foundation out of a small warehouse near his apartment on Eddy Road. Up to twenty-eight workers and volunteers came daily to record tapes, work on computers, package materials, and ship them all over the country. The Kolbe Foundation was unusual in that it conducted no fund raising campaigns and didn't require donations for its materials. Joe had insisted on this policy from the beginning, after having studied the lives of Saint Maximilian Kolbe and Mother Teresa of Calcutta. People seemed willing to send in enough to cover costs. Joe believed this contrarian policy forced him and the workers to be especially efficient.

The "new" church Nathan wanted to see was actually quite old. It had served local Catholic farmers in the Mishawaka area for over one hundred years. It was aptly named Immaculate Conception Church. Immaculate Conception had suffered from dwindling attendance for decades because of the gradual takeover of much of Mishawaka's farmland by housing developments. A large and relatively new parish in Mishawaka put the final nails in the little church's coffin. The bishop reluctantly closed down the church when the one priest assigned to Immaculate Conception died a year earlier. The priest had been over eighty years old. Only four families (including the Huey Browns) remained on the rolls at the time it was closed. The lack of vocations in the Fort Wayne diocese, combined with the growth of the two nearby parishes, had forced the bishop's hand. The little wooden church could barely accommodate one hundred people and came with ten acres of land, including a small country cemetery. There was a tiny, two-bedroom rectory for Father Chet, and a small groundskeeper's farmhouse which Joe and Becky planned to move into after their wedding. There was also a dilapidated barn. There was no central heating—the church and the rectory were heated by woodstoves.

Immaculate Conception was less than two miles from the Wheat's home and was surrounded by farmland. It was set on a dirt road a quarter mile from the nearest paved road. The bishop of Fort Wayne was happy to "unload" the property to the Kolbe Foundation. The bishop had mild reservations about the activities of the unconventional apostolate, but cash was cash, and Jackson had cash on the barrelhead for Bishop DiPetro. It also didn't hurt that Joe and the bishop were both Notre Dame alumni. The church and land cost $101,000— furniture and an ancient tractor included.

Joe had dreamed of buying Immaculate Conception since the time it had been abandoned. As they drove up the dirt road in the minivan, Nathan and Joanie were only mildly surprised to see construction equipment on the land. The basement for a huge warehouse and shipping facility was already dug. The workers had gone home for the day.

"Wow!" Joanie exclaimed excitedly, "What have you been up to, Joe?"

"It's late in the season to be digging, but we don't have time to wait through the winter," Joe explained. "The bishop gave me permission to dig before the land was deeded over to the Kolbe Foundation, which technically occurred two days ago. The construction firm is owned by the husband of one of my workers—I gave him the basement dimensions before the building plans were even printed up, and he got started over a week ago. I even worked out a perfunctory fine with the town because we started construction before receiving a permit. Your dad helped pull a few strings with the zoning board. Fortunately, this land has few zoning restrictions. I doubt we could have pulled it off if we had started six months from now. It seems the whole town is being rezoned for residential developments."

Joe had obviously been busy working out the details. He had been on the phone several times a day with Karl Slinger. Both men thrived on two-minute conversations.

"Nathan, I want you to go over the numbers with me as soon as you're able to work," said Joe. "I want to build three more shipping facilities like this one in the next six months. This first one is the prototype. Each one will have state of the art computers, shipping lines, printing presses—the whole ball of wax. This one is going to have a small radio and television studio with uplinks to an SLG satellite. We're going to have similar facilities in Utah, another in North Carolina, and one in New Hampshire. Lee is closing a deal on a warehouse outside of Salt Lake City today. We'll be able to ship millions of books, videos, and audio tapes by next summer!"

"Joe," Becky pointed out, "aren't you asking Nathan to do a little too much, considering his condition?"

Nathan replied for Joe, "That's okay, Beck, I'm feeling fine. Nothing's more boring than sitting around in a hospital. I can't wait to get to work. Why don't we all get out and take a look around."

They all followed Joe into the church. The setting autumn sun cast rainbow shadows through the stained glass windows. The tabernacle was empty and there seemed to be a lot of dark dust on the walls. Joe told them that it was soot, leaked for decades from the huge old stove set in the middle of the church. He planned to install a modern heating and cooling system and to repaint and clean the building thoroughly. The ancient stove was actually a valuable antique that could be sold at auction to pay for most of the repairs.

It was cold inside. Joanie looked around the abandoned house of worship and wondered why she had never visited Immaculate Conception, despite growing up so close to it. She had scarcely known it existed. She had a wistful feeling of being transported back in time, imagining herself among the hard-laboring farm families who had come here by horse and buggy. She looked at Nathan, who was standing next to the altar. His eyes were transfixed on the most elegant piece of art in the building: a wooden crucifix. A single tear streamed down one of Nathan's cheeks. He wiped it away casually, trying to hide his contrition from the others. Only Joanie saw. Nathan turned and limped back to her side.

Joe noticed how gracefully Nathan maneuvered around in his cast and remembered their football game with Becky and Joanie on the South Quad. *So many things have changed since then,* Joe thought.

To each one of them it almost seemed blasphemous to pray in the church without the missing person: Jesus in the tabernacle.

After an awkward silence, Becky cleared her throat and spoke up, putting words to all their thoughts, "I can't wait until Father Chet gets here. This place needs a priest's touch."

Nathan turned and slowly left the old wooden House of God. The others followed.

✝ ✝ ✝

They stood at the cornfield behind the church. It was late in the season, and the corn they saw should have been harvested a few weeks earlier. Joe explained that a neighboring farmer was sharecropping the church's land and had been having trouble getting to it. Becky held Joe's hand while Joanie held Nathan's hand as they watched the sun set in the west. A cold but slight wind chanted through the fields. The sound of combines could be heard low and steady in the distance.

"I grew up in farm country, although the farms in Louisiana are different than up here—smaller, different crops," Joe said to no one in particular. "But one thing is the same; when harvest time comes, there's no tomorrow. There's only *now*. That's why they have lights on combines. Night harvesting. It doesn't matter if you're sick, or tired, or if it's too hot or too cold. When harvest time comes, you got to get after it.

"That's what it's like for Catholics who understand the signs of the times. We have to be like farmers before the harvest. There's not a minute to waste. Jesus once said, 'No one who puts his hand to the plow and looks back is fit for service in the kingdom of God.'"

Joe looked out at the cornfield as if he could see more than just corn there. Dark clouds were quickly forming in the bleak Indiana sky. One more cold rainstorm and maybe this corn would be useless.

"The harvest is great, but the laborers are few," Nathan added, surprising everyone except Joanie with a scripture quote. Nathan had been reading and memorizing the Gospels during his hospital stay. His demeanor was calm, his words reassuring as he continued, "I think we should make a commitment to keep our eyes on the harvest plow, all of us, together. Here, do this…"

Weather in Indiana is known to turn on a dime. As if on cue with Nathan's command, the wind started to kick up. The whispering in the cornfield turned to whistling. Nathan gestured for the foursome to face each other in a circle. Nathan then reached forward and grabbed Joanie's right wrist with his right hand. He then guided Becky's right hand to his own right wrist. Likewise, Joe clasped Becky's right wrist and Nathan closed the square formed by the two couples' hands and wrists. Their grips instinctively tightened as the first large droplets of rain began to fall from the suddenly dark sky.

Nathan closed his eyes and began to pray with a deep, surprisingly loud voice, "Dear Mary, we consecrate our hearts, minds, and lives to the harvest. Your Son said that those who sow the wind shall reap the whirlwind. Let us sow souls. Let us reap a whirlwind of souls."

All four opened their eyes as they sensed Nathan was finished with his short prayer. A tremendous gust of wind whipped up and almost knocked them over. Only Joe Jackson's physical strength and balance kept them all on their feet.

The wind was so loud that Joe had to shout to be heard, "It's going to be a nasty one! Let's get Becky out of the cold! Bruno's Pizza next?" Joe engulfed Becky with one large arm around her shoulders.

Nathan and Joanie nodded; Joanie helped support Nathan in the wind as they all found their way back to the minivan.

3

Friday Evening
27 October
South Bend, Indiana

They ate in the front room of Bruno's. The bad weather had kept the usually packed restaurant empty. Joanie was dressed up—for Joanie. She wore a solid green sweater, a black wrap skirt, and black loafers. Nathan was wearing his casual, usual uniform of forest green Polo cords, a Brooks Brothers button-down without a tie, and a blue blazer. The left leg of his cords had the stitches let out to accommodate his cast.

The rain had stopped. After the main course was finished, Joe gave Nathan a look and abruptly excused himself for a fresh-air walk with Becky. Nathan was completely silent as he moved a piece of crust around his plate.

Joanie eyed Nathan suspiciously. The Warning had profoundly changed him; she believed that Nathan was much more unpredictable. She could not read his calm expression. He was a different man in a way that went beyond his newfound and deeply held faith in Catholicism.

Nathan is mature, she thought. *The Warning transformed him into a man. The brooding, dark side of his personality is gone. He's calmer, and more taciturn than ever. Does he still love you? Did he win Pascal's Wager and lose me?*

Joanie's thoughts made her heartsick. It was the most acute anguish she had ever experienced—even worse than the insanely charged night of his accident. Her immense relief over his physical survival, and her jubilation that he had "returned" with an abiding faith in God, had been severely tempered by his coolness towards her. He was not cold—in fact, he treated her as a best friend. But only as a friend.

Joanie took another large sip of wine and averted her eyes from Nathan. She filled her glass again.

He had not uttered a single romantic word to her since their first conversation after the accident. In the hospital they had discussed the Church, his incredible mystical Warning, and made small talk. Her intuition told her to give him time, to let him think through whatever it was that was keeping him from her. Even the way he held her hand was somehow not the way a *lover*—in the chaste sense of the word—would hold hands.

He's been treating me like I'm his sister, she thought. *I don't want to be his **sister.** I want to be his wife.*

Gloom settled, a cape over her heart. She forced herself to accept the conclusion she had been avoiding for more than two weeks: *I'm going to lose him. Once he's made up his mind, he'll never change, and he's decided to forget about me as a potential spouse. And to think that I was setting conditions for marriage with him just three weeks ago.* She felt too bitter for tears.

She made herself look up at him. Nathan was appraising her with ever so slightly squinting eyes. *Here it comes,* she thought, *he's going to let me down easy.* Syrupy Italian music was being piped into the room, distant, mocking her emotions.

"I'm sorry, Joanie," Nathan whispered. "I know you've been suffering. I asked Joe to give us some time alone so I could talk to you."

He's going to tell me that it's over, she thought darkly. She felt her back stiffen; instinct was preparing her for the blow which she was so certain would come next.

"This isn't the right place, but you see, Joanie, we don't have much time, and I wanted to be certain before asking you to marry me that—"

"What did you say?" she cut him off, practically shouting the words.

"I said, before asking you to marry me, I wanted to—"

"That's what I thought you said!" She quickly and deftly reached for her wine, downed the entire glass, rose from her chair, threw her hand linen on the table, and went to him on the other side of the table.

"I do!" she flashed. A joyful smile brightened her entire face. "I do! I do! I do!" Oblivious to his ribs, she climbed onto his lap and slipped her arms around his neck, kissing him all over his face and neck. "Don't you dare take it back, Mister, do you hear me?"

"I suppose I have no choice! Hey, that hurts!" he protested, laughing despite his pain, pointing to his ribs.

"I'm sorry, sweetheart, did I hurt you?" Joanie asked, suddenly concerned.

"No, I mean, yes. I mean, it doesn't matter." He put his arms around his true love, ignoring his pain—somehow pain would never be the same to Nathan—and hugged her tightly. "I love you, Joanie. I want you to be my wife. I want you to have my children…" With the last sentence, Joanie heard the emotion fill his voice. He buried his face in her warm embrace. He felt the wool of her sweater on his cheek.

"Can I explain?" he suggested.

"This better be good, Mister."

"Like I said, I know you've been suffering. I haven't given you too many positive signs that I was still romantically interested since the Warning, Joanie. I had a long, terrifying debate with myself since the accident, a debate about *you*.

"I didn't think I deserved you. I didn't tell you all the things I saw when I stood before Jesus on the Cross. Some of the things I've done are too horrible to say out loud. I think that was the point: God wanted me to face those things before He showed me His merciful love.

"After I came back, the more I looked at you and saw how innocent, and good, and kind, and loving, and wonderful you really are, and how much you loved me, the more I thought you need a good man, not a guy like me.

"Then Joe came to the hospital yesterday and had a little talk with me. I guess Becky could tell that you were upset; she could read between the lines that you were losing hope regarding me and you as one."

He paused, and looked into her eyes for a long time. He could see that some of the hurt was still there.

"Go on, Mister," Joanie whispered. "Go on, lover."

"Joe told me to decide either way. He said that if I really cared about you, I would make up my mind to marry you or not. I told him that I didn't feel worthy of you. He told me that no one is worthy, and that if I learned anything about the Cross of Jesus, it's that the *only* worthy one *is* Jesus. Without quite saying so, he let me know that I was being selfish and that I was indulging in a kind of twisted pride.

"So I kept talking with him, and it became clear after about three minutes that only a fool would let a wonderful girl like you out of his sight. I decided to marry you last night with old Hoss sitting on my bed. We prayed a Rosary together, and then we set up this little romantic evening.

"Besides, like I said, we don't have much time. Joe and Becky are getting married on December eighth, the Feast of the Immaculate Conception, and Joe thinks that a double wedding would be nice. What do you think? I take it that you were referring to my as yet unspoken marriage proposal with the thousand and one *I do's?* Should I do it up right, formal and all, now?"

"Then propose, Mister," she commanded sweetly, tears welling in her eyes.

Nathan surprised her with his strength as he lifted her gracefully off his lap, and then, less gracefully, got down on his one good knee. He pulled a jeweler's box out of his blazer pocket and carefully opened it. It was the largest diamond Joanie had ever seen in her life. Her eyes widened. Her mouth dropped open, and she shook her head in disbelief.

"Joan Angela Wheat, daughter of Thomas Edward Wheat of Mishawaka, Indiana, will you leave your parent's home to cleave unto me; to become flesh of my flesh; bone of my bone; blood of my blood. Will you become one body with me, my wife and my love before God and before man, till death do us part?"

"I will, Nathaniel Timothy Payne. I will."

Nathan was still Nathan—there was a preternatural grace and smoothness to his movements as he took the ring from the box and gently placed it on her finger. He took his time, and Joanie burned the act into her memory. The act of placing the ring on her finger was as important as his noble, scriptural proposal. The moment stood still in time until Nathan broke it with a one word question.

"Well?" he asked.

"Well what, Mister?"

"Double wedding in two months with Becky and Joe sound good to you?"

"We can talk about it. Later, okay? Right now, Mister, I want to go home and show Mom this beautiful diamond!"

Little bells on the door rang as Joe and Becky returned. Joe looked at Nathan and smiled. Nathan nodded, then blushed. Becky ran over to Joanie, who held up her ring. The two friends embraced.

Becky pulled away and gave the ring a second, closer look. She tilted her head, pursing her lips before addressing Nathan, "Nathan, really! This ring is bigger than the one Rhett Butler gave Scarlet O'Hara! Emerald cut, too—very classy. You New Jersey boys are something else!"

Joe looked uncomfortable, but Nathan and Joanie thought she was hilarious.

Becky went on, a playful smile on her lips, "Where are you going for the honeymoon? The Grand Tour—London, Paris, Rome, Athens, Djibouti?"

"Djibouti? Where's that?" Joe asked.

"Africa, Joe. Djibouti is in Africa," Nathan answered. "Actually, Beck, Joe and I were thinking of the Palmer House in Chicago."

"I'd love to go to the Palmer House!" Joanie chimed in. She was so openly happy that Nathan briefly thought that if he suggested they honeymoon in Bayonne, New Jersey, Joanie would say "Fantastic!"

"Why is Joe going on your honeymoon, Nathan?" Becky demanded. Before Nathan could answer, Becky turned to Joe and asked, "Is this some kind of Catholic thing you haven't told me about? Are you going to chaperone Nathan and Joanie?" Becky was only half-kidding now.

Joe looked at Nathan. Guilt crept over the big man's face. Becky read him like a book. He opened his mouth to explain, but Becky beat him to the punch, "Have you been planning our wedding again without consulting me, Joe Jackson?"

"Becky, it was supposed to be a surprise! I was going to bring it up to you after I saw what happened tonight with Joanie and Nathan. Honestly, I just had the idea for a double wedding with Nathan last night. I wasn't in Chicago on business this morning. I was in the diamond district. I bought that ring in Chicago for Nathan this morning!"

"You so-called Catholic guys can be real sly dogs," Joanie observed.

"I might remind you that you just called your future husband a sly dog," Nathan lectured cheerfully.

"Let the chips fall where they may," Joanie rejoined regally. "I want another drink—and a toast!"

"And a smoke!" Becky added. Joe rolled his eyes.

The foursome found their glasses and Nathan topped off Becky and Joanie's with wine.

"To love and marriage!" Joanie toasted.

"Goes together like a horse and carriage!" Becky added.

"Hear, hear!" the men chorused.

4

Saturday Afternoon
28 October
Salt Lake City, Utah

Lee Washington sat at Karl Slinger's desk in the den of Slinger's home. Lee was reading a text on New Hampshire real estate law. His brow was furrowed in concentration. Lee was coming to the conclusion that multiple shipping facilities might not be the best way to organize the Kolbe Foundation. *I'll have to give Joe a call tomorrow.*

Slinger and Washington had developed a close, warm, but rather odd relationship. Even though he was older than Lee and had a more forceful personality, it was Slinger who constantly found himself turning to Lee for guidance regarding the faith.

Using his heart condition as a pretext, Lanning took a leave of absence from his public relations duties in the LDS and began to meet Lee at Karl's house for instruction in the Catholic faith. Lanning enjoyed learning from Lee. There was no false holiness or pride in the young man. Lanning often thought of the attribute the world considered a weakness but Catholics have always considered a strength: meekness. Lee Washington was meek.

Even before the heart attack Lanning loved to go for walks. Now the doctors prescribed it. He began telling Elena that he was going to exercise for a few hours. Slinger lived less than a quarter mile away from Lanning, making it easy for John to duck into Slinger's house to meet Lee for an hour or two.

Lanning and Lee spent hours poring over the teachings of the Catholic Church. They prayed silently together facing in the direction of the Cathedral of the Madeleine, which was visible on the bottom of the mountain from Karl's den.

Slinger helped Lanning find a Catholic priest in Saint George—three hundred miles south of Salt Lake City—who agreed to baptize the influential Mormon. More importantly, the priest was willing to keep the conversion secret until Lanning chose to go public. He had already taken the long drive down to Saint George to visit the priest two times. The baptism was scheduled to take place in secret one week from now.

Lee was fascinated by the circumstances of Lanning's conversion as well as disturbed by his explanations of Mormonism. When John and Elena were married, he explained, they agreed to put off having children to give themselves time and freedom to serve the Mormon church. She insisted on using the pill "to make sure" she didn't bear children. This practice never set well with his conscience, even though Mormons were allowed to use contraception—they were even allowed to have abortions if deemed necessary. There was no official teaching on either contraception or abortion. Mormonism had a curious lack of well-defined moral theology. A "moral" Mormon was one who kept the rules outlined in the Word of Wisdom—no drinking, no smoking, and so on. In this sense the practice of Mormonism did not involve an interior life and was much more concerned with keeping rules. In this and other ways it resembled Islam more than Christianity, and had, for that reason, been called the "American Islam" by scholars.

Seven years into their marriage the Lannings changed their minds and decided to have children. Sadly, before they could conceive, Elena developed ovarian cancer and was required to have a hysterectomy.

Lanning's harrowing journey to hell opened his mind to this universal teaching of the Catholic Church regarding the inherently immoral nature of artificial contraception. Elena's

barrenness had embittered and scarred her. After the hysterectomy, a coldness had entered their relationship. Over the
years the sweet, talkative woman he had married became cold
and distant, throwing herself with a vengeance into the myriad
activities sponsored by her ward.

Lee began to do odd jobs for Karl Slinger and the Kolbe
Foundation from Salt Lake City. Slinger had immediately
recognized Lee's abilities in negotiating and expediting business transactions. Consulting with Lenny Gold and using
Slinger's den as an office, Lee procured the perfect facility
for the western division of the Kolbe Foundation. Lee was
also helping Lanning plan his "going public" with his conversion to Catholicism. It was a bold plan. Lanning had a
flair for the spectacular…

Chapter Sixteen

1

Saturday Evening
28 October
County Galway, Ireland

On the day Luigi Cardinal Casino of Milan became an antipope, Dr. Barnard Soames operated on Pope Patrick to remove the bullet from his side.

Sister Mary Bernard called Doc Soames after watching the reports of Casino's election on the television. The nun now forced herself to watch daily newscasts. The ersatz election convinced Sister Mary Bernard to act decisively. Doc Soames, who had been prescribing some unusual drugs on behalf of Sister Mary Bernard in the last few weeks, didn't seem too surprised to receive her call.

Sister Mary Bernard invited the doctor to her office at Holy Blood Monastery. When the abbess told him the identity of the patient, he reacted with silence and a raised eyebrow. He merely nodded his agreement when Sister Mary Bernard asked him to promise to keep it under his hat. He followed the nun to Angus's room. The other three nuns were waiting for him there. Doc Soames examined Angus and his bullet wound for several minutes. He grunted and muttered something about lacking the proper equipment.

"Which one of you is the nurse?" he inquired brusquely.

"I am," Sister Elizabeth murmured.

"You've done a fine job, considering. But the wound *is* infected. You were right not to put off calling me in. I'll prescribe antibiotics for the infection after I cut the bullet out.

"It's been a long time since I've performed surgery, but I've done worse. In my youth I was quite a magician with the knife. You know, I'm not a good Catholic, but I *can* cut. I used to *love* to cut. Back in medical school, one professor told me that cutting is a gift that could be improved, but not taught. I should have been a surgeon. I'll never know why I chose family practice. Then again, maybe the reason why is now lying before us on this bed," the doctor said directly to Sister Elizabeth as if the other nuns were not in the room. He held up his gnarled, wrinkled, but steady hands.

"Because the patient is comatose we don't have to worry about anesthesia, at least," he added to himself.

He proceeded to ask several questions regarding recent changes in Angus's vital signs, grunting at her answers. Angus's temperature, which had been below normal when the pope arrived, had risen above normal during the last few days—indicating infection.

He asked all the nuns except Sister Elizabeth to leave the room. After they left, Doc Soames pulled a flask out of his breast pocket and took a long, slow gulp. He breathed out loudly, looking at Angus's wound, a pensive expression on his face.

"Doctor, do you really think you should—" Sister Elizabeth began to question him, but he cut her off mid-sentence with a glare. He returned his flask to his pocket. Then he scrubbed his hands in the sink, donned a surgical mask, and gave a mask to the nun. He pulled on surgical gloves. She followed suit.

Holding his gloved hands up like a television doctor, he said simply, "Shall we, Nurse Elizabeth?"

She opened his bag, sterilized his instruments, and laid them out on a silver tea tray covered with an altar cloth. She debated with herself whether she should pray for the pope or concentrate on helping Dr. Soames. She battled a feeling of uselessness.

In the end Sister Elizabeth did a little bit of both—except she prayed for Dr. Soames and concentrated on Pope Patrick.

✝ ✝ ✝

The operation lasted but a few minutes. Doc Soames hummed the entire time. It took less than thirty seconds to make a simple incision and reopen the wound. He then poked around until he found the bullet. After he was convinced that the bullet was not lodged inside Angus's spleen, he used a surgeon's version of a pliers to pull it out. Then he dropped the bullet unceremoniously into a small steel mixing bowl from the convent's kitchen. The bullet made a loud ping. The piece of lead seemed amazingly tiny to Sister Elizabeth.

Neither they nor anyone else would ever discover the fact that the bullet had been slowed down by Angus's mattress as he lunged behind it to avoid being shot.

During the operation Sister Elizabeth gently dabbed a cool washcloth on Angus's forehead. The pope's expression was so peaceful that it seemed to the nun as if she were consoling a sleeping child.

Most of the surgery was spent cleaning, dressing, and sewing the wound closed. As she watched the old doctor's fingers move with speed and precision, Sister Elizabeth was reminded of a documentary she saw years earlier in the States about an octogenarian piano virtuoso. The doddering Russian pianist became animated and young as soon as he sat down and placed his hands on the keys. Leaving the piano, he could barely walk or even bring a teacup to his lips without spilling the tea.

"That's that," the doctor chuckled. "Don't look so shocked, Nurse. He might be the pope, but a wound is a wound. Call it luck or call it grace, but now that the bullet is gone, the concussion on his head is more dangerous than the wound. Perhaps I can find an anti-inflammatory drug to relieve the swelling in the brain cavity. We wouldn't want to do brain surgery," he observed coolly. "I didn't see any damage to his innards, though, which I find so unlikely as to be miraculous. The antibiotics should take care of the infection. Nevertheless, I'll return on a daily basis to check on the patient. Call me if you observe anything unusual, Nurse."

Sister Elizabeth was stunned by his nonchalant demeanor. Dr. Soames was enjoying himself.

Just as long as he does a good job!

Soames quickly washed his instruments, packed his bag, and left without saying good-bye, still humming.

✝ ✝ ✝

Doc Soames spent the afternoon after the surgery at Matthew's Tap House. He said nary a word to his longtime drinking buddies about his unusual activities.

However, that night before going to bed, he did tell his wife about the pope's surgery. She thought her husband was out of his mind and advised him to give up medicine, as she had urged a thousand times before. He didn't try to convince her that he was telling the truth—it amused him to no end that she wouldn't believe him unless she saw "the pope and the wound in the pope's side," as she put it.

Two weeks later Mrs. Soames told the ladies in the sewing club about her husband's "fib." The old women in the sewing club got a big laugh out of it. One of the women told her daughter. The daughter, a reporter's wife, told her husband. Her husband brought it up with his editor at the Galway newspaper during the daily meeting. The editor humiliated the reporter by pontificating that the *Galway Standard* was not the *Galway Supermarket Rag*. The reporter put his notes into the circular file and forgot about the sensational, unbelievable lead—for the time being.

2

Monday Morning
30 October
Salt Lake City, Utah

"I want to resign. I'm retiring," Lenny Gold stated with perfect seriousness.

"You're kidding, right?" Karl Slinger asked in reply. He threw a folder down on his expansive desk.

"No. I'm serious, Karl. I'm not a Catholic—as if I had to point *that* out to you. Hell, I'm not even a good Jew. I don't have any idea what you're up to with this…this *crusade* you've embarked upon. SLG is not a media company. We help ranchers raise cattle and farmers raise crops. I don't know what I'm doing here. I'm like a fish out of water." He now had Karl's full attention.

"Lenny!" Karl shouted, dumbfounded.

"Karl, I'm serious. I'm getting old. I've been working with you for over forty years. You're too good a friend—I don't want to leave with hard feelings. I want to resign quietly. I'm tired. "

"You can't, Lenny."

"Why not?"

Karl smiled. "Because we're just getting started, for one thing. I can't do it without you, for another. Sure, you know I'll press on without you—but both of us know that we're five times as good at whatever we do if we do it together. Lenny, I need you. God needs you."

"But I don't believe in God. At least I think I'm pretty sure I don't believe in God."

"Now it's my turn to say 'so what?' Faith is not a job requirement for this project. While I wish you had the faith that I've rediscovered, I'm not foolish enough to think you can go pick up a bottle of belief down at the 7-Eleven."

Lenny chewed on Karl's last remark. Karl got up and went to the bar and poured two drinks. He didn't ask Lenny if he wanted one—Karl just handed him a glass.

"Look, Len," Karl continued, "all I need is one more year from you. You're right—you are old enough to retire and enjoy yourself. But Gwen is gone, what, eight years now? What will you do? Paint again? You're a lousy artist and you know it. Don't think of this project as a crusade so much as a change of direction. We're embarking on a great media challenge— a real long shot. Unlike the old days, we're not starting from scratch, sharing the same desk in a dingy office on the third floor of a cruddy building. It's going to be fun! We've got tens of millions to blow down the hole."

"That's what I mean, Karl. You never talked about blowing money down a hole before. Never! I thought the idea was to make money, not lose it. I've already disbursed over five hundred thousand dollars to the Kolbe Foundation—"

"Only half a million!" Karl angrily interrupted. "Joe Jackson's moving too slowly! He should be paying more attention to Lee Washington—that black boy knows how to get things done! Not that Joe's a bad guy—he's as much as admitted that he doesn't know what he's doing!" His bald pate turned a shade of red. Lenny mused that Karl always gave the same telltale sign when blowing his top. A smile crept to Lenny's lips, and he took a sip of his Scotch.

"Karl," Lenny said softly, "you've gone stark naked crazy."

"I swear, Lenny, too many people have told me I'm crazy in the last few weeks for me to have to hear it from you. Have I really acted any differently? Sure, I've been trying to spend more time with Dottie since my change of heart, but I scream and scheme just like the old days. And the old days were only three weeks ago!

"Another thing. You're wrong about SLG not being a media company. We always were primarily a media company. Oh, nowadays they call it 'leveraging information' and so much gibberish, but you balked when I wanted to blow money down the hole for short wave networks, and more recently, satellite uplinks for the bigger ranches. We're just switching from cows to Catholics."

"Listen to yourself, Karl. Cows to Catholics! Where you gonna set up the meat packing plant?"

Karl stopped short, then roared with laughter and spilled his drink.

"That's why I love you, Lenny. I'm just saying we've got to apply sound business principles to this project. We've got to move fast, innovate, use process engineering. Really, SLG has very few employees—everybody's on the ranches. I need somebody to act as a liaison between SLG workers here and Kolbe Foundation workers. You can do it, Lenny. Only you!"

It was true. Despite its size on paper, SLG Industries had less than two hundred workers in Salt Lake City.

"Admit it. I'm right. I was always the smart one—the ideas guy—you were the implementation guy. Like I said, the sum is greater than the parts."

"Always the diplomat, Karl! And you always express yourself with such sweet sensitivity, Big Mister Ideas Man." Lenny countered with practiced ease. "Dumb Polack," he added under his breath.

Even though Karl was worked up, he could tell Lenny was returning to form. *He's starting to come around,* Karl thought optimistically.

"Tell me something, Lenny—do you think that this Jackson guy, Nathan Payne, Becky Macadam, and Lee can pull off what we're planning without you?"

"Maybe."

"Give me odds," Karl demanded.

"Ten to one," Lenny indicated quickly. The lawyer *had* been thinking things over.

"And *with* your priceless guidance and experience?" Something in Karl's tone relayed to Lenny that Karl was not being sarcastic.

"Eight to one," Lenny responded just as quickly and certainly.

"More like five to one," Karl rejoined.

"But I don't understand what you're up to, Karl! Really, I'm lost. Maybe if I did, we could get those odds down. They're young, but it's a talented team you've put together. They work hard. I like Washington. You may claim to be a convert, Karl, but Lee is the real thing. I don't know what happened to the boy out in LA, but he's a black Moses come down from the mountain. He was explaining Torah to me the other day on the phone—Old Testament stuff—and I was actually listening until another call came in. It was just like being back in Hebrew School."

Karl took a minute to mull over Lenny's last statement.

"You know, Len, I believe you catch a lot more than you let on. Tell you what? Why don't you put off your resignation for a few months. Don't tell me that the challenge isn't exciting—you know it is. Take a few days off. Think it over. Fly out to South Bend and spend some time with Jackson. Let him talk to you about the 'philosophy of the Kolbe Foundation,' as he calls it. You don't have to convert—all we need is for you to be a part of the team. According to Jackson—and I agree with him—we don't have to force-feed Tom Wheat down anybody's throat. We're not 'selling.' We're just trying to give as many folks as we can an opportunity to listen to the warnings from heaven and to digest them. Even Jackson expects most people to reject the opportunity. The key is to get as many people to start praying as quickly as we can. Jackson calls it looking for the Ten Just Men.

"Tell me, do you really think that with all my money I could possibly spend it all? I don't care about money any more. In a certain sense, I never did. I just cared about winning. I've got a hundred times what you have and you couldn't spend all *your* money if you tried. Jackson says it's not about money, it's about effort. Somebody's got to give this a grand effort. You can help us do it! You can top off your career with one wild ride, buddy boy."

Karl could tell his words were working their way into Lenny's psyche. Karl stopped, returned to the bar and got the

Scotch bottle. He topped off the lawyer's drink. It was another old habit.

"You know, Karl," Lenny admitted finally, "I know you're liquoring me up. I know you're appealing to my ego. You're putting a challenge before me. You've even sunk to playing on my innate Jewish sense of being an underdog—all so you can blow your millions on this Don Quixote Catholic Crusade. And I hate it whenever you bring up the part about us sharing a desk in that tiny office."

"Well, it is working, isn't it?" Karl said with a piercing look, raising his glass to Lenny Gold.

"It always does, Karl, it always does. Okay. I'll give you three months. Then I reevaluate. Capishe?"

"Capishe, Len," Karl echoed, raising his glass. "We're just getting started, my friend." They clinked glasses.

Lenny just looked at Karl. He didn't smile as he might have done in years past, but he drank to Slinger's toast nevertheless. *Karl's "project" is dead serious,* Lenny thought uncomfortably. He had listened to Wheat's "Marian Apparitions" tape. It was scary stuff if it was true.

Karl broke the silence. "Okay then. Get that Jackson fellow on the phone and light a fire under his boots. You flying out there?"

"Sure, partner." Now Lenny *was* smiling. "I'll take the corporate jet tomorrow."

✝ ✝ ✝

Five minutes later, Karl's secretary informed him that Nathan Payne was on the phone. Karl hadn't spoken to the younger man since the accident. However, the largest flower arrangement in Nathan's room had been from Karl Slinger with a simple note attached: "Get Well. Slinger." Tom Wheat had kept Karl informed of Nathan's progress.

"Payne here," Slinger heard before he could speak. *The boy just beat me to the punch,* Karl thought self-consciously. *How often does that happen?*

"Slinger," Karl replied. "Joe tells me you're working for the Kolbe Foundation now. I also understand congratulations are due. Tom's daughter is a lovely girl. One of a kind, son."

"Thank you, sir. The wedding is December eighth. You and Mrs. Slinger are invited, of course. Mr. Gold, too."

"I'll be there. Dottie's already excited about meeting Joe and Becky."

A barely perceptible pause ensued. Karl was acutely aware that he was waiting for instructions from Nathan. *Strange, I don't mind,* Karl thought. *I haven't taken orders from anyone since the Corps.*

"Three items, Mr. Slinger—if you don't mind."

"I'm all ears, son," Karl replied, a bit curtly.

"I think you should send Lenny Gold out to see Joe Jackson. Lenny could give Joe some guidance. And I think he could benefit from being around Joe, too. Joe's a great guy, but he's getting bogged down with details. Joe knows it, too. I'm sure Joe won't mind working in areas that are more suited to his strengths," Nathan suggested diplomatically.

"Done. Lenny just left my office with plans to fly to South Bend tomorrow—how's that for a coincidence? What else?"

Coincidence? I don't know if I'm a step ahead of Nathan or if he's a step ahead of me.

"Mr. Slinger, can I be perfectly frank with you?" Nathan asked tentatively.

"Shoot. Don't mince a word. You don't have to dance around with me, although I appreciate your thoughtful consideration of your friend Joe. I also gather you've figured out that Lenny has been having second thoughts about our project. He just agreed to three more months of service."

"That's a relief. I was worried after talking with Lenny on the phone yesterday. I could hear it in his voice. We'll bring him around before three months are up." Slinger found himself taking consolation from the certainty he heard in Nathan's voice.

Nathan continued, "Mr. Slinger, I want SLG to contact its associated ranches and farms—except for the ones owned by

Mormons, of course. Offer them credit to purchase legal fire-arms, along with ammunition and resources to cache the weapons in hidden storage."

"Weapons?" Karl asked. "You really think it's going to come down to that?"

"I sure hope not. But we should be prepared for the worst."

"I don't think Jackson and Wheat will go for that."

"I don't think they will either," Nathan agreed. "In fact I know they won't. But I've been reading up on what Augustine and Aquinas say about Just War."

"You're talking about legitimate self-defense?"

"Right. We're not starting an army, Karl. We're not going to start a war. But we have an obligation to protect our families, and our freedom to communicate with each other.

"Even if the odds are one in a hundred, I couldn't live with myself if Joanie were hurt because we weren't ready for anything and everything. I'm not a Marine. I much prefer being a stock analyst."

Karl paused. "Hmmn. I think the analyst in you has been speaking all along."

"This is one time when the analyst hopes he's wrong."

"Me too, Nathan," Karl said gravely. "How should we get the ball rolling?"

"Becky is working up some language now for the 'offer,' and I'm sure Lee Washington can figure out how to get it all done in less than a month," Nathan replied. "Becky says we should consider the increase in crime nationwide, as well as SLG's concern for its associates to provide their own security. Unofficially, your ranch owners can let their neighbors know that SLG is willing to 'share' resources.

"You and I both know that prayer is going to win this battle. But if Professor Wheat's summary of Marian apparitions is true, then part of what's coming down the pike is unprecedented economic and social breakdown."

"When do you think it's coming?" Karl asked.

"I don't know. Nobody does. I'm just trying to foresee what we'll need. Social breakdown means no rule of law.

Severe economic troubles in a culture with weak moral values
will exacerbate social breakdown.

"I studied the documents Lenny Gold sent me a couple of
days ago. I'm glad to see that SLG properties have a redundancy of communication channels—telephones, land-based
computer cable networks, satellite uplinks, Internet stuff, and
perhaps most importantly, short wave radios. As long as
money is no object, Mr. Slinger, I want to double or triple
that redundancy. Uplinks on every property—not just the big
ranches. Two extra short wave radios hidden on each property. Maybe you know of a better kind of radio system? Oh,
and we should get mobile antennas—we may have to work
with a manufacturer to fabricate something to fit our needs,
based on existing technologies.

"Along the lines of our self-defense project, we should
offer comsystems to SLG ranch neighbors, in the context of
all the bad weather in recent years and our desire to be neigh-
borly." Nathan paused. Slinger's silence prodded Nathan to
continue. "Do you see the big picture, Mr. Slinger? Do you
know what I'm driving at?"

"I believe I do, but explain it to me anyway," Karl replied
soberly.

"I've been reading American history, Mr. Slinger—"

"Call me Karl, son."

"Call me Nathan," Nathan replied confidently.

"Touché, Nathan. Go on."

"There have been three major wars on our continent—the
Revolutionary War, the War of 1812, and the Civil War. The
primary lesson of wars fought on American soil is that while
enemies controlled the cities and every major port, no one
has ever controlled the countryside. Americans will fight for
their land. The British won every major battle except one in
the War of 1812 and controlled every city and port, but they
still lost. The South held off the North for four years with
one-tenth the men and one-twentieth the resources. During
the American Revolution, an ill-equipped and outnumbered
citizen army held off the regular soldiers of the mighty British

Empire for eight years. Again, the British controlled the major cities and ports for practically the entire war.

"In my opinion, the radios are more important than the guns. Joe says that the truth will set this country free, and if there *is* widespread breakdown of the rule of law, we want to have the ability to broadcast the truth with systems that can't be knocked out no matter what the enemy does. We'll control the countryside if we win the battle of the airwaves. If our peacetime media blitz fails to avert massive social breakdown, we have to be ready to get the word out in the worst case scenario. This country might just turn into one enormous Vietnam. If you've read the papers, you know that the Russians are already having the same problems—the social upheavals are already happening over there. I know, I lost my job over it before the accident."

"You lost your job over Russian social upheaval?" Karl asked, genuinely curious.

"Remember TDC?"

"I lost a few bucks in TDC myself, Nathan. Not much. Fifty grand or so. A dicey play—when I bought in I figured I might lose my shirt, so it didn't bother me when I did lose it," Karl fell into business small talk.

"But you rolled the dice, didn't you?" Nathan was leading Karl.

"Sure did," Karl answered amicably.

"These guns and radios are the same thing. It's like buying gold in a bull market."

"A good investor always hedges, Nathan."

"Speaking of hedging, Karl, have you considered transferring a significant portion of your wealth into gold—"

"It's already been done. We think alike."

"I'm glad we're of the same mind, then. I've got to go, Karl. Sorry to take up so much of your time. Say hello to Lee Washington for me. I can't wait to meet him in person."

"I will. My time is your time, Nathan. See you at the wedding if not sooner. God bless!"

"God bless you too, Mr. Slinger—I mean, Karl."

Both men hung up the phone at the same time.

He just gave me two multi-million dollar projects and I didn't bat an eyelash. Nathan didn't even confirm that I would go ahead with his ideas, which I have to admit, are sensible, if not brilliant. He knows I'll do it. Boy, I'm glad that he's on our side. Nathan Payne might just put us over the top before it's all over.

For a reason that Karl couldn't fathom, he had a sudden and strong urge to light up a cigar—even though he didn't smoke cigars. He pressed the intercom for his secretary. There was no screech or crackle in SLG's intercom system—it was completely digital.

"Sarah, get Lee Washington on the phone. Tell him I want to meet him for lunch. I've got a couple of projects I need to outline for him."

"Right away, Mr. Slinger."

"Oh, Sarah? See if you can procure me a fine cigar before I leave for lunch."

"Right away, Mr. Slinger," Sarah replied through the crystal clear hookup.

"Thank you, Sarah. Keep up the great work!"

"Thank you, Mr. Slinger!" *Wonder what he's so happy about?* Sarah thought.

3

Monday Evening
30 October
New York City, New York

Harlan Gello sat on the floor in his tastefully appointed office at the Omega Institute. He was in a lotus position. He was lean, but powerfully built, surprisingly limber for a man of forty-six. He emptied his mind of all thoughts—a technique mastered after years of practice. He pictured a completely blank white wall with a television screen in the center. In his mind's eye the screen came on and his spirit guide appeared to him. The spirit guide, who called himself Rangor, had been deceiving Harlan for several years. The conversation began. Gello believed that Rangor was the reincarnated spirit of a Hindu mystic from the third century, as the spirit guide claimed. In fact, Rangor was a demon. Gello was looking forward to Rangor's advice as to what to say on the taping of the Tonight Show scheduled for later in the afternoon.

Gello was a famous man. He had written a *New York Times* best-seller detailing his journey to the other side. In the book (with the help of an expensive ghostwriter) he had chronicled his life before being struck by lightning in 1976. Growing up, he had been a bad guy by his own account—a violent juvenile delinquent in high school; an abusive, womanizing alcoholic; a former Army special forces soldier and CIA operative. Before lightning struck, Gello had killed forty-seven people during covert missions for the CIA. He wasn't exactly an assassin but the nature of his missions in Nicaragua, Kuwait, and other places had been extremely dangerous. Gello had thrived. He enjoyed being a bad guy for a good country. Until lightning struck.

In 1976, while Gello was working on the transmission of his classic car in his driveway in Athens, Georgia, it started to rain. He was underneath the car and he didn't want to stop working when the rain began. What was a little water to a tough guy?

The bolt of lightning struck Gello in the feet and melted the metal pins holding the heels on his cowboy boots. His ears burned. He died. A neighbor called the paramedics. Like John Lanning, Gello went to hell while he was dead. Unlike Lanning, Gello didn't know it was hell. Lucifer himself appeared to Gello as an angel of light in the form of Jesus. "Jesus" told Gello that he was loved by God and that all men are destined to be embraced by the light. "Jesus" led him to a room filled with faceless beings of light who showed Gello what was going to happen to the world in the coming years.

When Gello was revived, he was a changed man. He asked for and received an honorable discharge from the CIA due to his medical condition. He could still walk and talk after the lightning, but he suffered occasional fainting spells. He carefully wrote down all he had been told by the beings of light, had his predictions notarized, and began meeting Near Death Experience (or NDE) experts to try to figure out what had happened to him. He began to explore various meditation techniques that fell under the general category of the New Age Movement, including Transcendental Meditation, Mind Control, and others. He became an expert on NDEs, and was currently preparing a second book chronicling the experiences of hundreds of other people who also met the understanding beings of light at the end of a tunnel before being revived. Accounts of people experiencing hell similar to John Lanning's—rarely reported by terrified survivors—were written off by Gello as inauthentic brain wave nightmares.

While using the television screen technique in his apartment one evening, Harlan was visited by Rangor, who claimed to be one of the faceless beings of light. Rangor revealed his face on this particular night. His face was beautiful, peaceful, and strong. He gave Gello unfailingly accurate business advice for the Omega Institute. Gello felt privileged to be serving a being so bent on helping mankind.

Many of the predictions given to Gello during his NDE
came true, which fueled sales of his book. For example, he
had predicted "a nuclear disaster in the Soviet Union at a
place called Wormwood" in the mid 1980s. The word for
Wormwood in Russian is "Chernobyl." (Wormwood is also
the name of the deadly star cast to earth in the eighth chapter
of the Book of Revelation—a fact never mentioned in Gello's
book.)

He moved to New York after making a fortune from his
book, and began to lecture—for larger and larger fees—at
colleges and before New Age groups. He appeared on Oprah
and Donohue, and was an occasional guest on the Tonight
Show.

Harlan Gello had a winning personality and a knack for
self-promotion. Everyone liked him and his positive message: Mankind, after a series of trials, would be transformed
to a higher level of existence. Peace and Love would rule the
world. Above all, Gello preached, there was no need to fear
death, because all men and women were powerful spiritual
beings destined to live in light forever. Traditional religions—
Protestantism and Catholicism—were scaring people into outmoded conformity by preaching about hell and sin. "Jesus"
himself had told Gello that we are all Jesus, all part of the
light. Gods. Everyone was destined for the light.

That's why Harlan Gello named his organization the
Omega Institute. The "omega point" in New Age circles was
shorthand for the final merging of all sentient spirit beings
into one vast, wonderful, shared godhood of light.

Harlan had abandoned his brutal, murderous ways after
the lightning. He truly believed he was helping the people of
the world.

He was nice. He cared.

He was *special*.

4

Friday Afternoon
24 November
Mishawaka, Indiana

Tom Wheat, Nathan Payne, Becky Macadam, Father Chet, and Joe Jackson stood up to greet Lee Washington and Joanie Wheat in one of the meeting rooms at the newly constructed Kolbe Center. Lee had just flown in from Salt Lake City for the meeting called by Joe. Joanie had picked him up at the airport.

After saying hello to the group, Lee took a look around the room. A new computer, not yet hooked up, sat on the floor next to its shipping box in a corner. The chairs around the cheap utility table in the center of the room were all different styles. Joe had picked up most of the furniture at the Goodwill near his apartment on Eddy Road. The Kolbe Center had been open for only a few days. Commercial carpeting had not yet been installed on the concrete floors. Wires, boxes, computers, and audio tapes were scattered everywhere. Shipping operations were being carried out in a hodgepodge manner in a huge central room that could be seen through a large window in one of the meeting room walls. Some of the workers were sitting on the floor while packing materials. Others worked on computers, entering the day's requests using cardboard boxes for tables and chairs.

Joe watched Lee take his look around. The disarray bothered Joe. He knew that temporary disorder was part of the much-needed expansion. He was a stickler for neatness and consistency. Before Karl Slinger started financing the greater portion of the Kolbe Foundation's operating expenses, Joe had built the foundation into the largest producer of Catholic audio tapes in the world by imbuing it with a philosophy of what he liked to call "charitable efficiency." Every worker was required to spend weeks in training. Everyone soaked up

Joe's philosophy. The Kolbe Foundation was run like a disciplined football team. He had no intention of wasting a dime now that Slinger's money was available. He planned to have the Kolbe Center humming within a few weeks. If Slinger's money ran out or his generosity came to an end, Joe wanted to be able to continue the work of the Kolbe Foundation.

At Joe's invitation, leaders of Catholic lay apostolates from around the country had been coming to benchmark the Kolbe Foundation for years. Most were surprised to find that Joe had a detailed, printed "philosophy course" which drew on the examples of such diverse models as Chuck Noll (former head coach of the Pittsburgh Steelers), United Parcel Service, Southwest Airlines, Mother Teresa, Saatchi & Saatchi, Land's End, baseball great Ted Williams, and State Farm Insurance.

"Our work is our prayer," Joe was fond of saying, "so our work must reflect the Divine Order." Another favorite saying was, "The money we receive belongs to the Blessed Mother— we must spend it boldly to help save souls, but wisely to avoid losing souls." Lee was already familiar with Joe's philosophy after dozens of phone conversations with him over the past two months.

Slowly but surely, Joe had delegated the day-to-day planning, purchasing, and operations to Nathan. Lately, Nathan had come to rely on Lee to do more and more work from Salt Lake City, prompting him to ask Lee to move to South Bend. Becky was already in charge of several workers in the informal advertising department. Joe spent most of his time training new workers, and making sure everyone was on track.

It was time to start the meeting. Father Chet led the group in a prayer, calling on the Holy Spirit to guide their discussion. Then the entire group prayed the Saint Michael Prayer composed by Pope Leo XIII in the previous century:

"Saint Michael the Archangel, defend us in the battle; be our safeguard against the wickedness and snares of the devil. May God rebuke him, we humbly pray; And do thou, O Prince of the Heavenly Host, by the power of God, cast into hell

Satan and all the other evil spirits who prowl through the world seeking the ruin of souls. Amen."

The brain trust took seats around the table.

Joe cleared his throat, then began, "I'm not used to running meetings. As most of you know, we don't have regular meetings at the Kolbe Foundation. I just wanted to get everyone together so we could be on the same page over the coming months, and before the weddings that follow in two weeks. I only wish Karl Slinger, Lenny Gold, and John Lanning could be here.

"Tom, could you tell everyone what you told me earlier today."

Wheat was uncomfortable sitting after spending years lecturing on his feet. He rubbed his hand on his crew cut before taking a sip of coffee.

"Thanks, Joe. I won't speak long. I called Joe this morning because I've been on the phone with my contacts in the Marian Movement around the country."

Wheat paused and swallowed hard.

"Since the new pope has been elected, nine of the top ten cardinals and bishops most loyal to true Catholicism in the United States have been given instructions by the Holy See to quote, unquote, 'retire early.' One of the bishops was only fifty-seven years-old and in perfect health!

"Two of these de facto forced retirements have already become public knowledge, including Cardinal O'Donnell of Chet's diocese. O'Donnell's going to be replaced by Bishop Brookings, the one who so generously gave Father Chet to the Kolbe Foundation two months ago."

Everyone in the room looked to Father Chet, who did not smile. Chet slowly nodded his head.

"Father Chet has told me that Brookings 'tipped his hand' when he ran Father Chet out of the Newark Archdiocese," Tom Wheat continued, "and there have been rumblings in Rome that the vote for our new pope, the former Cardinal Casino, was somehow fixed. Cardinal O'Donnell told me two days ago that practically all the bishops he knew at the conclave had voted for Cardinal Nugumbu of Africa—a very holy man by all accounts. The secular media around the world has played down rumors of a fixed vote, if not ignored them altogether. The media is more interested in celebrating the new pope as a progressive who is finally in touch with the average Catholic, especially regarding contraception and women priests."

"I can't give you any certain answers. My gut feeling is that the Great Schism foretold by Our Blessed Mother through Father Gobbi has begun. The new pope has said very few things publicly—practically nothing at all. Maybe he's a pawn and the forced retirement of solid bishops is the work of others. I don't know if similar forced retirements are occurring in other parts of the world. If Casino *was* validly elected, a rumor that the vote was fixed is harmful to all Catholics.

"So I will reserve judgment on the new pope for now. Is Casino an antipope? Who knows? But we're in for months, perhaps years of confusion. The work of the Kolbe Foundation and other Marian apostolates around the world takes on a greater urgency. No matter how bad the trials get, we must keep in mind the promise by Our Lady of Fatima of a period of unprecedented peace after it's all over."

Joe noticed that Wheat had trouble calling the new pope by his papal name, Pope John XXIV.

"But how could this be?" Becky asked. "Isn't there a guarantee that the Church will always have a real pope?"

"Yes, there is," Wheat replied calmly, "but there is always an empty Seat of Peter when a pope dies. And there have been several antipopes in history. Or, the reigning pope is in hiding. They never did find the body of Pope Patrick. I'm not saying he's alive. It's just a hypothetical possibility. There wasn't much mention in the American press, but the body of the seminarian in the pope's car disappeared from the morgue the night it was recovered. The whole story is beyond strange.

"So those are the scenarios for an empty Seat of Peter."

A pregnant silence filled the room as the group mulled over the implications of Wheat's words. Faithful Catholics deeply and sincerely love whoever is pope, as a person as well as the holder of an office. After all, the pope is the living representative of Christ on earth. To even consider John XXIV as an antipope was a terrible thing.

Joe cleared his throat and spoke up, "Becky, could you outline the status of advertising campaigns?"

Becky opened a folder and began to speak in a professional tone of voice, "Our ads in the ten major secular daily newspapers and the five secular news magazines are set to run starting next week through February. We can track the response as the ads come out when requests for 'Marian Apparitions' tapes start to roll in. We've also produced a simple television ad at a local television station with Father Chet offering the free tape, but we haven't picked out the programming to run it on yet. I'm still working on it, but we want to be on network television before the end of February. We're also setting up sixty-second spots to run on major national radio talk shows.

"Then we'll have an idea of how much we need to tool up for the shipping facilities, and so forth. Nathan is going to be working with Lee on having the computer systems and shipping lines ready before we get overwhelmed—that's going to be a lot easier now that Lee is living here with Father Chet. We'll need a lot more workers. Then we can prepare more ambitious campaigns in the spring when we have some idea about response rates.

"The response rates from secular media ads will be much lower than the 'Free Tape' ads you've been running in major Catholic publications over the last two years, but we're offering the materials to tens of millions of people instead of hundreds of thousands. It's useless to rush to place ads if we can't ship tapes for months, because we'd get overwhelmed by orders. We need more information to coordinate marketing with production and we'll have it soon.

"The whole project has been overwhelming. We're not an advertising agency, but in the long run we can actually do things much faster, and at less cost, if we do them ourselves in this first stage. We can even decide to farm out advertising to professional agencies once we have the capacity to meet requests for tapes. We'll have more control, too.

"Finally, we're buying mailing lists of Catholic households. I'm talking about millions of addresses. We're going to have a Chicago company that specializes in mass mailings send a simple, tasteful letter offering 'Marian Apparitions' free of charge, no strings attached. I used to work with this particular Chicago mailing house. They're very professional and our first mailing goes out next month. Somewhere around 500,000 letters—"

Lee whistled softly when he heard the large number.

Becky smiled pleasantly, then continued, "Of course, we'll have to figure out the response rates just like we'll do with the television and print ads. Then we'll gear up production accordingly.

"As you can see, reaching the whole country isn't that complicated. It's simple, really. It just takes a little planning, hard work, and lots of money." Becky took a deep breath as she finished.

"Thank you Becky," Joe said softly, smiling with closed lips. "You're doing a fine job. We'll have to figure out how to get more workers in here and trained. There are over a thousand Knights of Immaculata in the area, and we'll continue to call them for help. We're planning to hire, what, twenty more part-time workers? I've already trained fifteen new volunteers in the last four weeks." Joe tapped a pencil on the table top as Becky nodded.

"Nathan?" Joe asked.

Nathan cleared his throat. His report was typical Nathan— short and sweet; facts with few opinions: "SLG Industries has been doing a great job setting up the backup comsystems, thanks to Lenny Gold. Over seventy-eight percent of SLG ranches have taken up the offer to stock arms. Fortunately, Karl tightly controls the board of SLG so there's been no protest in that area.

"We're hiring a full-time computer or 'MIS' manager from a local Novell firm—also a Knight of Immaculata who has done piece work for the Kolbe Foundation before, Hal King. We'll have over one hundred workstations up and running here before Christmas to handle requests. We don't have fifty workers ready to use them, however.

"We're set for the January ninth weekend retreat for Marian leaders. I offered plane tickets for those who couldn't afford to come, and most took me up on the offer. Incidentally, at Lee's suggestion, we've hired a multiple fax service so we can contact all of them in less than five minutes whenever we wish.

"As Joe and I discussed last week, Lee's suggestion that we scrap plans for several branches around the country and concentrate on making the Kolbe Center here a 'supercenter' has made planning a lot simpler. We simply don't have the workers or the time for organizing branches. We'll keep the building in Salt Lake City that Lee leased as a 'mini-shipping' center to speed deliveries to the western half of the country, but with much fewer workers there. It should be up and running in less than two weeks. A satellite burst line between here and Salt Lake will merge our computer systems in real time. That way, Lee can move here and work here.

"We can supply and train existing Marian Centers around the country with our materials in the meantime. We can refer people who want materials we don't stock to Marian Centers which do stock them. A Marian distribution network is already out there. It only needs to be developed, and we can help coordinate things. Why reinvent the wheel? Our focus will be to take the existing wheel and make it spin faster."

Nathan stopped to take a sip of Snapple.

"Can I say something?" Lee asked.

"Sure," Joe said, "just jump in. You don't need my permission, Lee. Without your knack for cutting corners, we wouldn't be here today. Every time you think of an idea, it's like mining gold." Everyone at the table nodded.

Lee looked down, embarrassed. Privately, he prayed to Jesus for guidance in what he was about to say.

"I don't want this to sound negative…" Lee started, hesitating, "and I think that all the stuff we're doing is great, and needs to be done, but the only answer to the problems we face is spiritual.

"You all know that. You know that the enemies we face, as Saint Paul wrote, are powers and principalities. When we get down to it, the only weapon we need is prayer. All our materials, especially 'Marian Apparitions,' are designed to get people to pray, live a sacramental life, evangelize, and to do reparation for sin.

"It should start with us. While we can't require workers to do these things, our example should inspire them. Father Chet agrees, and wants to set up perpetual adoration of the Eucharist in Immaculate Conception, twenty-four hours a day, every day. Joe and Nathan, you already pray before the Blessed Sacrament for an hour each day. Even if all our other activities fail or amount to nothing, at least we'll have obeyed the first request of the Blessed Mother. Prayer." Lee failed to mention the three or four hours he spent before the tabernacle every day in one hour segments. Everyone in the Kolbe Foundation knew they could always find him in Immaculate Conception when he wasn't working.

"I agree with Lee," Chet said simply.

"We all do," Wheat added. "I'm sure Anne would want to sign up for an hour a day, and I'm going to add an extra hour a day here after work, in addition to the hour I spend at noon at Notre Dame."

Everyone looked to Nathan, who nodded agreement. This seemed to seal the matter.

"Thanks, Lee," Joe said sincerely. "With all the disorder and activity, as well as planning the wedding, I have to admit that I've been tempted to justify not praying as much on the excuse that I've got work to do. Prayer is the measure of our love for God.

"I believe with all my heart that this little team was assembled by Mary as a direct answer to tens of thousands of Kolbe Foundation benefactors who pray for us daily. I've been praying for a Karl Slinger to show up for years. The real workers are the dedicated benefactors who distribute our materials to their friends and relatives at great personal sacrifice. Our success will be measured by how many more evangelizers and prayer warriors we add to the Marian Army. That's always been our goal—to substantially expand the remnant," Joe finished and took a breath.

"If there aren't any more questions…" Joe paused. No one had questions. "Then let's get to work. Chet, if it's okay with you, can we start Eucharistic adoration tomorrow morning at six? I'm there anyway. I'll fill in whatever hours are needed until we get people to sign up—"

"We'll all fill in, Joe," Nathan interrupted gently. "I'm usually awake before five, so I'll come in before you. I'll go out to the shipping floor right now and start signing people up." Nathan usually went to sleep before midnight and rarely slept more than five hours a night.

"Sign me up from midnight to two," Lee told Nathan.

Nathan made a note on his legal pad.

"I'll go in at seven, before school—write that down, honey," Joanie, who was sitting next to Nathan, volunteered, tapping his notepad.

"I'll take from eleven to twelve, as preparation before I say noon Mass," Chet added, smiling.

"And I'll come in at five after my last lecture—" Wheat said.

"Hey Chet, let me finish writing this down," Nathan protested amiably.

"Okay, okay. I see it's going to be a snap," Joe observed, standing up. "Maybe we should build an enclosed walkway from the Kolbe Center to the side door of the church—" Joe suggested half-seriously.

"I've already called the contractor," Lee pointed out.

Joe opened his mouth to say something but stopped himself. After a moment he said, "Let's go for it, Lee."

Chapter Seventeen

1

Thursday Afternoon
7 December
Mishawaka, Indiana

Two women stood next to each other in the stockroom of the Kolbe Center.

"I just can't *imagine* what Joe sees in her," Kelly Jones told a new volunteer in a conspiratorial tone. "She's such a cold fish. You've only been here a few days, and you can tell that. The way she orders us around like she's God's gift really bothers me, too."

"I kind of like Becky," the newer worker said. "But she does expect everyone to work super hard. That's not right. I mean, I'm a volunteer. I don't need to get bossed around."

Kelly Jones moved in for the kill, whispering loudly, "I hear she's pregnant and that Joe Jackson is definitely *not* the father, that's what I hear. Joe is so naïve, really. He's a child being led around by his you-know-what because Becky used to be a fashion model or something. And I heard her talking with Joanie Wheat about her wedding dress. A white dress." Kelly said "white" as if it was a dirty word. "The nerve of her. The least she could do is wear something that doesn't make a mockery."

"What's wrong with wearing a white dress?" Naomi Adams, the new worker, asked quite reasonably.

"You're only supposed to wear a *white* dress if you are a *virgin*, dear," Kelly answered in a kind but slightly patronizing tone. "Joe is so sweet, I really worry that she'll drag him down. Oh well, I'm not going to let Becky Macadam ruin *my* day. I've got to get these new forms to everybody's desks, even if Miss America did tell me to do it."

Kelly Jones finished her assassination of Rebecca Macadam's reputation. Kelly had only been working for the Kolbe Foundation for one month. She was quite pretty, but not nearly as pretty as Rebecca Macadam. She was also infatuated with Joe Jackson. Kelly spent much mental time and energy thinking up ways to be around him during the day. When Kelly's mother, a longtime Kolbe Foundation worker, suggested to Kelly that the foundation needed extra workers, Kelly had volunteered reluctantly—until she got one look at Joe Jackson. Kelly was between jobs and needed to kill time. Her mother had hoped that volunteering at the Kolbe Foundation would help revive Kelly's faith.

So Kelly stayed on and was eventually asked to work full-time for a small hourly wage because of her secretarial experience and apparent dedication.

Kelly walked out of the stockroom, leaving the poison to settle into Naomi Adam's system. Kelly did not see Rebecca Macadam, who had heard every word of the conversation, behind the room divider in the makeshift stockroom.

✝ ✝ ✝

Becky tried to put Kelly's words out of her mind, but found it difficult to concentrate on her work. Finally, overcome with emotion just thinking about it, she ran out of the Kolbe Center. *How many of the other girls think about me the way Kelly does?*

Lady, Joe's new collie, ran up to Becky as she hurried out the front door of the Kolbe Center. Tears were in her eyes as she struggled to keep her composure.

"Oh Lady!" she called as she picked up the puppy and held it. Lady's warmth made Becky realize that she had forgotten her coat. It was quite cold outside. She hugged Lady to herself all the more as the puppy tried to lick her face.

"You don't care who the father is, do you, Lady? You like me no matter what I am!"

Becky looked up and saw Father Chet pull up in his old Chevy. There were over thirty cars in the unpaved lot. She quickly fished a handkerchief from her pocket and tried to dry her eyes and make believe she was blowing her nose. Lady jumped from her arms and ran to Father Chet.

Too late. I can tell by the look on his face that he knows I'm upset. Indeed, there was an expression of concern on Chet's face.

Since moving to South Bend, Chet had made a habit of meeting weekly with Becky to give her spiritual direction and to go over questions she raised as she worked her way through the *Catechism.* He had also given Becky and Joe (along with Nathan and Joanie) their required marriage preparation course. Immaculate Conception Church was not officially a parish, but the overworked pastor of the church in Mishawaka had gladly delegated the marriage preparation job to Father Chet. The pastor, Monsignor Wilson, had taken a liking to Chet, and convinced the bishop of Fort Wayne to let Chet fill in for Sunday Mass at Wilson's parish. Wilson was a steady old priest and not at all like Monsignor Whelan of Notre Dame du Lac in New Jersey.

Chet was comfortable in his new job as chaplain of the Kolbe Foundation. He was able to hear confessions for two hours every day in Immaculate Conception. Penitents were already starting to come to him from all over the area. Lee Washington's suggestion to begin perpetual adoration was a stunning success—Chet was more than pleased that there were up to ten people in Eucharistic adoration in Immaculate Conception at any given time during the day. In the confessional and during his daily work at the Kolbe Foundation, he observed the effects of perpetual adoration first hand. Slowly but surely lives were being transformed through the Eucharist. Immaculate Conception would soon be too small to hold all the workers and local Catholics who attended morning and noon Masses. Starting next week, he planned to add an evening Mass after working hours.

Because Chet wasn't saddled with the daunting administrative duties of a pastor, he was able to fill his day meeting Kolbe Foundation workers for spiritual direction and catechetical teaching. He also taught a half hour lesson on the *Catechism* after noon Mass. When the priest found spare time, he worked in the packing department with the workers and kept everyone laughing. Along with Lee and Nathan, Chet ate most of his dinners at Joe's farmhouse across the yard from the tiny rectory. The past three months had been the happiest of his priestly life. He had also tried to cut down on his drinking. He knew he didn't have a "problem" with booze, but cutting down helped keep his head clear for prayer and work. Twice a month he met with Father Duffy at Notre Dame for confession and spiritual direction. The old priest had long since retired from teaching, but was overjoyed to have Chet back in his life.

When he saw Becky trying to hide her emotions, he instantly began to pray for her: *Dear Mary, please let me help your daughter Becky on the day before her wedding. It's probably just the jitters. I'll leave it up to you and to her whether she needs to talk.*

"Hi Beck!" he called loudly, trying to sound cheerful, petting the puppy jumping on his leg. "Down, Lady. Down girl!"

"Hello Father, how are you? Back from town?" She tried to smile naturally, but her lips felt cold and tight. A small sadness crept into her voice.

"I'm doing great. Just picking up a few groceries," Chet replied, holding a brown bag in one arm. "With Joe going out of town for the honeymoon and you moving in, I'm going to have to start cooking my own dinners."

"You can eat dinner with us every night of the week! You can count on it, Father," she said.

Father Chet knew better. Newlyweds needed their privacy. The truth was, Chet could have dinner with any number of Kolbe Foundation workers most days of the week if he wished.

An awkward silence followed. Chet was reminded of the first time he met Becky in the coffee shop in Chicago.

"Remember when we first met, Beck?" he asked, trying not to sound like he was fishing for an opening.

"You don't have to hint. Don't worry, I won't burst out in tears this time. I guess I need to talk. Maybe I should talk to Joe about it. I'm so confused. And I'm also cold." She looked at Lady, who was now romping near the harvested cornfields. She avoided Father Chet's eyes.

"It's up to you. We can talk in the rectory if you want," he offered equably, also watching Lady. "I've got to bring these groceries inside either way."

Becky thought of the terrible things she had heard, shivered, and answered by taking a step toward the rectory.

✚ ✚ ✚

Father Chet led her to his favorite counseling room—the kitchen. After putting away his few groceries, he put a pot of tea on the ancient woodstove. He preferred to give advice at the kitchen table. His father had often gathered his sons around the kitchen table to discuss life and its problems. James Sullivan would smoke his pipe and often served hot toddies made with bourbon. The discussions would range from politics to authentic Christian sexuality. Chet often wondered if his high school friends—frequent guests at Mr. Sullivan's bull sessions—liked his dad more than they liked Chet himself. Mr. Sullivan was cool. He even allowed the older guests to smoke cigarettes!

Once they got settled at the little wooden table, Chet began with the same words he had used in the coffee shop in Chicago, unaware of the repetition, "Sometimes it helps to just start, Beck."

"I know. I know. I was in the stockroom this morning, thinking about the rehearsal dinner tonight, when I overheard the most horrible things from two foundation workers…" Becky related the conversation between Kelly Jones and

Naomi Adams. "I felt like going up to that Kelly Jones and ripping into her! I'm so angry! What should I do? Am I allowed to fire people?"

Father Chet rubbed his forehead and took in a deep breath. He prayed to the Holy Spirit for help.

"Becky," he began, "I know this is going to be hard advice for you to take, but I don't think you should confront Kelly at all." He saw a look of surprise come to Becky's face.

"It would only make matters worse," Chet continued. "Kelly is a relatively new worker, and I honestly believe that she doesn't know any better. Believe me, I know that destroying another person's reputation—especially by slanting the truth—is a grave sin. But Kelly doesn't have a problem with you so much as she has a problem with Jesus and the commandments.

"The best thing you can do is to treat her with as much consideration and kindness as you can manage," Chet advised, thinking of the brutal treatment he had experienced from Monsignor Whelan and Sister Margaret.

"But she's trying to hurt me! She's spreading lies about me! Indirectly, she's trying to hurt Joe and that *really* ticks me off," Becky fumed, now so angry that her tone of voice was lower and harsher.

"And Christ said to turn the other cheek," Chet replied evenly.

"I don't get it...it's just not right," Becky protested, confused but still indignant. She took a sip of tea and put the cup down hard on the saucer.

"Settle down, Beck," Father Chet said, looking at her cup and saucer. "Look, we normally think of suffering as dealing with illness or poverty or stuff like that, right? But the worst suffering by far is mental anguish. You've just been heaped with a truckload. This is your cross. I know it's not going to be fun for you to be wondering what terrible rumors are being spread about you. Even if Kelly Jones were to leave the Kolbe Foundation tomorrow, the rumors are going to persist.

"Gossip is poison. The antidote is humility, meekness, and charity. Being kind to Kelly is probably going to make her meaner in the short run. But your example to the other workers who know the *real* you will be an inspiration in the long run."

"Okay, I get it," Becky said doubtfully, "I'm supposed to let myself get walked all over by some petty b—" Becky, who was working on her language, cut herself off before finishing the word. "But I'm still not buying it, Father. If anyone treated me this way back at the ad agency, I would have dealt with the situation fast."

"I know you would have. But this isn't an ad agency. The fact is, you are pregnant by a man other than Joe. The word is out, and unkind people are going to say and think unkind things about it. And you *are* somewhat bossy." Father Chet winced, bracing himself for her reply.

"I am *not* bossy! And you don't believe Kelly, do you?" Becky turned an angry gaze on Father Chet.

"Let me explain," he said softly.

"I'm listening—very carefully, Father," she said, folding her arms.

Chet knew that Lee was praying in front of the Eucharist at that very moment in Immaculate Conception. Before he answered Becky, the priest prayed quickly for a share in the grace Lee was bringing into the world.

"Let me put it this way. One of the reasons I think we get along so well is because you've got a lot of New Jersey in you. You're brutally direct. You don't try to put a rosy spin on problems, yet you're always an optimist. You've got a sarcastic, biting sense of humor. You take every job you do seriously and you expect everyone else to fall in line. You're a fighter. I like that, I really do. Where I grew up, that earns a person's respect. Around here, some people think the same behavior is bossy."

Becky was surprised at Chet's strange list of compliments. "You make me sound like I'm a drill sergeant or something!"

"Right," Chet replied, a gleam in his eye, letting his words sink in.

He got up and refilled his tea. He pulled a bottle of bourbon out of a cabinet and poured a nip into the tea. He offered the same to Becky. She nodded, so he made her a hybrid toddy, thinking of his dad. They both lit up a smoke.

"Still haven't quit?" she asked.

"One of my few remaining vices," he acknowledged, arching an eyebrow.

"I'm trying to cut down—for the baby. Bossy? Do I really come across that badly?"

"Hey, I don't think it's bad. That's my point. I hate clichés, Beck, but I like you just the way you are. Let me play amateur psychologist for a minute." He gave her a blithe smile.

"I can't wait to hear this pearl of wisdom, O Great One," she said unenthusiastically. "Oh, there's that wonderful sarcasm you love so much, Father Sullivan. How dainty!" She smiled wanly, squinting her eyes and tilting her head slightly.

Chet laughed and sipped from his cup.

"Oh Becky! You remind me of something I read about Gabriella Sabatini, the tennis star from Argentina. She was such a national hero down there that when she went for training runs in the streets of Buenos Aires, people came to their windows and yelled, 'Don't die Gabriella! Don't die!'

"Please Beck, don't die!"

"Seeing how much it means to you, I suppose I could continue breathing for several more minutes," Becky said, stifling a smile.

"Okay, okay. Do you want to hear this or not?"

"Go ahead, Father Freud. Tell me, what am I? Let me guess—I'm a man trapped in a woman's body, right?"

"Nothing of the sort," Chet replied, playing it straight. "Let's put it this way. You lost your dad when you were young, and your relationship with your mom was ice cold—polar. Like most kids in that situation, you developed—how should I put it—a hard edge. On the positive side, instead of retreating within yourself, you developed a certain toughness. I see the same thing in Nathan—don't you?"

"Yeah, I guess so," Becky agreed. "Nathan's quiet on the surface, but tough as nails underneath. He's not going to change his mind, either, unless you give him excellent reasons. Am I really like that?"

"Sort of," Chet replied, relieved that he had been able to bring up a sensitive topic successfully. "Why do you think most of your friends around here are men? With the exception of Joanie, who's pretty tough herself, haven't you gotten along better with men most of your life? Maybe that's why you gravitated to one of the most cutthroat industries in the country—advertising? You could have been a model, but you chose a career that depended on your brains. Quite the opposite of your mother, by the way, who's been trading on her looks her whole life.

"That's why Nathan likes to work with you and why Joe wants to spend every minute of his life with you, starting tomorrow. Contrary to the feminist party line, strong men like strong women. I've known Joe for years, and he never so much as had a crush on a girl 'til he met you."

"He tells me all the time that he likes my 'Sherman tank' personality— "

"Right! And some of that toughness comes out when you're working at the Kolbe Foundation. I'm not advising you to lighten up on your standards, Beck. I'm telling you not to let whatever Kelly or anyone else says get under your skin. Sure, it wouldn't hurt for you to be extra courteous and kind around the office, but keep your high standard of excellence. The only one in the whole place with higher standards is Joe, which is why he gives you so much free reign. Regardless of whether or not you're engaged to him, you've earned your working stripes with Joe. He's told me that. Nathan agrees.

"In the meantime, offer up your suffering for souls in purgatory—say a little prayer to the Sacred Heart or 'I love you

Jesus' whenever you get miffed or bothered by thoughts about Kelly.

"My guess is that Kelly will either conform to the charitable atmosphere around the Kolbe Foundation, or leave it, eventually. It's good for her to be here. She doesn't practice her faith, you know. I think her mom was hoping that working here would help her out—"

"She's always hovering around Joe, you know," Becky interrupted, anger and realization creeping into her voice.

"I know," Father Chet said sympathetically.

"You do?"

"Yes. Joe's mentioned it, but I'm not at liberty to say more." Chet could see the look of surprise in her eyes. "Let's just say that Kelly has been bothering him. He's very sensitive, as you well know. I *can* say that Joe told Nathan to have Kelly do work that keeps her in other areas of the foundation. That's why she's been working for you more and more lately. None of us knew she was trying to hurt your reputation. Sometimes you're not like a woman at all, Becky, because women generally pick up on these things better than men. It's obvious now, isn't it, that Kelly has a crush on Joe? Her attack on you is a childish way of trying to get him to pay attention to her. And *that* will never, ever happen, knowing Joe."

"What's going on here, Father? I thought this was a Christian outfit. I thought I left office politics back in Chicago."

"The Kolbe Foundation is not immune to this kind of stuff. Considering how the work it does helps save souls, these kinds of things are to be expected. It's the evil one's backdoor way of trying to destroy us. As the chaplain, I see it and hear it more than anyone else. Joe is well aware that infighting and subtle attacks on the peaceful atmosphere of this place are ways the evil one will try to undermine our work. That's why Joe wanted me to come here—to help fight this unseen war with spiritual weapons like the sacraments, prayer, and spiritual direction for those who are willing to take it."

"Joe calls you the black robe," she observed.

"And that I am. Just because what we're doing is good doesn't mean we're all magically going to drop our faults and weaknesses when we walk in the front door. So Joe tends to get bogged down in details. Sometimes I tip the bottle a bit too much. You tend to overwork yourself like you did in Chicago—what other woman would come to work the day before her wedding? And gossips like Kelly will do their kind of damage."

He saw that his reasoning was having its effect on Becky.

"The Kolbe Foundation is different now," he continued, speaking as much to himself as to Becky. "It used to be that Joe could pick and choose his paid workers from volunteers who had proven their dedication and value over months and years. That's not possible anymore. And volunteers aren't as willing to follow instructions as paid workers—that's just the way it is with volunteers. I'm not running volunteers down, either; volunteers do much of the drudge work around here. In the old days—lo three whole months ago—everybody was involved with everything and everybody knew everyone. That's over. You, Lee, Joe, Hal, and several dozen others— each with unique and sometimes strong personalities—have come together rather quickly, and we're under a lot of pressure. This kind of expansion is hard enough to pull off in the secular world. It's much harder to accomplish for a spiritual endeavor. Lee is right; prayer is our best weapon."

"So that's why you want me to turn the other cheek? For the good of the Kolbe Foundation?" Becky asked, clearly much more willing to follow through on his hard advice.

"And for your own sanctification and for Kelly's good. For Kelly most of all," he added, taking another puff on his cigarette. "I'm also going to give a few lessons and homilies on gossiping over the next few weeks. The next time Kelly approaches a worker with her jealous lies, the person she talks to is going to be aware of the sin of assassinating reputations. We chaplains have our own ways of fighting this kind of battle.

"Within a month or two, I wouldn't be surprised if you overhear a conversation where someone sticks up for you, Beck."

"That would be a pleasant experience after what happened this afternoon," she said, much more at peace with the situation. She looked at her watch. "Look at the time! I've got to get ready for the rehearsal dinner. Joanie's waiting for me." She stood to leave.

"Don't let this incident bother you, Becky, not with your wedding tomorrow. Let it be like a fly buzzing around you. Shoo it away," he advised, taking another sip of his hot toddy.

She thought hard for a moment. Until she heard the conversation in the stockroom, Becky had been walking on air. "I really let it get to me, didn't I?"

Chet said nothing in reply. *Let her think for herself,* he thought.

"I'm not going to let this ruin the biggest day of my life. No way," she continued, thinking out loud.

"That's my girl! Turn the tables on it, Beck. Let your hard edge cut Kelly Jones out of your mind—"

"Right," she agreed happily. "Cut her out! Chop her into pieces. Put her on toast. Roast her in the oven! Take her out and lightly baste with butter and sprinkle a little dill weed...No! tarragon, yeah, tarragon—"

"That's not exactly what I had in mind," he interrupted, noting her impish smile.

"I know, Chetmeister. I'm just having fun. Believe me, I'm going to have a great time tonight and a better time tomorrow. I feel better already. I'm not even going to bother Joe with this. Thanks, Chet! You've got a gift, you know."

He said nothing. He took a sip of his toddy and a drag off his Marlboro Light, thinking to himself for a moment.

Eventually he said, "I'll offer some special prayers, asking Our Lady and the Holy Spirit to give you peace. They were married too, you know. Well, sort of. Saint Joseph wasn't exactly wallpaper."

Becky thought about that for a moment. She gave him a look. "You don't mind if I just take off, Father. I really do have to get ready for tonight. I want to look special for Joe, and Joanie is waiting for me."

"Not at all, Beck. See you tonight. I've got to get over to the church anyway." He gave her a wink.

He noticed an athletic lightness in her gait as she walked out of the kitchen toward the front door. *I love being a priest,* he told himself. *Joe's got a real blessing in Becky. And she in Joe.*

Chet finished his hot toddy. Joe had sometimes shared his concern over Becky's "hard edges." The two men agreed that her conversion was basically irreversible. Her mind and heart were committed to Catholicism forever. But like most people who return to the faith—especially those who were not raised watching the example of devout parents—Becky could not be expected to have her bad habits and imperfections disappear like magic. Virtue takes years to develop. Fortunately for Becky, Joe Jackson was a very patient man. Rather than constantly point out her faults, Joe decided to remain silent and wait for her to slowly and gradually recognize her own problems and then decide for herself to work on them. Through prayer, grace, effort, spiritual direction, study, Joe's unconditional love, and virtuous friends—an all encompassing Catholic atmosphere which Becky herself recognized as "layers"—she would grow into a saint.

Joe doesn't mind waiting, Chet reflected happily. *The big lug can wait for years. He loves her just as she is—hard edges and all. He realizes that the best way for him to improve Becky is to forget her faults and concentrate on his own.*

2

Thursday Evening
7 December
Mishawaka, Indiana

"Wasn't it great meeting Jimbo Sullivan and my brothers and their wives tonight? They really liked you, you know," Joanie told Nathan as they rested alone on the old leather davenport in the den of her parent's home. Joanie had changed out of her dress and into jeans and a sweater after the rehearsal dinner at Bruno's. Nathan was still in a rather expensive suit from his trading days, his jacket and tie on a rocking chair next to the couch. Their feet mingled on the ottoman before them. In front of the ottoman a fire that Nathan kindled was just beginning to rage. The engaged couple could hear conversation and laughter coming from the Wheat's large country kitchen, where most of Joanie's brothers and their wives were hanging out with her parents.

"I like your brother Greg. Good man. I had a long talk with him. I liked Mindy, too. You know they live only a few miles from where I grew up?" Nathan asked mellowly. Joanie nodded.

"And I always pictured Jimbo Sullivan to be a lot bigger after Chet told me that story about Jimbo's right hook. I really haven't seen Jimbo since I was in grammar school, except for pictures that Chet has lying around." He mused.

A long silence ensued as they relaxed together. Joanie rested her head on Nathan's arm, which was draped around her shoulder. Nathan talked even more infrequently, but there was an easiness and peacefulness in his conversation since his return from his Warning. Joanie was comfortable with his silences. They were a natural couple—so much was understood between them without talking. *We're like a couple of old fogies,* Nathan often thought. Joanie and Nathan were almost the opposite of Becky and Joe, who seemed to have regular, almost amiable arguments and discussions.

"I love you," he said simply.

"I love you too, Mister," she replied softly.

He sighed. They sat in silence for a few minutes.

"Got something on my mind, Joanie. Not about us. About the world. About the Kolbe Foundation."

"Shoot," she replied.

"I feel in my guts like we're in a calm before the storm. For the last several years these Marian prophecies have been building up, like Our Lady was mustering her troops. Slowly but surely the enemy has been gathering his troops, too. The natural disasters, the worldwide recession that never seems to end, the wars and rumors of wars, the gradual breakdown of families—everything has been building up so slowly that only those with a special grace from God can see it. Especially those who are consecrated to Mary. That's what Chet and Lee say.

"I feel like we're part of an army gathering in a field, waiting for marching orders. No bombs are going off yet. No shots are being fired. But you can feel it coming. Like I could put my ear to the ground and hear the metallic rumbling of tank treads, far off—"

"You're scaring me, Nathan." It was his tone as much as his words.

"I've seen the preview, Joanie. I've seen my sins. I've also seen God's Divine Mercy. Or I felt it, or whatever you want to call it. Every day I sit in front of Jesus in the monstrance and I don't say anything to Him. I just look at Him, and think about how He was innocent and they killed Him anyway. I think of how sad Mary must have been holding Him in her arms after they took Him down from the cross. It comes down to a mother holding her son—a son who never did anything but preach about love, heal the sick, and give solace to sinners.

"And I think of how grateful I am that He let them crucify Him. If that sounds selfish, so be it. I was lost, and Jesus came to get me. And after it was over, He gave me you. I'll never understand it," Nathan was becoming exasperated trying to explain his thoughts.

"Keep trying, Nathan," she said softly, knowing that it was wise to let him speak once he was rolling. She snuggled her head on his chest. She was briefly distracted by a natural curiosity about what he would be like tomorrow evening. *That can wait,* she told herself. *Listen to him.*

"I've racked my brains," he continued, "trying to think of why people won't listen to your dad. That's pretty much my job now—to get people to listen to your dad. Your dad is really like Noah. Very few people are going to pay attention until it starts to rain. I know I didn't pay attention until I had the accident.

"What I'm trying to say is, I think…" he paused, "…I think the whole point is to recruit an army for Mary that's willing to do what Jesus did. An army so unselfish that it's willing to shed its innocent blood for the sake of others. Lee is right—all this evangelization is all well and good and has to be done, but no human effort is going to stamp out the evil I saw when I went to hell. There's no arguing with that kind of evil. It made up its mind a long time ago and isn't going to change. Chet calls it 'lacking all good.' It's worse than the vilest, most evil man—because a man, no matter how evil, can still change.

"That's why people won't listen to your dad, which is the same as saying they won't listen to Mary or Jesus, because he's just repeating their words. They're afraid. Afraid to even *listen*. To listen means to start on the road to belief. To believe means to be ready to take up the cross for real. It's much easier to hide your head in the sand," he finished his sentence, almost breathless. "Before it's all over, there will be a lot of martyrs. A lot of sacrifices.

"The paradox is, I guess, that the resurrection will come. The Son will rise, pun intended. At the end of my suffering was light, and love, and you. You were worth all the suffering. I would have the accident and the Warning again tomorrow if I knew you would be waiting for me on the other side. The war that's coming is the same way. Whatever suffering is required is worth it."

"I know, sweetheart," she reiterated, taking his hand. "I've known it for years—about the suffering, I mean, in an intellectual sense, because I always believed my dad. It wasn't until I suffered along with you that I experienced it in my heart. Suffering is worth it. I'm just glad that no matter how bad it is, I don't have to live through it alone. I'm going to be one body with you. We can share the joy and suffering together. I'd rather think about the Resurrection. You talked about Mary holding Jesus in her arms at Calvary and her intense sadness. Sometimes I think of her joy when she first embraced Jesus after the Resurrection. That's something that's not described in the Gospels. Maybe it's too private. At least we'll have each other, Nathan," she turned her delicate eyelids up and looked into his eyes. They were no longer as inscrutable as they once had been. They shared a slow, light, tender kiss.

A log burned out and dropped from the stack, breaking the moment.

"Hey, hey. I've got a big day tomorrow," Nathan said.

"Yeah, Mister? What's up?"

"Gettin' married," he said playfully.

"Me too!" she replied.

"Then you need your sleep. Who's the lucky guy?"

"You, silly," she smiled. A moment passed.

"Joanie?"

"Yeah?"

"How can we talk about a supernatural worldwide battle one minute and have the stupidest conversations the next?"

"Don't know," she replied, standing up and stretching her thin frame.

"Me neither," he stood up and hugged her tightly.

"Take it easy, Arnold Schwartzenegger; save some for tomorrow."

"That's right, got a big day tomorrow," he said again.

"Gettin' married, silly?" she led amiably.

"Let's not start, Joanie!" he said, laughing. They held hands as they walked out into the kitchen.

3

Friday Evening
8 December
Indiana Tollway, Indiana

The wedding was over and the newlyweds were driving to Chicago's finest hotel, the Palmer House, for a four-day honeymoon. The Kolbe Foundation was too busy to have three of its top workers gone for much longer.

The big Buick LeSabre rolled down the highway at ten miles per hour over the speed limit. As he drove Joe's car, Nathan replayed the events of the day quickly in his mind like fast-forwarding through a video tape in a conscious effort to seal the day permanently in his prolific memory.

The night before the wedding Nathan had trouble falling asleep at Joe's house because of his excitement. He overslept the alarm. He rushed to get dressed. Chet came over for breakfast and they all prayed a Rosary together in Immaculate Conception Church before people started to arrive.

Joanie, Becky, and Joe had many friends and relatives in attendance, Joanie especially. *Even Becky's mother came. What a surprise!* Nathan thought. Nathan had only the Wojtals, Father Chet, and Chet's family. Joe looked unbelievably out of place next to his diminutive parents and his two blond sisters, but there was obviously a genuine affection among them all.

The nuptial Mass was kind of a blur. Only the vows slowed down in Nathan's memory. Nathan remembered thinking as he spoke his vows that he was starting his own family, a new family. Then a pleasant image from his Warning came into his mind's eye; Nathan saw King Sobieski III, his royal fore-father.

"You are my queen," he whispered to Joanie Payne before he kissed her at the end of Mass.

"I know," she replied calmly as she looked out over the packed church, "I know." Joanie had been calm and confident during the entire day. *She was, what? Regal. Yeah, that's the word. Regal in the best sense of the word. She seemed to be in her element. Like a real queen.*

Joe and Becky were a study in opposites to the relatively sedate Paynes. Joe seemed especially out of character. He talked loudly, laughed easily, and throughout the Mass and sacramental vows, he smiled brightly. It was like he was on a football field. Becky could not stop smiling. Nathan spied her winking at Father Chet twice.

Becky was absolutely radiant. There was a singular inno-cence about her beauty that made it difficult for any man in the church to keep his eyes off her. She did not look skinny and sultry like the pouty models who adorn the magazines on grocery store racks. Her beauty was pure and full—a perfect bride.

The reception was quite a mix of styles. It took place in the local VFW hall. Nothing fancy. Live band. Lots of free liquor and huge plates of roast beef served family-style on each table. Father Chet's mom made the cake at the Wheat's house the day before the wedding. Chet and Nathan did much of the planning, promising a "New Jersey Blowout Style Re-ception." There hadn't been much time to plan. Nathan gen-erously insisted on paying for the entire reception. Six dis-posable cameras were placed at each table—the guests were encouraged to take as many candid photographs as they pos-sibly could. At the end of the reception the cameras were collected in a box for later developing by the newlyweds.

The Sullivans and Wheats got along as if they were long-lost relatives. The brothers seemed to take a special pleasure in testing the morally acceptable limits of alcohol consump-tion and raucous dancing. Even Nathan thought it got out of hand when the Sullivan and Wheat brothers grabbed their wives—the ones who weren't pregnant—and started tossing them in the air along a dance line during a rousing rendition of "What I Like About You." Joe's relatives, teetotalers all, stood watching with their jaws open. Joe put one hand over his eyes and couldn't bring himself to join the line despite Becky's tugging. Lee, normally calm and invisible, danced with verve. But he seemed to hold back a little, and spent a lot of time talking with Joe's relatives about the Bible.

Karl Slinger, Lenny Gold, James Sullivan, and Tom Wheat smoked cigars over Maker's Mark and talked shop at the parents' table. In general their wives rolled their eyes at their juvenile husbands while exchanging friendly stories about children, grandchildren, and the two newlywed couples. Dottie, Anne, and Mary Sullivan got along well. Father Chet had taken Becky's mom around the room for introductions and spent much time talking and laughing with her. Husband Number Three had stayed behind in Seattle.

Slinger's booming laugh was heard often as it echoed off the worn wooden floors and cinder block walls of the VFW hall. Later on, when the Sullivan and Wheat boys were worn out, he surprised everyone by putting on a polka showcase with Dottie. They also performed a wonderful two-step to the straining rock band's version of a western tune.

The band took a break and put on a tape. A waltz came on the speakers. Joe and Becky amazed everyone except Chet by performing a wonderful, inspirational waltz. They had practiced. Chet had suggested they take lessons, figuring it would be great marriage preparation for the two strong-willed individuals. There was a grace, unity, and strength to the couple that seemed to be most perfectly expressed in the classical dance. After a minute or two, everyone else stopped dancing to watch them in a kind of awe. They were given a standing ovation when the song ended. Becky blushed and looked up at Joe. He surprised her with a wink.

Nathan spent most of his time talking to Joanie's college friends and to her relatives. She was so proud to introduce

her new husband to them all! He tried to be as perfect a gentleman as he could be. He kept his arm comfortably attached to
her thin waist in a conscious effort to build common memories of the day's events. As he now drove toward Chicago, he
remembered the unique feel of her perfectly-fitted satin dress
on his fingertips as he escorted her around the room.

Toward the end, Chet, Nathan, Lee, and Joe locked arms
with giant cigars in their mouths. Someone took a Polaroid
which Nathan slipped into his jacket pocket.

As happens at all weddings, the time slipped away. Tie-
less, sweaty men left with their exasperated wives after con-
gratulating the two couples. Many were headed to the Wheat's
farmhouse for that other great Irish tradition—the All-Night
Post-Reception Party. Somebody came up to Joe and stuck a
video camera in his face, asking Joe for any final thoughts or
advice. Joe took two full minutes to think before speaking
into the camera in his calm, soft voice, "I've been waiting a
long time for this day. My advice to anyone watching this is
simple. Hold out for beauty." Joe turned and smiled at the
beaming Becky.

Before getting into the car, each newlywed gave Father
Chet a hug. The priest smelled of cigars, yet was the most
sober of all male Sullivans within several square miles. Becky
was last and gave him the longest, most affectionate hug by
far.

"Thanks, Father," she whispered. "I wouldn't be here and
so happy if you hadn't called me that morning. I'll love you
forever for that. You saved me."

Becky left Father Chet speechless as usual. She never
looked more lovely or more content. Chet looked over her
shoulder to Joe and winked. *I'm jealous, you big lug,* the
priest thought, although he was not really jealous. *You take
care of her. Your souls are in each other's hands.* Joe read
Chet's thoughts and nodded gravely before allowing a smile
to come to his deep brown eyes. The Jacksons got into the
back seat.

Nathan powered down the window. "Thanks, Fadda Chet-meister. Don't let the place burn down while we're gone."

"Don't worry, Nathan, I will." Chet replied.

Nathan pulled out, kicking dirt and stones with the Buick's tires.

✛ ✛ ✛

Nathan held the steering wheel of Joe's car with one hand and Joanie's hand with his other. Joe and Becky were gig-gling and kissing in the back seat, not quite making out. The radio was off. The only other sound was the low hum of the Buick's big engine.

Nathan looked in the mirror. "You guys are like two high school kids," he commented in a friendly way. "Check that. You look like one normal high school girl and one incredibly oversized high school guy."

Joanie noticed how Nathan said "you guys" with a slight New Jersey accent. Unlike Father Chet, Nathan rarely revealed his childhood accent—until he had a few beers in him. Nathan was mildly buzzed after the wedding reception.

"Oh Nathan, leave them be!" Joanie chided him amiably. She was much too happy to care, really. Both women had decided not to change out of their wedding dresses for the ride. Before the wedding, Nathan had convinced them this was the way to make a proper entrance into the Palmer House. The two men were in identical tuxedos. Joanie and Becky wore similar but slightly different dresses. Joanie's was sim-pler than Becky's. Becky's was more elegant, shoulderless, and had more lace. Both had taken off their white elbow-length gloves for the car ride.

Joe stopped kissing Becky long enough to say, "You want to switch seats and let me drive, buddy? Beck and I have the rest of our lives for this kind of stuff. That is, if you don't rack us up like you did in your Mustang."

"Joseph, that's terrible!" Becky scolded. Nathan laughed.

"Okay," Nathan said simply. He slowed the Buick rather quickly—just short of dangerously—and pulled it over to the shoulder. The wives laughed as they switched seats, front to back. A passing trucker blew his horns when he saw their wedding dresses billowing in the wind.

As soon as they were settled in, Nathan and Joanie commenced with kissing. But there was no giggling. Joe and Becky heard no sound from them.

"I love you, Nathan, but you always drive like you're leaving a bank robbery," Joe teased as he pulled out into the cruising lane, keeping below the speed limit.

"Love you too, Joe. Now shut up, I'm busy," Nathan replied with feigned antagonism.

"Yeah, shut up," Becky said, mocking Nathan, "they're busy, darling." Becky felt for her husband's free hand and held it tightly on her stomach, clasped between both her hands. Her thumbs gently stroked his fingers. She looked at him, just loving him as he concentrated on the road. He gave driving his full attention.

Becky thought about something Joe had proudly confessed to her early on, something most people in the world would find extremely difficult to believe. During their entire courtship Joe had not kissed Becky on the lips—until Father Chet pronounced them man and wife. Rebecca Macadam was also the first woman Joe had *ever* kissed on the lips! Joe had chivalrously reserved his entire body and soul for her. It was the ultimate proof of his love. Rebecca Macadam was truly the first person to enter the garden of his heart. She was convinced that her husband was the finest man on the earth. Her emotions welled up like waves in her breast whenever she looked at him on this night. *He's not real,* she thought. *But he is real,* she answered herself.

Even her mother's surprise attendance at the wedding had failed to disturb her equilibrium. Her mother had actually been quite dignified at the reception, if not a bit aloof, and had cried during the vows. Becky noticed that Father Chet corralled Mrs. Jane Standish at the reception, making a point to introduce her to everyone. Chet had been able to make Becky's mom laugh. *Probably going to get her to confession before she flies back to Seattle,* Becky thought briefly, before consciously pushing all thoughts and sentiments out of her mind—except for those which directly concerned Joe.

Another noble sentiment arose in her, pushing aside for the moment her elation and joy: gratitude. Gratitude to God for Joe.

✝ ✝ ✝

In the back seat Nathan cried openly—but silently—for the first time since he was a small child, as he slowly and gently kissed Joanie on the forehead. Then he kissed her on the eyelids. And then he kissed her flushed cheeks. Joanie held his face in her hands with tenderness, feeling his tears on her fingertips. Although he had thrown away his physical virginity, in his heart Nathan was as much a virgin as Joe was. His former life seemed as if it had been lived by a different Nathan Payne.

Nathan looked at Joanie as he kissed her, then pulled away. Then he moved close to kiss her again. He did this over and over, mile after mile. He tried not to think; he tried to not let words cloud the purity of the love he felt for her. He was not fool enough to believe that the emotion of the moment would last forever. He received these emotions as a gift from God. He lived in them as they came forth from his heart. Somehow, unexpressed in his mind, he was aware that he was in a state of grace, and that he had made his peace with God, and that the world was all right. He was convinced that his wife was the finest woman in the whole world. Like Becky, he felt a sublime gratitude to God—not only for Joanie, who was the crown jewel of God's gifts, but for *everything*. All these things flowed out of Nathan in his tears, as he said *I love you* and *Thank you* to God and to Joanie with his gentle, lingering kisses.

Body and soul, he loved her. Body and soul, she loved him. The two were forevermore one flesh, one body. Just as Jesus was the perfect union of God and man, so in a real way Nathan and Joanie were a living symbol of the Incarnation.

After a lifetime of suffering, there was redemption for this man of sorrows in the grace of the Sacrament of Holy Matrimony. Nathan was finally abiding completely in the Moral Universe.

In the Beatific Vision, a man named Blaise Pascal rejoiced.

✛ ✛ ✛

Becky Jackson had never stayed at the Palmer House. Considering that she lived in Chicago her entire life, this was not a surprise. But her father had taken her to see the lobby when she was a little girl. She had forgotten how beautiful the hotel in the Loop truly was. The Palmer House had one of the most spectacular lobbies in the world, featuring a Romanesque ceiling.

Nathan liberally tipped the concierge, who seemed to recognize the two couples as they walked in the door. *I bet Nathan's greased the skids all the way up to the honeymoon suites,* Becky thought with a certain admiration.

Becky's grip on Joe's hand tightened as she looked around the lobby. She let go and took his muscular arm. All eyes were on the couples as they made their grand entrance. She and Joanie both knew at that moment that Nathan was right to insist on going to the Palmer House in full regalia. The moment would stay with each woman forever.

Becky thought of Father Chet's discourses on Beauty as she walked across the room on the arm of her handsome groom. *I feel like a princess. This is Good. This is Beautiful.* She looked up at Joe. He was holding his head still and his chin high as he walked. His dignified bearing reminded Becky of an enigmatic knight from some age long past, as if Joe had crossed time itself to find her.

Joe, did your incredible chastity preserve your unique-ness as a person? she asked, surprised at the sophistication of her theological insight.

Who are you, Joe Jackson? She felt a wave of love and a tinge of fear. *It all happened so fast. I guess I'm going to find out who you are. I can live with that. And with you.*

✝ ✝ ✝

The two couples stood in the hallway at the door of the Jackson's suite after the bellhops deposited their luggage in their rooms. For a moment they just looked at each other, soundlessly, with a nervous kind of seriousness.

"Well," Joanie said, stepping to Becky and giving her best friend a hug. They embraced with eyes closed for a long time. Joe looked at Nathan sheepishly. Nathan held his gaze, nodding slowly. Then Joe looked down at the red and blue patterns on the plush carpeting.

Nathan cleared his throat and pulled his plastic electronic key out of his pocket. "Let's go, Mrs. Payne," he said kindly. *Time to finish what we started. No more numbers. You are my number one from now on.*

Joe considered making a joke to break the ice, about meeting for breakfast tomorrow at three in the afternoon, but thought better of it. He looked at his bride's cream-colored shoulders, set off by her white dress, and suddenly remembered what came next. He took a deep breath, then opened the door. Becky wiped a tear of joy from her eye as she left Joanie and entered the suite, already locking her gaze on her husband. *This is the room,* she thought, excited and afraid and happy and ready.

✝ ✝ ✝

"I guess Joe forgot something," Nathan said mischievously, facing Joanie in front of the open door of their suite.

"Like what, Mister?" Joanie asked, having a pretty good notion of what Nathan meant.

He answered by deftly lifting his bride into his arms and carrying her across the threshold to another universe.

✝ ✝ ✝

Sacraments were consummated.

✝ ✝ ✝

Afterwards, the husband asked a question, "Do you think, you know, that we could have made a baby tonight?"

"I don't know, lover," the wife replied honestly. "I guess so."

He looked away, the inscrutability back in his eyes.

She looked at the scar on his cheek. *So much pain,* she thought sadly.

"What is it, Mister?" she asked kindly.

He hesitated. He looked back, directly into her deep blue eyes. He stroked her cheek slowly.

"I want you to know everything. Now that we're one," he replied, a note of resolve in his voice. He felt quick, biting sorrow as he saw a storm of hurt pass over her eyes. *She's hurt because I kept something from her.* The storm passed quickly and he saw a more familiar expression: understanding, forgiveness. *So quickly you fight and win your battles,* he thought.

"Only if you want to, lover. Is it about your Warning?" she guessed correctly.

"Yes," he replied in a raspy voice, emotion stirring like the tides, having no desire to hold back the waves.

She waited, patiently.

Nathan Payne told his wife about the children he saw standing on fields of gold. His children.

✝ ✝ ✝

Later, in another room, the bride had fallen asleep. The groom gracefully pulled himself up on one elbow, gently resting his other hand on her stomach, so as not to disturb her sleep. Her face was peaceful, almost childlike.

The thoughtful man, the Knight of Immaculata, reclined motionlessly for an unmeasured time and admired his wife, the most beautiful woman in Chicago. As was his habit, he burned the image into his memory for present and future meditation.

He thought. For this man there was often no discernible line between thought and prayer. His thoughts ran like gazelles through fields. He thanked God. He looked at her and thought of their mother, Mary. He felt a deep gratitude to his adoptive parents for teaching him about chastity and the Bible.

Joe had given much thought to why he had decided to love Becky. He cherished his thoughts and kept them to himself like a boy collecting favorite baseball cards. Despite his melancholic nature, he was not a romantic. He appreciated her singular beauty. He loved to look at her and anticipated a lifetime of enjoying her physical loveliness. But he did not ignore her faults—her hard-edged personality, her smoking, her quick temper. The same biting humor that could make him laugh could also cut him and others. She was stubborn. She was always willing to argue for days or weeks for something she really wanted.

Joe reflected that these same traits attracted him to her. Her humor had an intellectual quality that made him think— and how Joe loved to laugh and think! The fact that she smoked wasn't attractive, of course, but he also realized that one cigarette could calm her in the middle of a heated discussion, thereby smoothing her hard edge. She was trying to cut down for the sake of the baby, too—which was a more difficult sacrifice for her than for others. As for the hard edge itself? Joe had spent the greater portion of his life battling and overcoming men who were society's toughest warriors on the football field. Joe Jackson had never, *ever* been attracted to women who were pushovers—this he had known about himself since high school. He *liked* to battle and enjoyed verbally sparring with Becky. *She might look like Grace Kelly, but she argues like Maureen O'Hara.*

Joe was almost preternaturally self-possessed. Becky's temper didn't bother him the way it might have bothered other men. Her angry outbursts hardly registered. She was a lion and he was a bear. It was a standoff. And he thanked God for the psychological fit between them. The way Joe saw it, he had to love all of Becky or none of her. He could not remain true to himself and take just part of her. Isn't that what the vows he took this morning meant? For better *and* for worse.

He thought about the better. When they were alone and Becky let down her guard, she had a childlike innocence that was as unique as her beauty. Perhaps only one other had seen this part of her—Father Chet. Joe saw it in her eyes during wordless private moments. Like her anger, Becky's joy had a way of overtaking her entire self. Her unbridled joy energized him.

Becky had never told him explicitly, but he knew that she trusted him without reservation. She was incapable of anything other than total commitment. He had found his way into the secret garden of her heart, and he cherished the importance she placed on having only Joe in that exclusive place. He knew that losing her father had hardened her, so he loved her all the more for preserving her childlike trust behind the walls of her heart.

A scripture that he had memorized for the occasion came to him, from the Song of Songs:

You have stolen my heart, my sister, my bride;
You have stolen my heart with one glance of your eyes,
with one jewel of your necklace.
How delightful is your love, my sister, my bride!
How much more pleasing is your love than wine,
and the fragrance of your perfume than any spice!
Your lips drop sweetness as the honeycomb, my bride;
milk and honey are under your tongue.

The fragrance of your garments is like that of Lebanon.
You are a garden locked up, my sister, my bride.
I am my lover's and my lover is mine.

4

Saturday Morning
9 December
The Loop, Chicago, Illinois

The phone rang. Becky leaned across the bed to pick it up. It was Nathan.

"You guys busy or hungry?" Nathan asked cheerfully.

"Famished! Hold on," Becky replied. Then she held her hand over the mouthpiece, calling to her husband, "Jo Yo Ma! Wanna grab a bite with Nathan and Joanie?"

Joe, just finishing tying his shoes, nodded. He mouthed the word "Mass."

"Joe's game, Nathan. We're starving. But Joe wants to go to Mass first. Okay by you? Meet you in the lobby in, say, twenty minutes?"

"Sure. Mass sounds great. Twenty minutes. We can catch Mass at Saint Peter's. Later, Beck." Nathan hung up.

Twenty minutes later the newlywed couples met and walked to Saint Peter's Church. Afterwards, they walked to the lakefront and prayed a Rosary together, bracing themselves against the chill wind coming off Lake Michigan.

They had lunch at Trader Vic's. Joe ordered two steaks for himself. They had gone to Mass, prayed Rosaries, and eaten meals together many times in the past three months. Now, however, there was something different, something extra that went beyond their shared nuptial joy.

It's the layers of love, Becky thought, listening to Joe and Nathan talk about car repairs, of all things. *There's more.*

Marriage, Eucharist, Mary, the Kolbe Foundation, friend-ship—man to man, woman to woman, and man to woman. Meals and walks, and later, loving. I hope it never ends.

Becky looked at Joanie, who read her thoughts and said, "It's hard to believe, isn't it, Beck?"

"I know," Becky replied. "Don't wake me up if I'm dream-ing."

PART THREE
The Tribulations

See my marvels everywhere in the world! My beloved
children are responding with ever increasing
generosity and I am bringing them together in my
cohort, which is now drawn up for battle.
Our Lady to Father Gobbi, 13 May 1978

The king is gone but he's not forgotten.
Neil Young

Toward the end of the world, tyrants and hostile mobs
will rob the Church and the clergy of all their
possessions and will afflict and martyr them.
Those who heap the most abuse upon them will be
held in high esteem. The clergy cannot escape these
persecutions, but, because of them, all servants of the
Church will be forced to lead an apostolic life.
John of the Cleft Rock, Fourteenth Century Prophecy

Polytheism was never to the pagan what Catholicism
is to the Catholic. [To pagans] all the world was
a tissue of interwoven tales and cults, and there
ran in and out of it…that black thread among its
more blameless colours; the darker paganism
that was really diabolism.
G. K. Chesterton

Chapter Eighteen

1

From *Dark Years History*
(New Rome Press, 31 R.E.)
by Rebecca Macadam Jackson

...and so the Schism came gradually while the economic turmoil came in a flash. The whole world seemed to change overnight...

2

Tuesday Morning
11 June
County Galway, Ireland

Pope Patrick rested peacefully in his coma. Every day Sister Elizabeth came in to bathe him, and to do passive physical therapy. She often sang or hummed hymns while caring for him; she always spoke to him as if he were awake. There is a theory that these activities help bring the patient back to consciousness. Sister Elizabeth did such things out of love.

Once a week Doc Soames came by to check on his patient.

This morning while Sister Elizabeth was singing a traditional Irish song—one of many that featured a forlorn fisherman's wife begging the sea to return her long lost husband—something happened to Angus. Sister Elizabeth did not know that it was a song Angus's mother had sung to him in his youth. Deep in the recesses of Angus's mind a tiny electrical current sparked, beginning the first tenuous synaptic voyage toward consciousness. It would take a long time, but the fisher of men was returning to shore.

3

Saturday Morning
15 June
Mishawaka, Indiana

Saturday sunlight streamed through the window of the kitchen. Joanie had been surprised when Nathan took a strong but limited role in decorating the modest home they purchased after the wedding. The ranch house was in a development less than a mile from Immaculate Conception Church. He had bought the house with cash. He had insisted on light colors and big windows—everything else he left up to his bride except for the window decorations. Nathan forbid her to buy thick draperies. Short tasteful valences adorned most of the windows in the house and Nathan always kept the blinds open during daylight hours. He was a light freak.

Joanie enjoyed her coffee and the silence of domestic tranquillity. Her days during childhood had been happy but filled with the noise of energetic brothers—until Tom Wheat came home. Her mother had insisted on quiet time so the professor could relax in peace and study his history books. Evenings in the Wheat household were therefore notable for their lack of television; the boys and Joanie sat around reading books. She took a sip of coffee and turned to her battered copy of Hilaire Belloc's *The Crisis of Civilization.*

Nathan took a sip of Snapple as he read *Investor's Business Daily*. He looked up to make a note in his unreadable handwriting on a yellow pad.

"How do you do it?" she asked, still reading.

"Do what?" he asked.

"Make money without trying. Half this town is struggling to make ends meet. You've paid for this house three times over by taking a few notes every Saturday from that paper and making a few phone calls every Monday."

It was true. He had done quite well as a part-time investor, leaving himself plenty of time to run the bulk of the operations at the Kolbe Foundation for Joe Jackson. He also gave over ten percent of all his earnings to the foundation and other charities. Joanie, off for the summer from teaching, was his assistant.

"Oh, that. I'm not sure I can explain it. I read things, see the numbers, and play the percentages that come into my mind. I've been investing since I was a freshman in college. Despite our great returns lately, I'm quite conservative. I don't gamble. I invest—there's a difference. I've been doing a lot of contrarian stuff lately that's come up pretty good."

"Contrarian?" Joanie asked, thinking of Hilaire Belloc— the contrarian Catholic historian she was reading.

"Yeah, the economy has gone down so steadily for so long that most analysts are predicting a cyclical upturn. Taking a page from Dad, I've bet that it's going to get worse, and have invested in a range of things that go up when most things go down."

She was still not used to her husband calling her father "Dad."

"For example," Nathan explained, "I've got stock in a growing chain of car repair shops that make house calls. People hang on to their cars longer in tough times. I've got junk bonds in a little company in Indiana that's invented an electrical generator that runs on wood as fuel. That kind of thing might be a big seller in a depressed economy where utility services are not available everywhere.

"In another area, I have over forty percent of our stuff in Krugerrands, gold futures, gold stocks, and mutual funds that invest predominantly in precious metals. They've gone through the roof lately, especially with the war in Russia and the depression in Europe. But you've got to be willing to risk

losing your money or waiting out a storm. I held on to pharmaceuticals that hit rock bottom several years ago when they
tried to nationalize healthcare. With the new, weird diseases
that keep popping up—again, stuff predicted on Dad's tape—
certain pharmaceuticals are hot again. I cashed them in for a
respectable gain two months ago when I thought they became overvalued. Patience. Guts. Numbers. Guesses. Common Sense. Experience. It's a combo."

"Combo, eh? What happens if the European depression
comes to the United States?" she asked, getting up to pour
another cup of coffee.

"Buy land. Deflation. That's a tough nut to crack for the
cash poor. People with hard money assets picked up some
steals during the Great Depression. It's simple."

"Simple. A depression is simple? You're a cool one in a
crisis, aren't you?"

"Yeah," he said, unperturbed. He couldn't bring himself
to worry about money after his accident, the memories of
which were finally starting to fade. Except for the images of
his five unborn children. These never faded. Looking at her
lithe figure from behind as she poured the coffee, he thought
of more current events. "When will you start to show the
baby?"

"In a couple of months, lover," she said, smiling sweetly.

"How do you do it?" he asked.

"Do what?"

"Make me love you without trying," he said romantically,
if not a bit sheepishly. She turned to face him.

"Oh that? I'm a contrarian, darling. It's simple. But I'm
not sure I could explain it," she answered cheerfully, raising
an eyebrow in a now-familiar expression—an expression
familiar only to Nathan.

"But you could show me?" he asked in a certain tone of
voice and with a certain gleam in his eye.

"Yes," she replied, nodding.

He put his paper down and finished his Snapple in a gulp.
Joanie had already left the kitchen.

4

Early Saturday Afternoon
15 June
Mishawaka, Indiana

When Becky Jackson walked into the kitchen of the Wheat's house, it was with a pronounced wobble. She was already two weeks past due. Her natural beauty was only slightly marred by the significant weight she had gained over the months. Becky had cut down on her cigarettes but had not quit by any stretch of the imagination. Joe followed her into the big kitchen carrying a pineapple upside down cake.

Nathan, Joanie, and Joanie's parents greeted the couple with smiles and hugs.

"What does the doctor say, Mrs. Jackson?" Wheat asked. He made a habit of calling brides by their formal names for a year after the wedding.

"The doc says Amy is due any minute—same thing he told me three weeks ago…" Becky replied lightly. Ultrasound had revealed the sex of the unborn child. Joe had insisted on pre-naming her Amy—after Mary, Mother Most Amiable. He explained that Amy means *lovable.* "Oh great, you want me to name my baby the Love Child. That's rich," Becky had said at the time. Joe hadn't "gotten" the implications of her remark until three days later when it struck him out of the blue. Still, for months he had everyone at the Kolbe Foundation addressing the unborn baby as Amy. Becky found it confusing at first that he was completely oblivious to the fact that his wife was pregnant by another man. All the workers followed Joe's lead and she had not heard another unkind word at work (Kelly Jones had quit a month after the wedding, giving no explanation). At Father Chet's suggestion, Becky began meditating in front of the Blessed Sacrament on Saint Joseph's role in the Gospels. It dawned on her that perhaps her husband was a saint, too.

"Hi Birthday Boy!" Joe called softly to Denny, who was watching a small television on the kitchen counter. It was a CNI Special Report on the big experimental aircraft show in Oshkosh, Wisconsin. Most years Denny flew up to the show, but he had decided to skip it this year. He had been laid off from his cargo pilot job. The deepening recession was the culprit. Denny needed to be ready to pick up odd cargo and crop dusting jobs.

"Hi Joe! Hi Beck!" Denny called back, rising to shake Joe's hand. "Thanks for coming. I should've guessed Mom would make a big deal out of this. Upside down cake—my favorite."

"…after your favorite flying position, no doubt, Lindy," Becky said in a friendly way. She had dubbed him Lindy after Charles Lindbergh, but it hadn't stuck with anyone else yet. The nickname didn't bother Denny in the least.

"You bet. Nathan and Joanie brought me a bottle of Scotch. I bet you can think of some kind of flying pun for Scotch, Becky…"

Becky scrunched her eyebrows together and looked up, trying to think of something. She came up empty.

"Scotch gets you high without leaving the ground," Chet said behind them. Everyone turned to the doorway where Father Chet was standing. "Happy Birthday, Denny! How are you—"

"Oh my God! Greg and Mindy! The children!" Anne shouted in horror, cutting off Father Chet. She was referring to her son Greg, who lived in a New Jersey suburb, not far from New York.

✝ ✝ ✝

Everyone turned to Anne Wheat, who was watching the television screen. Nathan quickly leaned forward to turn up the volume on the set.

The image on the screen was apparently from a camera in a helicopter. The graphic on the screen was "Eyewitness News 11 Shadow Traffic." A female voice described the carnage:

"…pictures come to us from WPIX in New York. Our satellite feed is not picking up sound. Details are sketchy, but a massive earthquake has just struck the city minutes ago. CNI is having trouble contacting our local affiliate. Preliminary reports from the United States Seismic Research Center in Scranton, Pennsylvania, estimate the quake at 9.1 on the Richter Scale. That would make this the largest earthquake east of the Mississippi in recorded history. Wait."

There was a pause in the voice-over. The shocked families watched the herky jerky video of the Queensboro Bridge, which was no longer standing. The bridge's enormous steel supports had collapsed into the East River and onto Roosevelt Island. A crumpled, burning bus could be seen in the wreckage. The cameraman lifted the camera from the East River and an amazing science fiction view of Manhattan opened up on the television. Buildings were collapsed everywhere. People were running in First Avenue around overturned and crashed cars. It looked more like a huge bomb had gone off. Becky remembered photographs she had seen years before of the earthquake in Kobe, Japan. As the camera panned toward midtown, it was clear that another bridge had been destroyed. Nathan recognized it. It was the Williamsburg Bridge.

"We have a cellular phone connection to a correspondent in Times Square. We're patching in to Ricky Hodges now…"

A map of New York City appeared on the screen with a star on Times Square and an inset, candid photograph of the reporter.

The voice on the line was hysterical: "…can't get out of my car! People are running everywhere, screaming, covered with blood, crying. A mounted police officer just galloped by my car screaming 'Forty Second Street is gone! It's under water!' over and over again and…Oh my God! I just heard gunshots! Gunshots very close! Gunshots!…"

The voice on the line stopped, then began again: "Huh. Huh! The shots are fading. Oh. All the signs on Times Square are out. The building with the ball on New Years Eve with that young-looking old guy that Bandstand music guy that Publisher's Clearinghouse guy is, is…rubble! Oh, no…"

The line went dead.

A talking head came on from the CNI newsroom in Atlanta. The female announcer's voice trembled. She was clearly shaken, fumbling papers on her desk. Her husband worked in New York and commuted by plane to Atlanta on weekends. "Uh, we've been cut off from Ricky Hodges. Phone lines are out all over the New York-New Jersey metropolitan area. Officials from FEMA, the Federal Emergency Management Administration, have called our studio to ask us to urge viewers with friends and relatives in New York to please refrain from using cellular phone lines, which will be needed by rescue workers—"

Nathan switched channels. Reports of the quake were on every network.

+ + +

No one noticed Denny leave the kitchen. He came back just as Nathan began to flip channels. He had donned his leather flight jacket and was carrying the keys to the Cessna in his hand.

Anne was on the phone, hitting the redial button. "I can't get through! Tommy! What about Greg and the kids! I keep getting a message! What about Greg and Mindy? The children? They're only twenty miles from New York!"

"Settle down, Annie!" Tom shouted with more than a little bit of fear in his voice. He grabbed his wife's shoulders and held her. "Settle down. Losing control won't help Greg. I need you…to…settle…down…**now!**"

Anne stopped yelling and began to cry. Joanie came over and held her mother. "Give me the phone, Mom. I'll keep calling. I'll try some other number." She gently took the phone from her mother, who was weeping and shaking.

Nathan lit one of Becky's cigarettes—his first since before his Warning—and talked quietly with Denny, Chet, and Joe in the corner near the door.

"No!" Nathan said with eerie calm. "You can't go. Look at your wife." When Nathan said the final word, Becky turned from the television across the room and looked at the men.

"You can't stop me! And don't look at me with that look, Nathan, buddy," Joe fired back, raising his deep tenor voice. With the exception of Becky, no one in the room had ever heard Joe Jackson shout before. The room quieted down.

Nathan said nothing in reply.

"What's going on, son?" Tom Wheat asked Denny.

"We're going to North Caldwell to get Greg's family," Denny said bravely.

"Who's going?" Tom asked.

"Not you, Joe!" Becky shouted before Denny could answer, awkwardly running over to her man, grabbing him around the waist.

The television droned on about collapsed buildings and bridges...

Suddenly, everyone in the room except Chet and Anne started shouting at once, raising the overall noise level.

"Shut Up!" Chet hollered above the din in a thick New Jersey accent. That did the trick.

"Let's pray one Hail Mary and Our Father for Greg and Mindy and the kids. Hold hands."

Everyone, including Anne, prayed with Father Chet.

"Thank you, Father. I'm sorry I lost control," Anne said, a sniffle escaping between words. "Now, what's going on, Denny?"

Denny looked at Nathan.

It was Nathan who spoke up, "We'll help them. We'll bring them back. Nobody knows how bad it's going to get over there. There could be looting. Or worse. Somebody's got to go. Nobody's going to get in on commercial airlines. Denny and I are going," Nathan spoke calmly, but with steely determination and a fierce look in his eyes.

Joanie gasped.

"I'm going too," Joe added.

"No!" Becky shouted again.

"No, you're not," Nathan said evenly.

"Now hold on a minute—" Tom ordered quickly.

"Joe, you can't go," Father Chet interrupted.

"Why not?" Joe asked defiantly.

"Because *I'm* going," Chet replied. "My parishioners are there. I've got family there, too. And a Catholic priest can come in handy in tight spots—"

"—besides, you weigh too much, Joe, and I'll need to load supplies in your seat and—" Denny added reasonably.

"But—" Joe started.

"—But nothing!" Chet interjected, "your wife is due any minute now. For God's sake, take a look at her!"

That got Joe's attention.

Joe looked at Becky. Her arms were folded. She squinted in studied anticipation. The wheels began turning in his head.

"Go if you want to go," she said with pristine contempt. "But don't expect me to say God bless you and kiss you goodbye. *I* don't want you to go—but that doesn't mean anything to you, does it?"

Father Chet winced.

Everyone waited while Joe thought.

"Okay, I'll stay. I'll do what I can from here," he said finally in his regular soft voice. Becky hugged him, awkwardly negotiating her embrace around her full womb—but she was still angry.

"Now it's my turn to raise a few objections, Mister," Joanie said. Everyone seemed to have forgotten about her. She had stood watching her husband during the entire, absurd conversation while still holding Anne. She carefully let go of her mother and put her hands on her hips.

"What?" Nathan asked, his expression softening. Somehow he was never able to work his will on his wife. Not ever.

"What if I don't want you to go, either? What if I *forbid* you to go, Mr. Hero?" she asked, tilting her head. Her tone had an almost academic quality.

"Then I wouldn't go," Nathan answered with that odd calm he had exhibited during the entire conversation. He nonchalantly pulled another Parliament from Becky's pack and lit it. He inhaled deeply and leaned against the wall. "Remember what you told me this morning?"

Time seemed to stop as everyone else in the room watched Nathan and Joanie conduct their conversation without the tension that infused everyone else. Wheat felt particularly powerless, as if his entire generation had been passed to younger, stronger men and women. In Korea, *he* had been the warrior, ever ready to move with determined confidence toward the enemy.

"What did I tell you?" Joanie asked, honestly uncertain where Nathan was leading.

"You said I was a cool one in a crisis. Well it's true, I am. It might be dangerous—extremely dangerous—over there. Or everyone might be doing fine and we'll drop off some supplies and fly back before tomorrow afternoon. Either way, it's perfectly reasonable for me to tag along. Denny and Greg are going to need me. It's as simple as that. It's my old stomping grounds, too. Don't you think Denny could use someone who knows the neighborhood to guide him around?

"Just remember, no matter how hairy it gets, *nothing* is going to stop me from coming back here to you and our baby." His tone made the trip sound so—ordinary.

"You're pregnant?" Tom Wheat asked his daughter. She just nodded without taking her eyes away from Nathan.

Tom looked at Anne, who raised her eyebrows and shrugged her shoulders.

"Promise me you'll steer clear of danger," Joanie demanded.

He considered lying but found, as usual, that he couldn't lie to his wife. "No, I can't promise that," Nathan answered, taking another puff. "But I'll try. How's that?"

"Deal." Joanie gave in. In her heart of hearts she knew that Nathan could be the difference between life or death for her brothers in a bad situation. Nothing bothered him. *It's not that you're complex, darling,* she thought rather distantly, *it's that you're simple.*

"Joe?" Nathan turned to his friend.

"Yeah, little buddy?"

"Call my broker in Chicago tomorrow—his home number is on the computer. When the bell rings on the Nikkei on Monday, Tokyo time, tell him to sell everything in my B and C files and put it into the A file. All of it. He'll know what it means. Got it?"

"Yeah, got it," Joe replied. "B and C into A."

"You guys are out of your minds," Joanie observed to no one in particular.

"Tell me about it, Joanie," Becky agreed. "I feel like I'm in a bad war movie or something."

Anne Wheat, failing to see any humor in the situation, went to the refrigerator to pack food for the plane trip.

"May I use your phone, Professor Wheat?" Chet asked politely. "I want to see if I can get through to my folks. Dad has a cellular phone in his car."

"Sure, Chet. Help yourself," Wheat replied. The old man pulled his rosary beads from his pocket. *Time to pray.* That reminded him of Karl Slinger. *Karl'll pray, too.* "Chet, if you can't get through, let me have the phone so I can call Karl."

"Sure thing, Professor Wheat," Chet answered, punching numbers into the phone.

Nathan looked back at the television screen. A devastating earthquake in one of the information centers of the world could not long keep images of carnage from rolling onto the screen in waves. The most gruesome images were already starting to transfer from newsrooms into living rooms around the country.

Nathan knew, however, that within a few days images of wreckage and bloodied bodies would be replaced with graphics portraying numbers. New York was the financial center of the world. He had worked with its numbers for many years. They were *his* numbers. European banks, racked by recession, would surely call in the incomprehensibly massive notes borrowed by the United States Government over the past thirty years. Only God knew how the Japanese would react. The house of cards was finally going to come down.

He shook his head and took a long lazy drag off his cigarette. *So it begins,* Nathan thought. *So it begins.*

5

Saturday Morning
15 June
Salt Lake City, Utah

John Lanning, Dottie Slinger, and Karl Slinger knelt in silent prayer before the Blessed Sacrament in the Cathedral of the Madeleine. They met each day at eleven to make a Holy Hour with Jesus, followed by noon Mass to receive His Body and Blood. The routine set well with the three senior citizens. They all felt at peace with themselves and the world. It seemed as if Lanning had always been a Catholic, though he had only been one for seven months. His highly publicized conversion in January had turned the city on its ear for several weeks.

Lanning had carefully planned his coming out of Mormonism to have the largest possible impact. The first press conference had been on January ninth. He told Elena about his conversion thirty minutes before he spoke to the cameras, and faxed his resignation to the LDS office building fifteen minutes later. Except for some of the Kolbe Foundation leaders in South Bend, only Karl, Dottie, and Lee knew about his conversion to Catholicism. Every weekend, Slinger had flown Lanning to Saint George in southern Utah to enable him to attend Sunday Mass without exposure.

With Slinger's help, Lanning had carefully timed the dissemination of press releases. The very minute the press conference began, they were faxed simultaneously to the most influential news desks around the country. The local television, radio, and print media in Utah did not know the nature of the press conference—but they all knew and respected John Lanning. The headline read:

TOP MORMON OFFICIAL BECOMES CATHOLIC. CLAIMS HE CONDUCTED MISLEADING PUBLIC RELATIONS CAMPAIGNS FOR DECADES.

The facts revealed in the press release were all available in the public domain and could be garnered from numerous sources with careful research. The genius was in the presentation. All sources were verifiable. Many of them came from Christians who were former Mormons. Some of these Christians had written books and had produced exceptional videos—but few of these materials were widely circulated.

Lanning gave the press conference at the SLG Institute press room with Karl Slinger standing behind him. Lee had flown to Salt Lake City to intercede for John in front of the tabernacle in the cathedral, less than a block away. A digital video copy of the press conference was instantly available to all satellite wire agencies and through them to television news stations across the world. A transcript was uploaded onto the Internet and all the major computer on-line services. Lanning picked a slow news hour on a slow news day.

The primary purpose of John Lanning's effort was not to attack Mormonism. Revealing the truth about the LDS was a noble but secondary goal. Lanning knew that his sensational conversion—he described his trip to hell during the press conference—would cause a stir but would soon fade away, as all news stories eventually do. He knew that a hot story usually becomes cold in less than three days.

His primary goal was to reach out to Mormons who had doubts about their faith, just as he himself had doubts for years before his trip to hell. He looked into the cameras and addressed this sizable minority. He urged them to leave a faith they knew in their hearts was not true. He gave them an 800 number to call to get confidential information on joining a self-help group for ex-Mormons. He announced the establishment of a legal defense fund for ex-Mormons who were subject to economic retribution from Mormon employers.

"The real Jesus is not a spirit child," he explained in his practiced, grandfatherly voice. His gray hair, short stature, and bushy black eyebrows all gave an impression of calm trustworthiness. He was well aware that he looked and sounded a bit like Walter Cronkite.

"The real Christian Jesus is the Eternal God who called forth the entire universe from nothingness. I believe the real Christian Jesus is calling you and He's waiting for you in the tabernacles of Catholic churches around the world. He's calling you today! Listen to Him as He speaks in your heart! Go! Go and talk to Him. Ask Him to show you the truth! You will not regret your prayers. You will feel the *authentic* burning in your breast of His real Christian Spirit!"

Mostly, though, Lanning appealed to his isolated brothers by setting a courageous example. Only Mormons trapped in a suffocating faith they didn't believe could truly appreciate the bravery it took for Lanning to publicly denounce the sect in the center of its power, Salt Lake City.

For several days his face and voice were everywhere in Salt Lake City. A firestorm raged throughout Utah in the papers and on the radio talk shows. Lanning made himself available for interviews twenty-four hours a day. The fact that it became national news prevented local Mormon-controlled media outlets from squelching the story at the outset. For once, he was able to play to his advantage the dominant national media ambivalence toward religion. The story made CNI and two network news programs—their editors were happy to "bash" a religion—any religion. The fact that Lanning provided only truthful data about the LDS seemed to matter little to these secular program directors. A documentary was independently produced and aired on the show *Newsmakers*. He was also interviewed by *60 Minutes*.

Three days after his press conference, the LDS issued a terse, official written statement branding Lanning a crazed apostate, hinting that he was mentally unstable. Even worse, it was announced that an internal investigation was underway to determine if he had embezzled money from the LDS—an outright lie carefully worded to plant a seed of doubt in the average person's mind.

The following day he filed a defamation of character lawsuit which had been prepared by Lenny Gold ahead of time. The lawsuit revealed that he had passed an extensive battery of psychological tests with flying colors. The lawsuit gave more media attention to Lanning, who continued to appeal to disillusioned Mormons with every sound bite. The LDS was forced to issue an official apology in the face of publicity that portrayed them as a big bully attacking a recent heart attack victim.

He knew his "onslaught" was not much more than a simple ten-minute speech and a few sound bites. He let the media do his work for him by creating an "event" and a series of follow-up "events." And the LDS no longer had the formidable John Lanning in *their* public relations department. This exquisitely rich irony buoyed his resolve as he won one media battle after another. It greatly amused Karl Slinger.

By fighting back intelligently and quickly, Lanning was able to publicly demonstrate that the LDS was not much different from many large institutions. The LDS appeared more imposing than it really was. He graphically proved that one man could stand up to the monolithic organization. This gave even more courage to disillusioned Mormons.

During the first few weeks the story dominated a popular local Salt Lake City radio talk show. The station was not LDS-owned. Many outraged, believing Mormons called in to condemn Lanning. He was called names. He was called a tool of the devil. He was called a liar. He was called an adulterer and a thief. One woman claimed that she was a prostitute who had slept with Lanning several times.

Some of the callers, however, voiced their agreement with Lanning and related how they were terrified to leave the sect for fear of losing their jobs and families. The fear in their voices was palpable. They told listeners that defamation was a typical Mormon reaction to those who left the sect. Fear of defamation was just one more trap that kept many Mormons in a religion they didn't believe was true. Ex-Mormons called and confirmed that they too had been persecuted.

Except for the lawsuit, Lanning generally ignored public criticism and tried to keep a high media profile for as long as possible. Thousands of Mormons called his hot line and hundreds joined the self-help group, which formed several new chapters all over the state. Dozens converted to Catholicism overnight—most had been contemplating their conversions long before Lanning gave them the courage to follow through.

One month after the press conference he published a short book. It detailed his conversion and described most of the stranger teachings of Mormonism. Many bookstores in Utah refused to sell the book, but Lanning took out ads in Utah newspapers and magazines and sold the book direct through a fulfillment company in South Dakota. Over thirty-thousand copies sold in the first six weeks, and major Protestant and Catholic catalog book distributors picked it up. It was titled *Out From the Pits of Hell.* He donated the proceeds to the Truth Society, the self-help group for ex-Mormons which had been established years before.

The Kolbe Foundation produced a free audio tape by John Lanning, similar to the book, and over 100,000 copies were distributed all over the country before June.

Retribution came swiftly. Karl Slinger and SLG Industries became targets. Seventy percent of the Mormon ranches associated with SLG severed ties within three months. Twenty-seven devout Mormons resigned from SLG the day after the press conference. Thousands of Mormons sold their stock in SLG and the stock took a dive. The undervalued stock was soon snapped up by savvy buyers—including Nathan Payne. Within a few weeks SLG stock rebounded nicely. Then local offices of federal regulatory agencies such as OSHA and the

EPA began to call on SLG properties for "spot inspections." Slinger, no stranger to regulatory harassment, called in his chips with several local non-Mormon or nominally Mormon politicians. SLG Industries' largest department was the legal department. It fought ferociously and successfully against the trumped up "violations." Most of this activity occurred in Utah and southern Idaho. Slinger, on Lanning's advice, kept a low profile. He laughed it off. "Nothing's worse than Guadalcanal, John! And we're just getting started!"

The attacks on Lanning were more personal. Elena moved out immediately and sued for divorce within a week. Mormon friends refused to say hello to him on the street. One restaurant refused to seat him for dinner. No matter how many times he changed his unlisted phone number, threatening messages piled up on his answering machine. He carefully made notarized copies and sent them to Lenny Gold. Months later, Lanning was still receiving up to four messages a day. A typical message claimed that he was in league with the devil. Sometimes he recognized the voices—"friends" he had associated with socially or professionally for decades. Someone left a dead cat on his front porch, and rocks were thrown through his windows. An unmarked white van with darkly tinted windows appeared at odd hours, parked several houses down on his street. Karl had a private company check the house for electronic devices and a phone tap was discovered. This was documented by Lenny Gold.

Lanning was afraid but undaunted. He told Karl that his best insurance against physical harm was to keep a high public profile. Nevertheless, Lenny Gold composed a simple private letter detailing some of this documented harassment and sent it to the LDS on John's behalf. Gold reminded the LDS that nothing Lanning had publicly stated about the LDS was misleading or false, and hinted that he knew many more "facts" that could be released to the public.

"Let'em quake and wonder exactly what it is you know, Johnny Boy," Slinger remarked. "Lenny can play hardball with the best of them."

For his part, Lenny was energized by the whole affair and genuinely enjoyed working for Lanning. Lenny told Slinger that he would stay on with SLG indefinitely.

The harassment abated immediately, but never quite went away altogether. Lanning eventually sold his home as part of the divorce settlement. The spectacular property was purchased by an American Express executive who had transferred to Salt Lake City from Seattle. Lanning moved in with Slinger, who hired a full-time security guard. Whenever the mysterious van showed up, the guard set up a video camera on a tripod on Slinger's porch. The van stopped showing up.

By June several thousand Mormons had followed Lanning's lead and left the sect—a tiny segment of the Mormon population. Hundreds entered the Catholic Church—these converts tended to be more like Lanning in temperament and determination. They formed a core group to continue his work in their own spheres of influence. He was their hero and liberator. Hundreds of thousands of Protestants and Catholics became irreversibly aware that Mormonism, on the merit of its own teachings, had very little in common with authentic Christianity. A convert to Protestantism from Mormonism took over control of the Truth Society. Ironically, the convert's name was Joseph Smith; he began to organize chapters in all fifty states. Across America millions of ordinary people briefly wondered if the Mormons really were what they claimed to be. Seeds of doubt were sown.

Lanning's conversion eventually played itself out as a media event. Nevertheless, few people in Salt Lake City did not know who John Lanning was. The Catholic chancery had kept a very low profile throughout the affair—at Lanning's request—and quite properly, in his opinion. He took a part-time job in the public relations department of SLG Industries, splitting his time between SLG and helping Becky Jackson over the phone at the Kolbe Foundation. Both Lanning and Slinger mistakenly believed that the worst was behind them.

Chapter Nineteen

1

Saturday Afternoon
15 June
Notre Dame, Indiana

A summer afternoon at Notre Dame is a wonderful thing—if the humidity is low. Today was such a day. A group of thirty students and teachers along with a few religious brothers and two priests were gathered under the Grotto's gray stone overhang. It was a bigger crowd than normal. *Are others here to pray because of the quake?* Joanie asked herself.

"You really shouldn't have come, Beck," Joanie said. She had noticed that Becky was walking with difficulty. Joe was practically holding her up as they made their way toward the Grotto.

"I'm fine, I think," Becky said without her usual directness.

The daily Rosary was beginning. They joined the group, and prayed for Denny, Chet and Nathan, who were already flying to New Jersey. Before the fourth decade was finished, the threesome had to leave. Becky's contractions were less than five minutes apart.

2

Saturday Afternoon
15 June
The skies over Pennsylvania

"Reach into my bag and grab the bottle you see there," Denny said to Nathan, without taking his eyes away from the clear skies in front of him.

Nathan pulled the unopened bottle of Scotch out from the bag. He held it up for Denny to see.

"Open it!" Denny said loudly over the din of the engine. He was really pushing the Cessna. Nathan opened the bottle and handed it to Denny, who took a small swig and wiped his mouth with his sleeve.

Nathan followed suit, taking a bigger swig. He offered the bottle back to Denny, who shook his head, saying, "Can't. I don't drink when I fly."

"But you just did," Nathan pointed out. Denny smiled.

"I know. Wish me a happy birthday, Nathan—I didn't get to have any upside down cake or anything. And thanks for the Scotch—great present. We'll save the rest for medicinal purposes."

"Happy birthday, Denny," Nathan said with little enthusiasm. "Now that you mention it, I do feel a bit under the weather—or over the weather," Nathan added. He took another sip, looking out the window at the clouds below.

Denny had climbed high when the first mountains in Pennsylvania appeared. He explained calmly to Nathan that downdrafts on the backsides of mountains caused a lot of crashes for new pilots. Nathan, who was still a rather daring car driver himself, almost felt comfortable with Denny at the stick. He rarely felt comfortable if someone else was "driving." After recovering from the accident, he drove cautiously for about two weeks, but quickly reverted back to his old ways. Denny also seemed to enjoy skirting the fine line between safe speed and reckless speed, always leaning toward the edge of safety—although Nathan, relatively ignorant of aircraft piloting, had no way of knowing for sure.

Nathan turned to offer Father Chet a swig of Scotch, but the priest was asleep with his Breviary in his lap. Chet was leaning against several bags of groceries in the cramped back seat.

To kill time, Nathan asked Denny to explain the numerous gauges and gadgets on the dashboard.

✠ ✠ ✠

Father Chet was jolted slightly and woke up when Denny dropped down to land in a small private airport near Bellefonte, Pennsylvania. Denny pulled the plane close to the ancient-looking hangar behind the control hut. An old mechanic in oil-stained Dickeys waved at them from the cab of a fuel truck.

"Wait here," Denny said, as he jumped out onto the cracked macadam. He walked briskly to the fuel truck. The mechanic obviously knew Denny because he smiled when they shook hands.

The old man hooked a hose up to the Cessna's tank. Nathan and Chet watched the two aviation buffs talk. The weather was beautiful and the mechanic squinted as he pointed westward then eastward a few times, then held up four fingers.

Less than five minutes later, Denny was back in the pilot's seat and pointing the Cessna toward the runway. He radioed to the tiny control tower for permission to take off. Chet barely felt the wheels leave the ground.

"What gives?" Nathan asked.

"We're the fifth plane headed for New Jersey old Charley's refueled in the last hour and a half. Apparently, we're not the only ones doing what we're doing. The FAA is discouraging private flights into the counties near New York, so we might not get permission to land at Essex County Airport. The word is that Newark, La Guardia, Kennedy, Teeterboro, and most of the county airports are shut down. I could radio in to get more information, but I want to keep a low profile.

"Charley says the whole place is a disaster area. Bridges gone, fires everywhere, highways turned to rubble—the whole nine yards. The quake lasted for over a minute and was close to the surface, according to Charley, whatever that means. One thing is for sure—the infrastructure on the East Coast wasn't built for California-type earthquakes. Charley says he heard that there was a tiny quake in the 1980s from Montreal down through New York City. Rattled some dishes upstate on Thanksgiving day, but barely made the papers. Scientists didn't even know the fault was there until it happened."

"Unbelievable. So, can we get permission to land somewhere?" Nathan asked, feeling quite ignorant.

"No problem. My flight plan takes us to a private airport near Lake Hopatcong."

"Lake Hopatcong? That's over forty miles away from Essex County Airport, isn't it?"

"I know," Denny replied.

"Can't you get into Essex County?" Chet asked from the back seat, shouting mildly to be heard.

"Probably not. Then again, we're not going to Lake Hopatcong, either," Denny said mischievously.

"Quit beating around the bush, Den. Where are we going to land?" Nathan insisted.

"Don't know, exactly. Close to Greg. Don't worry—I'll find a place to land."

"I feel much better now knowing that. No, wait. I just started to feel much worse. I think I'll take some more of that medicine," Nathan said, grabbing the bottle of Scotch and taking a gulp. "Happy birthday, flyboy! My worthless life is in your practiced hands. We're probably gonna land in the parking lot of the local A&P, right? Hey, do you want some medicine, Chetmeister?"

"No thanks, Nathan," Chet replied. "I think I'm a little airsick."

"So you'll mind if I light up?" Nathan inquired.

"Go ahead and smoke if you want. It's up to Denny," Chet said judiciously.

"Normally, I don't like smoking in my cabin," Denny said, "but I'll make an exception as long as Father Chet makes sure he barfs into a bag."

Nathan lit a Parliament. There were only a couple left in the pack. The flight—more than the destination—was making him nervous. "Sorry, Chetmeister. You're a smoker. You understand."

"I do. Go ahead. I won't barf," he promised charitably. "I was exaggerating."

"Thanks buddy," Nathan replied sincerely, a little disappointed with himself for not being strong enough to hold off. He took a deep pull off the cigarette and closed his eyes, willing himself to relax.

"A little under two hours, folks, and we'll be landing in New Jersey at dusk," Denny said cheerfully. "I hope the skies stay clear—we'll need the light if I have to, ah, improvise the landing."

He's having fun, Nathan thought with admiration.

"Let's say a Rosary, Lucky Lindy," Chet suggested.

Nathan and Denny pulled their rosaries out of their pockets and waited for the black robe to begin.

3

Saturday Evening
15 June
South Bend, Indiana

Joe said very little during the relatively short delivery. His mind was overloaded by stimuli. He had to sign a waiver—some kind of incomprehensible legal thing—to get the hospital to let Joanie help in the birthing room. There was a doctor on call but a midwife supervised the delivery.

Joe regretted skipping the Lamaze classes. He had read a book on fetal development and delivery—pretty dry stuff compared to the real McCoy, he now realized. He watched in wonder as his wife's body and temperament changed. During the most violent pushing he tried to console Becky by taking hold of her hand. She scolded him through clenched teeth in a polite but extremely agitated way: "Please take your hands off me! I don't need that right now, Joe!"

Joanie took Joe aside and explained that a woman in labor will sometimes say things she normally wouldn't say due to stress, rapid hormonal changes, and sheer pain. Her brothers' wives had told her as much, Joanie assured him.

At one point the curiously taciturn midwife turned to Joe and ordered in a pleasant tone of voice, "Come around front, Mr. Jackson. The head's coming out. Time to catch her."

"Me? What? Catch the baby?" Joe asked.

Becky looked up at her husband and said rather forcefully, "You've caught a million stinking footballs! Catch my baby like the lady says!"

Joanie put her hand on the small of Joe's back and gave the overwhelmed father-to-be a small push. Becky gave a rather bigger push of her own.

4

Saturday, Dusk
15 June
The sky over North Caldwell, New Jersey

"Suburbia is not the greatest place to land a plane, fellas. Especially in the wake of an earthquake," Denny said, looking around for five flat, straight acres. "I need five or six acres, but I'll settle for four. Pavement is great, but grass is okay, too."

The sun was just dipping behind the horizon. They could now see the horrific damage with their own eyes. Every other house was twisted or broken. Traffic jams of abandoned cars were everywhere. Gaping crags of broken pavement jutted at every angle. Whole streets had become a maze of cracks and fissures. Fires burned everywhere. A huge cloud of black smoke formed over a gas station that had blown up on Bloomfield Avenue in Essex Fells.

They flew over Essex County Airport, which was less than a mile from Greg's house, but Denny was unable to establish radio contact with the control tower. He had been flying low since ten miles before Lake Hopatcong. When the control tower at Lake Hopatcong Airport called, Denny "faked" radio problems and dove low—below five hundred feet—for the last brief leg of the flight.

Essex County Airport was gone—a jumble of split wood and metal and glass. An abandoned corporate Citation jet blocked the middle of the runway; its passenger door hung open. *Must have been starting its takeoff when the quake hit,* Denny surmised.

"Here goes. Wish we could beam down," he said casually. He saw the ashen look on Nathan's face. "Sorry, didn't mean to make light of it."

He brought the Cessna around to face the landing strip.

"But there's a plane on the runway!" Nathan shouted, and then gulped.

"No problem, I'll land parallel to it—on the grass. It's flatter and nicer than Dad's backyard. I just have to avoid those annoying little lights they always put next to the runway," Denny explained, using layman's terms for the sake of his passengers.

"So we don't have to worry?" Chet asked, noticing how quickly the ground was coming up to meet the Cessna.

"Worry all you want; it won't matter either way…" Denny said calmly as he touched down on the grass, as light as a sandpiper on a beach. He ran the Cessna directly over a string of signal devices. They went right between the Cessna's wheels until he got the plane past the Citation. He let his tail down, and steered onto the runway. He came to a stop and turned the plane around to face in the opposite direction to which he had landed, just to the side of the runway. He shut down the engine and began checking the instrument panel. He made a mental note that half a tank of fuel remained. *Just in case we need to get off fast,* he told himself. Denny logged his hours out of ingrained habit.

Denny looked at Nathan, whose color was returning now that the plane had come to a stop. *You should stay out of the air, Nathan. Cool in a crisis, eh! Anyway, you'll never know how easy I just made that landing look, brother-in-law. I was pretty sure I had a few inches clearance over those signals— but I wasn't completely sure. It had to be less than two inches. One midsize bump and bammo! Flip City!*

"A piece of cake, wasn't it, Lindy?" Chet asked naïvely.

"Piece of cake," Denny lied smoothly. "You're in more danger gettin' outta bed in the morning."

There was a long silence.

"Let's find Greg," Nathan said, clearing his mind of all things relating to planes, unfastening his seat belt. "He lives up on the hill, right, Chet?"

"Right. How we going to get there?"

"Considering the roads around here, it might just be easiest to walk. We can carry the groceries," Nathan suggested as he climbed out and jumped to the ground. He surveyed the landscape. *Not many people around, are there?* Then he heard the first, far-off gunshot. The first of many.

Denny pulled his Colt 1911 from under the seat of the Cessna. He checked the safety, put an extra clip in his pocket, and jammed the gun into his belt. Father Chet watched but said nothing.

5

Saturday Evening
15 June
South Bend, Indiana

"Here she comes!" the midwife shouted to Joe. Amy's head was already out.

Becky gave a deep groaning shout during the final push, and Joanie watched in awe as the baby slipped into Joe's big, soft hands. The baby was quiet, but squirmed. He felt the tiny creature pull in its first breath.

"A girl!" he called softly to his wife. "Becky you did it! A girl! We have a daughter!"

The midwife quickly clamped and cut the cord. A nurse took the child from Joe and began to rub the natural fluid that a baby is born with into its skin. Then she wrapped a blanket around the infant and gave the newborn to her father. Joe carefully handed Amy Jackson to her mother.

"My baby!" Becky cried with relief and joy. Her arms were fatigued but she didn't mind. Turning to Joanie, she repeated, more softly, "Look, Joanie! My baby!"

Joanie was speechless. She prayed a quick mental prayer of thanks, and thought of the new life in her own womb. "God Bless us all," she told Becky and Joe finally. The midwife smiled politely.

Joe came around to Becky's side. His senses were heightened to a degree he had only previously experienced on the football field. He looked at his wife, noticing the dark circles under her brown eyes, and the many tiny blood vessels which had come to just below the surface of her neck and cheeks due to the strain of pushing. He thought of Jesus sweating blood in the Garden of Gethsemane.

Becky had already attached Amy to her breast for the first meal of her life—at Joanie's urging, Becky had read two books on natural breast-feeding and had decided to give it a try.

Joe put one hand on Becky's head and another on the body of his daughter, intoning solemnly, "Dear Jesus, I consecrate this child to the Immaculate Heart of Your Mother."

"Amen," Joanie whispered.

"Amen, Joseph. Amen," Becky repeated.

The midwife cleared her throat. "Whenever you're ready, Mrs. Jackson, just buzz the nurses' station. They'll need to weigh the child and do a few things."

6

Saturday Evening
15 June
North Caldwell, New Jersey

It was dark by the time Chet, Nathan, and Denny loaded food, water, and first aid supplies into knapsacks. The walk to Greg Wheat's house took less than ten minutes. There was very little traffic on the streets. When they first climbed up a residential street across from Essex County Airport, it seemed like there was no one around. Then they began to notice the dim light of candles in the homes which remained standing. One family was cooking a meal on a portable grill in the backyard. Two children huddled in blankets even though the temperature outside was quite warm.

Nathan thought better of walking up the driveway when he noticed the shotgun leaning on the tree within reach of the husband. The father smiled and waved at them.

Two teenagers were shooting baskets in the moonlight in another driveway. They ignored Chet, Denny, and Nathan. Several men were at another large house, trying to move debris from a Jeep Cherokee in a garage, shouting and cursing as they lifted a large wooden beam.

Water streamed down the center of the street. It must have been coming from a broken main.

This is surreal, Nathan thought. *It's like a science fiction movie.*

They came upon an overweight man in a dirty business suit who was sitting on the curb, sobbing. Chet approached him and asked if he needed any help. The man waved Chet away. When Chet persisted the man began to scream at the top of his lungs, "Leave me alone! This is all your fault, you filthy priest!"

Chet felt instant confusion. The man stood up and took a step toward him. Chet backed away.

Nathan stepped between them; the man stopped in his tracks, looked at Denny and Chet, and collapsed on the ground. He began to sob again. "Leave me alone," he cried softly.

"Let's go, Chet. Remember why we're here, buddy," Nathan said, taking Chet's arm firmly and pulling him away. "Greg and his family are just around the corner—one more street."

"The whole world has changed…" Chet said distantly.

"Get a grip, Chetmeister," Nathan said firmly.

Chet shook his head back and forth, but said nothing.

After what seemed like an eternity they reached Greg Wheat's house. It was a modern colonial set back from the street. The remains of the unattached garage, where Chet had stayed briefly after getting kicked out of Notre Dame du Lac, sat at the end of the long driveway. The garage had collapsed. Mindy's Taurus could be seen in the rubble, covered with broken wood and white dust from drywall. A couch from the apartment rested on the roof of the car.

Greg's Ford Explorer was parked in the driveway next to the house. The back gate of the vehicle was open. An oak tree had crashed through a wall on the opposite side of the house and there was a large crack in the foundation next to the front steps. The steps themselves were damaged. The whole house looked a bit off-kilter.

"Look! Light!" Denny called as he ran up to the side door of the house. He had seen a flashlight flicker in the kitchen window on the side of the house near the Explorer.

"Greg! Greg! Mindy! It's me! Denny! It's me, Denny!" he yelled, his voice echoing off the damaged homes surrounding them.

"Denny!" Greg shouted as he came out the door, holding a stuffed suitcase in his hands. Greg dropped the suitcase and embraced his brother. Mindy and the two children, Billy and Beth, came running out the door behind him, calling, "Uncle Denny! Uncle Denny!"

"Father Chet! Nathan! What are you doing here?" Mindy cried. She was a tall woman—taller than Greg, with dark hair. She was wearing a clean white skirt and a button-down shirt which must have belonged to Greg. Beth, the three-year-old, was holding her leg. Billy, five, ran up to Denny, who lifted him, kissed the boy on the face, and gave him a bear hug.

"We're here to help. We flew into Essex County Airport in Denny's Cessna," Nathan explained.

"Get the kids inside," Greg ordered without raising his voice. "Now."

Mindy shared a knowing look with her husband and then bent down to pick up Beth. "Come on, sweetheart. Daddy says we've got to go back inside."

"But it's dark inside!" Beth complained in a whiny voice. Mindy ignored her and turned to the men. "Let's all go in."

Nathan took the knapsack off his shoulder and searched through it before pulling out an electric lantern, which he turned on and showed to Beth.

"Turn it off, Nathan," Greg said. "Not outside. It's not safe."

"Okay," Nathan replied, flicking off the lantern.

They went into the house through the side door.

Father Chet and Mindy took the children into the dining room with Nathan's lantern and distracted the children while Denny, Nathan, and Greg had a powwow in the kitchen. Greg lit a holy candle for light and closed the window shades.

Greg told them what had happened during the earthquake. He and the children had been outside playing in the front yard when it hit. Mindy was working in the garden in the backyard. Greg dove to cover his children as the earth itself shook abruptly. "It rolled like the ground was one gigantic water bed."

All around him Greg heard the sound of buildings creaking and cracking. The neighbors on either side were out of town—on vacation down the New Jersey shore. He spent much of the afternoon helping his neighbor across the street climb out of the rubble of his house. The man, unmarried and not a close friend of Greg's, had a broken arm and walked off to find a hospital.

Other neighbors had gathered in the street to exchange notes. Water was out. The phone lines were also out and the cellular phone lines—those that were working—were jammed with calls. Cellular phone relay stations were apparently down in the area. One neighbor brought out a portable television and played it off the cigarette lighter of his car. No New York stations were broadcasting and the reports from the two local New Jersey stations were spotty. The governors of both New York and New Jersey declared a sundown curfew for non-rescue workers. According to the radio stations, the National Guard had been called in to assist. Only one New York radio station—an FM light music format—was on the air, and it was playing "Feelings" over and over again.

Estimates of casualties were already in the tens of thousands for New Jersey, and hundreds of thousands in New York City. Neither Greg nor his neighbors found it easy to accept the radio reports that most of the taller skyscrapers in New York were no longer standing—including the Empire State Building. There was an amazing, unsubstantiated report that the rock that was Manhattan Island had split right down the middle of 42nd Street, which was completely filled with water. Apparently, the epicenter of the quake was within a mile or so north of Manhattan Island. New Jersey had suffered relatively moderate damage. The quake had been felt all the way up the Hudson River Valley and there was serious damage in Albany. Buildings as far north as Montreal had suffered minor damage.

"If it hadn't been a Saturday, I might be dead—or worse," Greg observed coolly. He worked in New York for a large law firm. "I believe with all my heart that God inspired me to take the kids out to play ten minutes before the quake. Who knows what would have happened if we were inside? That tree crashed right into the room where we were playing before we went outside.

"I'm kind of disoriented. The quake hit less than seven hours ago," Greg said. "What should I do next? I've been hearing gunshots for several hours. I'm scared. This is the only candle in the house. I don't have a gun. I haven't seen a cop since this happened. One radio report said that looting has started in Newark. I was loading the Ford to see if I could make a break before things get worse. I wasn't sure where to go, though. I was thinking of driving west 'til I found a hotel. Somehow I don't think I'll be going to work on Monday. I doubt the building is still standing…" Greg trailed off after the rush of thoughts were expressed. His voice had started to tremble.

Nathan noticed how much Greg looked like Denny. Greg had darker hair that was tinged with first gray, and an almost identical build. Greg had a small paunch. *You've done a good job holding things together, Greg. I fell apart on a simple plane ride while you were keeping your family together here. What I'm going to suggest next is going to be a hard pill to swallow…*

"I have a suggestion," Nathan offered calmly.

Greg looked up, waiting.

"I suggest we take you, Mindy, and the kids and get as far away from here as possible. It's relatively calm outside right now. I think people are in shock, wondering what to do next, listening to radios for information. But that's going to wear off. The emotional shock won't last forever.

"I don't know this for sure, but I think the financial repercussions of this quake—if it's as bad as it sounds—are going to plunge the country into an instant depression. This might trigger the social unrest predicted on your dad's tapes. Business is shut down indefinitely around here, and food might become scarce. It's going to get dangerous.

"Driving might not be the answer. The roads heading west are going to be jammed by sun up, and many are not functional right now from what we saw on the way in. Flying is the only way out for now. You and Mindy and the kids can fit in the Cessna—Chet and I can stay behind—"

"No, wait!" Denny said loudly, taking hold of Nathan's arm, "I have a better idea—"

"We can't drive out, Denny. You saw the streets—" Nathan interrupted.

"Not driving. Flying," Denny said with a certain thoughtful look on his face. "And we can all get out together. With more people if we want, too, maybe. Let me explain…"

✝ ✝ ✝

One hour later, Greg gave Nathan a new pack of Marlboro Lights, and Nathan left alone in Greg's Explorer for Bloomfield. He had Denny's gun tucked in his jacket pocket. Driving as fast as he could, it took him an hour to complete what was normally a fifteen-minute trip. More than once he had to throw the Explorer into four wheel drive and leave the road to drive around car accidents, trees, and debris in the road. Twice he was forced to backtrack when he ran into huge crevices which he could not cross.

He finally found his way to the condominium where Chet's parents lived. It was just off of the main street in town, Bloomfield Avenue. It was not far from where Nathan had attended grammar school at Our Lady of Lourdes.

It was strange—this section of Bloomfield seemed untouched by the quake and had suffered relatively little damage. Nathan had encountered such "pockets" of normalcy several times during his trip. One street would be perfectly free of confusion or damage; the next would be utterly destroyed, every building turned to rubble.

James and Mary Sullivan were not in their condominium. Nathan found them with a young married couple in the condominium next door. The newlywed couple, the O'Briens, were close friends of James and Mary. The O'Briens often attended daily Mass with the Sullivans. Ronnie O'Brien worked in a bagel shop he owned with his wife Gloria. After a moment's deliberation, Nathan offered them a chance to leave with the Sullivans. He explained Denny's plan.

At first, James and Mary Sullivan didn't want to leave their home. Nathan was confused because James was retired and none of their children or relatives lived in New York or New Jersey. James and Mary had grown up and married in Boston before moving down decades earlier.

Nathan persisted. After an hour's debate, he finally convinced James and Mary to come with him. He persuaded them that they could always return after things settled down—though in his heart he doubted things would ever be the same. Near the end of the discussion, the five people were interrupted by the sounds of running on the street outside. There were gunshots, shouting, and cursing. It was a gang of young men.

Nathan watched through a slit in the curtain, his .45 drawn. He saw one of them fire a pistol at Greg's Explorer from twenty yards away, shattering the back window. Nathan felt slightly foolish holding the gun. He had never fired a gun, although Denny had given him last minute lessons.

They waited for ten minutes until the gang moved on. The Sullivans and O'Briens packed a change of clothes, some personal papers, and many photographs into a few boxes. James and Mary also brought a small strongbox filled with four dozen gold coins—representing over half their life savings. They quickly loaded the Explorer and jumped in. It was now past three in the morning and eerily quiet. Smoke from fires clouded out the moonlight. Nathan started the utility vehicle and quickly pulled away. James began to lead everyone in the Rosary. Nathan, distracted by the darkened streets and obstacles, was only able to pray half the responses.

A few minutes later, he took a left hand turn onto a side street and stopped suddenly. Mary screamed. Nathan ordered everybody to be quiet and get down. He felt adrenaline drop into his spine and chest like cold electricity.

Ahead of them, less than forty yards away, was the street gang they had seen earlier.

They were pulling television sets out of a storefront and loading them into a gray stepvan. One turned and shouted when he saw the Explorer. A few more youths came out of the store. Suddenly a dozen of them were facing Nathan and his passengers. Two or three had handguns. It was hard for Nathan to see clearly in the dark.

Nathan quickly kicked into reverse and spun the Explorer around in a driveway.

Gunshots rang out. "Get down!" Nathan shouted. Mary and Gloria screamed, clinging to Ronnie. James crouched next to Nathan in the front seat and continued praying his Rosary, but louder. Nathan hit the gas and drove away from the gang, which was now running toward the Explorer. A bullet ripped through the windshield to Nathan's right, causing a spidery web of glass to blur his vision on that side. He could hear the wild cries of the pursuers behind him.

Cursing under his breath, he resisted an impulse to stop the Explorer, get out, and beat the tar out of the hoodlums. *Why are they coming after us? Why don't they just leave us alone and go back to stealing their televisions?* The answer came to him: *Because they can. Because they think it would be fun to kill us. Because they're not afraid of being stopped.*

Then his mind's small still voice suggested another reason: *Because the evil one is guiding them.*

He prayed.

He tried desperately to remember which street was which. *I grew up around here!* he shouted in his mind.

The street came to a quick end and he had to turn either right or left. The gang was now only fifty yards behind him. He turned left, up a hill, and stopped short before a pileup of cars. The road was completely blocked. He quickly computed the odds of getting over the rubble, and despaired. He couldn't drive around the wrecks because the houses on either side had collapsed, leaving rubble on the sidewalk. It was an old neighborhood with houses built closely together and set in a few yards from the street.

Nathan cut his lights and quickly turned the Explorer around to face the other direction. *Think! Pray!* Nathan began a desperate prayer to his guardian angel: *Angel of God, Enlighten me—* He stopped in mid-prayer.

Enlighten. A plan, unlikely and bold, formed quickly in his mind. *Execute the plan,* he thought.

How far away are the bad guys from the turn I just took? Nathan calculated, willing panic out of his mind.

He chambered a round in the Colt .45.

"Wait here, stay down—they might not realize you were in the car with me," he whispered quickly to the others. "If something happens to me, your best bet might be to play possum. Be ready to drive, James. I'm going. When you hear me hit the car with a pebble, hit the high-beams. Keep your hand on the switch, right here."

"What are you—" James whispered back.

"No time!" Nathan whispered harshly, giving James a determined look. He slipped out the door and disappeared into the dark toward the sound of the men in front of them.

✝ ✝ ✝

Where are they? Denny asked himself desperately, huddled in the dark kitchen of Greg's home. Billy Wheat was sleeping on his lap. *They should have been back by now.* A cold chill whispered down his back. Denny began to pray, for there was nothing more he could do.

✝ ✝ ✝

Joe held the child in his arms as he sat next to Becky's bed. *You're here!* Yesterday, Amy was hidden in the womb. Today she had exploded into the world, causing an avalanche of thoughts to tumble down the valley of his mind.

"Joe? Joe?" Becky asked anxiously, calling him out of his reverie. He surfaced from a world of abstract connections.

"Yeah Beck?"

"Do you think they'll ever come back?" There was a line of concern on her forehead.

"Yes," he replied simply, still looking at Amy.

"How can you be so certain?" Becky asked, as much to hear the answer as to have Joe say something that would give her hope. She was sure he had thought of something that would give her hope.

He turned to look at Becky directly. "Because Nathan's not like the rest of us. A guy like Nathan doesn't come around very often," Joe explained serenely. "If you were the one in danger, I'd send him to get you, if I couldn't go myself. Maybe I'd send him even if I could go."

✝ ✝ ✝

Nathan reached down and found a smooth stone in the rubble.

He was wearing Levis, and his leather jacket covered a burgundy polo shirt. *Hard to see me in the dark.* It was the same jacket he had been wearing during his accident last October. He gambled that the gang wouldn't expect him to leave the Explorer; they wouldn't be looking for him on the street. He could hear them coming around the corner. Their forms came into focus. Nathan's eyes were well-adjusted to the darkness. All the lights in the neighborhood were out. He looked around and saw flickers of candlelight in the few undamaged homes surrounding him.

Stay cool. Check the angles. Execute the plan, he ordered himself, ignoring the sound of his own heartbeat. He counted eleven of them. Eleven enemies. Hunters. As he studied them, he realized that they were teenagers.

Sometimes the prey is dangerous. And sometimes the dangerous pray. Saint Michael the Archangel, defend us in the battle...

When the gang members were twenty yards away, Nathan stood up slowly, halfway hidden behind a telephone pole. He carefully unclipped the safety on the .45. He gripped the handle hard—a secondary safety mechanism disengaged. Denny's words rang in his ears: *Aim lower than you think. This sucker really kicks. It's not like a toy gun or Nintendo.*

Nathan aimed at the feet of the point man—a powerfully built, short teenager wearing a red bandanna. The gang was walking slowly now and had quieted down. This street was dark.

Time for part one, Nathan thought coolly.

He carefully threw the pebble with his free hand at the Explorer, and in one seamless movement returned his throwing hand to steady his gun. He aimed quickly, just as he saw the point man's gaze turn toward the darkened Explorer. The high-beams came on suddenly, ruining the night vision of the hunters.

He fired once, and dove forward to the ground behind a Toyota, *toward* the gang members, who were less than fifteen yards in front of him.

He hoped that they would look toward the sound and muzzle flash of the gun and not where he dove into the shadows. Prone on the ground in a crouch which he remembered from his days in the dojo, Nathan surveyed the scene erupting before him:

The thug in the red bandanna screamed, but he wasn't hit. Red Bandanna fired his handgun at the Explorer wildly, but missed.

It's hard to shoot anything farther than ten feet away with one of these things, Denny's words echoed in Nathan's mind.

Nathan heard a scream from the Explorer, then it was muffled. The gang was now parallel to the car Nathan was hiding behind. It was clear that they were confused and thought the first shot had come from the vehicle. Two were firing their guns at it.

Calmly—almost casually—Nathan stood up. He took careful aim at one of the shooters. This time he aimed for the thigh, adjusting slightly, learning from his first shot.

His target saw Nathan out of the corner of his eye and turned to fire...

Nathan shouted "Ambush!" at the top of his lungs, in a heavy New Jersey accent, and emptied three shots at the leg of his assailant, who collapsed while firing at—and missing—Nathan. One of Nathan's bullets had found its target.

Two, three, four, Nathan counted his rounds, remembering a trick from reruns of *Magnum, P.I.*

Another hoodlum, watching his comrade go down holding his shattered knee, repeated Nathan's shout of Ambush and ran in the other direction. Six or seven followed him. Nathan crawled backwards and then rolled into the street, firing the rest of the bullets as he rolled, concentrating with all his might on continuing his movement. Only one thug saw Nathan—Red Bandanna. He tried to shoot at Nathan, missing the rolling target, blinded by his fear of return fire. The rest of the gang ran away, leaving Red Bandanna to fend for himself.

Nathan reached the other side of the street and crawled with speed and agility to the window well of a house. He hit his shoulder hard as he dove into the deep pit. He fumbled mightily to get the extra clip out of his pocket.

Is Red Bandanna coming? He heard an odd-sounding gunshot ring out above him. *Is that Red Bandanna?* He prayed a Hail Mary as he continued to fumble with the extra clip.

He put the wrong end of the clip into the handle of the .45. He flipped the clip over quickly, then heard the distinct sound of it sliding in with a metallic click. Summoning his courage, he poked his head up over the window well and saw Red Bandanna stretched out on the street, writhing and bleeding. Nathan heard another gunshot and looked up. He saw a muzzle flash as he heard a third shot come from the second-story window of the house across from him. Red Bandanna lay motionless.

An ancient man with a white crew cut stuck his head out the window and shouted, "Better git yer butt outta here, sonny boy. Never know if'n they'll come back!"

Then the old man chuckled and said a curious thing to himself that Nathan barely heard in the still night air, "Semper Fi, sonny boy."

Nathan didn't spend much time pondering the dizzying events of the last two minutes. He looked up and saw James Sullivan getting out of the Explorer. There were two bullet holes in the grill.

"Get back in, Mr. Sullivan," Nathan called softly, feeling pain in his shoulder for the first time. "I'm okay—we're getting out of here."

He ran to the car and was behind the wheel barely a second after James closed his own door. "Everybody okay back there? Better stay down for the rest of the ride if you can stand it." No one said a word.

Nathan thanked God when the Explorer started right up. He drove down the hill, steering around the body of Red Bandanna. *The thug with the gunshot in his leg must have limped off.*

Seconds later he came to the street where the gang had run. He slowed and saw that the gray stepvan was gone.

No one in sight. Where are all the cops? He had heard a few sirens but had not seen one police officer. He *had* seen a police car that wasn't working—abandoned and smashed into the side of a building.

Most policemen and firemen were struggling to save their own relatives and friends. There were too many fires to put out and too many crimes occurring for their relatively insignificant numbers to make a difference on this night.

Did I shoot Red Bandanna first, or did the old Marine get him? Nathan would never know the answer.

Before taking every turn, he imagined gangs of hoodlums standing in a picket line, weapons ready and aimed at him and his passengers. Having been afraid for hours on end, Nathan had no choice but to drive through the imaginary foes.

Toward the end of the trip, James finished praying his second Rosary with the other passengers and cleared his throat.

"You're not the same boy who used to come over to play at our house," Chet's father said with a tinge of regret—and gratitude.

"It doesn't matter," Nathan replied tonelessly, remembering the dead body of Red Bandanna. But it did matter. Silently he prayed for God to have mercy on the soul of Red Bandanna. Having seen hell, Nathan feared for Red Bandanna. But he thanked his guardian angel for giving him the plan that had saved their lives.

Chapter Twenty

1

Early Sunday Morning
16 June
Mishawaka, Indiana

Lee Washington knew what Father Chet had planned. Chet told Lee about it before leaving. Lee was praying with extra fervor in front of the Blessed Sacrament in Immaculate Conception Church. Prayer had become like breathing. It was the only certain way to be with the God Who had saved his life.

After moving to Mishawaka to live with Chet, Lee confided to the priest that all he really wanted to do with his life was pray. And maybe become a priest. Chet had enthusiastically agreed. "You're real monk material! I can see you as a Trappist."

It was common knowledge that Lee had a gift for prayer. Many people came to ask him to pray with them and over them. Chet often asked Lee to sit in on the informal counseling sessions he had with foundation workers and local Knights of Immaculata. No one seemed to mind the presence of the quiet black man. Lee rarely spoke during the meetings, but when he did, Chet was impressed. He believed that Lee had the gift of counsel.

With Lee's permission, Chet told Joe Jackson about Lee's possible vocation. Joe encouraged Lee to spend more time in prayer and less time cutting deals for the Kolbe Foundation. By June the Kolbe Foundation was humming along nicely. Chet dubbed Lee "the white robe" and began searching with him for the right seminary to enter in the fall. It was not an easy search; there were only a few American seminaries that were loyal to the true faith. For the moment, Lee was a kind of lay chaplain for the Kolbe Foundation.

2

Early Sunday Morning
16 June
Fairfield, New Jersey

An hour after Nathan returned to Greg Wheat's house, everyone crammed into the Explorer and Nathan drove to the airport. The ride went without a hitch. It was still dark when they arrived. Denny wanted to move his Cessna to a far corner of the airport, away from any trees or buildings that could crash down on it during aftershocks. Greg unloaded the luggage at the abandoned Citation jet in the middle of the runway. Then he parked the Explorer while Denny moved the Cessna. Everything seemed to take too long.

"Are you sure you can hot-wire this thing—it looks sophisticated," Nathan now said as he settled into the copilot's seat of the Citation. The windshield of the jet seemed small to Nathan.

"It's easier than you think," Denny replied, pulling a Swiss Army knife out of his pocket. "Not many people know how to hot-wire these things, much less fly one after they get the engines wound up."

Denny unscrewed a metal plate beneath the instrument panel with the knife. He then carefully stripped three wires (out of about fourteen he had to choose from) and paused, saying to Nathan, "Go say good-bye to Father Chet. He's not coming with us."

✦ ✦ ✦

"I'm not getting on the Citation," Chet calmly told Nathan. "Don't even try to talk me out of it. I made up my mind back in Indiana."

Nathan looked at him. Chet looked back gravely—as if he expected Nathan to whack him.

"I thought you might pull a stunt like this, Chetmeister," Nathan replied with a note of resignation. "You packed too many clothes and books for a one-day trip."

The turbines of the Citation started to wind up behind them.

"Just tell me why," Nathan shouted in the darkness.

"I'm a parish priest. I belong to Notre Dame du Lac. My people need me," Chet shouted over the engines. "Do I need complicated reasons? Can't it just be simple? I'm a parish priest. That's all I ever wanted to be! I already talked to Lee about taking over for me at the Kolbe Foundation. He's praying for us right now."

Denny stuck his head out the door of the jet and yelled, "Let's go!"

Nathan shook his head at Denny and held up a hand. Chet and Nathan moved away from the Citation so they could hear each other better.

"You could get yourself killed out here—" Nathan argued.

"So what?"

Before Nathan could say anything more, the earth began to shake lightly beneath their feet. Aftershock. One of several they had felt since taking the Explorer from Greg's house. The shocks seemed to be coming at closer intervals.

"Come on!" Denny shouted behind them.

"Okay!" Nathan shouted back. He turned to his friend.

"You stubborn Irishman. I love you, you know. I never told you that," Nathan said hoarsely.

"I know," Chet said, smiling. "I love you, too, buddy."

The two men embraced tightly, awkwardly.

"Don't burn the place down while I'm gone," Nathan joked.

"Don't worry, I will."

Nathan turned, ran to the Citation, and climbed in. Denny secured the door. The Wheats, Chet's parents, and the O'Briens were already strapped in, filling all the passenger seats. Nathan looked at James and Mary Sullivan. James nodded. *So they know that Chet's staying.*

Nathan looked out the window. The priest was already moving away from the runway, carrying a large duffel bag over his shoulder. Nathan wondered if he would ever see his best friend again. The sun was not yet over the horizon, but its glow was growing in the eastern sky beyond Chet.

Probably would have made us wait an hour for that Hollywood background, Chet. You always had a knack for the melodramatic.

Nathan went to the front and took the copilot's seat. There were a lot more instruments on this dash than on the Cessna.

✝ ✝ ✝

"So you're sure nobody's going to be ticked off that we're stealing their corporate jet?" Nathan asked Denny as they taxied toward the end of the runway.

"I never quite said that," Denny replied with a smile.

Denny was reminding him more and more of Father Chet by the minute. *Unlike your sister, getting a straight answer from you is like pulling teeth. One of these days, I'm gonna haul off and pop you...*

"So what *did* you say? I mean, did Father Chet check off on this?"

"Sort of," Denny said, looking at various instrument gauges, avoiding Nathan's eyes.

"Sort of? Look, Denny, before you go stealing a million dollar jet—"

"We're not stealing it, Nathan. We're *borrowing* it. It's not like I'm going to keep the damn thing. The papers here say it's owned by a New York leasing company called Streamline Jets. That's New York *City*. There's a good chance that Streamline Jets doesn't even exist anymore. And, we're going to take this million dollar jet and we're going to land it in a very safe place compared to the middle of this airport with its doors wide open. It'll get trashed here. Streamline will probably give us a reward, even if we do offer to pay for any expenses we incur. I can fly it back to wherever, after we contact them from South Bend. All we have to do is avoid crashing it. *That* would cost us a lot of money. But of course, if we crash, we'd all be dead, so it really wouldn't cost us—"

"Okay, okay. You're giving me a headache. You sure you know how to fly one of these things...?"

"Don't worry," Denny replied.

"How come you always say 'Don't worry' when I ask you yes or no questions?"

"Don't worry about that, either." Denny grinned.

"There you go again!"

"What? That wasn't a yes or no question, was it?"

"Forget it," Nathan said, exasperated.

They reached the beginning of the runway. First dawn was starting to light up the tarmac. Nathan saw Father Chet standing next to the remains of the control tower. Chet waved. Nathan felt a familiar knot in his stomach.

Another airplane trip. Great.

"Strap yourself in," Denny suggested, noticing the pale look on Nathan's face.

"I don't wear seat belts," Nathan said dryly.

"Suit yourself," Denny replied casually. "It's not like this is an FAA approved flight or anything. Well, here goes—"

Just as Denny began to push the throttle forward, the second largest earthquake in the history of the East Coast began to rumble...

3

Early Tuesday Morning
18 June
An empty beach on the Gulf of Mexico, Texas

An average looking, middle-aged man with a crew cut sat wearing sunglasses and a fisherman's hat on a beach chair. Beside him, a fishing pole with its line leading into the surf was upright in a stake. A bucket and a tackle box were nearby.

He hadn't caught a thing. But Chip Williams didn't care. He wasn't here to fish. He had flown back to his boyhood city of Austin from Washington on the pretense of visiting his ailing mother. Then he drove several hours to this deserted spot on the Gulf to meet a friend.

After several minutes a big man with a bald head walked down from the roadway onto the beach, and wordlessly set up a beach chair next to Chip.

"Aren't you dead yet, Williams?" Karl began.

"What? And let you outlive me, Sarge?"

The two men chuckled. Karl offered Chip a cigar. Both men took a few moments to light up correctly.

"Anything catching?" Karl asked after a while.

"Didn't even put bait on the line."

"So, it's that serious," Karl said.

Chip didn't reply. He took a long pull on the Macanudo.

"There's some Maker's in the box, Sarge," Chip offered.

"Now we're getting somewhere." Karl reached over and opened the tackle box. He pulled the bottle out, uncorked it, and took a hefty gulp. "So why all the cloak and dagger stuff, Chip?"

"The New York quakes were the last straw. Word is that the president and Congress are going to join the European Union to stabilize the dollar…"

"And suddenly you're not so sure who the Commander in Chief is anymore?"

"I swore to uphold the Constitution, not the president, Karl. I feel like an ass." Chip looked away and threw the cigar in disgust. "I'm not the only one, Sarge. Some strange scuttle-butt is going around. Some of my friends in the Corps have been cashiered for no reason at all. Some of our best men. Rumor has it I'm next in line to walk the plank."

Karl snorted at the native Texan sitting next to him. Slinger had been in business for decades. He had no love for the regulators, politicians, and bureaucrats who had sunk the massively debt-ridden nation into an endless recession. Like many Americans, he had come to regard the government as an enemy of freedom.

A long silence passed.

"Sarge?"

"Yeah, Chip?"

"They've had foreign tanks on our soil for over a decade. Not many at first. Hell, I thought it was a good idea. We trained against them in our own exercises. Three days ago, I received photographs in an unmarked envelope. Photos of six giant cargo ships filled with the same kinds of tanks. I can't tell you the source. Let's just say that the cargo ships are coming out of the Gulf of Finland. With troop carriers in convoy. They're going to use the riots from the quakes as an excuse. They know American troops won't fire on Americans. But foreign ones will."

"Let 'em come," Karl said with a dangerous edge to his voice.

"Huh?" Chip replied, confused.

"Chip, can we dispense with the crap?"

"Sure, Sarge."

"Ever wonder what George Washington and Tom Jefferson and Sam Adams and all those guys felt back in the good old days?"

Chip shook his head.

"They felt what you feel right now, Chip."

"But Karl if you're talking about what I think you're talking about—foreign armies working in concert with the might of the United States military—we can't win!"

"Didn't the Founding Fathers face the same thing? And against worse odds—"

"—but the bad guys have all the money and the military assets this time around."

"Stop talking like a damned Army puke, Commandant! I remember something about the signers of the Declaration of Independence pledging their fortunes and their lives. Our side will have the truth, and the land, till the bad guys spill our blood taking it. I don't care if they nuke every city in America with their stinking tacticals. They can't nuke Nebraska. They'll run out of bombs. Then it's back to good old-time warfighting. Remember, they're just a bunch of bureaucrats when it comes down to it. We're going to be fighting the military equivalent of the Post Office, and they can't even deliver a friggin' letter."

Slinger paused, squinting at the breakers. He took a puff through clenched teeth.

Without a trace of bravado, he continued, "I wish I was a young man, 'cause I'd take the old Garand out of the closet tomorrow and start training."

"What are we really talking about here, Karl?" Chip asked soberly.

"Revolution. The American Revolution, Part Two."

Both men shared a few swigs of the country's best bourbon, contemplating the unimaginable.

"Then I'll get in touch with a few good men," Chip said at last with a note of resolve.

"Good. We're just getting started, you know," Karl said with little enthusiasm.

4

Sunday Morning, Dawn
16 June
Fairfield, New Jersey

Father Chet was thrown from his feet as he watched the Citation begin its sprint down the runway of Essex County Airport. *Hey, this ain't no aftershock!* he thought crazily. *Dear God, don't let them crash!*

As the ground became a moving ocean of rock beneath him, he struggled to lift himself up to a crawling position and yelled, "Go Denny go!"

✝ ✝ ✝

Denny had never flown a Citation. Aircraft are not like cars. A typical pilot could not just climb into any model and fly one. Denny was not a typical pilot, however. He was *born* to fly. Years later, people would tell stories about him, saying that perhaps Denny Wheat was born to fly this particular flight.

Nathan was horrified when he saw Denny smile as the earthquake hit.

Denny did the aircraft equivalent of "flooring it." The runway was a mildly sloped roller coaster. But the rails on a roller coaster don't move. Nathan struggled to click his seat belt together but couldn't figure out the configuration of the locking mechanism.

"Don't worry about your belt," Denny called out.

"Don't worry about the belt?!" Nathan wailed. "Just get us off the ground!"

"You're such a spoilsport Nathan, why don't you—" Denny cut himself off to adjust the throttle as they hurled over another dip and the tires of the jet rumbled across a crack opening in the tarmac.

It's this next slope or never, he thought to himself. Then he did something he had never done in an airplane—he asked for help. *Dear Jesus, don't let me crash this sweet little lady...*

As it approached the moving crest of the next wave of runway, the nose of the Citation lifted and the jet left the ground.

Wow, Denny thought, *this baby's got power. I want one of these!*

Open-mouthed, Nathan felt the G-force of the climb press his body to the seat. Then he threw up.

"We're okay now," Denny calmly informed his copilot. "No thanks to you," he added amiably.

"Where's the medicine?" Nathan croaked.

"In the barf bag under your seat, buddy."

5

Sunday Morning
16 June
South Bend, Indiana

The flight home took less than two hours. When Denny radioed ahead to the air traffic controller at Michiana Regional, permission was granted for landing because of the unusual nature of the unauthorized flight. Denny asked the controller to get someone to call his parents. With an impish smile on his face he also asked the controller to call the local newspaper. "It's all part of a plan," he confided to Nathan.

A reporter and a photographer from the *South Bend Tribune* met them on the tarmac. The story was picked up by the wire services and Denny Wheat had his fifteen minutes of fame. Photographs of Joanie hugging Nathan, with Denny in the background next to the Citation, made the front sections of newspapers around the country.

The offices of Streamline Jets had indeed been destroyed in New York City, but a member of the board of directors who lived in Shreveport was quoted in the papers the next day. He refused to press charges and thanked Denny for saving a company asset. Streamline Jets had five Citations before the earthquakes. Three were destroyed at Kennedy Airport.

The FAA made some noises about suspending Denny's license for violating over thirty regulations, but the investigation was dropped after a few days. Denny Wheat was a hero. The FAA had more pressing problems at the numerous airports destroyed or damaged by the Quakes, as the two earthquakes came to be called around the country.

✛ ✛ ✛

Everyone, including Denny's family and the reporters who had made him an instant hero, assumed that Denny had given up his Cessna to rescue his family and friends. Two days after the flight home, Denny left for New Jersey at three in the morning with Huey Brown in Huey's Cessna 150. No one else was aware of this second trip. Late that afternoon they returned separately—Huey in his 150 and Denny in his 172.

In order to retrieve the 172, Denny had been forced to land Huey's 150 on an access road in a huge industrial park near Essex County Airport. He came close to crashing during takeoff on the churned-up grass next to the same runway he had used two days earlier. Denny swore Farmer Brown to secrecy, and the press never discovered anything about this second daredevil trip.

The only one who wasn't surprised when Denny landed in Tom Wheat's backyard was Nathan Payne.

✛ ✛ ✛

Slinger bought the jet from the bankrupt Streamline Jets at forty cents on the dollar one month later and gave it to the Kolbe Foundation. Denny now had a Citation in his fleet.

6

From *Dark Years History*
(New Rome Press, 31 R.E.)
by Rebecca Macadam Jackson

...the second great New York earthquake obliterated any chance the United States might have had to avoid slipping into a depression. When the Quakes destroyed the financial capital of the world, the nation was already mired in the worst recession since before World War II...

...happens in times of severe economic uncertainty? Within a week of the second quake, several major insurance companies declared bankruptcy because they couldn't cover their policy holders in New York. Banks from around the world called in notes for businesses based in the New York region. Runs on banks began on the East Coast and spread across the country. Foreign banks, alarmed by the falling dollar, called in their outstanding notes. When some of those notes were not paid, the dollar went into free fall...

...Wall Street was physically gone. Along with the buildings and computers (and almost a quarter of the professional workers in that sector), the Quakes also destroyed the "institution" that existed in investor's minds. Money could not be entrusted to it. Millions of transactions had occurred there every day. Now it was a ghost town. Apart from Wall Street, banks in the region processed over seventeen percent of all the checks and electronic financial transactions which occurred in America every day. Accounts all over the country were in sudden and complete disarray. Lawsuits were filed in courts all over the...

...the Market was temporarily "transferred" to Chicago, using the information stored on "earthquake proof" Wall Street backup computers. The Market dove long and deep and hard the day it reopened. The president of the United States declared a national financial emergency and called a "banking holiday." The Market was closed down for over two months. Publicly held companies around the world came to a standstill as business decisions were delayed, pending the opening of the Market...

...the financial details are chronicled elsewhere. Our concern is to convey what happened to the so-called "average American." In the absence of a gold standard what was the real value of a dollar? Economists would answer by stating that the value of one dollar is the amount of goods or services a person is willing to exchange for it. A week before the Quakes, the average person was willing to work one hour in exchange for an average national hourly wage of fourteen dollars. One week after the Quakes, the average worker was willing to work one hour for less than three dollars.

The average person living in the New York region sat in his damaged home and said to himself: "Hard times are here. Money is going to be scarce. My stocks are valueless. My job is gone because my building is gone. My business's customers are gone. My insurance policy on my damaged home is worthless. My mail won't be delivered tomorrow and maybe not for months. My utilities are gone. There are not enough police to protect what I do own. I have to conserve what I have, so I will buy less starting right now."

This is deflation. Consumers are less willing to part with dollars. Retailers drop prices to stimulate demand. Buyers buy fewer goods and services to preserve their dollars. Fewer goods and services are produced because demand is radically lower. Therefore fewer workers are employed to produce goods and services. *Fewer* workers are able to buy even less and prices drop again—and more workers are laid off. Workers become desperate for work and are willing to work for less; and employers are desperate to lower costs to stay in business; by mutual agreement workers and employers both take a pay cut. And so on...

...and so the damage the Quakes caused was unprecedented. In monetary terms the Quakes were fifty times more costly than any previous American natural disaster. New York effectively ceased to exist as a living city. Over two million people died in three weeks. All the tunnels to Manhattan Island were destroyed in the first earthquake. All the bridges collapsed by the end of the second earthquake—except for the Brooklyn Bridge. Rescue workers and the National Guard were forced to use boats and helicopters to reach the island which had split in half (the 42nd Street River is a grim monument to the Quakes). The effects of the Quakes in terms of human devastation were horrifying. In one building alone, over three thousand people perished when a gas main blew...

...was tremendous devastation for thirty miles in every direction outside of the city. One of the largest ports in the world was closed indefinitely. Rioting on an unprecedented scale took place, and tens of thousands were killed in street fighting. At first the riots were motivated by the criminal element taking advantage of the confusion and lack of law enforcement. Soon riots began to break out over scarce food and water. Eventually, United Nations "peace-keeping" armies were called in to restore order...

...meanwhile, more natural disasters struck the world every month, confirming Marian prophecies which predicted that "America will be brought to its knees by natural disasters." A huge earthquake practically destroyed half of San Francisco, but the damage and loss of life paled compared to the Quakes. Thirty percent of the buildings in Tokyo were severely damaged in a large earthquake four months after the New York earthquakes. The most bitter winter in recorded history wracked the country. Severe autumn floods on the Missouri and Mississippi Rivers spilled over levees weakened by floods earlier in the decade. Canada was also devastated by freezes, minor earthquakes, floods, depression...

...within three months the United States became the last industrialized country to join the World Depression. Unemployment rose above thirty-five percent as the depression spread across the country. Riots broke out in almost every major city. Armed groups of thugs began to leave the cities to prey upon the better pickings available in the suburbs. The president declared martial law and begged Congress to join the newly-formed European Union of States, in order to stabilize the dollar and to restore peace. After the United States surrendered its sovereignty, the European Union was renamed the World Union of States. The World Union operated under the aegis of the United Nations and several levels of regional bureaucracies...

...when southern and western states balked, the Second American Revolution (SAR) began. At the time, it was known as the Conflict for Peace in America—a euphemism no doubt conjured up by a bureaucratic committee. At first the SAR didn't seem like a war. States simply began ignoring the increasingly burdensome and tyrannical taxes levied by the bankrupt federal government. The taxes were supposed to pay for the national disasters and the enormous debt now "owed" to the World Union. These taxes were part of the New Constitution, which was ratified by Congress and signed by the president. The New Constitution was never sent to the states for ratification...

...The United States effectively became a socialist state with over seventy-five percent of all income turned over to the World Union. (In our day and age of taxation below three percent, a seventy-five percent rate is no doubt beyond comprehension for many readers. Refer to Appendix D: Overall tax rates in the early 1990s were a whopping fifty percent! A seventy-five percent tax rate to appease the World Union was considered reasonable by many politicians in the months following the Quakes.) The New Constitution was a requirement for entering the World Union...

...and established a new currency, called the World Dollar (WD). Europeans were already accustomed to the new cashless system which promised to save that continent from economic disaster. Shell-shocked Americans in eastern states accepted a universal debit card with little protest. Plans for an identity chip (to be implanted in every person's hand at birth, and already in use in Switzerland) were unveiled when counterfeit debit cards became widespread in the "test state" of Massachusetts...

...in western and southern states, millions of people struggling to make ends meet during the World Depression simply stopped paying their World Union income taxes. Many refused to use the debit cards. Bartering and the black market flourished. The shooting started when relatively prosperous Texas declared itself an independent nation. Russian and German armored divisions were sent to take over Austin. According to the World Union, this First World Union Army (under United Nations command) was purportedly in the former United States to help with disaster relief and to quell periodic rioting in the cities. When the invasion of Texas failed miserably, a rash of other states declared independence or formed confederations with neighboring states...

...exploits of the Lone Star Army, under the command of General William Williams, became known to every revolutionary in the former United States through the information network of short wave radios, the Internet, direct TV, and satellite cellular phones originally established by SLG Industries and augmented by Resistance Movements as the regional wars dragged on. The World Union was never able to incapacitate all the satellites which enabled the system. The satellites were controlled from Houston at the former headquarters of NASA...

...the Red Death added salt to an already wounded world. This new virus literally ate the flesh of its victims from the inside out. Death rates in Europe reached ten percent. No one knows how many died in China—perhaps hundreds of millions. The name came from the physical state of the bloody victim at the end of the three-week cycle of death. To this day, no one knows where the Red Death came from, why it spread, or why the Red Death passed over most baptized Christians and Catholics, especially those consecrated to the Immaculate Heart of Mary...

...In the midst of this political and economic confusion, the Great Schism was barely noticed. The antipope Casino continued to force orthodox bishops into retirement and replaced them with members of the Society of Builders or ignorant dupes of the Society. Society priests were raised to the office of bishop or cardinal in a matter of weeks. Religious congregations and orders loyal to the universal teachings of the Catholic Church were brutally suppressed. Women flocked to seminaries to become the first crop of female priests. Confession and weekly Mass were suddenly declared "optional" sacraments. Use of artificial contraception was declared a matter of conscience. Even abortion was condoned by new schismatic clerics as a necessary evil in a world torn by war, poverty, and depression...

...many were converted by the astounding Eucharistic Miracle of the Quakes—not one Catholic church in the entire metropolitan area where Jesus was in the tabernacle suffered any damage. In some areas, the church was the only building standing, and a natural locus for relief activity. This mass miracle was highly publicized in the Marian Movement. Marian apostles were filled with hope. These tangible Eucharistic signs served to foreshadow and prepare Marian apostles for another major development lost on the secular world: as prophesied, authentic Marian apparitions around the world stopped on the day of the second earthquake...

7

Saturday Morning
27 July
Newark, New Jersey

Father Chet woke up. He prayed his morning offering: *Dear Lord, I don't know what will happen to me today. I only know that nothing will happen that was not foreseen by You and directed to my greater good from all eternity. I adore Your holy and unfathomable plans and submit to them with all my heart for love of You, the pope, and the Immaculate Heart of Mary.*

Plaster chips from the ceiling littered the floor but the walls and roof were mostly intact. The old rectory was solid. Saint Agnes Church next-door was undamaged.

He wondered if there would be water in the shower today. He doubted it. Fortunately the pastor shared his clothes with Chet—almost a perfect fit. He couldn't avoid smelling badly in the confessional—but there was plenty of cologne left in the medicine cabinet to help with that.

Maybe I'll see if I can get Donny Fabrizio to pull up Joe Jackson on the ham radio, he thought. Donny was a local teenager who had been a ham radio junkie before the Quakes hit. Chet had already talked to Joe once since coming here. Chet smiled sadly. He missed his Kolbe Foundation friends.

He wondered whether there would be bread in the cupboard. He doubted it. There was still some canned food left. Last night he had cherry pie filling for dinner. At least the gas was still on and the pie filling had been warmed up. Sometimes parishioners brought food. Most of the rectory's supply had been given away by the pastor, Father Montini, in the first few days after the Quakes.

And there was still plenty of soap. He could keep his hands clean using the water dropped off by the National Guard a few days ago. Saying Mass with clean hands was a priority.

Chet would make the rounds in the neighborhood today, as he did every day. Maybe today he would spend a lot of time helping some of the Italian families rebuild their homes with broken bricks, split boards, and used nails. Maybe he would preach on a street corner. He always kept a small vial of chrism oil, and another of holy water, in his pocket. Yesterday he had baptized twenty-five people.

Maybe he would do something else. He was certain to have the distant knot of hunger in his belly during most of the day. Saint Anthony would find him a meal. Chet had lost several pounds since the Quakes.

The weather had been cool lately, which was a blessing. Cool weather mitigated the smell of dead bodies which sometimes hung like small pockets in the air as he made his rounds.

The pastor of Saint Agnes, old Father Montini, had agreed to "delay" informing the diocese that Chet had returned to Newark. That was fine with Chet.

The Ironbound Section was relatively safe. It was not safe. But it was relatively safe. There was a tacit agreement among the men in the neighborhood—many of whom had connections with the Mob—that all bets were off concerning law enforcement. A Gatling gun on a tripod was set up on one of the iron lattice balconies overlooking most of the main street. It was manned twenty-four hours a day. Several looters had been shot after the first quake. Bad guys had their own grapevine and avoided the Ironbound Section.

Father Chet faced hunger, fatigue, and suffering. Most of the suffering came from seeing the trials his people were undergoing. It was depressing at times—although many, many people seemed more open to receiving the sacraments and the Gospel than ever before. Another day. Another Cross. Father Chet wouldn't trade his for the world. *Your burden is light and your yoke is easy,* he repeated often.

Chet jumped out of bed toward Calvary.

Chapter Twenty-One

1

Sunday Evening
24 November
Salt Lake City, Utah

A man picked up a special phone. The line could not be traced. He punched in a memorized number.

At the other end of the line a phone rang in Chicago. A man with a thick Chicago-Italian accent answered.

The man in Utah gave an address. Then he said, "Fire. The big building only. Leave the church alone, for now."

"Got it. Fifty grand. Half up front. Half after. You know the drill."

The man in Utah, a member of the Council of Fifty, hung up the phone. It was so much easier nowadays. *The Council of Fifty doesn't officially exist,* he thought. *And we don't have to do our own bidding. Thank God for the Mob. We'll teach Lanning and his friend Slinger and their precious Kolbe Foundation a lesson they won't soon forget...*

2

Sunday Evening
1 December
Mishawaka, Indiana

Becky found herself woolgathering as she looked at Amy, who was sleeping peacefully in a baby hammock on the kitchen table. She looked out the window of her home toward the Kolbe Center. Joanie sat next to her, chopping away.

Joanie put the knife down on the table. She was preparing carrots which her mother had given her for a new kind of cake she knew would not taste very good: carrot corn cake. Indiana didn't have much sugar, but it had plenty of corn. Joanie noticed that Becky had lost some weight in the past few months. There was an added dimension of starkness to her beauty.

Joanie was due in less than two weeks. Her slight frame was dominated by the baby in her womb. Her back had a permanent, dull ache.

"Penny for your thoughts," Joanie asked.

"Oh," Becky said, shaking her head. "Nothing. Well, I mean, I was just thinking that for better or for worse, little Amy is never going to know what it was like for us. Either they'll kill us all or it'll turn out great like Joe says it will, and she'll grow up happy. Anything is better than this limbo. I shouldn't complain. At least we still have freedom in the good old Hoosier state—for now. But I miss hot showers." Becky looked from Amy to Joanie, and back to Amy. "Isn't that right, Amy Girl?"

"I miss hot showers, too, Beck. And I miss my favorite shampoo. I miss chopped meat. I miss Taco Bell. I miss that feeling that wasn't a feeling…" she trailed off.

"Huh?" Becky asked, putting her hand on Joanie's. She noticed that Joanie's hand was getting rough. Farmer's hands. Joanie had been doing a lot of gardening. There had not been many vegetables on the table the past couple of months.

"You know—that feeling that's not a feeling," Joanie tried to explain, her tone distant. "It's the feeling you used to get when you woke up in the morning and you know that today would be like yesterday. And that tomorrow would be like today. That's gone."

"Yeah, I get it—" Becky stopped for a second while she picked up Amy, and gently attached the baby to a breast. Nursing had become second nature, and a godsend, because baby formula was no longer available, except on the black market. "I remember thinking every night when I went to bed with Joe that life was going to be great as long as he was there next to me. Now I think: Oh, I better hold on tight. We might get some World Union paratroopers in the backyard tomorrow and they'll take Joe away to some prison and pull his fingernails out one by one like they did to those Jesuit priests in New York—"

"That's disgusting, Beck," Joanie made a face. Becky was liable to come out with a graphic image in any conversation.

"Sorry," Becky apologized. "I guess I just got carried away. Click your shoes together three times and repeat after me, Becky Jackson: Don't be so macabre. Don't be so macabre.

"Anyway, I hold on tight to my man at night. I just don't know if Joe…if Joe…" Her eyes suddenly filled with tears.

They held each other's hands more tightly. Becky pulled herself together. "I'm such a mess. You know, Joanie, sometimes the best part about having a good man in bed isn't the sex. It's the company. The warmth. The having and holding. Not being alone. That kind of security isn't there any more. I have nightmares." Becky sniffled one final time as she finished speaking.

"I know, Becky, I know," Joanie said softly, sympathetically. "I have nightmares, too. I feel the same way. I feel selfish. I don't know how Mom was able to live with Daddy away in Korea for two years. You want to hear something weird?"

"Me, wanna hear something weird? Do you really have to ask my permission, Joanie?"

They shared a nervous laugh.

"When the depression first started, I was glad—because I was able to spend more time with Nathan. He was really working long hours after the Quakes. I don't know how many times he slipped into bed at three in the morning and put his arms around me while I was half asleep. You know what I mean, Beck. Joe and Nathan burned the midnight oil together. When the money dried up and it became practically impossible to send out stuff, it was like a strange, stay-at-home vacation.

We'd go on long walks, and sometimes he would talk to me like he never did before—"

"We both married the strong silent types, didn't we?"

"Yeah," Joanie replied. "We married the mute brothers."

"Yeah," Becky said. "It's funny, but I'd rather starve to death than not have Joe. It looks like I may get that chance. If corn stops growing in Indiana, that is." She smiled slightly, releasing the baby from her breast and holding her up for a burp. "But I'm sure those carrots are going to help make corn bread all the more delicious," she added with the perfect kind of sarcasm—completely false sincerity.

"I hate corn bread, too," Joanie admitted. "And cold showers. But I love warm beds. Corn breads for warm beds. Hey, Beckmeister, I made a pun, or a rhyme! Or whatever."

"Cool, Joanie. We'll make you a city girl, yet. First puns and rhymes, then, biting jibes and quips. Stage one, which I'm already working on, is to wring all that farm girl wholesomeness outta ya. That takes time. It's especially hard for Hoosier women, who seem to be infested—"

Becky stopped when Joanie started to laugh. The baby burped.

"Can I practice?" Joanie asked, looking at the baby.

"Sure," Becky replied, raising an eyebrow as she passed Amy over to Joanie, "but only if you promise to not make me eat carrot corn bread tonight at dinner.

"Deal!" Joanie said, playing along, cuddling the child. She had come to cherish the quirky back and forth of conversations with Becky. *It's another one of those things that might not be here tomorrow if the paratroopers land in the backyard tonight,* she thought sadly, hugging Amy a little bit tighter.

Becky leaned over and gave Amy and Joanie a little kiss on the cheek. She grabbed a few carrots and the knife, and began to chop.

3

Early Monday Morning
2 December
Mishawaka, Indiana

Joe slept, cradling his wife in his arms. Baby Amy was next to Becky, having an early morning snack of breast milk while Becky dozed lightly.

Joe Jackson's dream was lucid. He found himself in Saint Joseph Church during Sunday Mass. The church was packed with people whom he knew personally, but didn't know personally, in that strange paradoxical way of dreams. The order of the rites in the Mass were all out of sync, and Joe found himself unable to concentrate on the readings. He couldn't hear the readings. He turned to take Becky's hand, but she wasn't there. He heard a crying baby…

…the Mass ended and a smartly dressed woman with "cat's eye" sunglasses and huge calves slowly walked up to the podium carrying a bright red knapsack…

…she was speaking and Joe heard every word distinctly. She said, "As you know, the Future Church is now. Starting next Sunday, attendance at Mass will be optional. Come if you want to. I'll be the priest, reader, printer, and candlestick maker. It doesn't really matter. All that matters is that we have a good time. If it feels good, then feel it. Whatever floats your boat digs your moat."

Joe tried to call out "No!" but he couldn't find his voice. He looked to the man sitting next to him. The man was wearing a nice Brooks Brothers suit which had lottery tickets in all the pockets. The man was smiling in a copacetic trance— as if the woman at the podium were making great sense…

"From now on, Joe Jackson," the woman with the huge calves (Joe could see her calves through the glass podium…) continued, "the new ways are the old ways. You want to use condoms—fine by me and McGee," she smiled with good humor. "You want to stuff your face? Fine with me. Whatever you be, don't say pope to me. No confession. Snow confession. Blow confession…"

The whole congregation was eating it up, except for the mute Joe. They loved what this woman was saying! He felt paralyzed as he struggled to stand up. With all his considerable might he willed his legs to stand! To no avail.

"Are there any objections? Any questions? Any extra fish in your pockets, people?" The fat-calved woman's face melted into a blank with no features as she kept babbling.

No one had questions. Joe was finally able to stand but he still could not speak…

Why don't they object? Why don't they speak up? Nooooo!

"Then great. See you next week—if you come! So long and thanks for all the fish…"

Joe looked around the congregation and every face had turned to a blank, sickening beige (beige was a sickening color in this dream).

Joe found his voice and began to croak, "Lukewarm! Lukewarm! God will spit you out! Lukewarm! Believe me I love you. Lukewarm…lukewarm! I'm not lying—she's lying!" But no one paid attention to him. They stood in unison and laughed—cackled—with one huge voice and applauded…

…the side of the church (which was now Immaculate Conception Church and not Saint Joseph Church) turned into glass. Joe saw the Kolbe Foundation building and had a sudden horrible foreboding. *I'm too lukewarm and too late…*

✠ ✠ ✠

A thin man opened a briefcase. His car had Illinois plates. He was sitting in his Cadillac Seville on the shoulder of a back road less than two miles from the Kolbe Foundation. He pulled a small remote control from the briefcase and extended the antenna out twenty inches. The remote had one button. He pressed the button. A second later he saw the explosion in the rearview mirror. A few seconds after that he heard the explosion. He put the car in gear and drove off.

✝ ✝ ✝

Becky and Joe woke up together when the Kolbe Center blew up. The window panes in the side of their little home facing the center instantly shattered. The Jackson's bedroom was on the opposite side of the house.

Like many new wives, Becky was amazed at how quickly her husband was up and out of the bed and across the hallway to the window. Lady was barking loudly in the living room downstairs.

"Joe, what happened!" she cried, sitting up in the bed. Amy began to cry.

"The Kolbe Center's gone," he said evenly. He came back to the bedroom and called the fire department using the memory dial.

✝ ✝ ✝

The rectory was closer to the Kolbe Center than Joe and Becky's house. Fortunately, the rectory and the Jackson's home were upwind from the center, or else fiery ash might have carried in the brisk winter wind and burned the two ancient wooden structures to the ground. There was more explosion than fire. Lee Washington's ears would ring for days.

✝ ✝ ✝

Lee was watching the fire from his bedroom window when he heard the doorbell ring. When he opened the door less than two minutes after the explosion, he saw Joe, wearing pajamas, towering before him.

"It's gone," Joe said.

Lee said nothing. *No kidding,* he thought.

"Do you have the computer backups?" Joe asked, squinting in the light from Lee's tiny foyer.

"Sure. The tape's in my room. We've got an extra in the Salt Lake City office, too."

"Good," Joe said calmly. "We'll find a place to rent in town tomorrow. You can do it better than I can. I wish Father Chet were here."

"Me too," Lee said softly. Then, "Aren't you upset, Joe?"

"Why? Should I be?" Joe said with a pleasant smile.

"Well I might be upset if somebody jus' blew up my foundation," he observed. The conversation was becoming surreal. The Kolbe Center was in flames behind Joe as Lee spoke.

"Oh, that. Yeah, it's disappointing. But it's not my building. It's Mary's. If she let somebody blow it up, then there must be a good reason. I'd like to say that we'd talk about it in the morning, and I'd tell you to go back to bed, but with the fire department coming, we'll be up all night."

Lee stepped outside, tilted his head and gave Joe a skeptical look.

"Are you acting or something? Should I get ticked off for you?"

"I'm not acting. We'll start rebuilding in the morning. Or whatever. I'll give Karl a call," Joe said. "It's just a building and we have the backup tape."

"What about Becky and Amy? Aren't you worried about them?"

That seemed to give Joe pause for thought.

"I'll have to think about that," was all he said.

Becky was dressed by now and out the front door, watching the Kolbe Center burn from the porch that circled three quarters of the farmhouse. She had Amy in one arm, still crying. Lady was at her side barking like mad. Becky shook her fist in the air.

"I don't know who you are but you're a bunch of bastards and I'll personally rip your hearts out if I ever find you!" she screamed at the top of her lungs at the wind and the fire. Lady started barking even louder.

"I don't know what she sees in you, Joe," Lee observed, before yelling to Becky, "Right on, Sister Becky! Right on!"

4

Sunday Evening
8 December
South Bend, Indiana

The whole gang was back together again to celebrate the first wedding anniversary of the Paynes and the Jacksons, as well as the Feast of the Immaculate Conception. Denny had flown Slinger up from Dallas that morning. The atmosphere was not festive.

A fire burned in Bruno's fireplace. Delivery of heating oil had been spotty for months. There was talk of trading food for oil with the Nation of Texas, but it was just talk.

The restaurant was practically empty. This was becoming common at Bruno's, even on weekends. People had long since cut back on luxuries such as dining out. Bruno had been forced to lay off most of his workers.

When good pizza can't cut it, the end is near, Becky thought sardonically. *Another sign of a world gone mad.*

Becky held sleeping Amy in her arms. She looked at her man and Joe looked back at her. She felt that familiar fire in her belly when she looked at him—familiar, but still plenty hot. He winked at her awkwardly, somberly.

I'm in love with a dork, she thought without regret. *Why didn't I realize that the first time I came in here? I guess I did...**and** that I was in love with him.* She briefly wondered where the word *dork* came from. She looked at her wine and realized that she had barely touched it. *Can't blame it on the booze.*

She looked at the baby and realized that she didn't care as much about the world outside as the men in the room did. She cared about Amy. Becky was in from the cold.

Still, Tom Wheat could talk about grass growing and keep an audience in rapt attention. She turned when she heard Joe's name come up.

"…being much too hard on yourself, Joe. You're wrong if you think the Kolbe Foundation failed in its mission. So what if you didn't reach every single Catholic in six months like you wanted? You reached as many as you could. Millions heard the words of Mary and acted upon them. Nathan's idea of referring everyone who requested tapes to local prayer groups really worked.

"The Quakes were a tragedy beyond words, but in the big scheme of things they were a blessing. More people are going to listen now. More people are going to turn to God now that their material world is collapsing. You yourself said that requests for tapes hit an all-time high in the first weeks after the Quakes. The depression barely slowed you guys down until recently. You were shipping tapes and books within days after the explosion, too. Things aren't so bad in that area."

Joe did not seem consoled by Tom's words. The Quakes had hit just as the Kolbe Foundation was getting ready for a media campaign of major proportions. Even though the response from the general public to the test campaigns of the spring was not encouraging, at least they knew the response rates and had the production set up to meet demand. The firebombing of the building had been a severe blow. Joe felt that he had done too little, too late. *We needed one more year,* he thought dejectedly.

Lee had rented a new warehouse, and arranged for a skeleton computer system to be installed within days of the explosion. But the big jump in demand after the Quakes quickly tapered off as the economic depression and the self-destruction of the Church accelerated.

"The real problem is the schism," Tom continued. "That's why you feel so helpless. But there's nothing you can do about it except to stay on course."

Joe was disappointed over the way most bishops in the country "rolled over" when the new guidelines came in from Rome regarding accepting women into the seminaries and relaxing the requirements for Sunday Mass. The dream Joe had on the night of the explosion was coming true before his very eyes. The liberal media hailed the new "modernization" of the Catholic Church as a religious earthquake. The reaction by most Catholics in the country had been: "Well, it's about time."

The bishop of Fort Wayne had been "retired" when he failed to go along with the new guidelines, and over half the priests in the diocese were suspended by the replacement bishop. Confessions were no longer being heard in nine out of ten churches in the area. Penitents who called on rectories were encouraged to schedule appointments with "lay counselors" to discuss and explore their guilt. Things were changing at dizzying speeds. Liturgies around the South Bend area barely resembled the Mass. Younger priests were being encouraged to make up their own Masses. Some priests no longer consecrated the Eucharist, imitating the Protestant model. Now that Sunday Mass was optional, church attendance had dropped by over seventy percent.

Father Duffy (Chet's old professor from Notre Dame), now in his eighties and retired, came secretly to Immaculate Conception Church to say Mass on Sundays. The old priest had a heart condition and it was wearing him out. Someone would report him eventually and then even Father Duffy might be suspended by his congregation, which was rejoicing in the changes.

"What I wonder about is why there have been no encyclicals or official statements from the pope, if he is a pope," Tom Wheat observed wryly. "Everything seems to come in the form of 'guidelines.' It's weird. If I were an antipope, every day I would issue a new encyclical contradicting the teachings of the Church. I just don't get it."

Nobody else did either.

✝ ✝ ✝

Most married people do the bulk of their talking in bed. Joanie and Nathan were no different. Joanie was glowing. She found herself looking forward to Nathan's comfortable habit of opening up afterwards. Nathan had said nothing during the meeting at Bruno's, which was not unusual for him. He gently rested a hand on her womb, waiting for the occasional kick from their child.

"I'm joining the Resistance," he said soberly.

"I know," she said. "I saw you talking with Karl after dinner. I guess I don't have much say in the matter."

"It's not that," he said, surprised by the testiness in her voice.

"Then what is it?" she asked, the tension rising in her voice. The baby kicked again.

"This," he said.

"This?"

"The baby kicking in your womb," he explained. "For the baby. I don't remember everything from the Warning, but I do remember Mary calling me a warrior. It's what I am."

"I don't understand you," she told him angrily, disappointed that the conversation had taken this turn.

"Yes you do," he said after a moment.

"Well I don't think the Blessed Mother meant for you to pick up a gun and go out and start killing people. Maybe she was talking about being a prayer warrior or something," she said bitterly.

Nathan suddenly remembered Red Bandanna, bleeding. Dead on a street in Bloomfield. After returning home from the harrowing trip to New Jersey, Nathan hadn't known whether to confess the shooting or not. Father Duffy told him it was self-defense. James Sullivan had described the incident to the older priest. Nathan tried to hide the pain of the memory, but found he couldn't. Since marrying Joanie, he found it harder and harder to keep his thoughts or emotions from her.

She hurt him. She could see it in his eyes. He became distant—something he rarely did anymore.

"Joanie…" he trailed off, not knowing how to finish.

She resisted an urge to turn away and then gave into the urge.

She felt his hand on her shoulder. He didn't force her to turn around. He was gentle. She could not—would not—listen to his silent, gestured command. But she was not like that. She had never been like that. Selfish. She was Joan Angela Wheat, daughter of Thomas and Anne Wheat, and she had been raised to take the good with the bad. She wrestled with anger and guilt.

The wordless argument continued for a moment longer.

Nathan finally broke the silence, "The time for talk is over. Now is the time for action." He had said the same thing to her at the Father Sorin statue after their first dinner at Bruno's. In another universe. Then, as now, Joanie did not understand what he meant by it. *Is he defining himself?* Something inside her soul reached out for his soul.

She turned back and looked into his eyes. "Can't you see that I don't want to lose you to some stinking Revolutionary War Part Two? I fell apart when you flew to New Jersey! I can stand cold showers, depression, poverty, no toilet paper, starvation—anything but not having you next to me."

"Joanie—" he tried to interrupt but she wouldn't let him.

"Now that the tribulations are here I hate it! I hate it! Suddenly all that stuff in Revelation about woe to mothers and pregnant women isn't just a bunch of words anymore. I love you! I don't want you to die in some damned war! I'm sorry, but I'm not you. I'm not a hero type. I want you here, *with me.* I thought angels would appear and save us when the tribulations came. You're the only angel I see right now.

"I can't even go to confession or Mass when I feel like it. Jesus might not be in the tabernacle next week if they find out what poor Father Duffy is doing. Don't you understand? You're the only sacrament I have left. You say you're leaving for the baby's sake, and that may be all well and good—but why don't you just admit it—you were made for war. All you damned men are. Daddy was too. That's what you bastards do—spill blood every chance you get. Maybe God's gonna punish—"

"Joanie stop," he said. He held her, trying to console her.

She let him keep his silence, knowing she had no choice. *Why is everything left unsaid with you, Nathan?* A small voice that was her own answered: *Because that's the way he is. You married a warrior. And war is a punishment for sin.*

5

From *Dark Years History*
(New Rome Press, 31 R.E.)
by Rebecca Macadam Jackson

...Indiana finally joined a loose confederation with Ohio, Western Pennsylvania, Michigan, Kentucky, and West Virginia and seceded from the United States, refusing to take part in the new monetary system. They called themselves the Midwest Confederation. Their economies were in a shambles. Minor rebellions *against* joining the Confederation broke out in the capitals of Indiana and Michigan— but were eventually quelled. Rumors abounded that the World Union would crack down on the Confederation as soon as the Nation of Texas was brought to heel...

...Indiana and Ohio became the breadbasket of the new Nation of Texas, exchanging foodstuffs for oil and meat. Michigan hurriedly retooled its auto plants so it could provide much-needed military vehicles, including tanks...

...The Fall of Chicago rocked independent free states and regional confederations. The surprise invasion from

Canada, across Lake Michigan, brilliantly conceived and led by General Blatovsky, was one of the more spectacular World Union victories. Illinois's efforts to remain neutral had failed, cutting the industrial center of the United States in half. Blatovsky brutally suppressed all opposition to the World Union, and will forever be known as the first foreign leader to authorize and construct concentration camps in North America. Special Psychological Warfare battalions worked hand-in-hand with CNI Media correspondents to broadcast what was happening in Chicago and Illinois around the world. It was obvious that Illinois was being made an example of the fate planned for states which rebelled against the World Union. Nevertheless, regional battles with Iowa, Nebraska, and Missouri lasted until...

6

Thursday Morning
12 December
Mishawaka, Indiana

Joanie Payne gave birth to Jonathan Thomas Payne while Nathan was out training with the Indiana Resistance.

The baby was delivered at home by Sarah Brown, a midwife. Sarah was Huey Brown's wife. The maternity ward at Saint Joseph Hospital had been closed due to lack of funding. Rioters had set fire to one wing of the hospital. The few doctors and nurses who showed up for work did so without pay. There was very little medicine available. Many professionals had fled to the western confederacies—which seemed to have better economies—or to the east, where they were promised jobs in the universal health care system of the World Union. Some had gone to Texas. Health insurance companies based on the East Coast had long since ceased doing business in non-World Union Territories.

Nathan joined the Indiana Resistance, and was assigned to Jimbo Sullivan's staff. (Jimbo had moved his wife Doris and his three sons to Mishawaka when Virginia went along with the World Union. Slinger had introduced Jimbo to Chip Williams at a secret meeting in Texas two months earlier. Jimbo agreed to try to set up a citizen's army in Indiana.)

Jimbo gave Nathan the low-profile but important responsibility for coordinating materiel and supply lines. Nathan's genius for numbers was his primary asset for the job—but he had little experience and did not really know what he was doing. Jimbo didn't have any choice. There were not many men from whom to choose. The Resistance had not received much support from the general population. The Governor of Indiana was all for the World Union, the state legislature was against it, and the people of the Hoosier state generally wanted to remain neutral.

The World Union and the various free states vied for Indiana's industrial and agricultural resources. Terrible weather had played havoc with harvests in Nebraska, Iowa, Kansas and other western agricultural states—and getting food to the cities was no longer a certainty, given the chaos of the railroad and trucking infrastructure. Hijacking and corruption were rampant. The mighty economy of the United States had more and more come to resemble that of the former Soviet Union. The black market was becoming a significant part of everyday life.

✝ ✝ ✝

Joe Jackson didn't join the Indiana Resistance. He remained at the Kolbe Foundation instead. Slinger had run out of money, donating the bulk of his wealth (in the form of gold) to Texas to help set up reserves for the new nation's banking system.

The Kolbe Foundation shrank in size. Postal systems were in disarray and there was no money to purchase supplies even if supplies had been available. No shipments could be sent to the World Union states, and service was expensive and spotty west of the Mississippi.

The Kolbe Foundation now faced many problems: Most of the blank audio tapes they used had come from China or Europe before the tribulations began. There were no suppliers in the Midwest Confederation. There were laser printers but no toner cartridges. There were no Japanese replacement parts for computers that broke down. And so on for a hundred other kinds of business goods.

Instead, the Kolbe Foundation became a center of prayer. Every day, thousands of people showed up in good or bad weather at six o'clock to pray the Rosary and to hear Lee Washington preach from a platform set up on the charred remains of the Kolbe Center. Joe had decided not to rebuild it. Thousands were baptized—sometimes whole families at a time. Everyone prayed for peace.

The Catholic Church in America was in utter confusion. Priests who had been thrown out of parishes from around the state came to the Kolbe Foundation to say Mass and hear confessions. Authentic Catholics no longer doubted that the Great Schism was in full force, but found themselves in a minority.

7

From *Dark Years History*
(New Rome Press, 31 R.E.)
by Rebecca Macadam Jackson

...Texas seceded from the United States and the World Union. The Lone Star State had a major economic trump card: its own oil supply. The National Guard was renamed the Lone Star Army and William "Chip" Williams was appointed Supreme Commander by the new President of Texas, a descendant of Sam Houston. Tens of thousands of unemployed men enlisted in the new army within a few weeks.

Texas immediately began signing non-aggression treaties with neighboring states: Alabama, Oklahoma, Louisiana, New Mexico, and Arkansas. The effect of Protestant Christianity on this development can not be underestimated. Texas's conservative, Christian legislature immediately outlawed abortion, repealed no-fault divorce, and rejected almost all the liberal social nostrums of the World Union and the secularized United States. Prayer was allowed in public schools in Texas for the first time since the early 1960s (and now the whole state had something to pray for—survival)! Refugees flocked to Texas from all over the country.

These events rocked the world. Texas was immediately condemned as a rogue nation in the legislature of the World Union in Amsterdam, and the president of the United States was instructed to bring it into line.

Two months after the Declaration of Independence of Texas, Utah followed suit, declaring itself the Mormon Nation. When the LDS took control of the state government, the first theocracy in the modern history of North America was born. LDS rank and file members buzzed with the rumor that the beginning stages of Joseph Smith and Brigham Young's famous White Horse Prophecy were at hand.

According to the White Horse Prophecy, the Constitution of the United States would one day hang by a thread and would be saved by members of the LDS, who would be appointed by God to take control of the federal government. All good Mormons keep a year's worth of supplies in their homes in anticipation of this period of trial. A new government would eventually be established in Independence, Missouri (according to the prophecy), and the LDS would await the Second Coming of Christ...

...The East Coast never quite recovered from the Quakes, but everyday life slowly but surely took on a semblance of normalcy. Massive graves were constructed for the dead. Military vehicles with blue United Nations insignias became a common sight in American cities. German and Russian soldiers brutally suppressed criminals. Many U.S. troops were transported to Europe to help keep peace there. U.S. dollars—worthless in the deepening depression—were exchanged two to one for World Dollars and debit cards. Precious metals in the form of old coins, jewelry, and the like were exchanged at three World Dollars to one U.S. Dollar. On October twentieth, roughly four months after the earthquake, U.S. dollars were declared illegal—no longer legal tender. People rushed to beat the deadline with the few dollars they still had. Swedish-made debit card machines, hooked up via satellite to a central computer located in Brussels, began to appear in those stores able to open their doors after the Quakes. The transformation was relatively smooth—the World Union had learned a few tricks in similar switch-overs in Europe during the previous few years. Europe was held up by the media as a model of peace and prosperity. (It was not widely known that this was propaganda. Europeans, in turn, were rarely aware of the truth of events transpiring in the former United States.)

In accordance with the mandates of the World Union, eastern states began setting up euthanasia centers for elderly people. Older folks were encouraged in media campaigns to go to "Omega Centers" for the good of their nation and for the sake of the futures of their children. When the postal service began to deliver again, form letters were sent to those over the age of seventy-five who were deemed to have a "low quality of life" by State Health Departments. These letters offered huge World Dollar credits to heirs. Senior citizens could submit their case to a panel of "independent" medical professionals to find out if their children qualified for the credit. Brochures and television commercials hailed the Omega Centers as a solution to the debt problems of the United States. "Don't Be a Burden: Be A World Patriot" the campaigns urged...

8

Sunday Evening
5 January
Newark, New Jersey

Harlan Gello appeared on a CNI news program as a spokesman for the Health Ministry of the World Union. He told
about the light that awaited those who allowed themselves to
be injected with pain-free, deadly drugs at the Omega Centers.
He was passionate and eloquent. "You have nothing to fear.
You are a powerful spiritual creature. Your godhood awaits
you." He pointed out that his own book had prophesied great
tribulations such as the Quakes, to be followed by a period of
peace—the omega point.

Almost all the propaganda—slickly produced in Europe—
had underlying New Age themes. The World Union constantly
promoted itself as being accommodating toward religion.
After all, if the governments of the world could unite in peace,
why couldn't the religions of the world? Toward that end,
candidates for Omega Centers were encouraged to invite their
clergy members to participate in the "final act of love."

As Father Chet watched Gello on the tube, the priest
resolved to do whatever he could to expose the Omega Centers for what they truly were: abortuaries for the elderly.

9

Saturday Morning
18 January
Newark, New Jersey

Chet knew that he might end up in jail when he began to publicly protest the Omega Center next to the remains of the Prudential Building in downtown Newark.

The Special Police came in a van, arrested him, and brought him to a temporary jail building. They punched him in the face with gloved hands. They struck him in the ribs with a billy stick covered by Chet's own jacket. They gave no explanation for the beating. Eventually, Chet was put in a room in an old school building with twenty other Christians and Catholics who had also been arrested for resisting various World Union proclamations.

Ignoring his pain and the hunger in his belly, Chet began making the rounds of his new mission territory.

He thought of Saint Maximilian Kolbe and decided to imitate him—no matter what the cost. To love his captors. To minister to the people in this room with him. To bring Christ to them through the sacraments. To keep his sense of humor.

Chet reminded himself with a wry smile: *When Kolbe found out that the Nazis were about to send them to Auschwitz, Kolbe told his friars, "Wonderful, we're going on a trip and our fare has been paid by someone else!"*

You signed up for this. They might kill you tomorrow or in three years. Don't waste a minute.

He walked over to a woman holding a sleeping girl in her arms. He lowered himself into a catcher's crouch. The sleeping child could not have been more than five years old. He asked the woman, a blond with dirty hair, if she was a Catholic. She nodded.

"Would you like to have your confession heard?" he asked gently, smiling. No amount of hunger could take the gleam out of Chet's eye.

She nodded again.

"Good. Great! You're not going to be confessing to me, you know. You'll be whispering into the ear of Christ…"

The woman carefully handed her child over to her husband. Father Chet made the sign of the cross and began…

10

Tuesday Morning
21 January
The Loop, Chicago, Illinois

Five days after the Fall of Chicago, the Russian general who masterminded the lightning strike across Lake Michigan surveyed his new city. He had a patch over his left eye. He had lost the eye in combat during his years in Afghanistan. He had instructed a field surgeon to cut a notch out of the bridge of his nose. That way, he could still see to his left past the notch using his right eye. The loss of his eye had forced him out of combat and into the War Strategy Department, where he flourished.

General Ivan Blatovsky liked to ride tanks. He was atop the turret of his favorite tank in the world. He knew everything about tanks in general and this tank in particular. He had helped design this model, the K-45, the fastest tank in the world. It was not heavily armored, but it flew like the wind during battle. It had a small gun—but this gun was extremely accurate, had the longest range in the world, targeted quickly, and took advantage of the high-tech ordnance he also helped design.

Blatovsky had lobbied for his tanks. After Tbilisi, the fools from Amsterdam finally decided to start churning out K-45s in big numbers in a huge factory outside of Saint Petersburg. Traditionally, Russians preferred slow, simple, heavily armored behemo，ıs. Blatovsky was considered a maverick for pushing the Ƙ 45 and for following the tradition of World War II German ɭanzer commanders. Blatovsky was a speed freak.

If they had K-45s down in Texas, this war would be over, he thought. *Those morons in Amsterdam! When will they begin listening to me? They want me to go west when we should be going east. Fools!*

After this they will listen, he told himself as he scanned the blackened, smoky ruins of the Chicago skyline. He looked over his shoulder and saw the huge supply ship unloading K-45s by the hundreds. He smiled.

It took only a few thousand soldiers and less than two days to win the battle of Chicago. *Boldness, speed, surprise, and planning won this great city for me. The City of Big Shoulders—Hah! These Americans don't even know their own history. Washington did the same thing at Trenton during their so-called Revolutionary War—*

He heard an electronic beep inside his helmet.

"General, sir, we are ready to take you to River Forest, sir." The voice came from a man in a staff car parked in front of the Palmer House, less than a hundred yards away.

"River Forest?" The general had trouble pronouncing the name of the Chicago suburb.

"Yes, sir. River Forest. To inspect the detainment camp. Commander Gelitsin chose the location. You approved it three days ago. It will be ready to hold over 100,000 prisoners in less than a week. Ahead of schedule, sir."

"Yes, of course. Bring the car here," he ordered curtly, flicking his mike over his helmet. He saw the staff car leave its parking spot in front of the Palmer House.

America's first real gulag—and fate has given me the honor of building it! There's one for the history books!

Chapter Twenty-Two

1

Early Thursday Morning
1 May
Salt Lake City, The Mormon Nation

Sandra Brixton walked past the Cathedral of the Madeleine every night after leaving the radio station. She was a producer of a late night, live talk show. Sandra rarely looked at the cathedral on her way to her apartment. Tonight was different. For some reason she felt compelled to glance up at the roof of the Gothic church.

When she did, she saw the Blessed Mother. The Mother of God did not look real. She looked more like a bright white hologram than flesh and blood. Sandra shook her head and blinked her eyes to make sure the vision was not real.

But the lady floating on the church roof was still there, her arms outstretched at her sides, facing the city center.

Sandra felt goose bumps over her arms and legs. She stood entranced for several minutes, awestruck. Distracted, she dropped her handbag. This broke her reverie. She turned and ran back to the radio station. Maybe she could catch Billy Corcoran, the host of the show she produced, before he left for the night.

2

Thursday Afternoon
1 May
Anderson, Indiana

There was a picnic table in the center of the war room. Two laptop computers and a map were on it. Faxes and satellite photos of Indiana and Ohio were tacked to the walls next to a picture of the Sacred Heart of Jesus. The "war room" was the living room of a farmhouse owned by the White brothers of Anderson, Steve and Joe. At the moment, Steve and Joe White were down at the bottom of the long hill, part of an infantry unit. The old bachelors had given their home to the cause. The farmhouse had a big bay window with a panoramic view of Interstate 69. Sandbags were lined up all around the concrete walls of the farmhouse, leaving only the bay window exposed.

Satellite photographs faxed from Houston and reports from the short wave network placed the huge Second World Union Army just outside of Columbus, Ohio—only a day or two away on Interstate 69. Ohio had held off the World Union Army for almost two months before falling, making a desperate last stand just east of Columbus.

Jimbo Sullivan looked gravely at Nathan and shook his head. It was not in the grizzled Marine's nature to turn tail and run.

We can't run anyway, Nathan thought dejectedly. *They'll catch up to us in a matter of days—and annihilate our armored assets. Then it's guerrilla war. Unless there's a miracle in Anderson.*

"Short wave out of Columbus says scouts see evidence that they've split a third of the Second Army off to send it up I-71 to Cleveland," Nathan reported. "It seems like they're trying to secure the industrial sector, Commander. Maybe we can hold them off a bit longer here in Anderson if they're a smaller force. We've got good positions over the Interstate. We've set up antitank missile positions here, here, and…here, just like you said." Nathan pointed.

The four other men on the staff—a former lawyer from LaPorte, two farmers (veterans of Vietnam) from Terre Haute, and a radio operator from Evansville—grunted as they looked where Nathan indicated.

Jimbo looked at Nathan, then down to the map. Jimbo's neck was beyond tan. It was dark brown from long days and nights outside in the winter wind and the summer sun. He spent up to twenty hours a day training officers and setting up the Resistance's limited assets. Nathan supposed that this was why Marines were called *leathernecks*. (In this, he was mistaken. Marines are called leathernecks because their original uniforms had collars made from leather.)

Nathan had driven from Indianapolis this morning, where he had tried, unsuccessfully, to get more tank and artillery ordnance from a former National Guard Depot.

Nothing doing. Can't blame them. They're just as scared as we are. He had taken his Mustang for its speed, using up precious gasoline. Fortunately, several refiners in Gary had been willing to supply Jimbo's little army with gas and diesel. Nathan had bartered Mishawaka corn for the fuel, which he split between local farmers and the Resistance.

Half my job is bartering. Slinger had donated several million dollars to the Resistance, but that had run out a long time ago.

Nathan's most important procurement came from Camp Atterbury to the south. In the basement of an old field house, he had found a large cache of long-forgotten, hand-held antitank missiles. Jimbo had deployed over forty men with the weapons on either side of the anticipated battlefield.

Jimbo was proud of Nathan. He had told him so this morning when Nathan arrived with the bad news from Indy.

"I'm proud of you. You've done all you could do, little brother," Jimbo said, trying to cheer him. Jimbo had called Nathan "little brother" ever since their days on the playgrounds in Bloomfield, New Jersey. "We wouldn't have been able to field this army without you."

These words had given Nathan a boost. It was practically a speech for the elder Sullivan. Jimbo led with a minimum of words.

Jimbo looked at his watch. Time for the daily Rosary with the troops. He picked up his rifle and Nathan followed him. Even some of the Protestant soldiers joined in the "voluntary field Rosary," as Jimbo called it.

"Jimbo? What do you ask for when you pray the Rosary? Do you pray for victory?"

The short, barrel-chested Marine seemed surprised by the question.

"I never pray for victory, little brother. I pray for God's will. For me and for my men. For you, too."

They jumped over a wood fence on the White's property. Nathan felt an urge to say what had been on his mind for over a month. "We're going to get our clocks cleaned, aren't we?"

Jimbo kept his eyes on the tanks and troops at the bottom of the hill.

"Maybe. Probably. Then we'll move on to the next thing. Ever read about the battle of Thermopylæ, Nathan?"

"Yeah, a long time ago, at Our Lady of Lourdes. I still remember it. A couple hundred Spartans lost a battle to the Persians. Spartans were tough as nails. The original Marines. Every one of them died, including their king, but I can't remember his name. Begins with an *l*—"

"Leonidas," Jimbo filled in.

"But they bought enough time for the rest of Greece to prepare for battle. Eventually, the Persians lost."

Jimbo was not surprised at Nathan's memory. He said nothing.

"You mean we're like the Spartans?" Nathan finally asked.

"Yeah. Those weren't Ohioans who bought us time with their blood in Columbus. Those were Americans. One of my best friends, Michael Whitmore, commanded a Buckeye Battalion there. He might be dead for all we know.

"We're fighting for America. We're fighting for Maine, for South Carolina, for Montana. For freedom. I'd rather be dead than not have freedom. That might sound simpleminded to you—"

"No it doesn't," Nathan interrupted, a certain fire in his eyes.

"I'm sorry. I was out of line," Jimbo apologized. "You're here. That's enough."

"Forget it," Nathan said quickly. "Go on."

"Well, I've never been much of a mystic. I just say my prayers and do my job. I've tried to do good by Doris and the boys. God knows she's put up with a lot, sharing me with the Corps and all…" Jimbo trailed off.

Nathan had never heard the man open up so personally before. Then it struck him. *Jimbo is ready to die. He's not afraid. He's just ready. Willing. He's telling me this for a reason beyond giving me a military lesson.*

"Like I said, I'm not a mystic. But I'm not a doubter either. Every night before I go to sleep, I talk to Mary. I've done that since I was a little boy. In the morning, at Mass, I talk to Jesus, but at night I talk to His mother until I fall off to sleep. I taught Chet to do that, too. Last night, I was having second thoughts about the Resistance, and I told Mary. I asked her why. I know we're going to lose. She knows, too. And we can't run, either. The terrain is too open. We can't hide tanks."

Nathan realized that Jimbo's mind was like a computer; it was constantly evaluating data. It caused him to run off on tangents. *Maybe that's why he doesn't say much,* Nathan thought. *Just listen. The punch line is coming.*

"Then I dreamed I was in the battle of Thermopylæ. It was so real. I was a Spartan. I saw men falling on either side of me. Blood was everywhere. I must have killed a hundred men with my sword, which was exactly like my Marine officer's sword—you know how dreams are.

"I saw Leonidas up ahead, battling scores of Persians. There were huge rocky cliffs on either side of us. At the end of the dream, I was the last Spartan standing. Leonidas was dead at my feet. When the last Persian raised his sword, I saw it was Xerxes himself, the King of the Persians.

"But Xerxes was frowning, like he knew killing me wouldn't win the war. Even though the Persians had won this battle, they had lost. We won. He lost. I woke up as he ran his sword through me. My rosary was in my hands.

"It might sound like a nightmare, but it wasn't. I was having the time of my life. I know what I am. I'm a Marine. That's all. It doesn't have to be more than that for me. You're different, Nathan."

Nathan felt an urge to protest. He opened his mouth to speak but Jimbo waved him off. He recalled his last conversation with Father Chet. The Sullivan brothers had a sense of purpose. A willingness to be true to their vocations without counting costs ahead of time.

"Don't say anything—let me finish. The dream was a sign. It was an answer to my question to Mary—the question *Why?* She's saying that there's a reason for everything—even death. I don't know why we're buying time for tomorrow. But I do know there's a good reason. I just don't need to know what it is. Maybe Mary is planning something big. I want you to tell Doris for me—"

"You're not going to die!" Nathan snapped, gesturing with a clenched fist.

"Nathan," Jimbo said evenly. "That's out of our hands. You'll tell Doris?"

"Tell her what, man?"

"Tell her I'll take care of her from heaven if it comes to that. She'll understand."

Nathan dropped his hand in resignation.

"Sure, I'll tell her. But you're not going to die. All you Sullivans are rockheads, you know that?"

"Then why do you always hang out with us?" Jimbo asked without a trace of humor in his voice.

Nathan did not reply. At the bottom of the hill, a former autoworker atop the turret of a tank spotted the two officers and waved.

3

Early Thursday Morning
1 May
Salt Lake City, The Mormon Nation

John Lanning was awakened by the ringing phone at his bedside.

"There's something incredible happening at the Cathedral of the Madeleine," said the voice at the other end. "Some kind of phenomenon. A vision or something. There are almost four hundred people watching it right now."

The voice was Billy Corcoran's. Lanning had been a guest on Corcoran's show several times during the brouhaha over his conversion.

Lanning rushed to the window overlooking the valley, carrying the phone with him. On top of the cathedral, over a mile away, there appeared what looked like a glowing white bulb—like a Christmas light.

"I see it," Lanning said.

"Tell me, Mr. Lanning, you seem to be Salt Lake City's expert on all things Catholic—" Corcoran began.

"—well I would hardly call myself an expert—" Lanning interrupted.

"—whatever, Mr. Lanning. In your experience or research, have you ever heard of such a phenomenon?"

"Let me think," Lanning said, buying time. Then he remembered reading about something in a book called The Final Hour by Michael Brown. "If it's not a cruel prank or a hologram or something, what all those people are watching is similar to what happened at Zeitun, Egypt, in 1968, on top of a Coptic church there. Hundreds of thousands of Muslims, Eastern Orthodox Christians, and Western Christians witnessed the Mother of God almost nightly for a year, and less frequently for several years afterwards. Come to think of it, Mary also appeared over a church in the Philippines, witnessed by hundreds of thousands, in the early nineties. I have a book with documentation," Lanning paused. "I'd be happy to come down to the station and show it to you…"

Corcoran gladly took the bait. "Sure, John. You're no stranger to the Billy Corcoran Show. Come on down the hill! Time for a commercial folks. We'll be back with John Lanning, controversial ex-Mormon convert to Catholicism, within the hour. Don't touch that dial."

Lanning heard a change in the electronic tone of his line. Billy Corcoran came on the line, off the air.

"Thanks John. What a wild night! Sandra Brixton, my producer, was the first one to see it. I can't believe it. But I watched it with my own eyes. What's going on?"

"I don't know what's going on. I know Sandra from her days at WXYX—good producer. Knows her stuff. Look, I've got to get dressed. We can talk when I get to the station."

"Fine. How long?"

"Fifteen minutes, Billy. I want to see this for myself. The similarities to Zeitun are startling. One other thing…"

"What's that, John?"

"Aren't you afraid of the authorities?" Lanning asked. "I hear rumors that they might be cracking down on stations that aren't broadcasting according to the teachings of the LDS. They've already closed down that rock station in Provo—"

"Look John," Corcoran cut him off, "they'll never do that to a talk format. The Mormon Nation has promised religious freedom and freedom of speech to all citizens. Non-Mormons will go bananas if they start pulling licenses. I'll broadcast whatever I please, whenever I please. It's surprising to hear that kind of thing from you, of all people. You stood up to those stuffed shirts pretty damn well yourself once upon a time—"

"But that was when Utah was part of the United States, and before the depression," Lanning interjected. "There's really nothing to stop the LDS from doing whatever it wants to those who, ah, disagree with the aims of the Mormon Nation. Things are different now."

"Tell me about it, John. The Mother of God is appearing on the roof of the church across the street! See you in fifteen." He hung up. Billy Corcoran, a transplant from Sacramento, was neither a Mormon nor a Jack Mormon. He was nothing when it came to religion. But he was always willing to pursue a good story. Lanning admired him, but got the distinct impression that the broadcaster didn't quite understand the Mormon Nation.

4

Sunday Afternoon
4 May
Anderson, Indiana

It was humid and cloudy on the day of the battle for control of Indiana. Most residents of the state had not supported the Resistance. Most doubted that a band of expertly-trained but poorly-equipped citizens could hold off the powerful Second World Union Army.

After Mass, Jimbo decided to attack at three in the morning. The battle of Anderson lasted almost twelve hours. It was raining and foggy—which helped. The Indiana Resistance was outgunned and outnumbered, but not unprepared and not without courage. They were fighting for their own land, on their own land.

The enemy expected the battle to last an hour. Indiana had only a few dozen National Guard tanks and limited artillery. There were ten Guard fighter jets—outmoded 1980s models. On the plus side, there were several sophisticated antitank helicopters which had fled from a Marine Base in Georgia early in the wars (Jimbo knew the commander personally).

Using a bold strategy which he adapted from studying the battles of the legendary Duke of Marlboro (the forefather of Winston Churchill), Jimbo concentrated his forces and attacked the heart of the startled Second World Union Army. During the first hour, Resistance antitank missiles destroyed dozens of enemy tanks in a deadly cross fire. The Indiana Resistance poured through the gap and created massive confusion in the ranks of the enemy. Nathan believed there was a chance—a small chance—of pulling off a stunning upset.

The Indiana Resistance did have good communications systems, but information alone was not enough to overcome superior force. The air power of the enemy began to pick off Indiana's tanks one by one in the pandemonium.

That night, during the thick of the battle, Nathan watched the stern face of Jimbo in the yellow light of an old lantern

Jimbo's courage stirred him.

The bold attack wasn't a suicide mission—it was their only hope of winning. *Jimbo figured he owed his men that much. A chance—a thousand to one—of winning. But a chance.*

Jimbo's face betrayed no emotion as his friends died on the battlefield. Nathan wondered what King Leonidas' face looked like at Thermopylæ.

Finally, the field HQ was bombed by French fighter jets that came out of nowhere. Jimbo Sullivan was killed instantly when a cluster bomb burst through the roof of the White brother's farmhouse and exploded, sending fragments of shrapnel in every direction for several minutes. If Nathan had not been standing outside behind a thick brick wall, having a smoke, he surely would have been killed.

He now watched helplessly as enemy tanks and infantry rumbled in the direction of Indianapolis. A detachment of infantrymen and two French tanks were already heading toward the farmhouse.

Nathan quickly carried Jimbo's bloody body to the car. A scapular dangled around Jimbo's neck. There wasn't time to take care of the other bodies in the wrecked farmhouse. He jumped into his battered Mustang and drove north, recklessly, as fast as he could, retreating along the back roads toward

South Bend. He expected to be blown off the road by an enemy jet. There wasn't much to defend in riot-torn Indianapolis, where the World Union troops would probably be welcomed.

Maybe Joanie was right, Nathan thought as he streaked down a farm road. *Maybe Mary doesn't want me to be this kind of warrior.*

He hoped the troops on the front escaped, too. It was suicide to try to help them. If they were caught, they would be murdered. World Union forces took no prisoners. He thought of Jimbo Sullivan and began to cry. Nathan cried easily now.

5

Sunday Afternoon
4 May
World Union Health Ministry
Hackensack, New Jersey

Harlan Gello felt a strong urge to dwell upon the dossier in front of him. The name on the dossier was William C. Sullivan.

He's a priest—how interesting.

He felt a stronger urge to ask this prisoner a few questions. William C. Sullivan had been languishing at a World Union detainment center in Newark for months.

Perhaps I could find out why the priest has defied the Omega Centers. The Omega Centers were the vanguard of the New World Order. After the elderly were done, the centers would open their doors to the retarded, the criminals, and the unenlightened. Gello had been given the honor of seeing the plans.

All this Sullivan has to do is make a public statement endorsing the Omega Centers and he can be a free man the next day. That's fair, isn't it?

Gello noted that Sullivan was scheduled for "involuntary processing" at the Omega Center in Newark in just two weeks. The idea was distasteful, but Gello accepted the practice of involuntary processing as necessary and inevitable. Rangor, his spiritual master, had confirmed it many times. Rangor had eased his mind by pointing out that one could destroy the body, but one could not destroy the spirit. Sullivan would be reunited with the Great Light after processing, and would be reincarnated with a clean slate, free of the misconceptions of Catholicism. In the big picture, processing would be doing Sullivan and those like him a cosmic favor.

Maybe I could gain a few insights into the psyches of these fanatics and learn how to better serve the Health Ministry in the long run.

Gello suddenly remembered the one-week public relations trip he had to make to London to promote the Omega Centers. He opened his time-planner and frowned. His flight was scheduled to depart this evening. He picked up the phone to call the makeshift prison where Sullivan was being detained. *I'll have them bring this case over after I get back from London.*

6

Late Sunday Afternoon
4 May
State Highway 19, Indiana

In that odd Indiana way, the weather suddenly cleared about fifty miles south of Mishawaka. The sun came out, and the air was becoming more humid.

The smell in the car convinced Nathan to pull over and lower the top of the mud-covered Mustang.

He pulled back onto the highway. There had been a few refugees on the road, so Nathan wasn't surprised when he saw a thin old man walking along, carrying a raincoat and a small leather bag. He was wearing relatively clean chino pants and a red cotton shirt.

"Pick him up," a voice that sounded like Sister Lardo said inside Nathan's head.

He hesitated—the old man was not hitchhiking—then pulled over, opened the door, and offered him a ride.

Suddenly Nathan was filled with fear, remembering Tommy Gervin and a knife. That night seemed like years ago.

"Can I help you?" the old man asked.

The old man had an American accent but Nathan detected a hint of an Irish lilt in his voice.

"Need a ride, old man?" Nathan heard himself ask, still worried by an undeniable fear.

"I need to get to South Bend…" the old man replied. He noticed the fear in Nathan's voice and added, "Be not afraid, young man. I once had a brave Polish friend who used to say that all the time. Be not afraid."

The words soothed Nathan. True to his nature, he ignored his fears and chose to act.

"Hop in. I'm going to South Bend. There's some food and shelter there, too. Friends." Somehow he knew that he could trust this old guy.

Now that the man was up close, Nathan noticed that he was exceptionally thin. He had been limping, but there was a lithe spring in his motions as he opened the door of the car.

The old man looked toward the back seat of the car before getting in, and noticed the body of Jimbo Sullivan for the first time. He grimaced, and noticed the scapular on the dead man. In these times such a sight was no longer unusual.

"Catholic?"

Nathan felt like crying again. He nodded.

The old man raised his hand and prayed a blessing over Jimbo, and then over Nathan. Then he sat down.

"Be not afraid, young man," he repeated. "Lo, though I walk through the valley of the shadow of death, I will fear no evil."

And then, he added, "Would you like me to hear your confession, my friend?"

Nathan thought of his ongoing arguments with Joanie about joining the Resistance. Maybe he had been wrong. Maybe not. But there was still grace to be had in the sacrament. The young warrior nodded to the old priest.

When the old man opened his bag to retrieve his stole, Nathan noticed the scar on his neck.

There was something very familiar about him. There was an accent. Nathan had a vague feeling that he had seen the old man on television.

Do I know this man? he asked himself. *Irish accent. Scar on his neck must be from a bullet wound. Knows somebody who's Polish. He's a priest...Oh my God!* Nathan suddenly realized who was about to hear his confession. *It can't be!*

7

Sunday, Dusk
4 May
Mishawaka, Indiana

Lee sat rocking on the porch of Joe's house rereading one of Father Chet's books. The humidity was finally dissipating as the evening air became cooler. He was surprised at how easily he had become accustomed to the lack of air conditioning. Even his mother's tenement had been air conditioned when he was a child. Now, heat was more important. There had been very little electricity in Indiana since the winter. The ancient woodstoves in the church, rectory, and Joe's house had proved to be incredible blessings during the brutal winter. Lee had taken many people into the rectory during those cold months. Relatively speaking, a little humidity was nothing to endure.

I wonder where Father Chet is? Is he alive? he asked himself. In January, the pastor of Saint Agnes Church had informed Joe by ham radio that Father Chet had been arrested, and that World Union authorities refused to disclose where they were incarcerating him. Becky had taken the news particularly hard.

Lee was fasting. He had found a battered copy of Father Chet's *The Life of the Curé de Ars,* and had become fascinated with the patron saint of parish priests. Saint John Vianney had fasted on potatoes and bread almost every day of his priestly life except for Easter Season following Lent. Lee had been fasting for weeks now. At first it was difficult, especially because rich food had become scarce. It was tempting to eat the occasional chocolate bar or pie that found its way to his table. Becky still turned an egg into a piece of charred mortar, but she had learned how to bake a right good apple pie, using the apples from the trees that surrounded the cemetery.

When Lee noticed a marked increase in his ability to concentrate during contemplative prayer after the first week or two, he stepped up his mortifications. Now he fasted on bread and water four or five days a week. Local farmers delivered wheat to Ronnie O'Brien, who had set up a makeshift bakery in the barn. The O'Briens were great bakers. They had moved into the rectory with Lee after coming from New Jersey with the Sullivans, who now lived with the Wheats.

James and Mary Sullivan started a school for the children of refugees and local families. It was housed in a small building that Joe put up where the Kolbe Center used to stand.

Lee's heart leapt when he saw Nathan's battered Mustang pull into the long drive leading to Joe's farmhouse. He had heard about the battle of Anderson over the short wave network earlier in the day. He jumped to his feet and banged on the wall of the house, "Joanie, Becky! Joe! Nathan's back! He's alive!"

Lee ran down the steps to meet Nathan as he pulled up to the house. Then Lee stopped dead in his tracks when he looked at Nathan's car. There was a tall man standing next to the car. The man was wearing a beige tunic and had curly red hair…

"Raphael!" Lee called out jubilantly.

As soon as Lee cried out, the angel smiled and disappeared. Joanie, Becky, and Joe came running up behind Lee. They had not seen Raphael. A wiry old man got out of the car and began to limp toward Lee.

Lee watched with a strange detachment as he saw Joanie run by him and hug her husband, who lifted her into the air and spun her around.

Joe saw Jimbo's body and collapsed onto his knees, overcome with emotion. Becky knelt next to Joe, holding him, crying herself.

"Oh," Joanie whispered weakly as she saw the reason for Joe and Becky's grief. She also began to cry, her joy instantly turning to sadness. *Will these awful times never end!*

Lee was paralyzed as he watched the old man get out of the car. As the Woman had promised him in the Motorman Motel so long ago, he was given a certain knowledge that the wiry man limping toward him was a consecrated soul. *The* consecrated soul. There was a flash and Lee saw a white cross on Angus's forehead. The cross disappeared as soon as he noticed it.

Lee knelt down before the pope.

"Rise, my son," Pope Patrick said calmly.

Lee stood, then heard himself say, "The archangel who helped you was named *God Conquers.*" The young black man looked directly into the Irishman's eyes.

Angus smiled. *So that's what **God Conquers** means.* His smile grew. *I always wondered about that.*

"What do you desire, my son?" the pope asked his apostle. The words seemed to come out of the pope's mouth of their own accord.

"I desire to be a priest," Lee replied simply.

"And so it shall be, my son," Pope Patrick replied solemnly, placing his hands on Lee's head. "The Holy Spirit moves me. I do not know your name. But I do know you. We are brothers."

Angus paused. By now Nathan had revealed the pope's identity to the others. They stood in awe, watching the Vicar of Christ pray over Lee Washington.

Angus turned to the small flock before him. They reminded him of the Gospel passage in which Jesus, feeling an intense sadness, looked over the people, saying, "They are like sheep without a shepherd."

Perhaps... Angus thought. *Yes! That's it!*

He had been spared from death in the Tiber and forced to endure the endless, terrifying journey from Albano to Ireland to Boston and then across the badlands of Pennsylvania to this little church in Indiana. He thought of the brave sacrifice of Thomas Phillips and was briefly overcome with grief.

This meek black man kneeling beside him was one of the reasons he had been spared.

Pope Patrick raised his voice: "These are extraordinary times! Like the Son of Man, your weary vicar has no place to rest his head. Extraordinary times call for extraordinary decisions!"

He turned back to Lee. His next words were a prayer:

"By the authority granted me by the merits of the Cross and Resurrection of Jesus, and in His All Powerful Name, *you* shall have a new name. Your priestly name will be Phillip, after a martyr and saint who gave his life, so that you may give life to others. May you be a Bearer of Christ in humility, bravery, and obscurity."

As Angus finished his words, the last wisp of sun disappeared behind the horizon.

The pope turned to his flock, his remnant, and said, "Let's take care of James Sullivan. Ladies, the men will prepare the body while you prepare whatever is in your cupboard for a meal. Select the finest foods, however poor or humble they may be, in his honor.

"We'll do this right—an Irish wake! I hope there's some good whiskey stashed here someplace. I'll say a funeral Mass for him tomorrow morning. I am weak. I need to rest while you prepare things."

And that is how the first and last Irish Pope came to celebrate the death of Jimbo Sullivan with the Paynes, the Jacksons, and a former drug dealer named Lee Washington in the darkest days of the tribulations.

✟ ✟ ✟

The pope slept on Becky and Joe's marriage bed for three hours before rising to preside over Jimbo's wake. During the pope's nap, Lee drove over to Tom Wheat's farm to tell Jimbo's parents the tragic news. He then drove James Sullivan to Nathan Payne's house, where Doris and the boys had lived since moving from Virginia. James told Doris about her husband's death. She had three sons. The oldest, James III, was ten. Lee then told everyone about the unusual guest who would say the funeral Mass the next day. Neither Doris nor James III shed tears over Jimbo. The younger boys cried inconsolably.

✟ ✟ ✟

Angus remained silent after being introduced to the inner layer of Paynes, Sullivans, Wheats, and Jacksons during the first hour of the wake. As much as the guests tried, they found it difficult to act naturally. Jimbo was dead. The pope was alive. It was all too strange. There were no rules or previous experiences to guide emotions, actions, and words. Everyone kept glancing furtively over to the pope, thinking in unison: *How did he get here?*

Finally, Nathan Payne stood up and raised a toast to Jimbo: "To Jimbo Sullivan, son, husband, father, Catholic, patriot, Marine. Semper Fi."

They drank Maker's Mark, including Jimbo's seemingly shell-shocked wife, Doris. Her two oldest sons sat silently next to her on the couch. Her youngest son, Mark, who was three, slept in the arms of Mary Sullivan.

No one knew where Tommy and Mike Sullivan were. They had both moved from Boston to Texas at the beginning of the wars to fight in the Lone Star Army. One letter made its way to Indiana after the battle of Austin; both had survived to that point. But that had been months ago.

Nathan Payne told how Jimbo had stuck up for him on the playgrounds of Our Lady of Lourdes Grammar School. Then he retold the story of Jimbo's Right Hook. He took his time. He recounted Jimbo's bravery and leadership in Anderson. "He told me to tell Doris that he'll take care of her and the boys from heaven."

When Nathan was finished, James Sullivan, remaining in his seat, talked about what a fine son Jimbo was, and how the boy had been like a second father to Chet, Tommy, and Michael. He spoke with trembling voice at first, growing stronger as he went on.

Others took turns. Joe silently went around the little living room, refilling drinks from the last two bottles of Tom Wheat's stock of Maker's Mark.

Throughout the stories, Doris sat silently. She shed no tears. Finally, she spoke up in her almost gruff, matter-of-fact voice, "I knew when I married Jimbo that this might happen, and I've tried to prepare for this day. But I guess nothing could prepare me. Jimbo told me not to expect him to come back from Anderson.

"I appreciate all your wonderful words about him. I really do. I just…" she trailed off.

Nathan realized why Jimbo had chosen Doris. She was tough. Tougher than Jimbo. She was taking this better than anyone else.

"I'm just thankful that he died doing what he loved, and that he died in a state of grace," Doris continued, regaining her composure.

Amazing, Joanie thought, *she's so much stronger than I am. These times really are separating the wheat from the chaff.* She felt a tinge of shame for resisting Nathan's participation in the Resistance, and for her first reaction when she saw Jimbo's dead body: *Thank God it wasn't Nathan.*

A heavy silence followed Doris's words.

Becky broke it: "Holy Father?" she began tentatively.

"Call me Father Angus if that's more comfortable, dear," he said. "Or just Father. Pope means father."

"Father," she began again, "tell us what happened. Tell us how you got here, and why you're here."

Everyone was looking at the pope as Becky finished her question. After so many awkward silences during this astonishing evening, it seemed like the pope might be justified in waiting a long time to answer her bold question.

But Angus didn't hesitate.

"I'm not completely sure of why yet, Becky, but I'd be happy to tell you how. It's been so long that I've kept it inside, feeling, as it were, until tonight, that my silence was required by the Holy Spirit."

They were struck by the energetic life in Pope Patrick's eyes—and how uncannily he reminded them of another Irish priest, Father Chet.

"But it begins with a seminarian, hero, and martyr named Thomas Phillips..." For the next two hours, Angus recounted the incredible story.

He told them about his efforts to reunite the Eastern Orthodox church. The night of the assassination. His fantastic rescue from the Tiber by an Archangel.

"His name was God Conquers," Angus said, smiling at Lee.

The harrowing journey to Holy Blood Monastery. The coma. The shock of discovering how much the world had changed in the months he had been unconscious. And how he came out of the coma just as a journalist from Galway began pestering the Carmel regarding a wild rumor that the pope was alive. His long journey across the Atlantic in a passenger ship, always incognito, to Boston Harbor. Hitchhiking and walking across Massachusetts and Pennsylvania in disguise for two weeks. Regaining his sense of God, like an Old Testament prophet entering the wilderness to fast and pray for forty days. Saying Mass in a small Catholic Church in Emlenton, Pennsylvania, for several Catholics who did not know that he was the pope. And finally, demanding to be dropped off by a truck driver on the back road on which Nathan found him.

"I've come to rely more on the Holy Spirit and less on my intelligence, which at times misled me before the assassination attempt. It was the Holy Spirit who persuaded me to get out of that truck so Nathan could pick me up and bring me here. It was the Holy Spirit..." he trailed off, looking down at his battered shoes.

Contrition had crept into Angus's voice. "I may be a pope, but I don't have a secret book of instructions to turn to in this situation—besides the Holy Scriptures, of course. In some ways, I'm more confused than you are. I'm afraid that I've been a failure as your pope. I failed miserably shepherding the Church during these times of great trials."

They were shocked by the self-castigation in his voice. Angus had always been hard on himself. The pope's spiritual director from days gone by, the Bishop of Belfast, would not have been surprised.

The only one in the room who was not surprised by the pope's dismal summary of his papacy was Nathan Payne. This was partly because he had sensed the pope's dejection during the car ride to Mishawaka.

But he was not wholly listening to the pope. A part of his mind was filled with joy and hope. And a plan. A simple plan.

I have to talk to Joe about this. I have to talk to Pope Patrick... he thought. *I have to talk to Karl Slinger!*

It was a unique part of Nathan's nature that he was not intimidated by the presence of the pope. After Nathan confessed his sins, there had been a connection between the two men. Both were natural leaders. Both were men of sorrows. Both needed the other in order to fulfill their destinies.

Nathan decided that he would try with all his persuasive might to convince the pope to execute the plan.

He downed his last shot of Maker's Mark, excused himself and Joanie from the room, and went out on the porch to have a smoke and tell his wife that he finally realized what the Blessed Mother had meant when she called Nathan Payne a warrior.

✛ ✛ ✛

The following day, Pope Patrick presided over the Requiem Mass for James Ronald Sullivan, II. They buried Jimbo in the cemetery next to Immaculate Conception Church.

The day after the funeral, Pope Patrick ordained Lee Washington as a deacon in the morning, and a priest in the early afternoon.

Father "Phillip" Washington began hearing confessions that evening.

8

Sunday Morning
4 May
Salt Lake City, The Mormon Nation

John Lanning stood on the steps of the Cathedral of the Madeleine, baptizing. He had been baptizing for three straight days.

Months earlier, when the LDS had declared Utah the Mormon Nation, Slinger had packed his bags and moved to Houston with Dottie. He had also resigned from the Chairmanship of SLG Industries. Lenny Gold went with him. At Karl's request, Denny Wheat flew to Wyoming and picked up Karl's two daughters and their families and followed him to Texas. Since the secession of Texas, Karl had spent most of his time in Houston.

Lanning had refused Karl's offer to leave Salt Lake City, and stayed behind in Karl's house on the hill. Before the Mother of God began appearing, he had spent most of his time praying at the Cathedral of the Madeleine, writing a second book on Mormonism, and meeting with fellow Catholic converts at the Truth Societies around the state. He did not expect religious freedom to last long in the Mormon Nation.

As in Zeitun, the Mother of God appeared every night, between one and four o'clock in the morning, and always in the "holographic" image. She never addressed or acknowledged the crowds which gathered there in ever larger numbers. She seemed to be looking directly at Temple Square. At times, a shining dove appeared to be flying over her head—a symbol of the Holy Spirit. One time, a young man tried to climb up on the roof of the cathedral and the vision quickly disappeared.

An investigation by the Salt Lake City police department found no evidence of holographic or other electronic devices on or near the church. An official report by the police declared the apparition "unexplained phenomenon not caused by human agents." The crowds grew larger.

The LDS remained silent about the growing spectacle. Mormons believed that Mary was the mother of Jesus. But Mormons did not believe in the Holy Trinity. They believed that Jesus and the Father and the Holy Spirit were separate beings. In fact, they taught that the Father was Adam, the original husband of Eve, and *also* that the Father later came to earth from his own planet and sired Jesus through Mary! The Father was not even the creator of the universe—"God" was a god no greater than the god every good Mormon believed he too would become after death. (Mormons also believed that Mary had other children, including a son who was the direct forefather of Joseph Smith.)

In short, Mary played a small, almost inconsequential role in LDS theology. She was not considered the Theotokos—the Mother of God. To Mormons, she was just someone who was randomly chosen by the Father to bear the physical body of the "spirit child" Jesus.

When Lanning began preaching on the balcony in front of the Cathedral of the Madeleine, certain members of the LDS shadow hierarchy became nervous. Then thousands of Mormons—most of them Jack Mormons—began to ask to be baptized by Lanning.

Without the legal restrictions of membership in the United States, the LDS was planning to publicly resurrect the teaching of Blood Atonement. According to this teaching, "sins against the Holy Spirit" could not be forgiven by God; they could only be atoned by the shedding of the sinner's blood.

More and more, Lanning came to be seen as just such a sinner. John kept baptizing.

9

Tuesday Evening
6 May
Notre Dame, Indiana

The Holy Father and his four new friends sat together under the Father Sorin statue. The late evening sun was just beginning to set, casting a beautiful glow on the statue of Mary on the Golden Dome. Nathan looked over to the pope, who was dressed in black with a simple Roman collar. Angus was wearing Chet's clothes. The resemblance to Father Chet was uncanny. It was more than the pope's slight build and strong Irish features—it was the spring in the step, the twinkle in the eye, the willingness to listen. And the collar.

The campus was practically empty. Few people had the money to send their children to college. Word spread quickly that the pope was alive. Hundreds of people had come to Lee's ordination several hours earlier. His first act as a priest was to enter the confessional. Angus heard confessions himself for almost three hours.

Earlier in the day, before the crowds came to Immaculate Conception Church, Nathan had asked the pope to set aside some time to discuss "a plan of action." The pope had agreed enthusiastically. It was a chance to get away for a relaxing, restful walk with his new friends after a physically draining day. His joints still ached as a result of the coma, despite the physical therapy he had received from the Carmelite nuns. He found during his long journey to Indiana that constant movement helped keep him from tightening up. That, and five aspirins a day, allowed him to limp along.

They all crammed into Joe's Buick and drove to Notre Dame. Anne and Tom Wheat were watching the two babies back at the farm. The pope had never seen the beautiful campus before, but he was well aware of its existence, because the university had played a major role in undermining the teachings of the Church since the early 1960s. The administration was now actively lobbying for Indiana to join the World Union so it could reopen its doors in the more vibrant, peaceful economy promised by the New World Order, its debit cards, and its World Dollars. Tom Wheat had been laid off. His tenure meant nothing in the existing legal and economic chaos.

Joanie explained the significance of Sorin as a founding father of Notre Dame, and how the statue had been a talisman of friendship for the two couples. Angus was eager to hear their stories in more detail, and reclined on the grass as he listened, sipping a cup of water from a thermos Becky had brought with them.

Angus led them in a Rosary. As they prayed, they appeared to be a simple gathering of friends with an old priest. *Often, the best disguise is the truth,* Angus thought.

As a small precaution, Angus had kept his hair dyed dark black. His extreme loss of weight and his "death" kept him safe from recognition.

Nathan found himself concentrating on the Sorrowful Mysteries of the Rosary. Since his Warning, he never mumbled the words, but strove to meditate on the mysteries: the Agony in the Garden, the Scourging at the Pillar, the Crowning with Thorns, the Carrying of the Cross, and the Crucifixion. It was not hard for him to imagine being an active observer at Christ's Passion.

A heavy silence hung in the air after they finished praying. Joe was deep in thought. Becky was absently picking at strands of grass. The pope kept his gaze on Mary atop the dome. Joanie nervously fumbled with Nathan's hand, gripping it tightly, then caressing it, then gripping it tightly again. She looked into Nathan's eyes. He couldn't read her thoughts. Joanie was the inscrutable one now.

Without looking up from the grass, Becky broke the silence. More than ever, it seemed to be her calling—to be the one to speak up, the one to vocalize the group's thoughts.

"Go on, Nathan. Tell the pope what you think he should do. That's what we came here for," she said. The words were a command, but the tone was a plea. She shifted her weight and leaned back on Joe's chest. He wrapped his arm around his wife. It was a warm day, but Joe's affection was more than welcome. Becky looked directly into Angus's eyes. Then, she smiled. It was just the right thing to do. Her beautiful, innocent smile broke the cloud of doom that had settled on them all.

"Speak up, son. Providence has brought us together on this lovely day, in this beautiful place, in front of this inspirational Father Sorin. May the Holy Spirit enlighten us all!" The pope finished with a disarming laugh.

He's smoother than Father Chet, Nathan thought, saddened and hopeful at the same time. He had been watching the pope very carefully since the plan came to him at Jimbo's wake. With every word and intonation, he became certain that Pope Patrick could pull it off. The Sorrowful Mysteries had clinched everything. *What is the imitation of Christ?* Nathan thought. *To lay down one's life for a friend. But who am I to counsel a pope?*

"Go on, Nathan," Joanie gently encouraged. "The Holy Father doesn't have to do it, you know."

Nathan looked at Joe briefly, then at the pope. "It's not a plan, really. It's an idea. It requires…" Nathan hesitated, but never broke the pope's gaze, "a willingness to die. A willingness to fall and rise, like Jesus did. When Jesus triumphed over Satan by his death and resurrection, only the apostles recognized…"

Nathan stopped. *It's not my place to tell him this. The pope knows all this.*

"Don't worry about preaching to a pope, son." Angus winked. "I put my pants on one leg at a time, and a lot more slowly than most folks. And I'm alone. I've been alone for a long time. As you were saying…"

"Okay." Nathan took a deep breath. "When Jesus died and rose from the dead, only the apostles recognized that the show was over for Satan. They were commissioned to go out and tell others. Most of them ended up like Jesus—dead. Martyrs.

"But this time around, we need to crush the evil one in a public way. In a way that everyone in the whole world can see right before their eyes. We can't do it with guns. We can't do it with money. We can't do it with worldly power. All we have are several hundred thousand short wave radios, a few satellites operating out of Texas—and a pope. You. And millions of beleaguered Catholics and Christians all over the world praying for the Triumph of the Immaculate Heart of Mary. We're supposed to be her instruments to crush Satan."

Nathan was gaining momentum. Joe, Joanie, and Becky were stunned to see him bearing down on the Holy Father with *the look.* And they saw the light in Pope Patrick's eyes—so reminiscent of Father Chet—growing brighter with every word Nathan said.

"In less than a few weeks—or sooner—the bad guys are going to track you down, aren't they?" Nathan asked with a note of sadness combined with a strange, distant excitement.

Angus nodded. "Yes. Go on, my friend."

"So let's beat them to the punch. Let's leverage everything we've got. And we've got all we need. We have you—and a communications network inspired and named after the man who was the greatest example of Marian sanctity in the whole history of the world. Maximilian Kolbe."

Becky briefly felt like clapping. The air was thick with grace.

"You've got to do it, Holy Father! You've got to," Nathan pressed. "Like you said, Providence has brought you here."

Then all his enthusiasm drained away as if it had never been there at all. Nathan felt as if he were hanging motionless off the side of a cliff.

"There's only one catch…" Nathan choked on the last word. He couldn't finish.

Angus didn't say a thing.

Joe completed the thought for his friend, "The catch is, Your Holiness, like Saint Maximilian, they'll kill us all. Nathan is asking you to lead us to martyrdom."

"I know, lad," Angus replied. There was a wistfulness in his voice combined with anguish.

Becky was struck with a realization similar to her earliest impressions of Father Chet—that the pope wasn't a demigod, a superman standing in for God. The pope was real flesh and blood, emotion and soul. A man.

The pope looked up at Father Sorin, then, oddly, to Joanie. "What do you think, young lady?"

She looked at Nathan.

"This is yours, Joanie. Don't ask me what I think." Nathan told her with his eyes. *"Tell the pope what **you** think."*

She gripped Nathan's hand so hard it hurt.

"With all due respect," she began, "I think you should listen to my husband, Holy Father. I don't want to speak out of turn but…but whenever Joe and Nathan agree about something, well, you can be sure Our Lady is behind it. I have a newborn son, and I don't want to leave him—but I don't want Jonathan to grow up in a world gone insane. If we do nothing, he probably won't grow up at all. It's not much of a choice, I guess. But I'm willing to do whatever you ask of me. I am."

Angus nodded and turned to Becky. "As for you, Beck— you let your friends call you Beck, don't you?"

"Me? You want to know what I think?"

The pope nodded again.

Oh no! Joe thought. *Becky's going to come out with a real winner.* He could see it in his wife's eyes and the way her cheeks rose ever so slightly, forming a squint.

"Father Angus," she began earnestly. For a second Joe hoped she might say something serious. "You really don't know these guys very well, do you? I do. They're out of their minds." She paused.

Everyone laughed.

"But I love them dearly. And as Father Chet, the original Irish priest in our little circle used to say, 'It's like throwing sand against the tide, but I knew that it was going to be tough when I got into it. That's what I signed up for.' I agree. Let's go for it! I'm sick of sitting around waiting for things to happen. That's not what I signed up for. If we're going to go down, let's go down fighting, with a smile on our faces!"

Becky looked around the group with a raised eyebrow. She had not been practicing her faith long enough to have that instinctive awe for anything papal. There was something peculiarly American about the way she spoke—and something profoundly right.

Now is the time for action! Joanie thought jubilantly.

"Well spoken, Becky!" the pope replied. "I'm with you." The decision had been made. Everyone felt it.

"Well now, Nathan," Angus continued, "what exactly do you propose we do?"

"Joe and I have some pretty specific suggestions, Holy Father, and a tight schedule to follow right up to the big event…"

Chapter Twenty-Three

1

Thursday Morning
8 May
Mishawaka, Indiana

Tom Wheat found his preparation for today's weekly short wave radio program more difficult than ever. Usually he spoke for an hour on the "SLG Network" about the apparitions of Mary and how they fit in with the turbulent times. Today he would speak for less than one minute. His show was called "Mary's Army."

Recordings of the program were usually made and circulated on audio tape to those who did not have short wave radios. The talks would then be transcribed and printed by underground newspapers around the country—even inside World Union Territories. Word of mouth did the rest.

Tom Wheat felt an affinity for the historical figure, Thomas Paine, whose pamphlet *Common Sense* had electrified and mobilized patriots during the first American Revolution.

The SLG Network had also championed the cause of any state which defied the World Union. Its program, "Radio Free America," was rebroadcast several times a day. After Utah became the Mormon Nation, Radio Free America began to be broadcast from Houston instead of the SLG Communications Institute. Slinger was managing to stay a step ahead of events—and was having the time of his life.

Nathan Payne had been correct. In the long run, radios proved to be more important than guns—although more than a few Resistance Movements around the fractured country were armed with weapons that came from SLG farms and ranches, especially in the western states.

The SLG Network was capable of beaming television programs through its satellites. The broadcasts could be picked up by anyone in the world who owned a digital satellite dish.

Wheat sat in his living room, ready to begin his program, facing a television camera hooked up to wires leading to a van in his driveway. The van was white and had three words painted on its side panels: The Kolbe Foundation. Its engine was running, supplying electricity to the digital transponder that was aimed directly at one of the unseen SLG satellites.

The room was crowded with trusted friends and relatives. They had all just finished a Rosary with him. Father Phillip Washington was not in attendance. He was offering Mass in Immaculate Conception Church.

Joe hung up the cellular phone in the kitchen and came to sit next to Tom on the couch, saying, "That was Houston. Karl says they're praying for you and for all of us up here. The satellites are ready. You've got eight hours. Good luck and God bless, Tom."

Tom nodded and cleared his throat. He took a sip of water. It was time to launch Nathan's plan. It was time to take the battle to the airwaves.

After Tom heard the introduction music, a techie in the van whispered "three, two, one" in Tom's earphone.

"I welcome all soldiers in Mary's Army, Catholics loyal to the universal teachings of the Catholic Church, baptized Christians of all denominations, fellow Americans, lovers of freedom everywhere, and all those listening to my voice."

And then he veered from his usual script.

"Mark my words. This day will be remembered for the rest of human history. You are a part of it. If you have a digital satellite dish and VCR, an audio tape recorder, or any other kind of recording device, I urge you to begin recording now, for I have an amazing guest for you to meet. We don't have much time. I'll let the guest tell you how he came here, and why he came here to talk to you today."

Wheat paused and lowered his tone while raising his voice at the same time…

"The name of my guest is…Pope Patrick!"

Tom Wheat and the camera turned to face the leader of the Roman Catholic Church, the Vicar of Christ, who was dressed in the traditional white papal cassock (hastily sewn from bed linens by Anne Wheat and Joanie during the past two days).

✛ ✛ ✛

Pope Patrick, raised Angus Bartholomew O'Hara in the poorest section of Dublin, looked directly into the camera and told the world the Truth. He began in English and continued for two hours. Then he gave the same address in Spanish, French, and German over the following six hours.

Angus gave a stunning performance; the mastery of languages alone proved to the world that this was indeed the real Pope Patrick. He did not use complicated theological language, often called "popespeak." He spoke simply and directly, fluidly weaving his amazing story. He was a master storyteller. At one point he pulled open his cassock and showed the world the bullet wound in his side. The world discovered the heroic truth about Thomas Phillips.

He urged people everywhere to pray for an end to the troubles in the world, and, winking into the camera, specifically asked his "Carmelite Prayer Army" to deploy themselves in force.

"Please, I beg you, pray for a special Mass which I will soon celebrate in public. I will offer the Mass for the Triumph of the Immaculate Heart of Mary, and for the Divine Mercy of the Sacred Heart of Jesus to descend upon the world. I will announce the time and day of the Mass when I broadcast tomorrow. Come, join me in prayer!"

Toward the end of the talk he released all the clergy in the world from obedience to any bishop or person in Catholic authority who had been appointed by the antipope. It was also clear that he rejected "those governments which do not respect basic human freedoms, and I urge all men and women of good will to use every possible, morally acceptable means to resist such godless regimes." Without quite mentioning it by name, Pope Patrick had effectively defined the World Union as the enemy of God and His people.

2

From *Dark Years History*
(New Rome Press, 31 R.E.)
by Rebecca Macadam Jackson

...Pope Patrick's stunning electronic resurrection literally changed the world overnight. Because the schismatic antipope Casino had closely and publicly aligned himself with the World Union, it became suspect and lost what little moral authority it had earned as the purported economic savior of the world...

3

Friday Morning
9 May
Amsterdam, The Netherlands

"I want him alive!" the dark man screamed at the men gathered around the mahogany table. "I don't care how you do it! Use every asset we have. Converge upon that...that town in Indiana and get Patrick! I want—"

The dark man stopped himself short. He had never screamed in front of these men before. He saw their shocked expressions. Shock, but not fear.

Not fear. The dark man and his allies still controlled most of the industrialized world, its armies, its currency, and its institutions. Even with that damned Angus O'Hara alive, the Catholic Church was in ruins, a shell of its former self. That fool Casino would still do whatever the dark man told him to do.

What did the dark man have to fear from a wrinkled old man? Why was he losing his composure? Why were the five men around the table no longer afraid of him? Was there something they were more afraid of?

Perhaps even *they* believed in the power of God.

And the dark man felt *his* power draining away like murky oil flowing out a crankcase.

The only thing left to do was play out the string—and to drag as many souls down to hell with him as he could. Even evil men have pride.

"Bring Patrick to me," he ordered coldly. "Send that butcher, Blatovsky, to get him." He looked around the room to regain whatever measure of fear he could salvage. He turned and walked out into the marbled hallway.

✝ ✝ ✝

The dark man and his allies made their phone calls, sent their memos and emails, and issued their orders. Two powerful World Union armies (one from Chicago, the other from Indianapolis) turned from whatever grisly business they had at hand and converged on South Bend, Indiana. The Second World Union Army, licking its wounds from the costly battle of Anderson, was unable to mobilize immediately, giving Blatovsky's Third Army a two-day jump. They met with no resistance from what was left of the rag tag Indiana patriot army.

It was clear from the daily broadcasts by Pope Patrick that he was content to stay indefinitely at Joe Jackson's home next to Immaculate Conception Church. Hundreds of thousands of people from around the Midwest raced against two World Union Armies to meet this one man. Pope Patrick.

Within a few days, the crowds became so large that Pope Patrick decided to address them, and pray with them, and say his pre-announced Mass with them on the Main Quad of the University of Notre Dame. The Mass would take place on a day shared by the Feast of Our Lady of the Blessed Sacrament and Our Lady of Fatima.

4

Tuesday Morning
13 May
Newark, New Jersey

Chet removed his rosary beads from the hiding place in the seam of his prison uniform. They consisted of eleven tiny beads, made from spit and bread hardened onto a sturdy piece of string the priest had culled from his filthy cotton pants. Lately, he had found it difficult to concentrate on the mysteries. His migraine was back. Lack of food and water were the cause.

I thought I knew what hunger was after the Quakes.

He tried to think of Saint Maximilian for the hundredth time in the last few days. For the ten thousandth time in the last four months. *Max, how did you do it? All the biographies made it seem so easy. And this isn't nearly as tough as you had it.*

A week ago, they had stopped feeding Chet a regular ration. The priest now got one meal a day—tasteless soup and a piece of bread.

It was pretty clear what that meant. *Involuntary processing, the case workers call it. Death in an Omega Center.*

A prolife Protestant minister, Jimmy Sisler, had been processed last week after two weeks of low rations. Chet had become very close to Sisler during their time together, and missed him dearly. *They don't waste food on a dead man.*

I have to hang in for a couple more weeks. Go out like a man. Like a Sullivan.

Inspired by Saint Maximilian, Chet had shared his meager rations with other prisoners, especially the ones with children. At any given time, there were over three hundred in this holding center. They slept together on the floor of the gym. Most were political protesters. During the winter, they huddled close to keep warm. Since then, several had died after receiving last rites from Chet. He saved bread from his meals so he could rise in the middle of the night to say Mass with the other Catholics. A few Protestants had converted to Catholicism in order to receive Jesus at Chet's Masses. Others attended, but didn't receive the tiny hosts.

Before the night Masses, a French guard had reported Chet for saying Mass during the day. That had merited a beating. Chet thanked God that he couldn't remember pain. He tried to pray as the big German "case worker" beat him with a rubber hose.

The prisoners seemed to be lost in some kind of giant shuffle of World Union cards. Once a week, a hard-faced Belgian woman would show videos—mostly World Union propaganda. Afterwards, she would offer them a chance to sign some papers saying that Omega Centers were a wonderful idea, or something to that effect. In return, the prisoner was free to go. There was a document attached giving the World Union permission to use the statements in the media. Occasionally, a few prisoners would sign. Most didn't.

The center had been converted from an abandoned high school. Late one evening last week, the twelve-year-old daughter of two married prisoners managed to escape by climbing the pipes on the walls of the gym to the roof. From there she crawled on the steel rafters until she reached a skylight. Her name was Nancy Biehl. After reaching the roof, Nancy jumped two stories to the asphalt and climbed the hurricane fence, no doubt cutting her hands on the barbed wired attached to the top. The girl had been a gymnast. The next day, Mr. and Mrs. Biehl disappeared for processing.

Four months. It seemed longer. The first month was the worst. The shock. The cold. The stink of bodies. The lack of privacy. The lousy food. The weekly, cold shower without soap. The endless boredom. Next to the hunger, the boredom was the worst. Chet found some consolation in his vocation. It allowed him to fill the time. There were twenty-seven little kids here. Each one knew Father Chet's Saint Stories by heart.

He gave a daily lesson on the *Catechism* from memory to about fifty prisoners. One guard, an American, allowed this during the day. *Maybe he reported me. Maybe that's why I'm going to be processed.*

He had long discussions with the Protestants about the faith. They were trying to pass the time, too. Two-thirds of the prisoners filling the gym were Protestants—evangelicals who took the prolife fight more seriously than most Catholics. They missed their Bibles. Some said Rosaries with Chet.

This is not as bad as Uncle Max had it. They used to beat him senseless every other day. I've only been beaten a few times. I can say Mass. I can hear confessions, though the people in this room are mostly saints, sinless. It's like having a special parish without having to travel or even walk down the street to see my parishioners!

There, now that's more like how Max would look at it! Thank you, Uncle Max. I offer this Rosary and the migraine up for the souls of the case workers. Jesus, help me love my enemies.

Chet managed to smile. Ignoring his hunger and his headache, he held up his rosary when he saw that the guard wasn't looking. Mr. Reginald Johnson, a Baptist, casually tapped the gym floor three times. Several prisoners noticed the signal. The black robe was going to pray. Looks were exchanged. Chet saw a fourteen year-old-boy, Hank Noble, grabbing his thumb—the first bead of a human rosary.

Father Chet began, whispering, "I believe in one God, the Father Almighty…"

✝ ✝ ✝

After the Rosary, the door at the end of the gym was unlocked, then opened. Two guards and a case worker marched in. A guard pointed to the corner where Chet was sitting on the floor. The other guard removed plastic handcuffs from his belt.

Reggie Johnson stood up and cried, "No! Not the priest! We need the priest!"

The guard whacked Johnson on the side of the face with a billy stick. The black man fell to the floor, bleeding. A few prisoners came to his side. The other guard held up his machine gun in a menacing fashion. *They've come early,* Father Chet thought, feeling strangely relieved.

"It's okay," Father Chet said, hearing his knees crack as he stood up. He raised his voice to sermon level, "Pray for me, all of you. I'll see you in heaven!"

"Be quiet!" the case worker ordered in a thick Cockney accent.

Ignoring the case worker, Father Chet raised his right hand and blessed his parishioners out loud, before the guard could apply the handcuffs. Men, women, and children began to cry. *I'm a Sullivan. I'm a priest. This is what I signed up for,* he told himself, trying to control his fears and tears.

5

Tuesday Afternoon
13 May
Salt Lake City, The Mormon Nation

The gunman lined up his scope and made himself comfortable on the roof of an apartment building on East South Temple Street. The target was less than three hundred yards away. *You filthy apostate. You servant of the devil...*

John Lanning was preaching and baptizing with more vigor than ever, now that Pope Patrick had resurfaced.

The gunman was one of the many great, great, great grandchildren of a close friend and contemporary of Porter Rockwell—the nineteenth-century personal bodyguard of

Brigham Young. This gunman was proud of his heritage. He was an accountant for a respectable firm in downtown Salt Lake City. As a young man—after he had proven an excellent marksman in the Army—he was recruited to be available to the Council of Fifty for "special" jobs. This was his second one. His first had been almost eight years ago.

There. To the right. Good. Breathe in, the gunman told himself. *Torso shot. No head shot.* Those were the instructions.

Lanning's heart lined up in the cross of the hairs etched on the crystal of the gunman's scope.

On three. One… two…

6

Tuesday Afternoon
13 May
Hackensack, New Jersey

Father Chet waited alone in the empty room at the Regional Administration Building of the World Union Health Ministry. The handcuffs were hurting his wrists. He tried to distract himself from a mood of impending doom. Despair knocked on his door.

Was it worth it? Was it worth it being a priest?

He thought of all the sacrifices he had made in order to find himself shackled in an empty office after months of freezing and starving in jail. Even before the tribulations, his had not been an easy life.

Then an image of Becky came to his mind. The image was crystal clear, which surprised Chet, because the faces of his relatives and friends had been fading in his memory. In the past few weeks, it had frustrated him that he couldn't imagine a clear image of his mother, or Nathan—or anyone.

Rebecca looked so beautiful in the image he now saw. He remembered the time and the place well. She was with him at the Grotto at Notre Dame. Her face had a curious but wonderful expression of innocence and determination.

*Determination to do the right thing—no matter what. She had just decided to be a Catholic. Because of my priesthood. We used to talk about Beauty all the time. Now, **that** was beautiful!*

Her resolve and her goodness complemented her physical beauty. For Chet, her faith was a glimpse of heaven, then and now. It was just one example of the fruit of his labors, but an example close to his heart. It gave him the grace he needed.

For Becky. For all the Beckys. For Nathan and Joe, and for Mom and Dad and Tommy, Mike, Jimbo. Suck it up, Chet. Finish strong!

✝ ✝ ✝

Harlan Gello closed his appointment book. Absentmindedly, he opened the drawer in his desk, took something out, and slipped it into his jacket.

The hour had come.

He strolled into the room and closed the door. The building used to be the headquarters of a now-defunct insurance company. It was quite modern. Quite spiffy. The Health Ministry often had first choice of appropriated buildings.

Gello pursed his lips and sat down across from the priest.

The two men were alone. They sat facing each other on modern leather chairs. There was no table between them. There were no windows in the room, but there was a fine blue carpet and a Picasso print on the wall. Chet's hands were cuffed behind the chair. They were the kind which tighten if the prisoner struggles. Chet was bleeding from one wrist—the guard had clamped the cuffs extra tight before putting him in the van to take him here.

Not exactly a dungeon with moldy walls and a shadeless light bulb hanging from the ceiling. You watched too much television as a kid, Chetmeister.

He managed to smile at Gello, but his humor was forced. Goose bumps rose on his arms. That constant companion, hunger, made room for fear.

"Mr. Gello. I've seen you on television. Are you going to offer me a cigarette or something?" Chet asked bravely, half-joking. He looked like a skeleton. His skin was white, pallid.

Gello had healthy skin, a small paunch. He wore neatly pressed Dockers with a blazer over a Polo shirt. Penny loafers, no socks.

Gello smiled. "Smoking is bad for you, William Sullivan. No one will be allowed to smoke in the New Age." Gello had a gleam in his eyes. A priest's gleam, but of an entirely different priesthood.

The room was silent.

Gello looked at a dossier with "Sullivan" on the tab. He sighed and threw the dossier casually to the side. The papers settled all over the carpeted floor. He shook his head and looked at Chet with a practiced sort of compassion.

"What exactly don't you like about the Omega Project?" he asked, as if he were taking a survey. As if Chet were not cuffed, filthy, and destitute.

Chet decided to ignore the question. He had been praying to the Holy Spirit since Gello had come into the room. Gello frightened him.

Gello is crazy, Chet's inner voice told him. *Find out why,* grace prompted him.

Chet asked the Blessed Mother to use him as her instrument. *I'm yours. I'm yours. Let your Son speak through me.*

"You can still turn back to the Father, Harlan," Chet said. He wasn't sure why he used those particular words. They did not strike Chet as especially eloquent. Yet, just for a second, the smug gleam in Gello's eyes disappeared, and Chet saw the child within the man connect to the grace.

Have mercy on him, Lord, Chet prayed.

Then Harlan disappeared. Chet saw the whites all around
the man's eyeballs. *We called that "bugging out" back in grammar school,* Chet thought.

The sinister gleam was back and now Rangor spoke using
Gello's voice, but not Gello's tone or facial expressions. Chet
came to complete attention, like a deer looking at headlights.

"Harlan is dead," the thing inside Gello croaked viciously,
"I will destroy you and all your priests!"

The look in the man's eyes was utterly evil. It was Chet's
first encounter with a possessed person. The demon speaking through Gello screamed insanely and began to laugh.

"I have been given the power to begin with you. Today! I
am Legion!"

Gello's hand reached into his jacket and pulled out a long
silver envelope opener.

7

Tuesday Afternoon
13 May
Notre Dame, Indiana

"Crowd estimate?" Ivan Blatovsky demanded, speaking curtly
into his microphone.

"Two hundred thousand, General, sir," came the reply from
a man in a helicopter hovering above.

The general flicked his mike up on his helmet. His lead
tank rumbled down Notre Dame Avenue, closely surrounded
by infantry, with a seemingly endless line of armored vehicles
behind it. Blatovsky was certain that it was safe enough for
him to ride with his upper body exposed atop his Russian K-
45. He was keenly aware that he looked like a throwback to
the great World War II panzer commanders. It would look
good on television, too. No staff car for Blatovsky. He drew
the line at makeup when the CNI correspondent suggested a
"bit of powdering." Makeup was for simpering politicians.

The Ukrainian had grown up despising the arrogance and prosperity of Americans. Many of his relatives had died in Stalin's forced starvation of Ukraine, which had killed millions. As a little boy, he had heard stories from aunts and uncles who had eaten corpses to survive. He had rejected the secret Christian faith of his weak mother; he had embraced the Communist Party in school, at camps, during sports, and with his friends. Soviet propaganda blamed the starvation on the Enemy. The Americans. Fat, lazy, corrupt, greedy cowboys and bankers.

He had endured Russian prejudice against Ukrainians during his long rise to the upper echelon of the Soviet military. In the process he had eschewed anything Ukrainian, just as Stalin had rejected all things Georgian during his rise to the top. Ivan Blatovsky had suffered humiliations as a battalion commander in Afghanistan. He had chafed at the dishonor of the breakup of the Soviet Union. For him, the debacle in Chechnya was the last straw. He made his mark with the battle plan that worked so well in Tbilisi. Recovering those TDC oil fields had made Russia a player in the World Union. The command of the Third World Union Army was Blatovsky's reward.

He was insanely jealous that the invasion of Texas had been given to the krauts and frogs in the First World Union Army. The Third World Union Army had sat on its hands in Canada while the Germans and the French fell to pieces in Texas! Blatovsky had proposed the daring invasion of Chicago and took full advantage of the opportunity. Before the Fall of Chicago, the World Union had been looking for a propaganda victory; Blatovsky was looking for a real, strategic victory— a military victory. And a chance to spill American blood on American soil.

His worshipful staff had reported that Blatovsky was now being mentioned in the same breath as Rommel and Patton in Amsterdam.

I am a man of destiny! Lenin may be long gone, but his theory that capitalism would corrupt America from within

*still holds true. They will burst beneath the treads of my armor
like ripe, rotting melons.*

It was rumored that he would soon replace the German,
General Rahner, who had screwed up so incredibly in the
Texas debacle. Blatovsky recommended using tactical nuclear
weapons in Texas. Rahner was against it. It was known that
seven out of nine ballistic missile submarines (part of the
former United States Navy) patrolling the seas had aligned
themselves with the Texans. Just one submarine could
annihilate all the capitals of Europe in less than thirty minutes. Blatovsky didn't think Chip Williams had the guts to
start a nuclear war. The defining principle of these American
rebels was their softness. Blatovsky prided himself on being
hard.

Take this job, for instance, he told himself, looking around
at the multitudes gathered for Mass on the campus of Notre
Dame. *These people are sheep.*

But they had a shepherd. The shepherd was now preparing silly little bread wafers for his sheep on the steps below
the Golden Dome.

Arresting Pope Patrick was a minor headache for the commander of the Third World Union Army. A photo-op.
Blatovsky planned to shackle the skinny Irishman in full view
of the Third Army's CNI cameras. The Psyche-Ops guys had
gone ballistic last night when Blatovsky revealed his plan to
personally handcuff and arrest the pope. Blatovsky ignored
them. The atheist Blatovsky, the representative of real power
in this world, planned to show everyone who was in charge.

*The answer to Stalin's question about how many divisions
does the pope command is **none!***

Blatovsky laughed out loud. He put his gloved hand over
his visor in mock scrutiny. *No. Not a tank in sight that doesn't
have my name on it.*

He chuckled. Some of the infantrymen walking near his
tank wanted to look up at their one-eyed commander. But
they knew better.

One of his staff had mentioned during the cultural briefing this morning that Notre Dame was an institution whose athletic teams were known as the Fighting Irish. That had greatly amused the general.

The crowd parted to let his tank through. They tried vainly not to look at the tanks, which were crunching and grinding the pavement on Notre Dame Avenue. Many in the crowd succeeded in keeping their attention on Pope Patrick, who was continuing to say Mass on a makeshift altar on the steps of the Administration Building. Above him was the Mother of God in gold.

The general looked through his binoculars at the pope.

That bastard. He is ignoring me, Blatovsky thought, angered beyond reason. *Well, let's get his attention.*

He pulled the microphone down from his helmet and ordered his tank to stop just as it reached the Father Sorin statue. He was about sixty yards from the Pope and the Golden Dome.

"One shot for the folks watching on the television back home," Blatovsky told the gunner. "Destroy the statue on top of that damned dome."

The gun on the K-45 aligned itself with a few mechanical hums. "Statue on dome targeted, sir," the gunner responded quickly.

"Fire!" Blatovsky screamed.

✢ ✢ ✢

John Lanning lifted a baptismal cruet in one hand and made the sign of the cross with the other, gently intoning the most beautiful words in the world, "I baptize thee in the Name of the Father, and of the Son, and of the Holy Spirit…"

The gunman in Salt Lake City pulled the trigger and John the Baptizer died for the second time. This time around, however, he did not go to hell.

✢ ✢ ✢

The report from the K-45's gun was tremendous. Many in the crowd surrounding the tank suffered permanent hearing loss. A unified gasp of shock and surprise surged from the people.

The statue of Mary atop the Golden Dome disappeared instantly. Suddenly all eyes were on the pope.

Angus barely flinched. His server, Father Washington, was paralyzed with fear. Angus, no stranger to gunfire, slowly nodded his head to Lee to continue to bring the water, bowl, and towel to the altar, even as the debris fell off the roof in golden chunks around them. No debris fell on the altar. Most of the statue was strewn on the ground on the opposite side of the building.

"Lord, wash away my iniquity; cleanse me from my sin," Pope Patrick prayed, raising his voice. The entire crowd could hear him on the loudspeakers. The pope looked directly at Nathan Payne. Their eyes met. Nathan nodded gravely.

Do it, they both thought. *Now is not the time for talk. Now is the time for action,* the pope remembered the young man's words.

Angus glanced at the tank heading toward the altar, then looked back at Nathan. The pope drew strength from his steady gaze. Then Nathan smiled.

Angus reached for the chalice and continued with the Mass as Blatovsky's tank continued to roll toward the front of the crowd in an absurd armored procession.

Why arrest him? Blatovsky thought. *Why not just shoot him? This crowd of sheep will be too stunned to react, and if they do the infantry can cut down any resistance. I'll go down in history! Screw Amsterdam. After it's done, they'll take as much credit as they can!*

✝ ✝ ✝

The possessed man raised the silver letter opener over Chet's head, and paused. Gello's eyes looked as if they would burst like tiny balloons! He shrieked an incomprehensible, gleeful scream that filled the shackled priest with fear beyond fear.

Hail Mary! Chet began to pray. A Psalm came to his mind immediately.

"Though I walk through the valley of the shadow of death, I will fear no evil…" Chet muttered, turning his head, feeling pain in his wrists, looking away from Gello and the knife.

Chet received the certain knowledge that he was about to die. He had anticipated his martyrdom since being thrown in jail, imagining that he might have a chance to make a holy speech like Saint Polycarp or some other great martyr. But he would not have his chance to give a speech. No one would hear it, anyway. Not even Harlan.

In his last act of courage, Father Chet forced himself to look up at his enemy and prayed for both himself and the poor possessed man.

"Hail Mary," he started tentatively, "Full of Grace," his voice grew stronger, "The Lord is with thee!" Chet prayed with a deep timbre that reminded him of Tom Wheat.

The demon inside Gello gave one last, bloodcurdling scream and brought his dagger down into the priest.

"Blessed art thou…among women…and Blessed is the Fruit of thy womb, Jesus…" Chet continued, keeping his eyes on his tormentor, avoiding the urge to watch the blood pour out of his body onto the blue carpet. *Don't stop,* he told himself. *Finish strong.*

Time slowed as Chet looked with supernatural calm as the sword descended for a second time. Even as the blood flowed out of it, a grace filled Chet's heart beyond all time and all movement—the unique Grace of Martyrs.

As Chet's heart was pierced by the sword for a third and final time, he finished his life's prayer. "Holy Mary, Mother of God… pray for us sinners…now and at… the hour… of our… death… "

Life left Father Chet's eyes. His head dropped. He was dead. It was finished. Father Chet prayed "Amen" in heaven. In the arms of his mother.

✦ ✦ ✦

Becky grasped Joe's hand, and Joe grasped Nathan's hand. Nathan was already holding Joanie's hand. They tried to ignore the man in the World Union uniform as he dismounted from the tank with the blue insignia of the World Union on its turret. The general exuded power, arrogance, and contempt. Joe considered storming the altar to fling himself in front of the pope. Nathan, reading Joe's mind, tightened his grip on the big man's hand, sending a clear message. *Stay. Follow the pope. Follow the pope.*

They kept their eyes on Angus and the consecrated Savior in Angus's holy hands. The crowd surged forward, making it difficult for the four friends to balance.

The old priest's eyes focused on the Sacred Host as he solemnly raised it above his head, praying, "Take this, all of you, and eat it. This is my body, which will be given up for you."

The priest held up the Body of Jesus for almost half a minute before gently lowering Him to the altar. He genuflected reverently. Then he took the chalice, ignoring Ivan Blatovsky, who was standing only a few feet away.

The General pulled a pistol from its holster and arrogantly pointed it at Pope Patrick as the chalice was raised...

"Take this all of you and drink from it. This is the cup of my blood, the blood of the new and everlasting covenant."

Something delayed Blatovsky from firing his weapon. Perhaps he felt it would be rude to interrupt a condemned man while he was speaking such words, which Blatovsky had to admit, were almost hypnotic...

"It will be shed for *you* and for all so that sins may be forgiven. Do this in memory of me."

He elevated the chalice.

Pope Patrick's eyes remained on the Sacred Blood.

Blatovsky steadied his aim, preparing to shed blood.

I will not allow myself to be hypnotized by this skinny witch doctor!

✝ ✝ ✝

Then the Great Warning came.

✝ ✝ ✝

The demon surrendered control of Harlan Gello. The Warning then came to Harlan as he stood holding a bloody dagger over the dead body of another Christ...

...after the Warning, Harlan dropped the letter opener to the carpet.

"What have I done!? What have I done?!" he repeated, stunned, looking back and forth from the blood on his hands to the dead priest.

He left the room and collapsed on the couch in his office, sobbing and moaning.

Words from the Bible echoed in his ears, each word a judge and jury of his life:

Father, forgive them, for they know not what they do.

The words seemed to be spoken with the voice of the priest he had just helped murder.

The Christ on the Cross in the Warning had spoken the one Word that could save his soul.

Mercy, he thought desperately. *Mercy.*

Then, a sinister voice taunted Harlan. It was Rangor's voice: *Say that word all you want. But do you have the courage to pray it?*

Rangor laughed. *I don't think so. You made your choice a long time ago, Harlan.*

The demonic laughter came again and filled Harlan's head.

Did I? Harlan asked, uncertain.

✝ ✝ ✝

Swords were pounded into plowshares.

When General Blatovsky came out of his own harrowing Warning, the gun dropped from his hand. Sweat covered his face. He slowly looked out into the crowd, many of whom were collapsed on the ground, coming out of their own Warnings. Some of the older people in the crowd appeared to be sleeping, but had actually died from heart failure caused by the trauma of their Warnings.

The General looked to the Pope, who was just lowering the Cup of Blood. Angus was obviously shaken. He turned to the man in uniform.

Blatovsky dropped to his knees, whispering emotionally in Russian, "Father forgive me, for I know not what I have done. My mother! My mother taught me about Jesus when I was a child in the Ukraine. She baptized me! I didn't know! I am so sorry…so sorry. I am a murderer. I am so sorry." The tears began to flow uncontrollably from his one eye.

Angus looked with compassion on the weeping man. He held up a wrinkled hand, and prayed in perfect Russian, "Through the ministry of the Church, I absolve you of your sins in the Name of the Father, and of the Son, and of the Holy Spirit."

Blatovsky fell forward, grasping the pope by the legs.

Angus put his arms around this prodigal son. The first of many.

✝ ✝ ✝

The Warning came for everyone except Nathan Payne. Nathan was almost alone during the Great Warning. He could not move. He was not breathing. Time stopped. Everything stopped. His gaze was locked in place for a second—for an hour—for an eternity.

He was looking at his wife. Joanie was perfectly still, the expression of fear for Pope Patrick fixed on her face like a living photograph. Beyond her, he could see the motionless crowd. There was a soldier on a tank, exhaling a cigarette. The smoke from his mouth sat in the air—fixed. There was no sound. A bird was suspended in the sky, as if held in place by an unseen string.

And there was peace. Nathan remembered his own Warning, and the words of the Woman, the Mother of God.

I will always be at your side.

✝ ✝ ✝

Becky, Joe, and Joanie came out of their Warnings and looked at Nathan. Now they knew.

"The Warning!" Joanie cried. "I saw the Cross! I saw the Immaculate Conception! My sins! I'm so…sorry…"

Her words hung in space.

Nathan took her into his arms. "It's okay," was all he could think to say to his wife. He felt her whole, thin body shuddering with contrition.

Joe and Becky joined them in a corporate hug. They were all crying at the same time now, even Nathan.

People were weeping all around them. Nathan suddenly remembered standing in front of the cornfield with Joe, Joanie, and Becky on the night of his engagement, the day he left the hospital, all four holding each other's wrists.

Solidarity. Solidarity, he thought over and over again, confused and bewildered and…somehow happy. *The walls are going to come down now,* he thought. *If only—*

Then they heard the pope's voice.

"We shall finish Mass now," he said with a firm, gentle voice which echoed out onto the quad of Notre Dame.

The first to receive Communion was Ivan Blatovsky.

8

"In the Pines"
Garabandal, Spain

Within one year, on a Thursday, in the mountain village of
Garabandal, Spain, a giant cross appeared in the sky above
the pines. It was the Great Miracle of Garabandal. Millions
present were instantly healed of mental and physical infirmities, as prophesied. The Cross was two stories tall, surrounded
by an illuminated cloud, and was suspended thirty feet in the
air above a patch of pine trees. Satellite television beamed its
image around the world. People could walk up to it, look at
it, but could feel nothing when they reached out to touch it.

It was similar to the Cross every person on the face of the
earth had seen during the Great Warning. There was one difference; there was no corpus on the Garabandal Cross. Suspended above it was a Sacred Host. Streams of heavenly red
and white light came forth from the Host. The Body of the
Risen Christ. The misty cloud illuminated the Cross and
Sacred Host at night.

The Cross remains there to this day. Over two billion
pilgrims came from all over the world to see it in person during the decade following its appearance.

✝ ✝ ✝

In a room in a building in the Vatican, an old man put the
barrel of a revolver into his mouth, and pulled the trigger.
Luigi Casino's heart stopped...

...in a room in a rectory in New Jersey, an old priest pulled
the barrel of a revolver out of his mouth.
*The image of Father Chet's face, weary after hours in the
confessional, faded peacefully.*
Monsignor Timothy Whelan placed the gun on his desk.

He stood and walked out of the room to find a priest to hear his confession.

✝ ✝ ✝

After the Great Warning, there were still those who continued to imitate their evil master, vowing, "I will not serve."

The Great Warning did *not* eliminate human free will. After the Great Warning, however, no one could fool himself that there are other than two choices for each human soul: Good or Evil.

The Great Miracle at Garabandal was a public, supernatural sign that every person of every language could read with perfect clarity. The Great Miracle spoke clearly to every heart and mind, saying, "This is Goodness Personified. This is Salvation. The Cross. The Eucharist." In addition, *everyone* "met" the Immaculate Conception, Mary, at the foot of the Cross during their Warnings.

The World Union did not dissolve immediately. Those dedicated to evil redoubled their efforts to enslave and destroy God's people.

It would take more space than is contained in all the computer hard drives in the world to recount all the events...

9

From *Dark Years History*
(New Rome Press, 31 R.E.)
by Rebecca Macadam Jackson

...General Blatovsky's Marian Armies crushed the Second World Union Army in the cornfields near Lake Waxinkuckee several days after the Great Warning. The Second Army was fighting at one-third strength due to the mass desertion of troops immediately after the Warning. The First World Union Army surrendered in Texas without firing a shot. French, German, and Russian soldiers joined the Marian Armies. The reconquering of the World Union territories in North America took less than four months.

Most of the more horrific wars occurred in China and Europe, where the Great Warning had less effect on the populations. Months after the Great Warning, millions had either decided to serve evil without reserve or had convinced themselves that the Great Warning had been a worldwide mass hallucination...

...nuclear weapons were used frequently on the Continent and in Asia. It is beyond the scope of this history to go into great detail regarding events in those places. However, it would be remiss not to point out that the spiritual and cultural treasures of Saint Peter's Basilica were utterly, senselessly destroyed when the Society of Builders abandoned the Vatican and detonated a nuclear weapon rather than surrender control. The Pieta Miracle—the perfect preservation of Michelangelo's masterpiece at "ground zero" of the nuclear detonation—stands as a supernatural symbol of God's mercy to the world...

...as the Lord Himself promised after the Great Flood in Noah's times, the next time He punished the world would not be by water. In this next section we will recount the Three Days of Darkness (TDD), which destroyed all those who did not heed the Great Warning. Supernatural fire fell from the sky for three days, consuming all those who refused the immense grace of the Warning...

...corpses were everywhere after the TDD. Because of the disease generated in the corrupting bodies, certain cities became uninhabitable for years afterward. These cities stand as gruesome monuments to the Dark Years...

...first president of the re-formed United States, Karl Slinger—and others like him such as General Williams—can rightly take their place as the second wave of founding fathers. Slinger is often referred to as "the Second George Washington." More than any other man, President

Slinger fearlessly led his people with faith, guts, example, piety, and sacrifice during the darkest days of the Dark Years. Few observers believe that Texas would have held out until the Great Warning had not Slinger inserted his forceful personality into history. The whole world came to know and love his booming laughter.

The author of this historical survey openly exempts herself from any pretense of objectivity regarding President Slinger. He was the godfather of my first daughter, Amy Jackson, who was born on the day of the first of the Quakes...

...therefore, the Vatican was temporarily relocated to Assisi, where the Great Pope Patrick reigned after his triumphant return from the re-formed United States. Plans are already in place for the reconstruction of Saint Peter's Basilica in Rome in the next decade, when the radioactivity will have dissipated enough for human habitation...

...it took more than five years for missionaries to baptize the survivors in China...

...refer to *She Shall Crush Your Head* by Thomas Wheat. It is hard to discount Wheat's central thesis that the United States was spared nuclear disaster because millions of prayerful Catholics and Protestants (who converted to Catholicism by the tens of millions after the Great Warning) mitigated God's punishment. According to Wheat, these millions were the "Ten Just Men" who formed the heel that crushed the head of Satan. These millions enabled the re-formed United States to play a pivotal role in bringing order and peace back to the world after the Three Days of Darkness. Pope Patrick the Great, in his first worldwide satellite television address from Assisi, praised the United States as the country which responded most generously, if imperfectly, to the messages from heaven in the years leading up to the Great Tribulations...

...so the unprecedented peace the reader enjoys today is owed not only to martyrs such as Saint John Lanning, but also to millions of men, women, and children who prayed in response to the urgent pleas of the Blessed Mother and Jesus. Perhaps readers born after the Dark Years will find it easy to imagine that they would have responded well to heaven had they lived during the tribulations, but the fact remains that the vast majority of people claiming to be Catholics and Christians at that time *did not* respond, or responded in a lukewarm fashion. Had the whole world responded the way a remnant of Americans did, perhaps countless souls would not have been lost. The generous response of humble Catholics in Poland, and to a lesser extent, in Ireland, seems to bear out Wheat's thesis. These countries suffered greatly, but did not suffer nearly as much as others. England, for example, lost millions to a massive flood which wiped out London. The rest of the population centers of England were nearly obliterated during the final stages of the nuclear exchanges...

...even hindsight is blurred. One thing is clear: it was through the merits and sacrifices of a handful of obscure, humble, and unknown heroes that God's Will was accomplished on earth and in heaven. And the humblest, most obscure, and unknown hero of all was the Virgin of Nazareth, Mary. May we forever serve the Eucharistic Son of the Immaculate Queen of Heaven!

Rebecca Macadam Jackson, M.I.
Feast of the Immaculate Conception
Marytown, Indiana

✚ ✚ ✚

Father Chet's body, like Maximilian Kolbe's, was taken to a crematorium, mixed with the ashes of other sinners and saints, and scattered to the winds on a golden field of grass.

PART FOUR
After the Triumph

Days turn to minutes and minutes to memories. Life
sweeps away the dreams that we have planned.
Johnny Cougar Mellencamp

For although our Savior's cruel passion and death
merited for His Church an infinite treasure of
graces, God's inscrutable providence has decreed
that these graces should not be granted to us all at
once; but their greater or lesser abundance will
depend in no small part on our good works, which
draw down on the souls of men a rain of heavenly
gifts freely bestowed by God.
Mystici Corporis (On the Mystical Body of Christ)
Encyclical Letter of Pius XII

The heart has reasons that the reason does not know.
Blaise Pascal

Chapter Twenty-Four

1

Five Years Later
13 May
Mishawaka, Indiana

The big man knelt before the Blessed Sacrament in Immaculate Conception Church. He was perfectly still. Joe Jackson had been praying for half an hour. The old football injury in his back was beginning to cause some pain. He only had a quarter of an hour before he had to go back to help Becky with the children (they had one daughter and two sons now). It had been five years to the day since the Warning, and more than four years since the Three Days of Darkness.

His Warning had been different from most—because Joe was a saint. There had been very few mortal sins to review— only three—and relatively speaking, very few venial sins. Nevertheless, these few sins had been terrifying things to re-experience. Overall, his Warning had been a wonderful experience. Especially meeting Mary. Despite his melancholic nature, he rarely dwelt upon his Warning. But on the anniversary of the amazing day when Pope Patrick celebrated the Mass that saved the world, Joe allowed himself to remember…Tape Number 33. It still gave him chills.

Joe was too humble to think about Tape Number 33 often. Even now as he prayed, he reminded himself that he was only a link in the chain. After all, Professor Wheat had spent decades developing his speaking skills and years researching the talk. Joe realized that he wouldn't have produced the tape if some dedicated Catholics hadn't taken the trouble to put the "Metairie Family Rosary" on the radio when he was a youngster. And most of *those* people had been Catholics because their families had passed on the faith down through the centuries. It was a chain that stretched all the way back to the apostles, and found its origin in the Holy Trinity. The first link was Jesus.

The tape.

Like Nathan, Joe was also shown the ramifications of all the *good* acts of his life. There were too many to chronicle, and he had begun to forget. He could not remember Mary's face very well, which was disappointing. He accepted this with equanimity. But he could not forget Tape Number 33, which would always remain capitalized in his mind.

It was "Marian Apparitions" by Thomas Wheat—the audio tape which Joe had produced at the Kolbe Foundation. During his Warning, Joe was shown that he had been inspired to *conceive* the idea of recording Professor Wheat in part by the grace merited by his real mother, Mary Johns. (The first thing Joe told Becky after the Warning was that he had seen his birth mother.)

By the time of the Warning, more than eight million copies of "Marian Apparitions" had been produced. What happened during the Warning seemed an impossibility, but Joe had seen every single person who had heard the tape. He saw each person, all at once, each individually. The good the tape had done in individual lives was stunning, to say the least. He could only remember a small fraction of those he saw. His mind could not hold that much information.

But Joe Jackson remembered Number 33 now, as he did every year on the thirteenth of May. It was the thirty-third tape he had given out at the Marian Congress in Chicago. He didn't even remember handing it to Mrs. Hannah Carle until the event was shown to him during the Warning.

Hannah loved the talk by Tom Wheat. She listened to it seven times in two weeks after the congress. She wrote to the Kolbe Foundation and received twelve copies, which she promptly distributed at her Rosary Society meeting. One of the ladies at the meeting, Mrs. Dorothy McLain, also liked the talk, and decided to give a copy to her son, Randall. She was so excited that she didn't write to the Kolbe Foundation. Instead, Dorothy made a copy of "Marian Apparitions" on her home tape recorder. Randy McLain took his sweet time before listening to it—four weeks—and was only mildly impressed. He gave it back to his mother, who left it in the back of Saint Jerome's Church. Dorothy said a little prayer to the Holy Spirit when she put the copy on a table next to the bulletins with a note that said, simply, "Free Tape About Mary. Real Good." Two days later, after Sunday Mass, Mr. Hal Werthlin picked up the tape out of curiosity.

Hal went bananas over it. He ordered a grand total of four hundred and fifty-eight copies from the Kolbe Foundation over the next six years. One of Hal Werthlin's tapes went to his accountant, Jim Rice, who eventually gave a copy to his best friend, Sam Fisk, who lived in Cleveland. Sam didn't like the tape—it was too scary. Sam gave it back to Jim, who gave it to Rosanne Hawley. Rosanne got ten copies. She gave one to Helen Anthony, who gave it to Mary Collins, who gave it to Richard Tiant, who gave it to Bill Conigliario. Bill Conigliario didn't listen to it, but he left it in his car, where it sat for three weeks until his wife Sandy played it while driving her daughter home from Franciscan University of Steubenville. Sandy's daughter, Rebecca "Reba" Conigliario, had been forced to go to Steubenville by her devout mother (Bill didn't care where his daughter went to college).

Reba had hated the solidly Catholic school for the first few months, but made some great friends—the first truly Catholic friends of her life—and gradually came to love the place. Reba was praying a daily Rosary by her senior year and liked the tape enough to give it to her friend, Juan Rivera (no relation to Father Juan Rivera of Tule River Indian Reservation), a fellow senior. Juan wrote for several copies and gave one to his mother four months later. Juan's mother also liked Tom Wheat's talk and began attending daily Mass after hearing it. Mrs. Rivera ordered several Spanish translation tapes from the Kolbe Foundation.

By then it had been almost two years since Joe Jackson had given out Number 33 in Chicago.

Mrs. Rivera lived in Youngstown, Ohio, but she sent a Spanish copy to her childhood friend, Roberta Sanchez, who lived in San Antonio, Texas. The chain almost broke with Roberta, who was a good Catholic, but threw her copy into an open trash can by a bus stop, several weeks after listening to it. She just wasn't the type of person to give tapes to others. It was taking up space in her pocketbook.

During his Warning, Joe saw the guardian angel of a man named Pedro Martinez urge Pedro to *look* at the trash can for almost twenty minutes before Pedro's bus arrived two hours after Roberta had thrown it away. Pedro spotted the tape and snatched it up just as his bus pulled to the stop. He listened to *«Apariciones Marianas»* on his Walkman the next day while doing his janitorial work at the IBM building in San Antonio. It had a profound effect on his life. Pedro, who was sixty, returned to the sacraments after a twenty-five year absence. He became a faithful man of prayer. Pedro immersed himself in the sacramental life. He also distributed fifty copies of *«Apariciones Marianas»* (and more than one hundred copies of the English version) over the next eighteen months.

The very last Spanish copy he distributed (before he died of a heart attack) was a tape he sent to a friend, Felix Morales. Felix and Pedro had gone to school together in Mexico City before crashing the border in the 1950s. Felix had eventually moved to Los Angeles and had done well as a computer technician. Even though they had lost touch during the past decade, Felix had been praying for Pedro for years. By the time he received the tape from his old friend, Pedro was in heaven interceding for him to *really* listen to it.

Felix did, and gave out several copies. He gave one to his parish priest, who sent an English copy to his nephew, Diego Baerga, who worked on a ranch in Wyoming. Diego's mother had been very worried about her son, who had stopped practicing the faith as a teenager in the barrios of Los Angeles.

The tape transformed Diego's life. It really wasn't the tape that changed him. It was the grace of Jesus distributed through the Mystical Body of Christ. Before listening to the tape, Diego was unhappy working in what he considered his dead end groundskeeper's job. He was uneasy about the sorry state of his spiritual life. He was tired of the endless string of women he had slept with over the years. He wanted to get married. He was open to the grace. He came back to the simple, profound faith of his childhood after hearing Professor Wheat's talk. He rediscovered his boyhood love and devotion for the Mother of God.

Diego's fellow worker and friend, Manuel Ruiz, was already a devout Catholic. Manuel had been offering his daily Communion for Diego for months and was absolutely thrilled by Diego's return to the Catholic faith. Yet it was Diego who convinced Manuel to place the copy of "Marian Apparitions" in the limousine of Karl A. Slinger.

Which changed the life of Karl Slinger.

Who helped Pope Patrick change the lives of everyone. Everyone.

Chapter Twenty-Five

1

Eve of the Feast of the Immaculate Conception
7 December, 16 R.E.
Marytown, Indiana

The old man's laugh was not as loud, but it still boomed across the room of the Jackson's home. The children in the play-room couldn't help but turn their heads toward Karl Slinger, former president of the United States of America. Karl had finished his first term and didn't seek another. He didn't cotton to politics. He had been elected after running unopposed. He had been drafted by Chip Williams. Chip had practically forced Karl to run. Karl's political career was a distant memory—finished for almost a dozen years.

Chip and Christy Williams were presently in the air on their way to Marytown. Denny's son Zack had picked them up in Virginia in Denny's old Cessna 172. Zack was fifteen years old, and almost as good a pilot as his legendary father.

"What's so funny, you stupid Polack?" Lenny snapped with good humor.

Lenny was sitting in a rocking chair with a blanket on his lap. He was next to Karl, who sat in a big stuffed chair, his head turning red. It was the same chair Pope Patrick had pre-ferred during his annual visits until he passed away a decade earlier. Historians and laymen alike were already calling him Patrick the Great—the pope who saved the world with a Mass.

"You're what's so funny!" Karl replied. "Look at you! You're an old man. I saw you make a beeline for that rocker.

And that blanket on your lap—that's precious." Karl laughed again.

In the kitchen, Becky looked at Amy's godfather and shook her head. She whispered conspiratorially to Joanie, "If Uncle Karl laughs like that one more time, our statue of Mary is going to rattle off the mantelpiece and knock Lenny on the head. Watch," she nodded toward the two old men. Joanie giggled.

"You're just jealous because a skinny Jew can beat you across the room without even trying," Lenny quipped.

"Don't go using that old 'skinny Jew' routine with me, Lenny," Karl retorted. "You've been a Catholic for sixteen years already!"

"You're impossible! Big Mister President! Mr. Tomato Head, that's what I say. I don't know why I even bother talking to you…" and so the same conversation rolled on and on.

Since Dottie passed away several years ago, The Partners, as Becky dubbed them, had been inseparable.

Denny Wheat and his wife, Molly, had flown the two nonagenarians from Houston a couple of days ago. Down in Texas, they were Founding Fathers. Up in Indiana, they were just two old men looking for a barber shop where they could chew the fat.

And they were dearly loved by their adoptive families, the Wheats and the Paynes. Karl had just turned ninety. Lenny was ninety-one. Even dying was a contest between them. Joe had bet a newborn calf on Karl. Nathan took Lenny Gold—and gave Joe a two-year spread. Karl and Lenny were well aware of the bet.

Karl Slinger's goddaughter, Amy Jackson, was going to be married to Jon Payne the following morning. After the Dark Years, people started getting married at ages more typical of agrarian societies. Nathan's eldest son, Jon, was only seventeen. Amy was slightly older.

Jon considered himself more than lucky. In his opinion, Amy was by far the most beautiful girl in the state. His opinion was shared by just about every young man in Marytown (Mishawaka and South Bend had been merged and renamed

Marytown after the Great Tribulations). Amy had taken after her mother, except for her thick brown hair, which reminded Becky of Sudden Sam, the girl's father. Sam had died in a concentration camp after the Fall of Chicago.

Fortunately for Jon, Amy had also inherited her mother's choleric personality, and had fallen deeply and completely in love with him at age seven. For Amy, tomorrow's nuptial Mass was nothing more or less than the culmination of a decade of patience. Jon finally fell in love with "the brat," as he lovingly referred to her, four months ago. Engagements were much shorter in the Eucharistic Reign. Amy called him Jon-Jon, as she had as a little girl.

Bishop Phillip Washington was scheduled to arrive in an hour—on horseback (although automobiles were making a comeback, horses and airplanes were the preferred modes of transportation in the new world). The good bishop would preside over the wedding, of course. Until Pope Nugumbu tapped Phillip to be the Bishop of Fort Wayne, Father Phillip had been content to be the pastor of Immaculate Conception parish. Tomorrow, more than a few people at the wedding would wonder why Becky Jackson insisted on calling him Lee.

Outside, Joe and Nathan were just finishing quarterback-coaching duty for their older eight children in a game of touch football. All four boys were Jacksons. All four girls were Paynes. Billy and Beth Wheat were also playing. Two more Jackson boys were inside playing at the feet of Karl and Lenny. Three more Payne girls were in the house helping their moms prepare the rehearsal dinner.

Tom Wheat and James Sullivan watched the game from the sideline, chatting amiably with Greg. The game was being played behind the cemetery of Immaculate Conception Church. Immaculate Conception was still heated by the ancient woodstove in the center aisle.

It was chilly, but clear and sunny. Good football weather. Everyone except Nathan wore homemade sweaters. Nathan wore an ancient, ragged Seton Hall sweatshirt—a gift from Father Chet over two decades ago. Nathan always wore this particular sweatshirt for the traditional touch football game on the eve of his wedding anniversary.

Joe had put on a few pounds over the years, and his bad back had slowed him down. Back surgeons were in short supply in the new world, but Joe never complained. Nathan looked the same, if a bit older.

He's catching up to his eyes, Joe thought suddenly, looking across the line, preparing to rush the smoothest quarterback in the new world. *Nathan always looked younger than his eyes.*

It didn't seem to bother Joe that Nathan's team was winning big. (Nathan's team consisted of two of Joe's incredibly tall sons, two of Nathan's redheaded daughters, and Beth Wheat.) Whatever it was that Nathan had, he still had it. His teams always won. Even Joe's kids knew it, and always lobbied to be on Uncle Nathan's team when sides were chosen. His younger boys had to take Nathan's stories of Joe's Super Bowl heroics on faith. There was no such thing as professional sports in the new world.

Nathan faded back, looking to the right side of the field for Joe's son Joey. Seeing Nathan's gaze, Joe took an outside rush around Catherine Payne, who smoothly guided her Uncle Joe around the pocket with surprising strength for her pixie size, laughing the whole time. Nathan smartly stepped up in the pocket and released a touch pass to his twelve-year-old daughter Bridget, who had slipped under the zone. She caught the ball with a lazy, casual kind of ease, then quickly reversed her direction, leaving Joe's son Chet to slip and fall. Bridget picked up the first down before Helen Payne tagged her.

I saw Joe Montana do that a hundred times, Joe thought with a familiar kind of admiration for Nathan.

"Feel the Pain, Old Man," Nathan whispered, a playful smile on his face, as he passed Joe, walking toward the new line of scrimmage, clapping his hands to huddle up his team.

✝ ✝ ✝

The kids and the older folks were in bed. It seemed like only those who grew up with electric lights wanted to stay up more than a few hours past dusk. In the new world, people lived more by the sun than the clock. It wasn't so bad. Electricity had been back for over a decade, of course—but it didn't mean what it used to mean. Even Maker's Mark was back. Denny Wheat made an annual flight down to Loretto, Kentucky, to stock up for the whole town.

The Paynes, the Jacksons, and Bishop Washington sat on the big porch of Joe's house. Joe and Becky had never moved out of the farmhouse. Like Tom and Anne Wheat, they simply added on as the family got bigger.

Nathan, Joanie, Becky, and Joe were covered with blankets on a huge old davenport. Lee eased back and forth on his favorite Adirondack rocker. Becky and Nathan were sharing one of Nathan's homegrown cigarettes. A bottle of Maker's Mark was being passed around. No one got drunk in the new world, either. That wasn't missed at all.

Lee went down the list in his head: *No drunkenness, no heresy, no fornication or adultery, no sects, practically no mortal sin. It's heaven on earth. All because of the superabundance of grace flowing through the Immaculate Heart of Mary. The Eucharistic Reign is a superabundance of grace! I got a foretaste of it after Our Lady came to me. After that, I would rather die than reject God's grace by sin. It all comes down to grace.*

Children simply didn't believe what happened in the Dark Years. *You mean they used to actually kill babies in their mothers' wombs?* they asked all the time.

Amazing Grace! You'd think they wrote that song just for me.

"You know," Becky said to no one in particular, "how come we still call the New Kolbe Center the *New* Kolbe Center? It's fourteen years old, isn't it? It's almost thirteen years older than the *old* Kolbe Center at the old Kolbe Center's oldest age."

Joanie sighed pleasantly. Nathan chuckled. Becky nodded toward the "new" Kolbe Center, which needed a fresh coat of paint. There wasn't much paint in the new world. No one missed it.

"Huh?" Joe asked. "Could you run that by me again, Beck?"

"I don't think I could," Becky answered honestly.

"Nathan could," Lee suggested.

"But I don't want to. I want more medicine."

Joe passed Nathan the bottle of Maker's.

A long silence ensued.

Joanie looked at her watch. "It's past midnight. It's the Feast of the Immaculate Conception. The whole world will celebrate. It's almost as big as Christmas and Easter, and tied with Divine Mercy Sunday. But for me, it's the day I married you, lover."

"You're the queen of my heart," Nathan replied sheepishly. Joe was amazed at how much more Nathan spoke from his heart since he first met him.

"Aren't you going to say something mushy to me, Joe?" Becky asked sweetly, and without a trace of sarcasm.

"I'm thinking, Beck," Joe replied. Everyone waited for two minutes while Joe Jackson thought.

"After all these years," Joe said finally, "I still feel honored to be your husband. During the Dark Years, when everyone was hungry and thirsty, I could always look at you and quench my thirst with my eyes." No one had ever seen Joe cry, except for the few moments after the Great Warning, but his eyes were misting over. He was remembering Becky sleeping on the bed in the Palmer House on their honeymoon. It seemed like yesterday. *I am my lover's and my lover is mine.*

"That's beautiful, Joe," Joanie whispered kindly.

Another silence passed.

"I miss you guys," Lee said softly.

Chapter Twenty-Six

1

A Warm Evening
13 May, 30 R.E.
Notre Dame, Indiana

He laid the roses at the foot of the Father Sorin statue and sat down with his back against the cold marble pedestal.

Remembering Chet.

Nathan pulled out a dog-eared Polaroid someone had taken on his wedding day. Chet had his arms around Nathan and Joe, with Lee at the end on Nathan's side. They had cigars in their mouths. Joe—looking so young and fit—with a rare, open grin. Lee with a peaceful smile. Just before the Polaroid was taken, Nathan had looked over at his best friend. The photo caught the side of Nathan's face which bore the scar on his cheek from the accident. The scar from the Warning. Even now, Nathan remembered taking that look at Chet.

The joy!

Nathan looked at the picture for a long time.

Thirty years. Nathan had grayed early. But he was still lean and strong. Every year he came here alone. He always started the memories at the same place. First grade. The skinny Irish kid behind his desk. Cracking a joke about Sister Lardo, puffing out his cheeks. Laughing. Smiling with his eyes. The vacations together in Chicago. The time Chet brought those two kids out to visit from New Jersey. When Chet heard his confession the day after he met Joanie and agreed to Pascal's Wager. Hearing Chet's voice from the Cross during his personal Warning. Presiding over his wedding at Immaculate

Conception Church. Saying good-bye on the tarmac at Essex County Airport.

Thirty years. Nathan realized that he was as old as Tom Wheat had been when he first met Tom here at the statue. That was before the Warning, before the Dark Years.

In another universe.

He missed his father-in-law, too, of course. But Nathan knew when and where and how Tom died—gracefully, in the midst of his family, at the Wheat farm. Tom had died a peaceful death six years ago, and knowing how he died made the mourning easier. Sure, in the years after Chet's death, a few of those who had known him in prison came from New Jersey. Even his old pastor, Monsignor Whelan, came to visit. They told Nathan about Chet's Kolbean charity before he was taken away to wherever they took him. And murdered him.

Nathan was certain that Chet was in heaven because Chet always answered Nathan's prayers. Maybe that had to be good enough.

Nathan lit a cigarette in honor of the priest. *Nobody smokes anymore,* he thought, feeling like an old man. Nathan had to grow his own tobacco.

Thirty years. The mourning never really stopped, despite all the joy and happiness he had experienced during the Eucharistic Reign.

✝ ✝ ✝

"Mind if I sit down?" Becky asked politely. Nathan shook his head. She sat down next to him. He saw her wince a bit at the arthritis in her knees.

She held up a homemade cigarette. "Got a light?"

Nathan nodded and popped his ancient Zippo for her.

In the light of his Zippo, he looked carefully at his friend. Rebecca Jackson's beauty had not faded over the years—it had only changed.

"Thinking about him?" she said evenly. It was not really a question.

"Yeah," Nathan replied.

"Mind if I remember with you?" she asked.

"Now that you're here, no. Not at all. Maybe you can come next year, too," he told her mellowly.

She sighed, then inhaled deeply. She was Nathan's biggest and only tobacco customer. Thirty years ago, after the news came of Chet's mysterious death, she vowed to remember her priest every time she had a cigarette. She had her own memories. The first phone call. Crying on the beach in Chicago. The first confession. Good times at Bruno's Pizza. His wonderful stories. Those heady days at the Kolbe Foundation before the tribulations. The wedding.

Tears streamed down her lovely, wrinkled cheeks. She tried to put words to the thoughts that Nathan could never quite formulate out loud.

"Sometimes I think," she began softly, "that when he died, however he died, the whole universe changed. I mean, he wasn't always holy, but Father Chet was always faithful. He used to tell me that Beauty and Sadness were related. I like to think that as sad as it was when they killed him, it was beautiful, too. Beautiful enough to change the whole world. Maybe it did. Maybe it did. Maybe none of us would have made it if he hadn't shed his blood for all of us. Do you ever think that?"

Nathan was crying silently as she spoke. *Yeah, Beck. I think that all the time.* But the man of sorrows could say nothing to the beautiful woman.

There was nothing more to say.

Did You Enjoy Reading
Pierced by a Sword?

Would you like to introduce Nathan, Father Chet, Becky, Lee, Joe, Joanie, and Karl to your...

Parents

Brothers and Sisters

Friends

Relatives

Prayer Group

Church or Parish

Business Associates

Local Bookstore Owner

Neighbors

Local School

Local Library

Pastor or Priest?

Saint Jude Media would like to help you.
We're ready to send you as many copies as you want for a nominal donation. Use the convenient Request Form on the next page and write to us today. Available at Catholic retailers everywhere. May also be ordered through most bookstores.

REQUEST FORM #1

Dear Saint Jude Media:
Please send me **Pierced by a Sword** and/or other novels by Bud Macfarlane Jr. I understand that a donation is **not required** for one copy of each book. I am not asking you to send a book or books to someone other than myself.

Signed: _____
(Please Print)

Name: _____

Address: _____

Town: _____

State: _____ Zip: _____

Suggested **Optional** Donation for one copy of each book: **$1 to $12**
Donation for **more than one** copy of each book, any quantity: **$2 - $8 each**
(For more details about Saint Jude Media, see next page.)

Quantity *Pierced by a Sword*	+	Quantity *Conceived Without Sin*	+	Quantity *House of Gold*	=	Total Number of Books
_____		_____		_____		_____

X Donation Per Book _____

= Donation for Books _____

+ Extra gift for shipping (Canadians: Add US$5) _____

+ Optional gift for Saint Jude Media _____

TOTAL DONATION* = $_____

*Your contribution to Saint Jude Media is tax deductible. Sorry, no phone requests for books accepted. We'll ship your book the day we receive your letter. Please make checks payable to "Saint Jude Media" and send to:

Saint Jude Media • Box 26120 • Fairview Park, OH 44126

How Saint Jude Media Works

- If you do not have a request form, writing a simple letter to receive our books is okay. Request forms are also available at www.catholicity.com on the Saint Jude Media homepage.

- Personal correspondence is encouraged. Tell us what you think of our books. We also welcome typographical, grammatical, and fact-checking suggestions for future printings (please include page and line number). Email us at saint.jude.media@catholicity.com

- We will send one free copy of each of our books to each person who writes to us directly. A donation for one book is not required, but you may send a donation if you wish.

- Using the honor system, we ask that you please refrain from sending us the addresses of people other than yourself. Please ask others to write to us directly. We will only send materials to those who personally ask for them, whether a donation is enclosed or not.

- At the present time, we only accept requests for materials by mail. Sorry, no phone requests. Only requests from the United States will be honored unless a sufficient donation to cover shipping is enclosed.

- Saint Jude Media will gladly absorb shipping charges on all requests, but feel free to add extra for shipping if you wish.

- Fast Delivery—all requests will be shipped on the day we open your envelope!

- Under normal circumstances, we are not able to "advance" quantities of books before receiving a donation.

- We will periodically write to let you know about new books and developments, but you will never receive a "fund raising letter" from us. We will not sell or lend your name to other groups—ever.

- These details apply to individuals as well as organizations such as bookstores, etc. Individuals, bookstores, gift shops, schools, and other organizations may accept donations for our books no greater than $5 each. A promotional retail display is available upon request.

REQUEST FORM #2

Dear Saint Jude Media:
Please send me **Pierced by a Sword** and/or other novels by Bud Macfarlane Jr. I understand that a donation is **not required** for one copy of each book. I am not asking you to send a book or books to someone other than myself.

Signed: _____

(Please Print)

Name: _____

Address: _____

Town: _____

State: _____ Zip: _____

Suggested **Optional** Donation for one copy of each book: **$1 to $12**
Donation for **more than one** copy of each book, any quantity: **$2 - $8 each**
(For more details about Saint Jude Media, see next page.)

Quantity *Pierced by a Sword*	+	Quantity *Conceived Without Sin*	+	Quantity *House of Gold*	=	Total Number of Books
_____		_____		_____		_____

X Donation Per Book _____

= Donation for Books _____

+ Extra gift for shipping (Canadians: Add US$5) _____

+ Optional gift for Saint Jude Media _____

TOTAL DONATION* = $_____

*Your contribution to Saint Jude Media is tax deductible. Sorry, no phone requests for books accepted. We'll ship your book the day we receive your letter. Please make checks payable to "Saint Jude Media" and send to:

Saint Jude Media • Box 26120 • Fairview Park, OH 44126

How Saint Jude Media Works

- If you do not have a request form, writing a simple letter to receive our books is okay. Request forms are also available at www.catholicity.com on the Saint Jude Media home-page.

- Personal correspondence is encouraged. Tell us what you think of our books. We also welcome typographical, grammatical, and fact-checking suggestions for future printings (please include page and line number). Email us at saint.jude.media@catholicity.com

- We will send one free copy of each of our books to each person who writes to us directly. A donation for one book is not required, but you may send a donation if you wish.

- Using the honor system, we ask that you please refrain from sending us the addresses of people other than yourself. Please ask others to write to us directly. We will only send materials to those who personally ask for them, whether a donation is enclosed or not.

- At the present time, we only accept requests for materials by mail. Sorry, no phone requests. Only requests from the United States will be honored unless a sufficient donation to cover shipping is enclosed.

- Saint Jude Media will gladly absorb shipping charges on all requests, but feel free to add extra for shipping if you wish.

- Fast Delivery—all requests will be shipped on the day we open your envelope!

- Under normal circumstances, we are not able to "advance" quantities of books before receiving a donation.

- We will periodically write to let you know about new books and developments, but you will never receive a "fund raising letter" from us. We will not sell or lend your name to other groups—ever.

- These details apply to individuals as well as organizations such as bookstores, etc. Individuals, bookstores, gift shops, schools, and other organizations may accept donations for our books no greater than $5 each. A promotional retail display is available upon request.

REQUEST FORM #3

Dear Saint Jude Media:
Please send me **Pierced by a Sword** and/or other novels by Bud Macfarlane Jr. I understand that a donation is **not required** for one copy of each book. I am not asking you to send a book or books to someone other than myself.

Signed: _____

(Please Print)
Name: _____

Address: _____

Town: _____

State: _____ **Zip:** _____

Suggested **Optional** Donation for one copy of each book: **$1 to $12**
Donation for **more than one** copy of each book, any quantity: **$2 - $8 each**
(For more details about Saint Jude Media, see next page.)

Quantity *Pierced by a Sword*	+	Quantity *Conceived Without Sin*	+	Quantity *House of Gold*	=	Total Number of Books
_____		_____		_____		_____

X Donation Per Book _____

= Donation for Books _____

+ Extra gift for shipping (Canadians: Add US$5) _____

+ Optional gift for Saint Jude Media _____

TOTAL DONATION* = $_____

*Your contribution to Saint Jude Media is tax deductible. Sorry, no phone requests for books accepted. We'll ship your book the day we receive your letter. Please make checks payable to "Saint Jude Media" and send to:

Saint Jude Media • Box 26120 • Fairview Park, OH 44126

How Saint Jude Media Works

- If you do not have a request form, writing a simple letter to receive our books is okay. Request forms are also available at www.catholicity.com on the Saint Jude Media home-page.

- Personal correspondence is encouraged. Tell us what you think of our books. We also welcome typographical, grammatical, and fact-checking suggestions for future printings (please include page and line number). Email us at saint.jude.media@catholicity.com

- We will send one free copy of each of our books to each person who writes to us directly. A donation for one book is not required, but you may send a donation if you wish.

- Using the honor system, we ask that you please refrain from sending us the addresses of people other than yourself. Please ask others to write to us directly. We will only send materials to those who personally ask for them, whether a donation is enclosed or not.

- At the present time, we only accept requests for materials by mail. Sorry, no phone requests. Only requests from the United States will be honored unless a sufficient donation to cover shipping is enclosed.

- Saint Jude Media will gladly absorb shipping charges on all requests, but feel free to add extra for shipping if you wish.

- Fast Delivery—all requests will be shipped on the day we open your envelope!

- Under normal circumstances, we are not able to "advance" quantities of books before receiving a donation.

- We will periodically write to let you know about new books and developments, but you will never receive a "fund raising letter" from us. We will not sell or lend your name to other groups—ever.

- These details apply to individuals as well as organizations such as bookstores, etc. Individuals, bookstores, gift shops, schools, and other organizations may accept donations for our books no greater than $5 each. A promotional retail display is available upon request.

For more on the Blessed Virgin Mary:

Audio Tape: **Marian Apparitions Explained.** Request form on last page of this book. No Charge. Optional donation accepted. Contact: Mary Foundation, Box 26101, Fairview Park, OH 44126. www.catholicity.com

Internet: **CatholiCity.** Contains homepages for numerous Marian organizations, national prayer movements, libraries, books, audios, chat rooms, links to other Marian sites. Contact: Box 26101, Fairview Park, OH 44126. www.catholicity.com

Newspapers: **Special Editions** available on Mary, Divine Mercy, Eucharistic Miracles. Summary of Marian apparitions. Contact: Pittsburgh Center for Peace, 6111 Steubenville Pike, McKee's Rocks, PA 15136. (412) 787-9791.

Book: **The Final Hour** by Michael Brown. Historical summary of Marian apparitions. Contact: The Riehle Foundation, Box 7, Milford, OH 45150. (513) 576-0032.

Medal: Handmade **Miraculous Medals** in silver, gold, and brass. Contact: Saint Catherine's Metalworks, 4289 Wooster Road, Fairview Park, OH 44126. (440) 331-1975. www.catholicity.com

Video: **Marian Apparitions of the 20th Century.** Contact: Marian Communications, Box 300, Lincoln University, PA 19352. (800) 448-1192.

Book: **To the Priests, Our Lady's Beloved Sons.** Contact: Marian Movement of Priests, Box 8, Saint Francis, ME 04774-0008.

Information: **The Knights of Immaculata.** World lay association of consecrated souls founded by Saint Maximilian Kolbe. Contact: Militia Immaculatæ National Center, 1600 West Park Avenue, Libertyville, IL 60048. (847) 367-7800. www.marytown.org

Book: **Our Lady Builds a Statue** by LeRoy Lee. The story of the statue of Our Lady in Butte, Montana. $13, including shipping. Contact: Our Lady of the Rockies, 2845 Nettie, Butte, MT 59701. (406) 782-9771.

For more on the Catholic Faith:

<u>Bethlehem Books</u>: Catholic children's fiction. 15605 County Road 15, Minto, ND 58261. (800) 757-6831, Fax (701) 248-3940.

<u>CatholiCity</u>: Internet site with chat rooms, dozens of Catholic organizations, free books and tapes, news, comprehensive links, more. www.catholicity.com

<u>Catholic Answers</u>: Apologetics books, *This Rock* magazine. Box 17490, San Diego, CA 92177. (619) 541-1131, Fax (619) 541-1154. www.catholic.com/~answers

<u>Catholic Marketing Network</u>: Professional association of Catholic suppliers, apostolates, and retailers. 7750 North MacArthur Boulevard, Suite 120-323, Irving, TX 75063. (800) 506-6333, Fax (972) 929-0330. www.catholicmarketing.com

<u>Envoy Magazine</u>: Apologetics and evangelization. Box 1840, West Chester, PA 19380. (800) 553-6869, Fax (610) 696-9977. www.envoymagazine.com

<u>Ignatius Press</u>: Theology, fiction. **Father Elijah** and other great novels by Michael O'Brien. Box 1339, Fort Collins, CO 80522. (800) 537-0390, Fax (970) 221-3964. www.ignatius.com

<u>The Mary Foundation</u>: Free Guide to 100 Catholic Resources, donation optional. Box 26101, Fairview Park, OH 44126. www.catholicity.com

<u>Saint Joseph Communications</u>: Audio tapes by Scott Hahn, others. Box 720, West Covina, CA 91793. (800) 526-2151, Fax (626) 858-9331.

<u>Saint Raphael's Bookstore</u>: Short wave radios, starting at $60, order by phone. (800) 548-8270, Fax (330) 497-8648.

<u>Tan Books</u>: Hundreds of titles, pamphlets, children's books. Catalog. Box 424, Rockford, IL 61105. (800) 437-5876, Fax (815) 226-7770. www.tanbooks.com

<u>WEWN 7.425</u>: Catholic short wave radio, 24 hours/day. Order program guide. 1500 High Road, Vandiver, AL 35176. (800) 585-9396, Fax (205) 672-9988. www.ewtn.com

For more on Catholic Family Issues:

<u>American Association of Prolife Ob-Gyns</u>: Provide referrals to prolife doctors nationwide. 850 Elm Grove Road, Elm Grove, IL 53122. (414) 523-6208, Fax (414) 782-8788.

<u>Couple to Couple League</u>: Natural family planning, chastity education program. Box 111184, Cincinnati, OH 45211. (513) 471-2000, Fax (513) 557-2449.

<u>Financial Foundations for the Family</u>: Responsible use of money, tithing, family budgeting. Box 890998, Temecula, CA 92589. (909) 699-7066, Fax (909) 308-4539.

<u>Human Life International</u>: Books, newsletters, audios on prolife issues worldwide. 4 Family Life, Front Royal, VA 22630. (540) 635-7884, Fax (540) 622-2838. www.hli.org

<u>La Leche League</u>: Natural child-spacing through breast feeding. 1400 North Meacham Road, Schaumburg, IL 60173. (847) 519-7730, Hotline (800) 525-3243, Fax (847) 519-0035.

<u>National Association of Catholic Home Educators</u>: (NACHE) Network of homeschoolers, annual convention. 6102 Saints Hill Lane, Broad Run, VA 22014. (540) 349-4314, Support groups (619) 538-8399, Fax (540) 347-7345.

<u>One More Soul</u>: Audios, videos, and other materials on the beauty of Catholic teaching on sexuality by Dr. Janet Smith, including the excellent audio tape **Contraception: Why Not?** 616 Five Oaks Avenue, Dayton, OH 45406. www.omsoul.com

<u>Saint Joseph Covenant Keepers</u>: Resources for Catholic fatherhood. Box 6060, Port Charlotte, FL 33949. (800) 705-6131, (941) 764-8565, Fax (941) 743-5352. www.dads.org

Come to where the Catholics are...
Come to CatholiCity®

Scores of Catholic Organizations
Free Chat Rooms • Comprehensive Links
Keyword Search • Discussion Groups
Prayer Movements • Free Books and Tapes
email • Publishers • Book Previews
Online Audio • Homeschool Groups
Gift Manufacturers • Lay Apostolates
Live Video • News • and More...

www.catholicity.com

An Internet Service of The Mary Foundation

If the coupon is missing for the free audio tape
advertised on the inside front cover, "Marian
Apparitions Explained," write to:

The Mary Foundation
PBS Offer
Box 26101
Fairview Park, OH 44126

An optional donation for this audio tape is gratefully
accepted but is not required.

FREE
Audio Tape!

Marian Apparitions: Explained.

by Bud Macfarlane, Sr.
Nationally Recognized Expert

Over two million people have heard this
riveting explanation of historical and current-day
appearances of the Mother of God.
Clear, concise, factual—never "preachy."
You will be on the edge of your seat from start to finish.

**Use the request form on the other side
of this notice or write to:**

The Mary Foundation
PBS Offer
Box 26101
Fairview Park, OH 44126

Donations accepted but not required.

Please photocopy and circulate this notice.

Clip or Photocopy Today to Receive Your **Free** Audio Tape:
"Marian Apparitions Explained"

Dear Mary Foundation:
Please send me a copy of the free audio tape, **Marian Apparitions Explained** and a list of your other free Catholic materials. I am not asking you to send a tape to anyone other than myself.

Signed: _____

_____ I understand the tape is free, but I have decided to enclose an **optional** donation to help with the manufacturing and shipping costs of this tape, and to help you supply tapes to my brothers and sisters in Christ. (Suggested Donation: $1 to $10)

_____ Also send me a free audio tape about the Knights of Immaculata (Militia Immaculata).

(Please Print)

Name: _____

Address: _____

Town: _____

State: _____ Zip: _____

Send to:
The Mary Foundation - PBS Offer
Box 26101
Fairview Park, OH 44126

www.catholicity.com

Make checks payable to: The Mary Foundation.
Your gift is tax deductible. Your tape will be shipped the day we get your letter! God Bless!